PRAISE FOR

Too Far Afield

"Any book by Grass is an event.... He remains the most prominent of the older German writers." —*The New York Review of Books*

"A witty, humanistic novel... now finely translated into English by Krishna Winston.... The many levels of history and memory all converge to create a neatly new, exciting and literary world in *Too Far Afield*." —*Los Angeles Times*

"A rich and complex book.... interesting and accessible. It is the work of a seasoned craftsman, certain of what he wants to do, completely in control of his gifts.... The narrative shifts, sometimes seamlessly, from the present (that is, 1989–91) to the characters' youth in the Third Reich, their lives in East Germany and back to the revolutions of 1848, the wars of national unification of 1866–67 and the first decades of Bismarck's German empire.... Despite its autumnal hues, this is not a book without hope and affirmation, which Grass finds in literature's enduring power to overcome the obdurate power of time, history and death." —*The New York Times Book Review*

"Grass's novel is a perfect instrument for tracing echoes and parallels across German writing and history... no other German novelist could have pulled off such a feat." —*The Economist*

"Not as brash as *The Tin Drum* but just as long and complex, this novel shows that the 1999 Noble laureate still can build a sweeping theme out of wry, telling details. Grass's ruminative yet accessible look at reunification through the eyes of two 70-year-old East Germans touches on the full history of Germany and spares no one in the process." —*Library Journal* (Best Books of 2000)

"Mr. Grass explores what reunification means not only politically but also socially and personally. And when he takes a look at reunification's impact on families long divided by the Wall, he shows why he's widely regarded as one of our most gifted living writers."
—*The Dallas Morning News*

"On the heels of Grass's Nobel Prize comes this graceful English version of his most recent and most controversial fiction: a potent criticism of German reunification, cast in the semi-fabulistic form employed so memorably in mega-novels like *The Tin Drum* and *The Flounder....* A rich, troubling work that offers incontrovertible evidence of this great writer's undiminished artistry, integrity, and passion."
—*Kirkus Reviews* (starred)

"*Too Far Afield* fulfills the great novelist's duty to voice subversive truth—the Swedish Academy properly cited this work in 1999 among Grass' acts of literary courage.... *Too Far Afield* burnishes Grass' reputation by meeting a prime requirement of enduring literature: It imagines a world, virtually parallel to the one we know, then sprinkles it with just enough novelistic glitter to illuminate insights grown dull through long repetition. The dead, if they're watching Grass, are surely doing so with respect."
—*The Philadelphia Inquirer*

"One can't help being impressed by Grass's literary ambition and the breadth of his latest effort." —*Memphis Commercial Appeal*

"The psychologically complex portrayal of a man's gradual relinquishing of his social position in order to keep his spirit intact is more than enough to maintain a reader's passion in the work."
—*Publishers Weekly* (starred)

Too Far Afield

ALSO BY GÜNTER GRASS

The Tin Drum

Cat and Mouse

Dog Years

The Plebians Rehearse the Uprising

Four Plays

Speak Out!

Local Anaesthetic

From the Diary of a Snail

Inmarypraise

In the Egg and Other Poems

The Flounder

The Meeting at Telgte

Headbirths

Drawings and Words 1954–1977

On Writing and Politics 1967–1983

Etchings and Words 1972–1982

The Rat

Show Your Tongue

Two States—One Nation?

The Call of the Toad

Novemberland

My Century

Günter Grass

Too Far Afield

Translated from the German
by Krishna Winston

A Harvest Book
A Helen and Kurt Wolff Book
Harcourt, Inc.
SAN DIEGO   NEW YORK   LONDON

For Ute, who has a thing for F——

© Steidl Verlag, Gottingen 1995
English translation copyright © 2000 by Harcourt, Inc.

All rights reserved. No part of this publication may be reproduced or
transmitted in any form or by any means, electronic or mechanical,
including photocopy, recording,
or any information storage and retrieval system,
without permission in writing from the publisher.

Requests for permission to make copies of any part
of the work should be mailed to the following address:
Permissions Department, Harcourt, Inc.,
6277 Sea Harbor Drive, Orlando, Florida 32887-6777.

This is a translation of *Ein weites Feld*

www.harcourt.com

Library of Congress Cataloging-in-Publication Data
Grass, Günter, 1927–
[Weites Feld. English]
Too far afield/Günter Grass; translated from the German
by Krishna Winston.—1st ed.
p. cm.
"A Helen and Kurt Wolff book."
ISBN 0-15-100230-4
ISBN 0-15-601416-5 (pbk.)
I. Winston, Krishna. II. Title.
PT2613.R338 W453413 2000
833'.914—dc21   00-029586

Text set in New Baskerville
Designed by Lori McThomas Buley

Printed in the United States of America

First Harvest edition 2001
A C E G I K J H F D B

"... und Briest sagte ruhig:
'Ach, Luise, laß ... das ist ein zu weites Feld.'"

"... and Briest said quietly,
'Oh, Luise, let it be ... that takes us too far afield.'"

—T. F. (1819–1898), *Effi Briest*

A Brief Chronology

1598	French king Henry of Navarre issues Edict of Nantes, guaranteeing the Huguenots (French Protestants) freedom to practice their religion, with some restrictions
1685	Louis XIV revokes Edict of Nantes; 200,000 Huguenots flee, chiefly to Holland and Prussia. Frederick William, "the Great Elector," welcomes the Huguenots with Edict of Prussia
1713–1740	Frederick William I, "the Soldier King," rules Prussia
1740–1786	Frederick II, "the Great," as king of Prussia, introduces modern agricultural methods, promotes manufacturing, undertakes revision of Prussian law
1756–1763	Seven Years' War. Prussia allies itself with England against coalition of Russia, Austria, and France; disunity within the coalition preserves Prussia from a resounding defeat
1764	Prussia allies itself with Russia against Poland
1772	First partition of Poland; Prussia receives West Prussia
1793	Second partition of Poland; Prussia receives Posen
1795	Third partition of Poland; Prussia receives New Silesia and Warsaw
1806	Napoleon invades German territory, establishes Confederation of the Rhine
1807	Napoleon marches into Berlin
1812	Emancipation Edict gives Jews equal rights as citizens of Prussia
1813–1815	Napoleonic Wars ("Wars of Liberation"). Napoleon defeated at Leipzig and Waterloo; Confederation of the Rhine dissolved

1815–1816	Congress of Vienna redraws European borders. Prussia's territory is extended as far as the Rhineland and Westphalia
1818	Prussian territory becomes a single customs union
1819	Assassination in Prussia of August von Kotzebue, anti-liberal playwright and spy for Russia, by a student, leading to Carlsbad Decrees, which ban student fraternities, call for persecution of "demagogues" (influential philosophers with liberal views), and impose censorship. Birth of "the Immortal" in Neuruppin
1830	July Revolution in France
1834	Prussia leads the way to establishment of the German Customs Union
1848	Revolutionary unrest in France extends to Germany. Barricades thrown up in Berlin. King Frederick William IV promises a national convention to establish a constitution. National Convention is dissolved by the military, and a constitution is imposed from above. Otto von Bismarck participates in founding of first conservative party
1849	National Convention in Frankfurt promulgates a constitution and elects Prussian king as emperor. Frederick William IV declines; National Convention is dissolved
1858–1888	William I. Bismarck becomes prime minister, unifies German territory through three wars (see following)
1864	War against Denmark; Prussia gains Schleswig and Holstein
1866	War against Austria; Prussia victorious in Battle of Königgrätz. Dissolution of German Confederation. Hanover, Kurhessen, Frankfurt, and Schleswig-Holstein ceded to Prussia
1869	Social Democratic Labor Party founded by August Bebel and Karl Liebknecht
1870–1871	Franco-Prussian War. In January 1871 Prussian king becomes kaiser, overseeing the second German empire, in which Prussia plays dominant role. Prussian prime minister, Bismarck, becomes Reich chancellor
1878–1890	Bismarck pushes through the Anti-Socialist Laws, banning the socialist press and party organizations
1888	Frederick III dies after a reign of only 99 days
1888–1918	William II becomes kaiser of Germany
1890	William II dismisses Bismarck. Anti-Socialist Laws are not

extended. "Free People's Stage," the first workers' theater, established in Berlin

1914–1918	World War I
1918	The Immortal dies in Berlin
1918	Uprising in Prussia; William II abdicates. Prussia becomes a republic
1918	9 November: First German parliamentary republic proclaimed, hours before a socialist republic is to be declared. Under Treaty of Versailles, Prussia loses territory, including Danzig and much of Posen
1920	Weimar Constitution is adopted
1923	9 November: Hitler and his followers stage Beer Hall Putsch in Munich. Some followers are killed; Hitler is sentenced to prison, where he writes *Mein Kampf*
1933	Reich President von Hindenburg names Hitler Reich chancellor; book-burning on the Opernplatz in Berlin
1938	9 November: Nazis orchestrate allegedly spontaneous "Kristallnacht," in which synagogues and Jewish shops and residences are attacked all over Germany
1939–1945	World War II
1942	At Wannsee Conference, held in SS-occupied villa on Berlin's Wannsee, Nazis commit themselves to the "Final Solution of the Jewish Question"
1944	20 July: Conspiracy to assassinate Hitler fails. Mass arrests are followed by executions of conspirators at Plötzensee Prison in Berlin
1946	Allies divide Germany and Berlin into four sectors
1948	France, Britain, and the United States decide to create an independent German state out of their occupation sectors. Berlin Airlift is undertaken when the Soviet Union blockades West Berlin
1949	Blockade is lifted after 11 months. Separate states are established in east and west Germany. East Berlin becomes capital of the German Democratic Republic
1953	17 June: Workers' uprising in East Berlin is put down by Soviet tanks
1956	At 20th Party Congress in February, Nikita Khrushchev criticizes abuses of Stalin's rule. Hungarian Revolution is crushed by the Soviet Union

1961	13 August: Berlin Wall is erected to prevent exodus of East German trained professionals and young people through West Berlin
1968	Prague Spring briefly raises hopes in Eastern Europe for political and cultural liberalization, before Soviet Union intervenes in August. Leftist-inspired student uprisings occur in West Germany, France, and the United States
1969	Willy Brandt, mayor of West Berlin, becomes first Social Democratic chancellor of the Federal Republic
1970	Brandt initiates his *Ostpolitik,* building relations with Soviet-dominated Eastern Europe
1974	Brandt resigns when it is discovered that a member of his personal staff, Günther Guillaume, is an East German spy
1976	East German regime deprives political folksinger Wolf Biermann of his citizenship while he is on authorized concert tour in West Germany
1980	Lech Walesa founds "Solidarity," an independent trade union alliance in Poland
1984	East German writer Uwe Johnson (b. 1934) is found dead of heart failure in his cottage in Sheerness-on-Sea, Kent, England
1989	Summer: "Monday demonstrations" in Leipzig spread unrest throughout the GDR, leading to fall of the Erich Honecker regime in early November. 9 November: Günter Schabowski, district secretary for (East) Berlin, declares the Berlin Wall open
1990	April: Social Democrat Oskar Lafontaine, candidate for the federal chancellorship, is stabbed by mentally ill woman who hid her knife in a bouquet; the wounds are life-threatening. 3 October: the two Germanys are officially united, under the West German constitution

BOOK 1

1

The Wallpeckers

We, the Archives staff, called him Fonty; actually many people who crossed his path would say things like "So, Fonty, heard from Friedlaender recently? And how's your fine daughter? There's a rumor afoot, and not just in Prenzlberg, that Mete's tying the knot. Any truth to it, Fonty?"

Even his day-and-night-shadow would exclaim, "No, no, Fonty! That happened years before the revolutionary stirrings; you recited something Scottish to your Tunnel brethren, some ballad, by flickering lamplight..."

Granted: it sounds silly, like Honni or Gorbi, but Fonty was the name. Even his insistence on the final *y* earns our stamp of Huguenot authenticity.

His papers identified him as Theo Wuttke, but because he was born in Neuruppin, and on the next-to-last day of 1919 to boot, there was enough material to mirror the vicissitudes of a botched life—one to which fame came late, but which was then memorialized in a statue that we, echoing Fonty's words, called "the seated bronze."

Undaunted by death and the grave, inspired, rather, by the larger-than-life statue, before which he had often stood as a child, alone or sometimes holding his father's hand, young Wuttke—be it as a schoolboy, be it in Luftwaffe blue—had so convincingly lived in his distinguished forerunner's footsteps that the elderly Wuttke, to whom the appellation "Fonty" had stuck since the beginning of his lecture tours for the Cultural Union, had a wealth of quotations on tap, all of them so apt that in various conversational circles he could pass for their originator.

He spoke of "my too well-known pear ballad," of "my Grete Minde and her conflagration," and time and again he referred to Effi as his "daughter of the ether." Dubslav von Stechlin and ash-blond Lene Nimptsch, cameo-faced Mathilde and wan Stine, along with the Widow Pittelkow, fainthearted Briest, Schach, who made a fool of himself, Opitz the forester, the ailing Cécile—they were his cast of characters. Not with a wink, but with convincing knowledge of past suffering, he would complain of the drudgery he had endured as an apothecary at the time of the Revolution of '48, then his ordeal as permanent secretary to the Prussian Academy of the Arts—"It's left me colossally limp and a nervous wreck"—going on to describe the crisis that almost landed him in a mental hospital. He was what he said he was, and those who called him Fonty took him at his word, so long as he chatted away, applying the razor-sharp wit of his anecdotes to the glory and decline of Branden-burg's gentry.

He made gloomy afternoons pass in a flash. As soon as he took his seat in the visitors' chair, he would fire his first salvo. He had everything at his fingertips, even the mistakes made by his biogra-phers, whom he would call, when the mood struck him, "the dis-tinguished obliterators of my earthly traces." And when it became clear to him that we were using him as a model, he exclaimed, "Ut-terly *ridicule* to portray me as 'hovering serenely above the fray'!"

Often he put us, his "diligent footnote slaves," to shame. He could reel off passages from the correspondence archived here—for instance, letters to and from his daughter—so word-perfectly that it must have given him enormous pleasure to continue this correspondence with undiminished epistolary fervor; in fact, right after the opening of the Berlin Wall, he penned a "Mete letter" to Martha Wuttke, who was off at the spa in Thale, in the Harz Moun-tains, for the sake of her frayed nerves: "...Mama, of course, had to open the floodgates, whereas to me, events like this, which insist on their own momentousness, mean little or nothing. I prefer to place my money on striking details, for instance those young fel-lows, among them exotic foreign types, the so-called wallpickers or wallpeckers, engaged in the undoubtedly welcome demolition of this multikilometer achievement, an activity in part iconoclastic, in part entrepreneurial; they're going at this pan-German artwork with hammer and chisel, so that everyone—and there is no shortage of customers—may have his very own souvenir...."

We have hereby indicated the bygone time in which we breathe life into Theo Wuttke, whom everyone called Fonty. The same applies to his day-and-night-shadow: Ludwig Hoftaller, whose previous incarnation appeared on the Western literary market in 1986 under the title *Tallhover,* began his career in the early forties of the previous century, but he by no means ceased his operations at the point where his biographer laid down his pen. Starting in the mid-fifties of our own century, we find him continuing to draw on his overextended memory, allegedly because of the many cases that remained unresolved, of which the Fonty case was one.

It was Hoftaller, then, who went to the Zoological Garden railroad station to redeem the tin coin of the East for silver, so that by the grace of Western currency he could invite his subject to a seventieth-birthday celebration: "Can't pass it over in silence. This calls for a libation."

"Like giving me the next-to-last rites."

Fonty recalled for his trusty old companion a situation that had arisen when a similar invitation had been issued by that venerable paper the *Vossische Zeitung.* A letter had come from Editor in Chief Stephany. But a hundred years ago the recipient had likewise shown little enthusiasm in his promptly posted reply: "Anyone can live to seventy if he has a tolerably sound stomach."

Not until Hoftaller promised that unlike the *Vossische* he would not gather close to four hundred of Berlin's notables, but would keep the circle of celebrants small, and even, if desired, restrict it to the elderly birthday child and himself, bringer of aid and comfort in sticky situations—not until then did Fonty relent: "Would rather huddle in my sofa corner—with seventy around the bend, a fellow's entitled to that—but if it must be, it must be something special."

Hoftaller suggested the Gull on Maternstrasse, a favorite haunt of artists. Next he submitted for his guest's consideration the

Ganymed, on Schiffbauerdamm. Kempinski's in the western part of the city was not to Fonty's liking either. "Have something Scottish in mind," he said. "Not with bagpipes, necessarily, but it really should be approximately Scottish...."

We, the footnote slaves still here in the Archives, caution ourselves not to rush ahead to the seventieth-birthday celebration. We must back up to report on a walk that took place several weeks earlier, in mid-December. It was only after they had been walking for some time that Hoftaller found an opportunity to broach the subject of the impending birthday and how it should be marked.

On a frost-crackling winter day, with a watery blue sky spanning the now undivided city, on 17 December, when the hitherto leading party was convening in Dynamo Hall to adopt an assumed name, on a Sunday when folks large and small were out and about, two figures entered the picture at the corner of Otto-Grotewohl-Strasse and Leipziger Strasse, striding toward their destination: tall and thin beside short and squat. The outlines of their hats and coats, of dark felt and gray wool blend, converged into a unit that grew larger and larger as it approached. The paired phenomenon seemed unstoppable. Already they had reached the Ministries Building, or, more precisely, had passed its northern flank. Sometimes the tall half gesticulated, sometimes the short half. Then both would wax eloquent, arms poking out of wide sleeves, the one with a long, swinging gait, the other with short, bustling steps. Their puffs of breath coalesced into little white clouds and floated off. Thus they remained ahead of and behind one another, yet grown together into a single form. Since this yoked pair never managed to march in step, it looked as though flickering silhouettes were moving across the screen. The silent film unreeled in the direction of Potsdamer Platz, where a gap as wide as a street had been opened in the wall once erected to secure a border. Traffic could now flow in both directions; yet this crossing point was so jammed that it allowed only a fitful stream of cars to pass from one half of the city to the other, between two worlds, Berlin and Berlin.

They crossed a strip that for many decades had been a barren no-man's-land and was now a vacant lot, panting for developers; already the first projects were underway, each striving to outdo the others; already the building boom was breaking out; already land prices were on the rise.

Fonty liked such walks, especially now that the Tiergarten's paths in the West gave him room to roam. Only now did his walking stick enter the picture. Hoftaller, tagging along, stickless but with bulging briefcase, was known to have in his possession, in addition to his thermos and sandwich box, a collapsible umbrella, which expanded to normal size at the touch of a button.

In its perfunctorily guarded condition, the Wall offered good buys on both sides of the opening. After a moment's hesitation they decided to strike out to the right, toward the Brandenburg Gate. Metal on stone: from far off they had already heard the peck-peck-peck. A sound like that carries especially far in the cold.

The wallpeckers were standing or kneeling cheek by jowl. Those working as teams took turns. Some wore gloves against the cold. With hammer and chisel, or in many cases only a cobblestone or screwdriver, they were chipping away at this bulwark, whose western side, during the final years of its existence, had been upgraded by anonymous artists to an artwork, with loud colors and hard-edged contours. It did not stint with symbols; it spat out quotations, shouted, accused, and as recently as yesterday had still seemed relevant.

Here and there the Wall already looked porous, exposing its innards: reinforcing rods that would soon begin to rust. And the vast expanse of the mural, stretching for many kilometers and still being extended until just before the end, was now yielding museum-ready swatches no bigger than the palm of a hand, wild daubs in tiny fragments: imagination set free, protest set in stone.

All this was supposed to serve as a form of historic preservation. Off to one side of the hammering, in what might be described as the second wave of dismantling by the West, business was already booming. Spread out on pieces of cloth or newspaper lay massive chunks or tiny chips. Some merchants were offering three to five fragments, none bigger than a one-mark coin, in Ziploc bags. Particularly impressive were larger details that had been painstakingly chiseled out of the mural—for instance, a monster's head with an eye in the middle of the forehead, or a seven-fingered hand—pieces with a hefty asking price, and yet there was no dearth of buyers, especially since a dated certificate—"Authentic Berlin Wall"—came with every souvenir.

Fonty, who could never let anything pass without comment, exclaimed, "Better in parts than whole!" Because he had only lightweight Eastern coin jingling in his pocket, a youthful merchant who had apparently already turned a tidy profit that day presented him with a gift: three penny-sized shards, whose traces of color— black clashing with yellow on the first, then blue jostling red, and finally three shades of green—were supposed to make them valuable: "Here you go, Gramps, only for my Eastern customers, and because it's Sunday."

Initially his day-and-night-shadow did not want to observe this popular pastime, which, although illegal, was tolerated on both sides of the Wall; Fonty had to tug him by the sleeve. He actually had to drag his companion past the arrayed pictures. No, this was not Hoftaller's cup of tea. This Wall art did not suit his taste at all; yet now he found himself forced to contemplate something that had always horrified him. "Chaos!" he exclaimed. "Sheer chaos!"

They reached a spot where the tightly joined concrete slabs with their crowning bulge allowed them to see into the East—a hole recently chopped in the border-guarding structure. There they stopped and gazed through the open wedge, from whose jagged edges reinforcing rods projected, some bent back, some hacksawed off. They saw the safety strip, the dog run, the wide field of fire. They stared across the death strip, saw the watchtowers.

From the other side, Fonty was visible through the widened fissure from his chest up. Next to him, Hoftaller entered the picture from the shoulders up: two men in hats. Had a soldier still been on patrol, out of the Eastern mania for security, he could have snapped a serviceable mug shot of the two for the files.

For a time they gazed in silence through the wedge-shaped crack, yet each kept his rush of memories to himself. Finally Hoftaller remarked, "Makes me sad, even though we've been predicting this dismantling ever since the *Sputnik Magazine* affair. It'll be published some day, our report on the collapse of government order. Wasn't taken seriously. The leading comrades refused to pay attention. No news to me: deafness always sets in when things start to fall apart. . . ."

More in a whisper than out loud, Hoftaller vented his professional dismay through the gap in the Wall. Suddenly he giggled. A fit of long-suppressed giggling, now dammed up to the point of overflowing, shook him. And Fonty, who had to stoop to hear his whispering, caught the words "Funny, actually. Typical case of power-weariness. Center can't hold. But wouldn't it be nice to know who unlocked the gate? I mean, who slipped Comrade Schabowski that script? Who let him use the PA system? Bellowing out sentence after sentence . . . 'From this day forward. . . .' Well, Fonty, who do you think remembered the formula 'Open Sesame!'? Who do you think? No wonder the West practically had a stroke when the ninth of November rolled around and tens of thousands—what am I saying?—hundreds of thousands came over, on foot and in their Trabis. They were dumbfounded, they called the whole thing crazy . . . crazy! But that's how it is when you've been whining for years, 'Tear down this Wall. . . .' Well, Wuttke, who was it who said 'Go ahead, swallow us up'? Has the penny dropped?"

Fonty, who had stood in silence, his head cocked, did not want to play Twenty Questions. He countered with a question of his own: "So where were *you* the day they sealed this place up, smack down the middle?"

They were still there, framed by the gaping hole that caught them at chest and shoulder level: a dual portrait. Because they both enjoyed submitting to the ritual of well-rehearsed interrogations, we assume that Fonty knew in advance the elements that would go into Hoftaller's litany: "Due to counterrevolutionary tendencies . . . Without the support of the Soviet Union . . . Purges soon followed . . ."

He enumerated neglected security measures, spoke of disappointments. He was still deploring gaps in the system. The seventeenth of June 1953 stuck in his craw: "Was punitively reassigned. Sat around at the State Archives. Slid into a depression. Had to get out of the Workers' and Peasants' State. Not a real crisis of values, though. No, Tallhover didn't call it quits, just changed sides, was in demand over there. Unfortunately, my biographer didn't want to believe that; he misjudged the freedom they take for granted in the West, saw me as boxed in, cooked up a death wish for me—as though my kind could ever call it quits. Our work, Fonty, it never ends!"

Hoftaller had stopped whispering. He was no longer posed in front of the gaping slab structure that forced confessions out of people, but was once more walking with bustling steps past the interminable mural. Now he sounded jovial: "All right to talk about it now: was received with open arms. Obviously: my special expertise! Went by a reversed name over there. I was on the books as 'Revolat.' The change of scenery did me a world of good. But no shortage of disappointments on the other side either. My warnings regarding the sealing of the border fell on deaf ears. I showed the agency in Cologne photocopies—bills of lading that documented all the large-scale purchases, stuff needed for the Peace Wall: cement, reinforcing rods, tons of barbed wire. Finally tipped off Pullach. Pointless. Eventually, when it was already too late, Agent Revolat realized that the West wanted the Wall, too. Made everything easier. For both sides. Even the Yanks were all for it. Couldn't get much more secure than that. And now it's coming down!"

"Nothing lasts forever," Fonty comforted him. In the diagonal rays of afternoon sunlight they strode and bustled toward the Gate. The sun, already low in the sky, cast a paired shadow on the Wall's painted surface. The shadow followed them, mimicking their gestures as they talked, hands poking out of wide coat sleeves. They assessed the recent breach in security either as a risk—"They'll want it back one day"—or as a "colossal gain": "Better without than with!"

A few wallpeckers were still practicing their handiwork with grim determination, as if for piece wages. One elderly gentleman was even using a rechargeable electric drill. He was wearing safety goggles and ear protectors. Children were watching him.

Lots of folks were out and about—Turks, too. Young couples were having their pictures taken with a backdrop, so that later, much later, they would be able to remember. Here long-separated families were meeting. Travelers from afar stared in wonder. Groups of Japanese. A Bavarian in lederhosen. A cheerful but not rowdy mood. And hovering over everything, that sound usually attributed to the woodpecker.

Two Western mounted policemen came toward them and proceeded to ignore the Sunday work scene. Hoftaller snapped to attention, but in response to his question as to the legality of the destructive goings-on, one of the patrolmen responded like a true Berliner, "It's not permitted, but it's sure as hell not prohibited either."

To comfort his day-and-night-shadow, Fonty gave him the three penny-sized chips off the Wall. And as he stowed the fragments with their one-sided color in his change purse, like pieces of evidence, Hoftaller continued his narrative: "At any rate, after August '61 it was time for a change again. My old department came calling. Didn't wait to be asked twice. You know, of course, that I was always pan-German...."

Their ritual had nothing more to offer. They continued along the Wall in silence. Their breath floated away, carrying only puffs of steam. One step after the other, and then the yoke-fellows were standing in the crush by the Brandenburg Gate, or rather by the wide curve of the concrete barricade where the world had been waiting for weeks, the camera teams poised to capture its demolition.

Massive, as if built for the ages. Only the embarrassment of several border guards, hanging around rather than showing their presence on the bulge atop the bastion, wide enough here to walk on, proclaimed the bulwark's imminent downfall. This much we are sure of: Hoftaller viewed the scene with mixed emotions. But Fonty was enjoying the sideshow to this Sunday idyll. Young women and children held up by their mothers were offering the soldiers flowers, cigarettes, oranges, chocolate bars, and of course bananas, the tropical fruit of the month. And wonder of wonders, these men in uniform, so quick on the draw until just the other day, allowed themselves to be showered with gifts. They even accepted Western bubbly.

And here—in the midst of the festive Sunday mood, surrounded by onlookers, including young folks shouting "Open the

Gate!" more beer-happily than aggressively, in that time of rapidly rising expectations and round tables, of big words and petty reservations, in that hour of toppled bosses and first hasty deals, on a windless, clear December day in the year '89, when stock in the word "unification" was rising hourly—Fonty suddenly began to declaim, at the top of his voice and refusing to be shushed by Hoftaller, that long poem entitled "Victory March" that had been printed on 16 June 1871 in the Berlin *Foreigners' and Classified Advertising Gazette,* specifically to mark the victorious end of the campaign against France and the founding of the Reich, as well as the coronation of the Prussian king as kaiser of all Germans, a poem whose many stanzas paraded all the returning regiments through the streets, the guard at the head of the procession—"And with them march, in closed ranks and coupled, / Their sabers in hand, fame and honor doubled, / The pale-blue riders of Mars la Tour, / But half of their number left, no more..."—and marched them through the Brandenburg Gate, then up the splendid avenue Unter den Linden in lockstep: "Prussians and Hessians in a welter of colors, / Also Bavarians and Badians and many others, / Saxons, Swabians, tall ones and short, / Spiked helmets, plain helmets, of caps every sort...."

This was not the first such celebration, for after Prussia's victories over Denmark and Austria, the first wars of unification, there had likewise been parades and rhymed victory marches—an eagerness to pay tribute, of which Fonty's first stanza had reminded the throng of onlookers before the barricade: "And here they come, the third time of late, / Marching through the magnificent gate; / The Kaiser ahead, the sun high in the skies, / Everyone laughs, and everyone cries...."

Despite the vigor with which he declaimed these verses, here out in the open the voice of the former lecturer for the Cultural Union, Theo Wuttke, whom everyone called Fonty, did not carry very far. Only a few laughed, and none wept for joy, and the applause remained sparse when, in the final stanza, he brought the victory parade to a close before the statue of the second Frederick, the monument to "old Fritz."

The echo of the verses had hardly died away when the two extracted themselves from the crowd. Fonty seemed in a hurry, and Hoftaller's voice hastened after him: "I assume this is your contribution to the coming unification? Nice spit and polish. Still have it in my ear: 'Down the Linden thunder their feet, / Prussia's Germany feels the beat....'"

"No need to remind me! Done for the money, and precious little of that..."

"There's more in the same genre, sometimes ramrod-straight, sometimes sloppily rhymed."

"Alas. But there's better stuff, too—and that will last!"

Meanwhile they were making their way along under trees stiff with cold. Their conversation on the value of occasional poetry soon petered out; we offer no comment. They walked along in strides of differing lengths, encountering Sunday strollers heading for the gate. The pair's destination was the Victory Column, whose crowning angel glittered in the evening sun, a freshly gilded monstrosity. Drawn to the intersection known as the Great Star, they struck out straight across the Tiergarten, which lured them to branch off to the left to Queen Luise Bridge, the Amazon, and Rousseau Island with its park benches. But they stayed on course. They barely slowed their steps at the Soviet War Memorial.

Seen from the Brandenburg Gate, they grew smaller and smaller. An unmatched pair. Now gesticulating again: one with his walking stick, which he called "my Brandenburg hiking staff," the other with the stubby fingers of his right hand, for in his left he was carrying the bulging briefcase. A silent film. One striding, the other bustling along. Seen from the Great Star, they were making headway. Coat merged with coat into a single silhouette, although they had not linked arms. At the end of the grand parade route, the two disappeared for a moment, for they had to duck under the ceaseless flow of traffic around the Victory Column, crossing by way of a tunnel built expressly for pedestrians.

Now that the couple is gone, we are tempted to utter some choice words about this Berlin landmark, which managed to preserve its full height through both world wars, but Fonty took the words out of our mouths, for they had barely surfaced and posted themselves at the base of the lofty column, which measured sixty-six meters to the tip of the victory pennant, when an opportunity arose for digressions into the field of history, undertaken either with the help of many-stanza'd poems or on the basis of a memory that reached back to Sedan Day and even farther down the steps of time.

It sounded as if they had been there for the unveiling of the column on 2 September 1873. At the time, the figure of Borussia as Victoria stood on a pedestal on Königsplatz, known today as Platz der Republik. Shortly before the beginning of the Second World War she was moved, on orders from on high, from the square in front of the Reichstag to the Great Star.

A relief mounted on the column at eye level is said to be worth seeing. It celebrates the wars of unification, one victory after another. Here a curly-headed lad brings his father his gun, as his mother bids the father farewell with an embrace; there members of the *landsturm* have just fixed their bayonets. A bugler blows the attack signal. The fighting men rush forward over the fallen.

They paced off the pedestal. Because the column—with its red Swedish granite, all-around metal casting, and crowning goddess of victory—had been damaged in the last, so wretchedly lost, war, Hoftaller's finger pointed out pockmarks everywhere; impossible to tell whether shrapnel had found its final resting place there, or, at the very end, grenade fragments. The breast of an infantryman pierced. Helmets chopped in half. This hand has only three fingers. Here a dragoon's cast-iron horse is missing its right front leg, there a headless captain storms headlong into the fray, at Düppel, or perhaps at Gravelotte. Looking dismayed, Hoftaller calculated the bottom line. He counted fifty and more direct hits, not including the damage to the granite base. But when it came to victories and the span of Prussia's history, Fonty had more to offer than the monument did.

He cited Count Schwerin and his flag, old Derfflinger, Generals Zieten and Seydlitz, and reeled off all the battles from Fehrbellin to Hohenfriedberg to Zorndorf. He was about to pin Prussia's victories and occasional defeats to the standards of various famous regiments and present Frederick the Great's fabled old troopers in terse quotations—"Herr Seydlitz smashes bottlenecks / When he settles down to drink; / His foes would fear for their own necks / If they could pause to think...." Suddenly Fonty—who was already gathering breath for the ballad, and had raised his arms, the walking stick in one hand—was nudged from behind.

A little boy, whom he later described to us as freckled, voiced a bold request like the little Berliner he was: "Say, sir, could you tie my shoelace? Don't know how yet. I'm only five, see."

Laying his hiking staff on the ground, Fonty bent down and tied, as requested, the right shoelace in a bow.

"There," he said, "that'll hold."

"I'll do it myself next time!" the boy exclaimed and ran off to join the other boys, who were kicking a football around the Victory Column—as the traffic circled incessantly.

"There you have it," Fonty said, "that's what really matters. Battles, victories, Sedan and Königgrätz, are null and void. All balderdash, *ridicule*! German unification, pure speculation! But tying your first shoelace, that's what counts."

Hoftaller stood there in his down-at-heels buckled shoes. He did not wish to be reminded.

Then the sun was gone. They ducked under the Great Star again by way of the pedestrian tunnel, walked down the long street renamed to commemorate the seventeenth of June, and headed for the Tiergarten S-Bahn station. Two old men deep in conversation. Their gestures more angular now. They no longer cast a shadow.

And only now, not prematurely, but barely two weeks before the round-numbered anniversary, did Hoftaller begin to lay the groundwork for his invitation: "Not an everyday occurrence, you know, turning seventy."

"For a celebration I'm a few tons short of conviction."

"It'll come, don't worry."

"And where from, if I may ask?"

"How about Friedrichsstrasse station, the Mitropa Restaurant? Used to be an agents' rendezvous. A historic venue, so to speak."

Fonty assumed a subversively noncommittal expression and lengthened his stride.

Short-legged though Hoftaller was, he kept close to his side: "No big deal, I promise. Just a pleasant little gathering..."

"Even so, it would cause too much uproar, as usual. . . . Besides, I can't bear..."

"Am I to take that as a refusal?"

"Am I to take it I have no choice?"

"Not to be too obvious: I think so!"

"And if I still refuse..."

"Would be a pity, Wuttke. You know—we can do this the hard way."

They covered the last stretch in silence. Fonty stopped in his tracks just before the S-Bahn. Now no longer looking subversive, he raised his right arm as if winding up for a speech, then lowered it again and remarked, gazing out over Hoftaller's head, "What did old Yorck say at Laon when the Russian troops failed to advance?— 'Ah, well, we must make the best of it.'"

This expression, as we archivists know, appears in a letter to Heinrich Jacobi, the Brandenburg pastor, where we also find the following passage: "I shall write nothing to you of my 'anniversary celebration.' The conservative papers, which pretty much have me down as a 'turncoat'—but do not really make much ado about it— hardly mentioned the subject. . . ."

2

Approximately Scottish

The letter to Pastor Jacobi continued: "I was feted colossally—and then again not at all. Modern Berlin has made an idol of me; but the old Prussia I have celebrated for a good forty years—in war chronicles, biographies, portrayals of the province and its people, folk ballads—the 'old Prussia' hardly lifted a finger, leaving everything (as in many respects) to the Jews."

Fonty came to see us a few days before Christmas to inspect the original of this letter, dated 23 January 1890, which does mention that Minister von Gossler, his old patron, "personally saved the day." "It's not the round-the-world trip it used to be, even if you can't get all the way to Potsdam by S-Bahn yet. But it's all right by bus!"

This he exclaimed while still on the threshold, handing the ladies, as was his custom whenever he called on us, a bouquet—or, rather, three sprigs of mistletoe with their pale, glassy berries. This, he assured us, was an English custom, still alive in Wales as well, and all the way up to the Orkneys. "Please take note," he said, and then, in English, "That's British Christmas."

When we asked how we could help him, Fonty responded with a question: "Why does a person live to seventy?" and then mentioned letters, including the one to Jacobi, all of which revolved around the birthday marked on 30 December 1889, and its official observance at the very start of the new year, on 4 January, at the English House Restaurant on Mohrenstrasse.

He did not stay long and took no notes. While reading he hardly so much as nodded or raised his eyebrows. In addition to the letters, he had us bring him several newspaper reports celebrating the graybeard; these he merely skimmed—even Eloge's tribute in the *Vossische Zeitung*. His interest extended no farther. Before leaving us, the Archives, that is, and after chatting a bit—about current events, among them the bloody unrest in Romania—he reverted once more to that birthday of one hundred years earlier. He was contemplating his own impending birthday, and not without trepidation, in fact almost fearfully: "Quite unnecessary, all this. Really not necessary."

And for that reason he turned down the celebration Hoftaller had wanted. Nothing went as planned. At the Friedrichstrasse station, where Hoftaller had reserved a table at the Mitropa Restaurant, no sense of festivity materialized. Although the three or four young men invited to gather around the aged birthday boy turned up on time, the guest of honor kept them waiting.

Presumably these were denizens of that part of town known as Prenzlauer Berg—never mind their names. Apparently there was no one in this particular group who would make the headlines later on when the files were opened for inspection. Since then much has been forgotten, if not forgiven; some matters stayed alive quite a while on the strength of suspicion alone. But at the time one could still speak without concern of "the young talents" Hoftaller had invited.

There were plenty to choose from. And Fonty, who always found it appropriate to compare budding talents with other poets who had recited their verses long ago in Leipzig's Herwegh Society or in Berlin's Tunnel Over the Spree, would liken the Prenzlberg talents to Wolfsohn, Lepel, or Heyse, especially in retrospective reference to revolutionary times. In his eyes, it was just a hop, skip, and a jump from the Metternich era before '48 to the Monday demonstrations in '89. In turn, since the young poets never made fun of the old gentleman as eccentric old Theo Wuttke but esteemed him as Fonty, they had no difficulty distilling his entertaining, time-defying understanding of politics and literature into dogmatic pronouncements or a witticism. In part they placed him on a pedestal; in part they reduced him to a mascot. And because he seemed to stand aloof from all contemporary happenings, the task had fallen to him of mediating between these young writers, with their anarchistic allures, and the ever-concerned Stasi.

We can merely surmise that the toleration practiced for years toward the restless and sometimes cheeky Prenzlberg scene could be ascribed not only to the innocuousness of its literary products, but also to Fonty. His reports—well-informed, to be sure, and characteristically sardonic—and his witty thumbnail sketches of the individuals in question satisfied the wishes of his day-and-night-shadow, and thereby cut down to medium size these young geniuses who had aroused the state's suspicions. They were suitably grateful, and viewed him as their guardian angel. But wasn't it natural that he, the mascot of their presumably conspiratorial gatherings, should in turn be the object of clandestine reports—reports by none other than the young talents themselves? These complementary reflections were part and parcel of a system based on mutually assured deterrence and preventive vigilance, a system to which someone like Hoftaller always remained indebted, even after its downfall.

The guests waiting for the guest of honor were crestfallen. Restlessness set in. We can imagine the concerned conversations. Hoftaller had to smooth the waters.

"What's up with Fonty?"

"Probably went astray in the Tiergarten."

"He's usually the soul of punctuality."

"Our friend will get here, no question. He said he'd come."

"We could be here all night. He's over there in Freedomland, blowing his welcome money."

"To him we're history, just like his Tunnel pals...."

"Listen! They're taking him out for a stroll over there in the West, around the Wannsee or whatever. A gala evening for Fonty on his seventieth—at the Literary Colloquium's Sandwerder Villa. And some bow-tied Western bigwig is spouting off on immortality: now available in throwaway form...."

"Bullshit! If anyone's making speeches, it's Fonty—something about Jenny Treibel. How she and her clan experience the fall of the Wall. And the profits to be made off it."

"Or they're passing him around from one talk show to another. You know how he likes to gab. We won't be seeing him again."

"I'll get him for you!" Hoftaller said, or could have said. "Our Fonty will have to admit where he belongs, even on his birthday."

With this final word he rapped his knuckles on the table and promised to return "posthaste" with the fugitive. He treated the young talents to a meal—meat loaf with fried egg and sautéd potatoes—another round of beer, and, as if for consolation, chasers of Nordhäuser schnapps.

"All right then, we'll stick around till he shows up."

Then Hoftaller must have set out, equipped for the search with his ever-alert nose. He took the S-Bahn straight to the Zoo station. And since he had always included the Western part of the city in his system of coordinates, he didn't have to feel he was getting off the train in enemy territory, no matter how often he had assured Fonty that he regretted the necessary opening of the peacekeeping border. Even to us he remarked, "Someday they'll wish they had that bulwark back, the Wall."

In those days, when world events were coming hot on each other's heels, when shots were flying not just in Romania, but also, as if to even the score, at the Panama Canal—in those days, the Zoological Garden station, or rather its drafty vestibule, as far in as the Heine Bookstore, had become one big *bureau de change*. Whole bundles of Eastern currency passed easily from hand to hand, while small sums in Western D-marks were harder to come by. The unstable conversion rate of 10.5 to 11 Eastern marks to one Western mark kept the trade lively, the more so now that many inhabitants of the previously cordoned-off half of the city were busy making themselves solvent for a visit to the other half of town: at the very least, they had to have enough for a movie and a beer.

And amidst the traders and their changing clientele stood a contented observer in a winter overcoat, with hat, scarf, and walking stick. Surrounded by the constantly enlivened swirl of transactions, Fonty remained rooted to the spot, enjoying the spectacle, which wasn't costing him a penny. He suspected sleight of hand, glimpsed fingers signaling in the din of voices, witnessed conflict that was quickly quashed. The swarm of traders and their mobile clientele astonished him. These envoys from a multiethnic land seemed harbingers of heavier traffic to come. Like merchants in an exotic bazaar, the traders intoned the fluctuating exchange rate of the bargain-basement currency in changing pitches—in whispers here, in loud accents there. At times the Berlin mouthworks predominated, in tones ranging from satiny-smooth to abrasive. But no one stepped forward to declare the station a temple and drive the money changers out.

In addition to the D-mark, American dollars and Swedish crowns were the currency of the day. You could get rubled for pennies. Fonty saw fingers fat and skinny counting bundles of notes with equal agility. Everywhere calculators were in use. Someone was wearing a hat with three foreign banknotes clipped to the brim with clothespins. Fonty saw plastic bags, rucksacks, and spanking new attaché cases—all stuffed to bursting—change owners rapidly, some of them more than once, as if following the rules of a universally tolerated ritual. Then a voice addressed him from behind.

"Your young friends have been waiting for over an hour. They're awfully disappointed, bitterly disappointed."

"Must be uninvited guests."

"Was supposed to be a surprise..."

"But if there's to be any celebrating, then *à mon gout,* if you please."

"Where then? I hope you aren't thinking of staying at this happy hour—the police could shut it down in no time flat."

"If I were in the money, I'd know exactly where to go."

Forced to foot the bill, the host turned to the nearest bidder and exchanged a quantity of Eastern banknotes for the round sum of fifty Western marks. But not until they found themselves on the equally busy square outside the station did Fonty name the establishment of his choice: Not on the Kurfürstendamm or on Savigny-Platz would they celebrate the round-numbered birthday of the Immortal and his epigone, but right nearby, not far from the Zoo's elephant house, directly across from the station, in a small place sandwiched between an electronics store and a *café dansant.* It called attention to itself with a neon sign. "Still don't think my seventy

years call for celebrating. But a hundred seventy—that's something. Don't expect me to put a festive face on it, though."

So this was what Fonty meant by "approximately Scottish." At Mc-
Donald's, things were hopping as usual. But they managed to find
a table for two, opposite the long counter with its six registers,
where they could see into the other dining areas. They marked
their seats with their hats, and Fonty added his walking stick. Hoftaller kept his briefcase with him at all times.

They joined the line at register 5 and had to make up their
minds quickly, because the cashier's expectant expression demanded their order, and fast. Like the rest of the staff at McDonald's, she was wearing a green visored cap, and below it a green
necktie with her green-and-white shirt. The name tag on the left,
above her heart, revealed that her name was Sarah Picht.

After scanning the easy-to-read menu board, complete with
prices, Fonty decided that the Super Royale TS was too expensive
at 5.95 West marks, and chose a cheeseburger and an order of
Chicken McNuggets instead. Hoftaller was having a hard time de-
ciding between the value meal—Hamburger Royale TS, medium
fries, medium drink, all for just 7.75—and a plain McRib, but then
settled on the double-decker hamburger called BigMäc and a
strawberry-flavored shake on the side. Fonty wanted a cup of Coca-
Cola. He made his choices as decisively as if McDonald's had always
been his regular haunt. He advised Hoftaller, who would be paying
for both of them, to order another item: French fries with mustard. When the trays were shoved across the counter to them, he
was entitled to two sauces for the Chicken McNuggets—one of
them known as "barbecue." Sarah Picht was already smiling at the
customers next in line.

They sat down, and each munched away. If one of them was
having some trouble with his BigMäc, the other was dunking his
nuggets like a pro, first in one sauce, then in the other. They
shared the French fries. They ate for a while in silence, looking
past each other, although they were seated on opposite sides of the
table. Soda and shake were dwindling. The straws were not real

straw, of course, but the meat was 100 percent beef, guaranteed, the breaded nuggets real chicken. Since they did not know what to do with their hats, they parked them on their heads. Fonty's walking stick or cane was hooked over the back of his seat. They heard themselves and others chewing.

Customers ordering takeout on the run kept the place hopping: lots of young folk, but also money changers from across the way. Yet the two of them were not the only ones advanced in years, or senior citizens, as they are called in the West. A scattering of rather bedraggled old men and women who usually hung around the station were in there trying to warm up; sometimes they even had enough for an order of fries. With so many customers, you might have expected a lot of noise, but the sound in all the dining areas was subdued.

Fonty did not wait to finish his cheeseburger and McNuggets. Between one bite and the next, still chewing, he delivered his commentary on the place: the brass lighting fixtures over the counter, the screened-off grill area, for whose offerings the price lists spoke eloquently—for example, a fish filet sandwich for 3.30 marks. He pointed out the double-humped company logo, which had conditioned people everywhere to salivate. It was even stamped on Sarah Picht's green visor. The name it stood for transported Fonty to far-off parts and back again. It was a name that had conquered the West and was now conquering the world, the name whose initial had come to symbolize salvation.

With the burden of time upon him, Fonty began with the historical MacDonalds and their mortal enemies, the Campbells. He described, as if he had been there in person, one frosty morning in February in the year 1692 when more than a hundred kilted members of the Campbell clan had fallen upon the still drowsy Mac-Donalds and almost wiped out the entire clan. And from the massacre of Glencoe, he turned to the present-day business empires of these two Scottish families, now household names known around the globe: "Hard to believe, Hoftaller, hard to believe. Scattered over the world are roughly thirteen million Campbells and at least three million MacDonalds. Just think of it. . . ."

And he was on his way, setting out from the ancestral home of the fast-food giant, Armedale Castle: rambles in the Scottish highlands beyond the Tweed. To the witches' rendezvous in the fog. On the trail of Mary Stuart, he proposed hikes from one ruined castle to the next. He knew every clan by name, could describe the tartan down to its subtlest hues. Fonty had nothing but Scotland on his mind. And that is why, after polishing off the last bits of chicken and rinsing them down with the last sip of Coca-Cola, he was drawn across the windswept heath, along deep, blue-black lochs, into the cascading stanzas of those almost interminable ballads, most of which the Immortal had read in the Tunnel Over the Spree to versifying lieutenants and assessors, his Tunnel brethren. Verses that Fonty described as "my somewhat musty ballads." Sometimes he spoke of "our ballads," as if they represented a collaborative effort.

The murderous quarrel between the MacDonalds and the Campbells led seamlessly to the feud between the Douglas brothers and King James. He began with snatches from the James songs, as though trying to get off to a running start—"The Duncans are coming, the Donalds are coming..."—then moved on to his cycle of romances on Mary Stuart—"Holyrood lies waste and still, / Nocturnal winds blow cold and shrill..."—wandered then through the cycle on the beauteous Rosamunde—"Woodstock Castle's an ancient place / From good King Alfred's day"—suddenly joined the cobblers of Selkirk, returned to Melrose Abbey to call up once more the Phersons, the Kenzies, the Leans, and the Menzies from the King James songs—"And Jack and Tom and Bobby come / And carry the bluebell away, away...." But then, after the pretty maid of Inverness had led him onto the bloody Drummossie Moor, after Lord Bothwell had slain the king, Fonty suddenly leaped to his feet, as if responding to a summons. He stood at attention, snatched his hat from his head, holding it off to one side, swept the table clean with his left hand, pushing away boxes, sauce containers, paper cups, straws, and all. Breathing evenly and in a clear voice, which, though sometimes shaky, rang out above all the other sounds, he launched into his "Archibald Douglas." Stanza followed stanza. Rhyme dovetailed with rhyme. He recited the ballad, a German schoolbook favorite, from its well-known opening lines—

"This life I've borne for seven years / I can no longer bear..."—through the old laird's request—"King James, oh, look on me with grace..."—and the king's harsh refusal—"A Douglas, stood he before my eyes, / A man undone would be..."—down to the conciliatory, still moving, though historically inaccurate final prospect: "Mount, friend, and we'll ride to Linlithgow, / And thou shalt ride by my side, / And there we shall fish and hunt with joy, / As we did in days gone by." Twenty-three stanzas without a slip of the tongue, without a stumble, full of expression. Even the dramatic climax— "And draw thy sword and strike me well, / Let me die without delay"—came across as soul-stirring. Yet this was no actor performing; this was the voice of the Immortal himself.

No wonder every table had fallen silent. No one dared bite into a cheeseburger, a BigMäc. Fonty was rewarded with applause. All clapped, young and old. The counter girl, Sarah Picht, shouted from behind the register: "Cool! Hey, that was cool!"

His performance had filled the crowd with such enthusiasm that two squealing girls sitting nearby jumped up, teetered toward him, and showered him with hugs and kisses like maniacs. And a beer-bloated skinhead, stuffed into much rivet-studded leather, punched Fonty in the shoulder: "Hey, old man, that was heavy!"'

The employees and the regulars were struck dumb with amazement. Nothing like this had ever happened at McDonald's before.

We archivists would have been less amazed. For years Fonty had been reciting "his" ballads for us, sometimes on request, more often unbidden, as well as occasional verse, such as "On the Steps of Sanssouci," written for Menzel's seventieth birthday, or even short dedicatory verses intended for Wolfsohn, Zöllner, Heyse. Unforgettable to the older ones among us was one dreary afternoon in the late autumn of '61, when we were all feeling that although the necessary measures taken recently along our border had created a protective shield between us and the enemy of the working class, they had also locked us in. Around that time—it must have been November—Fonty came to visit, now obliged to take a wearisome detour, and tried to comfort us with the late ballad "John Maynard," about the ship afire on Lake Erie: "And a wailing is heard, 'Where are we? Ho?' / And still fifteen minutes to Buffalo."

In those days, when Dr. Schobess was still director of the Archives, the heroic act of rescue performed by the helmsman— "In fire and smoke he kept his grasp, / Held fast to the rudder to his very last gasp"—may have helped us hope for better times, for freer speech, for a relaxation of restrictions; at any rate, Fonty managed to cheer us up a bit. And just as he had brought some sparkle to the grayness of everyday socialism, his shower of stanzas lifted spirits at McDonald's. Even Hoftaller applauded.

Afterward the two of them just sat there by themselves. Customers came, customers went. Fonty's hat was back on his head. Since the paper cups were empty, Hoftaller fetched Fonty another Coke, and a milkshake for himself, this time vanilla-flavored. At the counter the staff had changed: no more Sarah Picht. The two men sucked sparingly, meanwhile letting their thoughts hasten down the stairs of time. Having finally arrived at himself, Fonty said, "I read that ballad in the Tunnel to some acclaim, but under another title: 'The Exile.'"

Hoftaller remembered: "That was two years after your first trip to London, undertaken on our orders. Long after the revolutionary stirrings. To be precise: on 3 December 1854. We'd put you on the payroll again at the Central Press Office. Not easy to find a livelihood for the ex-apothecary. Merckel gave his blessing, of course. By then you were past needing surveillance. Friend Lepel had driven the last crazy Forty-eighter notions out of the would-be revolutionary. An aristocrat, like most of the Tunnel brothers—liberal yet conscious of class distinctions. At any rate, the amiably disposed young lord refused to put up with any more Herweghesque epic follies. That's how you fell in with the Prussians! And they liked the skillful rhymes you came up with for that tearjerker— 'Count Douglas took the reins in hand / And rode by his monarch's side...'—which still flows from your lips, as we've just heard. Nice job, Fonty, nice job! But that wasn't your first hit at Sunday gatherings in tobacco and coffee shops! Your stuff was well received even before that. One after the other, a whole procession of Prussian cutthroats—'Old Derffling,' 'Old Zieten,' 'Seydlitz,' 'Schwerin,' and 'Keith'—earned applause that they even recorded in the minutes. But in the so-called Pre-March Period you often fell flat on your face. At least so long as you were taking your cue from Herwegh—whom we had under surveillance, you know. Your adaptations of English working-class poets: a crashing failure! For instance, 'The Drinker,' recited in the Tunnel on 30 June '43. You probably meant to shake up your friend Lepel and the whole versifying gentry with that one. Portrait of a plastered proletarian. Not the kind of thing people wanted to hear. Nor was 'The Prisoner's Dream': 'The people are poor! Oh, why? Pray tell / Why the mighty squander their earthly goods!' Embarrassing, Fonty. I can still hear it, all that blatant social protest. Herwegh wasn't the only one I had under surveillance, you know. My biographer didn't think it worth mentioning, but I covered the Herwegh epigones, too. One of them was a twenty-two-year-old fop who hadn't taken his pharmacist's exam yet, but was already busy plotting against the authorities in Leipzig and elsewhere. Want me to jog your memory? 'Oh, the walls have ears to hear us, / And I hardly know your name, / And t'would be my sure undoing / Should the police o'erhear my game....' That was in '42. Wolfsohn, Max Müller, Blum, Jellinek were the friends who heard you recite. You traded them all for Lepel when things got too hot. And he was the one who took you to the reactionary Tunnel. National liberals—that's what those gentlemen Merckel and Kugler called themselves. Gave themselves fancy names; forgive me for laughing! Xenophon and Aristophanes, and Petrarch, of course. Friend Lepel was Schenkendorf. As a *nom de club* they assigned you Lafontaine, almost too close for comfort. Then the arch-reactionary editor of the *Kreuzzeitung*, a long-forgotten big cheese named Hesekiel, got me in, too, or smuggled me in, I should say. Though I'm more a passive admirer of literature, they decided to honor me with the name of a stone-dead playwright in the Russian service. And why not? His comedies weren't that bad, really. By the way, I was just being born when a student was stabbing Kotzebue to death. Without that assassination we probably wouldn't have had the Carlsbad Decrees, the demagogue trials, God knows what else. But that takes us 'too far afield,' as your Briest always said. On the whole they liked you in the Tunnel, in spite of those proletarian poems. Didn't young Heyse, who admired you, come up with a fitting couplet? Think I still know it by heart: 'This one's a true poet, as can clearly be heard. / Silentium, brothers, let Lafontaine have a word.'"

Fonty smiled over what remained of his Coca-Cola, but there was a touch of jaundice to his cheerful demeanor. With complete presence of mind and completely in the past, he remarked, "Yes, Hoftaller, you were superb as Tallhover. Even without the reference to Kotzebue, I remember your Nogoodnik tactics all too well. But my usually well-organized memory can't come up with any references to your reciting anything in rhyme, not even one of your police reports. Menzel, whom we called 'Rubens,' actually dashed off a few drawings, despite the tobacco smoke and guttering light, thereby immortalizing some of those versesmiths who've since been forgotten. But unfortunately you're not preserved on paper anywhere. Though it's possible that people of your ilk were systematically deleted from the sketchbooks. Cover your tracks. Stay under cover. Duck out of sight—that's your modus operandi."

Hoftaller was sitting with an empty cup before him, but he kept trying to capture the last dregs of vanilla flavoring. Again and again he felt the need to wipe his mouth with a fresh paper napkin. Fonty picked up the thread, recalling for him the fate of the members of Leipzig's Herwegh Society: "Weren't you the one who got Hermann Jellinek and Robert Blum executed by firing squad?" Hoftaller seemed to be concentrating on slurping up the last drops of milkshake, but finally exclaimed, "That's it! Not a drop left! But you're wrong, Fonty, that's a ridiculous exaggeration. I'm no bloodhound. Security was all I was concerned with. My biographer attests to that. The policies were made by others, just like today. We often didn't much care for their policies, whether under Manteuffel or during the reign of our leading comrades. Especially in the final phase—they lost their heads. What didn't we do to keep our Workers' and Peasants' State from falling apart? Why, just a little while ago you and I were having a look at the result of our efforts—it's destabilizing the enemy of the proletariat as we speak. That's the kind of thing you like, of course: wallpeckers! Just as we used to like your detention home for petty talents, the Tunnel Over the Spree! Real poets like Storm or Keller wanted nothing to do with it. Perfectly harmless, their 'clippings,' as they called the poems recited there. Even your own feeble Herwegh leavings, oozing social protest and pre-'48 revolutionary pretensions, were hardly worth reporting. Let's face it, you were in good hands there: chained to art and politically defanged. Reminds me of the Prenzlberg scene. That poets' squat turned out to be a useful detention and prevention home, too. And it got by just fine without aristocrats and the Prussian heritage—a typical product of our classless society."

Fonty said not a word. His face revealed nothing but the weariness of age. Now Hoftaller, too, fell silent. His face likewise revealed nothing but a watchfulness that had been around far longer than a hundred years. Since both of them were born in '19, Fonty had recently presented Hoftaller with a gift for his seventieth, a gift whose suitability Tallhover's biographer had already pointed out. And in fact the birthday child was delighted with it—a jigsaw puzzle, a genuine Western product. It portrayed a large filling station, complete in every detail. Spooled back a century, it could easily have represented a Prussian parade ground, Tempelhof Field, likewise complete in every detail; that was how timelessly Hoftaller had turned seventy on 23 March. It had taken Fonty a while to get around to buying the filling-station puzzle, which he found in the toy department of the Kaufhaus des Westens, affectionately known as KaDeWe. He used the Western "welcome money" that all visitors from the East received in those days, and delivered the gift ex post facto to his ancient day-and-night-shadow.

Because they were now sitting across from each other silent and dry, Hoftaller fetched a third Coca-Cola and yet another milkshake; this one promised chocolate flavor. They jokingly raised their paper cups and snapped to attention. Fonty said, "Frightfully true! We did want to drink a toast, even if I'm still in no mood for celebrating. Whose seventieth shall it be, then?"

The present birthday had already passed its climax. Fonty casually distanced himself from the whole thing: "Had a rather leisurely breakfast this morning—Red Riding Hood Champagne with the wife and daughter—about all I could handle, given my lack of enthusiasm for festivities. Besides, Mete is still under the weather, despite having been to Thale for the cure...." Not until Hoftaller bridged the centuries—"Well, then, let's celebrate the big hoopla, when the *Vossische Zeitung* threw the postbirthday gala on 4 January"—could they quickly switch costumes and sets. McDonald's and its customers grew fuzzy, receded far into the distance.

The event had been catered by the kaiser's chef, no less. The invitations went out in the name of the Literary Society and the Immortal's friends—Brahm, Stephany, Schlenther. As the longtime support of the theater critic who occupied corner seat 23 at the Royal Theater, the *Vossische* wanted to make a splash. All of Berlin was invited.

But Fonty found fault with the lavishness: it had been a dubious pleasure. The number of his enemies had doubled, tripled. The invitees, more than four hundred of them, had concentrated on polishing off the costly food and even costlier wines. Wherever one looked, medal-studded chests and entire jewelry collections on display. The whole scene overlaid with a rising and falling din, a mélange of mindless chatter and braggadocio. All colossally stuffy and self-important. "Nothing more ridiculous than receptions!" And when, near the end of this feeding-at-the-trough, his "Archibald Douglas" had been recited, the majority of the guests had revealed their ignorance by clapping before it was finished. Enough to make one want to sink through the floor.

"I must say, as far as the audience went, McDonald's just now was better than the English House that evening!" Fonty exclaimed. "But what am I saying? Your Royal Spyship, Earl of Eavesdrop, was there, of course, invited or not. Most graciously casting a shadow, the gentleman was in a position to observe how, during the entire recitation, I stared down in embarrassment at the lone radish on my plate, as if chicken shit had been deposited there. Most distressing, the whole affair! Should have turned down the invitation when Stephany, kind as always, broached it. Should have said no and much obliged, like my Emilie, and Mete, too, who weren't present, allegedly for lack of suitable attire, but more likely because my dear wife was terrified I might misbehave again in polite society and say something that would embarrass her. Wrote back to Stephany therefore, 'Must I describe the womenfolk to you? Mine are deathly afraid I'll make a fool of myself. No woman ever shakes off this fear; it must be something about us....' "

Fonty stared at the empty food containers, as if in their midst he could still see the lone radish from that 4 January 1890. The year of the young kaiser, who, cocky from the beginning, gave his chancellor his walking papers. And the previous year, the triumph of Naturalism with the Free Stage, to whose director the Immortal had recommended a play, Gerhart Hauptmann's first, *Before Sunrise*: "So, Tallhover, does that ring a bell? End of October '89? At the Lessing Theater: world premiere. Wrote two quite enthusiastic reviews in quick succession for the *Vossische*. And Emilie immediately began to worry again that I might go overboard where Hauptmann and his gang of anarchistic realists were concerned. I tended to get too involved, she said. At any rate, even you couldn't stop the advance of this de-clichéd Ibsen. And then, when the German Theater staged *The Weavers,* with Liebknecht and other Socialists in orchestra seats, it was curtains for Bismarck's anti-Socialist laws, which still didn't put you fellows out of work. There was no end to the snoopery. Still goes on today. Probably under contract for eternity. Take a bow, Tallhover! Take a bow, Hoftaller!"

Now Fonty's day-and-night-shadow stared at the empty containers, the paper cups, and the crushed paper napkins, as if crumpled among them were that playbill announcing the premiere of Hauptmann's *Weavers.* That had been more than a scandal. So much breached security. So many missed opportunities for injunctions, so many counterinsurgency laws that had died in parliament, so many reports submitted and advance warnings issued, only to be ignored—from the days of the kaiser to those of the Stasi. So much effort in vain.

"Let's go!" Hoftaller exclaimed. "Our young poets are still waiting at the Mitropa."

"Don't think I could tolerate any more blather."

"You aren't saying you want to back out?"

"No more festivities. My plate's full!"

"Come, come. You're not going to get around a little post-birthday celebration...."

"And if I say no?"

"I wouldn't advise that."

As he stood up, hesitating as if in the grip of inner indecision, Fonty commented, "By the way, I'd be interested to know whose payroll you'll be on when our Workers' and Peasants' State goes belly-up." Then he sighed and leaned on his walking stick: "No doubt there'll be no end to this. Why does a person live to seventy?"

They left some trash behind when they headed for the door, squeezing past fully occupied tables. Suddenly Fonty stopped, as if on command. By the counter, with its six cash registers and the green-capped cashiers, was a woman his own age staring at him. She kept closing her right eye as though trying to wink. Her stone-gray hair was plaited in two braids like Gretel's in the fairy tale, and tied with wrinkled propeller bows, one red, one blue. The braids stuck out from her head. Around her scrawny neck she wore a necklace of dried rose hips, looped around twice. She was wrapped in a blanket, into which slits had been cut for her arms. Gloves riddled with holes. Her feet in wooden clogs. The half-filled bag next to her revealed nothing about its bulky contents. A leather belt, the Red Army's emblem on its buckle, held the blanket in place. And with the two gloves, through whose holes her fingers poked, she was holding a BigMäc, which, because she had teeth missing, she was having trouble eating. But as she took a bite, then chomped with her gums, her eye was winking constantly, until finally Fonty winked at her too, several times.

She must have looked familiar to him. One of his old witches—Buschen from *Stechlin*, say, or Mother Jeschke from *Under the Pear Tree*. No, we would place our money on Hoppenmarieken from *Before the Storm*. She would have been able to wink that way.

Hoftaller dragged him toward the exit. "Come on, Fonty. We've seen more than enough of McDonald's."

Outside a gusty wind was blowing. It was not far to the station across the street. As they walked, they again formed a pair. The two coats interwoven. Seen from behind, they offered a harmonious image. And they leaned in unison into the wind blowing from the northwest.

3

From Liebermann's Hand

What did they look like? Up to this point, just shadowy outlines: coats, two hats, one with a high, dented crown, the other flat. To begin with this single shot means bypassing Hoftaller, at least for the moment, for he looked like no one in particular, or anyone, whereas Fonty made a strong impression, his distinguished countenance offering a likeness of a well-known personage.

Indeed, the resemblance was so close that you would have thought: It's him; for if immortality—or, put another way, the survival of an idea after its embodiment's death—can be said to have a describable appearance, his features, whether in profile or frontal view, certainly reproduced those of the Immortal. On the S-Bahn or on Unter den Linden, at the Gendarmenmarkt or amidst the Friedrichstrasse's bustle, people turned to look at him. Passersby were startled, hesitated. It made you want to doff your hat—he seemed like such a relic.

Several staff members from the Archives who had known Fonty since the fifties still insist that every time he appeared it was in a new edition. But not until that year when the Wall fell and he had entered everyone's field of vision as a speaker on Alexanderplatz did he begin to resemble the well-known 1896 lithograph by Max Liebermann. This work was based on several chalk sketches, in which the artist gave particular emphasis to the nose and eyes; yet the length of the slightly hooked nose can already be found in a relatively early pencil drawing that depicts the future novelist at thirty-five.

Hugo von Blomberg, a friend of the Immortal's from the Tunnel Over the Spree, sketched him between the two trips to England. It was shortly after the death of his third son. Writing to Theodor Storm, who had fled to Prussia when Denmark invaded Schleswig but was not enjoying his exile in Potsdam, the Immortal said of the little son he had lost, "Besides the father and mother, the burial was attended by a drunken hearse driver and the setting sun...."

This sketch by Blomberg, done in late Biedermeier style, shows a foppishly attired and fashionably coifed young man. It confirms the testimony of older staff members at the Archives, according to which Fonty sported a flowing mane and sideburns tending toward muttonchops when he appeared as an itinerant lecturer for the Cultural Union in the fifties. He must have made a vivid impression on the women in the audience, for one of these ladies, now of mature years, still raves about the "bourgeois decadence yet seductive elegance" of his performances in Oranienburg or Rheinsberg, wherever she happened to have seen him: "Really, he enchanted us."

That Liebermann lithograph, published in the journal *Pan*, offers nothing of the sort. In his 1910 essay, Thomas Mann, still young but, since the appearance of *Buddenbrooks,* already a highly successful writer, compares the "wan, sickly-visionary, and slightly insipid visage of those years" to the "splendid, firm old man's face, gazing kindly and cheerfully at the viewer," and asserts: "Around his toothless mouth, over which the bushy white mustache droops, plays the serene smile of a confirmed rationalist." It would seem that he, too, compared the Blomberg sketch to the Liebermann lithograph, where the almost white hair looks deliberately unkempt, forming a fuzzy mass around the mouth and ears and sparsely covering the head.

This same deficiency gave Fonty a high forehead. He, too, still had plenty of hair over his ears and down his neck. He, too, liked to let the silvery strands fall untidily over his collar. And his muttonchops were luxuriant, going from curly to fluffy as they worked their way down past his earlobes.

Certainly not twirled in Wilhelmine fashion, in fact hardly brushed, his mustache hung like an untrimmed hedge over his upper lip, concealing, along with the corners of his mouth, the frequent twitching caused by delicate nerves. The eyes framed by expressively curved lids. The gaze knowing and—albeit watery—firmly fixed on whatever he happened to be looking at, whether persons or objects. An observer and a listener, who found society gossip and ghost stories from old Brandenburg equally believable, no matter how firmly anchored he seemed in solid reality. He gazes out at us challengingly and a bit condescendingly.

His chin more on the anxious side, soft and receding. And the insufficiently developed willpower in the lower part of his face, which did not escape Liebermann's notice when he drew him, could hint at Fonty's frequently demonstrated weakness: Whether with Tallhover or Hoftaller, he caved in under pressure. We see evidence of this propensity in his erstwhile involvements with the censors during his employment in the Central Press Office, whether in Berlin or later in London; likewise in Fonty's assiduous service in the Ministries Building. Further phases of his posthumously continued biography—for instance, the many war bulletins from reoccupied France and all the lectures delivered for the Cultural Union—served the interests of the regime in power at the time. No matter how willing we are today to give him the benefit of the doubt for some choices, while condemning others as regrettable accommodation, his attempts during the years following the Eleventh Central Committee Congress to broaden the attitude toward literature by alluding to Prussian censorship were perceived at the time as evidence of death-defying courage. They got him in trouble. And trouble was something he always brought on himself, in one incarnation or the other.

Hoftaller's appearance is not documented in a single photograph, let alone a drawing. And since Tallhover's biographer has given us nothing we could cite, not even a shadowy phantom, we can only hope that if we capture Fonty's solid image, his day-and-night-shadow will also come into the picture, albeit merely by implication.

Whenever Fonty visited the Archives, he brought to life for us a description in rhyme that Paul Heyse had been inspired to compose by a reading in the literary gathering known as the Tunnel Over the Spree: "The door flew open and into the hall, / With the floating gait of a youthful god, / Strode the late guest with a spirited nod, / Greeted the company with eyes ablaze, / Tossed back his head as he met our gaze. . . ." The Immortal was capable of such an entrance and gait even at an advanced age. We have already seen that next to Hoftaller, whose steps had the tentative character of an old man's, as if always on uncertain terrain, Fonty's springy stride became particularly noticeable: a youth in an elderly husk.

That was how we saw Theo Wuttke. And Julius Rodenberg, who had encountered the near-octogenarian "in the Tiergarten, at dusk, with his historic thick scarf around his neck," noted elsewhere, "Despite the hoary mustache, he still makes the youthful impression that will live on. . . ."

Here immortality is addressed directly; and Fonty dedicated himself to the task of living on. For that reason we not only took him at his words, which spewed forth in the form of both casual chat and pages of gleeful quotation in prose and verse, but also were inspired, by the sight of him, with this conviction: He is not pretending. He is a genuine stand-in. He lives on.

Any doubts we might have had were banished by his appearance. And the many others who crossed his path also felt certain they were in the presence of the original, even when they tried to take refuge in irony, greeting him with the usual "So, Fonty, out and about again?"

Thus it happened that in the seventies, when several painters were expressing political protest through equivocal parables, the painter Heisig, or one of Heisig's many pupils, used him as a model for a mural. An expressionist variation on Socialist Realism, the work portrayed a gathering of important writers. Fonty found himself positioned as a surrogate between Georg Herwegh and the young Gerhart Hauptmann. There, in uncharacteristic harmony, were the brothers Mann, also an unmistakable Brecht, a stern Anna Seghers, and of course Johannes R. Becher. A few literary types of only contemporary interest were also incorporated into the group portrait.

The commission for this impetuous, riotously colorful painting is supposed to have come from the Cultural Union. One of its cultural centers, perhaps the new one in Bitterfeld, needed decoration for its walls. Unfortunately, this work, like so many others, foundered on the objections of the leading comrades. Self-criticism had to be practiced, the ideological platform invoked, the mural painted over, the preliminary sketches handed in at a government collection point—all because Heisig, or one of his pupils, had filled out this assemblage of literary giants with representatives from what was known as the "camp of imperialist warmongers."

Try to imagine: The face of Franz Kafka is said to have peeped out of a gap just big enough for a head; someone claimed to recognize, in a bearded apparition floating above the gathering, that cult figure of bourgeois decadence, Sigmund Freud; a few contemporaries insist they spotted Uwe Johnson, destined to die too young, gazing speculatively over the shoulder of the surrogate Fonty, who held a quill pen at the ready; ranked behind Seghers was Christa Wolf, recently reprimanded by the Party collective; at the feet of Heine, described as holding a slim volume of Wolf Biermann's poems, a bumptious little brat was pounding a tin drum; and, furthermore, a certain someone is supposed to have been concealed in the mural, visible only from certain angles, as in a trick picture: running here, crouching there, fossilized over there— a shadowy phantom.

Trustworthy observers asserted that one could recognize the multiple iterations of Hoftaller by his perma-smile, his persistent expression of menacing omniscience, and his obtrusive unobtrusiveness. The face attributed to him—more round than elongated—matches the reality, likewise the smile. Sandwiched in behind Herwegh, he was apparently exposed as Tallhover by a barely legible name tag on his lapel. In another part of the painting, those who saw it swore they had spied him piecing together a page from the official Party newspaper like a puzzle. The completed part spelled out the adjective *schädlich*, meaning "harmful." Since Hans-Joachim Schädlich's Tallhover biography did not appear in print until the mid-eighties, and then only in the West, it may be assumed that the painter was privy to inside information. A pity that the narrow-minded spirit of those far-off times could not tolerate the rich complexity of this mural.

As for Fonty, this much remains to be said: As a model and surviving image, he wore the scarf that Rodenberg perceived as "historic" and that the literary historian Servaes describes in the year of the Immortal's death as if it were a sacred relic: "...just off Potsdamer Platz. There he stood before the Palast-Hotel, his blue-green Scottish scarf draped loosely over his shoulders...."

This reference provides the ultimate explanation as to why, in both summer and winter, Fonty wore this flowing emblem of Celtic clan tradition—for instance, when he celebrated his seventieth birthday with Hoftaller at McDonald's and then was forced to participate in the postbirthday celebration held at the Mitropa Restaurant in the Friedrichstrasse station, a celebration that ended rather dismally. The scarf was integral to his continuation of the original's life. Yet Max Liebermann drew the seventy-six-year-old without the plaid, with a cravat tied high around his throat instead. The sittings took place either in the master's studio on Pariser Platz, or, at the subject's request, at 134C Potsdamer Strasse. In a letter dated 29 March 1896, we read, "It is fiendishly cold, and I take a chill so easily. I'd therefore make so bold as to propose that we have the final sitting at my place again...." Yet the studio sittings predominated.

He liked going there. Not only because, as he had written in a tell-all chatty letter to his daughter, who was off taking the waters for her nerves, Liebermann was "a real painter into whose hands I fall," but even more because the strain of sitting still was relieved by the painter's witty barbs, which spared neither the kaiser nor the chancellor, and certainly not the guild of court portraitists. Although the Immortal prized Menzel more, Liebermann was very much to his taste. The latter did not mince words. An echo of his method—which entailed passing through the fine-meshed sieve of his irony nouveau-riche philistines, debt-ridden lieutenants, dry-as-dust dogmatists, and privy councillors whose spouting of patriotic sentiments was not confined to Sedan Day—could still be detected in Fonty's method of scoffing at the Prussian aristocracy, although in the Immortal's tirades, injured, rejected, or unrequited love set the tone.

"The age of rhetoric is past. Now the watchword is 'Straight from the shoulder'!" he exclaimed at table to his shocked sons. The garret on Potsdamer Strasse was familiar with these sayings, whose pointedness his Emilie, ever fearful that he might overshoot the mark, likewise registered with alarm. Such "brashness" made for trouble, as had the recent commotion over his ballad "The Balinese Women of Lombok." The concluding lines, after the description of the massacre, had given offense: "Mynheer meanwhile, at his writing table / Dashes off a Christian fable." Likewise the couplet "Fellows equipped with Mauser guns / Hope to convert them to good Christians" had raised hackles in the Netherlands. He had been called a "master of the scoldsmith's art." Hairsplitting slyboots had discovered that the Dutch colonial troops were armed not with Mausers but with guns manufactured by Mannlicher, and were on a missionary expedition.

All this he recounted to Liebermann during the sitting, while he should really have been maintaining the mien of a dignified old man. "That's how the colonial masters are. No different in England, by the way. They say Christ and mean calico! Or, as my John Bull poem puts it, 'And for every hundred trouser pairs / Come fifty missionaries armed with snares....'"

He was venting pent-up anger, for a few days before this modeling session even the Foreign Office had voiced concern because his ballad, printed and reviewed in the *Börsenkurier*, had created an uproar, unleashing a battle in the press. "A full-blown diplomatic row. And of course not a word about any poetic qualities!"

Liebermann tossed off sketch after sketch, but not in silence. Now the conversation came around to Bismarck. The painter had heard that since his dismissal he was spending his days cursing all and sundry. Every time visitors came, the old man in the Sachsenwald would apparently pull out another stop on his invective organ. "And always aimed at the kaiser and his latest speeches, blunders, dispatches."

The model agreed, but was not content to let Wilhelm No. 2 be the only subject of mockery; he struck a blow for fairness, calling the Iron Chancellor "a dreadful crybaby, though certainly a gifted one."

Liebermann's elderly manservant, who was puttering around in the studio during these sharp-tongued exchanges, feared they would escalate still further, and remarked, "I'd best step out for a bit—I shouldn't be hearing all this." And Liebermann, just starting on another sketch, replied, "Yes, you run along now. I'm far from having it all off my chest."

When Fonty spoke of these sittings—for instance, among his Prenzlauer Berg friends during the postcelebration of his seventieth birthday—or responded to inquiries from us archivists, his memories had a curiously far-off resonance to them, no matter how close he brought the studio ambiance to his listeners—the skylight, pots filled with paintbrushes, palm fronds, horse studies lying about. "The latest in the art world, a wild man from Norway called Munch, came up for discussion. But for the most part politics occupied the forefront. The chap with the sulfur-yellow collar, of course. By the way, the most accurate assessment of Bismarck was penned by a Pole named Henryk Sienkiewicz; the rest is poppycock, even if it's hot off the press in *Der Spiegel*. Or the most recent abominations spewed forth by Court Chaplain Stöcker, who devours Jews for breakfast. Or Bebel's last speech in the Reichstag— simply grand the way that master turner whet his blade and went after the colonial powers till the chips flew. But when I breathe new life into certain phrases—'All interest resides with the fourth estate! The bourgeoisie is terrible, the aristocracy and the clergy utterly stale. Any new and better world has to begin with the people. They, the workers, take a fresh approach to everything. They not only have new goals, but also new ways...'—and sternly test my prophetic babbling from the mid-nineties, only a few years before my little light went out, against the imminent end of the Workers' and Peasants' State, which for forty years was called 'the first on German soil,' then the aristocracy and clergy from those days certainly come off no better, but as far as the workers are concerned, there's no more wind in those sails! Liebermann was already skeptical, and at bottom I was as well. That's equally apt today, my young friends.

Remaining skeptical is better than turning cynical. Everything's starting to slip and slide, in Russia and elsewhere, too. We can hardly guess the true dimensions of it. It's as in *Stechlin,* which was in the works from the winter of '95 on. There my Dubslav says, 'Nothing is impossible. Who would have considered the eighteenth of March possible before the eighteenth of March, possible in Berlin, that nest of dyed-in-the-wool philistines!' Or could anyone have pictured the fourth of November here, when I was called to the podium after a whole succession of frightfully clever speakers, suddenly all brave, intoxicated with freedom, and from there delivered my speech, which could not help being overcast with skepticism—'It's all fraud and sleight of hand!' It was clear to me that slogans like 'We are the people!' are inherently fickle. Change one little word, and poof! democracy was gone and unification took its place. That's how fast our most recent revolution ran out of powder...."

Fonty had often assured us, "Speaking in public has always been surpassingly dreadful for me, hence my aversion to the parliamentary system." Yet when he got into the swing of speaking, his face would flush, especially around the cheekbones. Making such appearances brought a sparkle to his eyes; his fuzzy gray hair looked windblown, his nose was bold in profile, his gaze soared out over the audience. And this is how he will be remembered by those among the five hundred thousand who were close enough to the podium on Alexanderplatz to see him. From head to toe a commanding presence, and speaking extemporaneously. "In Germany, unity has always made a hash of democracy!" he shouted into the microphone, and received applause. That is how someone should have drawn him, as a speaker, lightly tinted.

When we compare the portrait by Menzel's pupil Fritz Werner with Liebermann's sketches, it becomes obvious that Werner paid more attention to the ostentatious medal on the subject's jacket than to his head, which strikes us as somehow unfamiliar, more like that of a prosperous merchant. Fonty, who cared as little for his awards for cultural activism as the Immortal for his third-class medals, referred repeatedly to the sittings in Liebermann's studio, quoting the painter at every opportunity, especially when he was trying to stem the tide of blather from his Prenzlberg disciples or our archival reservations. "Replying to my query regarding art, the master said, 'Drawing is the art of omission!' I responded: 'But one must have sufficient material in hand to be able to omit something.'"

Whatever he said went far beyond mere quotation. His way of expressing himself, compelling yet casual, transfixed the listener. The concentrated triangle formed by his nose and eyes, the gaze, at once drawing one in and maintaining distance, with which Fonty inspected us whenever we ventured too close, held us captive. Therefore the question "What did he look like?" can be answered most tellingly by Max Liebermann's chalk drawings, which omit all extraneous detail.

"We could plaster them all over as wanted posters!" Hoftaller scoffed late that evening, after the birthday celebrations at Mc-Donald's and the Mitropa Restaurant, when he was settling scores in Tallhover fashion, and not only with the painter: "Liebermann this, Liebermann that! An important Impressionist: so what? Let's say it in plain German: Liebermann the Jew! Fine, he drew and lithographed you better than others, granted. But still, a Jew— even if he did do lovely illustrations for *Effi Briest.* And let's not forget all the other Jews you hung around with. The pen pal who supplied you with material, Friedlaender the Jew! For decades your chief publisher was Wilhelm Hertz the Jew! And when Cotta showed no interest, your first collection of lyrical outpourings was brought out by a Herr Katz—naturally. Add to that, Schottländer the Jew, who published *L'Adultera,* a novel in which the unfaithful main character, the bankrupt financial genius Rubehn, is a Jew— of course. And Rodenberg, who came from Rodenberg in Hessia and was actually named Julius Levy, who published the *Deutsche Rundschau* in his capacity as a Jew and serialized three of your thrillers, ending with *Effi Briest.* Dining with Jews, surrounded in Carlsbad by Jews, praised in the *Vossische Zeitung* by Jews, nothing but Jews. Jews underfoot everywhere. Even when your son Friedrich started a publishing company and published his father's books, not very successfully, the silent partner was a certain Fritz Theodor Cohn. A Jew like that Cohn you saw fit to toast at the end of your frivolous rhyme-smithing on your seventy-fifth birthday: 'Come along, Cohn!' And that's not all; when that family publishing house was founded, another Jew, referred to by you in certain moods as 'fat Lewy,' provided the start-up capital and thereby financed the novel *Frau Jenny Treibel,* which can't make do without its cast of Jews. Some picture! Tailor-made for a Cultural Union lecture: 'Jews in the Novels of the Immortal.' Or 'The Immortal and the Jews!' For example, that dreadful Ebba Rosenberg—you know, that scene in the burning castle in *Irretrievable,* where a Jewish veterinarian named Lissauer is mentioned but never appears. Or your Jewish commercial councillors, like Blumenthal, or the banker Bartenstein, who even rises to the rank of consul general. Or the firm of Silberstein and Isenthal, which plays just the role you'd expect at the end of *Mathilde Möhring,* when Isenthal affirms that the main character, a smart businesswoman, has an ear to the ground: 'She indisputably has some of our people's traits.' Which ones would he be referring to? Yammering in Yiddish? Talking turkey? Haggling? And in *Stechlin* it's the Hirschfelds, father and son, with their constant bickering. To the very end, Jews! A whole raft of Jews as super-Prussians! Not to forget your bosom buddies. Wasn't Brahm, your great patron, actually Abrahamson? And that Jew Theodor Wolff, who later, much later, had nowhere to go but the concentration camp, which would've been true of Liebermann's widow, too, if she hadn't put an end to it all. The pattern showed up right from the start, in your Herwegh Society days, when you were still grinding out revolutionary verse.... What was the name of that fellow from Odessa? Oh, yes, Wolfsohn was the Jew-boy's name—he had the gall to be called Wilhelm. And Moritz Lazarus was another one; his shady dealings would catch up with him later. And then heaps of letters addressed to Jews. There was no stopping you. To the very end, epistles to Friedlaender, time and again; and today you have a certain Professor Freundlich—or, rather, former comrade Freundlich—as your pen pal. In both cases, stacks of chatty letters to Jews. To one of them you confided your worries about the Prussian alliance between throne and altar, and to the other you just recently expressed your revisionist rage at the—mind if I quote you?—'monstrosity of Prussian socialism.' Friedlaender or Freundlich—with both of them you had a grand old time, slinging slander and acting the eternal turncoat. No wonder those of us in positions of responsibility weren't exactly thrilled to see you trafficking with Jews, at the expense of your once beloved Prussians, leaning on Jews, wanting to bamboozle us into acknowledging the Jews as the true sustainers of culture. It's true that one of your last letters to your daughter Martha contains the sentence, 'Time and again I am appalled at the total "Jewification" of the so-called most sacred goods of the nation.' But then you turn around and put your stamp of approval on this total Jewishizing with a paean of gratitude: '...for having the Jews in our midst. How would it look if the care of our "most sacred goods" were left to the German nobility! Foxhunts, whitewashed churches, Sunday-afternoon sermons, and *jeu....*' And accordingly your frivolous birthday poem—mighty clever, yes, yet basically perverse because it does in your reputation as a German writer once and for all—contains this snub of Prussia's nobility and an honor roll of Jews. Jews who flattered you. Jews who came to your aid. Jews you enjoyed chatting with over dinner. Jews who footed the bill. Your readers, the Jews...."

All this and more Hoftaller said on that New Year's Eve, dredging up his Tallhover memories, refusing to let himself be interrupted by Fonty; since the latter's wife and daughter were under the weather and preferred to slip into the new year in their sleep, his day-and-night-shadow had had no difficulty persuading him to come out for a "year's-end stroll": "What's the point of moping around the house!"

And Theo Wuttke, known as Fonty—of whom we now have a clear picture, thanks to Liebermann's chalk drawing—raised his eyebrows slightly when he observed that Hoftaller's appearance had changed as the two of them strolled at this late hour in their familiar configuration from Marx-Engels-Platz down Unter den Linden: His broad, dimple-generating perma-smile had been skewed by hatred into a rectangular grimace.

Fonty replied, "What was in that letter to my Mete, in what turned out, by the way, to be the last year, is still colossally true.

That's how it was, Hoftaller! Just think back, and try not to look askance. As my conversation with Professor Lasson confirmed—another Jew, you'll say—in those days the Jews were doing the Germans' cultural work for them, and in return the Germans gave them anti-Semitism. And what I wrote to my Mete about Stöcker, that Christian Socialist court chaplain, and that viper Ahlwardt remains apt—namely, that Ahlwardt was a no-good wretch—even if my fine sons and my fine son-in-law later thought they had to be considerate and delete the phrase 'no-good wretch' when they published my correspondence with the family. That probably explains why Mete refused to sign on as coeditor. Similarly, the late edition of my poetry omits that poem I wrote on the occasion of my seventy-fifth birthday. Yet it had to be said—straight from the shoulder!—that at the festivities, just as on the occasion of my seventieth, Prussia's nobility was conspicuous by its absence. As the pastor used to say from the pulpit: 'I see many who are not here.' Accordingly I rhymed as follows: 'Not a Bülow or Arnim, not a Treskow, Schlieffen, or Schlieben in sight, / Though in my books you will find them all, quite right. / But prehistoric nobles like Isaac and Abraham—Israel's patriarchs answered the call. / Kindly they placed me at the head of the line; / Who needs Itzenplitzes with supporters so fine!'"

Because Hoftaller remained silent, or was silently fumbling for his vanished perma-smile, Fonty, who had gained the upper hand by now, pressed harder, "You were there at the birthday fete, Tallhover! On assignment, no doubt. Saw you busily drawing up a list for your report. Yes, yes, Brahm, Lazarus, Wolff were all there. 'Those ending in "berg" and "heim" en masse, / Their numbers almost beyond one's grasp.' Even Liebermann, who, like me, finds such crowds distasteful, did me the honor. And of course copublisher Fritz Theodor Cohn at the side of my son Friedrich, not always the most successful of publishers. And therefore the poem I had on tap for this occasion concludes with a mannerly bow: 'To everyone present I was of note, / Each one had read some work which I wrote. / For many a year, to all I was known / And that is the main thing, so come along, Cohn!'"

In the meantime the two year's-end strollers had passed Humboldt University and the statue of horse and rider. They had already left the State Opera behind. Recent events had created a powerful undertow along Unter den Linden toward the Brandenburg Gate. This was not just any year coming to an end. And while the two now moved as though swept along by the Zeitgeist—"Go West" was a cigarette advertising slogan of the day—Tallhover, who had ducked out of sight and resurfaced as Hoftaller, retrieved his perma-smile: "Well, you're widely considered a hard-core philo-Semite, you know. Yet even your biographer Reuter has a tough time with this myth. Couldn't quite swallow that ballad 'The Jewess'—skimmed off Percy's rendition of a blood ritual: 'She had a silver dagger, / Its cut was smooth and sharp....' Was read in '52 in the Tunnel, but it took forty years for you to honor the wish of your Tunnel friend Heyse and dump the murder of that boy from the new edition of your poems. And furthermore: what a wobbly opinion on the Dreyfus Affair! All documented in those epistolary chats with your pal Friedlaender: 'Initially, of course, I was one hundred percent in agreement with Zola!' But then the other side has to be looked at. You're on the trail of a Jewish 'gazette conspiracy': '... the European press is a major Jewish force that has tried to impose its opinions on the entire world.' I swear, Fonty, that turns the well-meaning philo-Semite—'Come along, Cohn!'—into a run-of-the-mill anti-Semite. And then in '35, Himmler's *Black Corps* printed—in boldface, no less—your still apt condemnation of international Jewry. On the one hand you asserted, sweet as honey, 'From earliest childhood I have been a friend of the Jews, and myself have had only the best experiences with Jews...,' while on the other hand you didn't hesitate to make exorbitant prophecies—in one and the same letter. What you heralded on 1 December 1880 to your bosom friend and mother confessor, Mathilde von Rohr, today sounds like the final solution: '... nonetheless I have such a sense of their guilt, of their boundless presumptuousness, that not only do I say the Jews deserve a major defeat, but I even wish it on them. And it is clear to me that if they do not suffer it now and nothing changes, in times that we ourselves will of course not live to see, a great affliction will descend upon them.' How about it, Fonty? An accurate quote?"

Already they were standing in the midst of the crowd that was packed in by the open gate. Fonty aged visibly under the weight of the quotation: "We've lived them, these times. I know, Tallhover, I know. And you know even more. I'd give a great deal not to have written some of those letters, or to have written them differently. It must have been the times...."

"Forget it!" Hoftaller exclaimed.

"I'm afraid the shame will live on...."

"Oh, come off it, Fonty! We live with it. There are worse things ticking away—for instance..."

At that moment the first fireworks shot into the sky, even though it was still a good half hour to midnight. The crowd stared at the rockets, which opened up into blazing umbrellas and showers of gold; and with the rest of the crowd, the two looked heavenward. And now one could have observed how perfectly innocent Hoftaller looked as he gazed up at the sky: glowing in the reflected light, full of childlike joy. That, too, was one of his guises.

And only for the sake of these details, only to spotlight his wide, flat face, will we allow the New Year's festivities around the Brandenburg Gate to run their course, up to the stroke of midnight and a bit beyond; for as he stares into the sky, his large nostrils set into his blunt bulb of a nose are more important to us than this New Year's Eve that has ballooned into a jubilee. In those days people thought they had been handed a victory, if not achieved it themselves: It was victory rockets lighting up Hoftaller's ancient childlike face. His naive amazement at the sky bursting with rockets and this proclamation of world peace splashed across the heavens was certified by his round-arched eyebrows. And while the newly unfettered people had eyes only for the open gate, he gazed into himself, and we saw him standing there open-mouthed, showing off flawlessly aligned dentures. Stirred to the dregs in his depths by the patriotic churn, he felt unified, united, at one, and not only with himself. And he and the people waxed correspondingly raucous.

Unplanned impulsivity was still the order of the day. Everyone shouted whatever came to mind. Much pushing and shoving, because they all hoped to get a better view from a better vantage point. Yet other than the fireworks, which were intended for everyone, there was nothing to see but the gate towering mightily above them. No concrete bulge blocked the way anymore. The gate stood there in all its mass, bathed in light, promising to be open soon for taxi and bus traffic. This beloved postage-stamp motif was still crowned by the *quadriga*, the chariot that had sometimes ridden east, sometimes west. Hundreds had scrambled onto a scaffold erected next to the sprawling gate, and from there onto its flat roof; this had resulted in accidents, even fatal ones, yet not many in the crowd noticed.

Fonty stood indecisively next to his day-and-night-shadow. He wanted to leave: "I have a colossal distaste for crowds that are bound and determined to become an event."

Hoftaller grabbed him by the sleeve and shouted some nonsense like "Being there is everything!"

"Even back in '70–'71, when the victory march passed through the gate here, I felt no desire to watch. . . ."

"Yet that parade inspired a saber-rattling poem, as did every war we won."

"Was still *ridicule*, all that triumphant howling. . . ."

"Nonsense, Fonty! You recited it yourself not that long ago, verse upon verse, when we were with the wallpeckers on our Sunday stroll. . . ."

"Just a spasm of sentimentality. . . ."

Hoftaller did not spare him the brazen rhyme: "'And here they come, for the third time of late, / Marching through the magnificent gate. . . .'"

Fonty wanted none of it: "All a sham. And for the wrong occasion. It went to their heads—victory spawns stupidity! Wanted to puff themselves up bigger and bigger. Won't succeed any better this time. They're here already, the Treibels! They'll take their cut first. And that's exactly what I wrote to son Friedel when I proposed this novel as grist for his new publishing house: '. . . that's the Treibel style. Hollow, boastful, mendacious, arrogant, and hard-hearted— the quintessence of the bourgeois mentality. . . .' Naturally my Emilie was in a tizzy again. 'You're going too far! You're getting too involved!' 'You meddlesome fool!' she threw at me. 'You hothead! You child!' And me past seventy...."

Hoftaller had no chance to reply. Everywhere it was striking twelve. In East and West: twelve. On radio, on television: twelve. And at the stroke of twelve, there shot up in all directions, unfurling a magnificent display, the most expensive of the fireworks, held back with considerable restraint until that moment. Among the people gathered around the gate, champagne and beer bubbled over. The crowd jumped up and down as if just released. "Crazy!" they shouted. "Crazy!" The daring ones atop the gate's flat roof leaped into the air, wanting to go higher, higher.

And now from amid the general roar individual words emerged, sung by many voices at once. First sentimental beer-hall songs—"A day so fine, a day we'll all remember..."—but then the well-intentioned song by poor Hoffmann von Fallersleben that had had the misfortune to be promoted to the national anthem. Contagiously, compellingly, it began with the still licit third verse, "Unity, just rights, and freedom...," but then it was the fiendish first verse, banned since the last war, that was destined to point the way into the new year: *"Deutschland, Deutschland, über alles."* By this time there was hardly a breath of unity and rights and freedom; their voice was too faint to be heard.

Fonty tried to stem the tide with "good fortune's pledge," but close beside him stood Hoftaller, whose voice carried farther. His *"über alles in der Welt"* was on the winners' side. He belted it out as if freeing himself after holding back too long.

Now one could see that he was crying as he sang. Fonty saw the singing Hoftaller crying. He abandoned the third, futile verse and remarked, "Why, you're crying, Tallhover. Never would have guessed you had it in you to cry. Congratulations!"

With his gleaming round face, Hoftaller looked like a bawling child. Tears ran down his cheeks to his chin, forming beads that then dropped off. A joyful crying that ended only when the singing did. Yet no matter how passionately he sang and wept, his eyes remained uninvolved—gray, old, but not weary: Hoftaller's gaze.

Even before the crowd dispersed, Fonty and his day-and-night-shadow were in motion again: along Unter den Linden. Seen from the front they appeared as opposites, from behind as well matched, like interlocking pieces in a puzzle; yet from any angle they provided a dual portrait, made for an unending series of sketches.

4

Our Father Ad Infinitum

Here they are again, positioned in front of a grand portal that turns them both into small fry. This was no accidental effect; the building's architect had bowed to the will of a client who wore the bombastic like one of his beloved fancy-dress uniforms. In that bygone era, a Berlin ditty with the mocking refrain "Hermann is his name-o" made the rounds and was promptly banned; and the height and breadth of the portal were supposed to evoke the mighty figure alluded to in that song.

From then on, whenever anyone drew near, boldly or hesitantly, then mounted the front steps, he was first cut down to size by an architecture designed to diminish all those whom the building accommodated in the many offices and meeting rooms behind its tightly joined sandstone façades. To approach was to be humbled, whether as a ministry employee of any rank or as a visitor. Even undersecretaries pulling up in their official vehicles, even highly placed foreigners, like Italy's Count Ciano or Hungary's Admiral Horthy, had to submit to this instant minimalization, if only in the form of an inner cringing.

Thus the portal meted out leveling justice. All who approached could not help feeling degraded; only in the interior of the building, with its endless branching corridors, did the old system of rank prevail, its gradations of subordinates and superiors determining the direction in which official channels flowed.

Before experiencing such debasement and elevation, one first had to survive a dry stretch. On the side fronting the street, an open space had been punched out of the sprawling edifice, whose

52

several office wings extended far to the rear; anyone, whether in mufti or in uniform, who wanted to reach the portal had to traverse the court of honor.

Flanked by towering façades on three sides, it lay there, forming a sort of free-fire zone. After the war, when the court of honor was no longer called that, many still experienced it as oppressive, if not downright overwhelming. But as a young man Fonty had already categorized its dimensions as "too colossal." Granted that "colossal" was one of his favorite words and that he rarely hesitated to use it to characterize a thing—even a flowerpot could be "colossally cute"—we must admit that the court of honor was tailor-made for his brisk "Too colossal, Hoftaller! Won't ever get used to it. Simply too colossal!"

Only now did they draw near. From the fence that bordered the courtyard along the street, it looked as though the portal were sucking them in, indeed as if the pediment supported by eleven pillars were outgrowing its own proportions, while the two of them became gnomes of different sizes; and this dwarfing effect occurred in any season, even in the rain, when they approached under a protective umbrella.

Hoftaller, whose experience with the changed proportions had become second nature, did not suffer the same way Fonty did; the instant the latter exclaimed "Too colossal... simply too colossal," he heard his day-and-night-shadow reply: "Gives me a sense of stability. Whenever I swing by here, I know where I belong. And in times like these, which have a tendency toward instability as it is, I'm grateful to see the portal getting bigger and bigger. You should feel at home here, too, my dear Wuttke, or at least protected. A little humility can't hurt."

Fonty, still smarting from the Thousand-Year Reich, remained brusque: "It lasted only twelve years, yet it casts a colossally long shadow."

So we must run through their entrance again, shrinking the two of them and guiding them toward the growing portal. At a set number of paces before the first step, Hoftaller doffs his bashed-in hat, holding it off to one side, while Fonty keeps his on all the way up the steps and beyond. Thus they seek admittance: one full of reverence, the other full of revulsion. By comparison with others entering or leaving the building, both are special. It is true that for everyone entering or exiting on this 18 January 1990 it is a Thursday, yet for the two of them this date also marks the founding of the German Reich in 1871. Although they, like all the rest in service here, see themselves as subject to the Modrow government and the Round-Table resolutions, Fonty and Hoftaller were already acquainted personally with the endless suites of rooms in the Ministries Building when the massive complex was still new, was known as the Reich Aviation Ministry, and—like the He III, the most modern long-range bomber of the day—was of far-reaching importance; for, starting in 1935, this huge edifice, constructed in less than a year, made history. It was from here, in the flush of early victories, that Germany proclaimed itself master of the skies.

When the government district lay in ruins at the end of the Second World War, the colossus was still standing, free of visible damage, "as if spared." What a resource in a time of scarcity! Soon new masters moved into the more than two thousand offices in this building, which now lay close to the line separating the sector of the Soviet occupying power from that of the American. Soon the watchword was: Over there lies enemy territory.

Whenever the two entered—now Fonty would finally remove his high, broad-brimmed hat—both were aware that Otto-Grotewohl-Strasse, which ran past the building's long side, had been known as Wilhelmstrasse during the years of the empire, during the Weimar Republic, and as long as the Reich Aviation Ministry remained in operation. In those days uniformed guards in steel helmets had stood motionless to the right and left of the portal, their guns shouldered. Although chosen for their height, even the soldiers of the guard battalion looked like toys from a distance, against the backdrop of this piece of architecture they were guarding. And the Reichsmarschall himself suffered the same fate as his tin soldiers every time he appeared in full regalia, clutching his marshal's staff, and approached the portal across the court of honor, at which point the guards would awaken from their imposed motionlessness and present arms. For all his much-derided girth, he underwent the same degree of miniaturization that affected the adjutants in his entourage and the famous personages at his side, much-decorated flying aces, for instance; his appearances with Mölders, Galland, and Udet were filmed for the newsreels and today are stored as archival material, potentially available for playback.

And it was here that Fonty had come and gone as a soldier during the war years, with longish intervals when he was away on assignment. Often he came and went alone, rarely and only for special purposes accompanied by Hoftaller, who in those days, as Tallhover, maintained contact from his own office with Gestapo headquarters in the nearby Prinz-Albrecht-Palais—an address with a reputation, whispered only in a croaking voice.

As his biographer assures us, Tallhover was under contract during that phase of his career to the *Reichssicherheitshauptamt,* the Reich Central Security Agency. Among other things, he provided Agency 2 with a memorandum on the surveillance of churches of all denominations. From '43 on, at the behest of Agency 5, he monitored prominent prisoners in the Sachsenhausen concentration camp, including Stalin's son, held there as a prisoner of war. Yet Tallhover also found time for Airman Third Class Theodor Wuttke, assigned to his protective oversight and carried in the files as a special case.

Fonty was not yet twenty when they stuck him into uniform. Thus, when he approached the portal, it was in snappy Luftwaffe blue-gray. The visored cap perched at a cocky angle atop his longer-than-regulation hair. No one presented arms on his account, even though he entered the Reich Aviation Ministry in a not altogether insignificant capacity. Fonty in uniform was engaged as a war correspondent, and never had to expose himself to real danger, unlike the copilot in a dive bomber, the so-called Stuka. His reporting assignments did not require him to witness actual combat; instead he could take notes on French military airfields and their environs, notes that merged seamlessly with observations on art and history, generously sprinkled with literary references: Goethe and the cannonade at Valmy; Schiller and Joan of Arc; the contributions of Huguenot immigrants to German literature, including quotations from everything the Immortal had worked up. War correspondent Wuttke's accounts, enthralled by the Breton countryside, scaling the façades of French churches, focusing only obliquely on military matters, constituted such finely chiseled and enchanting mood pieces that they found readers not only in the military press but also in the culture sections of civilian papers.

It was Tallhover who had arranged this duck duty, as it was called at the time. But with the privilege went the obligation to keep an ear to the ground in officers' circles, to ferret out evidence of low troop morale, and to listen for undertones during boozy evenings in the mess hall. Thus there was ample pretext to change landscapes frequently, from air base to air base, from town to town, and to prove oneself an attentive listener and observer. Yet Theo Wuttke's supplemental reports, which were never published, must have provided little usable material for Tallhover or the Reich Central Security Agency. For Fonty tended to get caught up in anecdotes, and had no ear for conspiratorial undertones. With all this, his existence as a soldier remained out of shooting range.

Why was this soldier, first Airman Third Class, later Airman Second Class Theo Wuttke, particularly suited for this dual duty? We archivists surmise that while still a schoolboy in Neuruppin he had been prepared by the Immortal's collected works for undertaking the continuation or repetition of certain periods in that writer's career. When he filed his first articles on the occupied countries, on Denmark, for instance, the three war books came into play. In a rather long mood piece on Copenhagen, quotations from the novel *Irretrievable* seemed apt, as did episodes from the book occasioned by the war Prussia waged against Denmark in the year 1864. He worked into his otherwise peaceable account such details from the storming of the Düppel fortifications as "... on Easter Monday, when His Majesty's Regiment was caught in a hail of fire, one of the grenadiers was heard to exclaim, 'These Danes cook their Easter eggs rather hard.'"

And just as Germany's attacks on Norway and Denmark could be buried in chatty accounts of historical events, so too the 1866 war against Austria, the subject of the second war book, inspired the reports that Airman Third Class Wuttke penned from the Reich

Protectorate of Bohemia and Moravia, reports embedded in landscapes: "If we cut a segment out of the Plateau of Gitschin, its eastern side marked by the course of the Elbe between Josephstadt and Königgrätz, and its western side formed by the line stretching from Horitz to Neu Bidsow, in essence we have a square, two miles long and two miles wide, that we may describe in a broader sense as the battlefield of Königgrätz...."

We were familiar with Fonty's penchant for dipping deep into the past. The Archives knew which sources he was drawing from. And we knew that he had more than enough landscapes whose chief claim to fame was that they had become battlefields. For twelve long years, the Immortal, working in the pay of a miserly publisher, had written one war book after the other, each fatter and stuffed with more death-dealing information than the last. The war against France had yielded even more material than the Danish and Austrian campaigns. In two thousand pages, not one battle, not one siege, not one skirmish went unmentioned. Reference was made not only to armies and regiments but also to battalions and companies, so long as their losses in officers and soldiers were sufficiently large. Whenever the heap of war books makes claims on our editorial efforts, we archivists are tempted to speak of twelve years lost and energy squandered; yet young Theo Wuttke's hunger for detail drew nourishment from these mighty tomes. He had larded his *Abitur* essay with quotations from the final campaign report—for instance, the meticulous listing of war booty: "Starting at the Potsdam Gate, captured artillery pieces were lined up, distributed in such a way that Königgrätzer Strasse had 453, and Unter den Linden had 514, remarkable among them a twenty-four-pounder captured in Soissons, with rich ornamentation in relief, a relic from the penultimate year of Louis XIV's reign...."

No wonder such fanatical devotion to the past attracted attention and made the otherwise below-average student Theo Wuttke stand out. His essay was printed, somewhat abridged, in the local paper. And that must be how Tallhover, who specialized, after all, in immortals and their obsessions, got wind of this talent in the rising generation. A young man who could digest thick books so effectively that in the process German unification, the outcome of three wars, seemed compelling to everyone: such a talent could go far if steered in the right direction.

Regardless of how Theo Wuttke's career began, it is clear that he must have caught someone's eye; when in doubt, we can assume it was Tallhover's. The Polish campaign had just ended when the recruit was ordered to proceed from the Gross-Boschpol training grounds, where they had begun to drill him as an infantry soldier, to the Reich Aviation Ministry, Division of War Reportage and Propaganda. Fonty recalled later that he had made the switch as thankfully as thoughtlessly, for the terms of this relatively cushy duty were not obvious to him at the time: "The devil's kitchen smelled mighty good, at least at first."

We archivists reserve comment here. At any rate, in early 1940 the soldier Theo Wuttke was in the Government General of Poland, on assignment. His account of the eighteen-day campaign was somewhat wobbly, because on this terrain he had no war book by the Immortal to stiffen his backbone, and the chapters of *Mathilde Möhring* set in West Prussia yielded little in the way of a backdrop, having not a whiff of gunpowder or battleground; but with the onset of the lightning victories over France, he could draw not only on the thickest of all the war books but also on an incidental work in which the Immortal recorded the period from his capture in Domrémy to his release from the island of Oléron.

Without thorough acquaintance with, or even complete holdings of, his articles, we can nonetheless state the following: Theo Wuttke submitted reports from Sedan and Metz, from Northern France and Alsace, likewise from Neufchâteau, Langres, and Besançon, from the birthplace of the Maid of Orléans, naturally also from the fortified island off the Atlantic coast, and later even from Lyon—sensitive, retrospective reports, full of word-perfect quotations and always amusingly anecdotal, which soon found many admirers, for in them the daily humdrum of war was treated as incidental, while the past was brought to life in all its breadth and depth, and not only on battlefields. The Immortal's Huguenot origins provided an almost inexhaustible treasure trove; evidence of the search for historical traces turns up especially in the late reports from Lyon and the accounts of rather risky excursions to the Cévennes, including descents into the ravines of the Ardèche.

When we addressed this aspect of his work, he smiled sheepishly. Fonty did not like to talk about the wartime adventures of Airman Third Class Wuttke: "Well, at the time it was more than risky. Unfortunately, I couldn't get a special travel pass for a trip to Gascony. In the spring of '44 I even had Nîmes and the mouth of the Rhône in my sights. But Berlin was against it...."

Between assignments he was supposed to report back to the Reich Aviation Ministry for new marching orders. Time after time the young soldier saw himself posed before the "colossal" portal. Later he was privileged to escort a secretary named Emilie Hering across the court of honor into the colossal structure and introduce her to his superior, Colonel von Maltzahn: "With your permission, sir, my fiancée!"

Yet when the elderly civilian Wuttke, who as Fonty had only recently celebrated a double birthday, indulged himself in memories, he said, as he stood with Hoftaller, gazing up at the Ministries Building and its ever-faithful portal: "That monstrosities like this possess a certain immortality renders every laurel wreath suspect. If only it were all a few sizes smaller!" Even before the first step, Hoftaller doffed his hat, while Fonty kept his on until they were inside the vast double doors.

We regret to announce that the interior view of the structure along Otto-Grotewohl-Strasse will have to remain blurry until we reach the next phase in the history of the building's use. Only later, when the structure has undergone yet another renovation, will its endless succession of rooms recover their luster. For the time being, everything still looked shabby. Marble in different colors, its once polished surface dull, framed the doors to the offices of ten ministries that oversaw the various branches of industry. In the corridors grubby carpeting covered the original linoleum flooring. For forty years the Workers' and Peasants' State had administered its economy of scarcity from this place. Collectives had projected five-year plans, retouched their failures, then substituted new, equally unmeetable goals. All this had produced documentation whose inner life filled endless file cases; among these files were some that of late had cried out for review, and without delay.

And here Fonty comes into play again. Theo Wuttke delivered. As a file courier he had the job of hauling stacks of binders from one department to another. He mediated between ministries. And because he had found this position thanks to Hoftaller's solicitous intercession, and had been making his way along the corridors since the late seventies, the question arises as to how people moved from floor to floor in this building.

Immediately a mode of transportation comes into our field of vision that has been in operation from the beginning. We picture Theo Wuttke, the file courier, in an elevator that is open at the front and moves in two directions, a chain of cabins in constant motion, passing turning points in cellar and attic, rising and falling, never stopping, gently rattling, not without suppressed groans and sighs, yet as reliable as—well, all right, as a prayer wheel; for which reason this old-fashioned passenger elevator, which, despite heartfelt protests, has been decommissioned almost everywhere nowadays, was known as a "paternoster."

And it was in this paternoster that Fonty carried out his halfday job in the Ministries Building. They kept him on despite his advanced age, thanks to a special dispensation. Burdened with files, he traveled from floor to floor. No one else seemed so busily familiar with all ten ministries. He rose from the depths below, gradually came into view—his upper half, then all of him—and soon disappeared as he went up, first beheaded, then cut in half, finally showing only his laced boots. He seemed to have vanished, but insisted on appearing on the next floor up in the same guise, whiteheaded, with his bushy mustache, then as a half-length portrait, finally in full length, after having been only half there; or he descended from above, laced boots first, with a pile of binders clutched to his chest, first half of him, then the whole, showing his familiar face as if in farewell, was then completely gone, only to heave into view again one floor down and—if files were to be delivered and picked up on the third floor—to get off there, the binders still clutched in his arms.

And this is how we imagine Fonty's exits: As soon as the floor of the paternoster cabin was more or less level with the corridor, he would dismount with a little leap, then go on his way as file courier, with youthful stride and complete familiarity with the location of all the offices. The corridors seemed not to tire him. A tachometer strapped to his leg would have recorded the many kilometers he put behind him. He delivered, picked up, returned, laden with in-house communications, instructions being circulated, with still more file folders and binders. As he drew near, his long strides asserted his mastery of the corridors, and in marble-framed doorways he grew to the stature familiar to us.

When a crowd gathered by the elevator, he had precedence. Sometimes he caught it in a falling, sometimes in a rising trend, hopping into the descending cabin with a slight downward motion, into the rising one with an upward thrust; no one ever saw Fonty stumble or fall when getting on or off.

So much for his independent forays along the corridors and solo appearances in the paternoster. But since he owed his half-day position—which alternated from week to week between mornings and afternoons—to Hoftaller, and was therefore obligated to him, just as Airman Third Class Wuttke had owed his duck duty as a mere lad of a war correspondent to a certain Tallhover and was thus indebted to him, he often found himself in one and the same paternoster cabin with this particular person. They stood facing one another. And not seldom it came about that they passed the changeover points at the top or the bottom and continued on, up and down, many times over, which merely had the appearance of pointlessness.

Whenever the two of them occupied a cabin for the duration of many Our Fathers, Hoftaller was busy. He insisted on inspecting the mobile files. And Fonty had reason not to block this inspection. As long as he had been a file courier in the Ministries Building, this review of files had been routine. But now that the actual power center of the Workers' and Peasants' State, the State Security fortress on Normannenstrasse, had been stormed and then immediately sealed, new tasks presented themselves: Hoftaller often arrived with bulging briefcase to secure salvaged records. During these uninterrupted paternoster rides he would mention "transitional storage" when Fonty opened one binder or another for him. Later the stored files had to disappear, and Hoftaller knew where.

Much in-house traffic was occasioned by these circumstances. What seemed yesterday to have been rescued had to be moved to another level the next day. Often these preventive measures required both of them to enter or leave the paternoster at the same time. Fonty appeared more nimble at getting on and off. Hoftaller, who did not trust the open elevator but felt that *force majeure* compelled him to use the bi-directional cabins, sometimes stumbled when getting on or off. Fonty had to take his hand. Fonty could be relied on. He provided support. The file courier's surefooted familiarity with the ever-moving paternoster gave Hoftaller adequate security; after all, Fonty had been familiar with the elevator and its dangers for five decades.

He had been in uniform when he mastered the technique of leaping smoothly into the cabin or the corridor, for each marching order that recalled him to the Reich Aviation Ministry included practice time, which, however, was not an unalloyed pleasure to the airman third class. In those days, Tallhover was interested not in securing files but in receiving or delivering dispatches, which soldier Wuttke brought, without knowing what secret messages they contained, from the occupied countries, especially from France, or took back with him. And everywhere, whether in France, Belgium, or Denmark, intermediaries had turned up, among them not a few members of the Prussian aristocracy.

In this way Fonty made himself useful. In this way he was forced to make himself useful. For whether in Tallhover's or in Hoftaller's day, Theo Wuttke, aka Fonty, came under pressure. He was kept on a short leash. No, worse than that: we archivists know that from the beginning he was under surveillance. Even the Immortal's youthful follies bore time-released consequences. The conspiratorial circle in Leipzig, the love affair in Dresden, the years in Berlin as an apothecary and would-be revolutionary: nothing happened without aftershocks. Not to mention his work for the "Central Office" and as a government agent in London. A net had been cast in whose meshes the hero of the '48 barricades and the friend of the

Prenzlauer Berg "scene" were flailing simultaneously; that was how little freedom the crumbling of the Berlin Wall had brought. Supposedly everything was wide open now. Yet the incarceration seemed to go on and on. Sometimes we heard Fonty groan both retroactively and contemporaneously, yet he bore his double burden bravely through all times of changeover, an Archibald Douglas who was vouchsafed no mercy.

Of course the paternoster was also the scene of some unforced conversations. During the first year of the war, when Airman Wuttke returned in April from a tour of duty in the protectorate of Bohemia and Moravia, he hopped into a rising cabin where a dark-haired tousle-head was standing, an Adler typewriter in her arms.

Fonty confessed to us that he pegged "the young thing" at "eighteen at most" and that the typewriter immediately suggested an idea to him. Usually bashful, and anything but a ladies' man, he found it easy to strike up a conversation in the paternoster with the "colossally winsome young lady." "First you smile and get a smile in return, then you say something."

He offered to carry the heavy machine. This overly sudden advance was rebuffed. Not until the soldier had introduced himself was he allowed to take charge of the Adler. He clicked his heels as he identified himself in the paternoster. The young lady's name was Emilie Hering, but she wanted to be called Emmi. He wanted to know whether she was related to the writer Willibald Alexis, author of the famous novel *The Trousers of Herr von Bredow*. The writer's actual name, Häring, had once been traced back to the Huguenot name Hareng.

"Not even three times removed!" Emmi insisted that her origins were strictly Upper Silesian. "Besides, I don't read dirty books, about trousers and such."

They had already missed the seventh floor. The soldier spoke reassuringly to the young lady, for Emmi was rather nervous when they reached the changeover point in the attic, where their cabin swayed sideways for a moment, then began its descent. She described the experience as exciting. She had never dared to try it. "Kind of scary, but not bad, not bad at all."

And because the two of them kept talking, Emmi had a chance to enjoy the bottom and top changeover several times. "Over the course of many Our Fathers," Fonty told us, they had become better acquainted. At first his interest had focused on her secretarial skills, but then the chestnut-brown tousle-head had driven him crazy. "Love at second sight. Of course I insisted on calling her Emilie. Not to her liking at all. But then she allowed it, and a bit more...."

This was how Theo Wuttke met his future fiancée and the mother of his children, Emilie Wuttke, née Hering. After completing her apprenticeship she had found employment as a typist and steno girl in one of the many anterooms in the Aviation Ministry. And she was very willing to type "clean copy," as she called it, of war correspondent Wuttke's handwritten mood pieces, after hours. She said she was good at reading handwriting. She would be able to make it out. And at home, at her Aunt Pinchen's, she had a brand-new Erika machine.

Soldier Wuttke claims not to have kissed Emmi the secretary until the fifth Our Father, at the bottom turn, to be precise, when they were already headed upward again.

At any rate, their story began in the paternoster. And the report from Bohemia that Emmi turned into clean typescript had a nice flow to it. Very matter-of-factly the travel impressions were underlaid with portrayals of the long-ago war of '66 against Austria, including observations he had jotted down while viewing the former battlefield of Königgrätz. His report said almost nothing about civilian conditions in the occupied protectorate; instead, the historical battle was invoked. War correspondent Theo Wuttke was a master of the art of omission.

And two days later, when he had Tallhover beside him, waiting as usual for him to hand over the mood pieces from behind the front lines, he is supposed to have said, as he pulled the freshly typed version of the manuscript out of his courier's pouch, "Good Lord! How it all came alive for me again! The copse in Sadowa, for instance, or the village of Cistowes, where we found little destruction at the time, since the shells from the great battery in Chlum had passed right over it. In Lipa, though, which today looks wretched in an entirely different way, things were fairly bad. Whole rows of houses with nothing but the chimneys left standing. And here, too, children approached us, offering souvenirs. A virtual bazaar was spread out for us: feather plumes, caps, the double eagle, sashes with and without bloodstains. *Tempi passati!* This time no children. And the few we did see ran away, terrified. But the landscape was still magnificent. What a panorama! To the left the gleaming stripe of the Elbe and just beyond it the soaring towers of Königgrätz! All that, Herr Hauptkommissar, can still be sensed today, although time, like the current wartime, has passed over it. But in my report I managed to bring the past to life, a mighty tributary flowing into the present. Wonder what my colonel will have to say. After all, one of his ancestors lies buried with many others on the heights of Chlum: a Lieutenant von Maltzahn, a mere boy, like all the rest...."

On the fifth floor of the Reich Aviation Ministry, the war correspondent left the paternoster and went looking for his superior. This man prized Fonty and his artful omissions. We can imagine Fonty's relaxed chats with him in the office but also in the paternoster. The officer was said to be well read. Thus young Wuttke could have pointed out to the colonel, in the course of a rather long conversation continuing past the turning points, that the figure of Count Holk in *Irretrievable* and his affair in Copenhagen with a certain Ebba von Rosenberg were borrowed from a Mecklenburg scandal involving a Carl von Maltzahn and a lady-in-waiting named Auguste von Dewitz. And the colonel, because he knew his novels, could have said, "Terrific, Wuttke! I heard something of the sort myself. But this Ebba's behavior is rather off, no? From the tribe of Israel, though ennobled. Absolutely out of the question for the Maltzahns. Pure fiction, understood?"

And soldier Wuttke is bound to have exclaimed, "Yes, sir, Colonel!" and saved himself with a small leap—as fifty years later he entered the paternoster with a still youthful leap and pulled Hoftaller in after him; they had matters of current concern to chat about.

"Makes me sad, Fonty, all this wear and tear on the files."

"Things went awry on Normannenstrasse?"

"And because the Modrow government can't last..."

"Any records concerning my family sealed? Or shredded, perhaps?"

"...supposed to have early elections, by mid-March...."

Fonty made no comment, allowing inspection between floors of his load, a stack of binders. But Hoftaller, who found nothing of interest and put only a single record into transitional storage, stayed on the trail of the changeover: "It all depends on Bonn. They're in such a hurry, those fellows. Instant unification! But elections mean nothing to us, right, Fonty? Elections don't change a thing, at least not in theory. We'll stay in touch, one way or the other...."

The file courier Theo Wuttke took his leave with a little leap. What could he have said, he who never voted in elections, who had no vote or voice in any case?

He carried the stack of binders down the long corridors to offices from which he emerged laden with new binders, and strode back toward the paternoster. In the Ministries Building many employees were still there from the days of the now crumbling Workers' and Peasants' State. Yet one also saw new people who, although they had dealt the death blow to the decaying state, now showed little expertise in their handling of files. They were forever finding things they were not looking for—and vice versa.

That probably explained why so many employees were moving about the corridors and from floor to floor. Fonty, heavily laden, shared the paternoster cabin with hands from way back and those who had just come on board—whenever, that is, Hoftaller did not occupy the second spot. Now that the Ministries Building had been recast as a giant grid, there was much talk of networks, old and new. Certain ladies and gentlemen from the old network were known to Fonty from the many years he had worked there, but he was also acquainted with the new employees, whether from encounters in Prenzlauer Berg or from conspiratorial gatherings in the Church of Gethsemane. People nodded to each other. They exchanged a few words. They could intuit what they did not know for certain. And many who rode up and down with him in the paternoster called him Fonty: "No end in sight for the files, eh, Fonty?" "So what's new, Fonty?" "Doesn't get any lighter, does it, Fonty?"

5

Deep Down in the Sofa

Even if we are sure of both the primary and the secondary facts, this much must be conceded: the Archives did not know everything. Deeper insight into the realm behind his nervous crises was not vouchsafed us. And because the Immortal kept his lip buttoned, even in the journals, we compensated by focusing on Fonty's word-for-word continuation of the life, authenticated in quotations that seldom deviated from the original. We would put him to the test, more in jest than in earnest, and usually with stunning results—they left us shamefaced. When he visited the Archives, we would question him at length, secretly hoping he would fall out of character or spill the beans, revealing more than the Immortal had permitted himself.

But even in barren terrain—for instance, when we inquired about the *Likedeeler* project, which the Immortal had started late in life and abandoned time and again—he had an answer for us. According to him, the publisher Hertz had produced only run-of-the-mill material for the projected epic on "proto-communist levelers": Störtebeker's piracy from the Hanseatic vantage point, not a word about the ideology of Störtebeker's brotherhood. Yet he considered this draft a legacy and wanted to complete the fragment in balladesque style; he said he already knew how to go about it—certainly not with the crude pirate doggerel and Party-line pronouncements to which Barthel, whom the comrades called KuBa, had resorted. And queried about a marginal problem from the past, the scandalous case of Oskar Panizza, he commented that as far as Panizza's *Council of Love* was concerned, it had certainly been "arresting," but he still maintained that for this Panizza "either a stake or a monument should be erected."

He knew everything, and we could only surmise what secrets, and in whose intonation, he kept to himself; for the only glimpse of the dark side of his continued existence was provided by the flickering light of a speculative tallow candle—for instance, the recondite particulars he let fall, the striking details he struck from the record, the final refuges, the hiding place. Accordingly, we were merely groping in the dark for a long time as we pursued the question: Where was this hiding place at which he hinted several times? And what did he mean when he cast the baited phrase "upholstered furniture"? What style might this apparently commodious piece of furniture exhibit?

This much is certain: somewhere in the Ministries Building there must have been a special armchair or a most unusual sofa. Fonty's comment—"You have no idea how much of the past can fit into an upholstered piece"—offered enough of a clue. And since he could not be imagined in this building without his shadow, a chair was out of the question; but where the sofa might be was impossible to determine with any finality.

Either it was located in the cellar—in the furnace room, to be precise—or it was gathering dust in a corner of the labyrinthine attic. If we settled on the cellar, we next had to answer the question: Was the furnace suitable for carrying out Hoftaller's prophylactic operations? Certainly, but only if it had burned soft coal and had a large door, if, furthermore, there had been briquettes stockpiled and shovel-wielding stokers; after all, the Workers' and Peasants' State was often heated with this inferior fuel, and throughout the land the air smelled correspondingly gassy, if a polity can be said to have a characteristic odor.

Had we inquired, our question would doubtless have been answered with a curt reference to an off-site heating plant. The office to which we might have written for information would have deemed our follow-up query about a possible backup burner unworthy of either a Yes or a No; so the question would have remained open, and what could be envisioned was a heating unit inoperative since war's end, perhaps located next to the underground parking garage, which would bring trips to the cellar into the picture. The sofa would be standing in an alcove facing the backup burner, and a cozy refuge like this would match our suspicions. Because no soft-coal extraction in the Lusatian mining region had had to feed the furnace, and only an emergency heating unit was maintained, this burner, cold now for many a year, would serve to carry out a proceeding that Hoftaller, who sometimes liked to adopt the jargon current in the West, referred to as "environmentally friendly waste disposal."

The files with which Fonty left the paternoster on the lowest level originated with the ministries headquartered in the building. From mid-January on, these were joined by records that had been searching for a new home ever since the central facility on Normannenstrasse was sealed tight. The possibility cannot be discounted that photocopies of files released to the furnace room survived the "disposal." This sort of backup would have jibed with one of Hoftaller's principles: He always kept something up his sleeve; he never told us, "Everything was destroyed." Rather, he emphasized time and again that "almost everything was disposed of."

Fonty seldom glanced into the heaps of files thus transformed into furnace fodder. He knew quite well why this state, whose inner life was seeping out everywhere through fissures and holes, was reluctant to reveal its inner life to the bankruptcy administrators who were already moving in; since the elections in March, it had become abundantly clear that henceforth between the Baltic Sea and the Erz Mountains the shots would be called by supervisors trained in the ways of the West.

But occasionally Hoftaller insisted on his having a look. Even a hasty glance confirmed for the file courier that the powers-to-be had every reason to welcome any form of assiduous waste disposal, for the crumbling of the state in the east did not reveal only its own secrets; it uncovered another, previously hidden, inner life whose branching highways and byways eventually led to the state in the west. Commingled pan-German files of this sort had to be eliminated on the one hand, secured on the other. Hoftaller spoke repeatedly of a "proactive resource-recovery operation."

In conversation with us, Fonty asserted that the secrecy with which the files were exchanged struck him as ridiculous. He said that in the rising and falling paternoster, his day-and-night-shadow had made summary judgments as to which proceedings were to be considered explosive, which harmless.

We assume that the disposal technician hard at work in the paternoster and by the open furnace door put on a show of considerable self-importance, for Fonty told us later, "As certified archivists, you're certainly familiar with this quirk. Everything, even utter nonsense, seemed important to him. He would save things like the bill for two beers and two orders of bockwurst, or lengthy minutes of trivial conversations—intending either to dispose of them or to preserve them for some future use."

In this spirit Hoftaller admitted to us, "Ah, you're lucky! Nothing like a snug study. I do envy you sometimes. Just love old papers, even with mildew on them."

As the two of them stood yet again by the open door of the backup furnace, while Hoftaller let superfluous files go up in flames, Fonty remarked, "All this just because the Modrow government's been swept away? Why the farce? It's more ridiculous than after the fall of the Manteuffel government, when they tried to cover up its bungles by making files disappear. Meanwhile it was being shouted from the rooftops who'd been lining whose pockets. They even tried to rope me into something of the sort during my time in London.... Was supposed to grease the palm of a certain Glover... Count Bernstorff putting on pressure... My actual superior, Director Metzel... I sat there in the Café Divan writing my fingers to the bone.... But you know more about those transactions than I could even guess at the time...."

And Fonty doubled back, retreating to the fifties of the previous century: "*En famille* to Kensington... Emilie outraged at the 'English people'... A dispatch in the *Times*: Hinkeldey killed in a duel...." There followed a rather long conversation; it got underway by the furnace's open door but did not end until all the "top secret" materials had been incinerated and, thanks to the excellent draft, whisked out of the world. They chatted for a long time. First standing, then walking, finally both sitting down.

Assuming that the sofa was located in an alcove in the furnace room, its simple presence would have proved inviting; and assuming further that the file courier Wuttke had finished his shift and was free for an afternoon chat, and, because it was pouring outside, was willing to forgo his usual walk in the Tiergarten, the two of them could have spent quite some time venting their separate forms of indignation at the Prussian police system. Hoftaller charged it with "always letting things slip through—it leaked like a sieve," while Fonty had experienced it as "omnipresent." But then Tallhover's backlog of experiences came in handy: "The journals, if you know how to read them, are a treasure trove. Like us, you had specific directives from the Manteuffel government. Your friend and patron Merckel—who gave posterity the formulation, often confirmed, 'To put the democrats to rout / You have to call the army out'—had sent you to London, despite our reservations. After that a certain Metzel had you under surveillance. But when the government changed, even he couldn't cover all the traces. Your palm-oil operations, for instance. The two thousand talers in hush money paid annually to the owner of the *Morning Chronicle* are documented, even if your biographers, Reuter included, wanted to fudge the matter. They claim there was no receipt for any of the payments."

"You're exaggerating, Police Superintendent Tallhover! Or you still can't admit that I, although not a complete nonentity, was the wrong man for the part. Buying off that newspaper didn't work. . . . Berlin was too stingy. . . . I had to let Glover and Bernstorff down. . . ."

". . . because you had no perseverance. Even your first trip to England should have made that clear, if not to us, then certainly to the Central Press Office on Leipziger Strasse. But Merckel's judgment was clouded by his infatuation with literature. . . ."

"Nonsense! You were on the scene yourself and should have recognized how ill-suited I was. . . ."

"Too short an inspection tour. Had to look after Marx & Co.

Nothing went the way it was supposed to. Was taken in by a faked logbook. Ran hither and yon through Soho—the red-light district. From Gerrard Street to Dean Street. Went right past the house in question. We had to avoid bumping into the Marx party, if possible. Besides, Freiligrath was in London. He'd managed to uncouple himself in time from the Communist trial in Cologne. That's what counted; you were only small fry—though by today's moral standards you'd be finished. A case for the culture pages. Mercilessly unmasked. The Immortal with a skeleton in his closet! Pilloried! They show no pity, Fonty. If we were to reprint or quote what you said about Prime Minister Lord Palmerston, your declared enemy..."

"...whom my articles in the *Kreuzzeitung* didn't manage to topple, no matter how obvious the barbs. That I, of all people, had to splatter ink against England! And London was better than Berlin, too. Though what sense does it make to compare two metropolises of that size? Over there, courageous cosmopolitans risking all for profit; over here, pfennig-pinching provincials. A dry sense of humor on the Thames, spiteful jibes on the Spree. At any rate, Berlin paralyzed me and London educated me, even if I hadn't the foggiest notion of Marx & Co. Never mentioned him. You can look it up. Even Hegel was terra incognita.... Had enough trouble with Kant...At most Schopenhauer...I was clueless, and not just in philosophy. Hardly grasped what was expected of me in London and what malaise this Manteuffel mania would drag me into...."

"You knew who was paying you."

"And not very generously, Tallhover, not very generously!"

"And the German émigrés also knew whose pocket you were in. They cut you dead. Even Max Müller kept his distance. They took you for a spy, one who was agitating against Bucher's anti-Prussian polemics and trying to siphon off the funding for Schlesinger's *English Correspondence,* which didn't work...."

"I've already said it: You were throwing good money after bad!"

"...and soon after the Manteuffel government fell, you became completely worthless, at least to us. Hence the attempt to dispose of these trifles. Not thorough enough, as we know. There's always some residue...."

Both of them sat with legs outstretched, each hugging his corner of the sofa. Fonty gazed at his laced boots. Hoftaller was concentrating on his buckled shoes. In their minds both were presumably roaming the streets of London, be it in Soho or Camden Town. Everywhere dense traffic and crowds. They sat there deep in thought. Between them a gap.

At any rate, the sofa's wooden frame with its triple curve was wide enough for more than two. A piece from the Founders' Era, with upholstery that might once have been burgundy. Worn and frayed, it had little recognizable color left. The sofa's legs could have been turned by August Bebel himself. The padded armrests were adorned with Wilhelminian scrollwork. Only the curved backrest followed a simpler line, as if trying to recall its Biedermeier forebears. Both men sat there like relics from a bygone age. And from the depths of the sofa Fonty remarked, "At least Lepel and I got in our trip to Scotland before the Manteuffel madness was over. At the beginning of 'Beyond the Tweed' I wrote..."

But Hoftaller was in no mood for long quotations, and certainly not for confusing details about the Scottish clans. He hated Scotland, because this remote region lay beyond his control. "Spare me! I couldn't care less about your Campbells, Stuarts, and Mac-Donalds. It wasn't my assignment to correct your often sloppily researched travel narratives. By contrast, your forgeries of *Times* articles in the columns of the *Neue preussische (Kreuz-)Zeitung* were a real accomplishment: masterpieces of stylistic credibility, despite all the anti-English propaganda. But never mind. I'm satisfied with our current collaboration, you know. Developing nicely. By now I'm even prepared to take certain documents pertaining to you and feed them to the furnace. I'm thinking of informants' reports from your Cultural Union period, harmless for the most part, but in certain cases fairly explosive. For instance, the assessment you wrote of a play before it was even performed in Berlin-Karlshorst by a Free German Youth student group... Oh, well, that was dealt with. But your fawning comparison of the author, Heiner Müller, to the young Gerhart Hauptmann—placing his shoddy *Resettler* on the same level as *The Weavers*—verged on sabotage. And only a few weeks after the building of the antifascist bulwark, too. Unfortunately, we mistook informant Fonty's final sentence—'This play contains blast chambers full of socialist dynamite'—for a positive judgment. As a result, the play opened on 30 September '61—insulting the working class through its distorted portrayal of reality. Agricultural collectivization cynically dragged through the mire. Measures had to be taken. Exclusion from the Writers' Union. Interminable meetings. Even the Academy was called into session. Afterward the usual self-criticism. A national crisis! And all because we trusted your assessment, your 'socialist dynamite.'"

Fonty laughed from his sofa corner. "Well, you can't say it didn't explode!" And when Hoftaller drew the out-of-date piece of paper from his wallet, unfolded it, smoothed out the wrinkles, and finally read aloud the informant's report line for line, all the way down to "With socialist greetings, Your Theo Wuttke," not suppressing the code name "Fonty" in the letterhead, Fonty was still laughing. "Goodness me, and to think how our Müller turned out!"

Fonty didn't stop laughing until Hoftaller leaned forward in his sofa corner, holding the double-sided document away from his body with thumb and forefinger, pulled out his lighter, and lit it on the first try. Fonty's smile faded rapidly as he watched the evidence of his dual role with the Cultural Union burn, from the lower left-hand corner to the top, with no harm done to Hoftaller, who let go just in time. Between their laced and buckled footgear, the paper burned until nothing remained on the concrete floor of the furnace room. They both felt rather solemn.

That probably explains why Hoftaller did not dig into the depths of his briefcase and retrieve the thermos and tin box of mettwurst sandwiches that usually appeared during such breaks and are already testified to by Tallhover's biographer. Instead he conjured up a bottle of red wine, two paper cups, and a corkscrew.

Before Hoftaller could remark, "Let's give ourselves a treat," Fonty said quickly, as if determined to have the last word, "That I compared young Müller to the young Hauptmann is still frightfully right. Unfortunately, their late plays are cut from the same coarse cloth. Gussied-up theatrical effects. One of them tickles your funny bone with mystical hocus-pocus, the other offers muddled Shakespeare and cruelties by the dozen. It's supposed to come across as cynical, but it's nothing but a pose, a colossal hemming and hawing...."

We archivists know that even Hauptmann's early play *Hannele's Ascension* had rubbed him the wrong way. "I could go on japing at this angel-making for the next two days," he wrote in November '93 to his regular theater, where as critic he had occupied seat 23 for twenty years and had hardly missed an opening night. His comments in the *Vossische Zeitung* on Schiller's *Wilhelm Tell* and Ibsen's *A Doll's House* still read as though the ink were barely dry. He despised anything bombastic, such as Wagner and Bayreuth, where he left the packed festival shed immediately after the overture to *Parsifal*—"Another three minutes and you'll fall out of your seat, unconscious or dead"—and returned his expensive ticket for *Tristan and Isolde* at the window, requesting that an equivalent value be donated "to a worthy charity."

Fonty likewise. Anything too highly seasoned was not to his taste—as indeed the wine Hoftaller had pulled out of his briefcase was too sweet, too cloying for him; yet he had to drink it because he was under orders to participate in a "brief but convivial get-together." Hoftaller filled his cup again and again. Again and again Fonty invoked the infamous goblet of hemlock. "To your health," he had to say. "Here's to you...." And with every swallow, he feared he might die of a surfeit of sweetness.

The sofa had been through a lot. It had probably been standing in the cellar since the war. During the frequent air raids, it might well have served as a refuge. We picture it providing an illusion of safety, between the warning siren and the all-clear, to three or four secretaries employed by the Reich Aviation Ministry. Fonty's fiancée, the secretary Emmi Hering, was certainly among those seeking protection, especially since bombs fell on Berlin night and day. Even then the sofa must have been an inviting place for a chat, or whistling in the dark, and Emmi Wuttke, née Hering, is supposed to have been an inexhaustible chatterbox; her thread never ran out.

This was the only way she could appeal to Airman Third Class Wuttke; this was the only way she could be tolerable, even when in a bad mood; and this was the only way the soldier and later civilian could remain tolerable to her, for, as Fonty said, the chatty tone had become second nature to him, "including in my writing." He was chatting now with Hoftaller for the pure pleasure of it, but certainly also to counteract the sweetness of the red wine being forced on him. Anything to keep the conversation from flagging! The penultimate word had to flow into the one after next. Mixing time periods again and again, he leaped, without leaving his sofa corner, from one century to the other.

Several times he invoked Neuruppin, the birthplace. Of the two fathers, he devoted few words to the apothecary, but those words added up the man's eternal gambling debts indulgently. Then with Father Wuttke, a lithographer by trade, he lingered at extravagant length over the famous Neuruppin pictorial broadsheets, whose colorful continuing coverage, extending over a century, had guaranteed popularity for every military event, as well as such occurrences as conflagrations and floods. Fonty stressed the enrichment this bonanza of brilliant images had meant for one man's youth and for other's, the lasting impression the lithographer's art had made on him. He colored in some broadsheet narratives so bloodily, so gunpowder-blackly, that one would have thought that he still saw before him the forester's death at the hand of a poacher, that the slaughter of Mars la Tour was occurring at that very moment. And breathing life into lithographs from Gustav Kühn's workshop, he complained at the same time that nothing from the current changeover period offered such visually compelling material: "Picture the events of October. The Workers' and Peasants' State celebrating its fortieth anniversary. Great hullabaloo! The People's Army on parade. The working masses marching past the reviewing stand on Marx-Engels-Platz. In colorful succession we see comrades waving, and of course the chap in the little hat waving back, all smiles now, after his illness and operation. And next to our Honni we see Gorbi, who refuses to smile. Why the stony face? Then more pictures, showing the events in Leipzig. The Monday marches. The sea of peace-loving candles.

The forces of order, the police dogs, and everything bursting with wonderful tableaus. Motif after motif. We see a hundred or more pastors in Geneva bands and robes, in command of Luther's teeming images. We see Pastor Christian Führer in the pulpit of St. Nikolai, preaching nonviolence in compelling parables. We see crumbling Leipzig, city of heroes. Then Berlin again. Disappointed in the people, Honni resigns. His successor bares his teeth in laughter. More and more resignations and heart attacks. Then a series of images with speech balloons: remorseful comrades in conversation with the bearded men of the New Forum. Further resignations and demands. Round tables everywhere! And pastors everywhere; my Lorenzen could have been there. Let's not forget the fourth of November, of course, the day of a thousand banners and far too many speakers, launching a bit of hope in ever-larger balloons. Stefan Heym laments bitterly. Christa Wolf tries to cozy up to the people. Müller warns, 'Let's not fool ourselves....' Spira, the actress, recites a poem. And then, after a youngish writer named Christoph Hein has talked any euphoria to shreds, I am summoned to the podium: 'Let Fonty speak! Let Fonty speak!' Yes, I addressed the five hundred thousand gathered on Alexplatz. 'It's the imponderables that rule the world,' I shouted into the microphone. And then I recalled the Revolution of '48: 'Much cry and little wool!' I wonder whether anyone understood my warnings. And soon came the ninth of November, the Germans' perennial rendezvous with destiny, but this time with potential for a happy outcome. After all the horrors associated with this date, at long last it is joy's turn to strike up the chorus. The Wall opens wide, the bulwark falls, wallpeckers are at work, bananas are the fruit of the month.... At any rate, this would provide a series of images every bit as good as the Neuruppin lithographs illustrating the victory at Sedan, the proclamation at the Palace of Versailles of the kaiser's accession, even the days of the Paris Commune, but then, too, the victorious regiments marching through the Brandenburg Gate; as indeed for me, who was full of hope, the entire passage at arms provided two thousand pages of material. But no one wanted to read my war book; they were all reaching for the colored broadsheets. Yes, Kühn was as bold as his name suggested in bringing the general slaughter, drenched in color, to the populace. We could use such a Kühn today. I'll say this straight from the shoulder: We may be cutting down whole forests to turn into news-blotting-paper, the radio may be blaring round the clock, and television may glare till it blinds us, but what's missing, Hoftaller, what we lack, as Hauptmann's weavers' children lacked a heel of bread, is a Gustav Kühn from Neuruppin!"

He almost leaped from his seat. He tried to rise from the worn-down cushions, but only sank back into his sofa corner, deeper than ever. Before further images could rush to his lips, Hoftaller, who had been listening with a little smile, filled the paper cup again with sickly-sweet wine; and then Fonty reached far back into the past.

The years of apprenticeship as a "drug pusher" in various pharmacies were inextricably entangled with the front- and rear-echelon dispatches of Airman Third Class Wuttke. After traversing the apprenticeship and journeyman years on parallel tracks, he suddenly came to the awards and honors: "In the year '76 they tried to buy me off with the Order of the Crown, Fourth Class; not until '88 did I finally receive the Knight's Cross of the House of Hohenzollern...." But he had hardly dismissed his rather sparse collection of medals as "tinware" when his chest, which had remained free of medals during the Second World War, was studded with honor badges and merit pins, conferred on him during his years with the Cultural Union: "All third-rate! But still, two or three for 'meritorious activism.' Bredel personally recommended me for a medal. My colleagues Strittmatter and Fühmann repeatedly emphasized my service on behalf of our cultural heritage. But then my patron at the time, Johannes R. Becher, president of the Cultural Union, died.... If I'd been so inclined, I could have had a career as regional secretary, in Potsdam or Oranienburg....Just imagine, Tallhover: what if it had gone my way in the year of the Lord 1859; what if, after my halfway passable time in London, when things were looking pretty grim in Berlin, and Emilie could do nothing but moan and groan, my friend Heyse had succeeded in arranging a position for me at the Bavarian court. Me—librarian to the king! Me—with a steady income! Everything would have turned out differently. No rambles through the Mark Branden-burg, no war books; instead, the foothills of the Alps, Starnberg Lake, Berchtesgaden, Oberammergau, King Ludwig's castles, and novels in which people drink gentian schnapps and the Föhn is blowing. Alpenglow, poachers, mountain farmers, quaint Catholic customs..."

Here Hoftaller interrupted him to sum up: "Don't kid yourself, Fonty. Yours was and is a botched existence. Here, in this sandy region, you at least earned yourself a monument. In Bavaria you wouldn't have accumulated even a half-pint of immortality."

He, too, reached into the past, as Tallhover, then struck as Hoftaller while the iron was hot. The sofa seemed made for final reckonings. With smiling regret, he cited evidence, more in a whisper than a bellow, of the "botched existence." Only rarely did his voice acquire an edge. And even "that's that" statements such as "You were, and remain, an unreliable customer" were accompanied by that mild, indulgent smile. Benevolence was the prevailing attitude, as indeed Hoftaller's round face, which we have often described as that of a sly peasant, its little button eyes surrounded by laugh lines, reflected concern and solicitude rather than harshness.

We would not want to speculate on a specific resemblance to the Police Superintendent Rumpf mentioned in Tallhover's biography who was murdered by a certain Lieske, yet we can confirm Fonty's reference to the early novel *L'Adultera*, which is set in Berlin; in it a Police Superintendent Reiff appears as a minor character, and he exhibits a similarity to Hoftaller *qua* Tallhover that cannot be ignored: "...a stout little gentleman with rosy, gleaming cheeks, a gourmet and raconteur, who, as long as the ladies remained at table, looked as if butter would not melt in his mouth, but as soon as they withdrew excelled in anecdotes of the sort and quantity that only a police superintendent has at his command...."

We surmise that Tallhover must have stood still long enough to model for this minor character Reiff; and making the character Catholic in that Prussian Protestant setting also pointed toward Tallhover, even though Hoftaller, when questioned about his religion, claimed to be "a strict scientific materialist."

At the outset, he handled the "botched existence" indulgently. He glossed over the abandoned university aspirations, even praised the diploma earned from the Friedrichswerder trade school, which shortened the obligatory military service to a year, and went on to praise the apprenticeship at the White Swan Apothecary Shop, which, in spite of ceaseless rhyme-mongering, was actually seen through to certification as an apothecary's assistant—signed by Wilhelm Rose, Spandauer Strasse. But after that, Hoftaller's reckoning took on a stern and ultimately implacable tone: "Such restlessness! All that moving from place to place! I'll remind you only of the Dresden address—Salamonis Apothecary Shop—because there, in the course of selling cod-liver oil, a connection was formed over the counter that, far from being revolutionary, was actually more neo-Romantic, but whose consequences proved ruinous: Once and then again the apothecary's assistant and youthful poet became liable for support payments, to which a plaintive letter to Lepel testifies: 'My children are eating me out of house and home, before the world is even aware that I have any....' All right, we knew about the excessive, much lamented 'strength of loins.' But Emilie Rouanet-Kummer, the fiancée-in-waiting, was kept in the dark about the whoring that went on for years along the banks of the Elbe. All hush-hush. Lepel floated loans. Nothing came to light. But we had the fish on our line: the botched existence, the impoverished papa, the genius hammering out love poems.... I could tell you a thing or two.... I wouldn't mind providing more inside information than those flawlessly organized archives in Potsdam..."

Fonty was taken aback, and we with him. As more and more embarrassing details emanated from the other corner of the sofa, he sank deeper and deeper into the cushions, and we, too, were distraught at all this expertise. If what Hoftaller described as "Dresden and the consequences" had existed as a bundle of incriminating documents, it would have filled a painful gap in the Archives. He quoted from letters and the appended poems. He lingered over matters of dating. Apparently, thirty-seven love tokens in the Immortal's hand were still extant from the seven years before the "Revolutionary Dispatches" in the *Dresdner Zeitung* broke off, yet these papers, more heartrendingly poetic than politically radical, remained available, in the form of a secret dossier, only to those professionally authorized to exert pressure.

Even with us Fonty did not go into detail when we questioned him as to the whereabouts of the letters. As if still under orders to keep to his sofa corner, he took refuge in generalities: "Stuff and nonsense! What a person writes in postal privacy mustn't count. My epistles to Emilie from our unduly long engagement are also out the window. Were all burned. Nothing to weep over. All criminally insignificant anyway. Well—because love letters as a rule tend to be a repository for clichés. Secondhand sentimentality. And quotations from Lenau and Platen sewn on like trouser buttons. Yes, of course there were some original bits, too. It all just poured out. I had an easy touch and unremitting longing. The emotions were heartfelt...."

Our hunger for the Immortal's secret correspondence often drove us to extremes, and in our archival ruthlessness we actually grilled Fonty. Dig in! Probe deeper! Don't let up! As interrogators we may have resembled his day-and-night-shadow; at any rate, our greatest concern was the fear that Hoftaller might decide to wrap up the case "Dresden and the Consequences" in his usual fashion. For as the two of them sat in their sofa corners, he served up not only the sickly-sweet red wine but also even sweeter promises. We sensed the danger looming over the thirty-seven letters, the gap in our holdings.

Fonty shocked us with the admission that Hoftaller had introduced a dramatic pause, then leaned forward in his sofa corner, and said, in a voice dripping with benevolence, "Even we think enough is enough. Dresden shouldn't have any further consequences. We'll silence not only the bundle of hot-blooded letters and the appended poems, but also all the money orders, any bureaucratic stuff, whatever even hints at child support, including our own records. We won't do what your poor Effi, that silly girl, should have done with Crampas's letters and what your worrywart Botho did with the letters from Lene. No, we won't burn them; we'll dispose of them by a method that's close at hand: Everything—every sigh, every outpouring, every solemn affirmation in rhyme—will be torn up, ripped to shreds, and will disappear into this sofa. In its bowels, the poet and youthful apothecary's letter scraps can mix and—for all I care—mate with many thousands of other scraps, all vocal in their own ways, scraps disposed of at an earlier date..."

Thus the following can be established: the backup furnace was not involved. The sofa was not located in the cellar. We step into the paternoster, and are borne up to the labyrinthine attics extending over the entire building, which is four stories high in some places, seven in others. And there, in the seven-story wing along Leipziger Strasse, we see the sofa: simply mothballed, for whatever reason.

But upon close inspection, this piece of attic furniture turned out not to be worn to a sinkhole but instead well upholstered, stuffed with shredded papers once stamped top secret. As we have since learned, many of the files came from the Ministries Building, but the headquarters on Normannenstrasse had done its share of stuffing and cramming; in Fonty's words, you could hardly have fattened a Pomeranian goose more vigorously—so plump was the sofa with secrets.

Hoftaller's accomplishment. Or perhaps we should say Hoftaller's and Fonty's collective accomplishment. Both of them acted as manual paper shredders, ripping the files and poking the scraps through holes into the already riddled lining, using their fingers and Fonty's walking stick to help the sofa achieve that firm padding, a bit at a time.

They had been hard at work since mid-January. At it for weeks on end. At it likewise on that afternoon toward the end of March when Hoftaller conjured out of his briefcase the bottle of red wine, the paper cups, and the corkscrew. Hoftaller did not propose their treat until they had filled their quota, reducing to scraps a pile of personal files, several confidential payrolls, various contact reports, and probably also a bundle of West-Eastern correspondence, forcing them through seven holes and working them into the most remote hollows in the upholstery. "Makes a man thirsty!" he exclaimed.

After the second cup, Fonty found himself under pressure to down a third. Then came the fourth cupful. Obediently he swallowed the wine's syrupy sweetness in little sips, like a punishment. He allowed himself to be filled up, while his host, who merely pretended to drink, enumerated everything that had added to the burden of guilt: Dresden, Dresden, and no end in sight.

And here, in the attic and not in the cellar, the possibility was weighed of fattening the sofa further with this papery information. Information not catalogued in the Postdam Archives, a gap we feel painfully: here it found a voice, here stammered professions of love—unrhymed and rhymed—were quoted at length; here a clandestine love struggled along year after year, page after page, here a sofa was to be furnished with precious confidential information.

Our collection contains only that one special letter to Bernhard von Lepel with the "revelation": "...for the second time the wretched father of an illegitimate offspring." It also indicates the scene of the crime: "The interesting document in question (a letter from Dresden) I shall show you on Sunday...." But Hoftaller knew more, knew, indeed, everything Fonty seemed to know but wanted to keep under wraps: The mother of the two children was the daughter of a gardener in Dresden-Neustadt and was called Magdalena Strehlenow; the gardener's daughter had been a welcome customer at the Salamonis Apothecary Shop; it was cod-liver oil for her younger siblings that she had asked for time and again; the young apothecary's assistant who served her over the counter had persuaded the gardener's daughter to go rowing with him on the Elbe; at first the rower was inspired to celebrate Lena Strehlenow in revolutionary verses modeled on Herwegh; on a gently flowing branch of the Elbe, he eventually relapsed and—inspired by the gardener's daughter's name—could soon find suitable rhymes for his Lena only in the style of the Romantic poet Nikolaus Niembsch von Strehlenau; and the description of this person, who became pregnant again some years later—"slim, of medium height, ash-blond"—coincided suspiciously with that of a much later character in a novel. "We know who modeled in rowboats for Lene Nimptsch."

Hoftaller refused to let himself be silenced: "You can't say it was only fiction. If Lene in the novel didn't end up pregnant from the boat ride on the Havel, and the night spent afterward at Hankel's Depot, that merely proves that the author stuck to his stylistic principles, omitting the bed and the Dresden consequences. At most he ventures to play with the name a bit. But in reality the ash-blond gardener's daughter got pregnant for the first time after repeated boat rides, and then again six years later. The 'offspring,' another girl, died before she turned two. Only the first-born daughter escaped being whisked away by diphtheria. You should be happy, Fonty! Little Mathilde survived all the childhood diseases, grew up to be the kind of practical person who took things in hand, was conspicuously clever and resolute, and later married. ..."

Here Hoftaller broke off. And Fonty did not urge him to divulge sofa tales that would have led farther afield. This was enough. All this stored information—his day-and-night-shadow quoted not only love letters but also dedicatory verses in which *cod-liver* rhymed with *heart aquiver* and, in other cases, pointedly, with *rocked by the river*—filled him with a sensation of utter misery, to which too much red wine contributed. Sickly-sweetness rose in his gorge. Nothing came of Hoftaller's half-promise to stuff the sofa with incriminating letter scraps: "Later, Fonty, maybe later, when we've worked through the Dresden consequences."

That did it. File courier Theo Wuttke had had his fill. He was already gagging. And even if the Immortal, in a comparable situation, would have faded this scene out and spared his reader anything that smacked of vulgarity, we see ourselves forced to make a confession: Fonty had to throw up.

But where? Into what? If we were still in the cellar, our initial guess, and if the sofa were standing close to the furnace's iron door, Hoftaller could have exclaimed, "Come on, Wuttke: over here! Into the furnace, man!" But because it was not in the cellar of the former Reich Aviation Ministry but in its attic that Fonty got sick to his stomach, he probably threw up all over the freshly stuffed sofa.

After downing so much unwanted wine, and being forced to listen to all these depressing details, after having to choke down the concentrated brew of the past, the old man could hardly be expected to leap out of the cushions in time and dump his load somewhere off to the side, amidst the accumulated debris, for instance. He could have vomited on a pile of banners left over from the last May Day parade, still calling for socialist solidarity; he could have purged himself until nothing was left.

Hoftaller helped Fonty, who could barely stay upright in the paternoster, get from the attic to the ground floor, then in a beeline past the guard's desk, out through the colossal portal, and finally into the fresh air.

Outside it was getting dark. No rain, but beneath lowering clouds the damp air was oppressive. There was a sweet-and-sour gaseous smell of burning soft coal, the odor of the state whose sun was setting.

The file courier Theo Wuttke was breathing hard but did not want to lean on anyone; he strode under his own steam across the court of honor. In the punched-out square, every word spoken too loudly created an echo: "Let go, Tallhover! How much farther, Hoftaller, how much farther? The hell with your operational records! Go to hell with your pose of innocuousness, Police Superintendent Reiff!"

But his day-and-night-shadow stuck by his side. It looked as though they were glued together for eternity. No literary trick could separate them. We were not surprised; this practice went back well over a hundred years. After all, didn't the bankrupt banker Rubehn in *L'Adultera* say to his beloved Melanie, "One must be doubly on guard against this breed. Their best friend, their own brother is never safe from them...."

6

The Diving Duck

No one would ever have said "Comrade Fonty," even in jest; and because he had never been a card-carrying Party member, he made it a point of honor to be addressed as "Herr." Indeed, such boorish greetings as "Hallo, Fonty, what's up?" would usually elicit the irritable response, "Herr Wuttke to you, young man."

His civilian name protected him, and he liked to remind people of the file courier, still working well past retirement age, whose contributions were often cited and in years past had even been highlighted on the bulletin board. Whether at the Cultural Union or in the Ministries Building, Theo Wuttke had the reputation of being an activist. With grumpy glee, he claimed to have been committed from the outset to the Workers' and Peasants' State, a loyal citizen. But to be thought of only as Theo Wuttke was as difficult as it was easy for him to convince us all as Fonty.

He was both. And in this twofold guise he was dangling on the hook. We who saw him wriggling at first merely suspected what later became a certainty: too many open files weighed down his extended existence. And because each file was significant enough to make him the subject, over time, of more or less tight surveillance, all that paper resulted in his being constantly shadowed. There was ample reason for assigning to him a person who, like Theo Wuttke, wasn't born yesterday. Thus two wreaths of immortelles should be awarded—and even a third, for we hardly fared better ourselves; nothing is more immortal than an archive.

As anxiously as we tried to stay out of Hoftaller's way, ducking down did not help; we and Fonty were in the same trap, for, like him, the archival collective went under the name of the Immortal, though for decades we were protected by an official finding that categorized us as secondary, and harmless to boot.

Hoftaller did not take the Archives seriously. He sneered at the gaps in our catalogue, persisted in viewing Fonty as a subject, and probably for that reason refused to cooperate with his own biographer, who wanted to snuff him out after more than a hundred years in the service. If he had responded to the biographical summons—"Comrades! Come! Help me!"—and carried out his own sentence by placing his head under the guillotine, Fonty would have been better off, and we with him. We would have had more freedom of movement, just a little more. From 13 February 1955 on, the Archives would have been left in peace—by state directive. And along with the case "Tallhover, Ludwig, b. 23 March 1819, former member of the secret police," the Fonty case could have been filed away for good.

Or would this death, logical only in a literary sense, have provided no occasion for celebration after all? Might there have been reasons to mourn Tallhover's passing? Could it in fact be Fonty protesting toward the end of the biography, on page 283, demanding that it be continued—in a pinch even by us—because after being the subject of solicitous concern for so long he would have felt lonely, exposed, shadowless, like Peter Schlemihl, without his day-and-night-shadow?

Questions to which the facts have provided an answer. Fonty remained under pressure. He was dangling on the hook. And we, who sat in the Archives as though in house arrest, saw him struggling.

Nonetheless, the file courier Theo Wuttke managed to make little breaks for freedom. Time and again he slipped away from his pacesetter and overseer, the goad and barbed hook in his memory. He thought, at any rate, that after work he was free to take day-and-night-shadowless outings. Before the Wall came down, the Friedrichshain People's Park had offered him an outlet; but now, without having to take a running jump first, he could cross Potsdamer Platz, on whose cleared surface garish speculation was blooming, and not only since spring had broken out. After that he would stroll along the western end of Potsdamer Strasse, from shop window to shop window, as far as the pathetic remnant of Number 134C. There, in spite of the impenetrable traffic, he would hark back to garret-drudgery and the novels it had produced; or, indulging another habit, he would strike out from Potsdamer Platz, pursuing the repeatedly branching paths, punctuated by benches, that the Tiergarten had to offer, either to the goldfish pond or to the Amazon, or to the banks of Rousseau Island. Of course he walked with his stick. He had a youthful stride, as contemporary accounts tell us. And when he sat down, the walking stick lay beside him.

Most of the time Fonty sat there by himself, more furloughed than alone of his own free will. Had specific time limits been set for him? Had he had to wrest these solitary excursions from his day-and-night-shadow? Or is it possible that Hoftaller gave in for pedagogical reasons, granting him unconditional permission for abrupt turnabouts, often in midsentence—"Company is good, solitude better!"—because this was the only way Fonty could adjust to the new freedom peculiar to the West?

Their temporary partings usually took place right after work, on street corners—for instance, at the corner of Otto-Grotewohl-Strasse and Leipziger Strasse. Hoftaller intended to go straight, while Fonty was turning left. After a curt good-bye—"Till tomorrow, then"—he struck out on his own. Hoftaller stood still, confirming, "Right, till tomorrow." He gazed after his charge and his billowing scarf for a time, then went on his way; Fonty, meanwhile, was already putting distance between them.

Here we must admit that both of them sometimes succumbed to an urge characteristic of men of their age, and such was the case on this occasion, too, as they took leave of one another. Farting between one step and the next, each went in the direction he considered his own, one with the swinging gait of the eternal youth, assertively bouncing his walking stick on the pavement, the other with small, bustling steps. Even as they drew farther apart, they remained sure of one another. They would be reunited by the next day at the latest, when Hoftaller got onto the paternoster, for they had no lack of shared work. From floor to floor, the file courier

Theo Wuttke was in demand in the Ministries Building, and, all the way up to the attic, where the sofa stood, always obliging and accessible: "You're needed, Fonty—it's urgent. Room 718, Transportation Division, been waiting a long time, and in the Personnel Department some files are piling up, too...."

Only on Tiergarten benches was he alone. Even when a pensioner sat down next to him, and the two of them tallied up the afflictions of old age for one another or maligned their doctors as bunglers, solitude was assured him. Although he amiably countered "asthma" with "nervous prostration," the chatter remained on the surface, and he could keep his background to himself.

Nature, here tamed into an expansive park, helped him be alone, even in company. Yet that was not the only reason Fonty loved the Tiergarten. We shall see that within this artistically designed landscape he was unmistakable from the very beginning.

When Theo Wuttke had parted from the overseer he jokingly referred to as his "guardian angel," and had slipped out of his file-courier identity like a costume, he sallied forth, as he had throughout the month of April, now in splendid May weather. With the exception of a rolled newspaper poking out of his right coat pocket, he resembled, with his hat and walking stick, a caricature of his predecessor that had conveyed the latter's unique features so tellingly that a good twenty years after the Immortal's officially recorded death it could be printed in the satirical journal *Simplicissimus* as the latest thing; in the Archives we have preserved a copy as evidence.

Above the caption—"Is this how Brandenburg's aristocracy looks these days?"—there he is, in the flesh, striding along with his walking stick in his right hand. The left arm is crooked across his back. Without displaying its plaid, the often cited Scottish scarf is draped casually over one shoulder, falling to either side of the left pocket in his loose-fitting overcoat. His face shadowed by the curved brim of his artist's hat, he gazes into the distance, past his immediate surroundings. The bushy mustache beneath his boldly molded nose is matched by his hair, which hangs in strands past his ears and over the nape of his neck. An image suggestive of the lord of a manor, distantly resembling even Bismarck in the Sachsenwald or Dubslav von Stechlin, who is said to have looked like Bismarck. And that is why a bourgeois couple, descending a flight of stairs only few steps away, their two rambunctious children dashing on ahead, are posing the obviously parvenu question concerning the current appearance of Brandenburg's aristocracy.

All this the caricaturist T. T. Heine captured on paper, with a sure eye for contours and great economy of detail. He knew what an antiquated figure the Immortal had cut in the Tiergarten, and what amused astonishment he had aroused there. And we know that it is not only in *Stechlin* that the Tiergarten provides a backdrop for walks and coach rides. It also promises peace and quiet to Waldemar von Haldern; the young count, who lives nearby on Zeltenstrasse, goes to the Tiergarten in search of a bench, there to put his indecision to rest, an end to his relationship with Stine, and a bullet to his head: "A fresh breeze was blowing, tempering the heat, but from the flower beds wafted the delicate scent of mignonette, while across the way, in Kroll's Music Garden, a concert was just commencing...." The Music Garden and the Kroll Opera, built there later, no longer exist. Much has been cleared away, but the Tiergarten manages to renew itself time and again. Fonty was a witness to that.

His image was firmly established from the beginning; only the man-made landscape around him had been altered, either in cautious phases or at one stroke. Until the Wall went up, the Tiergarten was accessible to Fonty, in spite of the city's division into occupation zones. But then for almost three decades the walking paths had remained off limits to all those who, like him, had to make do with the eastern part of Berlin, proclaimed the capital of the Workers' and Peasants' State.

Now he was astonished to see how lushly the postwar plantings had branched and twigged out in both height and width. The fast-growing poplars and alders, the first plantings on the devastated expanse, had in the meantime given way to beech and oak, maple and weeping willow. Here single trees on tree-lined meadows, there grovelike stands of trees, elsewhere actual woods, lakeshore plantings, pruned shrubbery. Of course there was no shortage of the conifers and birches native to Brandenburg's sandy soil. And the entire park, which extended from the Brandenburg Gate to the Landwehr Canal and the Zoo beyond, was, as the urban planner Lenné had originally conceived it, crisscrossed by tree-lined avenues. In the northern part of the park, seven such avenues fanned out from Zeltenplatz, planted with chestnuts, elms, plane trees, and so forth; in the southern part, avenues crossed the Little Star and Great Star or else were shaded by double rows, like the Hofjägerallee, which likewise led to the Great Star. Yet among the traffic-jammed motorways and on both sides of the former Avenue of Victory, later renamed Avenue of the Seventeenth of June, a network of quietly meandering footpaths opened up vistas of meadows, ponds, and lakes. They led to the Rose Garden or over Queen Luise Bridge, and made it possible to stroll from monument to monument, from Goethe to Lessing, from Moltke to Bismarck, and on into the English Garden, which bordered the grounds of Bellevue Palace and the nearby Academy of the Arts, dear to the western half of the city. Until recently the Academy had preserved its peace and quiet, but since the fall of the Wall it had been roused by the spirit of the times and robbed of its smugness; the eastern half of the city likewise harbored an Academy of the Arts, and now that they were condemned to unification, both institutions, which had avoided each other for decades, were looking back, with an embarrassed grimace, to a Prussian institution whose secretary had once been the Immortal, although only for half a year—that was how quickly conditions at the Academy had come to disgust him.

Fonty returned again and again to certain spots. He liked to stroll from the Friedrich Wilhelm III monument to the Lortzing monument and try out various benches to see if he could find an unobstructed view of Rousseau Island. And as we know, there was a favorite bench, half in shade, with an elderberry bush behind its backrest.

Sometimes he walked to Fasanerieallee and the bronze sculptures that represented the rabbit chase and the fox hunt, then on to New Lake, which fed the Landwehr Canal and was alive with rowboats, starting in early May. Here he watched from bankside benches and was filled with thoughts of rowing excursions in which he had participated or which had found their way into literature— the Easter Monday boat trip in Stralau, for instance, or later the boat ride on the Spree at Hankel's Depot—but at the very beginning it was a quiet arm of the Elbe where a twosome went rowing; and always Lene Nimptsch was present, either as premonition or posthumous experience—that Lene whom Frau Dörr affectionately called "Leneken."

These were his favorite spots. Fonty seldom crossed Hofjägerallee to see a sculpture called "Folk Song," for near it, by the edge of the Tiergarten, he would have been forced to see himself, in the form of a marble statue, gazing out hatless from his round pedestal, with a damaged walking stick and an upright Prussian carriage.

He did not want to encounter himself as a petrified civil servant. Better to take the Great Way time and again to the quiet waters around Rousseau Island. There, after sitting still for a while— with the blooming or ripe elderberry at his back—he could enjoy this special contemplation of changing times; for example, those around 1836, when his apprenticeship in Wilhelm Rose's White Swan Apothecary Shop began. That was shortly after he, still in trade school, first laid eyes on Emilie Rouanet, at the house of his father's brother, Uncle August, that incorrigible money-borrower. Because of her illegitimate birth, she bore the sorrowful last name of Kummer, after her foster father. A child in a becoming poke bonnet, but with an air of wildness about her, whom he must have startled, as indeed the girl startled him at first sight. Even in those days he could have taken the girl by the hand and, if the child were willing, led her along sandy riding paths through the still-unfinished Tiergarten until they came in view of the island, named even that early for a philosopher; just as in the spring of 1846, the year after their engagement, he had searched with Emilie Rouanet--Kummer for a place to sit in the Tiergarten, and had found a bench with a view of the island dedicated to that raving pedagogue and practitioner of enlightenment.

Fonty saw himself in retrospect at the side of the young woman of twenty-one, who no longer resembled a wild, black-eyed goatherd from the Abruzzi but now sized up the world with gray-blue eyes like a normal citizen of Brandenburg and wore her chestnut hair demurely piled on her head: ripe for marriage.

At that time, the layout of the Tiergarten, designed by the landscape architect Lenné, was considered complete. According to his plans, the area around Rousseau Island had achieved its definitive form. Everything was greening on schedule. And the Great Way led past the lake to Great Star Avenue, in the same configuration as forty years later, when daughter Martha, known as Mete, would occasionally accompany her father through the Tiergarten to his favorite spots; but as Fonty rewound to this period and saw himself with Mete in several longer sequences, he could not stop a time shift from zooming in on nine-year-old Martha Wuttke as she dashed across the path, followed by Theo Wuttke, calling out again and again, "Come back, Mete!"

That was shortly before the Wall went up. Father and daughter had been visiting her grandfather, Max Wuttke, in his cellar apartment by Rabbits' Run. Then he saw himself again, tearing through the Tiergarten alone, this time in the guise of a distraught Young Turk. That was a few weeks after the funeral staged for those who had died on the barricades in March '48, at which even the king had been forced to doff his hat.

Incidentally, the marriage to Emilie Rouanet-Kummer took place a good two and a half years later, on 16 October 1850, and the reception was held on the edge of the Tiergarten, near Bellevuestrasse, in a restaurant called the Georgian Garden, a place that attracted many guests, both before and after the revolution, with its sheltered location and excellent food. The Tunnel brethren had taken up a collection for the gift. Of his friends from the early years in Leipzig and Dresden, only Wolfsohn was present. Three decades later, when the moment arrived to celebrate the anniversary at 134C Potsdamer Strasse, one of those tell-all letters noted, "Only a few friends showed any interest in what has become our 'Thirty Years' War.'..."

But from his favorite bench Fonty saw more than family comings and goings. He saw himself with Lepel at his side, saw Storm and Zöllner, bumped into Heyse and Spielhagen, swaggered about with Ludwig Pietsch; later, much later, he shared a bench with Schlenther and Brahm: endless theater gossip.

In changing seasons he saw himself, between and after those three military campaigns soon dubbed the Wars of Unification, weighed down by various manuscripts, each filled with battle and landscape descriptions—representing years of drudgery that earned him nothing but annoyance—whose hurly-burly of words he nonetheless hauled to the Tiergarten, whence he hauled it home again, rather the worse for the effort, to a succession of residences. Not until he had the Academy rubbish behind him and had finally, to Emilie's dismay, become a freelance writer, did he see himself setting out with cargo of a different sort: novels bursting with deftly captured conversations were the Tiergarten booty the Immortal now carried up to his garret on Potsdamer Strasse, a late bloomer at sixty, then on his way to seventy and beyond.

Before the Storm came to fruition here. During walks, his mind continued to tweak at whatever novellas and novels he had in the hopper: "I'm in favor of headings, which is to say resting places, and that goes for life as well; I have no use for parks without benches...." But when the family told him, "Chapter headings are old-fashioned," he suggested to his publisher that all the chapters in *L'Adultera* have numbers; but the headings remained. And when all the "ands" in *Grete Minde* and *Ellernklipp* came in for criticism, he replied, "...I consider myself a stylist who derives his style from the subject matter, and that explains the many 'ands.'..."

And so on to the very last. *Effi Briest*, appearing in serialization, had hardly met her sad end when he was already out roaming around with old Stechlin: in overcoat and with walking stick and hat, striding purposefully from Number 134C toward the Queen Luise Bridge, conversing all the while with Rex and Czako, keeping an ear out for witticisms, repeatedly pouring on Gundermann's "grist for the mills of social democracy," warning time and again of the "great worldwide conflagration," and provoking Domina Adelheid in Wutz Cloister with cutting remarks, for which she repaid her brother Dubslav, old Stechlin, in the same coin: "Keep your French to yourself. It always depresses me."

94

And then for a long time nothing more. The silence of the grave. Monuments. The literary estate unloaded by his son for a paltry eight thousand reichmarks. Assiduous professors parsing and paraphrasing. His devastating judgment on such pedants: "Bone-dry gibberers—they're supposed to support us, and instead just wreck everything. . . ." To some he was too Prussian, to others not Prussian enough. Each hacked out the slice that appealed to him: sometimes he was stylized as the "rambler through the Mark Brandenburg," sometimes abbreviated to the "serenely detached observer," sometimes celebrated as the balladeer, sometimes rediscovered as a revolutionary or dismissed on partisan grounds. Schools were named after him, even apothecary shops. And further misuse and abuse. Already he was dismissed in schoolbooks, consigned to the dustbin of the ages, threatened with oblivion, when at last this young man in Luftwaffe blue turned up, sat down on this particular bench in the Tiergarten, alone or with a companion, and proceeded to become a mouthpiece, for him, and for him alone, the "Immortal."

The name's Wuttke, Theo no less. Hails from Neuruppin and offers his date of birth, the thirtieth of December 1919, as proof of identity. Has tales old and new from France to tell his fiancée, Emmi Hering, who wears her hair combed high, and in her sprigged dress inclines to plumpness. Initially only Gravelotte and Sedan, but then, in quick succession, lightning victories, pincer operations, Guderian's tanks, air supremacy all the way to the Pyrenees, Sedan and Metz falling this time almost without a struggle, crossing the Marne, and on to Paris, Paris! And then the distant view from the Atlantic coast, across the beaches of Normandy and Brittany at low tide to England, the hated cousin. And, dotting the coast of France, the islands, one of which is Oléron, with special significance: many richly atmospheric mood pieces.

Time and again he returns, on leave from the front or on assignment, escorts his betrothed Emmi on his arm through the Rose Garden, past the Lortzing statue, and has already walked with her once around the pond and over bridges, succumbing completely to the pedagogic enchantment of the island: freedom and virtue clash, or give birth to committees of public safety and death by guillotine; Robespierre was Rousseau's most obedient disciple....

Yet the reports the airman gives his fiancée, who is pretty and something of a chatterbox, reports whispered in a style so polished you might think he was reading from a text, are out searching for traces in the crumbling hamlet of Domrémy. There he delivered literary lectures for enlisted men and officers: Where Schiller's "Virgin of Orléans" was born...Why "La Pucelle" is immortal... And how the Immortal, in search of Jeanne d'Arc during the war of '70–'71, with his Red Cross armband and that unfortunate pistol, was nabbed as a Prussian spy and ended up a prisoner of war.

Time and again he returns, with fresh travel impressions, which his fiancée types for him. Accounts from Besançon, Lyon, and finally from the Cévennes, where he tracked down Huguenot hiding places, putting himself in harm's way. Yet he continues to file those reports, confident of victory and devoted to things cultural, even though, before receiving his final marching orders, he found the Tiergarten badly battered, retreat on all the fronts since Stalingrad, his fiancée Emmi pregnant, and Aunt Pinchen nagging them to get married....

The moment came when the airman and war correspondent Theo Wuttke failed to return. Not until all the trees in the Tiergarten had been felled and all the bomb craters had filled with water, not until all the statues had been reduced to torsos, not until the benches, Queen Luise Bridge, and the Kroll Opera were destroyed, not until all the glories around Zeltenplatz lay in ruins, and only the Victory Column remained standing, like some kind of bad joke—not until the war was over did he return, from the French prison camp in Bad Kreuznach, emaciated and shaky in his tattered uniform, searching for his fiancée, whom he found, with his baby son, Georg, under Aunt Pinchen's bomb-damaged roof, and married retroactively in October of 1945.

Immediately after the ceremony, the young couple had to go off to scrounge for firewood, for Aunt Pinchen's coal cellar was bare except for blackish dust. And since all that remained of the

Tiergarten, for the Wuttkes and hundreds of thousands of other Berliners, was scraps of firewood, even roots were hacked out; nothing was left.

These and other flashbacks came to him on his favorite bench. Having first seen himself out in search of the last stubs and stumps with ax, handsaw, and rickety pushcart, he was moved almost to tears by a family tableau: Like ten thousand others, he and Emmi were digging up a plot with pick and spade, while baby Georg trotted back and forth between his parents with his toy shovel. They were planting potatoes, sowing turnip seed; from April '46 on, the clear-cut Tiergarten was chopped into allotments all the way from the Brandenburg Gate to the flak bunker by the Zoo.

This was done by official decree—that's how great the need was. And then came the terrible winter of '46–'47. Many died, including Pauline Piontek, née Hering. Only by two years did she outlive her younger brother, Emmi Wuttke's stepfather, who, along with his wife, had most likely met his death in encircled Breslau. Aunt Pinchen was not even sixty when she left her apartment to the Wuttkes: three and a half rooms, plus kitchen and bath, in Berlin's Prenzlauer Berg district, a circumstance that made them both happy for a while.

Only now, after the lean years, did Fonty return from his excursions into the past. With astonishment he observed that the dream of master gardener Peter Josef Lenné, which neither the skinflint king nor the Berliners' destructive frenzy had been able to snuff out, had finally been realized, after numerous stages of planting, plotting paths, channeling water: Round about him everything was clothed in its May finery; thousands of buds were bursting before his eyes; birdsong, so richly blended that even the blackbird had trouble making her cadences heard. Behind him the elderberry was beginning to unfurl its fans of bloom. And because the waters around Rousseau Island were similarly lively, Fonty found himself tempted to continue Lenné's dream in installments, as if nothing had happened, as if there had been neither war nor devastation, as if the park landscape would remain unscathed in its beauty, as indeed it had always been a feast for his eyes and a refuge. But suddenly everything seemed foreign to him: children from another world—two Turkish girls with sternly knotted kerchiefs—stood before him and the Tiergarten bench, where he thought he had been sitting since his earliest years as an apothecary's apprentice.

Both girls wore a solemn expression. They seemed to be ten or twelve. Both the same height and with the same solemnity; they gazed at him without wanting to take in his smile. Since they said nothing, he did not want to risk speaking either. Only birdsong and distant shouts over the water. Far off in the distance, the roar of the city. For a long time foreignness hovered between Fonty and the Turkish girls. The kerchiefs framed dark-skinned oval faces. Four eyes remained fixed on him. Slow blinks. Now even the blackbird was silent. Fonty was about to formulate a friendly question to break the silence when one of the girls said in German, with barely a trace of a Berlin accent: "Would you be so kind as to betray to us what time it is?"

At once everything seemed less foreign. Fonty fumbled under his coat for his pocket watch, drew it out with a glint of gold, read off the time without having to reach for his glasses, and betrayed it to the girls, who thanked him with a nice little bob, turned, and went on their way. After a few steps they broke into a run, as fast as if they had to get the betrayed time to safety as quickly as possible.

Alone with himself again, Fonty thought he would be able to gaze at Rousseau Island without wandering thoughts, or perhaps without any thoughts at all, and watch the ducks, two swans, and other waterfowl, among them a diving duck; but he wasn't alone for long.

Not that anyone plumped down beside him on the bench and began to talk about the weather. No pensioner, no arthritic grandma, and no wet nurse still in residence from the previous century—"The women from the Spree Woods all smell of sour milk"—turned up to prey on his nerves. No actual person had to sit down beside him to persuade him to recount anecdotes and pick to pieces entire dinner parties. Even sitting by himself, he was caught up in conversation.

This time the tone was not chatty. Compelled to listen, he had Hoftaller's droning clerk's voice in his ear, not so much stern as dryly calculating the weight of evidence. As Tallhover he picked up where it hurt: with the Herwegh Society. The Leipzig period. And already, without even having to leave Saxony, he was in Dr. Gustav Struve's Salamonis Apothecary Shop, and promptly brought up the initially revolutionary, later romantically inclined gardener's daughter Magdalena Strehlenow, rowboat excursions on the Elbe— Dresden and the consequences: "Come now, it wasn't as bad as all that. In a pinch, one could tap Lepel for a loan. One was free, had that year of sentry duty with the Kaiser Franz Guards behind one, likewise the unplanned holiday, that disastrous two-week detour to England. And the apothecary's license was finally in hand, the state boards having been passed with distinction—congratulations! A more or less happy engagement, without, it must be said, the future bride's having been let in on the Dresden secrets. Those boat rides were suppressed out of cowardice, likewise the love-crazed coupling and the squalling of infants. Instead our Forty-eighter brandished a rusty rifle. Being there is everything! Even so, we didn't step in. No matter how some of the Tunnel doggerel and later the conspiratorial Herwegh Society nettled us, nothing happened, not even a reprimand. Well, because we had our hands full, me especially. As superintendent of detectives I'd been assigned to the Georg Herwegh case. He was spawning epigones wherever he went, and that with an arrest warrant out for him that my biographer rightfully describes as 'ridiculous.' But when the *Dresdner Zeitung* published a series of political dispatches in twenty-nine installments, with the author identified only by a cipher, we found ourselves forced to start a file after all: code word 'Fontaine.' The pieces were partly overwrought, partly inflammatory, each and every one aimed at Prussia's police state—nothing new there, to be sure, but this flailing about was certainly dangerous...."

Fonty heard all this in his mind's ear. Any passerby who had noticed him on the park bench and paused to listen would have witnessed his head-shaking and grimacing: an old man at odds with himself and others. Now and then he exclaimed, "Balderdash!" And: "Autodidacts always exaggerate!" He protested: "Wrong, Tallhover!

Even Pietsch confirmed that I spared neither myself nor others in *Between Twenty and Thirty*...." He offered a detailed response: "Glad to hear your memory's so colossally faulty. Our first contact occurred not before but soon after my wedding. In the late autumn of '50, shortly before the 'Literary Cabinet' was dissolved. We met here in the Tiergarten, specifically at the In den Zelten rowboat-rental stand. You were bound and determined to go out on the water. But I was in no mood for rowing. So we went and sat in the Moritzhof beer garden. The last chestnuts were falling. White beer and falling leaves. And after I'd taken one swallow, my dossier appeared on the table, not thick, but thick enough...."

Even if Fonty fell silent after such explanations, or pretended to be interested only in mallard families and one particularly enterprising diving duck, he did not succeed in being deaf as well as dumb. Someone kept talking at him. If not Hoftaller, then Tallhover. His constant carping could not be switched off: "It wasn't in late fall, after your latest foolhardy adventure, your failed attempt to play the war hero on the side of Schleswig against the Danes, but rather at the end of August '50 that I had to reel you in. You're right about the Tiergarten rendezvous. What a hot day! At any rate, before the wedding the groom was already assured of our support. From September on, you were on the government payroll as a reviewer for the *Literary Cabinet*. High time you were taken under the wing. In every respect. In your private life, your strict Emmi saw to that, and officially you were supervised by Herr von Merckel, your patron, true, but also our man. The kindest censor imaginable, such as you hardly find anymore in our service. Knew a lot—well-rounded and cultured, a model I could never live up to. He could rhyme army with democracy, but also had other strings to his bow. His solicitous policy of paying sparingly but regularly worked like a charm. At any rate, your young wife was delighted to be able to count on a steady income at last. And just a year later George, the son and heir, was there...."

Meanwhile, out there amidst the mallards the diving duck was demonstrating an alternative. "Let him blither on," Fonty may have said to himself. "After all, my collected poems did get published. And as for Merckel, a friendly and collegial relationship was developing...."

"But of course. Family to family, later with regular exchange of letters. No one cared as lovingly for your poor Theo, neglected by his father, as the Merckels. No wonder, then, with that kind of protection, that a position became available, at the Central Press Office, to be exact, a minimally camouflaged censorship agency to which our botched existence had to adjust—despite all the yammering at home—especially since after Rastatt his last revolutionary cock feathers had been plucked. Hinkeldey was the name of Berlin's police commissioner...."

The tufted duck had dived out of sight, and suddenly resurfaced somewhere else. Fonty let himself be taken by surprise. After every dive he bet against himself—and lost. He would have loved to be similarly unpredictable, out of sight, now here, now there, at his will and pleasure—even if only for minutes at a time: "All frightfully true, Tallhover! Sold my soul to see a wish fulfilled. To escape from those dry strictures—finally. To London by way of Cologne, Brussels, Ghent, and Ostende, even with ministerial shackles on my ankles. My first real trip to England—the very first one, those two weeks on borrowed money, doesn't count. Even with commissioned reports to file, I had to do better as the breadwinner—gave German lessons! That's how poorly I was paid. That's how wretchedly Prussia rewarded my little betrayal. What more do you want, Tallhover! You eternal snoop! Why don't you just beat it? We're not on the interrogation couch now. You old regurgitator! Scram, sir! Keep your distance, will you! This is my Tiergarten. This was always my favorite bench. Rousseau Island is mine, mine to feast my eyes on. And that's my diving duck!"

With his left hand Fonty was making shooing motions, as if flies were buzzing around him. With his right hand he was clutching his walking stick so tightly that he trembled. An angry old man flailing in the air.

Turkish families passed in their appointed order: the men first, then the wives and children. A steady stream of Turks with shopping nets and plastic bags. From the women's and girls' head scarves—many of them black or white, some motley—Fonty tried to derive a significance analogous to the Scottish color spectrum.

But after yet another extended Turkish family had passed without a moment's glance at his struggle with his demon, he exclaimed, "Listen, Tallhover! Besides me, the Tiergarten belongs to those people. The paths, the meadows, the benches, everything. This is indubitably Turkish terrain. Read the paper: After Istanbul and Ankara, Berlin is the third largest Turkish city. And they just keep coming. Even you folks can't impose control on that many. Got it? The Turks are the new Huguenots! They'll create their own order here, they'll set up a system; yours capitulated yesterday, and mine long ago. To be sure, before I was made censorship's handmaiden, I wrote to my friend Friedrich Witte: 'I despise this cowardly, stupid, and mean-spirited policy, and three-and sixfold the wretches who lend themselves to defending this swindle, intoning daily: Herr von Manteuffel is a great statesman! You could offer me my previous position again: I don't want it...'—but six months later I had no choice but to confess to Lepel: 'Sold myself to the reactionaries today for thirty pieces of silver monthly. A decent person simply has no way to survive nowadays. I am making my debut as a hired hack for Adler's paper with a poem in ottava rima—in praise of Manteuffel. Contents: the prime minister crushes the dragon of revolution beneath his heel!' Yet when I was in London, and Ambassador von Bunsen, a liberal of course, wanted to incite me against Manteuffel, I resisted, despite my sympathies, and wrote to my Emilie, who was naturally terrified that I might just jettison all the rubbish, 'To live at Manteuffel's expense and write against him would heighten the moral shabbiness....' Then, back in Berlin, the second child died before I had a chance to see him. A wretched business. No longer a drug pusher but a scribbler under surveillance. And that for the duration, whether with the Reich Aviation Ministry or the Cultural Union. You folks always had your hand in, making sure my thoroughly botched existence...Even now, with the Wall gone... I'm graciously permitted to haul files around, and have to look the other way while you...And never alone, not even in the paternoster...And if it weren't for the Tiergarten, all these Turks, and the diving duck..."

After that Fonty just went on muttering to himself. He cut a fart, then another. Sitting there, his head with its wispy white hair bowed, he propped both hands on his walking stick, his nervously trembling lower lip covered by the upper one. Aged, as if the end were near; no thought seemed to animate him. Only flight—down, down, down into the past.

A person walking slowly past him would have been able to make out single words, even half-sentences; and we archivists would have been in a position to decode the flow of his speech. Much took the form of quotations from the Immortal's travel narrative "Beyond the Tweed," written after his third and longest sojourn in England, when he visited Scotland with his friend Lepel: "As we strolled down High Street...at every corner, sons of the highlands in kilt and plaid...presumably recruiters for the Highlanders...."

Then he was no longer pounding the sidewalks of Edinburgh but was living in the days of King James IV. The issue was chivalry and "Bell-the-Cat." With a schooled ear, one could make out some of the words: "At the court of King James was Spens of Kilspindie...In Stirling Castle as the sweet wine flowed...The House of Douglas's growing might...The blow was deadly, it struck to the heart...."

Then he merely watched the diving duck—now you see him, now you don't. The repetition never grew tiresome. Even when he got up, approached the bank, and fed the mallards bread crusts from his coat pocket, he was preoccupied with the tufted duck and its tricks. Nothing could distract him. True, stuck in his other coat pocket was a rolled-up *Tagesspiegel* with the election results from the provinces panting for annexation; but Fonty had taken leave of the Workers' and Peasants' State. Current events that he witnessed as Theo Wuttke—when they thrust themselves upon him—did not count in the Tiergarten; there he was on a journey backward in time; in Scotland again, from Stirling Castle to Loch Katrine...

7

The Double Grave

It's still quite a distance. It was no longer necessary to apply for a special permit to enter this particular cemetery, whose location by the border made it difficult to reach, but by the time Fonty decided to visit the grave, May had passed and June had arrived. The Tiergarten had taken precedence; he had sat on his favorite bench, chatting with the living and the dead, and a water bird had talked him into traveling down predestinate paths.

Why not France? Wasn't Gascony a viable destination? We archivists, familiar from thousands of letters with the ebb and flow of his wanderlust, had to ask ourselves this question. Why did every thought of ducking out of sight carry him to London, and then on across the border-marking Tweed? What drew him to the Scottish moors, to Macbeth's witches' heath? Did his escape plans, taking off from that Tiergarten bench, lead only to this far-off region, staked out by the clans? Shouldn't the diving duck's instruction have pointed in a more enlightened direction?

We remained of two minds on this question. True, there were the memoirs, in print, of two sojourns in England, and the London journals, as yet unpublished, but these were counterbalanced by other, more deeply rooted connections: Huguenot ancestry on both sides might well have exerted a decisive influence on this man who lived, after all, entirely in earlier footsteps. And family background aside, that mighty tome on the Franco-Prussian War, together with the slim volume on the captivity, should have been as compelling as the Scottish journey with Bernhard von Lepel, despite the fact that the war book garnered approval from neither military historians nor the kaiser; and as for the memoirs on his internment in France, his son George, who in '70–'71 served on the battlefield as a captain, reproved him for not hating the French enough; in a carping letter he complained of his father's lack of patriotic sentiment.

Yet precisely because he, who was close to the theater of war, though never directly involved, had ended up in captivity, everything spoke for France. After several way stations, they had interned him on the island of Oléron. They could have had him executed, which would have been their right under the rules of war. At least Prussian officers later assured him that in analogous circumstances, in other words as a Frenchman in German hands, he could not have expected mercy; even as a harmless person, "a mere writer," he would have been shot.

Aside from a certain gratitude—the Immortal's internment ended after only two months—Fonty could have found, in the course of his follow-up existence, further ties to France. As we know, two wars later he was already back in action there as a correspondent. In four years of rear-echelon duty, Airman Wuttke never ran out of ink as he diligently and retrospectively stayed on the trail, from the Atlantic Wall to the Cévennes; and we archivists really should have collected this material, for all the texts released by the Aviation Ministry were rich in quotations and scintillating cross-references—it was not only the war books that provided him with cues. Likewise we neglected to inform ourselves about Lyon and that love affair, allegedly with consequences that were destined to revive later on in wondrous fashion and catch up with Fonty.

On the subject of travel, to destinations that could merely be surmised, Hoftaller often "operated" with insinuations, and when he sought us out again, irritating the Archives by his mere presence, he commented, "Whether Dresden or Lyon, the airman equals the apothecary's apprentice. It wouldn't be far-fetched to describe their behavior as shooting from the hip; both of them behaved so impetuously as to be irresponsible. But I see that you people are quick to excuse anything in the name of youth."

The formula Fonty often repeated now—"I'm on the point of making myself scarce"—was, like many of his "that's-that" declarations, yet another quotation. He let us think he was yearning for the Cévennes, where he could have ducked under in the gorges of the Ardèche; yet he remained secretly fixated on England and the moors in the Scottish highlands. Nothing could dissuade him from leaping the Channel. He took his escape plans to work with him, but wherever he was occupied, whether in the paternoster or padding the sofa, he kept them to himself. The diving duck's lesson remained confidential. At home his wife and daughter found him taciturn.

Later, when we rang the doorbell on the third floor of the apartment house on Kollwitzstrasse, the two told us, "When Wuttke talks to me, he never tells what's really going on in his head..." and "So what else is new! Theoretically, Father's always been restless. And since he never belonged to the travel cadre, he dreams up trips for himself, here and there."

Even Hoftaller, who had guessed Fonty's outward-bound intentions long before we had, could find no pretext for an exploratory interrogation, no matter how often the two of them were out and about together; the big topic of the day—the imminent wholesale currency conversion—had people all across the country trotting around, not just our entangled pair.

They described their walks as "going shopping." Shortly before the new currency was due to come to power, clearance sales were announced everywhere. Products manufactured by the "people's own" factories flew off the counter at closeout prices. The idea was this: On the day of the promised monetary miracle, shelves in all the state-run grocery stores, in every department store, would be bare, making room for the vast selection from the West that would replace the usual scarce and drearily packaged goods. Hopes were high: at long last consumption would be possible. At long last the customer would be right, always right.

But as feverishly as people longed for the new currency, many also dreaded its hardness. There was still time to stock up cheaply on nonperishables. Along with Fonty and Hoftaller, the thousands of East Berliners with totes and shopping bags were not the only ones thronging the streets; West Berliners were also helping haul away the junk. The old money was burning a hole in everyone's pocket; people grabbed whatever they could. Everywhere the shelves were emptying.

On Alexanderplatz, Fonty snapped up several reams of typing paper—guaranteed pulp-free—and two dozen pencils. In a liquor store near Rosa-Luxemburg-Platz he got a bargain on seven bottles of brandy bearing the label of the People's Own Distillery in Wilthen, known in the Workers' and Peasants' State for quality; in years past its products had seldom been available. He also acquired at throwaway prices various household items for his wife and daughter. Martha Wuttke, his Mete, planned to marry soon. And because her future husband came from the West and was considered comfortably situated, if not wealthy, it would not do for her to be the poor Eastern Mouse, recognizable by her skimpy trousseau, when she moved to Münster in Westphalia. The future bridegroom, Heinz-Martin Grundmann, and his partner operated a construction firm there that had been active for years in the East Bloc countries, notably in Bulgaria.

So Fonty rather unselectively scooped up bed linens, a soup tureen labeled "authentic Meissen porcelain," tablecloths, even an assortment of thread, and a hand-held mixer produced by the People's Own Robotron Works. For his Emmi he laid in a supply of terry hand towels and scented soaps; as inadequately as the large textile combines had produced in the past, now, with the end approaching, they managed to deliver the goods. Heavily laden, Fonty set out for home. Hoftaller helped him carry his haul.

Hoftaller's final purchases had a different focus. We have neglected to mention that Fonty's day-and-night-shadow occasionally smoked, or rather that he was a connoisseur of cigars. In other words, we must picture Hoftaller on previously described occasions with a thick lung-torpedo protruding from his mouth, its white ash casually tapped off at the very last moment. Whether at the Wall amid the sound of picking peckers, or after the birthday celebration at McDonald's, wherever he had been with Fonty, indoors or out, among the young talents of Prenzlauer Berg or on a bench in the Tiergarten; even in the Ministries Building, he had smoked his steadily shrinking cigars, whether in the furnace room or on the initially sagging, then well-padded sofa that stood in the attic, providing room for smokers and nonsmokers alike.

Through all his years of service to the state, and even up to the pending currency union, Hoftaller had at his disposal the contents of wooden boxes originating in Cuba. He had his sources for this exquisite article, manufactured by a socialist ally. Even in times of scarcity, he was well supplied, and when was scarcity not the rule? From the mid-eighties on, he smoked not only Cuban product but also hand-rolled numbers from Nicaragua, of unusual length. No one ever saw him with a Brasil.

Tallhover was described by his biographer as a cigarillo smoker; and in turn we can vouch for Hoftaller as a cigar smoker: time and again he turned up at the Archives ostentatiously puffing Castro's trademark, as if to demonstrate the international reach of his connections, though it would not have taken that much smoke to convince us. As it was, we suspected assignments that took him, if not to capitalist countries abroad, then at least to allied ones, and why not also to Cuba? When one of our colleagues revealed in conversation that he enjoyed the occasional hand-wrapped cigar, Hoftaller put on a show of generosity; and of course our colleague would not have dared to turn down this rare treat.

But now the era of such privileges was past. There was reason for concern. In no time at all, the fragrant boxes would be a thing of the past. The radical slash in the currency threatened to cap a supply that was barred from the West's free market by a trade boycott. No wonder, then, that Hoftaller had planned a preemptive strike. Accompanied by Fonty, who had already finished his purchases—laundry detergent and sunflower oil—he sought out a tobacconist on Weitlingstrasse, close to Lichtenberg station, to secure the remaining stock. Fonty later characterized it as panic-buying.

A nonsmoker himself, Fonty stood there as if absent, yet could not help seeing Hoftaller pull out a wad of Eastern money—"A good two months' pay," he said—and buy out the entire shop, which seemed to be privately owned. In addition to tobacco products, the store carried newspapers, now from both parts of Berlin. Hoftaller's booty consisted of three boxes of Romeo y Julietas and two boxes of the unusually long Joya de Nicaragua cigars. Fonty bought the *Wochenpost,* the paper he had been reading for years, and the West Berlin *Tagesspiegel.*

While the smoker was paying, wearing a triumphant expression, the nonsmoker was reading, under the headline "New Currency to Arrive Overnight," the announcement of the end of the bargain-basement currency. The first of July would be the day. From Monday, 2 July, on, only the hard deutschmark would be legal tender. The Eastern minister of finance, a Social Democrat named Romberg, had voiced nervous reservations, then bravely signed his name to the treaty. Skimming over the details, Fonty focused on the table of exchange rates. After all, the principle demonstrated by the tufted duck had to be paid for. Secretly he calculated the contents of his savings account and came up with a sum that gave him hope: there was still a good week until the first of July, known as Day X.

Outside all was normal again. Weitlingstrasse gray on gray, two elderly gentlemen pounding the pavement. They chatted about their purchases as they went, then paused indecisively by a snack bar inside the Berlin-Lichtenberg station. Long-distance trains passed through the station, traveling from Leipzig to Stralsund, for instance, and on to Sassnitz on the island of Rügen, from which the ferry departed for Sweden.

His supply of cigars secured, Hoftaller invited Fonty to join him for a beer and a bockwurst. He wore a jovial air and declared himself happy. They ate standing at a bar table whose surface was marbled with streaks of mustard and ketchup. Because of the summery weather, neither had been wearing hat or overcoat. Hoftaller, however, had smartened himself up with some new acquisitions: his cap, with a transparent visor, had an American cut, as did his shirt, which had flowers superimposed on broad stripes. Thus decked out in approximately Western style, he gave Fonty to understand that it would be crucial now to recognize the signs of the new times. But Theo Wuttke just wanted to be Fonty: even in summertime, he wore the traditional scarf doubled around his neck; besides, the station was drafty.

Hoftaller had no sooner polished off his bockwurst than he wound up to deliver a monologue. He recalled an assignment Tallhover had received in connection with a sealed train traveling from Zurich to Sassnitz and its passengers, among them a certain Lenin; at the behest of the imperial German government, this train was to bring the revolution to Russia and thereby weaken the enemy on the eastern front. But before he began, he reached into his shopping bag and opened one of the cigar boxes. According to Tallhover's biographer, the special train from Zurich via Gottmadingen made stops in Mannheim, Frankfurt, and Berlin as it crossed the German Reich. That was in March '17. With considerable fuss and a great show of secrecy, Hoftaller opened the box inside the shopping bag, finally straightened up again, and was now standing, short and squat, at the table, a Romeo y Julieta in his hand. "Of course," he said, "it was from Stettin station, not from here, that the special train departed for Sassnitz." The cigar in Hoftaller's mouth protruded as far as the baseball cap's visor. "At any rate, everything that happened later began with Lenin passing through here." He said this as the cigar, expertly ignited, began to draw. Fonty was still working on his bockwurst, dipping bite after bite in mustard.

And now Hoftaller spoke into the cigar smoke, which lingered briefly, then wafted away on the draft: "What do you expect? What we see happening today can still be traced back to all of that: Lenin and the consequences. I still say: Starting with the first of July, the world'll look different. Sure, our products'll be good for nothing, and our factories'll be what the West's been calling them for months now: scrap. From Rostock to Karl-Marx-Stadt: one big scrap heap. But the shelves will be filled. And in no time flat. Western stuff, beautifully packaged. And before we know it, the hard currency—we can get some now at one-to-one, and exchange whatever we have left at two-to-one later—all that money'll be right back in the West, where it came from. That's what they call 'getting a bargain.' And with the hard mark, we'll see hordes of shoppers. They're already here, looking over the goods. You know the kind, Fonty. They're all from the Tribe of Greed, your Treibels & Associates. They're taking their cut here. For all these Parvenooskis, this is no-man's-land. All they see is real estate. Carve out a piece here, a piece there. They call it prime cuts. They're already nibbling at Potsdamer Platz. And not only the Japs. No doubt about it: Mercedes is leading the pack!"

In the meantime Fonty had finished his bockwurst. He wiped his mouth carefully with the paper napkin. The draft blowing through Lichtenberg station stirred his thin, whitish-gray wisps of hair. Without a hat he looked older. Yet his voice still sounded youthful: "Colossally ideological hogwash you're spouting there. Exploitation of the proletariat—we've heard it all before. Capitalists out to crush us—know it by heart, never believed it. It's just you, Hoftaller, faking the handwriting on the wall with your big cigar. And you know why? Because you and your comrades have nothing to report now. A disaster, eh? The Normannenstrasse fortress stormed. All the file cabinets sealed up. The state in receivership. And your years of paper-pushing, those decades of Nogoodnik work for the firm of Eavesdrop, Peep, and Pounce: up in smoke. True, there's still some sniffing about. And what the shredder doesn't take care of has to be stashed away somewhere, even in a worn-out sofa, but you can't call it real operations anymore, just a way of killing time. I know, I lent a hand, was even glad to. I'm delighted to see that poison disappear. But now it's all over, for good! What I said last November on Alexanderplatz, with hundreds of thousands standing there, still holds true: 'A new day is dawning! A better and happier one, I believe. And if not a happier one, at least one with more oxygen in the air, a time when we can breathe more freely. And the more freely you breathe, the more you can live!'"

Hoftaller's stumpy hands mimed applause. His cigar emitted smoke signals. "You can't fool me, Fonty. Vintage Pastor Lorenzen stuff. 'Democratic world view'—that's what he purred to the lovely Melusine. Don't make me laugh. Deceptive packaging, just new pressures in place of old—that's all we can expect...."

"Yet the first thing coming is freedom. I can almost smell it— smells like a beast of prey. Oh, yes, it always was dangerous, and to

my mind nothing was more ridiculous than the liberals, those perpetual freedom-mongers. But this time it's different. Freedom's
opening things up on all sides. No doubt about it: the world's beck-
oning to us. That awful, shut-in period of the elite travel cadre is
over, the lovely view's no longer blocked. Yes, indeed, Herr Krimi-
nalkommissar Tallhover! Yes, indeed, Hoftaller! Now, when even
you could be out of the service, a trip—to who knows where—
should be tempting. Italy, Greece! Travel broadens the horizons!
And what exactly were you until just recently—a captain? a major?"

Addressed thus by name and in defiance of time, Fonty's
durable day-and-night-shadow smiled. Miraculously, his cigar was
still drawing. He removed his baseball cap and wiped his brow with
the back of his hand. His matchstick-length hair, once wheat-
blond, now stone-gray, stood up all over his head. Hoftaller could
smile winningly. And his voice had no sharp edge to it: "Now, now.
Who's running off at the mouth about leaving the service? Believe
me: for us there is no end. Blow us away, and we're back in a flash,
and chock-full of information that was tucked away safely to hiber-
nate. Information that's in demand, by the way, and that has its
price. Clients are already knocking: Pullach, Cologne, to name just
the most obvious addresses. Have a bunch of colleagues there who
want to be brought up to date. But older expertise is also in demand. And since the services always did their planning and operations on a pan-German basis, a person likes to be helpful. But our
opportunities don't stop there. You, of all people, my dear Wuttke,
should be careful about dreaming up trips. Even though you've recently taken to nattering about freedom, I must remind you that in
the past, under one name or another, you thought freedom was for
the birds. Prussia always came first, then the king and the Junkers.
At least as long as you were indentured to the *Kreuzzeitung*, the
Hezekiels and Merckels, for a pittance. During the relatively stable
fifties and sixties. Always toeing the line, right-o, saving your grous-
ing for letters. Same thing with the Cultural Union. Honest, Fonty!
First you hailed the 'Volk community' in the Reich Aviation Ministry, then you celebrated the 'Workers' and Peasants' State' in capital letters. And the more snappily socialism emulated your beloved
Prussia, the less you gave a hoot about freedom. Didn't one of your

lectures on *Before the Storm,* that brick of a book, have the positively toadying title of 'From the Prussian Home Reserves to the People's Army'?"

"Colossal distortion! That was its title, but they banned it after I'd delivered the talk twice. Too much Scharnhorst and Gneisenau, too little Red Army..."

"Because your theories were premature. In the mid-sixties they couldn't amount to anything. But less than ten years later, Prussia was all the rage, and the goose step was back. And now, all of a sudden, freedom's supposed to set the pace. Out into the wide, wide world! Yet it's all about us, about Germany, about unification. That's the only reason we nudged things along, pressuring the comrades here, the gentlemen over there, to make a move. We were the ones who saw to it that in Leipzig and elsewhere that childish bawling 'We Are the People' was spiced up—all it took was exchanging one word, to make it 'We Are One People.' That's right, one little word. That's how unification was spelled out, with chants, and now it's actually coming. There's no other way. But first comes money, because that's a necessity. They'll have to pay, pay for years. And when the gentlemen over there are weak from pay-ing, the way our comrades were weak, just too weak, we'll lift the lid and open the box, the big barrel. All our information—and we've been diligent—will flood over them. Holy Mielke! Our efforts won't have been in vain. You, too, my dear Fonty, should realize that our operational records aren't closed yet. The files are push-ing their way into the open, all in their original order; they want to come alive and enjoy the freedom you're so keen on. That'll be some celebration, a pan-German celebration! In the end every-one'll know all about everybody else. We call it declassified unifi-cation. Germany must become transparent. That goes for you, too, Wuttke. Ducking under and disappearing for a while won't do a bit of good. We've known all about that since Herwegh's day, the diving-duck theory!"

The beer glasses empty. The two standing at their table in the drafty station. Hoftaller's cigar cold. The loudspeaker announced a departure for Sassnitz, via Stralsund. And Fonty said nothing. It wasn't until they were waiting on the subway platform for trains in the direction of Alexanderplatz and on to Schönhauser Allee that Fonty remarked, shortly before the train from Marzahn pulled in, "All frightfully right. But what's right needn't be true. The truth takes one far afield." They picked up their bags of closeout items and got on: Hoftaller behind Fonty.

Not long after this he came to the Archives, with flowers of course. He had no particular requests, just wanted to chat. Nothing struck us as particularly significant, except his repeated references to the French parish's cemetery on Pflugstrasse, which he intended to visit—"I'm bracing myself for hordes of tourists." Who would have guessed that what brought him to us, as to the cemetery, was the thought of departure?

"I'm having one of those quotation days," he exclaimed, and promptly began, applying the "Rütli method," to shoot down a number of literary colleagues much touted in their time: "Heyse still owes his renown more to his personality than to his poetry...." And after Storm's "incessant Husumantics," it was Raabe's turn: "He belongs to that category of Germans I find appalling. They're dissatisfied with everything, find everything wretched, mendacious, nonsensical...." Then he poked fun at lady readers, the typical "Marlitt-suckled knitting-needle lady from Saxony or Thuringia," and made a graceful transition with the exclamation, "Brachvogel should be read in the kitchen!" from the ebb of German literature to the flow of his beloved English writers, in which connection he rated Walter Scott above Dickens.

After we had chatted for some time about literature's ability to generate sympathy for deeds that were essentially criminal, comparing Thackeray's *Catherine* to the Immortal's *Grete Minde*, Fonty pointed out to us how the serialization of novellas and novels had put authors under increased pressure to devise suspenseful chapter endings. But no sooner had he reduced Tangermünde by way of quotation to ashes and embers—"The entire city below a sea of flame; destruction as far as the eye can see, and in its midst a scurrying and screaming, and then the silence of death..."—when he suddenly laughed and changed the subject. He wanted to know from us how the Archives would be funded after the impending currency union. "That will cost us dearly and bring no gain."

Utterly at a loss, like everyone else in those days, we mentioned the possibility of founding a research association that would charge dues, and told him that in December a conference would take place, here in Potsdam, in fact, and that Frau Professor Jolles planned to come all the way from London to deliver the keynote address. Fonty gave us to understand how highly he prized the old lady's scholarly efforts; her work on the sojourns in England was especially exemplary: "She knows almost everything. And perhaps she knows even more than she's revealed publicly...."

Our director remarked that Charlotte Jolles had promised in a letter that in her keynote address she would issue an unmistakable appeal for financial contributions. And Fonty had a quotation at his fingertips: "One has the purse, the other the money...."

After he had taken back or modified his initial, overly harsh chiding of various literary colleagues, had praised Heyse's sonnets and Storm's lyrical poems, had even called Brachvogel a "decent craftsman," and had put in a good word for Raabe's acerbic or sometimes merely quirky sense of humor, he left, waving from the doorway with his light, straw-yellow boater in hand; his daughter Martha had bought it for him years earlier during a vacation in Bulgaria on the Black Sea coast.

We were not the only ones filled with simultaneous hope and dread by the new currency. Altogether, it was a time for wishes that had been long deferred, perhaps too long. The Wuttke family was agitated, too, Fonty in his own way, obsessed as he was with thoughts of ducking out of sight. Well aware that the tin coin still in circulation would be worth nothing in the place he had in mind, he put his money on the new currency, doing the calculations in his head. He pinned his hopes on the current prime minister of the still-existent Nation Number Two, a figure who came across in public as caved in, but was in fact being propped up by the West since the last election. This man, who had taken over from Comrade Modrow, a leftover from the years of the Workers' and Peasants' State, was now practicing contrition, countrywide and in a representative capacity, manifesting an aura of strict Calvinism, even down to his name.

For this very reason, Lothar de Maizière became a repository of hope for Fonty. He may have said to himself that the West could not charge this man with socialist obstinacy, as it could his predecessor. This man would usher in a new, harder currency. His demonstrated humility could count on terrestrial rewards. Only with his help, and a halfway favorable exchange rate, could Fonty's program of ducking under here and surfacing somewhere else be financed. Calvinism had always enjoyed an intimate relationship with money. Yet he himself had never had a chance to revel in this proximity to Mammon, despite the Immortal's twofold Huguenot heritage. To the Archives he said confidently: "This de Maisière will sell us out, but he'll get a good price."

Speculations of this sort may have moved Fonty to visit the cemetery of the French Reformed parish, located in the north end of Berlin, near the Chausseestrasse checkpoint. The grounds, including the section belonging to the Catholic St. Hedwig's congregation, were bordered on one side by Luisenstrasse, which ran along the bulldozed death strip and the Wall. For this reason, the entire cemetery had been classified in '61 as border zone, and until '85 it could be visited only with a special permit, a privilege that even Fonty had seldom been granted. Yet now one could reach all the graves from the open entrance on Pflugstrasse.

Because the No. 6 subway line was not yet in operation, Fonty took the streetcar—the last stop was called Stadium of World Youth. He had succeeded in shaking off his day-and-night-shadow for a while. The last days of June were just around the corner. The weather could be described as changeable, but was kindly disposed toward the cemetery visitor. The puddles from the last downpour had seeped into the sandy soil of the paths.

Fonty came without flowers. His presence, so often thwarted in earlier days by red tape, had to suffice. Acquainted with the layout, he strode in his summer hat and with his bamboo walking stick past simple gravestones, monosyllabic by contrast with the aphoristic prolixity of the neighboring Catholic markers: only dates and names, names like Delorme, Charlet, Marzellier. He paused briefly in front of a pale red granite obelisk engraved with the names of several soldiers of Huguenot ancestry who had died for Prussian Germany in the war of '70–'71: Reclam, Bonnin, Harnier, Hugo, Sarre . . .

And then Fonty was standing before the grave of the man whose later fame went hand in hand with the concept of immortality, the man whose life he was continuing, down to the details of his outward appearance; he even brought with him his predecessor's susceptibility to nerves, counteracted, to be sure, by stoic bearing.

To be more precise: he was standing before a restored gravestone. Since the beginning of the century, there had been two ivy-covered mounds and two simple granite markers, slightly arched on top. Near the end of the Second World War, when the Battle of Berlin left no spot unscathed, these were destroyed and damaged: an artillery shell of either Greater German or Soviet provenance blew the Immortal's granite to bits and split a piece off the top of his wife's stone. Likewise, the iron posts and chains around the double grave were toppled, and later carted off by looters.

As Fonty stood, his mustache quivering slightly, before the stone that had been erected in the postwar period, he was probably recalling the double granite and the two mounds. This stone was less simple but still traditional in style: the engraved surface was coarse-polished to a lighter gray to lend emphasis to the letters and numbers, which stood out in highly polished relief. The rest of the front of the granite block, whose sides were artfully rough-hewn, was polished to a brilliant gleam. A stone taller than it was wide, which dictated the placement of one name above the other. Above Emilie, née Rouanet-Kummer, who had died on 18 February 1902, stood the name and birth date of the Immortal, with his date of death below: 20 September 1898.

"Soon it will be time to celebrate the centennial," we had often assured Fonty and ourselves. "We at the Archives are already making preparations; thanks to our collective efforts, something special should be appearing between book covers."

Hat in hand, he stood silently before the stone marker, yet the words in his mind could easily have been communicated as half-spoken remarks. Two withered wreaths, their bows faded by the weather, provided ample cues. The wreaths were reminders of the last birthday, the seventieth, which Fonty had celebrated at McDonald's, albeit in oppressive company. On the ribbon of one wreath, from the Archives, by the way, one could still read that 30 December 1989 should be dedicated to the "Great Humanist." The other wreath came from the Huguenot Museum. So much commemoration despite tumultuous times. Such an advance on further immortality.

Fonty demonstrated his head for dates. Since he was there alone, aside from a few visitors to the cemetery busy at some distance with rakes and watering cans, he praised out loud the fourth French Henry's Edict of Nantes—"That was in the year 1598"—and went on to extol Elector Friedrich Wilhelm of Brandenburg, who in prompt response to the revocation of the Edict of Nantes by France's fourteenth Louis had issued an edict of tolerance—"That was in the year 1685." Fonty could even quote the salient words: "By means of this Edict, which We have signed in Our Own hand, to offer a safe and free retraite into all Our lands and provinces to Our brothers in the Faith, being impugned and persecuted on account of the Holy Scriptures and their righteous doctrine..."

He reeled off further solemn promises like a poem; and it is not at all astonishing that among the five thousand "réfugiés" who settled as a result of the proffered tolerance among the barely ten thousand Berliners in Brandenburg, Fonty should have discovered and invoked direct ancestors, among them some belonging to Emilie Rouanet-Kummer: "Without us colonists, and, granted, the Battle of Fehrbellin, where the Swedes took a blow to the head, probably nothing would have become of Prussia. That is why I have always emphasized my Huguenot ancestry, as opposed to the dull Borussian element. Have no intention of changing that. My ancestral cradle stood in the Languedoc and in Gascony. My father a Gascognard to the letter: full of bonhomie, but also a dreamer... and they say I, too, am prone to the occasional gasconade: always on the point of vaulting over the fence and taking off, simply ducking out of sight...yet not without a touch of the braggart, empty purse or no....Yes, yes, here I stand before this substitute stone, see withered wreaths and permanently rooted ivy, but I'm ready to travel, because I have Gascony at my back, as well as before me... or another destination: Scottish heaths, blue-black lakes, beyond the Tweed....No surprise that in writing as in speaking I'm still a *causeur*, a chatterer par excellence, which guaranteed me a community of sympathetic listeners on my lecture tours for the Cultural Union. And even as a young smart aleck and airman I could lecture off the cuff in Domrémy to high-ranking officers—on Jeanne d'Arc and her literary afterlife....How ridiculous, then, and outrageous, that Julius Hart, one of those super-clever new-fangled critics, who love to skewer a writer, examine him up close, and then write him to pieces, described me as 'a dyed-in-the-wool philistine with a ramrod in his back.' Me, who went to bed with Mary Stuart and got up with Archibald Douglas, me, whose quintessentially French nature still causes him trouble....The Labrys, on my mother's side, were all involved in hosiery, in silkworm-raising, in silk in general. My grandfather Pierre Barthélemy introduced an artistic vein into the family—was even drawing master to the royal children. And later he became a cabinet secretary to Queen Luise, which is why I often seek out a bench in the Tiergarten with a view of her monument. All those who bore my name belonged to the French colony, like some of the women in my novels: in *Schach*, for instance, Josephine von Carayon along with her homely daughter. Even Corinna makes a point of her Huguenot heritage to the Treibels, although she has the family name Schmidt. By the way, Melanie van der Straaten was of Swiss Calvinist stock, but liked churches only for their atmosphere—as I, too, for all my loyalty to the colony, found all organized religion colossally suspect...and doubtless have a streak of paganism....At any rate, at home—we children sometimes found this rather silly— our last name was always pronounced with the accent on the first syllable and the final *e* swallowed, and Papa, especially on Sundays and holidays, when the dignitaries of Swinemünde came to call, pronounced it with a nasal *o*. Yet no one who belonged to the colony had any Parisian sophistication; on the contrary, they were all puritanical in bearing—stiff, solemn, touchy about their honor, you know, like that church mouse de Maizière, a little nipper who's prime minister now, despite his scrawny looks, so that, decked out and kept firmly on a leash, he can guide the undone Workers' and Peasants' State to unification. 'None of us should be worse off and some even better off,' he lisps, with his undertaker's mien. No more tin coin rattling in our pockets; with solid silver we can go far when travel fever seizes us—to who knows where. At any rate, this de Maizière looks Calvinist enough to have a knack for the pecuniary. And when it came to the elections, my Emilie, who always had a head for figures and even during the summer holidays would sit brooding our nest egg, put her X in the right box without hesitation.... Whereas to me all this election rubbish...But I've known this since I was little...pennypinching...scrimping and saving...In '63, in May, right after trade school, I was confirmed in the French Reformed church on Klosterstrasse, and married there also, to my Emilie, after far too long an engagement. Because money and secure employment were always lacking. No, I wasn't a churchgoer, but I still think like a Calvinist: all a question of grace. No matter what your upbringing, nothing happens without election by grace. As my otherwise vacillating Holk says in *Irretrievable*, "In this respect, good Lutheran though I am otherwise, I hold with Calvin!" And that's just what our de Maizière will say when he has to present himself in Bonn and take his place, in all his shabbiness, next to the booming ruling mass. You either have it or you don't— money and divine grace, that is, both of which I expect will bestow a little biggish trip on me when the conversion comes: I already know where to.... Want to duck away, even if Emilie opens the floodgates again, and Mete's shaky nerves, which she has from me...But can hardly set out without penning a letter of farewell... No need to get everything down on paper, of course...At any rate, a letter left behind is better than a lot of talk beforehand...."

Then Theo Wuttke, whom everyone called Fonty, stood there in silence before the double grave, whose enclosure had recently been improved by the addition of sandstone curbing and a low wrought-iron fence. To left and right in front of the marker stood a newly planted yew. And just as simply as the stone for the Immortal and his Emilie, the neighboring graves recited their names: on the left Gerhard Baillieu rested without any inscription; and under the right stone lay Georg Minde-Pouet. In the row of graves in front of them stood an elaborate obelisk, the height of a man, on whose polished surface grateful students paid tribute to their teacher, A. F. Arends, and the stenographic system named for him; a shorthand symbol was even engraved on the stone.

Fonty looked out over the graves. Beyond an iron fence on the west side lay a desolate stretch of land where one could still feel the presence of the death strip and the Wall. For a fleeting moment, retrospectively dated cemetery visits passed before his eyes. The old days, when he had stood here with his special permit and his stamped grave card, when the watchtower still loomed above the railroad bridge, when guards in pairs still patrolled the silence of the graves, and sharpshooters took aim at escapees, when the Immortal's grave seldom received visitors, when East and West battled each other with loudspeakers, when over there was enemy territory.

We archivists could add details from our own experience, for we, too, had had to go to Alexanderplatz every time and apply anew for grave cards at the Magistracy for Greater Berlin, Department of the Interior, Religious Affairs Division. Actually only immediate relatives were authorized to enter cemeteries in the border zone. But just as Fonty received a special permit through the good offices of his caregiver, the Archives were granted access to the French Cathedral's cemetery for birth and death anniversaries.

Likewise we could supplement Fonty's conversation with himself by the double grave, citing, for instance, the Immortal's essay on Willibald Alexis, in which the Huguenot sphere yields a wealth of quotable aperçus; but Theo Wuttke did not stay long enough. Once finished with his conversation, he turned away, donned his hat again, and followed the sandy paths past the rows of graves. Walking upright and never deviating from his path, he crossed the adjacent Catholic burial ground of St. Hedwig's, cast not so much as a glance at the side still flanked by an intact stretch of the Wall, ignored the row of nameless nuns' graves, and was finally in a hurry, as though fleeing, for meanwhile a warm summer rain had begun to fall.

A good thing that someone was waiting with an umbrella by the cemetery entrance on Pflugstrasse. As if by prearrangement, Hoftaller was there. He said, "Didn't want to bother you. Out of respect for the thoughts a person has in cemeteries. No stranger to them myself. Bit of reflection's necessary from time to time. At least at gravesides, it's good to be alone."

Then he took Fonty under the umbrella, whose protective span was sufficient for two. They headed through diagonal rain-hatching in the direction of Schwartzkopffstrasse, past apartment houses whose stucco fit them like a dingy yellow uniform. To the left, the street was still blocked off; only a western church spire rose above a stretch of the Wall, forgotten, or preserved for cinematic purposes. But toward Chausseestrasse everything was wide open. To the south, where no rain clouds hung low over the city, a tall chimney poked into the sky. It was fed by a large heating plant, padding the summery blue with white smoke. Completing the perspective, tenements framed a vista that included in the foreground the streetcar, waiting at its last stop. Under the umbrella the two men walked toward the skyscraping smoke signal. They got onto the streetcar, because the U-6 line, which today travels between Alt-Tegel and Alt-Mariendorf, did not go into operation until the end of that year of unification.

8

A Magical Journey for Cold Cash

If Fonty had been granted three wishes, we could change the tune of our narrative to something like this: Once upon a time there was a file courier. His name was Theo Wuttke, and he wanted to make himself scarce, for the moment had come. Day X did indeed take place on the first of July. The order of the day was no empty promise; rather, something that had been fervently wished for could now be called in, immediately and under the terms of the unification treaty. Because the ruling mass could think of no other way to shoulder the national burden and achieve a unified balance of effort, money had to compensate for the dearth of ideas. At least there was that—there was only money, money for the first wish.

And everywhere—in ten thousand and more branch banks, savings banks, post offices, and special payment centers—the first billion, with the dew still on it, was slapped down on the counter. The Federal Bank made sure that in the monetary accession territory, this state of workers and peasants whose total worth had been reduced to scrap, every backwater had its conversion counter. On the island of Rügen, in the Altmark and the Uckermark, on the coast of West Pomerania, among the lakes and water holes of Mecklenburg, in Brandenburg—not to forget Fonty's old stamping ground around Friesack and Ruppin—in sandy Lusatia and on the fertile soil of the Magdeburg flats, in the Oder Delta and along the Neisse and the Elbe rivers, at the base of the Thuringian Forest and in the land of the Sorbs, as far as the Saxon tongue extended, high into the Erz Mountains, in the Catholic Eichsfeld, where

Luther had wielded the Word on every occasion, at the outermost tip of the Vogtland, and of course in the now open semicity of Berlin, which in official documents still styled itself the capital of the German Democratic Republic: wherever, for forty years, the first German Workers' and Peasants' State had waved its ever-optimistic banners in all kinds of weather, in the East, in what the West called the Soviet Occupation Zone, in the other, the "quote-unquote" German Democratic Republic—everywhere the cash they had wished for, the cash they had voted in, the cash that promised to be hard and tough, made its triumphal entry.

The first billion came in guarded armored vehicles, whose routes were kept secret. Then another twenty-four billion was put into circulation, shoveled from West to East with similar care. Consumer wishes could be fulfilled, dreams converted to realities; the calculation seemed to come out even.

Ah, if only it really had! All that money, and even more money—yes, there was money, and plenty of it, in fact, only money—didn't produce the desired prosperity. Having quickly slaked some of the thirst for consumption, it hustled back to the West. There, with its freshly skimmed profit, it settled down again in bank accounts, or, as tax-fugitive capital, sought asylum in Luxemburg. It should have been toiling and moiling, working hard, working wonders, not lazing about, interested only in interest.

Ah, if only there had been a few more wishes. But as it was, the fairy tale soon came to an end. What was left behind was a wailing sinkhole of misery, a choking lump of worries. Only one old man did not blubber, did not choke; and so we may say: Once upon a time there was a file courier. His name was Theo Wuttke. His wishes did not collide with the speeding payment traffic. His list contained no consumer goods. He had no trouble reading the prettiest Western packaging, swindle included, and yet his plans, too, had their fair market value.

For many years Fonty, as the file courier Wuttke was known, had found his earnings quite adequate for the limited supply of Eastern products, and he had even managed to save. Now he was allowed to exchange up to six thousand marks at a one-to-one rate; anything beyond that—since his Cultural Union days Fonty had accumulated his surplus in a yellow postal savings passbook—was worth only half its face value. The file courier's wife and daughter were in a similar position. From Emmi Wuttke's pension and Martha Wuttke's teacher's salary they had always been able to put aside something for a rainy day. But the most favorable exchange provisions applied only to those past their sixtieth birthday; this restriction hit Martha hard, for she was thirty-eight. The regulation entitled her to only four thousand at one-to-one, which left the bulk of her savings cut in half.

This distressed the file courier's daughter. She was going to be married soon, and for her wedding outfit she planned to visit a department store in West Berlin, the legendary KaDeWe. Emmi had the same thing in mind. On no account did she want to see her daughter, as she is supposed to have said, "standing at the altar in the shoddy stuff from over here." Frau Wuttke had firm views: "Not every day a person gets married. If you're going to do it, better do it right."

Only Fonty viewed with equanimity the clothing he had been wearing for years. For solemn occasions he had donned gray pin-striped trousers and a jacket we referred to as his frock coat; the last time we had seen him thus attired was when he received the silver merit badge for his contributions to the cultural heritage. It was understandable that the file courier Theo Wuttke had no intention of renewing his wardrobe at the Kaufhaus des Westens. His wishes were focused on a ticket for a journey: he wanted to take the train to Hamburg and from there the ferry to England.

A magical journey was in the offing, but he was in no hurry. He sat out the first exchange day, a Monday, when after midnight the new money was welcomed everywhere, particularly on Alexanderplatz, with a din of honking horns, gun salutes, and choruses of joy, in the course of which a bank's windows were smashed and older people fainted in the general crush. It wasn't until a week later, on 9 July, that Fonty took his place at the end of a moderately long line on Schönhauser Allee. This was the first day when a person could draw on his entire bank account; until then there had been a two-thousand-mark limit on exchanges.

Here was something everyone had mastered during decades of a scarcity economy: standing in line. In the fifties for everything, and especially potatoes; in the sixties for bicycle tubes, fresh vegetables, nylon stockings; and later for lemons and oranges. Standing in line had become a pose perfected by an entire people, a people that took its time wherever time was to be had. So no one grew impatient and stormed the counter.

Emmi and Martha Wuttke had lightened their bank accounts before having full benefit of the favorable exchange rate. The moment had come for their visit to KaDeWe, where every department was prepared to make them offers. The two of them hesitated long over glittering fripperies and solid elegance; yet they must have followed Emmi's admonition "not to buy things that aren't needed," for aside from the wedding outfits only two luxury items ran into money: for Martha a stylish purse fashioned in Italy, and for Emmi a bottle of "genuine eau de cologne." Afterward the word was: "Well, if you don't watch out, these West marks go pretty fast."

Fonty was dressed for summer as he waited in line. He had a document certifying the sum recorded in his yellow postal savings passbook. At first he was curious to hear what was being said out loud, or whispered in the accustomed fashion, by those ahead of and behind him. But then he became engrossed in a series of mental calculations, calculations that imposed austerity on his planned journey; the volume of the talk around him seemed to be turned down low or muted completely.

In any case, this whining was all too familiar. It hardly differed from what he heard every day at home: hundreds of wishes hemmed in by a wall of worries and reservations. At one point there was talk of a Japanese-made hi-fi, then of an almost new Opel Kadett for Martha, who, however, turned down that idea because she did not have a driver's license. He was having a hard time talking Emmi out of her dearest wish, "a TV from the West, with all the features": "We got by perfectly well up to now without the goggle-box. Why do I need to be deluged with pictures? The Scottish moors in peepshow format—what nonsense!"

And just as in the garret on Kollwitzstrasse, while waiting in line he kept faith with his destination. All around him people were anx-

126

ious and filled with indecision. But he wanted to be daring, not despondent in advance like the single mother holding her small child by the hand as she stood in front of him. Like many others, she feared the new currency, because its very hardness might well turn against those who had called for the dream money so loudly: "Y'know, you wish for a thing, but when it comes it's like someone hit you over the head—God only knows what you were thinking it'd be like."

But even if Theo Wuttke in the role of file courier had shared these fears, Fonty would have remained fearless. He was prepared to risk all on one card, and could already see himself setting out. He did not want to join in the laughter when someone behind him started cracking jokes about the Party bigwigs with their villas in Wandlitz. He preferred to visualize himself again and again going on board. Years ago the white ferry to Harwich had been called *Prince Hamlet*; now his ship, according to the travel brochure, was called *City of Hamburg*, and apparently it cast off from the dock in St. Pauli.

The steady stream of jokes disgusted him. Far back in the line someone was discharging his pent-up anger by listing the Stasi networks he saw everywhere, but especially extensive and tightly knotted in the Ministries Building. Fortunately, a West Berlin travel agency was already holding a place on the ship, in Fonty's civilian name; trips to England were popular. Right behind him a bearded young man, who had kept his mouth shut until then, suddenly asked the rowdy Stasi-denouncer, who was still going at it, what network he belonged to: "It's standard operating procedure—folks always bitch the loudest about the outfit they work for!" After that he preserved a huffy silence. The jokester had run out of jokes. The mother with the small child stopped whining. No one was in the mood anymore to formulate those sentences starting with "you": You heard all these promises... You went on believing... You get used to... You never would have guessed... You always end up the sucker.... As the summer heat beat down on them, the line in front of the savings bank had nothing more to say. Only Fonty had an inexhaustible supply of conversation inside his head.

The hot, humid weather did not bother him. Along with his boater, he was wearing a light linen suit that had been through many washings. The wrinkles, which looked as if they had been born with him, lent an air of casual chic. *Sans* walking stick but wearing his trusty plaid scarf, he inched forward, while his thoughts sought a foothold in the past. Wherever he tapped his memory, the sources of his savings gushed forth. He crisscrossed the country, hitting every village and town with a Cultural Union center, shabby or pretentious. From all the lectures he had delivered from the early fifties until almost the end of '76, he derived a sum, reduced it by daily expenses, and still came out with a tidy surplus; for, in addition to the not exactly munificent honoraria the Cultural Union had paid him between Stralsund and Karl-Marx-Stadt, he had received numerous bonuses for particular contributions: Theo Wuttke was prized as a cultural activist.

True, he never attracted a mass audience, but he had a community of loyal listeners that proved self-perpetuating. Everywhere local-history buffs and nature lovers gathered, eager to hear his wittily abridged *Rambles Through the Mark Brandenburg*; there were plenty of patient souls for whom even the longest ballads were not overly long; everywhere devotees of the thousands of chatty letters waited with bated breath for the punch lines; and always the focus was on the works of the Immortal. Sometimes the novels—perhaps *Jenny Treibel* or *Irretrievable*—provided the topic; other lecture tours concentrated on women characters, who, rounded up to form a chorus—sometimes plaintive, sometimes commonsensical—pushed their way to the fore: Cécile next to Effi, Ebba arm in arm with Melanie, Stine hiding behind Mathilde, Lene between Corinna and the widow Pittelkow. A hen party at which each presented her case anew; for instance, Grete Minde the always latent danger of conflagration.

Of course at every public appearance the relationship of this older literature to socialism was supposed to be adumbrated. Every lecture, even one centering on adultery and duels, had to bring in humanism, specifically of the progressive variety. It was often a challenge to give proper emphasis to the social-democratic elements; "proper" meant viewing such figures as Torgelow the file cutter, winner of the election in Rheinsberg, or the "Bebelized" Junker Woldemar, through the lens of the Socialist Unity Party. Even more than *Stechlin*, the late letters could be mined for allusions to the working class or—as a letter to Friedlaender called it—the "fourth estate." With such material it was easy—or sleazy—to toe the line; on the other hand, the lecture in Hoyerswerda that described the apprentice apothecary's journalistic fulminations against the "Prussian police state" brought down major objections from on high, because comparisons with the practices of the People's Police lay close at hand. He was forbidden to repeat this lecture. A longish passage in another lecture, this one devoted to the apothecary's Tunnel friend Wilhelm von Merckel, met the same fate; Merckel's rhyme, used as the speech's motto, "To put the democrats to rout, you have to call the army out," had to be deleted because the itinerary for the late fall of '53 included Cultural Union centers in Merseburg, Bitterfeld, and Hennigsdorf, where the unrest in June of that year had been crushed by tanks. And after the troops of the fellow socialist countries had marched into the Czechoslovak Socialist Republic, the Immortal's book on the campaign against Austria and the Battle of Königgrätz could no longer be used as a topic because—well, because Bohemia had always been too close for comfort. Even Pastor Lorenzen's sympathy for the Christian-socialist theses put forward by Stöcker, chaplain to Kaiser Wilhelm, was considered suspect, and had to be glossed accordingly. Such headaches from one end of the country to the other. So much bickering, so many narrow-minded functionaries who knew nothing, but always knew better. "XYZ is Strictly Prohibited" posted at the entrance to every village.

Yet the pleasant memories predominated. As the line crawled toward the counter, Fonty heard himself delivering many lectures that got by without major cuts. His favorite, "Idle Chatter at the Dinner Tables of the Prussian Aristocracy," was a smash hit from the Baltic to the Riesengebirge. That was the kind of thing that drew an audience. Although the swashbuckling of Rex and Czako, of Bülow and young Poggenpuhl, sounded almost like a foreign language, it was entertaining, and provided a pretext for taking a swipe at aristocratic arrogance and bourgeois decadence. Similarly the lecture on the Ribbeck ballad, which he called "From Junker Estates to Agricultural Collectives," hit the spot. Altogether he was allowed to deliver this lecture nineteen times, unabridged and including a recitation of the entire "Pear Tree" ballad. That explained his savings. But neither Hoftaller nor Tallhover ever slipped him money—not for his richly atmospheric travel pieces or for the revolting effusion on the Immortal's collaboration with the Manteuffel government that he was directed to present in Potsdam and elsewhere. And, needless to say, he received no remuneration for the character sketches of cultural functionaries encountered on his lecture tours that he was expected to file; for the most part, they boiled down to insignificant comments these figures might let fall over a glass of wine, and the failings of local big shots, in places like Güstrow or Wittstock, portrayed in loving detail.

And the bonuses? These were handed out for particular achievements, for sheer length of service, for demonstrated loyalty to the Party line—between relapses. It was certainly not easy to depict the Poggenpuhls' aristocratic milieu, poor in both plot and pecuniary means, in a way that would prove exciting to weary working people in Guben or Neubrandenburg, Senftenberg and Eisenhüttenstadt: "All of them—though the mother less so than the rest—possessed the fine gift of never complaining. They were practical-minded and adept at calculations, yet without appearing calculating in a disagreeable fashion. In that respect, the three sisters were alike, although their personalities were very different...."

"No, no!" Fonty exclaimed suddenly. "We earned this money the hard way!"

And all those in front of and behind him voiced their agreement, for they, too—the woman with the small child ahead of him, the gruff bearded fellow behind him—were bringing their hard-earned savings to the exchange counter: "We worked like dogs for this."

"Not a single mark was just handed to me," Fonty said loudly, "thin and tinny though it was."

Again general agreement: "They didn't give us anything. And what little we got, we paid for, one way or the other."

And when Fonty exclaimed, "One to one is fine. But it's not

right to cut our nest egg in half!" comments like "Do they think we're worth only half as much?" and "Are they cutting us in half to punish us?" seconded his dismay at the fate of his retirement savings. Then he heard a shout from someone standing seven or nine places behind him: "Well, that's what the people wanted. Soon we'll be one people, sure, but essentially worth only fifty pfennigs on the mark."

Fonty had no need to turn around. It was Hoftaller, and his jocular contribution was rewarded with laughter. He had more on tap, too: "It's always been this way when we got down to the meat of things. They toss the people the scraps, and in bite-sized pieces, to keep them from making pigs of themselves...."

And then Hoftaller, who had apparently found an audience, quoted, as if spontaneously, certain key provisions of the treaty between the two Germanys. He pointed out that Article 6 permitted any documented right to the people's property to be asserted. "Listen up, folks! All that's supposed to be handled by a trust. Yessir, that's what they're calling it over there: the Handover Trust!"

Suddenly Fonty found himself at the exchange counter. He handed over his notarized document and his postal savings passbook, along with his identity card, and the new currency was counted out for him in large bills, with the change in silver. The passbook was returned with one of its corners notched. In addition to the 6,000 marks he was allowed to convert at the one-to-one rate, he had 3,582 marks that were halved. He left only a piddling sum, 20 marks, to be entered in his new blue passbook; the rest he withdrew, a pretty penny.

After the Cultural Union lecturer and later file courier Theo Wuttke had calmly counted all the banknotes and silver coin, had tucked the freshly minted stuff into his wallet and stowed the change in his purse, with what was left of the tin coin, and then vacated the exchange counter to make way for the bearded man behind him, Fonty felt rich, halved only to a lesser extent. Now he hastened to get away, past the line.

In fact everything happened as described, and yet as if in a fairy tale. A file courier—of whom it should be said that he lived once upon a time—exchanged all his money, after standing in line for quite a while, and, having nodded a greeting to his day-and-night-shadow, who was farther back in line, went on his way unshadowed. He made a beeline for the S-Bahn station at Schönhauser Allee, rode in the direction of Ostkreuz, changed there to the line that went to Friedrichstrasse by way of Warschauer Strasse, the main station, and Jannowitz Bridge, and stayed on the train, with the money in his wallet, as far as the Bellevue station, over in the West. From there he walked quickly toward the Little Star, then to the Rose Garden, and, passing the Lortzing monument, sought out his favorite bench, with its view of Rousseau Island. He exchanged the Federal Bank for the bank of the lake with such determination that one might have concluded he felt safe only here, in spite of the many Turks spreading out with their extended families on the Tiergarten's lawns to savor the delights of their Anatolian cuisine: a faint fragrance of shish kabob floated on the air.

It was no longer Theo Wuttke but Fonty who sat there watching the diving duck. How suddenly it disappeared. How surprisingly it popped up each time where it was least expected. And how all its underwater exertions left the diver's smooth crest unscathed: handsome and elegantly slicked back, it made for a striking profile. While this virtuoso of the unexpected among the waterfowl was out of sight, Fonty patted his swollen breast pocket now and then. It almost looked as if he were stroking the bulge in his jacket. The elderberry bush behind the Tiergarten bench had long since dropped its blossoms and was already unfurling fans of unripe berries. He was sitting there alone, as he had wished, against the summery green backdrop, when suddenly and without warning Hoftaller plopped down beside him.

That he showed up here was unexpected, yet no surprise. This time he was wearing Bermuda shorts with a short-sleeved shirt and his baseball cap. Since he had also stopped by the Archives in this getup, more catching us, too, unawares than paying us a visit, we were already familiar with his sturdy calves and padded knees, the dense freckles on his peach-fuzzy forearms. All over he displayed ageless rosy flesh.

This leisure wear, which included new, multicolored jogging shoes, did not prevent Hoftaller from lighting up a Romeo y Julieta, wordlessly and with much ado. As his eyes followed the smoke, his gaze appeared at once concentrated and relaxed. Now Fonty saw the lake through a slight haze. Both of them were sitting half in shadow. Behind them the elderberry bush was green. Now and then people passed by—individuals, couples, Turkish mothers with children. Hardly any birdsong. Silence, the hum of insects, two cabbage butterflies fluttering. They could have sat there a long time without exchanging a word, for all their secrets had been betrayed, every suspicion voiced.

It wasn't until the smoker in Bermuda shorts had tapped the ash off his cigar that Hoftaller broached the subject: "Added up to a nice little pile, eh, Fonty? Bet there's a tidy sum in your account. Quite tempting, a mini-fortune like that. But we're not going to do anything rash, are we? That's all behind us, right? Head-over-heels departures, ducking out of obligations and duties! Like back in '50, the hasty departure to seagirt Schleswig-Holstein, where the armed struggle was supposed to be taken up against the Danes in particular and the suppression of freedom in general. Nowadays a heroic number like that would just make us laugh. And nothing came of it, either. Fizzled out, like March '48—ha! Sounding the tocsin! But the minute the bit of revolutionary posturing had died down, old Goethe's 'America, you have it better' was supposed to hold out its arms to the down-and-out emigrant. And if I think of all the other attempted escapes...Fleeing without a thought for wife and children. Up and away. Flying the coop. Often saddened me. Utterly irresponsible!"

Fonty said nothing. The cigar-smoker emitted periodic puffs of smoke. As if outside time: two old men. Survivals from bygone days, they watched the doings on the lake, watched swans and variously feathered ducks, watched the diving duck, and yet had a wider view than that which the lake presented to the naked eye.

A windless day. When Hoftaller cradled his cigar between index and middle finger, the smoke rose straight up. Fonty had stopped patting the bulge in his jacket pocket. Once something rustled behind them in the elderberry bush, a rabbit, perhaps. And once a swan took off, only to return to the lake after a few wing beats, fixed to the water as if painted on.

"Just a moment of melodrama," Hoftaller remarked, and after heaving a few sighs sounded concerned. "Right, Fonty? We'll keep a cool head—won't we? No foolishness this time, like in '76, when you simply 'jettisoned the culture rubbish,' as you put it. Since then, off the air. No more lectures. And don't think I had an easy time making sure..."

Before they set out, both of them went down to the water's edge, but not to feed the ducks. With the tin coin of the devalued currency, Hoftaller, who had some of it rattling in his pocket, tried his hand at a children's game. The idea was to send these coins skipping across the water, the way flat stones could be made to take three, or even five hops with the right twist of the wrist. But not one of his tosses succeeded. This funny money wasn't even good for playing with. When challenged to try, Fonty had no better luck: what was left of the tin money wouldn't go very far.

But this might be the moment for the fairy tale to begin. At last we may be permitted to say: Once upon a time there was a railroad platform, which no longer smelled of acrid smoke, on whose tracks puffing, shuddering Borsig locomotives no longer stood, waiting for the departure signal. Gone were the years when steam sped everything on its way, even time. "Now that the railroad is here," old Stechlin said, "horses count for nothing...."

And Fonty recalled departures with his wife and daughter for Thale in the Harz Mountains, where later the ailing Cécile made her way on St. Arnaud's arm to the Ten Pound Hotel. Or arduous railroad trips to the Riesengebirge, where Friedlaender was a magistrate. No year without summer holidays. And what awaited them on holiday was available in print somewhere, having been captured in writing: "In many cases, sheer highway robbery. Innkeepers and coachmen outdo one another in greed and inconsiderateness.... The train comes to a halt. It is seven in the evening. Across the tracks stands the usual crowd of conveyances—omnibuses, charabancs, hackney cabs...." Then memories of hotel rooms that Fonty wanted to talk out of his system: "Away with the worn remnants of carpet, away with the gold wallpaper, grimy with tobacco smoke, away with the shabby plush sofa, away..." Yet he wrote from Thale, "I feel well here, as I always do (knock on wood) whenever I turn my back on Berlin...." And each and every time he traveled laden down with work, no matter what his destination. His luggage always contained the beginnings of something, along with stacks of books: "Have been reading a good deal, Lessing and Turgenev by turns. Yesterday one of the huntsman stories. He rather resembles a photographic apparatus, but is also the Muse in sackcloth and ashes, Apollo with a toothache. In his works, Life wears a grimace...."

And at every summer resort something was amiss; irritation was not long in coming; one had soon had one's fill. Someone—here Christians, there Jews—created bad blood. All this was recorded in letters: "I was startled whenever I saw a Christian—they all looked rather like pabulum by comparison. At least the Jews, even the ugliest among them, have faces...." But in the mail from Norderney, as if seared into the page, were the lines, "The Jews were atrocious; and their impudent swindlers' faces—for swindling is where they shine—swarm about one on all sides...." Not until later did the train transport him by way of Dresden to Carlsbad, and more and more frequently for the cure, rather than on holiday. There was no lack of Jews there with whom one could chat agreeably: "Just the day before yesterday we had the usual Goldschmidt-style *dîner* at the Bristol: various Friedebergs, Liebermanns, and Magnuses. All rich as Croesus, all very charming and worldly. That is to say, they were up on 'everything.' My Cohn poem came to mind again...." And his English correspondent James Morris likewise received a letter from Carlsbad: "...I can visit again the houses where old Goethe stayed, also the hotels where kings and emperors spent their days in Carlsbad during the—thank heavens—long-gone days of that alliance of police-states known in history by the pretentious name of 'the Holy Alliance.'...." But when the moment came to take the train back to Berlin, the cure had not helped a great deal, and his displeasure was on the prowl for enemies: "I only hope I have a Jew-free compartment...."

Thus overflowing with memories, tormented in heart and head, thus torn wretchedly hither and thither, and yet at one with himself, thus close to nervous prostration and at the same time serene in his yearning for distant parts, thus exposed by us, Fonty stood on the platform.

Lightly dressed, as if about to set out once again for the summer holidays, he waited. Only his old suitcase, a medium-sized piece of luggage with which he had traveled all over the Workers' and Peasants' State in the service of the Cultural Union, stood beside him as the train for Hamburg, the diesel locomotive at its head, pulled into the station and was no longer merely fairy-tale-like but actually came to a stop: Once upon a time there was an express train....

He took a seat in a second-class compartment: by the window, facing toward the front. Until shortly before the train's departure he remained alone, sitting there quietly, the tips of his mustache quivering ever so slightly. Then a woman, hardly younger than he, sat down across from him. Fonty had heaved his suitcase onto the luggage rack and propped the plastic bag on the seat beside him. The old woman looked as though she had been crying or had the sniffles, and her head kept jerking beneath her hat. Just to make sure he had his travel reading with him, he reached into the plastic bag with the KaDeWe imprint and felt, next to the *Tagesspiegel*, the potboiler by the old Brandenburg count Marwitz, who had modeled for Count Vitzewitz. Across from him, the skittish old lady hugged her large, shapeless valise to her bosom, unwilling to give it up.

"Marwitz I always found stimulating, and exemplary in his attitude," he had lectured the young would-be authors of Prenzlauer Berg. "A Prussian of the old school, conservatively progressive, a monarchist, yet in a pinch prepared to disobey orders, like my Vitzewitz in that first novel, too long delayed...."

The old woman's valise was of flaking black leather. "I was almost sixty when the unpleasantness in the governing senate of the Academy of the Arts finally left me free, after a few months of misery, free to breathe, free to write...."

Clucking on her lap, the flaking black bag, whose rounded handles lay flat. "No more minutes to record, no more intrigues. Once I became a freelance writer, *Before the Storm* just flowed from

136

my pen. After that, book after book, all the way to *Stechlin*. And if death hadn't blown out my little lamp..."

The old lady's hands restlessly patted the flaking leather. "But old Marwitz always prodded me. Yes, indeed, my most gifted but unsuspecting friends. A Prussian of the best sort. Always a straight shooter. And always at odds with the folderol at court. As I, too, advise you to resist the raucous spirit of the times and keep both eyes open..."

They refused to settle down, those hands on the flaking leather kept patting, stroking a living thing....

The plastic bag also contained a recent travel guide, with information on hotel prices, transportation, and the hours for museums and castles. Merely to distract himself from the old lady sitting across from him with the valise on her lap, he briefly leafed through the richly illustrated paperback, then sat up straight again, calm except for the quivering tips of his mustache.

Confident he had brought everything he needed, above all a freshly issued passport identifying him as a citizen of the Federal Republic, Fonty displayed that partly serene, partly feigned determination that many contemporary observers ascribed to the Immortal. And we archivists saw him this way, too: always ready to sally forth. Even his fits of nervous prostration accompanied him wherever he went, to theaters of war, to Düppel, Königgrätz, Metz. And the airman and war correspondent Theo Wuttke must have set out for France just as impulsively and nervously, easily distracted, because he kept both eyes open, and easily seduced, because he was instantly captivated by inscriptions on headstones, wreaths of immortelles, and other leitmotifs: Effi's fear of the Chinaman's grave and Frau Kruse's black hen—"Beware the hen, for it knows everything and keeps nothing to itself...."

Now Fonty was leaning back, his eyes closed. Across from him the much-stroked bag. The compartment felt hot, overheated. Suffocating July heat along for the ride. The train pulled out, and was just picking up speed when the compartment door flew open. Panting and dripping with sweat, the new passenger wrestled his suitcase onto the overhead luggage rack and threw himself down on the seat next to Fonty. "Whew! Just made it!" he exclaimed by way of a greeting. "Train was already moving; had to jump on."

He whipped the American cap off his head and with his hand mopped his damp brow and his sweat-matted spikes of hair. Fonty did not even have to open his eyes. Whatever came now, he would obey blindly.

We archivists have reason to doubt the alleged nonviolence of what ensued. Yet since the account we received spoke of a "basically sensible agreement," our doubts carry no more weight than an aside. This much is certain: The fairy tale was over almost before it had begun. After the next stop, at the Zoo station, the train went on without them. Even if no force was used, some form of duress must have helped things along. Hoftaller's contention that Fonty gave in of his own accord says it all.

Allegedly only a few words were necessary. It was sufficient for Hoftaller to point out that either they would travel on to Hamburg together, together take the ferry to England, and together, like the Immortal and his boyhood friend Lepel, see London and journey through Scotland—"There we shall merrily fish and hunt"—or the two of them would get off the train, have a cold beer, and thus, after a "sensible agreement," call off this pointless and expensive excursion.

He told us: "When it comes right down to it, you should have talked him out of this nonsense yourselves. The Archives must have been implicated in his travel preparations. Pretty irresponsible to let an old man undergo such an ordeal. But we have freedom now—is that it? Fools' freedom!"

It wasn't until he charged us with "passive complicity" and held out the prospect of "rather unpleasant repercussions" for the Archives that he dropped the accusatory tone. "Oh, well, forget it. I had to do a lot of coaxing. Since our friend didn't want me to come along, further arguments were superfluous. I pointed out to him, though, how irresponsible that was—his skulking away like that. I even used the expression 'cut out.' Told him again and again, 'You can't simply cut out, Fonty!' And then made it clear to him how shoddy it was to leave his wife and child in the lurch in hard times like these. Reminded him of Martha's approaching wedding, said, 'Maybe even your fine sons will come and want to join in the celebration. The moment to bury the family hatchet. Friedel's certainly coming, and maybe even Theo from Bonn. Your Emmi will be so happy, after all these years. Too bad Georg, your favorite, can't be there....' And then I wound up and hit him with a superannuated file: 'When I think of your trips to England! Good God! What your pregnant Emilie had to put up with, thanks to your escapades. The child no sooner born than he was carried off, while you were away doing who knows what in London. In dives down by the docks...with whores, for all we know...And when she came to join you, with two children clinging to her skirts, she was utterly miserable among "English people" and in that climate...always fog...always homesickness...' "

Hoftaller acted indignant as he filled in the details for us, the "accessories before the fact." He seemed driven by an inherited sense of duty: "In any case, I couldn't spare our Fonty. But no reaction. Just us and an old woman in the compartment. But she was no trouble. I talked; he didn't say a word. All the way to the Zoo station. He was probably thinking: Who cares about yesterday's news? Today we have freedom....Anyway, it came down to a test of wills. The train to Hamburg had a ten-minute stopover, so he thought he had time to mull it over. He stayed in his seat, took the whole time, and assumed I'd been bluffing—you know, that stuff about Scotland, and me coming along for the ride. I opened the *Berliner Zeitung,* and he read his *Tagesspiegel.* I read him something from the culture pages about the Prenzlauer Berg scene and suspected informants. He went on reading, the business pages, of all things. I have to admit, he was so calm it was getting on my nerves. He even seemed to be taking an interest in the stock-market quotations, underlining prices with a pencil. I was about to light up a cigar, just to make a point, even though we were in a no-smoking car and two younger women had joined us. I was already tapping a nice little number from my Cuban cache when he stood up, left the newspaper on the seat, reached for his hat, pulled his suitcase off the rack, picked up a plastic bag in his other hand, bowed briefly to the dolled-up young women, then to the old lady, and, already at the compartment door, said directly into my face, 'As you may have noticed, this is the nonsmokers' section. And if you can't show consideration for the ladies, then at least for that poor hen there.' Appalling! He pointed with a trembling finger to the black leather bag on the lap of the old woman by the window and whispered, for my ears only, 'Effi's afraid of the hen. The hen frightens her.' I had to rush like the devil—I'd barely got off behind him when the train pulled out. It wasn't until we were on the station steps that I could thank him: 'It's terrific that you always come to your senses, Fonty, even though you sometimes take your own sweet time getting there.' "

Hoftaller invited him for a snack. The two carried their luggage to a place very close to the station, diagonally across from it, where else? This time it was Hoftaller who insisted on McDonald's. With their Coke and milkshake, each of them consumed a cheeseburger and an order of fries. Around them, lots of young folk were busy fast-feeding themselves.

They ate standing at a bar table across from the counter, their suitcases resting peacefully at their feet. There was not much left to say. Hoftaller promised to try to get the travel costs refunded: "Let me see your ticket—train and boat."

Fonty handed over everything, except his new passport. His day-and-night-shadow pretended to be surprised: "Well, well, what have we here? This is one-way. Pretty expensive. You can kiss ten percent of that good-bye!"

Nonetheless Hoftaller did not make a big fuss over Fonty's planned one-way trip. As later to us, he spoke to the file courier Theo Wuttke with only a hint of menace: "I'll see if I can straighten this out, the consequences, I mean—at the Ministries Building, for example. I'll put in a word, even two. In periods of major change there have to be people like you, Fonty, people who are smart and come to their senses in time. People who've learned to be loyal to any system. You've demonstrated that often enough, even if it was sometimes hard to keep to the straight and narrow. As you admitted yourself, you were rebellious, but never a dissident. Were always true to yourself, whether in the Manteuffel years or with Reich Aviation. Your Cultural Union lectures prove that: critical, no doubt, but never destructive...."

It wasn't until his second Coke that Fonty loosened up a bit. He tried to take his aborted trip lightly, even jokingly. He folded three or four McDonald's napkins into a paper hat, popped it on his head, and exclaimed, over the din of the feeding frenzy, "Wouldn't have thought my excursion would wind up so soon in a Scottish milieu. Frau Kruse, now—the one with the hen on her lap, you know—still has hours to go before she gets to Hamburg."

Then he cited the names of several legendary Highlanders, the Percys and the Douglases, but was not willing—no matter how Hoftaller urged him—to repeat the public recitation of his famous ballad: "'Tis seven long years I've borne this load...."

BOOK 2

9

It's the Nerves

Kollwitzstrasse is an extension of Senefelderstrasse. It is crossed by Dimitroffstrasse, and leads to Kollwitzplatz. In earlier times, when Aunt Pinchen lived there, it went by a different name, as did the square; it did not bear the name of its erstwhile artist-in-residence, but was called Wörther Platz, and the street was called Weissenburger.

Käthe Kollwitz was the sort of artist who could not look the other way; she captured human misery on paper, which was reason enough for banning her name in one era, celebrating it in another. Over the years, the practice of renaming streets and squares to ape every change in the political system had a similar effect on the Prenzlauer Berg district and others. When Schickedanz in *Stechlin* says, "A street name outlasts even a monument," he had no inkling of how soon and how ferociously commemoration would become short-lived. Whether Kollwitzplatz and the street of the same name would survive was by no means certain at the beginning of this most recent period of revolution and revaluation. In other parts of the city, petitions were already circulating, passionately demanding that a Heinrich-Heine-Strasse here, a Rosa-Luxemburg-Platz there, be done away with. Yet in that summer of '90 people were still scrambling for names to cement the promised unification of Germany.

Number 75 was on the right as you walked toward the square. A passageway as wide as a barn door led to the rear courtyard. Halfway into the passageway, on the left, a staircase led up to the front part of the building. On either side of the entryway, the façade's crumbling stucco still displayed several advertisements from days gone by: on the right, black lettering, partially obliterated, indicated the availability of "Wood, Coal, Charcoal Briquettes, Coke," while on the left a cobbler had advertised his cellar workshop as a "Sole-Heeling Institute." The base of the façade belonging to the house next door offered even more: at one time "Dry Goods, Shoe Polish, Waxed and Toilet Paper" as well as "Tins and Preserving Jars of Every Size" had been sold there over the counter.

But only Number 75 concerns us here: a house with three stories above its elevated ground floor. In the rear courtyard, which was hemmed in by outbuildings, sheds, and fire walls, one chestnut tree had survived periods of war and postwar. As far up as the attic, where the Wuttkes occupied their three and a half rooms, the tree signaled the current season, letting wintry light though, flaunting its buds, casting broad-leafed shade, and in October dropping the spiky husks of its softly rounded fruits onto tarred shed roofs and the hard-packed earth of the courtyard. Children were not the only ones who collected them; year after year, Fonty carried newly fallen, still moistly gleaming chestnuts in both pockets, often well into December. And every year Emmi complained about the damage to the pocket linings: "Sometimes he's just like a child, my Wuttke. If he sees something, he has to pick it up."

But it was a hot day in July, with gusts of wind raising dust clouds, when Hoftaller escorted the thwarted traveler back to his front door. From the subway station at Senefelder Platz, he even carried both of their suitcases. Although Fonty, left holding only the plastic bag, forced himself to maintain his youthful stride for most of the last stretch, from Kollwitzplatz on, he had lead weights in his shoes, and once they reached the front of the house, he did everything he could think of to postpone his arrival. He did not want to go upstairs.

He paced. The apartment house and its smells, which varied from floor to floor, dismayed him. He refrained from his usual "Well, till tomorrow," invented a heap of excuses for prolonging the parting, trying out various topics—the weather, politics, the inscriptions on the façade, the bygone coal business on the right, the onetime cobbler's shop on the left—to buy time.

He remarked, "Actually I quite like hot weather." Or he opined: "Colossally *ridicule*: this bearded pastor as commander in chief of the People's Army. Always knew my country preachers had immense ambitions." The weathered sign for the Sole-Heeling Institute was repeatedly characterized as "frightfully witty." He trotted out anecdotes from the life of Aunt Pinchen and her chronically plastered Ernst-August Piontek, the cobbler who operated the Sole-Heeling Institute on days when he was halfway sober, until "the tippler finally tipped off his stool for the last time, whereupon my Emilie came to live with her widowed auntie. That was in '39, just before the war began...."

Actually Fonty wanted to talk neither about the youthful Emmi, already plump as an office trainee, nor about old Frau Wuttke, "aged," as he said, "before her time." Rather, while Hoftaller barricaded himself "behind Moltke-esque silence," he launched into a soliloquy that flashed backward and forward in time, his reel unwinding uninterruptedly.

In the course of this filibuster Fonty touched on all the planned stations of his prematurely terminated journey. In London he omitted not a single art gallery, in Scotland not a castle. All the horrors of the Tower of London were enumerated. He poked around every moor in search of legends, finally arriving—by way of the first lines of *Macbeth*, "When shall we three meet again," and the witches' gathering, "In the seventh hour by the bridge"—at one of his late ballads, where he lingered: "The Bridge on the Tay" was published on 10 January 1980 in Paul Lindau's journal *The Present Day*, and was based on a newspaper brief under the heading "Miscellaneous," which described a railroad accident in Scotland.

Standing in front of Number 75 Kollwitzstrasse, Fonty recited stanza after stanza. He began with the announcement of the Edinburgh train, punctual "in spite of night and pelting rain": "I see a glow on the other bank; that's it, I know"; then, in response to the bridge watchman's request, traced the date of the catastrophe invoked by the witches: "Light all the lights as for Christmas Eve"; then rhymed his way forward in dramatic escalation: "For wilder raged the tempest's play," had already reached the accident on the bridge: "Explodes in downward-plummeting glow / Into the night o'er the waters below"; whereupon he concluded with the three witches' commentary: "They crumble like sand, / The works of man's hand"; and had once more proved to Hoftaller how much he had at his fingertips. Just as the façade behind him bore witness to the disappearance of small business, he dusted off this much-anthologized ballad; yet he refused to quote from the letter of farewell he had left on the kitchen table for his wife and daughter—even so much as half a sentence.

His listener professed satisfaction all the same: "Splendid, Fonty! I always enjoy hearing such things, especially this ballad. It goes to show what an expert can do with a little news brief from the *Vossische Zeitung*. I doubt our Prenzlberg talents could come up with anything so spine-chilling. A lot to be said on the subject. True, the whole thing seems overly fatalistic to me, but your witches' hocus-pocus is right on target, no doubt about it. There's more confirmation every day—nothing lasts. 'Crumble like sand, / the works of man's hand.' Some swell rhymes you've got there, Fonty! I see it the same way. Need only look at my own area of expertise. What's left of our state security, besides the paperwork? What rock have the leading comrades crawled under? Writing their memoirs—that's what they're doing. . . . Not a shred of class consciousness left . . . crumble like sand . . . but enough whining. You and your suitcase here should start working your way up the stairs. Your Emmi'll be worrying. And duty calls me, too, as the saying goes. You know how it is. Have to grind out a report—purely routine. Can make it short and sweet, praise your sensible decision to turn back. Moors, castle ruins on Scottish witches' heath, all fine and dandy, but you're needed here, especially in times of change-over like these, when everything—I mean all the works of man's hand—is about to cave in."

Hoftaller departed abruptly. No glance over his shoulder. As he toiled up to the level of the weathered signs on the stuccoed façade of the house next door—"Dry Goods, Shoe Polish, Waxed and Toilet Paper"—Fonty could hear that his day-and-night-shadow, bustling away, could not put the witches' eternal verity behind him. But Hoftaller's tone was cheerful, not gloomy, as he repeated the phrase, like a tune stuck in his head—"Crumble like sand, / The works of man's hand"—and he was still chanting it as Fonty continued up the stairs with his luggage.

We archivists are accustomed to reviewing material that has already been evaluated, to casting doubt on received judgments, and channeling water from any number of sources to our paper mill, whether it bubbles up steadily or, after a brief spurt, slows to a trickle. We are inquisitive by profession. Contemporary witnesses deserve to be heard, and persons directly involved in events must be interviewed, no matter how subjective, and thus dubious, their interpretation may turn out to be. That includes family members, who would often rather take refuge in perplexed silence.

But Fonty's daughter Martha came forward with information: "What a scare Father gave us! Mama was beside herself when she found that letter on the kitchen table. And all the stuff he'd lined up around it, or piled on top of it, sort of like paperweights: all his old medals. I mean, the Johannes R. Becher Medal in bronze from the Cultural Union. And the silver badge for Contributions to Building Socialism that he got from the National Front—in '65, I think. And the Meritorious Service to the Fatherland, only bronze, of course. And a couple of other medals and badges for activism. Exactly: it was creepy. I'd left for work already, and Mama was still in bed when he sneaked away on tiptoe, without a suitcase or anything. He'd stowed one in the MB, probably in the cellar, or maybe in the attic. Anyway, when I came home for lunch—because Tuesdays I only teach half a day—Mama was sitting there looking like she'd been struck by lightning. Not a word; she shoved the letter across the table to me without a word. Theoretically I already knew what it would say when I saw that potpourri of medals on the table. Well, what do you think? The usual moaning and groaning: 'Can't take it anymore. This can't go on. Feeling walled in for so many years. Always on a leash. The only hope now is to say good-bye and duck under....' Exactly: here it is, word for word: 'I'm going to duck under and come up again in some place where it's quiet....' And then this: 'Let me just sit humbly on the rim of my Diogenes tub somewhere and besiege the world with silence....' And of course apologies laid on thick, and thanks a million to Mama for her much-tried patience. And for me 'all the best to my darling Mete,' and again he got my fiancé mixed up with the husband of the historical Mete. You know his name was Fritsch, not Grundmann like my Heinz-Martin. Look, here it is, in ink and his best handwriting: 'No matter that he has been widowed for only two months. The brief interval between funeral and wedding may cause all sorts of embarrassment, yet you have every reason to be happy. Your Herr Fritsch is a clever and sensible man, and of good character. . . .' And so on, leading up to this: 'To be sure, I know myself to be free of all pettifogging notions of marital bliss, yet for your wedding day I wish the two of you . . .' Of course I can't tell my fiancé, not something like this. And here: he's asking Mama to inform his 'faithful correspondent Friedlaender' of his departure— exactly, that was the Jew back then who was something in the Riesengebirge, a judge, I think—and who doesn't exist anymore. Exactly! Theoretically he means that professor from Jena—Freundlich's the name, another Jew, naturally. And Mama's supposed to write to that arrogant so-and-so, whom she never could stand, and tell him that Father's finally enjoying the privileges of the travel cadre. Which is true. After all, till just a little while ago Father was never allowed out, at least not to the West. But this Freundlich, he could do whatever he liked, till he got on the comrades' wrong side, on account of revisionism and deviationism. But even though Father was a cultural contributor and got scads of decorations, and even bonuses, he never belonged to the travel cadre. Of course before '68 he was allowed to go to Prague and the spas at Karlovy Vary a couple of times, but that was it. Unh-unh, Mama wouldn't have sent that Freundlich so much as a postcard . . . arrogant so-and-so that he is. And then this here topped it off, this really did us in. You can hardly even read it aloud, this last bit: '. . . by nine o'clock all will be over. Not in the spirit of a yearning for death, but only in the spirit of a profound yearning for peace. Such a fortunate and privileged life, so much freedom, whatever the constraints, so much lived immortality; and yet, what is the point of this nonsense!' Pretty confused stuff, but you Archives people must know what's factual, where he gets it all from, and what he throws in when he's in one of these moods and thinks he's something special. But Mama always takes everything literally, and she was a wreck. Well, because she's caught up in this damn role-playing with Father. All those years, the two of us had to go along with him, to keep him quiet. What a circus it was sometimes. The boys wouldn't join in, though, specially Georg. It embarrassed the hell out of them. That's why they stayed over there, with Aunt Lise. See, they were visiting her for the holidays when the Wall came. Well, because they couldn't stand it anymore. With me it was a different story. Even when I was little and Father took me along on Cultural Union tours, I was his Mete, a Huguenot, supposedly, like Mama, and him, too, goes without saying. Of course she was born a Hering and comes from Upper Silesia, just like Aunt Pinchen. And Father doesn't have a drop of French blood, at least not to my knowledge, even if he always says, 'Theo Wuttke is merely my official moniker—entitles me to a pension, that's all.' No, there's nothing to this French business. But because Neuruppin and the birth date matched—though a hundred years later—that was all he needed. And everyone went along with it, especially you people, the Know-it-All Brigade from the Archives. You get a kick out of it—right?—hearing the old man reel off everything by heart, and I mean everything. Give him a cue, and it comes pouring out. Exactly: as you say, ballads by the yard, whole pages from the novels, all that Brandenburg stuff, even the old war potboilers—he has them all down pat. And he forced us, not only Mama and me, but also the boys when they were still here—no, forced isn't the right word . . . but we had to go along and say yea and amen, at least theoretically. Mama because she had to, and me because I'm attached to him, damn it all, and looked up to him, even when I was a kid, when everyone clapped at the end, you know, in Oranienburg or Potsdam, where he had me along a bunch of times. You couldn't embarrass me. But of course the boys were older, specially Georg— and they couldn't take it anymore. As I say, that's why they stayed over in the West. Even today Friedel gags on the immortality tic, as he calls it. And I'm sure that's why Teddy doesn't want to come to my wedding. But Georg, his favorite, he was the one who really screwed things up, even from over there: pretty nasty letters. He made fun of him: Party mouthpiece, Comrade Wisenheimer, that kind of thing. But the fact is, Father never was a Party member, not like me—I believed everything, for much too long, of course.... No surprise, Father's letter on the kitchen table didn't say a word about the boys, only about Mama and me. I went on tour with him pretty often, even did those rambles with him on weekends, just like in the book. Was fifteen or sixteen at the time—I already had my blue shirt, at any rate. And after he lectured in Rathenow, the two of us went to see Katte's crypt in Wust. Real spooky in there. And Father talked about Katte as if it'd all been yesterday; off with his head, and so on. And how just before that, the crown prince kissed his hand. But nothing left of the manor house there. Like I said, we hiked all over the place, clear across the Uckermark or through the whole area around Freienwalde. Over Lake Schwielow, of course, taking the steamer from Caputh. Or from Lübbenau into the Spree Forest. Kossenblatt Castle. Still gives me the shivers, because Father always came up with these ghost stories... the lady in white, things like that.... And we hit the Ruppin area again and again: by train, by steamer, on foot.... Come to think of it, it wasn't half bad, wearing out the shoe leather with the old man.... All those parsonages—most of them falling down. But you got to hear some interesting things, even though it had nothing to do with politics, just church records, chronicles, boring old death registries. Not a word about socialism. Didn't even come up. And Father always so well informed, you know, on any subject. Sometimes he ran into folks who were as crazy about old stuff as he was. Exactly: all the generals, the whole frigging aristocracy. Reactionaries, every one of them, I thought, and that's why... I'll admit I turned in a few reports... well, about supposedly conspiratorial meetings.... I let myself be used by the—I'm sure you can guess who I mean. Sure, I was only fourteen or fifteen at the time, but still, it was a pretty cheap trick, even if I didn't write anything about 'antisocialist agitation' or such, just that they talked about pretty boring stuff. Sure, I'm ashamed of it today, but back then... Still remember like it was yesterday, Father arguing for hours with that writer in Kossenblatt—what was his name? Right, Günter de Bruyn—about whether the Soldier King forced Count Barfus to sell his castle, and whether this huge oil portrait of the von Oppens family was an original or just a copy. And then there was that business with the set of antlers that was sold to somebody in Saxony and is supposed to turn up somewhere in Karl May's books. Theoretically all perfectly harmless. That's why I didn't write anything about the castle that burned down with the dead birds in it—Father just made that up to scare the daylights out of me. Even so, those are my happiest memories. And he let me tag along when he had to 'sing for his supper,' as he said, with the Cultural Union, and sometimes I had a real good time. I still remember Cottbus and his talk on the women characters—Melanie, Effi, Corinna, Stine, Mathilde, and so on. Or here at the Archives in Potsdam, the talk on *Schach von Wuthenow*, of course, and how Frau von Carayon goes to see the king, and he has that clipped Prussian way of speaking: 'Recall children's ball. Lovely daughter. Long ago. Most devastating. Be seated, Madame...' Father could do that so well. They all clapped and laughed. Sometimes he talks that way himself, you know, like in his letter here: 'Don't like to play the moralist. Was always a singleton. Always a mere onlooker. Observing things is better than owning things. Want therefore to duck under...' And sometimes that guy—you know—his day-and-night-shadow, Father calls him, talks the same way: 'Let's be reasonable. Say so yourself, that the West's no good. Don't want to have to report... Can do it the hard way...' Anyway, it was lots of fun in Potsdam back then. First we had coffee and cake with the Cultural Union's district secretary. But to this day I haven't figured out why Father sometimes compared me to his Corinna Schmidt. I'd give a lot to have her sharp tongue—the way she gave that Jenny Treibel tit for tat, straight from the shoulder, like Father always says. Sometimes wish I could do that, especially to Father when he goes over the edge, like just now. But he's back, and that's what counts. So Mama's happy, in spite of everything. What that woman's had to put up with from 'my Wuttke,' as she calls him, you wouldn't believe. And since the Wall's been gone, it's been getting worse and worse. Always hanging around over there in the Tiergarten, coming up with these weird ideas. Fact is, though, that other guy has him under his thumb. Always did, theoretically. It really should stop, now that Normannenstrasse's sealed up and the outfit supposedly has nothing more to report. But no! Can't manage without him. Exactly! When Father didn't want to sing for the Cultural Union anymore and simply threw in the towel, he even got him that half-day job in the MB, and also made sure he could keep on working there after the changeover. Mama's being unfair when she grumbles, 'What's a file courier?' Theoretically he's just fine when he has something to keep him busy, and it's nice he can bring in some extra on top of his pension. Exactly: we think so, too. He's in great shape for his age...."

In this respect we had to agree with Martha Wuttke. And we could also have confirmed her doubts about the appropriateness of her father's comparing her to Corinna Schmidt in *Frau Jenny Treibel.* Martha had none of Corinna's innate light-footedness and quick wit. We saw her instead as big-boned and essentially taciturn, even if, in response to our questions, more came out of her mouth than her head wanted to authorize. Like her father, she tended to abbreviate her sentences, a style of speech that has recently begun to catch on at the Archives, parodying Prussian word-skimping: "Have a rough letter-writing day behind me."

No, she was no Corinna, yet certain family resemblances could not be denied. Martha Wuttke's sudden spells of depression often brought on violent, even feverish attacks of nerves, which not only interrupted her teaching for weeks on end but also allowed a comparison with her father's relived "nervous collapses" and the foul moods experienced by the historical Martha. She resembled the Mete immortalized in many letters and also familiar to us from archived photos, which show her as matronly even at an early age, gazing gloomily at the observer even when attempting a smile. The Immortal's faint sympathy—"Mete has something almost unscathed about her, which life has merely clouded"—suggested what he confirmed in another letter: "You sign yourself 'bird of ill luck,' and there's something to that...."

Yet despite the similarities, Martha Wuttke was a person in her own right. Arms crossed and head cocked to one side, her very posture signaling mistrust, she answered our questions in tones sometimes deliberately brusque, sometimes crude. Not that she indulged heavily in Berlinisms, yet she ran the local "mouthworks" with such perfect carelessness that no one would have suspected a seasoned teacher behind that vocabulary. She taught math and geography, and must even have been a passable pianist as a girl; at any rate, she let fall that she "could crank out a few things by Chopin": "Mama wanted me to stick with it, of course, but I didn't care to anymore. Makes me sick, music. I'm a lot like Father in that respect...."

And the ideological litmus test? Martha Wuttke revealed more about herself than one would have expected. For instance, even before the changeover—"from March '89 on, to be precise"—she was out of the Party, "at last," as she stressed, but its successor organization was out of the question for her: "When your faith fails you, you've got to make a clean break. And I was a believer, absolutely and far too long, in our common cause, I mean—socialism, solidarity with the international working class, and all that. Had a clear goal in sight...I toed the line....Undeviatingly, as they said, till it all came crashing down. Suddenly nothing made sense. Over and done with. That leaves you feeling pretty empty. Looked around for a long time, then went knocking at a different door. You won't ever guess, and maybe you'll even laugh. Well, it was St. Hedwig's. Because theoretically a person's lost without faith in something...."

She merely hinted at her newly awakened interest in religion— "You can't explain everything in strict materialist terms"—and proceeded to voice her concerns about her future as a teacher: "Because I was in the Party so long. Besides, from now on, the bottom line's supposed to come out capitalist, and I can't do that. How am I supposed to teach geography when all they want you to talk about is oil reserves and the Third World? Zero prospects, except housewife. We'll see what happens after the wedding. My fiancé's construction business is in Münster, of course, but now Heinz-Martin wants to invest over here, which theoretically is the right thing. No, not in Berlin, more in Schwerin and that area, where he got a house for us, just the other week...."

If you listened to Martha Wuttke holding forth on matters practical, she sounded more like a Mathilde Möhring, even if she lacked the cameo profile. Nor was she ash-blond; she had chestnut-brown waves, like her mother before she went gray. But perhaps she had her father's hair, although we always saw Fonty as white-headed. She kept coming back to his most recent escapade: "Imagine! He just stuck a five-hundred-mark note, hot off the press, in the letter: my wedding present! And when he came back with his suitcase and that plastic bag, butter wouldn't melt in his mouth. Blithered something about a 'little excursion': 'Fell through, I'm sorry to say.' And all because, so he said, an old woman got onto his train and sat down across from him. Supposedly had a black hen on her lap, a live one. You get it? Right: poor Effi, Kessin, the haunted house with the Chinaman, and old Frau Kruse in her overheated parlor—she always had a black hen like that on her lap, which scared the daylights out of Effi. And Father said that was why he got off the train, out of superstition, because the hen was bad luck. But of course that's not what happened, imaginary hen or no imaginary hen. Someone dragged him off the train at the last moment. You know who. 'I guess we owe him,' Mother said. And Father? He laughed when I wanted to give him back the five hundred: 'A gift is a gift!' Then he took his suitcase and went straight to his room...."

The next day in the paternoster Fonty remarked, "You were frightfully right, Hoftaller. Can't do that, leave wife and daughter in the lurch. Were both so happy when I got upstairs, all out of breath with my suitcase and bag. A veritable shower of kisses from Mete. And my Emilie in tears again. The old story. Still, I felt colossally weak in the knees when I saw the two of them at the kitchen table and began to envision the consequences of my suddenly ducking out of sight.... I'd been picturing a cottage tucked away behind alders, amidst heath and high moors, with a peat fire.... But not much chance this refuge for my old age could have been made palatable to my two ladies. Even London was just pea-soup fog to my Emilie.... I wanted to hurl myself alone and nameless into the jaws of dull approaching oblivion. To be mortal, Tallhover! I wanted to be mortal at long last.... Should have waited for Mete's wedding, and then I could have...Would have been practically

without company up there, except for Macbeth's three witches—
'At midnight up on the mountain's lee, / On the highland moors,
by the alder tree.' Far, far away, and lost to the world. If life is silent,
desire falls silent. . . . But it's better this way, Hoftaller! Acting re-
sponsibly. Following through. With both eyes open, straight from
the shoulder . . . Besides, I do want to see my Mete at the altar, finally. Always *engagée,* just not 'engaged.' It's high time, with the girl
approaching forty and no reserve lieutenant far and wide. Wrote to
her and wished her luck with her Herr Fritsch. Supposed to be a
decent architect, even has a university chair . . . Never got that far
myself. At the very end, before the lights went dim, an honorary
doctor of philosophy. Proposed by Schmidt and Mommsen, who,
on account of *Before the Storm,* had taken a liking to me. My Emilie,
who appreciated that kind of fuss and bother, was pleased, but not
I. Came too late. I stood there in academic regalia wishing I could
sink into the ground and come up somewhere else. Yes, indeed.
Pop up in a blackish brown water hole full of bubbling and blubbering. Would have dried myself in the hut by the peat fire, chuck-
ling to myself. . . ."

Fonty was giggling as he left the paternoster on the fourth
floor. Although weighed down by three file cases, he executed a
defiantly youthful hop. Hoftaller, who had had a quick look-see in
between floors, continued in a downward direction and did not
rendezvous with Fonty until half an hour later, when the latter entered the paternoster on the second floor with a new load of files,
whereupon both of them proceeded upward. Their often practiced cycle. Their ascents and descents, without fear of turning
points. They passed the time. A chance for a good chat. But on this
day their paternoster patter remained one-sided. Hoftaller was
content to listen, and only Fonty spoke—as if he had been drinking babble-water.

Overflowing, as after a long trip, he went on and on. For a while
he was off in Edinburgh with Lepel, the friend of his youth; then he
prattled on about the stages of his first, precipitate journey to England, which he had wangled out of his military service; then he
quoted from the London diaries: "Wrote letters at Café Divan . . .
Worked . . . Sadler's Wells: Miss Atkinson as Lady Macbeth . . ." And

finally the correspondence with James Morris, whom he claimed to have tutored in German during his second sojourn in England, served to bridge the centuries, intermingling them. Freed of inhibitions because beyond any temporal constraints, Fonty quoted from a letter written almost forty years later to Morris, the tone now that of an observant world strategist: "England's rule in India must collapse; it is nothing short of a miracle that it has survived to the present day. It will fall not because of its mistakes or its crimes—all that means little in politics—no, it will fall because its time has run out. . . ."

Toward the end of this letter—which he reeled off spontaneously—after deposing England, he thrust another world power into the historical foreground: ". . . the 'other one' is Russia, for the moment. But Russia, too, will be only an episode. . . ." And deliberately leaving America out of the discussion, he promptly arrived at the present and its succession of collapses: "What we are experiencing here as the fall of the Wall and the collapse of the Soviet Union does not mean the end; no: a self-aware life, nationalist and religious, consistent with its most ancient traditions, will ultimately triumph. Terrible, and inexcusably stupid, I know. But this evolution, merely hinted at here, is taking place wherever one looks, all over the world. I believed at first, my esteemed Mr. Morris, that it was a blessing for the world's peoples, among them small ones and even the smallest ones, but now I fear the worst, in view of the Balkans and the Caucasus. Should it be granted to me to sit by your London fireplace, a prospect for which I am still permitted to hope, I shall gladly let all the gloom that has seized me in its powerful grip be blown away, with the help of good common sense, a colossal advantage that England still has on her side. . . ."

As the two of them left the paternoster on the second floor, Hoftaller said, "Easy does it, Fonty. Your friend Morris can wait. The world is still holding together pretty well. You, on the other hand, shouldn't let yourself get too worked up. Why don't we call it a day? A little earlier than usual. You're looking peaked—sweat on your brow. Your delicate nervous system. Not worth putting at risk. We have to watch out, watch out damned carefully! By the way, I share your opinion as far as the most recent super- and mini-nationalism goes. But we don't want to forget America. And some day China... But enough of that. Man, Wuttke! You're shaking like a leaf. Not going to get sick on us, are you?"

Fonty's daughter shared Hoftaller's concern when he delivered his ward to the garret apartment. Fonty had the shivers. "The excitement of the last few days is taking its toll. Assume it's his nerves again."

Martha Wuttke did not invite her father's day-and-night-shadow into the parlor. Although she had learned in her youth to accept him as, in Fonty's words, his "faithful old companion," and to fear him as the "stubblehead," she got rid of Hoftaller in the kitchen, holding open the door to the stairwell. "I'm sure all the up-and-down and lugging those files around isn't doing him any good. Time they left him in peace. At his age, God knows, Father's earned some peace and quiet. Of course you must have seen him like this many times. You're supposed to know him from way back, since the war. Exactly! Old comrades! Whatever you say. But in that case, you should find him a job that's not so strenuous. An organization that big has to have something. And as before, half-days. Theoretically it's fine with us if Father has something to do. But you can't let it turn into real work. You see where that leads to. He's shaking all over. That's because he tends to overdo it. 'Father doesn't know his limitations,' Mama says. She has a point. Shouldn't be news to you, what with you knowing him so long. But show some consideration—oh, no! They're exploiting him, abusing him, using him. He looks like hell. Must be the nerves again. Comes on the same way with me. Have to call Dr. Zöberlein again. You wait and see—he's going to go and get sick on us!"

Hoftaller confirmed Martha Wuttke's fears without defending his own actions. When he saw he would not be invited to sit down, he left. Fonty had withdrawn into himself. He paid no heed to the dismay over his condition. He sat at the table, rocked by waves of trembling, and pushed a few crumbs of bread back and forth on the oilcloth. He sat there, his tie loosened, his eyes watering.

Hoftaller had hardly left when Emmi Wuttke opened the door from the parlor to the kitchen a crack: "Thought he'd never go!

You have to air the place out when that skunk's been prowling around. But he won't let go. Has to keep on my Wuttke's tail. And idiot that I am, I thought we were through with all that!"

We archivists would have liked to be of help, if only with apt quotations. But word of Fonty's nervous collapse did not reach us until later. The two women got him to bed. He put up no resistance. Not a word, not a complaint. Only when they were taking his temperature did he say softly, yet as if declaiming to an audience, "Crumble like sand, / The works of man's hand..."

When Emmi Wuttke heard that Scottish witches' formula, she exclaimed, "Now you're going to go and get sick on us, Father!"

10

Tugging at the Ring Finger

It was a difficult marriage—the one and the other—yet both held together. The marriage to Emilie, née Rouanet, whose biological father was called Bosse and whose adoptive father was a certain Kummer, lasted forty-eight years. And the bond with Emmi Balunek, who thanks to her stepfather was known in her secretarial days as Emmi Hering, likewise weathered many a crisis, whatever the cracks at the seams. Fonty tended to complain about the second marriage when he was thinking of the first, yet both in letters and in person, when he called on the Archives, he praised the long marriage to Emilie as "all in all a pretty hardy relationship," an example to him and Emmi: "We're too tangled up in each other to extricate ourselves...."

Fundamentally, he was attached to both women, for the occasional nagging of the Huguenot Emilie and the Upper Silesian Emmi was shrill yet lively music to his ears. In a letter he wrote later to Martha Wuttke, weeks after he fell ill, we read: "Mama is prone to a kind of ranting and raving; just slip in a wreath and you have Ophelia, or, *sans* wreath, Lady Macbeth; and two hours later she's polishing off a ham sandwich...."

And with quotations of this sort Fonty invoked both marriages. The longer the marriages lasted, the more often he had a double vision of the golden wedding anniversary, sometimes an alarming spectacle, sometimes a hard-earned triumph. Even though at the end of the seventies he had looked back on his married life as "our Thirty Years' War" and observed the occasion with very few friends, nonetheless he never hoped for a truce; and at the Wuttkes' there were also sour notes aplenty in the home-sweet-home.

Photographs show the historical Emilie as sternly buttoned up, her rigid dignity reflecting the technical limitations under which studio photographers labored in her day. Candid pictures exceeded their ability. But of Emmi we received such a lively and physical impression that we could easily imagine her in snapshots. She was an emotional, rather lachrymose person with a tendency toward stoutness—no, she was fat, in fact. If Emilie looked matronly and stately in photographs, when we visited the Wuttkes, Emmi seemed to be spilling over, sometimes with high spirits, sometimes with sheer misery. Usually we found her in a short-sleeved housedress and worn scuffs.

Almost as soon as we rang the bell on the fourth floor, she would be standing in the doorway, forearms locked across her bosom: a fleshy bastion who had to be coaxed into talking, which proved not too difficult, for Emmi Wuttke enjoyed chats with us about her aches and pains, always mingled with her dismay at her husband's almost incomprehensible existence. Whether she was complaining of bladder problems or trouble breathing, she would conclude any account of her latest infirmities with the sentence, "But my Wuttke always makes it even worse."

Yet the old woman's moaning and groaning evoked the image of young Emmi Hering. She veritably blossomed in her vocal lament. The little secretary must have been pretty, or at least winning. We pictured her hair, prematurely gray and now dyed an unfortunate blue-black, in its original brown—"chestnut brown," Fonty assured us. When Emmi laughed, a young girl was still laughing inside her. At any rate, it was not hard to see why Airman Third Class Theo Wuttke fell in love, in the spring of 1940, with the barely eighteen-year-old "saucy steno girl"—head over heels, in fact.

As we know, it happened in the paternoster. Later they sat, during furlough after furlough, spring or fall, in the Tiergarten, no doubt on a bench facing Rousseau Island, while behind them the elderberry bloomed or was ripe. The soldier regaled the girl with anecdotes from occupied France. The soldier invited her to go rowing. On the large man-made lake near the Zoo, they took turns at the oars. And soon, which means after his next assignment, they got engaged. Aunt Pinchen, with whom Emmi lived, did not object to the entertaining young soldier's coming and going in the apartment on Weissenburger Strasse, which only a few years later would be called Kollwitzstrasse.

The soldier brought gifts: apple brandy from Normandy, sausages from Lyon, sheep cheese from the Cévennes, even perfume and Brussels lace. The soldier returned time and again, whereas for many of the neighbors' sons only the death notice made its way home. And when the soldier Theo Wuttke came back late in the summer of '45, a newly released prisoner of war, he seemed only mildly astonished that his fiancée greeted him by placing his firstborn in his arms. The child was already teething; and soon little Georg was running around the three-and-a-half-room apartment, which had sustained only moderate damage. Aunt Pinchen had turned over one and a half rooms to the young family.

They lost no time getting married. The soldier earned an expedited teaching certificate. And the following year, when Aunt Pinchen died because the food shortages were compounded by bitter cold, the Housing Office could not force them to take in a lodger because Emmi was already five months pregnant with Theodor. And then she wanted even more children. After a miscarriage, she gave birth to their youngest son, Friedrich, always known by his nickname, Friedel—similarly, the children in the neighborhood all called the second-born Teddy and the firstborn Schorsch. Not until three years later, when the former soldier was no longer a teacher but a traveling lecturer, did Martha arrive. Her father christened her Mete as he held her in his arms, and Mete he would later call her in letters.

But it was not the many pregnancies that caused Emmi to put on weight. Nor was she a big eater or unduly fond of sweets. Fonty, and Fonty alone, was allegedly to blame for her piling on the pounds. When we expressed some skepticism at this explanation, her anger overflowed: "No, you just couldn't count on him. 'Cause after the war, when he had the chance to become a teacher and did the accelerated training and got a job right away, teaching German and history, well, it was just a couple years later, and he's teaching here at Senefeld Grammar, he goes and throws it all away, 'cause he was fed up, he said, with the 'pedagogical rubbish.' And because after that, see, he didn't make anything of himself. 'Cause he always wanted to do something 'freelance.' And 'cause from the start he had this bee in his bonnet. You know what I mean. That's why the boys stayed away, all three of them. Our Georg was already seventeen, but Teddy and Friedel were just fourteen and twelve, still children, when the three of them decided that everything was just hunky-dory at his sister Lise's in Hamburg. No, she took real good care of them, I've got to hand her that. School, university. Must've cost her plenty. At any rate, all three of them made something of themselves over there. And our Georg, he'd already made air force captain; if that thing with his appendix hadn't happened...But over here it kept getting worse and worse for me, 'cause I lost my job, and we couldn't go over even for a visit, 'cause the boys...well, Republic-desertion, they called it...And 'cause I had health problems after that, 'cause of my weight and 'cause my bladder's been messed up since then, and 'cause I have this trouble breathing, and not just when I climb stairs...That was bad enough. But my Wuttke always made things even worse. Well, 'cause he didn't amount to anything, not as a teacher, not with the Cultural Union, or in the MB...he never did get past file courier...."

What lends weight to this heavy burden of blame is the fact that whenever Fonty was driven out of the house by Emmi's reproaches, he would invoke the aspirations of the historical Emilie, née Rouanet-Kummer. His source was a sketch called "My Wife's Image of the Proper Civil Servant," in which the unfortunate state of affairs in the Immortal's household is enumerated in points, numbered one to ten. For instance: "A civil servant lives a long time. So as long as he remains alive, he draws a decent salary. Should he fall ill, a substitute is found. Taking the waters belongs to his perquisites. And mistakes are a matter of indifference, so long as the outward appearance of his own and his profession's infallibility is preserved...."

Similarly, though in a different tone, Emmi Wuttke would have had no trouble enumerating the advantages of permanent employment at a rank far above that of file courier. It was upon her urging, by the way, that the piano was purchased for Martha: "We had a piano in our villa in Oppeln, too...."

Time and again she reproached her husband for giving up teaching: "Why did my Wuttke—he was teaching back then—have to put his oar in on everything that was going on in politics?" And after the jeopardized career—"My Wuttke could've been a head of school for sure"—she dredged up all the missed opportunities that had presented themselves from the late sixties to the mid-seventies, when the deserving traveling lecturer for the Cultural Union was offered the post of Party district secretary. "But my Wuttke said every time: That kind of thing doesn't suit me—sitting at a desk all day and writing reports. Besides, he didn't want to be sent to Pasewalk or maybe even farther, way down to Saxony. But then when the comrades offered him Potsdam and Neuruppin, which is practically round the corner from us, and really put on a whole lot of pressure, he went and ruined everything again, with politics. Well, first he'd have to join the Party, but he didn't want to, and then in '68, when he was on tour, apparently he squawked about how our fellow socialist countries marched into Czechoslovakia. But in '76 they offered him the Cultural Union secretaryship on a platter, and again he blew it. Said in public, 'Singers have to be allowed to sing.' And then, to top it off, 'A Biermann in the hand is better than a Biermann in the bush.' And 'jettisoned the culture rubbish,' like he said. That's how he is, my Wuttke. He's always got to make things even worse. So bad they wouldn't let him speak any more. 'Cause when he had to do self-criticism in front of the Cultural Union, 'cause the comrades were trying to help him out, he took a pretty high and mighty attitude toward the Party collective: 'District secretary means nothing to me,' he said. 'I'm not suited to such a position, perhaps not to anything official. From now on I want to speak only as a freelance, as a free man....' That did it for the comrades, of course. And thank goodness someone stepped in again—don't make me say who—and helped my Wuttke get this file courier job."

We archivists can attest that the statement Emmi quoted gave evidence of modestly self-assertive arrogance, for the Immortal had used those very words when he gave up his post as permanent secretary of the Prussian Academy of the Arts in the summer of 1876. Three months of accumulated unpleasantness, mishaps, and quarrelsomely pursued intrigues furnished him with ample justification for leaving the well-remunerated position. He had taken up his duties not long after Easter, in response to his wife's wishes and at the urging of friends—and also because the kaiser had approved the appointment. Later he wrote, "Probably the worst period in my life. Nothing but annoyance and insults. When it was over, I was sufficiently humble to seek the blame in myself. But now I see the matter in a different light...."

And Emilie? She simply could not forgive her husband for resigning from the *Kreuzzeitung* or for throwing up this respected position, whereas he, unfit for any such office, breathed a great sigh of relief, as if liberated, and promptly sat down and finished *Before the Storm*, and from that time on had only one wish: to be a freelance writer. Emmi Wuttke could not refrain either from accusing her husband of knowingly talking his head into the noose, putting on political airs for the express purpose of escaping the tedious Cultural Union meetings and life as a paper-pusher. As usual, he hadn't cared a bit about his family, thinking only of his sacred freedom: "Well, traipsing around like a gypsy on those lecture tours. But then that was over. All he was good for was hauling files. We were so ashamed. And then Martha stopped in to see Father one time at the MB, and she saw how they had him going up and down those corridors and from one floor to the other in that old paternoster, loaded down with files. Afterward she just sat there and cried...."

That much is true: never again would Fonty be allowed to go on the road, giving the classic lectures celebrating the Immortal that he had delivered between the Baltic and the Erz Mountains, the Elbe and the Oder. But Emmi had even had her doubts about the itinerant lecturer, who at least had provided adequately for his family. She reproached him for making a fool of himself in public: "They make jokes about you, Fonty jokes!"

We could have protested; it wasn't really that bad. True, people smiled when in one of his lectures he plowed through all the novels from a horticultural point of view, and right after the heliotrope the immortelles sprouted symbolic significance. People smiled behind their hands when he used his amazing talent for word-perfect quotation to tuck in ironic allusions to contemporary socialist reality—for instance, when he let Party functionaries and travel cadres appear in the guise of typical Prussian privy councillors and reserve lieutenants. Because in those days we were still wearing ideological blinders, we shook our heads as he expounded theories according to which the future of the "fourth estate," although sublated in the Workers' and Peasants' State, remained uncertain. But we never laughed at Fonty, let alone made cynical jokes about him. It would be more accurate to say that his obsessively displayed cheerfulness left us feeling ill at ease. We never knew for certain whether we were witnesses to, or complicit in, a comedy whose author seemed to be doubled. Fonty toyed with us, and because this form of play provided amusement in often dreary times, we played along, even when his lecture on the reactionary *Kreuzzeitung,* "How to Suppress One's Own Opinion for the Good of Prussia," proved more than audacious; each quotation could apply to the Socialist Unity Party's chief news organ, without Fonty's having to quote a single passage from that state-sponsored soporific, *Neues Deutschland.* No, open provocation was not for him, nor for his grateful listeners. He drew an audience by remaining ambiguous; in his asides, he made time blur and rush on ahead, or drove the "white horses of Socialist Realism" around the manège like a ringmaster. He disseminated the Immortal's work more by chatting than lecturing; he made people laugh, yet never made himself a laughingstock.

But Emmi Wuttke viewed this adaptive imitation with alarm. The older he got, the more he resembled his model, down to the merest detail. Emmi hazarded a technical term: "He's personifying himself again." For she could never be sure, as they sat at the kitchen table, whether it was really her Wuttke she was hearing, no matter how conscientiously Fonty suppressed the Immortal's tendency to show off his esprit with a sprinkling of French expressions.

It did not help that Emmi was increasingly irritated by his appearance. True enough: he looked like a carbon copy, and in those films based on literary works, produced for cinema or for television—in both Germanys, by the way—he could easily have played several of the characters, so much had he come to resemble old Briest, old Stechlin, and eventually their much older originator. No wonder Emmi moaned, "That's not how my Wuttke talks. 'There's not much left of me, Buschen,' he said recently. And the way he goes around, always with that old scarf wound round his neck and that awful stick. And then his hair all wispy and down around his ears. And that hat! Well, maybe it suits him. But a Bismarck hat? That is not him. He isn't Bismarck, nor anybody else, either. Just my Wuttke, a raggedy old file courier who folks laugh themselves silly at."

We know from Fonty that even his wife's chronic dislikes were memories from a previous life—her annoyance at his hat and "Bismarck-brown overcoat": "My Emilie sees in me the complete proletarian, who goes around in a sort of disguise, and then on the other hand she expects me to comport myself as if I had issued from an unnatural crossing of Cato with Goethe. . . ."

Emmi's list of complaints went on and on. Even his lectures, which she referred to as "blabber," had been too laden with innuendo for her taste. She was in a good position to judge, she assured us; for years, the barely legible pencil scribbles had been handed over to her for typing: "During the war it was those mile-long reports from occupied France. Some of them were funny, about officers' clubs in castles and luxury hotels. And after the war, all the lectures. I typed up everything nice and clean on my old Erika. Couldn't get a new machine for love or money. Wasn't till much later that I treated myself to a real modern one, a Robotron. Through connections. A scarce commodity, as you know. Still have it. That I was good for—just his typist, all those years. But I didn't like the stuff he talked about, really didn't. Too unscientific, that's what Martha said, and she read every book his one-and-only ever wrote. Wall-to-wall exaggeration. 'What's this supposed to mean?' I kept asking my Wuttke. I remember—it must have been the early seventies—when he gave me something to type again, and I say, What's a person supposed to make of stuff like this: 'The Conflagration As Metaphor for Sexual Encounters.' 'Leave it be, Emilie,' he said. 'These are delicate matters, beyond your ken. It's old hat to me, and there's little harm in it. A novel like *Irretrievable* calls for an unfettered spirit. . . .' 'No, Wuttke!' I say. 'You're getting into something kinky again. You've got a thing for fire. Just take a sentence like this: "Fiery passion equals fiery conflagration"—that's scary. But folks just laugh at it. . . .' "

Emilie Rouanet-Kummer viewed her husband's literary production with a similarly critical eye. In conversation with Gerhart Hauptmann, the young playwright to whose theatrical success the Immortal had contributed by lavishly praising his first play, *Before Sunrise,* she is supposed to have admitted, as members of Berlin society swirled around them, "He considers himself a writer. Well, I don't believe it for a minute. He can't have the wherewithal. . . ." But for years she, too, copied all the pencil-scribbled manuscript pages into legible script, and her opinions—"Emilie thinks that as a rule I write better with non-material than with much material . . ."—even found a hearing.

It must have been love that kept Emilie and Emmi devoted for an entire lifetime. And both women compensated for their lack of understanding with solicitude, often vociferously seeking sympathy from others for their cares and worries.

Emmi Wuttke even came to see us at the Archives, to have one or another of her husband's lectures checked over "by real scholars," as she put it. Fonty was of course not supposed to know anything about these visits. She trusted us. We could not allow ourselves to disappoint her.

When Emmi came, she sat a little bashfully in our visitors' chair. While she waited, she leafed through a book of photographs— landscapes and monuments in Brandenburg. She looked sad as she sat there, sunk into her bulk. Even when we could provide reassurance—for even Fonty's audacious lectures proved absolutely accurate in their quotations and factual references, no matter how obscure the sources—concern for Wuttke dictated her suffering facial expression.

We should add that even dubious details, ones that irritated us as well, were confirmed by manuscripts that turned up only later. He quoted—in intuitive anticipation—from letters that came to light quite by chance, among them several to Mathilde von Rohr. He even gave us salient references to passages in lost journals. In case of doubt, Fonty was the better archive, because he had no gaps. And what he did not know or had repressed, Hoftaller could supplement, but his visits we found disconcerting.

When Emmi Wuttke left the Archives, nothing seemed to have raised her spirits, not even our expert opinion in Fonty's favor. Fonty was justified in complaining that he "often had to endure for weeks on end a sour mood and bitter face." She could be unbearable. Like Emilie, Emmi saw herself as "forced to bear a heavy cross," and both believed they were cut out for better things, for a life of happiness and prosperity.

This much is true: money was often in short supply, yet neither family ever went hungry. Of course one had to be thrifty, and even write on both sides of the paper; but in a pinch someone always stepped forward to help—kindly Lepel or the Merckels. And later, when things got particularly bad, because the Wuttkes had fallen victim to "nervous collapse," Hoftaller was there—like Tallhover before him—to play the role of family friend.

He immediately saw to it that Fonty was granted sick leave. He made sure that word got around in the Ministries Building that the file courier, well liked on every floor, was in a "worrisome condition." Everywhere, or, to be more precise, throughout the eastern part of the city, word of his illness spread. Thus we, too, heard about it, although Potsdam lies off the beaten path. Hoftaller suggested a visit, but only in a small delegation.

The first thing we noticed was that Fonty, whom we found feverish and restless, kept playing with the ring finger on his left hand. No, he was not actually playing; eyes closed, he would tug periodically at his wedding ring. Then he would sink back apathetically, lying there in the narrow room known as "Father's study," with its desk and overflowing bookcases. His bed, in which he was now tugging at his wedding ring, had stood here for years. Because the blame had been pinned on him, Theo Wuttke had had to vacate the conjugal bedroom right after the sons' defection to the

West; the breadth of the marriage bed was thenceforth reserved for Emmi. Little Martha had moved into the boys' room. And since then Fonty had lain in Georg's old-fashioned iron bed, which had posts crowned with brass knobs. The bed made the study even narrower. Now he lay there with nerve fever, trying so persistently to free his ring finger of its burden that it was embarrassing to watch.

Later we were invited by Emmi Wuttke to stay for a cup of coffee in the so-called good room, where Martha's piano stood, silent since her girlhood, the same piano on which she claimed to have been able to "bang out" some Chopin and Schumann. Furnished with a sofa, two medallion chairs, a delicate secretary, on which Emmi's electric typewriter perched incongruously, and a white enameled looking glass with gold inlaid border, the parlor could have served the Poggenpuhls—"an impoverished aristocratic major's widow with three daughters"—as a parlor. Indeed, we archivists called the room "Fonty's Poggenpuhl parlor," especially since framed engravings on the walls illustrated Prussia's history in military scenes, among them, directly above the sofa, the slaughter of Grossgörschen, in which Cavalry Major von Poggenpuhl had achieved renown. Often enough we had heard Fonty's modified self-quotation: "Thus we live, and give the world proof that even in extremely reduced circumstances one can live contentedly and almost in accord with one's station, so long as one has the proper outlook and also, to be sure, the requisite adroitness...."

And now he lay there in a fever and tugged at his wedding ring, while we drank coffee from Meissen cups. Actually the two women had wanted to settle the patient in the parlor, but Fonty had insisted with his last strength on the bed in his study.

They took turns caring for him until Martha, too, fell ill; like the Mete we know from the correspondence, she had a tendency to succumb sympathetically to her father's frequent indispositions—his summertime depressions and now his nerve fever—to such a degree that her mother now had to bustle back and forth between the father's little room and her daughter's. The two sickbeds, flanking the kitchen, kept the overweight and constantly sighing woman on her toes. While in one room her Wuttke was talking "complete nonsense" in recurring surges of fever, in the other her daughter was weeping, saying she wanted to call off the wedding, or at least postpone it: "I'm not ready. Just can't live without a perspective...."

No wonder Emmi, who sat at the coffee table with us in the Poggenpuhl parlor, saw herself as bearing "a double cross." To hear her tell it, her life was nothing but sacrifice. The worse she felt, the more she dwelt, between brief visits to the patients, on her Upper Silesian origins. Her parental home underwent a metamorphosis into a villa with seven rooms and a solarium, surrounded by a park, while her stepfather became a prosperous grain dealer and her mother a musically gifted pastor's daughter, who had unfortunately let herself be seduced "as a young thing" by her piano teacher. We learned that Emmi Hering had been hoping to take over her father's grain business after she completed her secretarial training. "If it hadn't been for the war..."

She felt betrayed by fate. The war had not only saddled her with Theo Wuttke, unfit for any respectable career, but also toward the end robbed her of her parents; and she spoke with particular relish of her losses: "Believe me: Fate had it in for us. First everything down the drain in Oppeln. Then Papa and Mama went to Breslau, and that was a living hell, encircled during the final struggle and all. They didn't make it out, either of them. Nothing left. All kaput. Our beautiful villa. And behind the park four grain silos. And we had three teams to pull the delivery wagons. All sturdy draft horses. And Mama played every day, on the grand, of course, like our Martha used to, back when she still practiced every day, till my Wuttke said: Enough's enough. See, I was in Berlin already when the war started. No, our Polish workers couldn't complain, not even later when we joined the Reich. And it was Papa who wanted me to do the secretarial training, 'cause I wasn't really catching on at the Lyceum, and 'cause his sister, Aunt Pinchen, lived in Berlin with her Ernst-August. Master cobbler, my foot—by noon he was usually completely lit. Well, no one thought it would end that way. More and more bombs. But in the Reich Aviation, where they hired me right after my training, you were pretty safe in the cellar. And that's where I met my Wuttke; no, not in the cellar—in the paternoster. It was funny. He was real shy, at least at first. Course it was love at first sight—you don't ask a lot of questions. And then it was all over and we didn't have anything, just barely a roof over our heads, and that's when he came back. Skin and bones and starving to death. But kind of pleased about the baby. There was love there, still is. What the two of us went through during all those bad years, see, we have that in common; a thing like that brings you together. But when he first got back, he had to lay down. Aunt Pinchen took care of him, 'cause I was mostly out in the Tiergarten with the wagon, hunting for firewood.... He was in terrible shape. Not just the weakness. It was something like now: his nerves were shot. Took a long time to get over it. I had to go to work, first clearing ruins, then as a typist at the Housing Office. No more Reich Aviation, where I'd stayed through to the end, but then soon we had the whole apartment to ourselves 'cause in '46, that awful winter, Aunt Pinchen died, and I was expecting again.... The front of the building didn't have any windows at first, just cardboard. And the roof leaked, too. And in that awful winter nothing to heat with. But at least it was a roof over our heads, and that's why we didn't go over to the West, where my Wuttke's only sister— right, Lise Neiffert was her name; her husband never made it back from Russia—she had a little stationery store, first in Hanover, then in Hamburg. They were childless. And that's why she didn't send the boys back to me when the three of them went visiting and then stayed 'cause here the Wall came, and after that everything was sealed up tight. But I've got to give her credit for one thing: Lise took good care of those boys. Teddy's working for the government in Bonn, section head.... Friedel did his apprenticeship as a bookseller, and now he's got his own publishing company in Wuppertal.... And our Georg would be a major by now for sure if he hadn't had that thing with his appendix; he was already training on the Starfighters in the early seventies, and that's why we ... Lord, what didn't we do—letters, telegrams. I wanted to go over and bring the boys back, but they wouldn't let me. All through those rough years they wouldn't let me. But then that thing happened, and my Wuttke took sick again, right after we heard. Nerve fever again... There wasn't a doctor could help him... it got worse and worse... Oh, well, it's the same old story...."

Every time Fonty's situation became critical, which usually oc-curred against the backdrop of a political crisis, he fell ill or took refuge in illness, or so Emmi Wuttke claimed. This must have been the case in '51; right after the Fifth Plenary Session of the Central Committee he lost his position as a grammar-school teacher; he had made negative comments on the officially mandated formal-ism debate. He also fell ill soon after the workers' uprising in '53, when his lecture on the revolution of '48 was heavily censored, starting with the title, "To Put the Democrats to Rout, You Have to Call the Army Out."

"That time he didn't get out of bed for four weeks," Emmi said. "And the minute the Wall was here and our boys stayed over there in the West, he crawled under the covers again. Four weeks that time, too. And it was always his nerves—they were done in."

It was also with nervous symptoms that he took to his bed when he forfeited his chance to be district secretary by making pointed political remarks, then turned his back for good on the "culture rubbish." And just as he had made the transition from traveling lecturer to file courier in bed, now, after the most recent crisis, it was not only his aborted trip to Scotland that put him flat on his back but also the collapse of the Workers' and Peasants' State. He was attached to that state. True, he would have liked to see it more traditionally Prussian, but he belonged to it, and its history had been his own for forty years, along with the parallel prerevolution-ary periods, repeated Carlsbad decrees, and lasting dependencies. At any rate, all this played a part in his feverish fantasies. Some-times he lay there restlessly, sometimes apathetically. He talked to himself in bursts, then fell into breathless silence; he looked dead.

Emmi Wuttke knew how to handle this. When she let us peek into the sickroom again after our coffee, she said, "No surprise to me—it's just all too much for him. First thinking the file courier job won't be there long 'cause the unification is coming and the place'll be shut down, and then he wants to leave, just disappear, but that doesn't work out. So now he lies there fiddling with his ring, but he can't get it off his finger. That's how my Wuttke is—always has to make things even worse...."

During the ride back to Potsdam, my colleague reminded me how in an 1892 letter, which she quoted to me, the historical Emilie speaks of a grave illness the Immortal has developed—diagnosed as cerebral anemia—and reports to her son Friedrich: "I cannot describe how difficult it is to live with this poor sick man, the days as well as the nights. We are waiting for the doctor, who more and more insistently recommends an asylum. Papa, who at first seemed agreeable, now acts utterly terrified, such that I would give my consent only under the direst circumstances...."

The family feared the onset of lunacy; as Emmi Wuttke said to her daughter, likewise bedridden with depression: "Both of you'll end up in the loony bin if you keep this up." And Dr. Zöberlein, summoned from the nearby clinic because the chills and fever had become so acute, issued similar warnings.

As their family doctor, Zöberlein had been familiar for years with the patient's delicate nerves. At first he thought he could contain the crisis with strong medication. But when Fonty refused to take any medicine, out of epigonic hatred for anything that reeked of an apothecary shop, the doctor recommended that he be admitted to the psychiatric unit of Berlin's famous Charité Hospital. He himself preferred the Buch Research Center, whose mental hospital had "an excellent scientific reputation, even in the West."

But no sooner was the word "mental hospital" mentioned than Emmi exclaimed, "You aren't taking my Wuttke there. Over my dead body!"

And Fonty reacted to this medical advice as if falling into a prescribed role: on our next visit we found him abysmally depressed between surges of fever. He had even stopped tugging at his ring finger; and he could not accomplish what his predecessor had done, despite exhaustion, gastric upset, and nervous fever, namely, write long farewell letters. The Immortal had lamented from his sickbed to his correspondent Friedlaender, "A man is the yellow leaf on the tree as autumn draws to a close. The overall mood is joyless, and convinces one hourly of the wretchedness of the situation. Incomprehensible that we place such value on what is worthless and balk against taking leave of such frills and trappings...."

Dr. Zöberlein said that now the powers of self-healing had to come to the patient's aid. And aid arrived for Emmi from the neighborhood. The single mother of three children, Inge Scherwinski managed to find time at least in the mornings to lend a hand. She and Martha Wuttke had been in the Free German Youth together, and she was familiar with Martha's susceptibilities. Her diagnosis ran as follows: "It's the migraines. Nothing to do but wait and try to buck her up a little."

So she sat in Martha's darkened room—half an hour or an hour at a time—gabbing about the good old days, about harvest duty and summer camp. And since Inge Scherwinski liked to show off her pleasant little voice, she sang or hummed Martha to sleep with songs once intended to shake her countrymen awake and promote the building of socialism.

Emmi continued to lay cold compresses on her husband's forehead. This time she was more worried than during previous episodes, even though she paid little attention to Fonty's feverish ramblings, which flouted all chronology. He had just been hiking from castle to castle on the thwarted trip to Scotland, when suddenly, and in midsentence, he would be overcome with annoyance at a disastrous summer resort in the Riesengebirge, where the family could not get a wink of sleep: "Mete because of her anxiety attacks, which are not unlike my own, Emilie because of the incessant storms..." But while the fever surged, it was the writing block that had befallen the Immortal during work on *Effi Briest* that found the most ample expression.

Weary of urban life and already under the weather, he had escaped with wife and daughter to Zillerthal, near Schmiedeberg, on the advice of the family doctor, Dr. Delhaes, who had recommended a "change of air." In vain he had sat down to work on the last chapters, doubting every word, doubting himself. Someone advised him to entrust himself to a new treatment in Breslau, electroshock. The ordeal produced nothing but expense. Despair, which still echoed in the ravings of the feverish Fonty: "And thus I take leave of Effi; the flame refuses to flare up once more; what remains is too far a field. . . ."

They decided to return to Berlin, where second and third opinions were to be sought. Eventually it was Dr. Delhaes who got the feverish patient back on his feet, without resorting to any apothecary product; he simply talked him out of the nervous crisis inflamed by the sufferings of the unfortunate Effi: "You're not sick at all! What's missing is your work routine! And if you say, 'My mind is blank, I've lost my breath; it's all over with this novel-writing,' well, I say to you: If you wish to get well, just turn to something else, your memoirs, for instance. Start on your childhood tomorrow!"

That helped, as we know. During the writing of the book *Childhood and Youth*, the Immortal recovered; and soon after that *Effi Briest* was finished. Fonty, however, was not roused from his bed by medical advice, nor could his wife and daughter shoo away the fever. When Emmi finally took to her own bed from exhaustion, it was Hoftaller who had the healing inspiration.

11

With Sharpened Lead

It was not always easy to disentangle their voices, patiently separate the overlapping layers—often we heard the mother and the daughter talking at the same time. They stood in the kitchen, a united front. The women crossed their arms defensively over or under their bosom. Only on special days were we invited into the good room, the Poggenpuhl parlor. But in kitchen or parlor, visitors were served coffee. Sometimes coffee cake or honey-nut bars went with it.

The women on the sofa under the framed Battle of Grossgörschen, we in the medallion armchairs. Here, too, they sat with arms crossed. Between sofa and chairs, a round pedestal table, on whose fancy cloth, in addition to the coffee service, stood a bowl from Karlovy Vary full of wizened apples, a reminder of a long-ago trip to Carlsbad.

On every visit, mother and daughter viewed us with distrust for a while. Both held back at first, but if we waited patiently, eventually they would begin to talk. It was not chatting of the sort Fonty enjoyed, more a fitful gush of pent-up sentences, fragments, and buried verbal waste suddenly coming to the surface. They went on and on, interrupting and contradicting each other: a duet composed for a lengthy run. Our role was to give them their cues.

The chestnut tree's summer foliage allowed only a little light to filter into the parlor, whose windows looked out on the rear courtyard. The dimness was kind to the women, one stout, the other gaunt, both bearing the marks of all the lean years—"You know, when things just kept getting worse here"—resentful and hardened.

It seemed wrong to stare at them as they unburdened themselves, and Emmi and Martha also talked past us; only rarely did the Archives and the Wuttkes have each other in their sights. My colleague usually kept his eyes fixed on the Grossgörschen engraving in its cracked frame, focusing on horrific scenes and heroic details, while my gaze slid time and again to the pier glass, a piece of furniture that catches one's eye in almost all the novels and is referred to as a *trumeau*. The Immortal had a predilection for the "salon style," dotted with French phrases and flourishes that nowadays require explanatory footnotes in every edition. And willy-nilly, mention had to be made of his idiosyncrasies, even if the conversation in the Poggenpuhl parlor purported to be about Theo Wuttke: "Theoretically, Father's reliving stuff that went up in smoke long ago...."

"You'd think they were still riding by outside in those horse trams. And just kerosene lanterns, no electricity at all..."

"When he was feverish, all he talked about was the same old stuff, you know, Effi and her letters and the way old Briest ducks out every time things get sticky...."

"That's my Wuttke. Like his one-and-only, exactly, can't ever pin him down, just slips away from you..."

Since the daughter smoked, we were allowed to smoke as well. The women resembled each other only in their perms, which probably originated with the same hairdresser. Their defensive way of crossing their arms also seemed to be a family trait, one they did not shed until later on, and never entirely. Eventually they both let loose: "This isn't something you like saying, but it's got to be said sometime or other: It was downright embarrassing when our Friedel sent us those care packages—chocolates, toothpaste, egg shampoo, things like that—and we couldn't even thank him. No letters at all, only on the sly..."

"Well, because that was West contact, and prohibited, because the Security had Father classified as a confidential, see, always did, not just when he got the courier job...."

We stayed for a good hour. In the depths of the parlor the piano lurked in the shadows, silent now for years, with the same Chopin piece undisturbed on the music rack. This was at the beginning of Fonty's recovery, a few weeks before Martha's marriage to Heinz-Martin Grundmann. Of course the impending marriage was discussed, without our having to probe much. Martha said, "We're neither of us spring chickens, and we've both given this plenty of thought." But then we touched on problems that the Wuttke ladies had had with Fonty's day-and-night-shadow.

"No, sir, we weren't letting him in here. At least not at first. Only when it kept getting worse..."

"We made an exception for you, well, because you're from the Archives. Besides, too many visitors would've been much too tiring for Father."

"'Cause our Martha also ended up flat on her back. That's how it always was. When my Wuttke keeled over, she always went down with him...."

"Even so, I heard him trying to wear you down...."

"Rang the bell every other day, no shame at all. What did he want, anyway? But I wouldn't even let him in the kitchen...."

"What did he want? You know—to eavesdrop, snoop around. That's why I yelled, 'Don't you dare let him in, Mother!'"

"This story goes way back. See, the two of them've known each other for ages. Don't know exactly when it started. My Wuttke doesn't say much, and me, I don't ask...."

"Anyway, they were already pals in the war, when Father—you know he never really got to the front—wrote that stuff he sent back from the Government General, and from Denmark, too, but mostly from occupied France. Exactly! You said it. 'Historical Perspectives,' he called it. Must have been pretty lousy, not really fascist, but still propaganda, the kind of thing you'd be ashamed of today. Ask Mama, she knows more about it...."

"Goodness me, we were just kids, didn't know anything about all the bad things that came out afterwards, which I'm still ashamed of today. When I went to the Aviation right after secretarial school and they put me in Major Schnöttker's outside office, I had other things on my mind, 'cause I was in love with my Wuttke. You should've seen him: slim and trim! Anyway, we got engaged secretly. Only Aunt Pinchen was in on it. In Oppeln they hadn't a clue. I'd just turned nineteen. And we celebrated at Café Schilling, on Tauentzienstrasse."

"Typical! Mama still doesn't want to say anything about that fellow—even in those days he had his hand in everywhere, didn't give Father a moment's peace...."

"Listen to you—it wasn't that bad, really. Besides, my Wuttke always managed to give him the slip when he came home on leave, and we had some lovely times and went out, to Haus Vaterland and such. But the best part was his letters. Too bad they were all burned, 'cause they were bombing more and more, so I sent them to my friend Erika in Dresden, about a hundred letters in two packages... all up in smoke, 'cause of the carpet bombing.... And the streets full of refugees from Silesia... Anyways, my Wuttke always put poems in his letters, his own and other people's. But I never could tell for sure what was by him and what wasn't. All rhymed... One of 'em, I still remember, was called 'In the Rowboat.'... But that fellow, his shadow, I mean, he could really give you the willies sometimes...."

"Exactly! Even as I kid I caught on to that, when I'd go on lecture tours with Father, to Potsdam, Cottbus, even Neuruppin. He'd always pop up. But theoretically I didn't catch on, was so slow on the uptake that I even wrote reports for him, you know, like school compositions, all the stuff they discussed afterwards over coffee and cake at the district secretary's. 'Be on guard!' is what they told us in Young Pioneers. 'The enemy of the working class never sleeps!' Perfectly harmless, the stuff I wrote, but even so, I'm ashamed. 'Stubblehead,' I called him, and that made Father laugh...."

"He ran around like that even back then at the Aviation: hair no longer than a matchstick. Hasn't changed a bit. But went by a different name..."

"And he'd smile for no reason at all, always could...."

"Course we figured out, and Major Schnöttker, too, that he was connected to Prinz-Albrecht-Palais somehow or other...."

"You better watch it, I told Father later. If you don't watch out, he'll have you on his hook before you can say boo. You could smell it—that his address was Normannenstrasse. Was clear to me, even though I became a comrade in the mid-seventies, and I was ashamed in front of the Party collective when they called me in because Father'd sounded off in reference to that loudmouth they banned from singing over here, and then that was the end of the lectures, only hauling files from then on...."

"Well, you know, our Martha was just deluded—that's what they call it today. But my Wuttke, he knew, and even so he kept making things even worse with his constant carping. That's why he couldn't shake the fellow off, still can't. He owes him, 'cause of favors from long ago. Well, he helped out a few times when things got really rough. But you never know for sure: is he protecting him or hauling him in?"

"...Because Father never says a word about it. And when he lets something slip, it's always pretty roundabout; you know the drill: the revolution of '48, the March casualties.... And always like he'd been on the barricades himself, with a rifle. Sheer fantasy, but Mama, who took care of him when he was down with that fever, sometimes believes it herself...."

"Too bad you weren't there to take notes on what my Wuttke was saying, all jumbled, not just revolution, and him wanting to sound the bells, but also all these conversations with folks from way back in the old days. You could've sworn he had that Friedlaender or some other total stranger sitting there on the edge of the bed: 'Lepel, my good fellow!' Seems he wanted to borrow money off him, two hundred talers; you'd have thought Kaiser Wilhelm still had the say around here. And sometimes he acts like the streets and schools aren't named after his one-and-only but after him, so you begin to think he has some screws loose and should be put away...."

"Stop it, Mother! You never know what might happen!"

"I'm just telling it like it is. All this started long ago. Though not when he was in the military, and not after the war, either; he didn't go off the deep end till he was with the Cultural Union...."

"Mama gets upset about it; not me. Doesn't do any harm. People used to clap when he did those lectures. Was there with him, plenty of times. I thought I was something special as a child because they gave Father a cultural-activist badge and he had his picture in the paper. And theoretically it would have been bearable, if that stubblehead hadn't..."

"'My faithful old companion!'—that's what my Wuttke called that skunk...."

"You can't shake him; he shows up everywhere. 'Comrade,' that's what he said to me, and grinned, 'you're not going to turn down my request to visit my sick friend, are you? That would have consequences, Comrade! I mean, just before the wedding. You know, we can do this the hard way....A glance at your cadre file, Comrade...'"

"Even though our Martha got out in time, in the spring of last year already, when we still had the Party..."

"Exactly! And a team of wild horses won't get me to join those crazies who want to keep the tradition alive. I don't care how witty that Gysi is.... It's over... over and done with...."

"And that's why I wouldn't let him into our kitchen...."

"When he came by and rang the bell, it knocked me over...."

"If only you hadn't got up..."

"It was only because you yelled, 'Martha, come out here!'"

"Well, because he was making these threats—about the asylum and involuntary committal...."

"And can you guess what that stubblehead brought us? Flowers, a bunch of asters, exactly..."

By the time Hoftaller was finally allowed in, Martha was spending only half the day in bed. For a few hours she could relieve Emmi, who was exhausted from attending to the two invalids. And sometimes Inge Scherwinski came by to lend a hand. She scrubbed the kitchen, changed sheets, and aired out the place, humming her way from room to room.

Meanwhile July had passed. Summer heat hovered over the city. Hoftaller smelled sweaty when he came to call on the patient. And this odor accompanied him when Emmi opened the door to the study: "But don't you dare get my Wuttke upset...."

Fonty lay there, his eyes shut. His visitor told us later, "He might've been dead—that's how far away he looked." Even when Hoftaller drew up a chair and sat down by the bed, the sunken eyes remained closed. The expression on the patient's face was so fixed that someone with artistic talent and a quick hand—the painter Max Liebermann, for instance—could have dashed off several chalk sketches, especially since the bony hands of the apparent corpse had come to rest, as if forever: they lay there on the bedspread with not even the ring finger twitching.

Yet Fonty seemed to know that his day-and-night-shadow was there. Without needing even a moment to make certain, he said in a weak, tremulous voice, "This heat, Tallhover. You really should take a holiday. Don't you ever go to the country? I've always said: In July and August one should get out of Berlin. This last time we were in the Riesengebirge, but the change of air did no good. Usually helped with the depression, at least sometimes. But now I'm supposed to be carted off to the mental ward, that's Delhaes's advice. You have to do something, Hoftaller; intervene at once. This doctor from the clinic, Zöberlein's the name, was also bound and determined to pack me off to the asylum in Buch. But I don't want to go. Better to lie here shaking like a leaf than to lie there tranquilized. Besides, too much remains to be done. Must get back to Effi and Kessin—that's Swinemünde, you know: the bulwark, the heavenly blue house, my hiding place up under the rafters, where no one ever tracked me down, not even the boys from the neighborhood. Can still hear Father putting on a show with his gasconades, on Sundays, when visitors come, so that Mama's embarrassed again...."

Hoftaller listened, his head cocked to one side. He had brought along his smile, as well as a small package that he held on his knees, still wrapped. For a while Fonty lay there in silence, eyes closed, but then the feverish causerie resumed. Interlocking names, Prussia's aristocracy, time and again the Bredows, long since forgotten Tunnel brothers, Hezekiel, Scherenberg, Kugler, victorious regiments at Gravelotte and Mars-la-Tour, or runoff elections for the Reichstag—"Torgelow the file-cutter wins!"—mixed up with elections to the Volkskammer—"This bone-dry ninety-nine percent!"—and Forty-eighters' barricade songs: "Much cry and little wool!" All of this flowed without punctuation into Alexanderplatz speeches: "Only the coward is always a hero. Yet today even the most courageous of comrades are making concessions: The citizens are coming! The citizens are coming! They will save the Workers' and Peasants' State...."

But then he drifted into a lamentation in which he repeatedly figured as the permanent secretary of the Academy of the Arts. Although in fact only Hoftaller was present, Fonty seemed to think he had his mother confessor and regular correspondent Mathilde von Rohr at his bedside: "Find myself in a pitiable state. Have been in the post for three and a half months now without experiencing a single pleasure the entire time. Everything irks me. Everything disheartens me. Everything disgusts me. I've the distinct impression that I am becoming deranged, depressed. I've been through some terrible times, notably in my own household. My wife is profoundly unhappy, and from her point of view she's right. On the other hand, the Academy can go...In that case, better a file courier in the Ministries Building.... That scoundrel Hitzig...The other day, in the paternoster with him..."

He broke off. His pupils moving restlessly under closed lids. His mouth twitching under the shaggy mustache. Veins protruding in his temples. But then, because Hoftaller just sat there and smiled without a word, he began to speak as though Emilie, née Rouanet-Kummer, were seated by his sickbed and had to be placated: "What do you mean—'This is how I pictured our future together!'—and all because on your sister's table two bottles of Médoc appeared, to the tune of twelve silver groschen apiece? And you make a face because I've turned my back on Prussia's Academy and am simply longing for the moment when I can escape from this mediocrity draped in self-importance? You say the world insists on having its idols. I've no quarrel with that, so long as I'm not required to worship them myself. Have no desire to dance to every privy councillor's tune.... What do I care what resolutions the Party collective passes?... Fare thee well, secretariat! Can do without the Cultural Union drudgery, too...Requiescat in pace! It's not true that a person can get used to anything.... Am I supposed to kowtow to that man Kant, who just happens to bear such a distinguished name?... Or cling to this official post, despite the blowup with Hitzig?... No! Besides, I have a ton of new work in the hopper...."

Only now, as if he had shouted orders at himself, did Fonty open his eyes, which instead of their usual watery shimmer had a dry, feverish glow. He looked around. "What's up, Hoftaller?"

No sooner had he resurfaced than he returned to the present. He poked his finger into his mouth, checking his dentures, was satisfied, and even had some jocular remarks in reserve: "What, no cigar in your mouth? No reinforcements from Cuba? Or has the paternoster ground to a halt? No longer creaking up and down? And how's the documentation? Anything missing? Or is unification not going so smoothly—wasn't it supposed to happen in a flash?"

Hoftaller retracted his smile only temporarily. With the small, longish package still on his knees, he brought the patient up to date: how quickly the new money was being spent; how greedily the West was taking hold; how energetically the "man with the ears" was pushing ahead the four-plus-two discussions; how promptly they had decided at the Round Table to establish something called the Handover Trust: "For the people's property, you see!" Yet no one knew what to do with the Normannenstrasse files. That was not his concern, however. He himself was faring splendidly. No cigar shortage, at least for the time being. And since the West was showing an interest in persons with timeless, comprehensive experience, new jobs were coming his way daily: "My colleagues on the other side need people who know the score."

And then Hoftaller rolled out various cases: little fish from Prenzlauer Berg, Lychener Strasse; the Social Democratic case of Ibrahim Böhme; and the still-pending case of a musical attorney who had become prime minister and whom Fonty had dubbed a "latter-day Calvinist." "There's a heap of suspicions that will have to be confirmed as facts at the appropriate point in time. For now he's being spared, because the chancellor still needs him for signatures. But his turn will come. We live in fast-moving times. Anyone who stays in bed too long will miss his chance. You know who punishes that kind of tardiness, right, Fonty? So? Still a nervous wreck? Or isn't it about time we started getting better?"

When the patient responded with a smile that seemed to signal a final farewell, raising his hands a few inches above the bedspread, only to let them fall back at once, Hoftaller reached deep into his layered memory banks for comfort and good counsel: "I'm not a monster; don't want to pressure you. Can imagine how you must be feeling. I know how hard it is to make light of things when the old gastric nerves are acting up—every bird a bird of ill omen, every rat scurrying off the sinking ship, every puddle a sewer. Yet life must go on, Fonty. You usually have such a positive attitude! You always got back on your feet, whether in the days of the Sulfur-Yellow Collar or the era of the Saxon Goatee. And didn't the Immortal's family doctor offer first-rate advice that time he was on the verge of giving up, after his Effi got away from him and all the novel-writing seemed utterly pointless? Didn't he grab the malingerer by the scruff of his neck, so to speak, and haul him out of bed with a galvanizing assignment? What if I play doctor for a change? Here's my tip: Get your childhood down on paper, in parallel versions if you like; and I'll see to it you have an audience. Could be a lecture series. There's still a bunch of Cultural Union Centers that want to be revived before they get closed down. Needn't be here in Berlin. I could picture Potsdam, Neuruppin, even Schwerin, where your esteemed daughter will soon be taking up residence as Frau Grundmann, lake view, best part of town. So what's your favorite saying—straight from the shoulder! Best start tomorrow. We don't want to conk out, do we?"

Fonty told us later that Hoftaller had risen to his feet for the last part of his appeal, but then, the last word spoken, he had unpacked his little gift. The longish package contained a dozen shiny green Faber-Castell pencils and a sharpener.

Fonty at once began to play with the pencils on the bedspread. He laid them out in formations, like soldiers. Out of the twelve green beauties he formed four companies. He shaped letters: capital *A*, capital *M*, capital *Z*. A very large *E* probably stood for Effi. He let them roll together in splendid disorder, and delighted in the delicately modulated woody tones that emerged when he made all ten hop, dance, crowd each other on his right palm. Then he took each individual pencil, clasped it in the writing position, and scribbled in the air: word after word, short and long sentences, quotations and original formulations, page after page, including a good deal of chatty dialogue. We can visualize beginnings: "Once I had made up my mind to describe my life..." Then: "The first chapter is always the crucial thing, and in the first chapter, the first page, almost the first line..." And then: "In a properly constructed work, the first page must contain the germ of the whole...." Such was his delight with the well-nigh inexhaustible gift, the "Russian greens," as Fonty called the dozen pencils.

When Hoftaller opened the bedroom window, overlooking the courtyard, and let in some lukewarm summer air, the now convalescing patient remarked, "Actually I still have enough pencils on hand from that last clearance sale with the old money. But these have something special about them. They're Western, with gold lettering. Gold on green. Nice effect, the scales as a hallmark. A. W. Faber-Castell 9000. And just the right hardness: 3B! Not too hard, not too soft for the youngest child of my fancy. You have no idea, Hoftaller, how much is concentrated in a column of lead like that. Drafts, first of all, whether it's a letter or a novella. Entire novels or careers, happiness and unhappiness in installments. Always freshly sharpened, till only a stump is left. Even with the stump you can dash off a brief interlude, provided it flows, rather than just dribbling out. Then on to the next pencil... My Emilie will see to clean copy.... True, I set little stock in immortality, that perpetual laurel-wreathdom, as Schiller called it, but you have to produce something that will last, right, Tallhover?! You're taking over Dr. Delhaes's role. I know, I know, no way to get out of it—we stocked up on paper in time—there may be shortages to come...."

We know that Hoftaller stayed no more than another half an hour. Reportedly they chatted about old times. But as they presumably exchanged anecdotes—Prussian, Scottish, Wilhelminian, then pan-German, and again and again actually existing socialist—Fonty never stopped playing with the Western pencils. He arranged them in staggered triangles, then squares. A semblance of happiness hovered over the game.

Whether, during this temporal hopscotching, reference was made again to the childhood, we cannot say, but we think it more likely that Hoftaller repeatedly brought up situations in which Tallhover leaped into action, for instance that awkward situation into which Airman Theo Wuttke is said to have recklessly written himself, starting in the spring of '43.

Word had it that he had not only contributed to the Resistance, albeit unwittingly, by performing courier services, but also incurred suspicion by corresponding with certain highly placed officers, among them a few whose fate would later be sealed by the failed assassination attempt. True, the wording of his letters to members of the Prussian aristocracy—those with the most resonant names—revealed nothing conspiratorial, for the letters dealt only with ancestors of the recipients who had played a role in the Immortal's literary works; but apparently Tallhover did not have an easy time protecting the war correspondent from the long arm of Freisler's People's Court. Eventually the prolific private letter-writer got off, while some of his correspondents, among them a field marshal, met their end in Plötzensee Prison at the hands of the hangman.

But it is also possible that the two of them merely chatted harmlessly, for Emmi Wuttke, sitting in the kitchen drinking herbal tea for her bladder, began to hear, more and more often, Fonty's bright laughter, its youthful ring restored. She knocked on the door of her bedridden daughter and hauled her out of bed. Emmi and Martha listened together as the laughter became livelier by the minute. The merriment was such that it drew them into the sickroom, soon to become a study again. Mother and daughter found a patient on the mend, playing with a set of handsome green pencils; and the doctor responsible for this recovery was called Hoftaller. This latter remarked, "Pretty bouncy, our problem child, eh? But let me get out of your way now."

The next day Fonty was at his desk. He wanted to try out the new pencils, just for an hour or so. After that he filled page after page, day after day. A dressing gown of an unidentifiable color, stitched together out of army blankets after the war and now thoroughly matted, kept him warm. He wrote about the master's style, about its dialogic quality and its anecdotal miniaturizing, about the subtle art of omission, and then about the consistently maintained narrative posture, illustrated with a quotation that unmistakably invoked English style—Scott or Thackeray: "To begin with the beginning." Next he came to the motto used by the Immortal when presenting his childhood and youth: "...in the first years of life lies the germ of all the rest..." and thus found an opportunity to compare his early years in Neuruppin, experienced as the son of the lithographer Max Wuttke, with the years endured a century earlier by his predecessor, whose father had been an apothecary; soon the two were so inextricably intermingled that we archivists would have had trouble telling the original from the copy wherever Fonty operated with two mirrors at once.

In the beginning it was still manageable. The apothecary Louis Henri and his wife, Emilie, who liked to emphasize that she was the daughter of a silk manufacturer by the name of Labry, were clearly differentiated, thanks to their Huguenot ancestry, from the Wuttke line, which pointed instead toward Germanized West Prussia; yet Fonty's mother was named Luise, after the queen in whose service the apothecary's father, Pierre Barthélemy, had been active, first as drawing master, later at the rank of cabinet secretary, in which position, however, he had incurred the mockery of the sculptor Schadow: "His paintings are terrible, but his French is good."

True enough, Luise Wuttke had been born a Fraissenet, and that at least sounded Huguenot, but there was much that remained obscure in the Wuttkes' genealogy, for on the paternal grandmother's side, one line fizzled out among the Saxons. But soon Fonty managed to stake out a shared, brilliantly colorful field on which he felt at home in any direction. Since the Immortal had come under the influence in early childhood of the widely disseminated "Neuruppin Pictorial Broadsheets," and in Gustav Kühn's workshop the lithographer Max Wuttke was still pulling impressions from Solnhof stone plates of sheets that had been in circulation a hundred years earlier, further possibilities presented themselves for his dashing pencil to suspend time, embellishing this Neuruppin specialty with anecdotes: child labor for the coloring, lithographers' secrets, broadsheet tales.

Altogether, the town in the Ruppin region invited comparisons. How did things look there at the beginning of the nineteenth century after the great fire, and how in the twenties of this century of ours, soon to be over? The garrison town, with its venerable regiments and sprawling barracks, provided fluid transitions from war to war, all the way to the Reichswehr and the Sixth Panzer Regiment. The church, a Schinkel design, and the centrally located Gymnasium had also survived the passage of time. The lake remained almost unchanged, with Neuruppin spread along one bank, diagonally across from Altruppin; as early as 1904, a steamer had borne the name of the Immortal, carrying passengers to distant excursion points, wending its way down the Rhine to Lakes Molchow and Tornow. If people raved about the "Little Switzerlands" in Holstein, Mecklenburg, or Kashubia, one could also speak of a Ruppinian Switzerland.

Fonty reveled in blending the smells of the paternal apothecary shop, the Lion, on Friedrich-Wilhelm-Strasse—later to be called, for an indefinite period, Karl-Marx-Strasse—with the smells of the paternal workplace in Kühn's lithography shop: sal ammoniac and gum arabic, cod-liver oil and printer's ink. With a new pencil, its point sharpened again and again, he let first one father and then the other return from a major war, the war of liberation against Napoleon and the lost war against the entire world, whereupon the two of them, barely released, married and begat sons, who came into the world on the same day, although separated by a hundred years.

If the early life of one of the sons was set in a spacious *bel étage* flat near the Rheinsberg Gate, the later-born son had little elbow room in cramped workers' quarters on the corner of Fischbänkenstrasse and Siechenstrasse. The former witnessed the hog slaughter that constituted a recurring household event, took to his heels in horror, and did not stop to catch his breath until he was outside the town on a hill where, to his further dismay, had once stood the gallows; for his entire life, the latter could not bear the smell of fish, even freshly caught.

But this they had in common: just as the former had long blond locks falling to his shoulders—"less to his own than to his mother's delight"—the second also suffered under a wealth of blond curls that enchanted only his mother. Thus both of them were teased in their early school years as "angel-heads," and regularly shed tears during the morning combing. And in both cases, the mother's "impatient hand" inflicted pain. And other beatings were administered, too, even though "Schoolmaster Gerber" in Neuruppin's one-room schoolhouse did not actually live up to his name and tan the students' hides, while in the later grammar school the bamboo cane had to be replaced every month. But above all, both sons stressed the mother's strictness: Emilie and Luise demonstrated their love by withholding it.

Painted miniatures and memory mosaics: as Fonty developed the comparisons, not obtrusively but behind a veil of discretion, and compressed the passage of time the way pictorial broadsheets are wont to do, leaping here, marching in place there, yet scarcely pausing as he traced with new Western pencils the early years in Neuruppin, the process of healing began and took hold. His wife and daughter looked on in amazement. Their neighbor Inge Scherwinski spoke in Catholic terms of a miracle. Martha Wuttke decided it was time to let go of her nervous exhaustion as well. Emmi exchanged her bladder tea for café au lait. And we archivists, when we came to call on the patient, found only recovery and a steadily swelling manuscript. Even Hoftaller, who had recently been given free access to the apartment and stopped by every other day, was baffled by the wondrous effect of the Russian green pencils, which the Nuremberg firm of Faber had already been marketing as a standardized industrial product in the days of the Immortal.

Of course the recovering patient sat there surrounded by books. To the left and right of his pile of densely scribbled manuscript, was a stack of the Master's works—the Aufbau edition supplemented by the Nymphenburg edition in paperback. There was also Reuter's biography, two volumes with illustrations, bristling with bookmarks and close at hand for cross-referencing quotations. And since the volume *Childhood and Youth* already contained the kernel of everything that came later, Fonty could tease out further parallels. There were two major conflagrations, the first of which sent the barns outside the Rheinsberg Gate up in flames, fol-

lowed by the huge fire in the mid-twenties that destroyed a lumberyard, including the sawmill, on the edge of town. These early
impressions found their way not just into several novellas, novels,
and poems; the chronicler of catastrophic blazes and smaller fires
was also aided by a speech that had made the Cultural Union's itinerant lecturer Theo Wuttke known throughout the Republic in the
early sixties; its title, "Conflagrations in the Immortal's Narrative
Works," promised all sorts of things, even the revelation of a flare-
up of passion otherwise painstakingly concealed.

A technique involving such bold leaps could move effortlessly
from Grete Minde and the burning city of Tangermünde to Ebba
von Rosenberg and the chimney fire in a Danish castle. Frankfurt's
burning bridge over the Oder became the scene of a vivid flame-lit
drama. And connections could be drawn between Lene's love letters, which spineless Botho burned in the fireplace, and the fateful
epistles in Crampas's hand that foolish little Effi unfortunately
failed to stuff into the stove. Since the early fire in the stables and
the torched sawmill, all this had been tinder; this and even more
crackled, came crashing down in a shower of sparks, turned to
ashes, or for years protruded with charred beams into the store-
house of mixed memories.

No wonder this material cured Fonty. Yet his visitors, who were
soon joined by some of the young poetasters from Prenzlauer
Berg, were astonished to find him so chipper, yes, actually happy at
his crowded desk. We were less surprised, but the two young men,
obstinately shrouded in black despite the relentlessly oppressive
summer heat, could not understand how Fonty managed to be so
cheerful when the world was almost in its last gasp. While their favorite cafés on Lychener Strasse, consecrated to the pursuit of
pure literature, were being overtaken by the past, and, worse yet,
denounced and retroactively unmasked, in the recovering patient's
study, anything from the past was worth its weight in gold. These
two, beaten down and subject to every suspicion, perched on the
edge of Fonty's empty bed and listened to him expound on the
pleasures of looking backward, on time shedding its layers like an

onion, on rediscovered objects, long buried but suddenly gleaming like new, and on the delights of lingering smells, when spring arrived and the Swine was free of ice, and everything sprang to life along the bulwark, the boats were drawn up on land and laid on their side, and pitch bubbled in iron cauldrons so that the damaged places on the hulls could be plugged with oakum, and potatoes and diced bacon roasting over the fire blended with the reek of pitch that hung over the bulwark.

Thus we heard how the apothecary's family's had moved to Swinemünde. It came as news to us when Fonty read us his version in manuscript. We: by that I mean my colleague and me, as well as the two Prenzlbergers, who, according to the files, had by now been more or less definitely exposed, and the inevitable Hoftaller.

No wonder the already cramped study seemed crowded. We sat on chairs, or perched shoulder to shoulder on the edge of the bed, or hovered, like Fonty's day-and-night-shadow, in the background. To this mixed audience was presented a play in installments, whose title was "Childhood and Youth" but whose subtitle was "Recovery." Fonty provided cross-references, connecting details of the family routine in Swinemünde, Effi's married life in Kessin, and the chatty memories of the stagestruck pastor's daughter Franziska in *Count Petöfy*. For the two poets in black, who cultivated a depressed air, he acted out the satisfaction he had felt upon running into that Lieutenant von Witzleben who in '31 had deployed a battalion from the Kaiser Franz Regiment to quarantine the town on the Swine against the approaching cholera epidemic, and much later had reviewed, in a military weekly, the Immortal's books on the three wars of unification. Hoftaller took this all in without comment.

"And of course," Fonty exclaimed from his armchair, "during my time as a soldier in occupied France I wrote to a descendant of that lieutenant familiar to me from childhood, Field Marshal von Witzleben, which led to an extensive correspondence. Almost cost me my head, that correspondence did. As you know, my living Witzleben was part of the failed officers' rebellion. He was hanged, after showing true Prussian dignity before the People's Tribunal. Ask my trusty old companion; he'll confirm these connections, which turned out all right for me; I had a guardian angel, so to speak."

Hoftaller smiled knowingly and puffed on his cigar, which he had Fonty's permission to smoke. We archivists kept silent. My colleague was busily jotting everything down in her notebook. The two woebegone poets, however, for whom the raucous world outside had soured poetry by passing summary judgment on them, tried to find comfort in this and similar anecdotes. "Let's hear another story!" one of them exclaimed. And the other begged, "How did that go, Fonty—when the fiery red house was painted azure blue?" Both of them swore, when their request had been honored, that they could never hear enough of such things.

But Hoftaller, who had the Prenzlberg scene—and us, too, in a sense—under control, admonished the young people not to be greedy: "Now we're going to leave our friend alone with his pencils so he can get back in tip-top shape. We don't want to squeeze everything out of him now—this isn't an interrogation."

Hoftaller left, with his wards. We stayed a while longer. Fonty aired out his study until nothing, not the faintest whiff, remained as a reminder of the Cuban cigar smoke. He bustled around, tidying up, looking in his matted dressing gown like a hermit who received pilgrims, then sent them on their way. He enjoyed having us there, his "archive slaves." And the moment they were gone, he expressed affectionate pleasure at the stylized gloom displayed by the two Prenzlberg anarchists.

Fonty, who lived surrounded by suspicion and culpable complicities—"It's a tradition," he would say—continued to stand by the youthful poets, whose products he prized as "bibliophilic rarities." Perhaps they reminded him of readings in the Tunnel Over the Spree. That was why he had approved of Hoftaller's favoring them with comprehensive and solicitous oversight, for more than a decade. As the cigar smoke eddied out the window, Fonty remarked, "Frightfully right to keep the young bloods and their still-effervescent talent well away from the curse of politics, though of course bare idolizing of form is as little to my taste as naked social protest. Yet all that playing at being avant-garde certainly did no harm. It's still a pleasure to see what they produced on Lychener Strasse, with considerable graphic skill. Dilettanteries for collectors!

At all events, it kept our hotspurs from committing follies of the sort we once specialized in! We ran riot in the Herwegh Society and all through the pre-'48 period, trying to force the revolution into rhyme and outdo each other in liberty-mongering. Still, those were exciting times: 'Escape at last from the rut of the past; / With peril, life's price is rising fast....'"

Shortly after the airing-out, when daughter Martha brought tea and biscuits to the recovering patient, his pencil was already dashing across the paper again. We, too, took our leave, now that the next steps seemed to guarantee the further pacing off of the dual childhood. He had turned his attention to the vegetable garden behind the azure-blue house in Swinemünde, contrasting its wild tangle to the allotment garden planted in Neuruppin by his lithographing father, where carrots and onions grew next to cabbages amid the spreading vines of fiery scarlet runner beans, and ever-increasing numbers of rabbits lived nearby in hutches.

The recreational gardening undertaken both here and there called for a chapter of its own; it began with beds of mignonette and larkspur, led to a barberry bush as tall as a tree, and finally brought a "rather rickety swing" into the picture, initially given a push by siblings and neighborhood children, but finally and causatively pointing to Effi, as the description has come down to us: "in her blue-and-white-striped pinaforelike linen dress, whose waist was marked only by a firmly fastened belt of bronze leather; and over her neck and shoulders fell a broad sailor collar..."

It speaks for Fonty's far-reaching knowledge, which made forays even into literary modernism, that right after the image of the swing, which became a motif in the novel, he brought in Samuel Beckett's one-act play *Krapp's Last Tape,* in the course of which the monologist Krapp, before he starts the next tape, mutters, "Scalded the eyes out of me reading *Effie* again, a page a day, with tears again. Effie... (*Pause*) Could have been happy with her, up there on the Baltic, and the pines, and the dunes. (*Pause*) Could I? (*Pause*) And she? (*Pause*) Pah!"

To this Fonty appended the comment: "There is no happiness that lasts longer than five minutes...." And immediately thereafter his Russian green pencil invoked an illustration engraved by the hand of Max Liebermann; with a few strokes, it captured the last promise of happiness for that lonely Mr. Krapp: that most unhappy daughter of the Prussian aristocracy, the girl with the sailor collar, young Effi, standing on the swing and swooping with abandon.

12

On the Chinese Carpet

Amazing, what was crammed into that study: to the right of the door stood a cast-iron stove, its pipe no more than a slender reed, and, to its right, with brass knobs on its four posts, the bed, which extended along the wall toward the window. From the head of the bed, Fonty could see through the window several branches covered with broad fans of leaves, rustled only rarely by a gust of wind. On the wall above the bed, within easy reach, was a bookshelf, filled with historical works and travel guides long since out of print, with Thackeray, Scott, Dickens, and also American literature—Mark Twain, Bret Harte, Cooper, and a volume by Kafka that probably owed its place there to its title.

One third of the desk, which had compartments with doors on each side and a drawer in the middle above the kneehole, stood in front of the double casement window, with its view in all seasons of the rear courtyard and the chestnut tree; its long side butted up against the exterior wall, which to the right provided barely enough room for the bookcase that took up most of the long wall. Lined up in the bookcase were literary works from the nineteenth century, mingled with later works, such that the brothers Mann, Émile Zola, and Anna Seghers stood side by side with Turgenev, Raabe, and the Czech Hrabal; between Wolf's *Pattern of Childhood* and Johnson's *Speculations About Jakob* rested the massive tomes of Freytag's *Debit and Credit,* and next to Döblin's *Berlin Alexanderplatz* lurked Storm's verses and the poetry of Ingeborg Bachmann, while Heiner Müller's early plays leaned against Hauptmann's *Weavers.* Herwegh's *Works of a Living Poet* cozied up to Schädlich's *Tallhover* in seemingly deliberate disorder. The last-named volume, which had been published around the mid-eighties, and only in the West, by Rowohlt, had been given to Fonty by Hoftaller, soon after it appeared, with the words, "Hard going, but worth reading. Accurate for the most part, except for the ending. Never expressed a death wish. Would have liked to contact the author personally, but subject Schädlich chose to leave us, the Workers' and Peasants' State...."

Opposite the wall of books—on its top shelf, stacks of magazines and journals and a globe, which, at a push, would send spinning a world partitioned into colonial empires—there was barely room, squeezed in at the foot of the bed, for a narrow bookcase with glass front and side panels, a Biedermeier piece, which contained the Eastern and Western editions of the collected works, various biographies, the memoirs of old Marwitz, Jes Thaysen's Danish translation of *Irretrievable,* as well as various antiquarian finds, among them first editions of the *Rambles Through the Mark Brandenburg,* and, as if they belonged there, several volumes of Willibald Alexis.

Above this cherry-wood display case, whose simple form was embellished only by a gently curved molding on the very top, hung a framed Neuruppin broadsheet from the Kühn studio; its subject matter clashed with the collected calm of the book display case, showing as it did the final melodramatic burst as Berlin's opera house went up in flames in 1843; only the crowd of bystanders packed into the foreground remained composed in the face of the hand-colored festal illumination; likewise the mounted officers of the Gendarmes Regiment were taking no notice of this grand finale. A handsome and carefully chosen print; Fonty had a thing, as we know, for spectacular fires.

Between the display case and the window wall there was just room for a grandfather clock, also Biedermeier, which still worked, without any raspy throat-clearing, although the chime remained silent because for some reason the weight had been removed. It was a handsome piece in light birch, serenely framing the passage of time. The window was hung with transparent muslin curtains, never entirely drawn, part of Aunt Pinchen's legacy, and over them draperies, held back in heavy folds, their border of braid and bobbles made with a raised ridge along the middle: dust magnets from way back.

In front of the desk, on gently curved legs, stood the armchair, its back forming an open oval. And between the chair and the door lay a carpet, more properly described as a runner, because it ran along the narrow passageway, only six paces in length, between bed and bookcase.

In the mid-fifties Fonty had brought this exotic piece back from Eisenhüttenstadt after a lecture tour: a new Red Chinese export whose alarming pattern had subsided over the intervening years along the portion of the rug that received constant wear. Only around the edges did vines and shoots intertwine, displaying pink, lemonade-yellow, washed-out blue, and toxic green. In the tangle of vines lurked demons, and dragons with flaming tongues.

Above the right half of the desk, between framed photographs showing the historical family—wife, daughter, and all three sons— hung a reproduction of the Liebermann lithograph that portrayed the Immortal, hence also Fonty. On the desk itself, the writing surface was hemmed in by piles of books, a stack of letters, and a concrete-gray perforated brick, whose round openings held writing utensils: many pencils, among them, in a separate compartment, the Russian green ones; scissors; and two swan feathers that a park attendant had recently given Fonty in the Tiergarten; trimmed into quills, they now awaited the writer's hand, but were seldom used, actually only when the fancy struck, or in special moods, and then on letter paper.

To the left of the perforated brick and next to the inkwell stood a narrow glass vase, in which Martha Wuttke would arrange, depending on the time of year, a branch of budding pussy willow, the first dahlias, late roses, or a spray of Christmas mistletoe. And balancing the flower vase, as if posed for a still life, was a brass postage scale on a marble base.

Behind the brick, where the desktop's miniature balustrade bumped against the wall, Meyer's *Family Lexicon* in sixteen volumes was lined up within easy reach. It matched the edition from the Immortal's estate preserved in Neuruppin's local history museum. To the right and in front of the lexicon stood a small box of index cards, usually hidden behind stacks of books, and a cigar box of Cuban origin, used for paper clips and rubber bands, stamps, an eraser, and a pencil sharpener. For years, Fonty's bad habit of dropping the curls of wood and graphite dust into this box when sharpening his pencils had caused friction with Emmi, who entered the study only when she had to clean it.

Perhaps we have neglected to mention some small items—sometimes a miniature plaster bust of Frederick the Great stood atop the book display case, in the middle, or was pushed to one side of the desk, as if in the way—yet one curio or another can be added at a later date, or brought to the forefront now if it seems important—Fonty's glasses, for instance, lying on a blank sheet of draft paper, reminding us of the round rimless glasses worn by the Immortal, who never allowed himself to be painted or photographed bespectacled.

All in all, the study resembled the study at 134C Potsdamer Strasse known to us from photographs, although its dimensions were smaller, and the bed and the framed engraving of the fire were additions. Yet all the quotations—the grandfather clock, the postage scale, the vase, and the book display case—were cast into doubt by the Red Chinese runner and its candy-colored pattern; but it may well be that the much larger Turkish carpet in the original room looked equally out of place with the furniture.

Because Fonty and the Immortal had a weakness for the exotic, they lived out this contradiction in their homes: the Chinese runner and the Turkish piece invited pacing; they substituted for travel. The carpet allowed expeditions, the narrow runner only flying visits.

That was not the only explanation for Fonty's constantly pacing the five and a half steps forward and back in his felt robe. As he paced, the right words came to him. He paced until he was ready to return to the desk chair for the next time period and the one that followed, filling page after page. Again and again he was driven from the chair to the runner. It allowed rambles in any kind of weather. He could pursue this path without his day-and-night-shadow. Short though it was, it carried him back to childhood.

Already the era around 1830 had him in its grip. Prussia was stagnating in police-state uneventfulness, while the rest of the world was reveling in sensational occurrences. The ten-year-old learned about all this from visiting booths at fairs, where stereopticon images modeled on the Neuruppin pictorial broadsheets—"time and again soldiers in yellow and red, or in green if Russians"—provided accounts of major events: how the French fleet turned up off the Algerian coast under the command of Admiral Duperré and fired on the city of Algiers; how, after a revolution as violent as it was brief, Louis Philippe mounted the throne as the citizen king; how, in the course of the wars of insurrection, the rebellious Poles were finally defeated... "No other war, not excluding our own," Fonty quoted in pencil, "captured my imagination like the Poles' struggle...." But then he relativized the Immortal's enthusiasm for Poland's freedom struggle and the pro-Polish works of poets from Holtei to Platen: "...I hasten to observe—in a sense to my dismay, and certainly in conflict with my poetic sensibilities—that I often stood on the Poles' side with divided sympathies, and at all times felt within me a certain *engagement* in favor of the established powers, the Russians' not excluded."

After a rather long march on the short Chinese runner, Fonty pounced on a quotation that allowed him to bring his own biography into correspondence with the ambiguities of his model's; while the Immortal continued into ripe old age to insist, in letters and at the family table, on his love for liberty, at the same time he tolerated the grinding servitude imposed by a succession of regimes. As a result, he eventually came around to condemning the Polish conflict and others as well, a general conclusion with which Tallhover in those days and Hoftaller in the present could have agreed: "A dwarf's victory against giants confuses me and strikes me as unseemly, insofar as it runs counter to the natural course of events."

And because Poland was lost, lost again, or—despite the giant—to this day is not yet lost, Fonty, ever faithful to his role, recalled visual confirmations of the major events peddled in Neuruppin's pictorial broadsheets; what the ten-year-old in Swinemünde had seen reduced to peep-show format corresponded to those moving images to which Theo Wuttke was exposed as a ten-year-old in the weekly newsreels in Neuruppin's movie house: he saw Black Friday, with agitated little men gesticulating wildly on New York's Wall Street; he heard and saw Poland's heroic Marshal Piłsudski and Mussolini's balcony speeches, complete with expansive gestures; he witnessed the senile dignity of Reich President Hindenburg; he let himself be swept away with enthusiasm for robust young athletes competing and for mass demonstrations driven by idiotic fervor—for the future belonged to the columns in black and brown that kept the newsreels turning more and more with the passing years. And when the Olympics summoned the world's youth to Los Angeles—for the duration of a Fox's Movietone reel—it was the equivalent of the world peace that the Holy-Alliance-by-the-grace-of-Metternich must also have intended. The Poles' repeated struggle for freedom, as portrayed on Neuruppin broadsheets, had its counterpart in a newsreel that, by showing mass gatherings in India, captured the spirit of Gandhi's nonviolent resistance to British colonial power. Fonty found a suitable quotation: "Even given the Empire's military superiority, the question still arises: 'Who is the giant here, who the dwarf?'"

Then he traversed the length of the Red Chinese runner again, and after a good hundred meters confronted the portrait of the Swinemünde family tutor, Dr. Lau, with that of his own teacher: Lau came away just as well as Dr. Elssner. And as he assessed the merits of one teacher or the other, it was time to look at the interior of the once new, then old Gymnasium, dedicated in 1791, soon after the great Neuruppin fire. Of course this conflagration had to light up both childhoods, too, for the city actually owed much to the fire's clean sweep: neatly rebuilt drill grounds, straight boulevards, and, besides the city hall and the Schinkel church, this school building of neoclassical austerity, made famous by one pupil, who suffered there for only a short time, opposite whose portal had once stood a statue of King Friedrich Wilhelm, replaced much later by a larger-than-life bust of Karl Marx in bronze that gradually darkened to black. "At present this bust stands there subject to recall," Fonty wrote, "like so many monuments to which longevity was promised in the name of the state."

All these rapid time shifts flowed easily from his hand; only when the pencil needed sharpening did he interrupt the streaming narrative. After three or four carpet runs and the bursts of writing that followed, wooden curls fell into the open cigar box from Cuba, and with them each time a pinch of graphite dust. Now, in mid-August, a barely opened dahlia graced the glass vase.

Let us pause here and venture a comparison. Fonty was writing the continuation, whether with pencils, steel pens, or swan feathers that he cut into quills, of the manuscript that for more than five decades has been carefully preserved in the Archives, a manuscript whose very penmanship cries out for interpretation. We are not graphologists, and, for all our archival thoroughness, can merely offer a layman's guess at the calligraphic significance of any letter and manuscript page at our disposal; let us make the attempt nonetheless.

On the pages written in ink, we notice especially the way the loops or the strokes—as in the double *s*, as it was written at the time—extend from above to far below the line. Quick pencil scribbles, as if dictated by haste, only rarely achieve such open loops, sweeping outward with alleged voluptuousness; thus on the page we have before us, in the word "balderdash" neither the final *h* nor the penultimate *s*, for instance, displays the lower loops that suggest a man in the grip of carnal urges. Perhaps this confirms the criticism offered by his eldest son, which the father alludes to in a letter to Emilie: "What George writes is very nice; that I cannot portray lovers is only too true. But who can do everything?"

When the Immortal writes in ink, in contrast to pencil, his penmanship consistently appears more ornamental. Thus the big *M* in the epistolary salutations "My dear Wife," and "Dear Mete" consists of two descending loops and one loop pointing upward on the diagonal. All the normal German squiggles over the small *u*'s almost curve into a circle, sometimes open at the top, sometimes at the bottom, sometimes on one side or the other. Altogether, the shape of small *u* turns out even more random in the penciled texts; often it is an actual circle; anyone may interpret these encapsulations as he wishes.

Whereas the ink script moves purposefully toward a full stop or a point, now with witty excursus, now boldly, the pencil script dashes along in a nervous rush, as if it had to record—before they faded—scraps of conversation snapped up on the horse-drawn tram, or chitchat overheard at tables in the Café Josty or at Stehely's, also exchanges floating on the air during an evening stroll up and down Unter den Linden; yet the ear witness actually heard most of his dialogue in his own study, while pacing back and forth on his Turkish carpet.

All that has been said here is equally true of Fonty's handwriting. When the Immortal pens a letter to his friend Lepel, and the second-born writes a report for his trusty old companion, when the former complains of constant money problems, or appreciates or depreciates the latest Tunnel reading, while the latter spares the literary manifestos and poetic outrages of the Prenzlauer Berg poets with gentle mockery, while urgently admonishing his addressees to beware of state-securing interventions, the lower loops on the *h* or double *s* are identical, likewise the ornamental deviations and the idiosyncratic rings over the lower-case *u,* whether written with steel pen or swan feather.

Nevertheless we doubt that what we are dealing with here is merely an imitated hand. It would probably make more sense to speak of a sequel, for a page of *Childhood and Youth* scribbled in pencil matches to a *T* the pages filled with Russian green scribbling. The same haste. This same nervous, driven tempo. The same jotting down of conversations heard in the writer's head. Two elderly gentlemen whose memories come faster than a pencil can capture them. Two old men recovering from a longish illness, both of whom see in their mind's eye their secret refuge; summer thunderstorms and wintry ice floes; birthdays falling too close to Christmas; Sunday guests and card games; and finally favorite teachers.

The firstborn oldster bade farewell to his departed Swinemünde tutor, Dr. Lau, who had encouraged him to compose his first birthday poem—"Dear Papa, You are no cat, / But rather a man who can eat no fat..."—with the following words: "I genuinely loved Dr. Lau, more than any other teacher I had in later years; yet my accursed histrionic vanity robbed me of any proper feeling for this man, to whom I owe so much." The second oldster likewise feels compelled to scribble a eulogy in hastening pencil—and therefore with truncated lower strokes: "Of all the instructors at the Gymnasium in Neuruppin, I have clear memories only of Dr. Elssner, for he had the intelligence to eliminate the meaningless separation between the subjects of history and German by incorporating historical quotations into the latter and literary evidence into the former. Elssner, whom we dubbed 'Professor Time-Lapse,' on account of his pedagogical method, could bring far-apart phenomena close together—for instance, the Migration of Peoples, as seen through Felix Dahn's Ostrogoth best-seller, *The Battle of Rome*, and social conditions in preindustrial Germany, portrayed in Hauptmann's play *The Weavers*. It is from him that I acquired that time-lapse view of history and literature that for me anchors things of the past in a present drenched in futurity—in other words, immortality; for this reason, by the bye, they have declared the now rare immortelles an endangered species; in *Delusions, Confusions* they could still be purchased in the form of dried wreaths...."

No matter who had held the pencil, the manuscript pages were difficult to read. We archivists had had plenty of practice, but Hoftaller, whose thoroughness did not fall short of ours, still had trouble deciphering these pages, crammed with writing as if in the face of a deadline imposed by age. How fortunate that Emilie, despite her lingering doubts as to her husband's talent as a writer, made fair copies of most of the pencil versions, rendering them suitable for printing; for which reason Emmi Wuttke likewise transcribed her husband's Cultural Union lectures on her typewriter, so that they would be legible for Hoftaller. Starting in the early sixties, when Hoftaller had just returned, disillusioned, from the West and had resumed his old position in the service, it was he who went through all the lectures checking for security leaks.

And now, after a long hiatus, a new round of pencil scribblings was on hand. Initially Emmi protested that she was out of practice.

But then she relented and typed this lecture on childhood and youth that had brought about Fonty's recovery. Its time-lapse technique brought into simultaneous focus the blissful extravagances of the Neuruppin pictorial broadsheets and the deluge of images in Fox's Movietone News, the apothecary's son and the lithographer's son. Emmi typed away in the Poggenpuhl parlor on her electric Robotron. Although she grumbled, finding everything too roundabout and—as she said—"awful farfetched," by the time Fonty inserted an intermezzo, "Forty Years Later," shortly before the end of "Childhood and Youth," more than half the manuscript had already been typed.

His subject was the fathers. Both of them weak and lovable. Each of them reliably undependable. Fathers who ran away as a matter of principle from gambling debts or from any job that interfered with their independence, and were always ready with convincing gestures of helplessness or surefire schemes for a fresh start. If one of them resorted to frequent changes of venue as the panacea for mind-numbing bourgeois stability, the other saw each new print shop as the best thing that could happen to him. If one felt compelled, after the hasty, and, to his mind, profitable, sale of the Lion Apothecary Shop, to strike out on sandy roads for Swinemünde, the other likewise saw his future in change: he left Kühn's printery on Ludwigstrasse and moved to the printing firm of Oehmigke & Riemschneider on Friedrich-Wilhelm-Strasse, and soon—after he opened his own lithography shop, only to see it go bankrupt—all that was left for him to change was odd jobs, whether as a stoker on an excursion boat or as a gardener in Knöller's greenhouses. In the end, both found contentment in raising pigs or rabbits. They enjoyed their modest share of freedom in the potato field and vegetable patch. But at that point they were living alone, left entirely to their own devices.

Both fathers botched their marriages. Both were thrown out of the house by their wives, for neither stern Emilie nor stern Luise could see the family's social decline or lapse into the proletariat in a positive light—as "liberation from constraints" or a "fresh, class-conscious start;" furthermore, it was a matter of protecting their still-dependent children from their fathers' dissolute ways.

By the time he experienced his parents' long-postponed divorce, the Immortal was already apprenticed to an apothecary, that is to say, already grown-up and observing from a distance; with the Wuttkes it happened sooner, no doubt sped along by the tempo of the new times: Luise Wuttke threw in her lot early with "our Führer and Reich Chancellor, who will raise Germany up out of shame and misery." In 1935 the adolescent Gymnasium student and Hitler Youth Theo Wuttke saw his father slink out of the house with only a few suitcases. Weary of domestic strife and finding that the SA-thronged streets of Neuruppin were getting too hot under his feet, the incorrigible socialist headed for Berlin to duck under.

Both of the fathers had married young, at the end of their respective wars. Both had little preparation for the world of work, but had had military experiences that shaped them. The older of the two, although an admirer of Napoleon, had taken the field against him, under Prussian banners. The younger, although a pacifist who despised everything that smacked of the military, had volunteered, and as a member of the 24th Infantry Regiment had been wounded several times, receiving the Iron Cross and earning the rank of noncommissioned officer at Verdun. If the former taught his firstborn son the names of all the Napoleonic marshals, from Ney to Rapp, the latter, now a member of the Reichsbanner, had his eleven-year-old son bandage his head when he came home from brawls in public places between this socialist defense organization and rowdy Nazi storm troopers. Both fathers had snatched remnants of revolutionary fervor from the jaws of defeat. Both failed in their professional lives and as husbands, yet they never gave up their visions for saving the world. They had a thing for principles. The former kept faith with Napoleon, the latter vacillated between Bebel and Bernstein, but remained undeviatingly dedicated to the cooperative movement.

Not until they were separated from their wives and children and were entirely on their own did they find their way to forms of activity that gave ample scope to previously unfulfilled inclinations;

the first father earned a moderate income raising pigs near Freien-walde, along the overgrown old bed of the Oder, and for a lucra-tive price sold the plentiful stones from his sandy fields to a road construction company engaged in paving miles of highway through-out Brandenburg with crushed rock; the other father, after much restless to-ing and fro-ing, interrupted only by six months of pro-tective custody in the Oranienburg concentration camp, found a refuge in Berlin-Grunewald as a caretaker and gardener. There he tended a palatial rococo-style mansion, which, although it lay hid-den behind tall trees on the corner of Königsallee and Rabbits' Run, was heavily damaged in the bombing, with the exception of the caretaker's cellar apartment.

Thus the two of them lived, and survived. Both of these single men, when they were already approaching sixty, one in the Oder Delta, the other in a once genteel part of town, took in women, one in his cottager's hut, the other in his homey cellar. When the sons came to visit at irregular intervals, these women would emerge to set the table, in the guise of "housekeeper" by the banks of the Oder or as "my comrade in old age" at 35 Rabbits' Run. Both women were middle-aged; the former was described as "a good person, at times terrible, but everything is terrible sometimes in the cold light of day...." Of the other the comment was made, "She doesn't say much, but what she does say has both feet on the ground, even when it makes a false step or goes off in the wrong direction...."

Both women liked to cook. The former made use of every part of the pig, from the snout to the trotters; the latter cooked rabbit: roasted, simmered, or jugged. There were rabbits aplenty. Max Wuttke raised Blue Viennas and other domesticated breeds, just as he had in his Neuruppin allotment garden, but this time in such large numbers that they covered the household expenses. The great lawn that sloped gently down to reed-choked Lake Diana pro-vided ample green fodder.

Thus both fathers had found peace at last. They had even sworn off gambling and alcohol. The one waited for his son in gray linen trousers and, under his twill jacket, a shirt that had not been changed for a long time. The younger stood by the garden gate wearing his much mended gardener's apron over blue-gray corduroys, his feet in wooden clogs.

As Fonty was writing his intermezzo about the Immortal's father, his own father seemed so close to him that after the usual pacing on the runner he introduced the two fathers to one another. Sometimes he confused them. And because he attributed so many common features to them, they resembled each other like elective twins. Now they even fooled their sons when the latter sat down to table with them. At any rate, it sometimes happened that Fonty referred to one when he meant the other, with nothing but good to say of the two departed.

So much understanding for two old loners. So many affectionate words for two eccentric blowhards. And so much accumulated gain at the expense of the more distant mothers, who received only respect, for he was still intimidated by their doubly demonstrated strictness; it was only to the fathers, botched existences like himself, that he always felt close.

When the firstborn visited his father in the summer of 1867 in the former sailors' colony near Freienwalde, he was almost fifty, but was greeted by the seventy-one-year-old as "my boy," and not until somewhat later acknowledged to be "a lad well along in years himself." The Immortal was still writing for the *Kreuzzeitung* at the time and was working on his second war book, which treated the war against Austria. The onetime apothecary and later pig-breeder smiled at his son's journalistic drudgery and his efforts on behalf of Prussia's shows of strength.

The last time Fonty saw his father, in 1961 in the cellar of the Grunewald mansion, whose upper stories had been burned out in the bombing and not yet rebuilt, he could not have guessed that the construction of the Berlin Wall was imminent, or that this edifice, sheepishly dubbed the "Protective Shield," would create such a lasting separation between father and son. They greeted one another jovially. And the rabbit-breeder addressed the Cultural Union lecturer as "Junior." But the onetime lithographer had only gentle mockery for the lectures his cultural-activist son went around delivering, and scorn for the socialism practiced "over there." "I call it state-sponsored capitalism, plain and simple," the old man said; in the years after the war, he had had his run-ins with the Socialist Unity Party. His attempt to go back to Neuruppin had been interpreted in the worst possible terms; "Party-subverting social democracy" was his offense; only by fleeing did he avoid lengthy internment in the once and future Buchenwald concentration camp.

By now the elder Wuttke was in his mid-sixties, and in addition to an enlarged liver was suffering from asthma, like the Immortal's father, who had died in October, after his son's visit, whereas Fonty's father shuffled off two years after the construction of the Wall, for the purpose, in his gardener's terminology, of "checking on the radishes from below." In the spirit of his Napoleon fixation, the Oder Delta pig-breeder had predicted his own impending demise as his "summons to the Grande Armée."

On this visit, instead of pork roast, there was breast of veal, for a change, braised in a Dutch oven by the "housekeeper" for the delectation of the weary *Kreuzzeitung* editor. It was served with red wine in two large goblets left over from Swinemünde days. The taciturn "comrade of my old age," on the other hand, pulled a rabbit roast in cream sauce out of the oven for the evening meal. It was accompanied by Thuringian potato dumplings; she came from that wooded region. Pear juice constituted the evening's libation.

The pig-breeder chatted after the meal about the world exposition in Paris, as if he had just returned from there, and then proceeded, as on every visit from his son, to speak of Napoleon's marshals. "Do you recall? Lannes and Latour d'Auvergne and Michel Ney, how they put him up against the wall in the bleak and lonely Jardin du Luxembourg..."; over dessert—stewed rhubarb— the rabbit-breeder brought up the brawls with the SA in Neuruppin, then moved straight to the infamous Berlin Transit strike on the eve of '33: "A disgrace! The Clubfoot and the Goatee at the same table. Communists and Nazis aligned against us Social Democrats. That was too much. Our resistance crumbled. And eventually workers faced off against workers...."

Both fathers cared only about the old stories. "I shan't be learning anything new," one of them admitted, and the other said, "Something like that you just don't get over." Both of them listened distractedly or impatiently to their sons' professional plans; what did they care about the journalistic blood, sweat, and tears shed for a reactionary newspaper or the lectures delivered by an itinerant spokesman for the Cultural Union, who allowed the critical barbs in his remarks, which otherwise hewed close to the Party line, to be pruned by the censors. To the fathers, all this was small potatoes: admirable but useless. Both of them, after all, had their heads full of world-saving schemes, which promised justice, freedom, and communal happiness. And their thoughts, always concerned with growth and progress, never rested, but found willing ears in the good-natured housekeeper and the taciturn comrade in old age, who had only to be summoned from the kitchen. Yet no real conversation ever materialized. "And when I get to the best part, and say, 'It's circumstances that make the man, eh, Luise?' she either jumps or sits there like a wooden post...." "But my Gundula just nods without a word, probably thinking about her dill pickles, while I take a leaf from Bernstein and lay out for her the evolutionary method for bettering mankind: 'The way is everything, the destination nothing....'"

Thus Fonty constructed a monument to both fathers. With dashing pencil he sketched them larger than life and placed them together on one pedestal. He loved them not least for their very lack of success and the modesty of their accomplishments. With one of the fathers, he went out to the barnyard to see the hogs and later to the sandy field where the stones lay in piles, waiting to be sold. With the other father he counted litters of Blue Viennas tumbling around in the hutches, then admired the vegetable garden with its prolific runner beans, its cauliflower and celeriac. They walked down to the belt of reeds around the lake that came up to the edge of the villa's grounds, meanwhile conversing in shifted time, in which connection Fonty, with his resharpened lead, recalled another lake, like Lake Diana part of the string of lakes in the Grunewald district. Along the banks of this lake, literary scenes had played themselves out: the participants in the excursion organized by Commercial Councillor Treibel had strolled there, chatting, and gabbed about two swan huts without swans. When the talk came around later in the walk to life's vicissitudes, Frau Jenny Treibel, who was walking with Professor Schmidt, exclaimed, "Ah, what a curse external appearances are! Happiness, happiness! And to think, Wilibald, that I must confess this to you, of all people, and at such a time: Happiness is to be found here alone!" And she laid her hand on her heart.

Fonty quoted a few other passages referring to the Halensee, the anecdote about the beer-drinking horse, for instance. At intervals he was in motion, five and a half paces back and forth on the Red Chinese runner. It cost him no effort to cover an entire century in his galloping thoughts. He had just celebrated the victoriously concluded war against Austria, complete with Moltke and the Battle of Königgrätz—"How modest that great laconic one appeared after doing the deed"—when he arrived without more ado at the precarious situation Berlin had found itself in shortly before the construction of the Wall: "Somehow the mass exodus had to be stopped. The Workers' and Peasants' State was losing its citizens. Yes, I was in favor of the Wall, even if it cut me off for years from the western part of the city, from the Tiergarten and, almost more painful, from my dear father and, to my wife's dismay, from his self-renewing supply of rabbit roasts. . . ."

And already he was rushing from reed-choked Lake Diana to the sandy banks of the Oder, from old Max Wuttke in his gardener's apron to the Immortal's father, to place this twill-jacketed hermit on a pedestal as well. This father remarked, the last time his son came to see him, "This is real Hohenzollern weather you've brought. I know you write a good deal about the Hohenzollerns. Personally, I hold with Napoleon. . . ." And the former lithographer bent down from his pedestal and addressed his son, when the latter had come from East to West Berlin to visit him at the Rabbits' Run address, "What a summer we're having, eh? When I was a boy, we called this kaiser's weather. And how are things going over there? Still lecturing on the immortality of Neuruppin's local celebrity? I know all about it, how he carried on about the future of the working class. Even had Prussian Junkers bebeling away. By the way, does Comrade Ulbricht really let you quote old Stechlin, straight from the shoulder? And that Treibel woman's bosom pal— what's his name, oh, right, Wilibald Schmidt—is he still allowed to say to his daughter, 'Corinna, if I weren't a professor, I'd probably end up a Social Democrat...'?" Whereupon Fonty, after a brief run on the carpet, responded to the rabbit-breeder's question in barely legible pencil: "Certainly, Father, but only if in the next sentence I hoist a banner celebrating the victory of Communism."

One could smile at such intense veneration for the fathers, or delve deep into its meaning, the more so since Fonty even ascribed a certain immortality to the wartime ruin at 35 Rabbits' Run. That was easy to do, for shortly after Max Wuttke's death, the old mansion was renovated, and a well-known Austrian poet took up residence in the ground-floor addition, although her time there was brief. Still, the largely unhappy days Ingeborg Bachmann spent in Berlin gave Fonty a pretext for smuggling the figure of this later tenant into the portrait of his father the caretaker, to combine the two of them as if they had actually met, to quote some lines from the volume *Mortgaged Time,* thereby taking poetic license with the now more comfortable Grunewald mansion, and to add wistfully, "Would have enjoyed chatting with Bachmann for an hour or two out by Father's rabbit hutches...." Here was his cue for a lament familiar to the Archives: "Have no colleagues anymore, not even six with whom I'm on speaking terms. Earlier, with Bobrowski and Fühmann, yes, but since Keller and Storm died—such a sea of mediocrity. What can you talk about with Müller? So he sings the praises of his whiskey and clamps his cigar between his teeth, parodying his master Brecht—otherwise there's not much there, at most some cute little cynicisms. And Christa Wolf has her tight little hen party; you're lucky if they'll as much as talk to you if you wear trousers and a necktie. I've no objection myself to women writers, and place Bachmann as high as Mörike, but that hundreds of bluestockings like Ludovica Hesekiel are supplying our literature with sixpenny morality and threepenny patriotism at three marks to the ell—that is indeed a curse...."

13

Of the Exchange Rate of Fixed Values

By the time Fonty had finished the intermezzo and was ready to insert the final thread into his double-woven "Childhood and Youth," he had recovered from his nervous fever. Dr. Zöberlein spoke of "strong powers of healing" and recommended a return to normal activities. "But we don't want to overdo it. Short walks: authorized; but the file-hauling can wait; in any case, the Ministries Building is terminal."

Emmi agreed wholeheartedly with the first part of this recommendation: "You've got to get some fresh air, Wuttke..." and Hoftaller, too, as Fonty's actual physician and friend in need, expressed the opinion that the time had come for a stroll down to Kollwitzplatz, followed by a *café noir* at a table outside the bistro on Husemannstrasse, where it would be safe to sit in the open, given the steady summer weather: "Let's get together for an hour or so, and let's do it soon. Time to size up the situation. Why? Well, because it's changing daily, and there's a whole lot of people who'd flock to hear a lecture of your special fabrication."

Fonty hesitated. He was in no mood for anything public. He shrank from the world outside his study: "Don't feel like being social. What's the point of standing around and catching the flu?" He would need time to think it over. Until walks became a daily routine again and delivering lectures straight from the shoulder at the rostrum could tempt him, he wanted to confine himself to the familiar five and a half steps on the carpet, and if he was to be on the move, talking out loud, then only to cover the final stretch of

"Childhood and Youth." So he paced off line after line in his felt robe. In Swinemünde, Christmas was once more just around the corner, likewise in Neuruppin. And here as there, the home-sweet-home had sour notes. The fault lay with the fathers and their chronic restlessness; or did it lie with the mothers, who harped on responsibility and breached the family peace by constantly invoking it?

Fonty was under pressure. He wrote so fast that his pencil hardly took the time to trace lower loops. His scribble became illegible even for Emmi. She threw open the door between the kitchen and his study and railed: "Knock it off, Wuttke! It's time to pay some attention to Martha and take care of the couple of things you promised Grundmann. That's the least you can do as the father of the bride. If you don't get a move on, she'll call off the wedding...."

We can confirm that Emmi had cause for concern. Because the banns had been spoken weeks earlier, the marriage had to take place by a certain date. Impatient letters were arriving from Münster, followed by telegrams. All the invitations had been issued, even one to Professor Freundlich and his wife. There was no longer any need to fear that the church ceremony might be awkward, for the previous year, or, to be more precise, months before the fall of the Wall, Martha had decided to do something about her loss of faith and adopt her future husband's religion.

That had been Heinz-Martin Grundmann's wish, though not a condition. Accordingly, for weeks Martha had made her way to St. Hedwig's, where a priest had taught her the fundamental tenets of this new doctrine. The source of these exercises, usually assigned to children, had been the catechism; but everyone, including adult converts, has to submit to this laundering process; no one is taken in without going through the wringer.

Because no witness of the right faith was available, and Grundmann did not warm to Martha's old girlfriend Inge Scherwinski, one of us recalled his Catholic origins, which he had never forsworn, more out of defiance than out of devotion.

It was not Fonty, but his daughter, who asked me to step up to the altar as a witness. Although we warned ourselves, "Beware of overzealousness," and recognized that as newly minted Catholics former Communists tended to take their old articles of faith with them, I agreed; the Archives owed the Wuttkes this favor.

But the father of the bride was not really paying attention. He should have had a location picked out for the wedding dinner long since, the table reserved and the menu selected. The bride had a right to expect this. Her engagement many years earlier to a first lieutenant in the People's Army had been broken off under unfortunate circumstances. She had hardly dared to hope that in her late thirties she would find a husband. Now it had worked out after all—except that the father of the bride could not be counted on. He kept his distance, sharpening his pencils again and again. Fonty confined his recommended walks to the Red Chinese runner, and could not seem to find the end of "Childhood and Youth."

Even our visits, which we thought would bring him pleasure now that he was on the mend, merely irked him. We had to wait in the kitchen or in the Poggenpuhl parlor, as if on call. Often we were left sitting there for an hour or more. Because he neither came out nor sent for us, Emmi helped us pass the time. Without our having to ask, she confided, "This might take a while. He just can't stop his scribbling—same old story. If he's feeling a little better, he goes and overdoes it again. You'd think he could wait till after the wedding. But when I say to my Wuttke, Go easy on yourself, I say, No need to get the whole thing down on paper right this minute, he says, Let it be, Emilie, what wants to get out has to get out. So I've been typing away. Just like all those years when he had stuff to turn in. But this time he's just scribbling into the blue, 'cause who's going to want to read this kind of thing nowadays? That's all over and done with, the Cultural Union and so on. Down the drain! Not for my Wuttke, though. Nothing's real to him but the things he dreams up. The world can be falling down around him, and he just keeps on going. Soon as he's out of bed, he's trotting back and forth, muttering to himself, then he sits down, writes a few lines, trots back and forth some more, and writes some more. This time it's not just about his one-and-only, no, sir, this time it's about himself, too, 'cause both of them come from that same backwater. But you know all this better than me—the old guy's sitting up there, the one he always stood in front of and stared at when he was just a little fellow, 'cause his father always took him to see that dumb monument and pounded it into him: 'Look at him up there: he's immortal, he'll be there for all eternity.' That's how the whole thing began, so when he talks about his one-and-only he always works himself in, like he has to parrot everything he said. If there's something in the man's books about fist fights with ragamuffins who go around Swinemünde beating each other up, he claims he had it out too with some rowdies in Neuruppin. One of them had a wooden sword he got for Christmas, and the other just had a roofing slat. And how the boys would hide so no one could find them: one of them in the attic, the other in the coal cellar behind those bales of paper that was all scrap, or wastepaper my Wuttke calls it. But there were pictures on all that paper, the printing just a little smudged. And then he keeps coming back to the fathers! I'm telling you: if one of them had gambling debts, the other one couldn't get the bottle out of his face, starting when he lost his job. But actually the father of his one-and-only, who got himself a proper monument with his writing, was just a pharmacist who never amounted to much, so he has to build him up and make him this kind daddy who was thrown out of the house by his mean wife, whose name's Emilie, what else. And my Wuttke's father also gets built up quite a bit—he's supposed to be this wise hermit, who's moved into a cold, damp hole of a cellar to get away from the cruel world. Makes me want to laugh. I visited him plenty of times, before the Wall came. Him and his bunny rabbits! Let me tell you: that was a fancy neighborhood in the old days. But that place where the old guy lived was in terrible shape. I'd take a haunted house any day. Upstairs everything still burned out from the war, and down below you'd be lucky not to catch TB. The walls were dripping, that's how damp it was. Must've had toadstools in the floorboards. And the beds clammy even in summertime. Smelled of rot, and no way to get things clean. Made you feel sorry for that poor woman the old man'd coaxed in there with that laugh of his. Gundula was her name, a plump little thing. She never said boo or groused about anything. My, oh, my, the old man sure was nice to her—Gundelchen this and Gundelchen that. He always was quite a talker. Full of socialist preaching, making the world a better place and so on. Pretty confused, most of it. But you should've seen that garden. We got cukes and cauliflower to take home and a rabbit every time, sometimes even two, slaughtered just for us and skinned, 'cause we couldn't get that kind of thing over here. Oh, there wasn't much we could get, hardly even fresh vegetables, 'cause over here—course you know this—the shortages, so I should've been grateful to the old man. He could be a real gentleman, he could, like my Wuttke, when he wanted to be, specially with the young ladies. And the same thing with the father of his one-and-only—he must've been another of those sweet talkers. Their wives had nothing to laugh about, though, neither one of them. But I say to my Wuttke: 'It isn't right to show his Emilie in such a bad light, or your papa's poor Luise, either, when she's been dead and buried so long. What they had to put up with—both of them had their cross to bear. One of them with her deadbeat, who could squeeze money out of a stone, and the other with her big talker, who was a drinker, and a secret one, too, and that's the worst kind. But not a word about how your father wrecked his liver that way, only about how kind and wise and lovable they both were....' So then my Wuttke says, 'Let it be, Emilie, you don't understand. What's real can't be found on the surface. It's deeper down.' And then I say, 'I know that, I've known that a long time. But does anyone ask what's deep down inside me? You and your Emilies. Nothing but Emilies. And if your Emmi, who no one's interested in, who's supposed to just sit at the typewriter, hadn't been christened Emilie, I wouldn't have meant a thing to you, most likely....' You know, of course, that the other Emilie had to copy everything, too, just like me, only a whole lot more: all those monster war books and novels, and on top of that those rambles, all of them. I've read most of it, but I don't like it much. Too much talk, and every castle described down to the smallest stone, even if it's a total ruin. But every time something happens, adultery or a real duel, with pistols, I mean, and you've got some excitement, he just stops, or starts a new section, with more walks and more talk. But my Wuttke always says, 'That's what makes it special. The art of omission...' Fine! But then he should've followed that example with this lecture he's working on. I'm telling you, he won't get to give it anyway, 'cause there's no more Cultural Union to pay for it. That's why I keep pushing him: 'That's enough now. Quit while you're ahead. Besides, you're forgetting about us. Pay some attention to your daughter, even if you're in a huff 'cause she's a Catholic now.' I don't care for it either. Let me tell you: it's like the time our Martha went and joined the Party, first as applicant, then all the way. 'She sacrificed herself for us, specially for you, Wuttke,' I say, 'because you were on the outs with the guys on top. When our boys all stayed in the West, you were to blame, they said, 'cause they were over there in Hamburg with your sister. . . . And the worst part: our Georg was with the Wehrmacht, 'cause he was dead set on being a pilot. . . . But now all that's over and done with. Pay attention, so our Martha doesn't just mope around and hide in her room bawling her head off 'cause you don't give a hoot about her wedding, just about your one-and-only. . . .' "

Martha Wuttke, who for Fonty's purposes was called Mete and who would soon take her husband's name, had by this time recovered from her own version of nervous prostration, but was still dragging herself around the house like a sackful of sorrow, hauling her misery from the kitchen to her shabby old girl's room, where the photos and memorabilia from her days in the Free German Youth had recently been cleared to one side and a nightstand-turned-altar now solicited devotion. From there she hauled her misery back to the kitchen. To make things worse, school was still out for the summer. There was nothing to distract her, no friction with the newly appointed principal, untainted by any trace of Party affiliation, no classes to teach in basic math, a subject so far removed from ideology that it allowed only indubitable results—right or wrong. She was considered a hard-working, reliable teacher—save for her frequent use of sick leave—and was neither beloved nor feared, although she did have problems with colleagues, especially female ones, who had failed to leave the Party in time: bickering in the teachers' lounge. Actually she should have resigned because of her impending marriage; but in this connection, too, we discovered that Martha was indecisive, assailed time and again by fundamental doubts.

She discussed these things with us archivists, especially with me, now that I had agreed to serve as a witness at her wedding: "Theoretically I wanted to quit teaching long ago—I'm not really into it anymore. And I'm not so sure I'll take up something else in Schwerin, even if Grundmann says it's all right for me to keep myself busy down there. He wants me to watch over his money men—right, the investors. Just because I can add and subtract? But can you see me as a housewife? Sitting around the villa, which is way too big, waiting...not me! Actually I don't really feel like getting married at all, maybe because I've been alone so long....Theoretically I do want to, and a couple of times I've said to Father, 'It's the real thing this time. You won't catch me backing out like with Zwoidrak. This time I'm going to make it to the altar. You've got to give some attention to the wedding. Grundmann just wrote again—he's pestering, like Mama. He wants you to reserve a table for twelve, over in the West, at an Italian place. There's supposed to be a good one on the Ku'damm near that theater, the Schaubühne—he gave me the name to pass on to you. Exactly! Why not in the West?' It doesn't bother me, but Father isn't giving it any attention. Grundmann would have taken it off his shoulders, you know, and reserved the place himself, if Father hadn't insisted, back at Pentecost when Grundmann was in town for a short visit. 'I'll take care of the wedding dinner!' Father said. But whenever I bring it up, Father stops listening. Just says 'Yes, yes,' and his thoughts are somewhere else. Of course I sometimes wonder if it's my fault he acts deaf, because I didn't lay it all out for him soon enough; I mean that we're having a church wedding at St. Hedwig's, and that I don't have any doubts left, or only sometimes, and in any case need a perspective. Can't manage without one...I'm not trying to fool myself....I still remember perfectly: When I was in the Free German Youth I didn't just sing the songs, I really believed them—'Lest in the world you go astray...' But I'm sure it's not easy for Father...his only daughter...Exactly! And a Catholic wedding, of all things...He'd prefer a Calvinist wedding at the French Cathedral, of course, even if on paper we're only Lutheran, or even less, and when my friend Inge and I wanted to do the Party youth consecration he didn't object. But Catholic? He just can't see it, even if last year in March, when the old system was still around and I left the Party, he said, 'Finally!' I guess it was my mistake that I didn't tell him about catechism class and the priest at St. Hedwig's, or not till much later. At any rate, he took it wrong and muttered something about the leopard changing its spots. He was really offended. Maybe that's why Father wanted to up and leave. Heading for Scotland, of course, but he didn't get past Zoo station. Theoretically, though, he must have accepted the idea, because shortly before he took off he sat here in the kitchen and made a friendly little speech to me; sure, it had a couple of barbs in it: 'What does it matter, Mete?' he said. 'Whether Communism or Catholicism, they both start with a *C* and are both convinced of their infallibility....' Then he brought up that tearjerker *Count Petöfy*, because it has a conversion in it, too. But he certainly didn't like me joining the Church. 'Better to believe nothing than everything!' he exclaimed, and then added: 'What's the exchange rate nowadays for people's beliefs?' Not till I'd told him the whole story—about how shortly after I joined the Party—exactly, it was in the early eighties; before that I was a candidate for three years—I lost my belief, first in Lenin, later in Marxengels; not till then did Father spit out 'You have my blessing,' and then he murmured, 'Each according to his own *façon*...,' you know, like old Fritz the Great. Theoretically, he's the soul of tolerance. But it hurt that it was the stubblehead who spoke up for me. 'That's a nice dome on St. Hedwig's. What do you expect, Fonty? This just happens to be a changeover period....' That's what he said when Father started to get better, when suddenly he found he could write the way he used to. No more talk of a nervous collapse. Exactly, it cured him. But give some attention, really give some attention to my wedding, that's something he still won't do, theoretically...."

We saw Fonty digging in his heels. He even turned down my offer to spare him the legwork and reserve a table to his specifications: "If it must be, let it be my concern!"

To make things worse, the father of the bride did not like the groom. True, one could have a halfway pleasant chat with Grundmann, but first of all he was too old, and a widower to boot, and second this Mr. Smartaleck came from the West: "We don't know what makes them tick. And even if his company, which, third of all, I would assert already reeks of bankruptcy, has built hotels in Bulgaria, and our Mete ran into him on the Black Sea, he doesn't have the faintest idea about us. To Grundmann & Co. we're East Elbians, heathen Protestants, heretics, basically, which is in fact true. Converting isn't going to do any good, no matter how fashionable it's become these days. And I would venture to doubt whether this holy hydrotherapy will have any lasting effect on our Mete."

He probably would have dug in his heels if his day-and-night-shadow hadn't shooed him out of his study: "It's time to call a halt, Fonty! Or do you want my little present, all those pretty pencils, to be confiscated as a subversive product from the West? You see? By the way, I have some great news. How quickly the situation changes. You're in demand. It's looking good for a presentation of your 'Childhood and Youth' in the old Schultheiss Brewery—which they're calling the Culture Brewery now—before an audience, of course. They're wild about that kind of thing, the young folks. Dying to hear about the old days, even olden times. They've had their fill of the current fare. At any rate, I've managed to pry loose a tidy sum: a grant! By the way, the whole deal's being subsidized from over there, and I had some say when the appropriations were up for discussion. So, Fonty, what about it? All this writing's not only made you healthy again; you can even cash in on it. The whole thing pays, just the way it did for your great predecessor. As we know, his *Childhood and Youth* was his first real hit. The little book sold like hotcakes. Not only in Swinemünde, where people were always greedy for gossip, panting for the latest news. At any rate, you should know better than me that the Immortal earned almost as much for his memoirs as for his famous *Effi*. Which, as soon as he'd recovered, he just dashed off. Exciting times those were. Began in '88 with the three-kaiser year. And just got crazier and crazier: the minute the Anti-Socialist Laws are repealed, Bismarck's toppled. Restless years. We were constantly on

duty. Even so, *The Weavers* got produced. First here on Schiffbauerdamm, but open to club members only, then in Paris. Finally a big
production at the Deutsches Theater, with Liebknecht and other
socialists in the audience. Social injustice! Poverty in Silesia! I can
still hear the factory owner's speech—Dreissiger was his name—
being drowned out by laughter. And the gentleman in corner seat
23 wrote a rave review in the *Salon of Arts and Culture,* like a Young
Turk. The play had quite a run, in Breslau's Lobe Theater, and in
Hanover, even though we'd doubled the prices in the upper mez-
zanine, so the workers wouldn't be able to...Did no good. We had
our hands full. Well, because the social order was in turmoil again,
and the socialists were getting cockier and cockier...Even the
young kaiser was carrying on like a madman. 'I'll lead you into glorious times,' just like today, nothing but hocus-pocus and massive
bragging. The mantle of history! That's what the chancellor over
there said the other day. If you listen to him, one historic hour
after another is striking. He's got another think coming, that man.
A new chapter, ha! Don't make me laugh. A little changeover, putting on another new shirt, that's all. We've seen it all before, these
costume changes, on stage, with the curtain open. That's human
beings for you. Always worrying about their looks. So you shouldn't
hold it against your daughter if she wants to be decked out in her
new faith. In your day, you slipped out of your would-be revolutionary togs and dressed up as Manteuffel's agent, then went from
one journal to the next, offering your services as a hack, first to the
Dresden paper, then to the *Kreuzzeitung,* finally to the *Vossische.* And
now your daughter changes from red to black. One's no worse
than the other. Besides, we're sure your daughter will be a few
prayers short of a Catholic. When it came to Marxism and Lenin-
ism, she always missed a few beads on the rosary, too. I'm familiar
with her cadre file. Always grappling with doubt...But enough
shilly-shallying, Fonty. With or without holy water: the wedding's
around the corner!"

There was no more wiggling out of it: the moment had arrived.
Once more, to buy time, he had sought out his favorite childhood

refuges—in Swinemünde the space under the rafters and in Neu-ruppin the blackness of the coal cellar, lit by the ghostly glow of a tallow candle. From these two refuges he had extrapolated the "ex-istential necessity of a child's hiding place." Then on to the years at the Gymnasium, broken off in one case, continued in a straight line in the other, in which connection he portrayed the two head-masters in a double frame. After he had checked off the trade school in Friedrichswerder as an ordeal that simply had to be with-stood, along came a lengthy concluding paragraph leading to that bronze monument, dedicated to the rambler, gazing calmly out over Brandenburg's landscape, rather than to the novelist. The fes-tive consecration took place on 8 June 1907, with much fuss—pan-egyrics and recitations.

Fonty saw himself standing in front of the monument and be-hind it, and running around it. Sometimes the bronze cast its shadow on him, sometimes his own shadow fell on the stone pedestal. His pencil wrote of his earliest encounters with immor-tality, of the "sacred shudder" he felt when, holding his father's hand, he was sworn to uphold the "eternal values of literature." He finished the memoirs, which had in the meantime earned him a grant and a place at the lectern, with the confession "Thus I have been, since my earliest childhood, wholly at one with him who sits, cast in bronze, on a stone bench in Neuruppin."

After that he granted himself another brief back-and-forth on the runner, then reached for his hat and walking stick. Outside, the dry heat of August awaited him. Fonty had been given back to the world; but for now he was allowed to go out only under escort.

When they had circled Kollwitzplatz three times, a conversation with Hoftaller took place under a table-umbrella. They were sitting on Husemannstrasse outside the Café Bistro, which together with the fronts of the buildings along the street had already been re-stored in the mid-eighties. They were having a drink—Hoftaller a Schultheiss beer and Fonty a glass of Médoc.

Façades like a picture book. Backdrops erected to fool them-selves and others. Sometimes Western tourists strolled by. They gaped at the illusion left over from Berlin's 750th jubilee. Old-timers hardly showed their faces here. Sitting there with his day-and-night-shadow, Fonty felt like a piece in an exhibition.

When the promised grant, five hundred marks in the still new-seeming currency, was counted out into his hand, he decided not to take this round sum to the Dresdner Bank on Dimitroffstrasse, to add to the remainder of his savings—his escape fund—but to invest the proceeds from his recovery in the wedding dinner.

In the course of their chat, which started out quite relaxed, he remarked to Hoftaller, "I still say the French Cathedral is better than St. Hedwig's. But if we must have a Catholic song and dance, I'll see what I can dream up. Have a soft spot anyway, not for black robes, necessarily, but at least for incense and glowing candles, and certainly for the Blessed Virgin. What would have become of Effi without the maid Roswitha, dyed in the darkest religious faith, who remained faithful to her when everyone else, even Briest and his wife, abandoned her? You can count on Catholicism as you can count on hell. Should make sense to you, Tallhover. Come to think of it, aren't you from the papal faction, also, like— well, you know whom I mean—that Police Superintendent Reiff in *L'Adultera?*"

Fonty gloated: Hoftaller hadn't seen that coming. And Hof-taller conceded, at first sheepishly, then with the relief that comes of unburdening oneself, that he had acquired his earliest profes-sional experience in confessionals. He lit one of his Havanas, as-sumed the expression of a father confessor, gleaming unctuously, and recalled, now with real gusto, "Can't get over it, that revelation of a person's innermost thoughts, halting at first, then just pouring out, the whispering on both sides of the wooden screen, the priest's ear and the penitent's mouth: Yes, I have sinned...in thought, word, and deed....Ah, and the final absolution, that feel-ing of being newborn, fresh as a daisy, so to speak. It's like a shower, first hot, then cold....I really owe a lot to the Catholic Church. The Church knows what human beings keep locked in-side them, and has developed a whole arsenal of techniques for loosening the tongue. The Church is always there. In her arms, everyone sings. And what an invention the privacy of the confessional is: even people who consider themselves hardened cases will talk. What a shame that my biographer, who otherwise held nothing back, was reluctant to show the formative influence the confessional had on me...."

"Frightfully true!" Fonty exclaimed. "Should have seen that myself—the Catholic underpinnings of your outfit, so secular in other respects..."

"Too late!"

"But tell me the truth, Hoftaller, are you still practicing?"

"It's something you never shake off completely."

"You mean we're all sentenced to the confessional for life?"

"The denomination isn't important. Your daughter, Fräulein Martha, may have changed her faith, but sins, our sins, are always true to themselves...."

The following day Fonty set out alone. First he stopped by the Skittles Club on Lychener Strasse, familiar to him from earlier days, though not his regular pub. As he stood with a small glass of beer at the counter, he found the newly installed slot machines annoying, likewise the music that filled every corner of the taproom with its pounding beat; only the dishes listed on the menu—ham hocks, cold-cuts platter, stuffed cabbage—appealed to him, likewise the prices, which had not yet been Westernized; but these Berlin specialties were hardly suitable for a wedding banquet.

He allowed his gaze to wander, resting on the cardboard images of local celebrities on the wall above the counter. He recognized Street-Corner Nante, the hurdy-gurdy man, Autoharp Julie, and the cartoonist Heinrich Zille in his milieu. Then he read the motto of all skittlers, in the form of a curlicued inscription—"Good Wood and All Nine!"—ascertained that both skittle alleys were still in use, and, as the proprietor said, were booked "straight through the unification and on into October." He dredged up passages that echoed his mockery of everything native to Berlin—"Every roll is pulpy, every slice of meat tastes of mold, and no bookbinder can bind a book handsomely; yet for all that, the most insufferable snobbery..."—but then he ordered a shot of Nordhaus brandy to chase the last swig of beer, and toasted himself: No, this is no place for Mete to celebrate her long-postponed marriage; but Prenzlberg it must be.

His home quarter. In this part of town he was known as Fonty; even children shouted the name on the street. Here the must was particularly thick, saturated with all sorts of secrecy. Here, in various bars and cafés, the scene had congregated, more self-referential than conspiratorial. In a part of the city like this everyone had informed on everyone else, and no one had gone unshadowed. Here poems had been hatched, and traded like munitions. Betrayal came and went, and suspicion remained in circulation like small change. Talent earned double interest. And already bars that only yesterday had still served as trading floors to the unfettered geniuses were now considered historic sites: That's where such and such happened, that's where a spy, who was traded as a major talent, and another spy who couldn't keep his lip buttoned... because that's where they met, that's where they always... that's where they're even supposed to have... that's where time passed... time has passed over that... Yet Fonty, who was at home here, wanted nothing to be past. He wanted everything to be present, on call. He remarked to the proprietor of the Skittles Club, "Berlin has changed colossally. We owe that chiefly to the paved streets and the horse-drawn trams." Then he paid and left.

From here it was not far to the brick walls-within-walls of the old Schultheiss Brewery, topped with crenellations and turrets. It had recently reopened as the Culture Brewery and was drawing a crowd with daily fresh spectacles. Crossing Senefelder Strasse, he reached Stubbenkammerstrasse, which branched off to the right, where he knew a restaurant located on the corner, Offenbach's, as well as the proprietor, who in the days of the Workers' and Peasants' State had managed to negotiate with the leading comrades, then still in full command of their absolute power, the right to operate a private restaurant; singers and actors from the Comic Opera and the Metropol Theater are supposed to have helped when it came to alleviating the customary bureaucratic chicanery.

And so costume sketches for Offenbach's operas hung on all the walls—for instance, those for Felsenstein's *Bluebeard* production. Fonty recalled that in the late fifties *The Tales of Hoffmann* and later, at the Metropol, *La belle Hélène,* as well as *Susanne the Chaste* had been performed. Offenbach's drew nourishment from these theatrical events.

The proprietor grumbled a bit about the rent, which of late had been rising by leaps and bounds, and about the absence of regular patrons who had once been big spenders. Fonty treated himself to a Calvados at the bar and responded in kind to the long-time waiter's wordplay. To the question "Anything new from your pen?" he replied, "Every day could fill a book!" And not until he got the proprietor to hand him a menu did he bring up the question of "Mete's wedding," turning the saying "If you're young when you wed, joy will rain on your head" into its opposite: "It's at least as true the other way around. That's the usual fate of such sayings."

As if he had suddenly reached a decision, he reserved a table for twelve in the so-called Music Room, on whose walls various old instruments hung—mandolins, violas, violins—for the fifth of September, at noon; because right after the church ceremony the wedding guests were to dine here with the bride and groom, as a private party.

Fonty also selected a three-course menu. He did not want to appear stingy. If he was defying his son-in-law's wish for a "good Italian restaurant," no expense should be spared at Offenbach's. As he went on his way, he was humming to himself, "When I was still prince of Arcadia. . . ."

It should be emphasized again, in conjunction with this decision made in the nick of time—and not devoid of obstinacy—that Fonty was perfectly capable of acting as Wuttke. If we archivists experienced him only as Fonty, that does not mean that elsewhere he played only this prescribed role, for instance when carrying files in the Ministries Building. Indeed, he made a point of being Theo Wuttke there, and insisted on being called that. Similarly, in the days of the Workers' and Peasants' State, he had presented his political views directly as "Herr Wuttke," venturing to undermine the official Party line only as Fonty. Thus from the outset he supported land reform—"Junkers' Lands in Peasants' Hands"—but disapproved of forced collectivization as "state-sponsored expropriation." And when his three sons stayed in the West after the building of the Wall, the loss hit him harder as Wuttke than as Fonty. Therefore the declaration by his second-eldest, Teddy—Georg, the eldest, had died in '78 of a ruptured appendix—that he would on no account come to his sister's wedding, pained him primarily as paterfamilias; his youngest son Friedel's acceptance of the invitation did nothing to soften the blow.

At the outset, Fonty followed the Catholic ceremony at St. Hedwig's with curiosity as Theo Wuttke. But when no censer was swung, no Latin mumbled, and all the customary mystification failed to materialize, he experienced the disappointment as Fonty. Later, at table, he remarked that he missed the "dazzling hocuspocus" that still echoes in the last lines of the Immortal's *Count Petöfy*, when the Madonna speaks from her niche, promising the widowed Countess Franziska heavenly protection, even though she has taken her own sweet time converting, altogether unlike his daughter, who had first not hesitated to renounce her commitment to the all-redeeming Party and then embraced the credo of the all-redeeming Church: "Well, that's how she is, my Mete, always colossally convinced. But no matter in what *façon* the marriage is celebrated, all's well so long as the 'I do' is genuine."

14

Martha's Wedding

Both spoke their vows loud and clear. Represented by me, we archivists were far more impressed than the father of the bride, who had expected God only knows what of the ceremony in St. Hedwig's. Immediately after the nuptials, he began to grumble, and later, when he gave free rein to his discontent at table, he let drop the expression "deceptive packaging." He scoffed when I protested, "Even the Catholic Church has to move with the times," saying: "The Pope holds with the booksellers: they, like the public, quickly turn to new gods. Nothing lasts more than a week!"

Fonty let fly even more barbs on Bebelplatz, where the bridegroom insisted that the wedding party pose for pictures under an overcast sky, first one group, then another, against changing backdrops, until showers drove them away. With some difficulty they rounded up four taxis, and the party finally arrived, "pretty well soaked," as Fonty said, at Offenbach's in Prenzlauer Berg.

There the table awaited them, set for only ten. After some milling around, people finally found their seats, with the help of handwritten place cards. Professor Freundlich and his wife had been unable to come; according to their telegram, and to Fonty's regret, they were unfortunately otherwise engaged—"pressing university business...." But a magnificent floral arrangement had arrived in time from Jena, pleasing even Emmi Wuttke, in whose eyes the Freundlichs could otherwise hardly do anything right.

The place cards were Emmi's idea, executed in her own hand. Since her school days, she had cultivated a variation on the Sütterlin method; its childishly correct loops impressed all the guests.

Someone exclaimed, "How adorable!" and even Fonty tucked a compliment into his toast—"Gratitude is owed to my Emmi, who defies all the vicissitudes of life." He waited to rise and deliver this extemporaneous toast, however, until the interval between the appetizer—house-marinated salmon with creamy horseradish sauce—and the main course, called *La belle Hélène*—rosy roast breast of duck *à l'orange*, served with vegetables and potato pancakes. He waited, even though the urge to make himself heard had already come over him in church, in view of the "colossally puritanical Catholicism" he had encountered there. To his son Friedel, whom he knew only as a child or from photographs, and who had resolved in advance to take offense, he said, as the two of them were sitting side by side during the ceremony, "All one can do here is keep still or come out with a peck of pickled nonsense. Just wait, all of you, something unsuitable will surely occur to me at dinner."

Had all gone according to Fonty's wishes, the main course would have consisted of *Orphée aux enfers*—pot roast in plum sauce, served with green beans seasoned with bacon, but Emmi had succeeded in talking him out of Orpheus and substituting Helen, as more appropriate to the festive occasion; as a result, the company was no sooner seated than the duck breast, crisp on the outside, juicy on the inside, inspired him to a number of daring allusions: "*La belle Hélène* is never out of place. But pink and tender need not signify virginity. Our beautiful bride, who has been waiting in the wings so long, understands what is meant."

Emmi worried about such flashes of inspiration. And because she had never been able to exercise a moderating influence on her Wuttke's speeches, she feared further lapses; as it turned out, there was to be no lack of these when he tapped his glass and rose to speak.

The father of the bride began with a rather coy apologetic flourish—"I am a good *causeur* but a poor speaker"—which actually paved the way for a series of verbal escapades. He first described his beloved daughter's resignation from the Party and entry into the Church as an "ecumenical sauna." Next he used her new perspective as a pretext for various backward glances at the darkest Middle Ages, "including the burning of witches," and prophesied, "the stake will soon come into style again." Then he became Fonty altogether, passing in review all the characters in his novels, and, after only a brief search, introducing the actress Franziska Franz to the wedding party, describing her as a "chatterbox—from Swinemünde, by the bye." Only now was the hero of the novel, the "somewhat bandy-legged" old Count Petöfy, placed at the side of his bride; and their wedding, held in Vienna—"at the beginning of Chapter 13, of course"—was celebrated in nuptial installments: "For the first set of 'I do's' was spoken in St. Augustine's, the second in the Protestant church on Gumpendorfer Strasse." And then he returned to the bride: "Franziska was no spring chicken, but in comparison to the decrepit, soon to be deceased Hungarian-blooded count, she was still a young thing, for whom the doors of life stood wide open...."

One did not need to be familiar with this largely forgotten novel to realize that the allusion to the age difference between the newlyweds, thirty-eight-year-old Martha and fifty-six-year-old Grundmann, was risqué, especially since Fonty, in referring to the "decrepit count's" imminent demise, invoked the novel's catastrophic ending and even praised its "skillful narrative technique": "Thus the author spares us the pistol shot, important only for its outcome, which moves the plot forward. Not a single drop of literary blood is spilled. All interest can be directed toward the young widow and her grief...."

But then Fonty rescued the bridal couple, the wedding party, and himself from the awkward situation into which he had so recklessly talked himself, just as Emmi had feared; he executed one of those about-faces we so greatly admired: "But what am I saying! An age gap need not be an abyss! An age advantage is an advantage all the same! Or, as old Petöfy speculated, in his capacity as bon vivant and therefore with gusto: the excesses and rapid consumption of youth can provide ample nourishment for the long journey of more easily sated old age. Therefore let it be said once more: All's well, so long as the 'I do' is genuine!"

This brought the father of the bride, who wanted to postpone the main course a bit longer, back to the subject of the altar and the general question of Catholicism, whose essence he praised as "a centuries-long exercise in staying power," and "as colorful as sin," while he attributed to Protestantism "greater clarity of line," which "against a whitewashed background constantly seeks out guilt and blackens its name." With that the speaker had found his way to the old count's sister Judith, as elderly as she was devout, and the omnipresent Father Fessler, and thus also to the heart of the treacherous signet ring question, which revolves, toward the end of the novel, around engraved mottoes.

Fonty, who was searching for a telling point on which to end his speech, fixed his eye on the priest, who had been included in the wedding party, and took a rhetorical running start: "Monsignor, I must admit that this priest—a black papist blackening the name of every erroneous belief, Lutheran or Calvinist— nonetheless made an impression, for although he was a certified *vir obscurans,* he was open-minded enough to adorn his signet ring with a Protestant inscription, the pithy motto of that famous sage Thomas Carlyle . . ."

Here the speaker inserted a dramatic pause, and of course the wedding party, and above all the bridegroom, wanted to hear how the inscription went. Heinz-Martin Grundmann exclaimed, "Enough of this guessing game! What did it say?"

"Renounce!" Fonty replied, quoting precisely as always, and raised his glass. Whereupon all the others hesitated, but then raised their glasses of Médoc after all: first Emmi Wuttke, who did not want an embarrassing silence to ensue; she was followed by Friedrich, known as Friedel, the bride's youngest brother, whom the building of the Wall decades earlier had turned into a young refugee from the Eastern Zone and who now managed a publishing house in Wuppertal; immediately after him the gaunt, tight-lipped sister of the first Frau Grundmann, dead these five years, joined in the solemn custom of the toast—the widowed Bettina von Bunsen had raised the contractor's two motherless children in Freiburg im Breisgau; one of these children, Martina, lifted her glass at the same time; she was studying German literature in Cologne and could pass for pretty, or cute; now Inge Scherwinski followed suit; she, who had been invited as the girlhood friend and neighbor of the bride, did not dwell on her hard lot as a single mother raising three boys but smiled cheerfully over her wine glass, showing her little mouse teeth; and now I, too, reached for my glass, I, the witness on loan from the Archives, who had, for professional reasons, been deeply affected by this speech by the father of the bride; next to last, the priest from St. Hedwig's, Father Bruno Matull, who had helped Martha with her conversion and had given her the nuptial blessing, clasped his glass with the fingers of both hands in such priestly fashion that it looked as though he were raising a chalice; and only now did the bride and groom reach, at the same moment, for their glasses; the bridegroom, by the way, had just succeeded in establishing a branch of his Münster company in Schwerin. Heinz-Martin Grundmann raised his glass to eye level and exclaimed, "I hear you! Renounce! Very clever! But my dear father-in-law, Martha and I certainly won't have this wedding motto engraved on our rings. Delightful, simply delightful—renounce. Let's drink to that: Renounce!"

At this point Friedel Wuttke raised his glass to his brother-in-law and laughed in his face. Inge Scherwinski laughed even louder and more contagiously as she clinked glasses with her girlhood friend. When the priest allowed himself to grin above his chalice, Grundmann's daughter, Martina, began to giggle, and that infected Frau von Bunsen. Eventually laughter coursed around the whole table, for neither Emmi Wuttke nor I could contain ourselves. What else could the bride and bridegroom do as the glasses clinked but laugh, too, at the single word that had unleashed such merriment. Only the father of the bride solemnly and ceremoniously saluted the bridal couple with his glass.

Until this moment I had not noticed that on the lapel of his black jacket, which had become somewhat too big for him over the years, Fonty was wearing a ribbon with a medal dangling from it. His lecture suit, decorated in the days of the Cultural Union. But as he stood there in his gray vest, jacket, and neatly bow-tied cravat, with his white head, and his mustache dangling over his tilted wine glass, his gaze traveling out over the newlyweds, he could have been wearing on his left breast an altogether different medal, signifying a belatedly jingling honor: the Order of the House of Hohenzollern, First Class.

We have had some disagreement as to whether the Archives have the right to flout the chronological order of events and cut straight to the toast. It would have been correct to begin, if not with a blow-by-blow account of the ceremony at St. Hedwig's, then at least with the appetizer, with marinated salmon and creamy horseradish sauce, and dry Chablis in old glasses. Along with Inge Scherwinski's tears of joy, which flowed copiously over the wedding ceremony, I would have been in favor of including the interior of the church. After that I would have had the proprietor of Offenbach's greeting the wedding guests and acquainting them with all the dining areas. That may now be done retroactively, for in fact we did not go directly from the taproom through the hall and past the kitchen to the Music Room, where each of the many instruments had a legend clinging to it and the festive table awaited us.

The program included time for an apéritif, "on the house." And with filled glasses the proprietor escorted the members of this "private party" from the taproom through all three of the adjacent dining rooms. The first was wallpapered in lime green. But the other two, done in English red and violet blue, projected that blend of frivolity and catchy tunes that the name of the restaurant promised its guests. I permitted myself a few references to Karl Kraus's one-man performances of Jacques Offenbach, and used the wall decorations in these rooms, framed costume sketches for Felsenstein's *Bluebeard* production, as the pretext for allusions to cultural history. "I hear you!" said the bridegroom. "Lighthearted entertainment with a contemporary twist."

The taproom was decorated with autographed and therefore valuable photos of artists, among them some who were still well known. There was a glass case with a coin slot; when you dropped in a coin, figurines of dancers no taller than your finger began to kick their legs in the air, dancing a cancan in their tutus, to the pertinent music. A collector's item that the proprietor seldom set in motion—as he did now, at Fonty's request, for Martha's wedding. Everyone clapped as the dance came to an end with a few last convulsive twitches.

Yet as attractive as the dining rooms at Offenbach's looked, with their invitingly set tables, they were almost empty. The proprietor bemoaned this fact: after the currency reform, his regular customers had left him. "It doesn't pick up till evening; at this time of day, around noon, business is pretty flat. Oh, well, there's nowhere to go but up."

Heinz-Martin Grundmann, who had already been introduced to me at the registry office, a compact gentleman, bald in front, in a custom-tailored suit, turned out to be a person who took an interest in everything, even mundane problems: "So who owns this rundown corner lot? I hear you! Former owners from Munich have turned up, and now they're raising the rent, of course. Good God, these people have no shame. That'll take deep pockets. Won't be easy."

He'd manage, the proprietor assured him. He was an emaciated man in his mid-forties who had wanted to be an actor himself but had nonetheless—"and that in spite of socialism"—succeeded in creating a popular artist's haunt, always full to the bursting point—"until just before it all caved in." "Took some doing, if you wanted to stay in the private sector."

Grundmann wished him luck and a good tax consultant. Friedel Wuttke stood there looking like a stranger, intentionally keeping some distance between himself and his family. Inge Scherwinski would have liked to see the figurines dance again. The priest looked pained. I tried to strike up a conversation with Frau von Bunsen. The bride stared grimly. The bridegroom's daughter called Offenbach's "cute." The father of the bride said nothing. Finally the proprietor led the wedding party into the Music Room, where Emmi Wuttke had determined the seating order with her little place cards.

The bride and groom were seated across from one another, halfway down the long table, with a floral centerpiece between them. Emmi had the priest beside her. Next to Fonty, whom the proprietor had repeatedly addressed respectfully as "Herr Wuttke"—"The Chablis on ice, but of course, Herr Wuttke"—sat Martina Grundmann, the young student. Next to the bridegroom sat the maid of honor, his deceased wife's sister. I had the bride next to me. A place had been set at the head of the table for Inge Scherwinski. That left the foot for Friedel Wuttke.

Most of those seated at the table were strangers to one another, or, in the case of Friedel, the prodigal son, had become strangers. Even when the appetizer was served—the marinated salmon cut in wafer-thin slices—conversation was slow to start. Frau von Bunsen repeatedly assured her former brother-in-law that she had done "everything conceivable" to lure his son, Thomas, who reportedly was making short work of getting his law degree, "out of his sulk": "He's still so attached to his mother."

"There was nothing we could do," Emmi confirmed from across the table. "Our Teddy still thinks he can't come over to see us 'cause he works on the Hardthöhe in Bonn, at the defense. But the wedding would've been the perfect time for us to sit down and have a good, long talk after all these years...."

"That'll come with time," the priest remarked. "We've all become strangers to one another, alas, even within families."

Inge Scherwinski, speaking loudly, and not merely out of embarrassment, asked Friedel Wuttke at the other end of the table whether he still remembered growing up on Kollwitzstrasse. "You've got to admit, we had a great childhood in the old heap, with the courtyard out back. Remember the shed, Friedel?" When she received no reply, she proved understanding: "Still, you did the right thing when you stayed over there, the three of you, when they sealed things up tight over here. But we missed you guys...."

The balding publisher finally admitted that he remembered "the chestnut tree in the rear courtyard," but "Teddy and I had no time to be homesick. And Georg least of all, because he went into the military, and later he was off in Aurich flying the Starfighters.... You had to have the right stuff.... You people over here can't begin to imagine.... But never mind."

A good thing that the bridegroom agreed: "Let bygones be bygones. Today we're going to enjoy ourselves!" Georg's career as an officer, so soon ended, would not have been a suitable topic for the wedding party, especially for Emmi and Martha, who in any case had done their best not to hear Friedel's allusions to the family's sore spot, instead seeking solace in marinated salmon and melba toast.

Martina Grundmann was having an easier time of it, jabbering at Fonty. She was expatiating on the hardships endured by West German students in their overcrowded lecture halls, leaving no room for Fonty to get an interested question in edgewise. Actually, the father of the bride was somewhere else entirely in his thoughts. The bride and her mother noticed this, and it worried them. Emmi whispered to her neighbor, "He's winding up, Monsignor. The minute they clear the plates, my Wuttke's going to speak. I know from experience. It was always pretty dreadful. I just hope he doesn't forget who he is this time."

But Fonty remained silent a little while longer. He almost seemed to be listening to the chattering student, who was not only pretty but also pleasantly stylish in a turquoise outfit. With a light-hearted remark I tried to calm the bride, who was sitting next to me, breathing hard: "What do you bet he serves up the wedding party from *Stechlin*, Rex and Czako and all?"

But Martha's suspicions were directed elsewhere: "Just so long as he doesn't start in on that architect who married his Mete— what if he confuses my Grundmann with old Professor Fritsch! I couldn't take it. Not today."

We were both wrong. The remains of the appetizer had been cleared and the proprietor himself had poured a drop of the Médoc for the father of the bride to sample. Fonty had nodded his approval of the wine, whereupon the glasses on both sides of the table were filled. Only Friedel covered his glass with his hand and called for mineral water. At that point Theo Wuttke rose to offer a speech that proved unsuitable in an entirely different way. As he digressed, then veered back on course, heading straight for the perilous topic, a minor work of the Immortal's played an increasingly important part: the work in which, alongside Count Petöfy and his sister, Austro-Hungarian Catholicism came into view; yet, as we already know, Fonty spoke so whimsically about the exchange rate of conversion and skirted various shoals so daringly that Emmi, who always feared the worst, made only sporadic attempts to dam the flow of his speech with exclamations like "Come on, wrap it up, Wuttke!" To her and Martha's relief, the bridegroom managed to find some humor in the revelation of the motto on the Catholic signet ring, that emphatically Protestant admonition "Renounce!" Grundmann remarked, after the laughter had died away and they had all toasted each other with red wine, Friedel sticking to his mineral water: "I hear you! We're supposed to tighten our belts, so to speak. But that's no motto for developers. We take what we can get. We don't dabble around the edge, Father-in-law, we dig in!"

The speech was hardly ended when the rosy roast breast of duck known as *La belle Hélène* was served. As mentioned before, it might just as well have been saddle of beef, named after Offenbach's *Orphée aux enfers*. On no account would it have been the salmon fillet with herb butter extolled under the name of *Barcarole*, though surely it could have been *Popolani's Magic*, namely rabbit stewed in Burgundy, if only as a tip of the hat to Max Wuttke, the socialist and rabbit-breeder.

As they all reached for their knives and forks, the father of the bride remarked, "Actually I'd decided on saddle of beef, but my Emilie was dead set against Orpheus. And Knight Bluebeard, the filet mignon, didn't appeal to her either, though that recidivist's story would have permitted all sorts of allusions—to the forbidden rooms, for instance, that exist in every marriage!"

The duck breast called Helen had less to offer, the more so since the bride's facial features, constantly at odds with one another, could not be described as beautiful in any classic sense. Throughout her father's remarks, as he neared dangerous precipices, her small anxious mouth had kept trying to talk her eyes, which remained fixed on her empty plate, into crying. But now there was no call for that. A buzz of conversation arose around the table, enthusiastic comments on the duck and even more on the orange sauce. Someone called the potato pancakes an original touch. Frau von Bunsen spoke of "Saxon influences on Berlin's cuisine," and Inge Scherwinski exclaimed, "Not that long ago we called those pancakes filler, no kidding!" Everyone recalled other delicious duck dishes. Martina Grundmann enthused about a weekend trip to Amsterdam, where she had recently celebrated her twentieth birthday with friends over "scrumptious crispy Peking duck."

"So, what did you have for your wedding?" Emmi asked her son. "You know they wouldn't give me a travel permit, all those years."

Friedel Wuttke did not want to go into the subject of how his marriage, now dissolved, had begun. "Let's not dredge up those old stories! But how about hearing how this rich Wessie Grundmann scooped up my sister Martha, the poor little East mouse. Out with it, Brother-in-law! But the truth. There's nothing we like better than sentimental tales, especially ones about the two Germanys, and with happy endings."

Friedel's publishing house was sponsored by a Protestant missionary society. Its list contained not only pious works of various kinds, including religious tracts, but also works on the Third World and its unredeemed poverty. He had posed his question not without ulterior motives and, I suspected, pietist malice, for the origins of the love affair between the Western developer and the socialist teacher were considered a family secret and therefore not known to everyone at the table; even to me, the witness, the bride had not confided any details. I could merely guess at the nature of this relationship, very risky in its time. It had dragged on for years, in the requisite secrecy. Even the bride's parents knew little about it. Only Monsignor Matull, as Martha's father confessor, was fully in the picture.

"Why not!" said the bridegroom. "We can talk about it openly now. I realize my dear brother-in-law has, shall we say, a certain amount of catching up to do. I hope he won't be disappointed if our story's not very juicy."

"Just the truth..."

"...and nothing but. It was about six years ago. Our tale of two Germanys, as you phrased it, began in July, on a fiendishly hot day at a beachfront hotel on the Black Sea. I was there on business a lot—we were putting up high-rises—but this time I had my family along, though at that time my wife was already..."

"Spare us, Heinz-Martin, would you? I'm begging you! Besides, it's none of Friedel's business. He never asked me anything. Not a letter, nothing..."

"And I'm asking you, dear, not to interrupt. Your brother wants to have all the *i*'s dotted and the *t*'s crossed. So here goes. July '84.

Bulgaria. The coast near Varna. Pretty overrun. In those days a favorite vacation spot, and not only for the shut-ins living in the Soviet occupation zone, which you, my dear Friedel, were lucky enough to leave as a teenager, but also for West Germans, ordinary citizens like my family. The children were with us, right, Martina? It was their school holiday, but I also had some projects I needed to keep an eye on. At any rate, we were looking to relax, and I certainly had an interest in talking with our fellow countrymen who were cut off from the West. To me the forcible division of Germany was always a condition that shouldn't simply be accepted; on the contrary, my belief in reunification was rock-solid. . . ."

"And Martha, when does Martha come in?"

"Hold your horses, Brother-in-law. We're getting to that. Can't tell a story without laying a proper foundation. Anyone in the building trade knows what I'm talking about. That's why I referred to the unjust division of Germany, though you may consider that superfluous. At any rate, the West German tables were served first—the two groups ate apart—that's how it was done at the time, because of the currency, of course. We were sitting—my wife, who unfortunately passed away the following year, my children, and myself—close to the East German section, and already had our meals—I don't recall just what it was, probably fish . . ."

"That's wrong, Papa! It was roast chicken with *pommes frites*— pretty greasy, too. . . ."

"I hear you. Martina's memory, as far as the food is concerned, is better. At any rate, in the section reserved for Easterners, but toward the edge, a woman was sitting alone, and her plate was still empty when we'd already got our dessert. Now I remember: the children had chicken, and we ordered shish kabob. At any rate, I couldn't stand seeing Martha—it was her, of course—sitting with that empty plate. . . ."

"Admit it, Brother-in-law, love at first sight!"

"My dear Friedel, you're the publisher of 100-proof pious books—you should give a man some credit for Christian compassion. . . ."

"But Papa! It was Mama who pointed out the outrageous favoritism they were showing the tourists from the West!"

"I hear you! See how my daughter—how old were you at the time, Martina? Not even fifteen—still remembers how outraged we were at the blatant discrimination. And that's why I didn't hesitate, but got up and went over to her table...."

"Wrong again, Heinz-Martin. I distinctly recall my sister telling me it was Thomas who showed the gallantry that I'm sure went through your head, and my sister Cordula also...."

"That's true, Papa! It was Thomas who brought Martha over to our table, because Mama insisted on it. Right, Martha?"

"What does it matter who came over to my table? It was pretty embarrassing, I must say. And even more embarrassing that the minute I sat down your father called the waiter—and he raced over."

"At any rate, her food came right away: soup, entrée, dessert, like clockwork, for a nice tip, of course. And soon we were talking comfortably—don't know how else to describe it—the way Germans should talk with Germans, though at the time Martha still spoke about 'our republic' like a good Party member, and the most she would admit to was 'certain problems with the building of socialism.' And Martha and Cordula got along great, too. Unfortunately that was her last trip abroad. But she was the only one who knew how sick she really was, and she didn't tell us, right up to the end. Still, when it was almost over, it was Cordula who urged me not to lose touch with Martha. She's right for you, she's more practical than you, she said, and smiled.... But our meetings in East Berlin weren't that easy... always in secret, and always too short... and risky, too.... We were certainly being watched.... But then every summer in Bulgaria... It dragged on.... Our major projects... But even there, it was only gradually that we... Isn't that right, Martha?"

Nobody said a word. Most silent of all was the Protestant publisher Friedel Wuttke. Frau von Bunsen's silence was aimed at the bride, and accompanied by deep-frozen distrust. No one was surprised at Martha's silence. We would have liked to hear more about the first Frau Grundmann, née von Wangenheim, who had died of cancer: her understanding, her generosity of spirit. It was probably for this reason that Fonty's silence included memories of

Christine von Arne of Holkenäs Castle, who had been brought up by the Moravian community to exhibit similar selflessness. As a witness I could have said a number of things, could have quoted from *Irretrievable*, could perhaps also have taken a deep breath and offered a toast, beginning with Holk, though of course he suffered under Christine's virtue; but I remained silent, as we all did, until Inge Scherwinski found something appropriate to say: "That's exactly how it was here in the East. Without D-marks you were hardly worth anything. It was just the same in Prague; I was there a couple of times with Wolfi—that's my ex—and folks gave you these funny looks. Wherever you went in our fellow socialist countries, the same story. But now it'll all get better, because we're getting the unification: Deutschland, one fatherland indivisible! I want to drink to that, for real! Come on, have a sip, Martha! This'll cheer you up!"

I could never have managed such a toast. Everyone drank to everyone else. Even Frau von Bunsen mustered a smile for the bride that was only partially frozen. And the cue "German unification" gave the assembled company plenty to talk about. Everyone had an opinion, and it included the new currency, that advance on future payment.

Monsignor Matull commented, "Money won't do it alone. We still lack the will to accept each other as we've come to be." The bridegroom warned against inflated hopes: "You're going to have to work hard, damned hard; otherwise nothing's going to happen here, things'll just continue to go downhill." And Friedel Wuttke demanded that the guilty be named, without mercy: "That goes for everyone over here who collaborated. For instance, I'd like to know—though maybe this isn't proper to bring up at a wedding—how my family—yes, Martha, I mean you—made their peace with the Big Lie. Why didn't I hear any frank statements in Father's speech? Nothing but ambiguities. That's not going to bring us together. We need to have the guilty parties named. That's why this fall, for the Frankfurt Book Fair, my publishing house is bringing out a book called *The Stain of Guilt*, a collection of powerful confessions from East and West. I'd like to hear such a confession, if not from Martha, then certainly from you, Father—and without your usual bobbing and weaving."

No one dared to look at Fonty, who had listened to his son attentively but also with some amusement. "All frightfully right!" he exclaimed. "But guilt takes us far afield, and unification even farther, and let's not even mention the truth. But if you want something in writing for your publishing house, I could offer you a selection from my Cultural Union lectures; of course, they aren't admissions of guilt or outpourings of truth, but they're about life, which sometimes goes one way, sometimes another. And as for unification, we hold to the old German view that when the fellow from Sondershaus gets a drubbing, the fellow from Rudolstadt rejoices...."

This time it was Martina Grundmann who jumped in when things got dicey and tried to keep the peace. She summed up her reservations about unification with the comment, "Well, Dresden means nothing to me. In Cologne we're actually much closer to Paris or to Amsterdam." Whereupon Fonty again remarked, "Frightfully right," only to sink into silence again, no matter how persistently his table partner tried to draw him into a discussion of life at the West German universities and her courses on German literature. Martina Grundmann admitted, without the slightest embarrassment, that she had read hardly anything by the Immortal, although she had seen Fassbinder's film version of *Effi Briest*. "But they give us plenty of secondary literature, at least enough so we have an overview and know where he fits in historically, as our prof says—somewhere between Raabe and Keller...."

When Fonty roused himself to ask what she knew about *Stechlin*, he learned how blithely self-confidence can rest on ignorance: "Of course I've heard that he's your one-and-only. Martha said so. But to tell the truth, I've only looked at a couple of the shorter works, the one about delusions and the one about that fellow called Schach something-or-other. I can't seem to get into them: endless strolls, and the dialogue just goes on and on. Oh, sure, it's fairly witty sometimes. And maybe that's his special narrative technique, as our prof says. But I don't care much for great authors, or immortals, as you call them. Oh, I'm just going to call you Grampa Wuttke; do you mind? Anyway, I'm more for minimalism, if you know what I mean. You know, the fragmentary, or, in art in general, stuff like conceptual art. But marginal figures can also be pretty interesting. Our prof's dug out a few. I guess some of them were even pretty famous in their day. Paul Heyse, for instance, if the name means anything to you. He even got the Nobel Prize at some point. Today nobody's heard of him. And that's why we find him interesting, because...well, because he can be rediscovered. Our prof is hoping to offer a whole seminar just on Heyse and a couple of others....Of course you don't have to read all of it, just the abridged versions....And besides, there's always the secondary literature..."

Actually I would have liked to join the conversation and suggest to Martina that she visit the Archives, but I refrained, first because the bride needed my attention, and then because Fonty seemed to be enjoying his chattering table partner. He quoted a few Tunnel verses by Heyse, among them the salutatory verse "Silentium, brothers, let Lafontaine have a word..." and tried to suggest the benefit one might derive from reading the original texts.

But Martina and Martina's prof knew better; apparently any original text was merely a pretext for the true purpose of literature, which was to spawn interminable discourse on everything not to be found on the printed page, a discourse that extended far beyond the original text, rendering it incidental and eventually entirely devoid of content. The discourse was thus elevated to the status of a primary phenomenon. "It's incredibly interesting!" the young student exclaimed. Fonty merely inquired whether all that secondary material wasn't "colossally dry." Then he added, in a tone that, far from being resigned, was actually cheerful, "If you want to, my child, you can shorten even the longest story. Take *Stechlin*, for instance—it can be summarized thus: In the end an old man dies and two young people marry; that's just about all you get in five hundred pages."

Perhaps Monsignor Matull took these words as an allusion to the wedding party seated around the table; at any rate, the remains of Helen the Beautiful had been cleared, the proprietor had promised an assortment of ice cream flavors christened *La vie parisienne,* and the priest thought the interval between courses should be used for a speech. Now he was tapping his glass with his dessert spoon, now he was struggling to his feet, as if fighting some resistance, now the company was all ears.

15

Why the Bride Wept

"At last," I whispered to Martha. "Now we'll get the apostolic blessing."

The bride had to bend down a little to whisper her reply to me, because even seated she was taller. "Don't expect too much. He has a rough time with himself as a priest."

"An occupational hazard."

"But he really agonizes."

"You can tell. . . ."

At last I could get a good look at Bruno Matull, who had been sitting across from us and had now risen to his feet. No longer distracted by the bride's parents or by the quite pretty student, I found myself reminded—by the priest's physical proportions, his coarse hands that kept restlessly hunting for a place to hide, his massive head on his squat neck, and the cleftlike dimple in his chin—of the torments and pleasures of my long-lost childhood in the Eichsfeld region of Thuringia, a region more permeated by Catholicism than any other, and on both sides of the border, too; for the Eichsfeld, like the rest of Germany, was divided, and to top it off, the incision that had carved Europe into East and West, an expensively guarded death strip, ran straight through my wooded homeland.

And in my town there lived a vicar who had the same kind of trouble with his hands and the same kind of cleft chin. I think I must have loved him in my childish way, even after wearing the Young Pioneers' neckerchief came to mean more to me than serving as an acolyte, a tradition in our family.

Our vicar's name was Konrad. I don't remember his last name. He had kinky black hair and smelled of aftershave. Until my confirmation I was devoted to him; but in the course of my initially rapid rise within the Free German Youth—my Party career didn't begin to flag until I got to the University of Leipzig, and then suffered a fatal interruption shortly after Professor Hans Mayer quit the scene, and I was sent off to the lignite mines—the last bit of Catholic magic faded for me. But Vicar Konrad, who had long since found a parish among the miners in Bischofferode, never entirely disappeared from my life. On the contrary, he was always there in the background, looking over my shoulder when I became a librarian in Cottbus and later a member of the Archives staff in Potsdam. Now he was sitting across the table from me in the guise of Bruno Matull.

Actually he had heaved himself onto his feet in the meantime, immense and ungainly, massaging his chin and its dimple. He had tapped his glass and was collecting himself for a speech, opening his rather softly outlined mouth, closing it, opening it, then pressing his lips together as if to knead them, to make them pliable for extended use. A fish preparing to speak. A person who, in Martha's words, had a rough time with himself.

I could not bear to watch his exertions any longer. I therefore turned to Fonty, in whom the priest's struggle was arousing considerable curiosity. Perhaps he was expecting an exorcism, or the sudden appearance of miracle-working relics, because to him anything connected with "ancient beliefs" was exotic, and as mysteriously attractive as the Far Eastern bric-a-brac in the Copenhagen house of Captain Hansen's widow or the grave in Kessin of that Chinaman whose recurring apparition kept poor Effi awake nights. And like the Immortal, he always saw fictional characters with Catholic underpinnings in an ambiguous light—whether a title figure like Grete Minde or a secondary character like Effi's maid Roswitha. Thus I was certain that Fonty, like me—though drawing on entirely different childhood experiences—was expecting the priest to utter, if not a minor revelation, then certainly something "colossally heretical." Ah, if only he would finally spit it out instead of endlessly kneading his lips. We were both hoping that the fish would begin to speak to us.

Bruno Matull was one of those rare shepherds who had no use for that mild perma-smile, that cosmetic pastoral certainty that masks all doubts. Or, to be more precise, he never managed to assume such an expression. Instead we saw before us a somber-looking man, an almost brutish figure, who stood there groping for words, came up with a few and promptly rejected them, tested others and found them wanting, swallowed entire sentences, chewed some big lumps to bits, a flush spreading over his face up to his cheekbones, until finally he hurled himself off the diving board with the opening phrase, "My dear bride and bridegroom, witnesses, and wedding guests...," plunging straight into the tumultuous events that were asserting their market value and exchange rate just outside the cozy confines of Offenbach's.

Clutching the edge of the table as though he were about to flip it over, he intoned, "Nothing lasts forever. All about us we see crumbling things that only yesterday considered themselves lasting. Yet what brought these walls tumbling down? No, a brief, liberating breath was not enough; more was called for. But only a few were prepared to rattle the bars of the citadel from within. And lo: the walls swayed and fell, fell into ruins, became a mockery to themselves. Only then did many step forth and say: The quake, that was us. Victory is ours! And thus they bore false witness. But verily, among the few rattlers at the bars who had refused to let go, there were several shepherds from the other congregation, whereas my Church kept silent, perhaps believing that she bore no responsibility for the tyranny of this world. I, too, remained silent, all those years. I, too, accepted what no man should have accepted. There was no courage on my side. Thus the shepherd lost sight of his flock, but he comforted himself and sought solace in his faith. And then there came to me, dear guests, a woman who had no faith but was seeking firm ground. Her faith had left her, although it must once have been great, inspired by a hope beyond all doubt. Now she cursed that faith, calling it deceitful and blindly partisan. She spoke of a faith that merely parroted itself, and thus sustained lies. Yea, she reckoned up for me the price she had paid for this faith, and at whose expense. She came to me bearing a great weight and begged me to ease her burden, but I was assailed with doubt. I knew not whether my faith, my tongue-holding faith, could grant her the certainty she sought. For indeed the ground had begun to quake beneath my feet as well. And so I stinted with comfort, told her that I, too, had lost touch with final certainty, that a barren field, a valley of dry bones, bristling with thistles, spread before me. But she compelled me to stand by the parched remains of my faith, and asked with great urgency, 'Priest, where is thy perspective?' Yea, dear wedding guests, thus she spake, and did not cease to importune me. She came to me so full of longing that today I must give thanks to the bride, for I am the true convert. The power of her faith, which needed only to be redirected—and the shepherd finds it all too easy to drive the straying sheep into the nearest fold—her fundamentally inexhaustible power of belief taught me to doubt. And what is more, her hunger for a clear perspective, prescribed by faith, gave me the courage to clothe myself in the obverse of faith, in dowdy doubt, as my daily garment, for which reason the bride's father just now uttered the truth in a literary parable and thereby salved my doubting soul. Just as Father Fessler, in a novel alas unknown to me, *Count Petöfy*, embraces a Protestant maxim—the categorical 'Renounce!'—so, too, the bride Martha impelled me, by virtue of her will, to henceforth renounce my faith. Yea, I shall be without faith! And more: this 'Renounce!' commands me to serve henceforth only the cause of doubt, and to sow doubt wheresoever I may go. For, my dear guests, was there not too much faith and for too long in this land? Was not faith to be had too cheaply, like a whore? And is not the new faith, this time in the all-powerfulness of money, now cheap to acquire, yet too highly rated? And are we not again having a perspective prescribed for us that promises anyone who cleaves unto it in faith short-term profit and the phantom of blooming landscapes, where previously grayness reigned? I can give our dear wedded couple little to take with them on their way, but at least this much: Do not believe blindly. Leave God out of it, for Heaven's sake. God exists only within doubt. Renounce Him! Weary of all worship, He now lives by negation. He thirsts for nothingness. Faith would long since have killed God and cast him into a black pit, were it not for the doubter's cry, 'There is no God!' which to Him was a thorn and a goad, salve and manna...."

At this point in his confession the priest was dislodged from his pulpit. The bridegroom from Münster—who, as a developer, viewed both his immediate and his more distant fields of operations as one vast building lot by the grace of God—and the bride's pietistic brother—who, as a publisher, exported missionary writings to the far corners of the Third World, thereby realizing profits both in this world and the next—both exclaimed at the same moment, "That's enough, Monsignor! We hear you!" And: "This is Jesuitical smoke and mirrors!"

Yet even this combined opposition did not dislodge the confessing priest. He remained standing and continued to clutch the edge of the table menacingly, a rock amid the pounding waves. Inge Scherwinski, who at heart was still an unencumbered Catholic and was therefore seated, at the bride's request, at the right head of the table, crossed herself repeatedly and exclaimed, "What's going on here? Honestly, Martha, Frau Wuttke, what's going on here?" Bettina von Bunsen, on the other hand, was outraged at "these tasteless remarks" and "this Communist in priest's clothing." Grundmann's daughter laughed like a hyena, but knew exactly what to think of all the excitement at table: "Hysterical, it's absolutely hysterical!" The only comment that occurred to me was "Pretty strong stuff." And the bride whispered to me, "Exactly what I was afraid of. He won't spare us a thing. All that counts for him is facts. Oh, God, he has such a rough time with himself."

Heinz-Martin Grundmann and Friedel Wuttke tried to prevail upon the priest, who continued to stand his ground: "Come on, time to sit down, Monsignor!" and "You've embarrassed us enough!"—but in vain. Emmi Wuttke, noticing that the priest remained on his feet as if primed to continue, and did not loosen his double grip on the table, turned to her husband, "Say something, Wuttke, for heaven's sake, why don't you say something?"

But Fonty maintained a stubborn silence, no matter how many

ribs his wife poked. The priest had to be forced, physically forced, by the bridegroom and his brother-in-law, to take his seat; they pried his fingers from the table, not carefully but one finger after the other, with a cracking sound: two men, both bald on top, huddled around a third man, whose hair, like mine, was also somewhat skimpy. Now the priest was finally seated, and Martha Grundmann, née Wuttke, began to weep.

The sobbing wasn't audible. Instead a silent river of tears overflowed its banks. Since the bride, in deference to her past—two engagements that had been broken off, the first to her school's head, the second to Zwoidrak, a first lieutenant in the People's Army— had gone to the altar bareheaded and in a mouse-gray suit, rather than in white and with a flowing veil, we could have counted every tear. And the wedding party fell silent in view of such visibly cascading droplets, marveling as at a natural phenomenon.

Grundmann, now the epitome of the solicitous bridegroom, handed her his handkerchief. But she did not want to dry anything, just wanted to let it flow and flow. And so the image of the weeping bride won out, as we watched wordlessly; I even caught myself feeling moved.

But what kept the wedding party silent was Martha's ability to smile through her tears. Her moist good cheer, a little blurry around the edges, made a pretty sight. She emitted a glow. The bride was radiant. She, who had so seldom shown the world an amiable face, but had seemed stuck in a rut of grouchy seriousness, smiled with unpracticed candor at each of us around the table, offering us her young girl's smile, which had not been seen for many years. First she smiled tearfully at her wedded husband, Heinz-Martin, then at her father and mother and the witnesses, at her brother and her girlfriend, then at the previously amused but now disconcerted student, and finally at the steadfast priest, sitting there in an unmistakably stubborn and unreconciled pose; for Bruno Matull, in contrast to the bride with her beautifying tears, was not unlike that Augustinian monk who had once stood before the assembled Reichstag and uttered his soon-to-be proverbial words: *"Ich kann nicht anders"*—I can do no other.

Then the bride spoke. Still sitting, she said, "Listen, people, and that means you, too, Friedel. Don't worry about me. I'm crying because I'm so happy. That was exactly what I wanted to hear, not some pious mumbo-jumbo. I'm so glad this is what came out, and not the usual clichés. Thank you, Father Matull. Theoretically, I was pretty sure it wouldn't go smoothly, getting out of the Party and into the Church. I'd been too true a believer for too long. Heinz-Martin knows I thought ours was the better of the two republics. For a long time I even believed in our revolutionary goals. Ideological platform, discipline, Party loyalty—I never doubted the need for them. That's why I told Heinz-Martin right from the start, I mean when things began to get serious, after we started meeting in Bulgaria and in hotels in other places: If I do this conversion thing, it won't be because your family insists, but because I've got to learn to doubt, in a positive sense. See, I know all about the other way, this damned believing to the bitter end, which eventually did us in, I mean to the point where our republic wasn't much more than a detention camp. That kind of belief I know inside out. Nothing more to learn there. Exactly! It's been pounded into me, like the times tables I taught the kids year after year. But when it comes to doubting, I need tutoring; theoretically, I still have trouble with that.... And maybe that's why I'm so happy now. I've never heard anything as crystal clear as what Father Matull just said to us all a minute ago, not even when I was going to him for instruction. 'God exists only in doubt!' People, let me tell you, if we'd allowed that kind of thing in our socialist system here, I mean, a healthy dose of doubt, maybe it would've turned out all right. What do you say, Friedel? You're usually such a fiend for the truth. What do you say, Father? He put that well, didn't he, the Monsignor? All your pastors—Niemeyer, Pastor Petersen, and Superintendent Schwarzkoppen, even Pastor Lorenzen, who's supposed to be a socialist—couldn't have said it any better or more elegantly. Exactly! Not even Schleppegrell, who was no slouch—or am I wrong?"

Friedel sat there looking inscrutable. But Fonty must have been visualizing the pastors she had named. He extracted each one, ending with Schleppegrell the Dane, who, let it be noted, had rejected the love of three princesses, from his respective novel or novella, summoned other good shepherds to join them, ordered them to pass in formation, a more or less Protestant guard, reviewed the troops, so to speak, and said, "Whether assigned to a cathedral or a country church, all of them had preached to the point of exhaustion, although as good Lutherans they had both Testaments and the wisdom of Solomon on their side. Lorenzen was the only one who might have spoken as openly as your priest.... No, not even Lorenzen...My compliments, and again my compliments! It all came out frightfully right and straight from the shoulder, just the way I like it. I must say—if you'll permit the comparison—that the Reverend, who has nothing reverential about him, reminds me colossally of that forlorn cluster of illegal nuns who made sure my Grete Minde's beloved had a proper burial when Preacher Roggenstroh refused to give the corpse his blessing, hard-heartedly, as only a Christian can be hard-hearted.... All right, let's drink to Mete's tearful happiness, and then raise our glasses again to doubt. May it stand guard over us to the end. Doubt is always right!"

He raised his glass to his daughter, then to the clumsy priest, drained it to the dregs, and exclaimed, "Mine host! Let's whisk the dessert onto the table and cool off these heads, which are all heated up from disputing questions of faith; otherwise the wedding will become a slaughter festival, and only Knight Bluebeard will be left to serve us after all."

The assorted ice creams known as *La vie parisienne* did what Fonty had counted on. Everyone's blood pressure went down. Harsh words or even final reckonings were swallowed or postponed. The conversations around the table found other, less precipitous paths. Even the brother-in-law and the bridegroom cooled down. Grundmann finally had a chance to display his expertise in the construction field. He wanted his company to expand into Schwerin, "on a solid foundation" as a "beachhead." "The real estate market in Mecklenburg is completely underdeveloped. I hear you—since everything came crashing down, people have no idea what to do, but we'll help, we have to help. The field's been lying completely fallow since the planned economy went belly-up. Even so, we've managed to identify a few local resources, and they've helped us appraise the situation. I'm still convinced the final solution to the ownership question is going to call for unconventional methods; otherwise the whole deal's a nonstarter. Not an investor in sight. Stagnation. The old rut..."

Friedel Wuttke had to agree: "You can't imagine the trouble we're having, Heinz-Martin. My publishing company's main office used to be in Magdeburg, so we can certainly assert property rights there, but no one wants to honor them. For now we're still negotiating pretty patiently, but at some point this charade with the so-called people's property has to stop. In any case, we really must get started now on cutting staff if we want to stay competitive; the market for theological publications is tight. That's why we want to target Eastern Europe with our 'Missions for a New Millennium' series, picking up where the admirable Moravian Brotherhood left off...."

Now Frau von Bunsen, too, wanted to pursue the matter of private property. She mentioned several "completely run-down estates" belonging to her husband's family in the eastern portion of the "Altmark," spoke of "rightful ownership going back generations" in the area around Rathenow, which on no account should be left in the hands of "kolkhozes and such networks." "That much I owe my poor, departed husband!" She was about to bring up the von Wangenheim family's ancient holdings in Thuringia, but Fonty came up with a question out of the blue that distracted her from the twelve hundred hectares of expropriated Junker land.

The father of the bride wanted to know whether her late husband was related to Karl Josias von Bunsen, the Prussian ambassador active in London during the 1850s, "before Count Bernstorff": "Didn't receive his patent of nobility until '57. Considered a liberal, and a self-described Manteuffel-hater." Fonty was also interested in the von Wangenheim family: "Made a point of their adherence to the old faith. Assertively anti-Prussian. Old Frau von Wangenheim went so far as to assure me, with the most Catholic expression imaginable: "Prussian Germany holds out no promise of salvation...."

Frau von Bunsen denied that her husband had been directly related to liberals of any kind, and she showed not the slightest desire to chat with Fonty about the ramifications of the Prussian nobility; like Grundmann and Friedel Wuttke, she wanted to stay on the subject of "legitimate property claims." But now Inge Scherwinski, who had been giving the priest an earful about her problems with the "three boys"—"honest, they're a handful"—did something entirely unsuitable; she put an end to the various localized battles over property rights by addressing a question to the bride: "Hey, Mar, remember when the two of us were on harvest duty? Remember those huge aggie collectives! We sure had a grand time, didn't we? Young Pioneers, with our neckerchiefs...And later the blue shirts...Sometimes you'd play the piano for us....And when the two of us were in that a cappella group...Honest, I miss all that sometimes...."

And before anyone could stop her, Martha's childhood girlfriend was singing in her pleasant little voice, "The goal shines bright before us..." and the bride chimed in, "Lest you wander off life's path...."

Now the two of them sang louder, as if carried away by memories. Who would have suspected that Martha could produce such dark yet warm tones?

Next they struck up Eisler's Free German Youth solidarity song, "Forward, never forgetting wherein our strength resides..." and would no doubt have gone through all the verses if Friedel Wuttke had not interrupted them with a shout of "That's enough!"

But neither his sister nor her friend was prepared to stop on command. Now they launched into a song that went straight to the heart, so much so that I was tempted to join in: "The skies of Spain unfurl their stars," and I daresay I hummed along—"Our homeland is far, yet ready we are"—as Martha and Inge showed themselves melodiously determined to fight for freedom and to triumph. No, damn it all, I did sing along. Like them, I had had every verse hammered into me. I heard myself singing and was astonished that my memory had stored everything that had made us believers from childhood onward.

But when the two pals began to sing, like overgrown Free German Youth girls, "Build up, build up, build up, build up!" meanwhile gazing at each other and summoning all those present to help build the Workers' and Peasants' State, now in the process of being dismantled, the cooling effect of the assorted ice creams known as *La vie Parisienne* could no longer be detected.

Friedel Wuttke displayed anything but pietistic patience. This was no Moravian Brother but a tartar who leaped to his feet and pounded on the table until the very dishes clattered. He did not shout; he bellowed: "Shut up! All that's over and done with! 'A better future'—don't make me laugh. Never! I never want to hear that again. Those criminals. They wrecked you. I tell you, it's over, once and for all!"

But the friends' musical cascade was not to be stanched. "What are you talking about?" Martha challenged him between verses. "I heard you were a pretty fanatical Sixty-eighter in your time.... Quoting from Mao's Little Red Book and all.... Before you got religion, you were even peddling Che Guevara posters.... What songs were you singing in those days, I wonder."

And on they went with their musical buildup. Friedel's outburst died away. Martina Grundmann found his high-decibel anger excessive: "This is fun!" And she tried to sing along: "Build up, build up, build up..."

When Frau von Bunsen, her foster mother, and Grundmann, her father, reproved the student, "Please, Martina, don't," and "That's enough of that!" Emmi Wuttke begged both of them, and particularly her son-in-law, to show consideration: "That's how it was over here all those years. Almost everyone sang those songs, including our Friedel and his two brothers, when Martha was still little and before the three of them stayed on the other side. We meant well, all that stuff about building up, even though things didn't really get better. But the boys sang those songs and believed them, at least in the beginning. And you, Friedel, were real keen on it, before you... always real fanatical... We had to watch what we said around you.... But now all that's over and done with, now we're supposed to get our unification so things'll get better and better. And I sure hope they do! But don't go telling us we got no right to remember how it used to be, when we were on our own... right, Wuttke?"

The singing had stopped. Around the table we all felt like strangers to one another. Friedel was hunting for God knows what on the tablecloth, maybe the theses he had nailed to the door in '68. A gulf had opened up between the bride and bridegroom. Inge Scherwinski had lost her perky expression and looked exhausted. I found myself wishing I were back in the Archives. Martina was probably longing for Amsterdam, and Frau von Bunsen for Tuscany, which she had been raving about earlier. Only Father Matull came up with a few fitting words: "We don't know one another. We don't recognize one another."

And Fonty? He sat there erect, but as if absent. Only once, when the wedding party had still been enlivened by bickering, had he been heard to say: "A pity the professor's not here. Freundlich would find all this colossally piquant. Would doubtless have anecdotes of his own to share. For instance, what the emigrés sang in the old days in Mexico. . . ."

Then he fell silent again; yet one could surmise that Fonty was collecting himself for a speech. Emmi recognized the signs and was worried. But before he could lay out for us his eternally retrospective thoughts, dwelling on the unfortunate period when the Anti-Socialist Laws were passed, quoting from Bebel's speeches before the Reichstag, damning the Prussian system of domestic espionage, and conjuring up the Immortal's hopes for the working class—"The future lies with the fourth estate"—memory appeared in person; and at once we all saw each other in a different light.

Just as the coffee was being served, suddenly Hoftaller was there in Offenbach's Music Room. No, he stood in the doorway, smiling. He had forced a very yellow tie to keep company with his dove-gray suit. He brought no flowers, but was holding a small package tied with red satin ribbon, its elaborate bow suggestive of chocolates. To Fonty he explained why he had come, though not invited: "I'm part of the family."

So he, too, was served coffee. There were liqueurs and cognac, even pralines. Quite exhausted from the three courses and too much table talk, people hardly took notice of the stranger. Only

Friedel commented to his father, "Couldn't this embarrassment have been avoided? I know this fellow. He turned up a few times to see Teddy and me. Way back in the late seventies. And from Georg I heard . . . Don't know how you can let this kind of scum . . . "

Fonty said only, "We had to put up with his type," nothing more.

Hoftaller moved effortlessly from guest to guest and introduced himself with his pasted-on smile as a friend of the family. As he added his little package to the other presents and bouquets on a side table, he said with a slight bow in the direction of the bride, "Wouldn't have missed this opportunity to offer my congratulations; you're starting a new phase in your life, if such a thing's possible. Just a token of my regard . . ."

Martha's happiness was spent, her momentary beauty vanished. She looked drawn, with a grim expression on her face. She plucked briefly at the shiny satin ribbon but resisted the temptation to undo the red bow. She managed to squeeze out a "Thank you," then tugged at the ring finger of her right hand, as if the gleaming new band there were already irksome.

Hoftaller mingled with the guests again, entering into their various conversations, even exchanging a few words with Friedel Wuttke, who had just begun to proselytize the uncouth priest. At one point Fonty took me aside, and whispered, "You people can write what you like, but don't go turning Grundmann into a caricature on me. We mustn't forget that he went all the way to the Black Sea to reel in my Mete. . . ." Thus admonished, I responded with the bridegroom's pet expression, "I hear you!"

Later I was entertained by the student Martina. As she sipped a glass of Amaretto, she gave an amusing account of the special freedoms for which Amsterdam was famous.

We archivists wracked our brains. Hoftaller's rectangular package inspired several hypotheses. One of us guessed it was the Schott, the Catholic missal that had been one of the presents on my gift table at First Communion. Someone else thought Hoftaller might have shown the bad taste to buy the bride a copy of *Troika*, by a former member of the Stasi high command who was now marketing his "reminiscences." One of our colleagues remarked, her voice frosty, "Maybe he bought her a pair of red socks." I stuck to my original suspicion: "Oh, come on, the package was flat. It was just a box of really expensive but harmless pralines." Eventually Fonty set us all straight with almost excessive good cheer during one of his visits to the Archives.

This was his account: Toward the end of the wedding reception, Fonty had had an urgent need to relieve himself. Hoftaller had been right on his heels, apparently feeling the same urge. As they were urinating, which of course takes a while with old men, a conversation got underway, initiated by Hoftaller the moment they both took up their relieving positions; we must picture him standing at the next urinal. As we knew, Fonty's day-and-night-shadow always came right to the point, and this time it pertained to his sinister package: "Took the liberty of presenting the newly wedded Frau Grundmann with the last traces of her Party membership, I mean her closed cadre file, with a small addendum, by the way, relating to her long engagement. A bunch of whispered conversations in hotel rooms... some of it pretty embarrassing... that kind of thing shouldn't fall into the wrong hands."

Fonty claims to have replied, "Frightfully considerate of you. Will be a mixed pleasure to Mete; not the most edifying reading."

Hoftaller, whose desire to follow Fonty to the men's room had probably not been motivated solely by a full bladder, said soothingly, "Only the usual. You know your daughter. Has a thing for theory, sometimes veering to the left, sometimes to the right. Still, nothing that bad, really. A few revisionist deviations. But always practiced self-criticism afterward. She would never let anything be said against her former fiancé, Comrade Zwoidrak. And even in hotel beds she declared that socialism was theoretically a good thing. By the way, to make the file a bit less sober, I tracked down a bookbinder. Looks quite nice now, leather spine and marbled endpapers."

Fonty claims to have laughed: "Colossally sensitive of you! Mete will think it's a book of poetry. When she sees the contents, which are dry as dust, she'll have a choking fit. Ye gads! Must be the Chablis that gives your kidneys such a workout!"

Now standing at the sink, Hoftaller apparently sighed, "You're still making fun of me, Fonty. Wouldn't you love to receive a gift with similar contents? I'm afraid the bookbinder will be billing me for a number of such volumes. Lots of information was gathered, starting with the Herwegh Society, not to mention Dresden, and then the London years...."

"Save your money!" Fonty is supposed to have told him over the running water. But while drying his hands he did ask for the bookbinder's address: "I've been wanting to get my Marwitz bound for a long time, also my *Effi Briest* first edition, which Friedel brought out in '95...in bad shape, the spines...I'd like to do the diaries, too, especially the London notebooks.... Come along now, Tallhover! Stop dawdling. The guests are waiting for us."

At the end of the reception, it almost came to a full-fledged confrontation. Heinz-Martin Grundmann, who had downed a number of cognacs, raised his voice and called for the check: "All together, and make it snappy!" He waved his credit card and cornered the proprietor: "Put it all on one, and I want it dated and stamped!"

When the father of the bride protested, "This is my treat!" the bridegroom acted hurt: "Look here, Father-in-law, what's this supposed to mean? I understand you'd like to...but for me this is pocket change, so to speak...."

"The father of the bride pays!"

"Let's not make a big deal of this!"

"A deal is a deal!"

"But in tough times like these, the old rules shouldn't..."

"Times are always hard, but my Mete gets married only once...."

"Now I'm insulted. Three measly courses. It's not as though I can't afford..."

Fonty put an end to this haggling over principles, speaking in a voice that was firm though not raised: "It's a matter of honor. Or is my son-in-law intent on a duel with me?"

He beckoned to the proprietor, who had been listening with a faint smile, and the check was his. Soon mollified, he put his arm around the stocky developer and explained to him, somewhat superciliously, that after a rather long illness he had again picked up his pencil and that now his, as well as the Immortal's, childhood and youth filled thirty pages: "With the help of my Emilie, of course, who has always produced fair copy for me. It brought a respectable fee. I'm somewhat flush again. Will be even more so if a lecture can be scheduled. Besides, Friedel will soon be issuing a small volume that could accommodate a slightly shortened version of the lecture, though of course his list focuses more on tracts. True, the whole thing is more chatty in tone than written for print, yet this kind of thing is bound to find readers. Nothing earth-shaking, only what remains to us: memories, a few scars, smells, colorful images. Then Fox's Movietone News again. And tears. Mother's chastising hand, Father holding forth at table. Later some discussion of raising pigs and rabbits. And again and again the sea, the Schinkel church, the barns outside the Rheinsberg Gate on fire. The monument, the seated bronze. It all starts in Neuruppin, by the way."

BOOK 3

16

To Stralsund and Beyond

His summer holidays, trips to the spa, moderately priced hideaways, sometimes beneath his station, but always with manuscript in his luggage—novellas repeatedly laid aside, essays commissioned by Rodenberg—and sets of galley proofs. We find complaints about musty hotel rooms, other guests banging about at all hours, yapping dogs, the weather. From any location he addresses letters to publishers, editors, and friends like Hertz, Stephany, and Friedlaender, and, when he travels alone, to his wife and daughter: "I am feeling well here, as always (knock on wood) when I turn my back on Berlin...."

Shortly before July '82, when the novella *Schach von Wuthenow*, drafted soon after the first novel went to press, began to appear serially in the *Vossische Zeitung*, he reports, from Thale in the Harz Mountains, to his son Theodor, whom he was forever trying to knock off his high horse, especially on the political field: "The Alsatians belonged to France for two hundred years, & if they now say, 'Erwin von Steinbach be damned, we prefer the French to the Germans,' there is not a great deal one can say in reply...."

In August 1883, on the island of Norderney, the sixty-three-year-old finished *Count Petöfy*, his second novel of infidelity, following *L'Adultera*. From there he writes to Emilie, "You complain about my long-windedness. Yet this long-windedness I indulge is inseparable from my literary virtues. I treat small matters with as much love as great ones...."

He had solutions to others' ailments—"If one is suffering from the gout, Berlin is better than Krummhübel"—but he himself felt drawn time and again, and often "in a state of nervous collapse," to the Riesengebirge.

From there—where he had done preliminary work on a manuscript entitled *Quitt,* based on facts his faithful correspondent Friedlaender had provided, a Silesian tale about a forester and a poacher—he writes in early June '85 to Emilie, who has stayed behind in Berlin: "Have sketched out the new novella, insofar as one can sketch out a thing which still lacks all sorts of material. This is half true of the first half, for it takes place in this region, & wholly true of the second, which takes place among the Mennonites in America. . . ."

It should be noted that the magistrate Dr. Georg Friedlaender lived in Schmiedeberg, near Krummhübel; they saw each other often. "With a Silberstein one can discuss questions thoroughly, with Prince Reuss not at all. So long live Silberstein! Or Friedlaender. . ."

When annoyances connected with his work catch up with him on holiday, in the form of galley proofs—"To read one's own words over & over again is not only taxing, it is mind-numbing"—his disgruntled mood finds an outlet in a letter written on 18 July '87 to Friedrich Stephany, who wants to serialize *Delusions, Confusions,* and must now endure the author's commentary on the wretched proofs sent by the *Vossische Zeitung:* "If getting it right creates twice as much work for them, well, so be it!"

In 1891, the year before his nervous collapse, he spends August in Wyk on the North Sea island of Föhr. "I have yet to encounter one person with whom I might want to exchange five words . . . ," he complains to his daughter Martha. Unfortunately the Archives do not possess her letters to her father; only from phrases of hers that he quotes, such as ". . . the expression 'multifaceted fakery' is felicitous," do we know that Mete adapted her epistolary style to his. When Fonty said of Martha Wuttke, "She is better in writing than out loud," we suspected a lost quotation.

Letters from Bad Kissingen, and again and again from Carlsbad. From there, where he was taking the waters for the last time with his wife and daughter—that was in early September '98—he replies to his son Friedel, who has been his father's publisher since *Stine* and *Frau Jenny Treibel:* "I've read through, or, rather, skimmed, the reviews you sent. Parts of Otto Leixner's in the *Tägliche Rundschau* were side-splitting. In one place he writes, 'He (T. F.) had to wait five years for his little bride.' That would indicate that Leixner is a Saxon. . . . "

Back in Berlin, Mete finally becomes engaged to the architect Dr. Fritsch. The critic Paul Schlenther, well disposed for years, reports: "To celebrate the engagement of his daughter, who greatly resembled him in spirit, a small, elegant meal had been prepared. Only nine guests. The old man, in his splendid, endearing elderly beauty, formed the heart and soul of the conversation. . . ." Four days later the old man, or, as we usually call him, the Immortal, was dead.

Following Martha's marriage to the developer Heinz-Martin Grundmann and the subsequent banquet, for which, since Professor Freundlich and his wife had declined, only ten people gathered, eleven counting Hoftaller, the newlyweds set out immediately, complying with the dictum uttered by the father of the bride: "However short, a honeymoon there must be."

They drove in Grundmann's BMW through Schwerin, where they stopped briefly to inspect their future lakeview home, then on to Lübeck and Puttgarden on Fehmarn. From there they took the ferry to Rødby, and two hours later they were in Copenhagen, for whose sights three days would have to suffice. They then stopped, as prearranged, at the Hotel Praestekilde in Keldby, on the island of Møn.

The bride's parents likewise managed to escape from the still-steamy city. The part-time file courier in the Ministries Building was eligible for convalescent leave at full pay; and his wife was to accompany him. And since their son Friedel stopped in only briefly to see them on Kollwitzstrasse and was in a tearing hurry to return to Wuppertal, there was no need to postpone their departure.

They did not manage to clear the air, much less achieve a reconciliation. They sat in the Poggenpuhl parlor, facing each other stiffly. Each vulnerable in his or her own way. Carefully weighed words. The parents received no invitation, for instance, to visit a spa in the Sauerland. Queries about Teddy and his wife, as well as about her children from her first marriage, hardly received a reply. Friedel dodged any familial feelers. Only on the publishing business did he wax talkative: Now that new markets were opening up, his publishing program had to assume a global orientation. A history of the Mennonites and their worldwide missionary activity was being compiled. Now, after the rout of dialectical materialism, humanity was thirsting for spiritual meaning. "Our hour has struck!" he exclaimed.

When the son departed, leaving only his catalogue behind, Theo Wuttke remarked to his wife, "We've lost him, too, I would say. When all is said and done, a person is on the same footing with his children as with any other people. You can knock yourself out trying to rear them properly. Well, perhaps he'll pull himself together and publish his old man's lectures, delivered in difficult times. But when I hear my fine son holding forth so self-righteously, I'm not sure. What was all that about an illegitimate state? Within this world of want, we lived in a comfy dictatorship. Believe me, Emilie, over there, whether in Wuppertal or in Bonn, they cook with water just like us."

Emmi wept for half an hour, then she started packing. We suspect she preferred their chosen destination to all the other spas Fonty must have considered. The little town of Krummhübel in the Riesengebirge, known as Karpacz since the end of the war, when it had gone to Poland, and Carlsbad, now Karlovy Vary, seemed to merit serious consideration; these days, with western money, you would be treated like a king there. Emmi was not the only one who rejected Thale in the Harz Mountains. Bad Kissingen, Norderney, and Wyk on the island of Föhr had to be excluded for budgetary reasons. But Theo and Emmi Wuttke agreed on one thing: sea air should be a priority. No matter how much things had been transformed in the course of the changeover, the Baltic was still within reach; besides, Fonty's rather long illness and the exhausting preparations for the wedding argued for spending time along the coast.

Sounding as forceful as he still could, Hoftaller, who was determined to be of help, expressed the opinion that Fonty's many years of service as an itinerant lecturer for the Cultural Union certainly entitled him to "an exquisite vacation spot." He offered to use his connections. He still had contacts, he said. And by way of proof he promptly laid a letter on the table. "Took the liberty—not that I want to be pushy—of making some preliminary arrangements. I'm assuming you, too, dear Frau Wuttke, will be satisfied with this Capri on the Baltic."

The message came from the island of Hiddensee, and announced that behind Villa Sallow Thorn, adjacent to this house once occupied by the dramatist Gerhart Hauptmann, a guest room with a hot plate and a comfortable sitting area was free, directly behind the beeches. Herr Wuttke, as the letter writer well remembered, had already spent several nights there, the last time being after he had surprised a large audience with tantalizing references to the practices of the Prussian censor. It would be a pleasure to have him back. The off-season had its particular charms, as everyone who loved the island was well aware.

Without mentioning Hoftaller's discreet services as intermediary, the curator of the much frequented memorial wrote, "The works of this great writer will survive this period of changeover, too. No matter how altered circumstances are, no matter how astonished we are to see who washes up on our shores, panting to buy everything in sight, we remain committed to the collective creation of culture. You are most welcome on our island!"

The Hauptmann house was an address with which we were familiar. The Archives had often received queries from there. It was not uncommon for our staff members to combine longer or shorter holidays on the island with research. One's thoughts could take wing there. On this dream of an island, at least the horizon seemed to open up. A nearby destination with a distant perspective. And as we usually did, Theo and Emmi Wuttke took the train to Stralsund and continued the journey from there by boat.

From Berlin-Lichtenberg by way of Pasewalk. The Reich Railroad was not yet called the Federal Railroad. Because unequipped for high-speed operations, this relic going back to presocialist days would not be taken over for a long while; and since as a Cultural Union lecturer Fonty had ridden the rails for many years, he could be considered part of the Reich Railroad—that was how backward he looked, how slow and worn he seemed to himself: "I'm ill-suited for rapid connections, whether in railroad stations or in politics."

Habitually thrifty, the Wuttkes traveled second-class. The train was late arriving from Leipzig. All the way to Stralsund they had a compartment to themselves. We would have liked to join them, but indirectly we were present, because Emmi later re-created the whole rail journey for us: "The landscape was pretty boring, always the same. Still, it was good to get out finally. The heat in town, more and more cars, and that ozone stuff they're always talking about. Besides, the wedding took a lot out of Wuttke, and me, too. All the fuss, and then our Friedel didn't have one kind word when he came by afterwards. Just looked down his nose at us the whole time. Started in at the wedding. Stuck-up, really stuck-up, that's what they all are. At the end there, they almost got into a fight over the check. But like Martha says, she says, Father wouldn't let anyone take that away from him. Where do they get off thinking they can treat us like beggars? And that Grundmann! My God, the way he talks! Like everything had to be explained to us three times. But friendly, you've got to hand him that. Calls me 'madam' and 'my dear Emmi.' Can talk about anything, even knows stuff he can't possibly know about. Why certain things were bad and others not so bad, and how it really was in the Cultural Union, I mean, sometimes world-class, like Martha always said, and why my Wuttke worked so hard for them and earned a lot of respect, so they even honored him a couple times with the silver badge. But this Grundmann always says 'I hear you,' even when he doesn't hear anything you've said, and what he really wants to hear is that we suffered day and night and felt like we were in one of those concentration camps. And his daughter—she's something—jabbers, too, about everything under the sun. Tells my Wuttke, who never got authorized to go anywhere in the West, about all the places she's been to—you guessed it, Paris, Rome, and oodles of Greek islands. And London a couple times, once all the way up north to Scotland. And just imagine: that girl's even been to Bali. Bali! At first my Wuttke was speechless, but then he recited his poem, you know, the one about the Balinese women, every last verse. Later, when they were all gone, including that woman with the *von*, he says, 'They're perfectly nice, those people from the West, but they're colossally wearing to be around.' And on the train both of us were laughing 'cause my Wuttke was saying 'madam' to me and a couple of other funny things that Bunsen woman came out with, like 'Quite decent, the wine here...' or 'This Frau Scherwinski is just adorable. So natural. We haven't had types like her in the West for ages....' Anyway, we had a good time. It was a real nice wedding! Even if Grundmann drove me up a wall with his ten major building sites and his cracks about our prefab buildings, like they didn't have crummy buildings over there, too. We could see them from over here: Britz, Buckow, and all over the place. And will you look at what they're doing to Potsdamer Strasse! No, no, I'm telling you! Course my Wuttke said our Martha'd whip her Grundmann into shape, now that she's a Catholic and has a right to speak up, but he was worried all the same: 'The grand plans they have for Schwerin, all these real estate deals and whatever else he has in mind—an industrial park and recreational park, all in an economic-ecological symbiosis: I don't like the sound of it one bit. All balderdash! Reminds me colossally of the year '71, when the horns the Prussians were blowing were gilded with melted-down French gold ducats. The Founders' Era, they called it. Grandiose façades, and behind them tenements. Scandals and bankruptcies. You can read all about it in the *Vossische*: the crash of '73. The city one vast construction site. And everywhere Grundmanns, even if they were called Treibel in those days, had the commercial councillor title, and dealt in Berlin blue....' You know my Wuttke when he's talking about his one-and-only. Says he had a word for every occasion. And sometimes it really does fit. Being from the Archives, you must've noticed how he worked his old Petöfy into that speech of his at dinner. 'Renounce!' And at a wedding, of all places! But on the train he kept going on about the Treibels, all the way to Pasewalk. He really made me laugh, acting out Berliners and Hamburgers trying to outdo each other: 'Which is more beautiful, the Alster at Uhlenhorst or the Spree at Treptow?' And he quoted that puffed-up Frau Treibel when she sighs, 'That dreadful Vogelsang man weighed on me like a nightmare....' That's his forte. And always so colorful, like he'd scribbled it down himself in pencil just yesterday and put it there for me to type. It sure made me laugh. The only thing that didn't sit right was that he kept comparing that Corinna Schmidt from the novel—she's a spunky young thing, y'know—with our Martha. 'Cause that just makes everything even worse. It's always Corinna this, Mete that. The thing is, they say this Mete, the apple of his one-and-only's eye, committed suicide in the end, threw herself off the balcony, the poor thing, 'cause her husband was much older and went and died on her, and she already had problems with her nerves, like our Martha.... Anyway, I say to him, I say, 'What's going to happen now, Wuttke?' Actually I was thinking of something else, I mean the unification, which they were all talking about and which that Krause bargained for us. But he thought I was asking about the marriage to Grundmann. 'What do you expect will happen?' he said. 'It'll drag on like every marriage, sometimes better, sometimes worse. In my speech, which I suppose didn't sit quite right, I'd meant to refer to the adultery lurking around every corner. Wanted to begin with *L'Adultera* and spin the thread from stout-hearted Melanie to ailing Cécile and on to poor Effi, but then I took your feelings into consideration, dear Emilie, and by citing that Protestant "Renounce!" sought to dispel any wishes my freshly converted daughter may have had for Catholic bliss. But to come back to your question, what do you expect will happen? Marital crises, marital quarrels, marital infidelity! An evergreen topic. I'll write something in that vein to our Mete tomorrow. I'll advise her to take to heart the profession of faith made by her priest, who wasn't at all bad, and embrace doubt. I stand by what I said: Doubt is always right!' And then my Wuttke realized I'd meant something else entirely. 'What's going to happen now? If you mean the one-fatherland-indivisible, I've no idea. As soon as we're back, you should ask my trusty old companion; he always knew in advance what would go awry, every time. As they say nowadays, he knows the score and is colossally up-to-date. I've guessed wrong far too often, but Hoftaller has a nose for these things. Even when he was still Tallhover, when the sealed train with Lenin crossed Germany...' I just let him talk, and didn't say anything. I kept looking out the window and was pretty bored. All ancient history. No, not only the landscape outside, also those old stories. When we stopped in Pasewalk, I reminded him he could've been a district secretary or something there. You should've heard my Wuttke then: 'Pasewalk—never! This was where that Austrian corporal lay in the military hospital and decided to take up politics. This is where it all began, and it's still far from over. Not even my trusty old companion could talk me into it. Pasewalk? Never, I said. Didn't even try to pressure me after that; he came around....' That made me laugh: 'No, sir, Wuttke, that one doesn't ever come round. Just wait, you can bet he's got his fingers in every pie again.' And that he showed up at Martha's wedding, too, that was no accident. There he is suddenly, in coat and tie, with a package all tied in fancy ribbon, and says, 'For you, comrade bride,' and grins that grin of his, like he knows more about you than you know yourself. Gave me the shivers the way he was suddenly standing by Friedel and blathering away at him like nothing bad ever happened... Like he hadn't spied on our boys, and on Martha, too, when she and her Grundmann had their secret...Anyway, when we got to Stralsund, it was still nice out, but not as hot as Berlin, 'cause up there they have a breeze off the water. You could take a good, deep breath...."

By a rough estimate, more than seven thousand letters were collected, some of which were lost again; for close to one thousand documents in his hand must be counted among the losses the last war brought us.

Occasionally some original manuscript or other turns up and fetches a handsome price at auction, but we are seldom in a position to bid. Fortunately, several journals were found in a safe—a Jewish one, of course—among them the London notebook, which is more than just a writer's jottings. Other things are irretrievable, such as the correspondence with Wolfsohn and the early letters to the fiancée; soon after Emilie's death, the family burned them all, in compliance with her wishes.

The problem is compounded by the stinginess of the Prussian cultural-heritage agencies; back in '35, when the heirs felt they had to auction off part of the literary estate, real treasures—for instance, rough drafts—were allowed to pass into private hands and out of sight. This was a particularly bitter loss to scholars, for many of the letters, even those that read like spontaneous outpourings and are rich in inspirations of the moment, were painstakingly crafted, down to the most minute fanciful detail, including those letters that seem to be dictated by political ire—for instance, the emotional eruption committed to paper on 6 May 1895, the birthday of that crown prince who, praise God, would never become kaiser: "My hatred for everything that stands in the way of the new era is ever growing, & the possibility, nay, the likelihood, that the victory of the new must be preceded by a terrible slaughter cannot deter me from wishing for this victory of the new...." Elsewhere he offers a commentary on this sentiment: "I've often talked my way to the brink of high treason...."

One of the biographers, Hans-Heinrich Reuter, who for decades maintained a quite peculiar connection with our Archives, made a point of highlighting these and similar passages from letters, extrapolating from their radical posture the existence of the first German workers' and peasants' state as a historically logical development, yet he did so without being more obvious about it than necessary; his primary concern was probably securing the cultural heritage. Like the Cultural Union's itinerant lecturer Wuttke, who never ended a lecture without invoking the national "cultural achievements," Reuter, who, by the way, carried on a friendly correspondence with Fonty, fashioned a bridge back into the nineteenth century, a bridge over which both of them could parade progress and humanism, and thus the "victory of the new," often employing slyly selected passages from the letters to carry the message.

And it was Reuter who formulated the following bold assertion about our epistolographer: "Even if we had nothing but his letters, he would still be one of the great figures in German literature." He places him above Storm, Keller, and Hebbel, and speaks of "letters of European stature" that merit comparison with those of Voltaire and Diderot, of Lessing, Swift, and Scott.

We archivists are happy to concur; with Reuter, we would point to the chatty style that he developed into a high art form—for instance, in the letter written to his wife on 12 May 1884 from Hankel's Depot, where he was working in strict seclusion. He comments in passing on the quality of his ink, "which keeps clotting in little gobs": "... the things we come to be dependent upon! My entire pleasure in writing has evaporated. My room here is charming, & the view of the front garden, with the fast-moving river & the heath beyond, is invigorating. The air is richer in ozone than necessary & makes me feverish; a strong breeze is blowing from the east, yet I feel it has a salutary effect on my nerves. If it weren't for the ink! If this continues, all the 'perfumes of Arabia' will not be able to heal me. I also have dreadful premonitions of the night here—it all looks rather mouse-ridden...."

And with similar seeming spontaneity he chats about political annoyances—as in a letter to Mete, where he conveys by means of an anecdote the clash between the kaiser and Bismarck, whom he sees as "The Great Trickster," remarking in conclusion, "He bears a striking similarity to Schiller's Wallenstein (the historical one was different): genius, savior of his country, & sentimental traitor. Always me, me, me, & then, when things come crashing down, bitter complaints about ingratitude, North German weepiness...."

Fonty echoed this judgment in a letter addressed to Martha Grundmann, née Wuttke; for almost as soon as he arrived on Hiddensee he felt the irresistible lure of pen and paper, while Emmi set about unpacking their suitcases; besides, a newspaper someone had left lying about aroused his political annoyance: "As you know, I seldom cock my ear in the direction of Bonn, but when the current chancellor of the Germans succumbs to hubris in regard to unification and, in his capacity as ruling mass, allows himself be placed alongside Bismarck, the comparison is certainly apt, insofar as I would characterize both of them as colossal tricksters...."

In this same letter to his daughter, whom he addresses as "my Mete," he remarks, "The beeches in front of our lodgings are as yet unharmed, and in other respects, too, one sees no trace on this island of the coming unification, unless one takes the cigarette advertisement by the dock in Kloster—"Go West!"—as a general signpost; as indeed it is for this letter, the fruit of my excellent spirits, which I shall dispatch, as agreed upon, to Stege on Møn, so that you shall find it upon your arrival, poste restante.

"In the meantime you will have 'done' Copenhagen, the Glyptothek, Thorwaldsen's magnificent cold marbles, and, by way of contrast, the lively Tivoli Gardens. Grundmann is no doubt interested mostly in the buildings. You, however, I can see following the trail of Count Holk, as charming as he was unsteady, and of the fiery-tongued Ebba Rosenberg, who, of course, was not a Rosenberg-Gruszczynski but a granddaughter of the Swedish royal court Jew Meyer-Rosenberg, and endowed with all the advantages and disadvantages of Jewishness, for which reason poor Holk was no match for her, the more so since he was distracted by the lascivious carryings-on of Brigitte, the captain's daughter who happened to be on close terms with the secret police. At any rate, I am burning to hear from you whether Copenhagen is still a den of iniquity and the Danes are as jolly as of old. (*Irretrievable*, by the bye, appeared in Danish under the title *Grevinde Holk*.)

"Mama and I reached Stralsund—or what remains of that once beautiful city, which not even Wallenstein could bring to its knees—at the leisurely old pace of the Reich Railroad, which gave us plenty of time to talk over your wedding and all the guests, but barely enough to catch the boat, *The Isle of Hiddensee*. In my day, one took the smoke-belching steamer *Swanti*. Because we were in a hurry, we saw little of the city on Strela Sound, which despite a few gold teeth smiled at us with noticeable gaps. For at 2:30 P.M. on the dot we pushed off, leaving behind the few warehouses still standing. Soon we were approaching Altefähr, on the island of Rügen.

"Thanks to the splendid weather, with hardly any waves to speak of, Mama enjoyed the crossing, which took us past green and red buoys and provided a view of the Gellen waterway. The first bow nets greeted us, with black, and later black and yellow, pennants. Cormorants were perched atop the fishing traps. After a crossing of barely two hours, we docked in Neuendorf and soon after that pushed on to Vitte, following the navigable channel marked by buoys. Between Vitte and Kloster, I pointed out to Mama Lietzen Castle, nestled among the wooded hills. It owes its fame less to the sculptor Oskar Kruse than to Käthe Kruse, who gave birth to the dolls that bear her name. And again and again cormorants, flying in ever-changing formations against the background of the long, narrow island, a delightful sight. Mama, who is actually opposed to sea journeys and fears storms even when the weather is fair, was filled with childlike pleasure. 'Look! look!' she cried, and was content to see nothing else.

"Once we arrived in Kloster, waiting on the dock was not a grandson of old Gau, whom they called 'Schipperöbing,' if you recall your visit to the island with Zwoidrak, but a taciturn fisherman's son who hauled our suitcases in a wooden cart to the old Hauptmann villa, a high-bourgeois structure that I find excessively massive. Our quarters were in the guesthouse on the leeward side, far enough removed from the curiosity of tourists. By the way, it is the same double room in which I survived a rainy weekend in the early seventies, after my lecture on 'Literature and Censorship in Prussia Before and After the Repeal of the Anti-Socialist Laws' had garnered only nervous applause, all the more so since I had allowed myself to smuggle in a comparison between Hauptmann's *Weavers* and Müller's *Resettler*. During the ensuing discussion with the audience, which included some people from prominent positions on the island, plenty of red flags went up, but no shots were fired.

"The two rooms have the same simple furniture as before, with a cooking niche where Mama can prepare her bladder tea, blue-and-white-checked curtains, and a leather armchair which could tell many a tale of visitors to the island, including some illustrious ones, who nowadays would certainly be reluctant to be reminded of the immortality certificates they once issued for a socialist system already in precarious health. It's there for all to see in the guest book. Various amusingly rhymed expressions of devotion. Paging backward, I found myself as well, my last entry being May '71: 'While Hauptmann gave the kaiser a thwack, our Müller's a tough nut to crack.' Reading this little verse, I should now like to add that in both cases what I had in mind was the young radicals, namely, the Hauptmann of *The Weavers* and the Müller of *The Scab*. In the later works of both men, pomposity often gained the upper hand; much theatrical hue and cry and little wool.

"At any rate, I felt at home as soon as the suitcases were unpacked. Mama, however, found the rooms too cramped, and claimed the place smelled mouse-ridden. As you know, she often blows things out of proportion and is prone to expect the worst, a tendency that irritates me because I do not subscribe to the pessimistic. Unlike her, I do not seek out pretexts for being sad, but strive, rather, to respect the proportions and percentages that life itself confers on its phenomena, including the married state. Therefore I hope that your 'I do' to Grundmann at St. Hedwig's expressed neither rejoicing to high heaven nor the depths of despair, to paraphrase Goethe. Mama and I learned rather late the old adage about making a virtue of necessity—after life handed us some depressing lessons. A difficult art: to look the other way now and then and yet remain honest, which is what we of course also expect of your Grundmann—when he feels the urge come over him to speculate with Mecklenburg's real estate in lordly developer-fashion and to slice himself the juiciest cuts, to use the current expression. As I happened to pick up at the wedding dinner, he has no doubt cast an acquisitive eye on Schwerin's Schelfstadt district; he was speaking of various 'extremely interesting projects.'

"Ah, well. One tries to dispense fatherly wisdom, and in the end it, too, proves a weak brew. I merely want to warn against too much gluttony!

"Here, by the bye, the people are heartwarmingly friendly, also toward Mama. The museum director remembers my efforts on behalf of the cultural heritage. She seems to be the kind of person who knows how to look out for herself. Whether in today's climate one can preserve one's integrity remains uncertain.

"The island has few visitors. Some Westerners, who peer over the fences, licking their chops. One can still find old ladies with bobbed hair and rakish berets who have been semipermanent residents since their salad days. And of course there is no shortage of Saxons, as determined as ever to prove to the whole world how indestructible they are.

"Fortunately for me, Professor Freundlich and his wife, who alas could not come to your wedding, have taken up residence in Vitte. I know you do not like him much, and Mama even less. I, however, have always profited from his world-encompassing wit. These émigrés—Freundlich *père* took the family to Mexico in his day—have managed to preserve a broad horizon. And when the Freundlichs, first the father, later the son, still wielded influence in the Cultural Union, my efforts on behalf of the cultural heritage always found support. Eventually both of them ran afoul of the Party. But as you know, that happened to everyone who had any self-respect. It killed old Freundlich. Freundlich *fils*, who is now heading for sixty himself, greeted the loss of his Party membership with noble sarcasm and did not take it amiss when I—coward that I am—stayed on in the Cultural Union; indeed, he rather approved of it. He advised me, 'Keep it up, Wuttke; things can't get any worse.' And he was pleased at my playful comparison of him with Friedlaender, which, drawing on our correspondence, I worked up into a lecture—"Repeated Friendships with Jurists"—when the Pirckheimer Society invited me to speak in Jena in honor of his fiftieth birthday. The fact that Friedlaender ran afoul of the army merely because he was a Jew is of a piece with Freundlich's problems with the Party; but at present it is professors from the West—who have taken it upon themselves to evaluate his merits as a scholar—who are causing him concern. They want to be rid of him; they've always wanted to be rid of him.

"Now Mama and I are about to sally forth on our first stroll on the island. Of course our first stop will be the cemetery, where lie buried not only Schlucks and Gaus but also the local author. Here, with a boulder marking the grave, in compliance with his wishes, they laid him to rest, 'Before Sunrise'. . ."

We must concur with the biographer Reuter when he enumerates the ways in which the letter writer and theater critic helped the young playwright Hauptmann. As Reuter points out, he had an ear second to none for this new style, but he also recognized the danger that Hauptmann might slither into mystical sentimentality or tedious swashbuckling, as indeed happened in the play *Florian Geyer*, set among medieval knights. Thus when Fonty visited Hauptmann's grave, called the boulder "colossal but fitting," noted with pleasure the ivy covering the burial mound, found fault with several withered wreaths, noted a firethorn and clipped yews on the left, a hawthorn on the right, and praised as "a proud assertion of immortality" the simple cuneiform inscription on the stone, which gave the name but omitted the dates, as if superfluous, we may presume that—entirely in Reuter's spirit—he would have liked to have on hand a wreath of dried immortelles; but this form of cemetery decoration had not been available commercially for a long time, for as things stand in the world, many plants, among them immortelles, are endangered, as indeed the very concept of immortality has become dubious.

Emmi and he walked along the rows of graves in the gently rolling cemetery, located at the foot of the gradual hills. Past yew hedges. Only a few trees, bent by the wind. Local residents buried next to summer people. Emmi remarked on the many Gottschalks, Gaus, Schlucks, Witts, Schliekers, and Striesows. He pointed to a slender stele, tapered to a point, and knew that the Sabine Hirschberg whose name was engraved closest to the top and whose dates covered only the brief span between 1921 and 1943, had belonged to the "White Rose" student resistance group and had taken her own life upon learning she was about to be arrested.

We see the Wuttkes standing hand in hand in front of various graves. Both enjoyed walking in cemeteries. Here, as they moved from stone to stone, many anecdotes occurred to him, whether about the old island pastor Gustavs, or about Solting, thus nicknamed because his two cows grazed in the salt marshes. When Emmi admired the Felsenstein family grave, close to the church, his response was that the "vast expense," but particularly the elaborate wrought-iron fence, resembled the stage set for a rather mediocre drama. "All due respect to the great director!" Fonty exclaimed. "But here he's directed himself colossally off the mark!" Then he looked around, as if in search of an unclaimed plot.

17

Island Visitors

The compleat rambler. We see Fonty making his way from Kloster to Vitte along the flagstone path, passing brier roses and ripening sallow thorn, now under the few, wind-buffeted firs that face the sea. Like many visitors to the island, who are driven by urban restlessness, we, too, are fairly knowledgeable about the place and can find our way even on the heath, but he knows every plant, and from his last visit still remembers the white thorn, the willows, and the elderberry bushes, which were luxuriant then but now look scrubby, with barely any fruit clusters.

He strides along with his stick, wearing a Bulgarian boater and a straw-yellow linen jacket with light-colored trousers, both slightly rumpled. His laced boots, in which he usually walks all year round through the Friedrichshain People's Park and more recently through the Tiergarten, are hiking shoes in any case. We know that he keeps a second and a third pair in reserve; just recently, at one of the fast-moving Polish markets, he purchased "for peanuts" a pair of sturdy laced boots, Soviet army surplus. "If you want to be quick on your feet, you can't be walking on insoles" is one of those maxims of his that we initially collected just on a whim, later purposefully.

He is making good headway. To his right, a structure with an exterior spiral staircase catches our eye; it is ascribed to the Viennese architect Adolf Loos. The village of Vitte begins with some houses roofed with tile, others with thatch. Here and there, owners who are still renowned, or who were at one time and have since been forgotten. To the left, the house in which Asta Nielsen, star of the silent screen, once lived. Like Ringelnatz before him, the singer Ernst Busch vacationed here. Einstein sunned himself on the island, even Freud. When Thomas Mann considered settling his family here, he found the island too small for two major figures. Everywhere names to which island lore clings like vines.

At the northern end of Vitte, Fonty recognizes a long, single-story, cozy-looking house where, shortly after the end of the war, scenes from the now classic DEFA film *Marriage in the Shadows* were shot: in black and white.

He stops now and then. Here he pauses a bit longer, there more briefly, but not to rest; no, from here he can see far into the distance, to the left across the inlet to Rügen, to the right out to the open sea.

Anyone who comes upon him on the path turns around for another look. But there are other visitors to the island who also have something timeless about their appearance: a number of them seem to be dressed in costumes, the fashions of the twenties, for instance, or hand-knitted regulation anthroposophic garb. A man blows toward him and is already gone, with billowing lion's mane and eyes afire, declaiming poetry to no one in particular: verses by Däubler, perhaps, or the Expressionist effusions of Becher. But for the most part Fonty sees day-trippers in the usual leisure wear. Snatches of sentences with Saxon coloration. A jogger comes panting up behind him, overtakes him.

In Vitte, the village without church or center, Fonty stops in front of a bourgeois house built of Dutch brick. Here the island's one doctor—who soon after the Wall went up obtained false papers for himself and his wife and followed their three daughters to the West—once prescribed some valerian pills for him that also contained hops and mistletoe—good for the nerves, and perhaps they really did help when he was feeling *abattu* again; at any rate, they had a soothing effect.

Fonty is remembering, or looks like someone to whom memories are flooding back: during her holidays, one of the doctor's daughters, who was studying music in Greifswald, would practice the organ in the fisherman's church—always Buxtehude. Only her narrow back could be seen up in the loft, and her island-blond hair pinned up in a braid and trailing in wisps on the sides. Such devotion to preludes and fugues. She could have been the granddaughter of Pastor Peterson in *Irretrievable*, but Elisabeth played the piano and sang, "Ye who hate are much to be pitied, / Even more so, ye who love...." Fonty could not bear the organ. His nerves were dead set against the organ. Indeed, against music altogether, for which reason the piano on Kollwitzstrasse had been forced into silence.... But in his memory, the daughter of that doctor who had prescribed valerian for him played the organ so softly that only the image remained: the heavy braid, a long neck—and a flicker of longing that did not subside until he was once again setting one foot before the other, now heeding another maxim: "It is wisest to give love stories a wide berth."

When he was not hiking to Vitte and on to Neuendorf over the heath, Fonty was out walking the hilly terrain that began just past Kloster. Uphill through undulating sheep pastures, through underbrush that gradually thickened into woods, to the lighthouse and the precipitous coastline. From here, when the air was clear, one could see the chalky cliffs of the Danish island of Møn jutting into the horizon. An image that promised heaven only knew what: for a long time the West, with its made-for-TV prosperity, and freedom to boot. Some sons of the island tried to reach this destination by night in canoes. Not all of them made it. The weather report would suddenly turn out to have been wrong; a storm would churn up the sea, bearing out the coast guard's warnings that no one could get away, no one could escape the Workers' and Peasants' State and reach Møn's chalky cliffs, that mirage of freedom. Later the rowers' corpses would wash up on the coast of southern Sweden and be punctiliously repatriated: island lore.

As Fonty stood on the steep coast of Hiddensee, he could merely sense the chalk cliffs, however good the visibility. Yet he was certain that there, or close by, his newlywed daughter was waiting for her father's letter, sent poste restante to Stege, meanwhile enjoying all the freedoms the West offered in any budget range.

Emmi never accompanied him into the hills, although she did walk with him halfway to Vitte and then to the breakwaters. Likewise to nearby Grieben for coffee at the Enddorn Inn, where they could sit outside under umbrellas recently donated by an ice-cream manufacturer, with an eye toward market expansion.

As a twosome they made slow progress. A couple who had already said everything they had to say to each other, yet still found things to chat about, once Emmi gave the cue, as they took their seats under one of the colorful umbrellas: "Will you just look at these prices here...." And: "Look, Wuttke, they've got fresh flounder...." Or simply: "Wonder how our Martha's doing? So far away."

But for the most part we saw Fonty out walking by himself. Or we pictured him on foot and alone; for no one was there to witness it as he gazed from the hills over the island—whose outline is supposed to resemble a sea horse—all the way to the Gellen and then, looking toward Stralsund, whose towers were fixed to the horizon like something dabbed on with a paintbrush, called out across that flat landscape framed by inlet and sea, the subject of many painters, "Come back, Effi! Effi, come back!" forming a megaphone with his hands.

On his third day on the island, once more on the path from Kloster to Vitte, the prearranged rendezvous with Professor Eckhard Freundlich took place; from then on, he had someone at his side during his rambles, someone with whom he could chat about this and that in the old accustomed way, as though no time at all had passed since their last meeting—"That was when the Wall was still standing." They discussed family matters—"Lately my daughters have been flirting with Israel, as though you could enjoy your free time there in particularly rich and varied ways"—then the general situation—"Who would have thought the person negotiating unification for us would have a name like Krause!"—then island gossip—"The Hiddensee folk have just brought in a mayor from Helgoland, on loan, so to speak"—then the weather— "Couldn't be more beautiful"—and finally their time together in the Cultural Union—"I'll never forget the lucid lecture you gave for us in Jena—pretty daring, I must say, thanks to various pitfalls:

'Why Effi Briest Is No German Emma Bovary.' That must have been shortly before the Biermann business; a display of self-righteousness in which no one came out the winner, and nothing but losses from then on..."

They spoke as if tuned to the same note, hardly stopping to draw breath. Each sentence provided the cue for the next. Yet as well as they knew each other, Fonty and Freundlich were still on formal terms: "I beg you, dear Herr Professor, brace yourself for the victory of the party of Court Chaplain Stöcker. After all, it was they who developed a knack for that Christian Socialist buzz. As we now know, Stöcker's anti-Semitism was not merely a passing fad. I should have taken much sharper aim at Freytag's *Debit and Credit* when it appeared...."

And the legal scholar Freundlich never called him Fonty, no matter how familiar he was with his recapitulation of immortality, quotations and all. Instead he remarked, "My dear Wuttke, following your temporal leaps certainly keeps the mind supple, but it's enough to give a person a charley horse...." Or: "Your thesis about the return of the Founders' Era is a typical Wuttkeesque reckoning; it explains how the Treibels and other such parvenus can go on raking in profits even after declaring bankruptcy."

Thus one of them said, as their paths crossed just outside Vitte: "Am generally opposed to sensation-seeking, but meeting you here is a fine example of sensation-finding." And the other replied, "You, dear friend Wuttke, succeed in making even this adamantly autoless island tolerable. Let's go and have coffee at our place. My ladies will be delighted, though they're sure to regret that you've left your good Emmi behind at some breakwater, or possibly buried in the sand. And then, after a schnapps to snap us to attention, we can set out again, across the heath down to Neuendorf, if you wish...."

Their hospitable house was at the northern tip, across from Puting. In the early fifties, Freundlich's father, who had headed a ministry for a while, had managed to obtain a construction permit and building materials. Despite his privileged status, the house that went up was rather modest; by now there was no longer anything about it that suggested prominence. On the veranda, Freundlich's wife, Elisabeth, a resolute biologist with cropped hair, served them the promised coffee; the Freundlich girls, Rosa and Clara, were down at the beach.

We do not know much about the constitutional scholar Freundlich, only what Fonty was prepared to tell us. He was considered an authority, in demand as a legal expert abroad, even in nonsocialist countries, and apparently belonged to the travel cadre until certain problems surfaced, after which, when self-criticism was slow in coming, he was expelled from the Party.

The visit to the Freundlichs, which lasted barely an hour, did not yield much. There was concurrence with the housewife's concerns about the future of the island, where land prices were rising rapidly; the latest island rumors were exchanged—who would be most likely to snap up the retirement home built for employees of the Stralsund People's Shipyards, and into whose hands the vacation cottages belonging to the Simson People's Bicycle Works in Suhl would fall. They touched only briefly on the situation at the universities—at Jena and elsewhere—for instance, whether Humboldt University would soon come entirely under West Berlin's control. Then Theo Wuttke and Eckhard Freundlich set out again, passing the thatched hideaways of once famous actors: through a number of regimes, the island had offered a refuge even to those who enjoyed the limelight only briefly. While they were still in the village, Fonty remarked, "I would assume that that little witch's hut over there still belongs to the widow of the murdered Social Democrat Adolf Reichwein, with whom my father, himself a revisionist of the first water, corresponded in the thirties. One of them an educational reformer, the other a staunch adherent of the cooperative movement. Two Bernsteinians who liked to invoke the Erfurt Party Congress. Yes, that was all long ago, and yet, my dear professor, these stories never end!"

From the southern tip and the meadows they reached the heath. Two ramblers deep in conversation. It was rare for both to be silent at once. Freundlich was a well-knit man in his mid-fifties, already bald on top, though not completely hairless. Next to Fonty he looked like a melancholy addendum, but he did his utmost to add a few bright spots to even the gloomiest prospect. He liked to hear himself talk, and could take inconsequential details, significant only to the island, relate them to the larger world, and infuse them with value by means of far-reaching analogies—the heather with its spent blossoms, for instance, or a little birch copse. A child of emigration, Freundlich was at home everywhere and nowhere.

For a time his father had enjoyed great distinction, and not only because of his antifascist pedigree. After the burning of the Reichstag, the Communist deputy, who narrowly avoided arrest, had managed to escape with his secretary, soon to become his wife, by way of Prague to Moscow, where Eckhard Freundlich was born, as he said, "in transit." He grew up in Central America, for which the family was allowed to depart soon after his birth, just in time to miss the beginning of the Show Trials. It took a while for them to arrive. They waited almost a year in Shanghai for a visa to enter the United States. Finally Mexico offered the refugees asylum. There they met other émigrés with whom they shared Party affiliation, but it soon became clear that the political and the Mexican climate heightened the factional tensions to the point of pure murder.

It has by now become common knowledge that tremendous hostility existed among the émigrés and their various factions in the shadow of Popocatepetl and Ixtacihuatl; yet Freundlich spoke of this dark side of his youth only indirectly, or with touristic casualness, as though Trotsky and the ice pick or Anna Seghers and her mysterious automobile accident hadn't really happened. Not a word about the renegade Regler and the Party watchdog Janka. At most he remarked, "Just imagine, Wuttke, after a while my mother couldn't stand the sight of palms and cactuses, and even in the face of Aztec pyramids would rave about heather, and brier roses in bloom. In Acapulco, where we went to refresh ourselves for the summer, so to speak, she would yearn for a birch grove like this one."

When the family returned to Germany, only to find the country in ruins, Freundlich's father brought with him a faith in Communism that was as yet unshaken, but he soon came to place more hope in the ersatz religion known as "international humanism," for which reason he became one of the founding members of the Cultural Union; later, after being stripped of his ministerial position, he remained active in this arena.

When the two ramblers left the sandy path for the flagstone walk just outside Neuendorf, Fonty commented, "A wonderful speaker, your father. Gave a colossally inspiring speech in '47, at the first Cultural Union congress in Berlin. At the time, I was serving briefly as one of the newly certified teachers, and I immediately rallied to his humanistic efforts; I couldn't be moved to join the Party, however. Never did fit their template of excellence. A vacillator from the word go, I was politically unreliable. You know I was neither a dedicated *Kreuzzeitung* man nor a freedom-crazed liberal; the *Vossische,* with all due respect, could not command my loyalty, either. And if the letters to Friedlaender contain halfway sympathetic comments on social democracy, that still does not suggest that my father, a trained lithographer who was a socialist, naturally, had brought me into Bebel's camp. Humanism, yes. Party, never!"

To this Professor Freundlich replied, "Of course, the Cultural Union existed precisely to accommodate such bourgeois wavering. It was a playground with little space but much activity. Everyone could ride his hobbyhorse more or less without a lead, as indeed you cultivated your Brandenburg garden for many years and were allowed to stretch the tiresome socialist stew by tossing in various Prussian ingredients. Others sang, as I did as a child in Mexico, "Ladybug, ladybug" and other such immortal children's songs. Even philatelists were allowed to focus on their miniature humanism within the Cultural Union; they corresponded with stamp collectors all over the world, since they weren't allowed to travel. Collected stamps myself under the palms and amid the cactuses, by the way. Our mail displayed a splendid internationalist array of postal stamps. Alas, the album was lost. But what wasn't lost? I swear, Wuttke! Does anything matter anymore? As I wrote you recently: Nothing is left. In the end we all stand here empty-handed."

Freundlich was not Fonty's only correspondent. We know that until the mid-sixties he corresponded with Johannes Bobrowski, for a while with Fritz Fühmann and other writers, probably even with Uwe Johnson before and after his departure. There are said to be letters extant to Stefan Hermlin and Erwin Strittmatter. Hermann Kant doubtless does not want to recall Fonty's epistolary niggling during the period when the consequences of the Biermann affair were still creating ripples. Even Anna Seghers and the dramatist Heiner Müller are said to have received lengthy communications from him, offering to work up the historical Katte case for one or the other of them; he argued that the pedagogically effective punishment of Crown Prince Friedrich, when he was caught fleeing and, instead of being sentenced to death himself, was condemned to watch his close friend Katte kneel beneath the executioner's sword, demanded to be interpreted from a socialist perspective, in the spirit of Brecht's *The Measure Taken*; in this fashion, Prussia's virtues would finally achieve progressive resonance. But this correspondence and others—for instance, the exchange with the author of *Tallhover*, Hans Joachim Schädlich—are not documented; their existence is a matter of conjecture. We archivists regret the existence of such blind spots, but have been able to ascertain this much: in the letters Freundlich and Fonty wrote to each other, everyday matters were intermingled with concern for the cultural heritage.

While still a student, the professor had been smitten with the Cultural Union lecturer. They had met through his father, who by then occupied only honorary posts. Whereas the father was now considered a deviationist, protected only by the designation "meritorious antifascist," the son was allowed to finish his university studies. He rose in the Party hierarchy almost by the bye, and from the mid-sixties on was teaching the philosophy of jurisprudence and constitutional law, first as a lecturer, then as a professor, at Jena, where he received letter after letter from Fonty, who never fell completely out of favor or climbed the ladder. The letters were mailed during his lecture tours, but also from Fonty's post as file courier: the so-called paternoster epistles.

We would surmise that Freundlich, to whom nothing eccentric was alien, enjoyed this documentary evidence of immortality personified, viewing his correspondent as a curiosity and a walking monument to boot; Fonty, for his part, prized the professor's witty upswings and melancholy downswings, a bobbing motion that grew more pronounced when Freundlich's career was nipped by a Party inquiry—the usual charges: subjectivism and deviationism—and then terminated by expulsion from the Party; the antifascist's son was left with only his professor's chair. Their last meeting had taken place on 4 November on Alexanderplatz, when Fonty made his great speech, and with the aid of several temporal leaps warned of a repetition of the Revolution of '48 and the hangover that followed. "There is no such thing as a velvet revolution!" he shouted. But the crowd of thousands merely applauded; no one was listening.

The subject came up again in Neuendorf, where the two ramblers were observed going into Franz Freese's Oceanview Hotel; in retrospect we note that they looked neither sweaty nor tired, merely thirsty, for Freundlich promptly ordered beer, fresh from the tap.

They sat outside in the garden, which was shaded by three linden trees. At first only bicyclists passed, in pairs or in packs, then a lady stooped with age, with a basket over her arm and a kerchief on her head, struggling along toward the row of gleaming white fishermen's cottages. The whole tableau looked like a painting—a painting of which Fonty remarked, "Such subjects are common in the work of the Worpswede painters. But they show up in Liebermann as well; think of the woman with the goat. And one of his most talented pupils, Luise Büchsel, made a name for herself not least with Neuendorf scenes like this. You see: the old woman seems rooted to the spot."

When the beer was served, Freundlich asked the waitress, "And what culinary delights does the kitchen have in readiness?"

"Just what's on the menu."

"And might we see a menu, please?"

"Coming up."

When they had asked for the grilled herring and parsley potatoes listed on the menu, the white-ruched waitress, who still cultivated that air of grouchy solidarity so characteristic of the Workers' and Peasants' State, told them, "We're all out." So the friends agreed to order what they did have: steamed cod with boiled potatoes.

After Fonty had commented at length on the "Berlin mouthworks" and cited the server here as "a typical combination of countess, soubrette, and beer-garden wench," Freundlich responded, already tucking into his meal, "The women of Berlin are malcontent by nature, like this waitress. For example, in Mexico, which you know is famous for its cuisine, my dear mama, a dyed-in-the-wool daughter of Wedding, would find fault with the most delectable dishes—for instance, that Puebla specialty *pollo con mole.* 'Give me cod in mustard sauce any day,' she would say. And when we were seated under the most magnificent palms, she would imagine linden trees, almost proverbially, like these old ones in front of this pleasant inn. That happened in Guadalajara, when we were guests of the painter Diego Rivera, to whom she sang 'Over by yonder fountain there stands a linden tree.' "

This at once brought Fonty to Effi, who while in Kessin, far off in Pomerania, always had her native Hohen-Cremmen before her eyes: "The park, the sundial, or the dragonflies hovering almost motionlessly above the pond. . . . And to make things worse, that unfortunate union with Instetten, a man of honor, no doubt, but also an incorrigible stickler for principle . . . Yes, if Instetten hadn't made a fetish of honor, Crampas would still be alive. . . . And poor Effi would . . . Well, when it comes right down to it, we all tend to make comparisons in which the foreign element, when measured against ours in Brandenburg, comes off badly—be it Mexico or Kessin, or even the most solitary Scottish lakes. And whether our Mete will be more content in Schwerin then in Prenzlberg remains to be seen. Marriage alone won't do it."

With that, the topic of conversation had been framed broadly enough to include Freundlich's Mexico and Fonty's pining for the Scottish moors, Effi's unhappy marriage and Martha's wedding, and to allow the early afternoon to be spent in pleasant chitchat in the shade of the lindens. The waitress gave them occasional opportunity to muzzle the infamous "Berlin snout," at least in a manner of speaking. Matters near and far were raked over. For a while they scrutinized the wobbly position occupied by Jena's Carl Zeiss Football Club, as whose avowed fan the professor waxed passionate. Then one stocky chancellor or the other was hauled over the coals for his trickery: "Fame is a newspaper tiger!" But soon politics was swept from the table again. Two gentlemen in shifting shade, who did not set much store by sticking to one subject. We shall leave them sitting there, for everything we could have picked up by eavesdropping can be found in a letter to Martha Grundmann, née Wuttke.

"The sandy path to Neuendorf through the heath was the epitome of peace and innocence; yet I did not undertake yesterday's walking tour alone, but was, rather, accompanied by a stream of sometimes sparkling conversation, which touched on every conceivable topic. For at my side was a man, quick on his feet, who not only has the name but also has proven himself to be just what his name promises, i.e., friendly; I am speaking, of course, of Eckhard Freundlich, my intimate from many years' correspondence, closer than anyone but Friedlaender, to whom the formula 'We understand each other' likewise applies. Today people speak of being on the same 'wavelength,' but when all is said and done, we understand each other because our pens, or, as yesterday, our mouths, share a proclivity for the clever turn of phrase.

"At any rate, we had soon taken flight from Hiddensee, and landed first in Mexico City, where Freundlich feels at home, with vivid childhood memories; then we saw ourselves strolling through Kessin, following the East Pomeranian shoreline, and hence in a region deplored by Roswitha, that most Catholic of all housemaids: 'And all they have is the dunes, and out there the sea. And it roars and roars, but there's nothing more to it.' After that we went on to take stock of Effi's vacillating moods, her terror in that haunted house, her susceptibility, born of boredom, and her yearning, both open and concealed, to get away from these alien Pomeranian parts back to the familiar little province of Friesack—weighing these moods against Instetten's essentially rationalist attempts to tame her. We could not get enough. Sometimes in one style, sometimes in another, sometimes even in old Briest's: 'It is so difficult to know what one should do, and what leave undone. That, too, takes one far afield.'

"You know that my style is always shaped by the material I happen to be treating at the moment. And since, after so much unhappiness, characteristic of my station in life, your wedding inspired thoughts about matters I cannot discuss with Mama, I launched into some frightfully fundamental observations on marriage, not only with regard to Effi, but also in light of Mete's belated union with the architect Fritsch, who, like your Grundmann, was connected with the construction business. He managed to get quite a bargain on those houses in Waren, lake view and all. And speaking of the real estate speculation of yesteryear brought us back to the present, without any need to go into the land-trafficking that has plagued Berlin for an eternity.

"Freundlich is terribly worried about his professorship in Jena. He says they plan to evaluate all the universities according to Western standards, which means have them appraised. And that, like the consequences of the currency union, will result in a bottom line of zero. Furthermore, he says, and I agree, that the rules of the impending unification demand—in order to justify this move as the victory of capitalism—that not only every product of our devising but also every last Eastern idea be proven worthless.

"Nonetheless, Freundlich did not fail to find humor in this evidence of a lopsided loss of value. He offered a delightful parody of the tone taken by Western professors—their condescending benevolence, their colonializing concern, their bragging about professional conferences, second homes, third marriages; and yet I heard an undertone of much unspoken bitterness. You know (and have often criticized sharply) his proclivity for presenting his sorrow in clown's motley. So, too, yesterday, on the way back, he tied four knots in his handkerchief—a glaring red one, by the way—to protect his always gleaming bald pate. And in this comical getup he sought refuge for himself (and us) in hair-raising island lore and ever-diverting island gossip. Since he speaks Low German to perfection, he was able to offer a splendid rendition of old Gau and his neighbor Puting, and also of the old island pastor, who in the middle of his sermon would exclaim, 'Me boys, the herring's coming in!' whereupon the fishermen's church would promptly empty out and all boats be manned for the catch. But then, after we had crossed the birch grove and had spelled out every local nickname, starting with Schipperöbing, moving on to Solting, and ending with Wichting, now, as the dunes lay before us, he burst out abruptly, 'Evaluated out of existence! Every trace of us is to be obliterated—all in vain, tossed on the scrap heap, as if we'd never lived or taught. Nothing left but eraser crumbs!'

"No matter how I tried to introduce some light into his gloomy vision, he remained in a most untypical funk. But suddenly he stopped dead, as if on command. With his fourfold knotted handkerchief he mopped his sweat-polished pate and uttered, more past me than over my head, several sentences that were so frightfully true that they still echo in my ears: 'Was always more a Marxist than a Communist. Even with all the annoyance, I still enjoyed it. But I was also a German, like my old man, who, Communist though he was, was German, whether in Mexico or on the Spree, though actually more Prussian than German. But now I'm something I'd almost forgotten to be, a Jew. First and last: a Jew! Now that they've decided to evaluate me, and my scholarship's supposed to be null and void, I'm a Jewish scholar with an additional small blemish: I'm still alive. So I'm a leftover Jew. And that's more or less what they told me recently to my face: "As a Jew you should understand that a person can't just repress what went before, your long Party membership, for instance, and the fact that you, as a Marxist, still... The mistakes we made in the West while coming to terms with our Nazi past mustn't be repeated in the East. Actually you should agree with me, dear colleague, if not as a Jewish Communist, then as a Jewish survivor, for that's what you are...."'

"After this outburst—or should I say outpouring?—he looked at me and—now smiling again—tried to revert to his customary tone: 'All frightfully true, isn't it, Fonty?' He, who otherwise addresses me as Wuttke or my dear Wuttke, and even begins his letters with 'Most Honored Herr Wuttke,' called me by the name the whole world uses, to your and Mama's chagrin. And I promptly replied, out of my extended experience: 'Nothing new under the sun, my dear and most honored Friedlaender! Everything that's currently on top in these parts, whether already in place or expecting to be so tomorrow, disgusts me no end: this obtuse, self-seeking, land-grabbing gentry, this mendacious and narrow-minded clergy, this eternal reserve-officer mentality, this gruesome Byzantinism....' And soon he was laughing again, and reminding me, with word-perfect quotations, as always, that in my day I had excepted Bismarck and the Social Democrats from my blanket condemnation, pointing out, however, that they were not worth much either. But to you, and to you alone, I must admit how lastingly certain utterances about the Jews, the moneyed Jews, Jewishness itself, and the general Jewification weigh on me, especially those inexcusable passages in the letters to Fräulein von Rohr, who liked to hear such things. Freundlich knows all this but does not comment; and I must live with it, nursing my shame in private.

"Over coffee at the Heath Rose—we were the only guests—we managed to recover our merriment, and, in thrall to memories, conjure up the old days in the Cultural Union. We spoke of the late Johannes R. Becher and the late Willi Bredel, naturally also of Comrade Kurella, the holy terror of all Party congresses. But we also recalled that at the founding of the Union, on the suggestion of the actor Paul Wegener, they elected the playwright Gerhart Hauptmann—stricken with years and waiting for his expulsion far off in Polish-occupied Silesia—honorary president; and Hauptmann, a year before his death, accepted the call. That brought our conversation around to the burial, or, rather, the tragicomic transfer of the famous corpse. It took days to transport it from the Riesengebirge by way of Berlin and Stralsund to Hiddensee. As a boy, Freundlich was there 'before sunrise' at his father's side.

"As you can see: a productive walk, which has indecently lengthened this letter to my Mete. The island climate is good for me, more particularly for my nerves. Dreamless sleep. Mama is also feeling well, or at least better. She has run into old acquaintances, whom I would rather avoid: a bunch of frightfully affable Saxon coffee-klatschers. I am well and amply served with Professor Freundlich. He puts up a brave front, but his family fears the worst for his professorship. Let us just hope that your Grundmann does not likewise evaluate you by Western standards. From the steep coastline I saw Møn's chalk cliffs in the morning sun, and was closer to you than is proper for a father during his daughter's honeymoon. I'd have liked to call out, 'Mete, come back! Come back, Mete!'..."

Let us try to reconstruct those events "before sunrise." Hauptmann's burial and his early plays were the topic of a lecture Fonty was permitted to give in the mid-sixties; the twentieth anniversary of the playwright's death provided the occasion. Our Archives' previous director, Dr. Schobess, was the only one of us in the audience.

In the Immortal's judgment, *The Weavers* and *The Beaver Coat* were among the very best things to come from Hauptmann's hand, matched by only a few other plays, decidedly not *Hannele's Ascension*. Yet the death of the eighty-three-year-old author and the subsequent ordeal of trying to procure a zinc-lined coffin, not to mention two pounds of plaster for the death mask, had affected the Cultural Union's itinerant lecturer Theo Wuttke so deeply that he was able to forge the details into a symbol of a war-devastated era: the lying-in-state of the princely writer in a peat-brown Franciscan cowl, complete with white rope belt; the pouch of Silesian soil placed on the dead man's chest; and the wrangling over the special train, which in the end consisted of eight freight cars and two passenger cars from the Reich Railroad; Hauptmann died when the peace was barely a year old.

In his lecture, Fonty did not stint on specifics. He did not fail to stress the merits of the Soviet colonel Sokolov, placing him time and again in front of the corpse laid out in the Villa Wiesenstein—Hauptmann's Silesian residence—to protect it from Polish marauders, of course. And because he transformed the Red Army officer into a hero, and a lover of literature as well, his always precarious position with the Cultural Union was shored up; he was allowed to deliver this lecture as a commemorative speech, first in Forst, on the west bank of the Neisse, then in the foyer of Berlin's People's Theater on Luxemburg-Platz, then in Stralsund, and finally in Kloster on Hiddensee, on 28 July 1966, to be precise. And everywhere surprisingly large crowds turned up. At all the stations of the dead writer's final journey Fonty spoke to a full house. Everywhere one heard which furniture had been designated as museum pieces, thanks to Colonel Sokolov—for instance, the enormous writing desk, which unfortunately was left out in the rain for a long time while waiting to be loaded. The clash with Polish officials over the number of sewing machines to be included among the goods being moved was merely touched upon, likewise the danger that the freight and passenger cars might be looted by gangs of youths, a danger averted time and again, sometimes with drawn revolver, by a Red Army lieutenant named Leo.

After the special train, the windows of whose passenger cars, incidentally, were hardly or only temporarily glazed, had slowly made its way from Agnetendorf through Lower Silesia, it was finally able to pass through the border station at Tuplice, formerly Teuplitz on the Neisse, and leave the Republic of Poland, shifted after the war from east to west. As soon as the train reached Forst, the little town on the border, memorial services began in this scaled-down Germany. Fonty listed the Party functionaries and occupation officers who were waiting there. Newsreel cameras were poised on their tripods. Actors, directors, professors, and journalists from all over the world had gathered, and the Cultural Union had assembled a large delegation to mourn Hauptmann, its honorary president. Recitations and funeral music were on the program. Speeches were given: in German, in Russian.

The reception of the special train in Berlin-Schöneweide was rather meager, a fact Fonty noted in his speech with the comment, "Here the local saint is still a character called Street-Corner Nante." Yet he characterized the People's Theater, now a burned-out ruin, as the ideal setting for the departed dramatist, whom he without reservations described as immortal.

In Stralsund, people were waiting with torches. The zinc-lined coffin, which had suffered minor but reparable damage in transit, was placed on a bier in the great hall of the Rathaus. A few university professors, several Party activists, and a small group of resettled Silesians kept the death watch. At the memorial service the speakers continued the tradition of glorification that the writer had enjoyed on every occasion while still alive: applauded in the empire because officially vilified; celebrated as long as the Weimar Republic held together; raised to the status of an idol in the Third Reich by the *Volk* and its Führer; and now the dead man's renown was being staged under Stalinist auspices.

Fonty the lecturer brought this unbroken tradition to life in an image: "Hauptmann always had pull, no matter what cart he was hitched to, or allowed himself to be hitched to." Yet because in the very next sentence he extolled the eulogy delivered by the chairman of the Cultural Union, the Expressionist poet Johannes R. Becher, in the process slyly invoking the recently implemented resolutions of the Eleventh Party Congress, the office that oversaw his lectures subsequently deleted the image of the ever-present cart, but without holding it against him in any lasting way.

Finally, after the obligatory references to German-Soviet friendship and to humanism's uniting the peoples of the world, when the only subject left to treat was the burial on Hiddensee, Fonty allowed himself a few remarks on the burial of another immortal on 24 September 1898 in the cemetery of the French Reformed parish on Liesenstrasse: "The funeral procession made its way under sunny skies from the building of the St. John's Order on Potsdamer Strasse along Invalidenstrasse, where Stine and the widow Pittelkow lived. Pastor Devaranne escorted the procession, friends, relatives. The critic Karl Frenzel spoke at the grave. That was all. Prussia's gentry was conspicuous by its absence!"

This, too, they discussed during their walk and over coffee. Fonty focused a while longer on the Huguenot cemetery, describing its current rather desolate condition, but since Eckhard Freundlich, accompanied by his father, had actually been present at the burial in the Kloster cemetery, Freundlich's memories, which had photographic clarity, soon moved into the foreground: the image of the coffin in the bow of the steamer *Hiddensee*; the image of the veil worn by the lonesome widow, Margarete Hauptmann, which blew in the same direction as the smoke plume from the death ship; and image after image of the six Hiddensee fishermen who served as pallbearers.

When Fonty, who had not been present, spoke rather vaguely of "Silesian soil stirred into the mix," Freundlich knew that "after every scoop of island sand a scoop of heavy earth from Agnetendorf," salvaged along with some of the refugee's posessions, had been shoveled "with quite a thump" into the grave. Fonty dwelled on the scheduling of the burial "before sunrise," in compliance with the writer's wishes. Freundlich was certain that the burial had been somewhat delayed. "We were all casting shadows, my dear Wuttke; that's how high the fiery orb stood over the Baltic horizon. I recall from my childhood seeing another such spectacle of nature in Mexico. Looked terrific!" He even knew the reason for the delay: "Oh, the fishermen got there late. Still corked, they were weaving so badly that they stumbled with the coffin; they'd raided the funeral feast the night before. And what a spread to go with the schnapps: sausage, ham, hard-boiled eggs, cold chicken, potato salad. And since the Gaus and the Striesows, the Schlucks and the Gottschalks were all not only thirsty but also starving, they dug in and stuffed their pockets. Quite a party, my dear Wuttke! No wonder the pallbearers still felt it in their legs!"

At this funeral reception, a screen actor from Saxony, known for portraying Frederick the Great to a *T,* is said to have been particularly assiduous at pocketing provisions for the next few days. This touch of local color was provided, however, not by Professor Freundlich, but on the following day by yet another visitor to the island.

18

Treading Water

We asked ourselves, in his oppressive presence and also later: Why did he come? Why so suddenly and unannounced? Did he think he couldn't afford to miss any more conversations between Fonty and Freundlich? Were rambles *à trois* his intention? Or was he simply in search of harmless rest and relaxation, an ordinary tourist?

One of us guessed it was jealousy. Another surmised the old routine was still driving him. We were all sure that nothing could keep him in Berlin. He must have been fed up with the city. He couldn't stand the persistent heat, the loneliness amid the crowds, the absence of his subject. He was suffering from withdrawal, for without Fonty he felt abandoned, if not lost. There was no substitute—certainly not the minor cases from Prenzlauer Berg. We realized that the day-and-night-shadow was capable of something akin to longing.

Did he just want to be there? At the very least he hoped to follow the faithful correspondents, at a distance, when they set out on their long walks. After all, the Freundlich case, as the files would reveal, fell within his purview: not only the past Party proceedings against the professor but also his present precarious situation were thoroughly documented. They even knew each other by sight, because in our solicitously restricted homeland no one could avoid bumping into anyone else. And since—according to Fonty—the magistrate Friedlaender lived on in Freundlich, whenever Hoftaller appeared, Tallhover was on hand.

In addition, he may actually have been trying to unwind. We base this supposition on his saying to the director of the Hauptmann house, shortly after his arrival, "I desperately need a couple of quiet days on an island like this. You can't imagine how trying it's become in Berlin, such a grind—it's hard to take."

We had to content ourselves with a nodded greeting as we made our way to Grieben. We were of no interest to him, as if outside the scope of his particular concerns. Later a brief exchange took place in the library of Sallow Thorn House: "How's the archive business?"—that was all. But he kept doggedly on Fonty's trail, panting along sandy paths up into the hills, all the way to the lighthouse and almost to the brink of the steep coastline. His appearance had undergone an unmistakable Americanization: along with baseball cap and T-shirt, Hoftaller was wearing not only shorts but also rubber-soled footgear very suitable for the island, "sneakers" by name. The brand was New Balance, as he informed us when we inquired later.

And since in these sneakers he persistently pursued his subject, making sure that Wuttke could not escape him on this visit to the island, and since a little accident with lingering effects had sidelined Emmi—on a walk to Lietzenburg she had sprained her left foot—Fonty thought he had enough material for a third letter to his daughter. He filled page after page, even though he could not expect a response, despite the proximity—as the crow flies—of one island to the other; in those days the borders were open, at last, in all directions, but in the Workers' and Peasants' State the postal service was proving unequal to this new openness. He wrote simply because he liked to write, and because he felt impelled to do so: "The weather is still splendid! Summery clouds from coast to coast. But because cloudy greetings, no matter how fluffy the packaging, are simply not enough, your old father wants to send you a letter, and this time it will be one that does not begin by measuring the length and breadth of the island but first reports on Mama, who has sprained her foot, the left one, of course. Sometimes she blames a spiteful root in the hilly part of the island for her *malheur,* sometimes an evil rock on the shore. She lies there moaning and wailing, overshooting the mark, as always. Reminds me dreadfully of earlier, when her so-called storm sickness would give way, after a period of silent suffering, to lamentations. Yet it would seem incumbent upon us, after our prolonged illness, to steer clear of anything smacking of a hospital, and not give in to boo-hooing, which, as I know, neither you nor I can bear.

"Fortunately Frau Freundlich and her daughters are very attentive, caring for our groaning but still voluble patient. They apply cool compresses and practice their skill as forbearing listeners. All three of them—though the mother more than the daughters—are clever enough for any conversation, and that includes such touchy subjects as the precarious situation in the Middle East, always a gauge for tolerance; only half-wits, of whom even this most paradisical of islands has no shortage, find the topic just too, too upsetting.

"Yet behind her exterior of calm cheerfulness (and at times forced matter-of-factness), Madame Freundlich seems extremely worried, and not only about her husband. In addition to the situation in Jena, her two daughters, who are at the University of Leipzig, want to emigrate—not to Canada, as their father urges, but to Israel. Ugly experiences are said to have motivated this sudden decision. Something that for a long time was suppressed, or could be uttered under Party auspices only as anti-Zionism, is now bursting forth in violent form, coupled with an impertinent insistence on free speech and that idiotic pride in 'Deutschland' that has always gone hand in hand with violence: in broad daylight, a howling mob surrounded the girls, although, as you certainly recall, Rosa and Clara have the most Nordic of blond locks. (Even you, despite your reservations about the Freundlichs, would be disgusted by such a naked display of hostility.)

"I, at least, was appalled by this story; the professor, however, is in fine fettle and remains so—which I view not uncritically—entirely in accord with his personality. Only his own experiences, in other words what is being done to him at the university at the moment—vicious enough in itself—affects and interests him. Besides, those wretched Party proceedings from earlier keep popping up. While they were underway, I advised him to do what I advised Friedlaender, a veteran of the '70–'71 war, when he was hauled before a court-martial: Dump the whole mess at the feet of those provincial Party functionaries, like those arrogant officers from

Friedlaender's regiment, thwarted in their own careers—as I did when the Cultural Union, like the Academy earlier on, began to stick in my throat. But no, as far as the magistrate was concerned, the wounded honor of a Jewish reserve lieutenant was at stake, a man who defended his quite well-bred if rather self-centered war memoirs more resolutely than the French defended the fortress of Metz; and obviously it was a question of class, for whose existence this Jewish constitutional expert argued on a scholarly basis, not merely an ideological one. Just recently he wrote to me: 'It was Marx's mistake to cast the pearls of his insight before the swine of a party.' He may be right, even if I must add that I didn't care one whit for Marx, not even during the time we shared in London; Dickens had more to say.

"But as pugnacious as Freundlich sometimes sounds, his wit never flags, and he remains open-minded, within limits, when, in the course of our extended rambles—yesterday we hiked past Neuendorf to the little lighthouse, though not all the way to the tip of the Gellen—we come around to the subject of father and mother Briest, or Instetten, as upright as he was loveless. He is an excellent listener, is always *au fait*, can do a delightful imitation of the swaggering Major Crampas, but also seizes the opportunity to make far-fetched analogies, as when I, to cite one example, trace the haunted house in Kessin back to ghostly occurrences experienced during the Swinemünde childhood. Thus he brought up his own childhood memories from Mexico, offering Trotsky's house, futilely fortified, as a haunted castle of his own, going on from there to speculate at length on the insides of the Stasi headquarters on Normannenstrasse, which can't stay sealed for long: 'A witches' pantry! The brew stored there will season Germany's soup for a decade and beyond.'

"Finally he even declared our rather innocuous Ministries Building to be a creaking haunted house. Some fear is lurking inside him, I suspect, for my professor, usually wedded to irony, has been on the alert for danger, with sweaty-palmed intensity, ever since someone turned up here in whom I recognize my trusty old companion. He is here on holiday, naturally: even day-and-night-shadows have to get out of the traces sometimes.

"Now I needn't explain to my Mete how colossally attached these Tallhovers and Hoftallers are. Under the beeches, clustered outside our quarters in smooth-skinned innocence, I received the following explanation: He merely wanted to stop by, not to disturb us, but he had to remind me that something big was in the offing. Even the best island location was no protection against an event of such epic proportions.

"Downright laughable. He was speaking of German unification, which, I am sure, will give even greater latitude to the No-goodnik activities that up to now have been contained within certain boundaries. The day is set for two weeks hence. The third of October is to be a red-letter day. But I have seen too many of these moments, with their claims to historic greatness, and I know that all we can expect is a lot of shoving and jostling. As a rule, this is what it boils down to: the report is better than the thing itself. This one will be mainly made for television. But I promised to have a look when they ring the bells.

"For without a doubt, while the people gawk—gawk and see nothing—some small, worthwhile, even striking details will be there for the picking: someone will be chewing the buttered roll he has brought along; another will be hunting amidst the crowd for a button that's popped off; a third will have a grain of sand in his eye and be rubbing and rubbing. . . . Or, as happened long ago at the Ten Pound Hotel in Thale, when I merely wanted to look up at the Rosstrappe from the balcony, but a couple of paces from me two English sisters stepped out onto the balcony, and the younger one was dressed as Effi would be later: a loose frock, blue-and-white striped cotton, with leather belt and sailor collar. . . .

"Yes, poor Effi! Perhaps she came out so well because the whole thing was written in a dreamlike mood, almost psycho-graphically. In other cases, the effort, the worries that accompanied each stage of the writing stick in one's mind—but not that time. It all came pouring out. That never happened again. Here, at any rate, there is no 'daughter of the ether' far and wide, no matter how many people this observant rambler sees coming toward him or dashing across his path as if chased by a pack of dogs. Worthy of a glance, at most, are the smartly dressed Westerners, who are on the prowl for real estate, sticky-fingered and unification-drunk; otherwise only distraught islanders, who have never felt at ease with the new—and of course my trusty old companion, whom it will hardly be possible to avoid.

"Today he insisted on tramping a number of paths with me— and without Freundlich, whom I would have liked to have along for support. You should see him in his casual 'look': an eccentric figure straight from the Panoptikum waxworks—an American baseball cap on his head, his feet smartly shod in parti-colored sneakers. And then his knee-baring shorts and the tight little jersey advertising in bold letters a drink that needs no further advertisement. Only this time he left his always loaded briefcase at home. One cannot really take him seriously, no matter how insistently attached he is. (Therefore I would advise you to view his unquestionably unsuitable wedding present as a trifle. A bad joke, that's all!)

"But he is thoroughly informed, that he is; he knows who built without a permit on the loveliest spot on the island; which original owners are registered in the town clerk's records in Bergen on Rügen, and which are not, and why. He even blew the cover of the vacation houses built in the mid-eighties by the Stasi, i.e., his own outfit, up in the foothills, in violation of all zoning regulations. He told me the whole inside story—a chapter unto itself.

"And when we—*nota bene*—were standing before Hauptmann's grave, old Tallhover suddenly became talkative, using Hoftaller as a mouthpiece: He had been present at the burial. Once the body left the Silesian village of Agnetendorf, his headquarters had stayed in constant touch with Comrade Leo, who was not to be pictured as a simple Red Army lieutenant. At the funeral reception, he had observed that actor—the one with the historical profile (as portrayed by Menzel) who had made a name for himself in various films as 'Old Fritz'—stealing food: cold cuts and hard-boiled eggs. He had vivid memories of those films, for which reason he had not filed a report. The dramatic flair, the embodiment of royal perseverance, and so forth. Finally he winked at me and pointed his pudgy finger at the colossal boulder: Much of what Hauptmann had written could still be performed today. But only the Immortal had perceived, and instantly, the young dramatist's subversive power.

He deserved plaudits because he had recognized not only the artistic skill but also the new, provocative, rebellious tone. And likewise the Immortal would certainly have been able—as I was in my day—to detect the dangerous new elements in the crude first attempts of that young playwright Müller, and would have brought them to the attention of interested parties when rehearsals for *Resettler* began.

"That is almost accurate, in one case as in the other. All the professional hacks, all the Landaus and Lindaus—with the exception of the drama critic Frenzel—merely vented their wit and sarcasm on Hauptmann, with malice but without thought. Ridiculous to dismiss this young fellow with the customary 'He has some talent.' Equally stupid the way they wanted to downgrade young Müller. Aside from me, only his colleagues Hacks and Bunge put in a good word for the play, still raw but deftly drawn from real life. To no avail! 'Talent without perspective,' and 'No Party spirit'— that was the kind of blather one could hear in both the Writers' Union and the Academy. But talent is nothing. Everybody has some talent. 'Believe an old wag,' I wrote to Stephany and later to Comrade Seghers, 'a man who can write like this has more where that came from....'

"By the way, after standing in front of Hauptmann's grave in his shorts and sneakers and doffing his cap, my trusty old companion assured me on the short way to the church that neither the island pastor Gustavs nor the island doctor Ehrhardt had participated in the freeloading during the funeral reception. 'Only the fishermen who later served as pallbearers and that actor with the profile really dug in!' he exclaimed. By then we were inside the church, where he gave me blow-by-blow plot synopses of various Ufa films filled with battle scenes, such as *The Leuthen Chorale* and *Fridericus Rex*. Shameless distortions of history, with which I am plenty familiar, God knows; as a young moviegoer I took an unpardonable pleasure in them, for this mime by the name of Otto Gebühr dished up the usual stereotypes: the king bent double with gout, the regal blue gaze, the frightful royal snarl: 'Dogs, would you live forever?!' Yet nothing about Katte kneeling beneath the executioner's sword while the crown prince is compelled to look on. Would have been material for Müller, perhaps even his answer to Brecht's *The Measure Taken.*

"Strangely enough, Professor Freundlich, who, as a boy of twelve, had been allowed to stand by Hauptmann's grave, because his father was a leading comrade, confirmed my trusty old companion's accounts, right down to the cold cuts and potato salad. But otherwise there is no love lost between these two. My companion refuses to accept my theory that the Jews have always shown themselves to be the better Prussians; way back, he already viewed Magistrate Friedlaender through those anti-Semitic Stöcker glasses (now once more in style). Likewise Mama, who is not pleased to see the professor by her sickbed. 'He's always so sarcastic!' is her explanation. Yet since she gives my day-and-night-shadow equally short shrift—'He always seems to be talking out of both sides of his mouth!'—I consider her judgment perhaps not just, but at least carefully weighed. I, on the other hand, have been familiar with both from so far back that I cannot deny a certain devotion, even when it degenerates into dependence.

"Now this little letter has turned into quite a long one again. Tell your Grundmann that for my speech at the wedding banquet I actually had a diatribe on adultery up my sleeve, but was afraid Mama would raise objections—just as Briest's wedding speech in the novel is wisely withheld, for fear of the usual ambiguities; Frau von Briest merely hints that on this occasion the old man came out with 'nothing very sensible.' No, tell your Grundmann that just as the technique of withholding is a crucial element in writing, so, too, keeping things to yourself is part of any marriage. Or, better still, say nothing. Mama, who sends her love, is already asleep. The only sound is from a moth. Otherwise it is colossally quiet here. . . ."

When they visited the cemetery, other visitors saw the two of them in front of the boulder. A pair seemingly made for appearing against a monumental backdrop. Later they sat side by side in the fishermen's church: Fonty stuffed to the gills with knowledge, Hoftaller a little ill at ease and struck with almost childlike wonder at the sky-blue barrel vault, whose firmament is wreathed in roses. With his stubby finger he pointed out the fleshy pink angel floating in front of the chancel and a swatch of blue drapery whose skillful folds hid the angel's own nakedness. Then his curiosity lit upon a small trawler with a reddish-brown sail suspended to the left of the altar, the type of boat used in the old days by Hiddensee's fishermen for fishing the bay. The Viking ship suspended to the right interested him less, but he let Fonty explain to him in great detail a painting mounted below the organ loft; it depicts a ship in distress in stormy seas. They both had to twist around in the blue-and-white pew, looking over their own shoulders, so to speak. As he was interpreting the ship's painted distress in piratical detail for his pew-fellow, Fonty was searching the organ bench for the former island doctor's eldest daughter. But the bench was bare. Nothing but memory, scantily equipped. Nothing but an old man's lingering longing.

Then there was nothing more to look at. They found diversion in neither the wooden baptismal font nor the sacristy, which protruded into the space to the right of the altar like a parlor. They were whispering. Soon only Hoftaller was whispering into Fonty's ear, while Fonty sat absolutely still, sagging in his pew, condemned to listen without whispering back.

We left the fishermen's church too soon, but were there long enough to see Fonty squeeze out of the pew and position himself under the fleshy pink hovering angel with gilded wings, as if seeking sanctuary. Then he pointed out a piece of ornate Baroque scrollwork above the sacristy, and loudly repeated the saying on the banner held aloft by the carved angels: "Holy, holy, holy is the Lord Jehovah!"

Several times he appealed to Old Testament authority, then said in a quieter voice, "The least you could do is show a little respect. We're on hallowed ground here, not on Normannenstrasse. This isn't a branch office of Prinz-Albrecht-Palais. Tell that to Herr von Puttkamer, your police commissioner. You hear me, Tallhover? You have no business being here. They don't follow dry-as-dust protocols here. I may be inexcusably unbelieving myself, yet I stand under special protection here!"

After waiting some moments with nothing to show for it, Fonty left the fishermen's church. Hoftaller did not follow him at once, instead making a point of hanging back. We were certain that they would not lose track of one another. The island was too small, their memory too amply supplied with reminders, the tangle that bound them too tightly knotted.

The two of them were repeatedly glimpsed close together: behind the broom in the hills, and on the spit of land extending into the old basin, now known as the new basin, the beach preferred by nudists. We saw them from a distance. The last time they were standing in the Baltic, which licks the beach, sandy between Kloster and Witte, weighted down with stones toward the dunes. But no matter how far they were from us, a gust of wind carried scraps of words, exclamations, beginnings of sentences in our direction, which allow us to consolidate mere conjecture into dialogue. Sometimes, however, the wind died down, and we merely saw them talking: empty speech bubbles for us to fill.

In and of itself an innocuous tableau: both of them standing in the tolerably cool low tide. Fonty in his boater, his trouser legs rolled up. Hoftaller had his baseball cap on and stood there in shorts, his knees bare. Farther off, other visitors to the island were having one last wade in this "Old Wives' Summer." Out past the last sandbank there were even a few swimmers. And this must be more or less what Hoftaller said to persuade his reluctant subject to take the plunge: "I know you approve of the Kneipp hydrotherapy method, Fonty. Just a half hour of treading water. Does wonders for the circulation. And ideal for a little chat."

Fonty's walking stick and jacket, a plastic bag, their socks, the laced boots and the sneakers with thick rubber soles were left on the beach. Wooden pilings had been driven into the sea at hundred-meter intervals to keep the beach sand from eroding. Little bays had formed, and one of these bays they made their own. At first they trod water in silence. Then Hoftaller, helpful as always, supplied the cue. This cue was one to which he was partial, as we know, and which he therefore used often: "Remember Dresden?"

Fonty, who was familiar with this trap since their last conversation on the sofa, and feared it, must have tried to call up his most recent association with that city: "You mean the Cultural Union conference in February '54? Remember it as if it were yesterday. Was the delegate from Berlin. The first time we were elected in regional conferences. Took the bit in my mouth in Dresden and warned of increasing clubbishness throughout the land..."

"When I say Dresden, we're talking about the period before '48, my good man. A certain young apothecary is trying to emulate a certain poet by the name of Herwegh. All of Saxony has fallen into the clutches of the demagogues. In Leipzig there's even a club where they're busily conspiring against the government. And this young apothecary belongs to that club...."

We are sure that Fonty clung to the Cultural Union as he trod water, and not without success, for when he persisted, "And that congress in Dresden—the fourth, by the way—turned out to be quite significant," Hoftaller could not refrain from responding, "Big surprise! After the unsuccessful counterrevolution in '53, it was thought that reformulating the basic mission would result in a degree of stability. But when I say 'Remember Dresden?' I don't mean the countless resolutions offered by the stamp collectors and aquarium keepers, and definitely not the wishes expressed by the 'Literature and Cultural Heritage' crowd, which theoretically was out to corner as many vacation slots as possible at the Cultural Union's Bad Saarow resort, and that included you, Fonty, by the way. Petty-bourgeois aspirations hiding behind allegedly revolutionary goals—it takes me back to the demagogic posturing of those eternal students in Leipzig, the pals of a certain young apothecary, who a short while later, in Dresden's Salamonis Apothecary Shop..."

"That's what I said. The delegates assembled there were disposed to let everyone ride his particular hobby-horse, though of course the rules of the race were set by the Party. I expressed my objections. It's all in the minutes. I'd think you'd be aware of that. But I can already tell what the Tallhover in you has in mind: our richly metaphoric dreams of freedom, our rhymes for spy and police, our sarcastic verses on armchair heroes of the liberal persuasion, our pathetic little conspiracy against the state. Wolfsohn and I, I and Wolfsohn. Wrote to him from Brühl's terrace...painful feelings...never mind. Who cares about that anymore!"

"I agree with you there. To us it was just fooling around. A relatively skinny file, long since closed. And if, later on, similar fooling around hadn't resulted in a veritable windfall of children, I'd have no need to keep bringing up Dresden. Well, what about it? Has the penny dropped yet?"

Treading water provides the perfect opportunity for a good chat, Hoftaller had promised. At the beginning of this Kneipp hydrotherapy session, Fonty must have suspected what was meant by the backward glance at Dresden; how could he forget that conversation on the sofa, when he was plied with sickeningly sweet red wine to celebrate the old couch's reupholstering? During that conversation he had learned that his day-and-night-shadow had in his possession a packet of love letters that we would have been delighted to get our hands on, for safekeeping in the Archives. Fonty's defense, accordingly, had something helpless about it: "I see our reluctant father is about to be tormented again." He concentrated on his exercises, assiduously treading the waters of the Baltic and feeling the invigorating effect working its way up from the soles of his feet, as a flood of speech washed over him—birth dates, the ominous letter to Lepel, punctual support payments, quotations from sentimental effusions addressed to a gardener's daughter by the name of Magdalena Strehlenow, as well as rowboat excursions on the Elbe, the death of the second-born, swept away by diphtheria, and finally the birthdays of the surviving daughter, Mathilde, celebrated without a single gift from the father, along with other embarrassing details—all simmered into a stew that Fonty had no desire to taste; no, he clenched his teeth as he trod water.

But when Hoftaller began to dish up further fodder—the lifelong obliviousness of Emilie, née Rouanet-Kummer, the onetime fiancée—the accused stopped treading water: "What good will trite confessions do? It's all there in the books, thoroughly worked over. The only reason I want to return one last time to the fourth Cultural Union congress is that I happened to speak there with someone thoroughly familiar with this material, the excellent biographer Reuter. I put forward the thesis that this unfortunate topic had been treated exhaustively in the novels: in *Ellernklipp* and

Grete Minde, as well as in *Stechlin*—think of little Agnes, who, although born out of wedlock, eases old Dubslav's last days; in *L'Adultera* there's the child born of marital infidelity, and then—if you'll show some pity for poor Effi—there's the child snatched away from her mother because of the mother's proven infidelity. Even so—as I know!—the question of guilt always remains open, as indeed the moral ground keeps shifting. Who wants to pass judgment? Who would presume to have the last word? Only philistines, who go sometimes by one name, sometimes another..."

Hoftaller remained silent for a while. Perhaps he hoped that Fonty's agitation would be cooled by the Kneipp water cure. We now observed that the two of them seemed intently focused on their health, treading the calm water with pedantic regularity. A pause followed, long enough for various speculations. But as we contemplated the many possible literary references, one title was missing; and we knew at once that this gap would not be left open.

Softly, too softly for us to hear in the dunes, but nevertheless quotable, because we, by profession clairaudient, caught wind of what he said, Hoftaller responded, "Oh, I agree. Only the Immortal showed such interest in the illegitimate child, also known as the bastard. Makes sense—his Emilie never said a word about her real father, a military doctor called Bosse; she preferred to be known by the name of her adoptive father, Kummer—which was bad enough, suggesting sorrow; and your Emmi has a similar blind spot. But I must admit, I'm amazed that you left one novel off the list. When it came out, it was denounced as a whore's tale. It's as if you were out to disown Lene Nimptsch, who is introduced on page one as an old woman's foster child; not one clue—except for a couple of hints from the gossipy Frau Dörr—as to the father and mother of the long-suffering beauty, whose lovable qualities were modeled on a certain Magdalena Strehlenow, and then, too, those rowboat excursions turn up again, except that this time it's the Spree, not the Elbe...."

"Wrong, Hoftaller! People can go rowing anywhere, and the only model for Lene was the daughter of the caretaker at the Academy of the Arts; during my short period as secretary there, I used to see her plying her needle..."

"...and she was a dark-haired beauty, whereas an ash-blond gardener's daughter and an ash-blond seamstress recall another ash-blond person, who was rowed on another body of water—by whom, do you suppose?"

"Is this absolutely necessary, Tallhover? I beg you..."

"A person who, let's say, was fatefully attached to Airman Wuttke, during the war, to be precise, in France—Lyon—the spring of '45. But this time we had an innkeeper's daughter in the boat...."

"Can't you people forget anything..."

"...who answered to the name of Madeleine. And this French girl, who wasn't even all that pretty..."

"This water's getting too cold for me."

"...soon cut a rather pathetic figure, because..."

"Besides, I see Emilie coming, look, over there, in the dunes...."

"...well, because a certain airman had..."

"Look—my Emilie's headed this way, leaning on the Freundlich ladies, who, so I hear, are planning to leave tomorrow already...."

"Oh, all right, let's show some mercy. But there's no help for it: Dresden and the consequences, Lyon and the consequences..."

"...and by the way, we're leaving tomorrow ourselves, sooner than we'd planned....We're worried because there's been no word from our daughter. Mete must have written to Berlin. My wife's very concerned, as am I...."

Thus ended the footbath in the Baltic. The Kneipp therapy and the embarrassing interrogation were broken off. As we went on our way, we saw that Fonty was the first to seek higher ground on the shore. His feet were blue, drained of blood. With a final statement—"We'll talk again"—Hoftaller followed, his feet and calves as red as lobsters. The two of them plodded in silence, Fonty with his trousers still rolled up, toward the Freundlich ladies and Emmi Wuttke, who gave the conversation a new turn, since her sprained foot offered ample material.

Theo Wuttke felt as though the ladies had saved him. He promptly began to jest with the daughters—who were twins, and therefore doubly charming.

Of the departure of the visitors the next morning, this much may be said: It started out cheerfully enough. Because our work was summoning us back to the Archives, we, too, departed for home, and thus became participant observers.

The Wuttkes almost missed the boat, for in spite of her handicap Emmi wanted to visit Hauptmann's grave again—alone—to lay a single rose at the boulder.

Fonty, who was waiting on the dock with their luggage, remarked, looking past us and Hoftaller, "That's how it is with the Emilies. Even Rouanet-Kummer preferred having a young whippersnapper at her side to the Immortal. 'My husband,' she said, 'is only a journalist, though he considers himself a real writer. But this Hauptmann, the one who wrote *The Weavers*—now there's a real writer for you.' That's how it was. She also preferred Raabe's *Hungerpastor* or Storm's Husumantics. Only Mete believed in me."

We archivists confirmed this anecdote. Fonty laughed. Professor Freundlich laughed. Both were still laughing as Emmi Wuttke, hobbling slightly, reached the pier. When Eckhard Freundlich explained the cause of the general merriment, Emmi laughed as well. The professor's wife and her evenly tanned daughters laughed with her. We smiled aloofly when we saw that now Hoftaller was laughing, too. So much merriment. But all the laughter would soon die away.

19

Alone in the Boat

In point of fact, the good mood should have accompanied the entire group as it took leave of the island and went on board, for in point of fact, all the visitors to the island could have taken the motor launch to Stralsund by way of Vitte and Neuendorf, as we and the Freundlichs did. But when the *Isle of Hiddensee* tied up, blowing its whistle to summon all on board, Hoftaller pulled out tickets for the Wuttkes and himself—for a boat leaving half an hour later for Schaprode on Rügen. He informed the assembled company: "Have a little surprise for our friend. Wouldn't want to throw off your plans. Anyway, best wishes for the trip. We'll wave from the shore."

He said this with a pasted-on childlike smile, and when Fonty, and, more emphatically, Emmi Wuttke protested that they had "not the slightest desire" to go to Schaprode, he had only one thing to add, this time withdrawing the smile: "I don't see how this wish of mine can be refused."

One of Hoftaller's usual conversation-stoppers, of which we keep a list in a special folder. He could also have said, "That would make me sad," or "Hope I've made myself clear." This time he had no need to be more menacing.

Emmi complained that she was in no condition for running around on Rügen, and she did not want to miss out on the train trip with the Freundlichs: "And I'm not letting anyone tell me which ship to take. That's over and done with now. We have our freedom now!" But Fonty had already been forced to swallow the bitter pill: "Afraid I must give in. No way around it."

We said nothing. And Eckhard Freundlich, who had likewise had plenty of experience with swallowing, offered a commentary on the imposed separation, "But of course, my dear Wuttke, we've learned to live with little vexations, or, to put it more mildly, certain travel restrictions. No one knows what deeper significance they hold. Your Briest said, in a similarly imponderable situation, 'This takes us far afield, Luise,' didn't he?"

But then the professor, already loaded down with luggage, added pointedly, "When my father left Mexico to return to Germany, he believed in something he liked to refer to at the dinner table, but also in public, as 'the good cause'; he should have reckoned with types like you." But Hoftaller was already flashing his dimples again: "Would have been a good idea, especially since we'd been watching your papa under the palms, which is why we came on board in Vera Cruz. But all joking aside: how are things in Jena? Disgusting, that whole evaluation process. Could make myself useful, if you wanted. Our contacts...you read me...don't want to be too obvious...but it doesn't have to be this way...."

The Freundlichs had to board the boat. We along with them. Both the daughters feeling anxious. The professor's wife kept repeating, "That pig!" As the *Isle of Hiddensee* pulled away from the dock, Hoftaller waved for a long time with a black-and-white-checkered handkerchief. The Wuttkes just stood there, their arms drooping. Emmi shed a few tears.

During the crossing to Stralsund, we tried to guess what compelling surprise could be conjured out of a hat in Schaprode. What did Hoftaller have to offer, other than the usual solicitude? Perhaps a trip to Scotland, of short duration, under supervision, of course? All sorts of things occurred to us, including the honorary directorship of the Archives. But we would never have guessed it would be one of those rattletraps manufactured in Zwickau, once coveted, now the object of scorn.

The three of them had been on board only a few minutes when Fonty was taken aside. Later he told us, "My Emilie absolutely refused to stay on deck. There was no persuading her. She spent the entire trip in the smoke-filled lounge. I, on the other hand, was assured of more fresh air than I wanted."

The two men stood in the breeze on the quarterdeck. Again black-and-yellow pennants, bow nets, cormorants perching on them, buoys along the navigation channel. Migratory birds practicing flight formations. The car-free island lay sprawled out, receding into the distance, a flat stretch extending from the hills to the Gellen, whose presence could be guessed, not seen. Neither spoke a word. Not until they were passing Vitte was the "little surprise" revealed to Fonty.

Hoftaller had not come by train but by car. And like other visitors to Hiddensee, he had parked his car in Schaprode, by the pier. He said, "My private car is waiting for you. I hereby take the liberty of inviting Herr and Frau Wuttke to join me for a drive. By way of Rügen, the Rügen embankment, and Stralsund, we'll soon be on the autobahn. I've always loved driving, by the way, since my earliest years in the service. Drove a DKW. Don't worry. I'm a safe driver. Besides, we'll get to Berlin much faster than that slowpoke train."

Only now, when it was too late, did Fonty demur. He said he refused to let himself be strong-armed, forced to ride in such a jalopy. If he could not share a compartment with the Freundlichs, he would have to travel alone with Emilie, as in the old days, when a railroad trip to the Riesengebirge or to Waren on Lake Müritz had still been an adventure: "Borsig's steam locomotives, fair enough, but not these tin crates..."

He dove into the past, reliving the rigors of the Immortal's summer holiday travels or trips to various spas; but Hoftaller was there waiting for him, even on the earliest journeys, cornering him with train schedules from before the '48 revolution: "You practically lived out of a suitcase. Constantly off to Leipzig or Dresden. This back-and-forth—we already discussed it—reminds me of the frequent official trips taken by a certain airman. Crisscrossing France to Lyon. All right, not a word—I promise—about Dresden and the ash-blond gardener's daughter, just a few clarifications regarding the repeated detours a certain someone, taking full advantage of the French national railroad, made to a city where a whole lot happened. Located on two rivers. Always a major trade hub. Filthy rich. And there was an innkeeper's daughter, who worked hard behind the counter, and in front of it, too, for which reason a travel-loving soldier soon became a kind of permanent guest in this bistro. Not without consequences, because the mademoiselle's brother was in the Resistance. But in other respects, too, what began in the spring bore, in the fullness of time, what I would call wintry consequences. See, after the soldier was forced to beat a retreat that summer... And because the abandoned Madeleine—yes, Madeleine was abandoned, for purely military reasons—and at this point no brother could help her...And after the invasion, there was a clean sweep everywhere, but particularly in Lyon....For which reason poor Madeleine's ash-blond hair was shaved off—buz-z-z...Well, Fonty, you get the picture? All began harmlessly enough with a rowboat excursion, just outside the city, on a lake where there were a whole lot of frogs, as everywhere in this region, which is also abundantly supplied with fish. There's more I could tell you. Could go on for hours. Have kept this to myself a long time, maybe far too long..."

Green and red buoys guided the motor launch to Schaprode. A ruck of gulls escorted them. Fonty let the breeze have its way with him, looking in his hat and light summer scarf like something from days gone by. Standing by the railing, he could have been a lead in the Ufa film *One Step from the Path*, directed by Gustav Gründgens. As much as he resembled old Briest, he was listening to an entirely different tale, watching all the while a formation of cormorants, those objects of all fishermen's hatred, as they flew toward the Gellen in a wedge, with constantly changing leaders.

Fonty said hardly a word, but Hoftaller seemed to have an inexhaustible supply of material. Up to the moment the boat docked in the narrows between Rügen and the island of Oehe, tucked between Rügen and the mainland, he continued to express his concerns in threatening tones: The recent contact and the years of correspondence with Professor Freundlich might prove harmful. A dossier still under wraps could, if necessary, compromise the scholar. Fonty should trust the inside information they had in storage: "Under changed circumstances, certain friendships become inappropriate. We don't want to get dragged into anything now, do we?"

Nothing remained of the Ufa flashback. As they were leaving the boat, Fonty had only one sentence for Emmi: "It'll be better if we go by car, better for your leg, I mean."

Emmi said, "I know what you mean."

They got to the car park and found there, squeezed in among Western chariots, the automotive signature of the former Workers' and Peasants' State. Hoftaller explained, "Lined this baby up just before the currency union, factory-new. Will run a long time. Believe you me, Fonty: unification, shmunification—some day it'll be cool again to drive a Trabi in Germany."

The trip in the two-stroker passed without incident. We archivists were also still making do in those days with the much-mocked cardboard box on wheels. Emmi told us later, "The two of them didn't say much. My Wuttke had to sit next to him. It was pretty cramped in back. And with my bad foot, too. But can't complain otherwise. Except that just past the Rügen embankment, no, not till we got to the autobahn, and that stubblehead—that's what our Martha calls him—wanted to light up one of his stinking stogies; well, I raised the roof. I'm not putting up with that. 'On the train I could've sat in the no-smoking car!' I yelled, and 'Let me out! Let me out of here!' So he put the stinking thing down and apologized. 'My little vice,' he whispered. 'How could I be so inconsiderate?' But not a word from my Wuttke. Only when we saw another of those wrecks on the side of the road, flipped over or completely burned out, he said, 'That's what you get for speeding. We're determined to imitate the West in every respect. But the hurrier we go, the behinder we'll get.' But no reaction. The other one, he just sat there, like an ape behind the wheel. Sulking, 'cause he couldn't have his cigar … But he didn't drive too fast. … How could he have, in a Trabi? Those Mercedeses and other speedsters kept passing us. No, my Wuttke didn't seem depressed at all, he just couldn't talk like he usually does. Somehow the atmosphere in that car was rotten, even though the weather was so nice outside. I say to myself, I say, He must've put some kind of pressure on him, but what? Could it've been our

Teddy, 'cause he's over there in Bonn doing something top secret? Or from the old Cultural Union, 'cause my Wuttke really did come out with some awful things at times? No, not aimed straight at the leading comrades, but kind of through the back door—you know how he always talks. I remembered Bad Saarow—that's where the Cultural Union had its recreation camp, but it was also kind of like a college—and my Wuttke said a whole bunch of awful things when he gave a talk there on that Lene Nimptsch woman. She's called that 'cause the poet Lenau was his hero. Anyway, there was a Lenau Club in those days where his one-and-only was a member before he joined that Herwegh Society, the one they banned. That's why they were all spied on, not only Herwegh, who got out while the getting was good. So my Wuttke talked about that, and about all the pharmacies in Leipzig and Dresden. And that the spying never ends, 'cause it can't. And that spies are immortal, like the poets they spy on. But that sometimes poets are spies, too, which makes them doubly immortal. And then, he says—and in front of an audience, too—he says, The top spy, the one who spied on Herwegh and his society a hundred fifty years ago, is still running around and spying—under a different name, of course, but that just goes to show he's immortal. When he got to that point, you could hear whispering in the hall. A couple of folks laughed. But then, in that Bad Saarow talk—we liked to go there for the holidays when Martha was little—my Wuttke shoots off a few rockets that weren't in his text—I'd typed it for him, you know—about how the spy from those olden times was there in the hall, pricking up his ears and taking notes on everything, just like he always took notes on everything before. 'He forgets nothing, he can forget nothing!' he said. When was that? Mid-sixties, when they suddenly clamped down on cultural stuff again. Must have been after the Wall went up, anyway, 'cause our boys were already over there... And Georg fully trained as a pilot...Friedel still doing his book-trade apprenticeship...Anyway, they held that against my Wuttke. They called him in a couple of times. Did no good when he tried to wiggle out of it with 'The enemy of the working class never sleeps!' and 'Always keep an eye peeled for Western agents!' Just made everything even worse. No more holidays for us in Bad

Saarow. And he couldn't lecture any more, till it straightened out again. But they didn't forget a thing. No-o-o, they never forget. That's why I think that stubblehead—that's what our Martha calls him—must've put pressure on my Wuttke again, 'cause he wouldn't ever have got into that Trabi on his own, not when he was looking forward so much to being on the same train with the Freundlichs. . . . Course I didn't care that much, 'cause . . . well, I just don't feel comfortable with them. . . . And like our Martha always says . . . But that's neither here nor there. Actually they were awfully nice to me when this thing happened with my foot, 'cause when I was climbing up to the lighthouse, a stupid root . . . Well, Frau Freundlich, she's all right. And the girls are nice, too. It's just the professor that I can't . . . Never could. When he says Meheeco, not Mexico like us, it gives me the shivers. But my Wuttke wanted to go on chatting for hours with his 'faithful correspondent'—that's what he calls him. 'Reichsbahn is better than autobahn!' he said. Anyway, we made it to Berlin all right, nothing bad happened. He took us right to our doorstep in that Trabi—it's some kind of yellow—and then—we'd already said 'Thanks for the ride,' or some such—he says, real serious to my Wuttke, 'The Lene Nimptsch case is still on the books!' and then he drops a couple of dark hints about France—'Lyon and the consequences!'—you know, that's where my Wuttke was in the military, but he doesn't like to talk about it. Even after the stubblehead went zooming off, not a word. I kind of think something bad must've happened there in France, 'cause his letters from the field were strange. When we finally got upstairs— three flights with our bags and the tote—and there was the mail, with letters from our Martha, one from Copenhagen and one from that Danish island—right, Møn's the name—my Wuttke seemed like a different person. Laughing and making jokes about honeymooners and such. Yet Martha's letters didn't say anything special, just that the weather's nice and her Grundmann has too much work along, lots of paperwork, and sometimes she feels so homesick for us and good old Berlin. Oh, yes, and Denmark's awfully expensive, especially Copenhagen. But my Wuttke was just beside himself. He's so attached to Martha, you know, thinks the world of her, but I . . . Well, I shouldn't say that, 'cause I do worry about her.... It'd be nice if she could be happy.... Exactly. That's the main thing. Anyway, my Wuttke goes jumping around the kitchen and keeps shouting, 'I feel like rowing! Around and around in a circle, for all I care. As long as I'm rowing! Would you care to come along, Emilie? That would be something. The two of us in one boat. You can rent them in the Tiergarten. Like Stralau in the old days. No, no rocking the boat. Nothing to be afraid of. Just drifting along...' And when he went on and on like that, I suddenly got the picture. 'Cause in his letters from the field in France he used to write about rowing all the time, too, and how nice it is to go rowing, even sent a poem... Well, well, I think to myself, something's fishy here, there's more to this than meets the eye...."

Emmi Wuttke was not to be moved to go for a rowboat excursion à deux. And it was not until the following afternoon that Fonty could act on his impulse. First he went to the Ministries Building to have his convalescent leave approved, a stack of paperwork. In the personnel office he was told, "That's fine, Fonty. Why didn't you stay longer? Far as we're concerned, you can take a break for as long as you feel like. Nothing happening here anyway. Only cleaning up and clearing out—housecleaning, new broom...you know what I mean. We're just paid to make ourselves superfluous. But stop by when you're back on track. There's plenty to do. You know, because of the one-fatherland-indivisible everything's got to be wound down in a hurry. But it'll be a while, don't you worry. Go take your walks, Fonty. Don't worry, we'll keep you on the payroll till there's nothing left, and then something new'll come along. It always has. They can't let this old place stand empty...."

Such prospects were reassuring. As if he wanted to stay in practice, Fonty went up and down a few times on the paternoster. He was greeted, greeted people in turn, enjoyed little chats between floors: "You lucky so-and-so. Holidays on Hiddensee! That's something folks like us could only dream of. Was usually booked solid by the big shots. What? You were in Neuendorf? I remember, the terrace of Franz Freese's Hotel, right on the water. Steamed cod they had. Oh, really? Are the lindens still there?"

Suddenly, or because the desire to go rowing swept over him again, Fonty quit the paternoster. Or is it we who want to see him on the move, impatient to get out on the water?

It is true: outdoors he seems more accessible to us than behind closed doors. We can see him now, striding with his youthful gait through the portal of the colossal edifice, turning onto Leipziger Strasse, crossing the future construction site on Potsdamer Platz, his walking stick shouldered like a gun as he advances unhindered into the West. We see him crossing the busy bypass, holding up the traffic for a few seconds, hear him whistling a spirited path-breaking march, something like "Prussia's Glory." He is in fine spirits, for now he is approaching the Tiergarten, always his favorite terrain for walks, whether to the Amazon near the goldfish pond, to Rousseau Island and his time-honored bench, or, as today, across Hofjägerallee, past the bronze evocations of the hunt, down the Great Way, twirling his walking stick now, striking the ground every second step, all the way to New Lake, whose tributary is fed by water from the Landwehr Canal—which borders the Zoo on one side—by way of the pumping station on Lützow Bank. Now he stops by the Lakeside Café, but with no intention of sitting on the terrace under the chestnuts.

On the spot for which he was headed there had hulked—until it was blown up long after the war's end—a huge flak bunker, in whose concrete bowels human beings and heaps of art treasures had survived the bombing. As early as 1840, New Lake had appeared in the third set of blueprints, an artificial pond for a natural park. Lenné had suggested that they avoid the expense of drying out the Elsbruch swamp by creating a body of water that could be linked later to the new canal and would be an inviting setting for boat rides. The park cost more than thirty thousand talers, including the bridges—a great deal of money for a thrifty king, whom some even accused of being stingy.

And on the very spot where, in the mid-nineteenth century, a Herr Alexander had begun renting out boats, there was a long pier, accessible from the left side of the terrace, with a good two dozen boats, made of plastic. Their rowing benches, however, as well as their hulls, were made of wood, as were the oars.

A form of recreation that could once be had for a song now costs twenty-two marks an hour; yet when Fonty asked about the rental price, he received the answer, in view of his wrinkled outfit—light jacket, linen trousers, boater, and walking stick—"That'll be ten for you, Gramps!"

As security, he had to hand over his identity card. After further questions, which in traditional Berlin style had to poke fun— "So where's Grandma today? And what've you done with the darling grandkids?"—Fonty got into the boat with a little leap, stowed his jacket and stick on the extruded plastic seat in the stern, sat down on the wooden rowing bench, and, as the boatman shoved him off with the cry "Ship ahoy!" dipped first one, then the other of the oars into the water. With a few strokes he had put distance between himself and the shore. One channel led from the café with the pleasant terrace to the middle of the lake and its island, which, however, according to a sign on the pier, was off limits: "Bird Sanctuary!"

Fonty was an experienced rower. He pulled evenly on the oars, his strokes never too deep or too shallow. As a boy he had felt at home on Lake Ruppin. Later he had rowed on reed-choked Lake Diana when he visited his father. The grounds of the villa at the corner of Rabbits' Run and Königsallee sloped down to the lake. There was not enough space for long rowboat excursions there, but he helped set the eel traps while his father explained to his taciturn lady friend for the nth time that the Social Democratic unions could serve as a model for the rest of the world.

Fonty enjoyed rowing alone on New Lake, even in a plastic boat. Yet all of his rowboat excursions, which included boat rides during the war—whether on Polish rivers and lakes, in the shallow bays off Danish islands, or on France's still waters—had literary overtones, for it was fictional experiences that shaped them. There was that boating party—on the Spree near Stralau—that Lene Nimptsch let herself be talked into in the prelude to *Delusions, Confusions*. "Because Lina Gansauge was determined to ride in a boat," and the adolescent Rudolf, "who was a brother of Lina's," took the helm.

That was followed, as we know, by the business with the steamer, which came from Treptow, making waves. Let us remind ourselves that Rudolf, out of fear and stupidity, lost control of the helm, "so that we spun around and around in a circle." Whereupon Lene and Lina began to scream, for the steamer was bearing down upon them. And surely "we would have been run over if, at that very moment, the other boat with two gentlemen had not taken pity on us in our moment of need...." Pulled in close with the boat hook and lashed firmly to the other boat, they were towed out of the vortex, and "only once did it seem again as if the huge wave coming toward us from the steamer were about to capsize us...."

This explains why Fonty, alone in the rowboat on New Lake in the Tiergarten, had other water under his keel, for it was a boat ride that led to the sad but beautiful love story of the ash-blond laundress and seamstress Lene Nimptsch and Baron Botho von Rienäcker, who, despite his imposing height, had a weak character. And later there was another boat ride, in conjunction with an excursion the two of them risked without Frau Dörr, who until then had functioned as their chaperone.

On the Görlitz train, they reached the vicinity of the inn at Hankel's Depot on the upper Spree, an ideal spot for rowing. Only after the boat ride did they take a room together. But the events of that night are not recorded. At most the innkeeper is allowed to express a touch of embarrassment. Just one of many omissions— or should we say gaps?

In a letter to Otto Brahm, written in '83, the Immortal confesses, "I can, it seems fair to say, portray the prelude to a love story and also the aftermath; indeed, for the latter I may have a considerable gift; but I will never carry off the love scenes themselves...." And Fonty defended his omission of the kind of "infamous descriptions" that he characterized as "the acme of tastelessness," reminding us of the telltale notes in Crampas's hand addressed to Effi that "say it all!" Lene's letters also had to pay the price; although Botho had perceived these tokens of her love as "at once rational and passionate," faulty spelling and all, in the end he had burned them, without quoting anything intimate, let alone passionate.

He rowed along the shore, the low-hanging branches grazing him, then back into the middle of the man-made lake and around the bird sanctuary, skillfully avoiding other boats. The island attracted many, yet no one actually stepped onto it; all respected the prohibition.

Fonty rowed with calm strokes. On the moss-green surface, flat as a mirror, a duck and later a swan created wedge-shaped wakes. Sometimes he rested the oars parallel to the water, letting the water drip off and the boat drift. He put his hat down behind him. We saw him maintaining an upright posture: his back straight and a little stiff, perhaps too posed; yet we were delighted with his deceptively authentic profile. The old man sat motionless, gazing out beyond the lake and its traffic. The sun, low in the late-afternoon sky, lit up his hair.

Perhaps the overhanging branches of the trees along the bank and the early autumnal sky of that September day deserve the credit for the rhymed quatrain Fonty composed during one such pause in his rowing; but we learned of this occasional poem only from a later letter, which enables us to transcribe it here:

> As I rowed, the weeping willow stroked my fev'rish head.
> Close by the lake shore I felt its tender hand.
> I saw us in the boat, a pair, so young, yet sped
> Too soon, alas, toward our love's sorry end.

Again he dipped in the oars and with listless strokes set out in another direction. He rowed along one of the arms of the lake, which, after a longish detour, delayed by one bend after another, took him back to the middle. He passed dense underbrush and twisted, knobby trees, their roots wading in the water. It was growing dark in a rather sinister fashion. On rocks along the shore, the remnants of a ripped dress sent a scarlet signal. Suddenly, on a bench, in the shadows, a man masturbating. The stagnant water smelled. Duckweed. There were no boats coming toward him. Treacherous silence . . . nothing to take pleasure in . . . No helpful quotation presented itself. . . . Not until Fonty rowed back into the open did he again have boating excursions in his wake that took place in favorable light and were captured on paper.

We assume that he relived the boat trip on the upper Spree: two boots were tied up by the dock when Lene and Botho took their trip to Hankel's Depot. "Which should we have," Botho asked, "the *Trout*—or the *Hope*?" And Fonty quoted Lene's reply out loud, in such ringing tones that he might have been proclaiming a philosophical position: "The *Trout,* of course. What good is hope to us?"

His oars resting once more, he listened as the quotation died away, then wiped his brow with the back of his hand, reached behind him for the straw hat, put it on, glanced warily toward the shore, ran his eyes over benches and a lawn that sloped to the water, saw couples and single individuals sunning themselves, saw a boy who kept a white ball bouncing uninterruptedly off his table-tennis racket, saw extended Turkish clans and clusters of bicyclists; but not until he rowed back to the Lakeside Café did he see what the present moment had in store for him: on the dock where boats were rented, someone was standing, waving to him with a baseball cap.

Hoftaller wanted to go rowing, too, or rather he wanted to be rowed. But Fonty was tired. He paid, even though the hour was not up yet, and reclaimed his identity card. "So, Gramps? All tuckered out?"

Hoftaller would not let go. "Just half an hour. At my expense, of course..."

"Tomorrow's another day."

"It's a deal."

Since Fonty seemed to have no choice, he raised his shoulders, then let them drop. If there was no way around it, early morning was best. The lake wouldn't be crowded in the morning. Of course he preferred rowing alone, but he would make an exception and accept this invitation. They went on their way, casting a coupled shadow.

We may presume that as they made for the nearby Zoo station they chatted about nothing in particular. Or should we see them on the

Lichtenberg Bridge, which spans the Landwehr Canal? They headed for the bridge because the Trabi was parked along Lützow Bank. Once again it was Hoftaller whom Fonty was forced to follow.

On the way to the car, a memorial plaque along the shoreline promenade brought them to a halt. It recounted how on the evening of 15 January 1919 the socialist Rosa Luxemburg had been killed on this spot by officers and soldiers of the mounted guards and thrown into the canal; only a hundred meters farther on, where the canal flowed into New Lake, Karl Liebknecht had been murdered.

They stood by the railing on which the commemorative casting was mounted. It was trying, in capital letters, to keep alive the memory of the victims' names. Hoftaller pointed out the mark of the foundry, the People's Lauchhammer Works, likewise immortalized in metal, with the date 1987. He also knew that the Workers' and Peasants' State had supported this late initiative—"Handled through our contacts in West Berlin." Fonty responded, "The services have always done thorough work. What the Tallhovers begin, the Hoftallers continue, even if this means that today the former murderers are dedicating monuments to their victims. Nineteen hundred and nineteen, the year we were born, by the way; I feel as if we'd been there."

Hoftaller had nothing to say to that. His ancient eyes gazed without blinking, the smile had faded. Nor was another word spoken later, when they were both seated in the Trabi. It was not until they had reached Kollwitzstrasse, where they had driven without stopping, that Fonty's day-and-night-shadow had accumulated enough material for a response: "Right again, Wuttke. Nothing's really over. Everywhere our derelictions dog us. No wonder Tallhover's biographer totes up nothing but bungles.... For instance, the Luxemburg woman should have had 'round-the-clock surveillance...Kautsky, too.... In 1910 Lenin comes to see him again.... And at Luxemburg's place on Cranachstrasse...We should have swung into operation, should have got down to business at the right moment; the story would've turned out quite differently.... Ah, Fonty, sometimes I wonder, like your Immortal: 'What's the point?' I'm getting tired...losing my grip...losing sight of the meaning...really need help....Yes, yes, we have to talk it all over, man to man. Best to do it tomorrow, in the rowboat...but don't want to get ahead of myself. Have a good rest, Wuttke. You'll need your strength...."

20

Changing Places

But he couldn't rest. All evening long and far into the night Fonty bore down hard on the Red Chinese runner in his study, refusing to listen to Emmi, who kept knocking from the kitchen: "You stop that pacing, now! Come out here and eat something, Wuttke. We're having cold cuts and tomato salad."

But he continued his back and forth. He had not paced so persistently since writing the therapeutic account of his childhood. True, someone else had set him going recently—poor Effi, whose too short life had been serialized in '94 and distributed the following year as a book, first in the usual tiny edition, then in printing after printing—by which time he was already at work on *Stechlin*. But now he felt thrown back, and as if on a rejuvenated carpet. Early memories revealed their pattern. And everything demanded to be named: "China pomade and sal ammoniac lozenges. Gustav Struve's Salamonis Apothecary Shop. Letters to Wolfsohn. Behind the counter with Richard Kersting. And one day that young thing came in, the gardener's daughter from the New Town, and wanted cod-liver oil for her little brother.... Ah, Lena Strehlenow... All shrouded in silence and secrecy... bays in the reeds... flaming kisses... But every secret was unearthed by that bloodhound, whose nose remained hot on the trail from the Herwegh Society in Leipzig to lovely Dresden... He sniffed out everything, even the birthmark under her breast and the thinness of her ash-blond hair. Ah, Lena! Her slender yet hard-working hands, always cracked from repotting and weeding. She liked to sing, despite her wispy voice, when the fancy for freedom or singing struck us, while rowing or on the grassy banks of the Elbe. Ah, what became of my radical friends? In Leipzig we were six or eight men weak. Two—Blum and Jellinek—were later executed by firing squad in Vienna. Two went to the dogs in America. Two others became Saxon philistines. Only Wolfsohn remained. And Max Müller—son of the poet who wrote those verses Schubert would later set to music—made a name for himself in England. Knew Sanskrit, tutored the queen, advised the Empire on all matters relating to India, for which reason the German cultural institutes, which elsewhere are named after Goethe, in India are called Max Mueller Bhavan. At any rate, he amounted to something, the only one who did, excepting the man memorialized in the expression 'shot like Robert Blum,' and the Immortal, who knew how to bob and weave, and survived all his freedom-crazed friends, for better or worse, but mostly worse. And with him hibernated poor Effi, as did, of course, the old man who chafed against his given name, Dubslav. Time and again the Treibels sprouted anew, overrunning everything like the local ribwort. Mathilde Möhring: indestructible. As for Schach, his fear of making a spectacle of himself has proven durable. A few ballads that seem determined not to die. But Lene also endured, a resonant echo—the scrupulous omission of any pillow talk notwithstanding—of a brief, or, rather, repeatedly prolonged bliss that lasted six or seven years, or at any rate blossomed time and again in Dresden, even shrugging off the engagement to Emilie as immaterial, escalating—if only out of fear of the imminent end—to the point that the bliss in the Elbe meadows accounted for two children, born in secret, of whom only the first, Mathilde, survived the childhood diseases, whereas Ernestine was soon whisked away, after two years of support payments: diphtheria.... Yet the mother, whose identity can be documented—yes, indeed, her name was Magdalena Strehlenow and she was eighteen when I took her—this mother was still alive forty years later when she underwent rejuvenation and renewal as Lene Nimptsch, through a kind of literary therapy; at the time she was in the care of her capable daughter Mathilde in the West Prussian town of Konitz. For the charming little anecdote about the Academy caretaker's daughter, who has black hair, by the way, is pure nonsense, spread by the family, including Mete, alas—but mainly by the sons. A strategic lie, by which my dearly beloved snooper was not taken in, of course; he sniffed out everything—the allusion in the name, the anemic moonlit verses—for we always had Lenau with us in the boat; actually he was called Nikolaus Niembsch Edler von Strehlenau, emigrated to America, came back, despaired of his times, and eventually went mad, yet his poems were immortal, so much so that when we were out in the rowboat we recited his reed poems and later the forest poems.... Yes, we rowed on still, almost stagnant waters. Sometimes we let the boat drift. Possibly it was at this time that a literary daughter was conceived, destined to come into the world under a title good for the ages. A rather slim novel that spilled out of my pen while *Cécile* and *Stine* were still in the works, or resting in a drawer; the first eight chapters were finished at Hankel's Depot, where the accursed rowing continued, for the Spree was no different from the Elbe.... But it wasn't until three years later, soon after *Cécile,* that *Delusions, Confusions* was serialized, from the end of June to the end of August in the *Vossy*; on the one hand I thought, Only the somewhat better audience of this paper—which calls itself liberal—will appreciate the Berlin milieu. On the other hand, I said to myself, Heavens, who reads novellas in hot weather like this? And it proved an utter disaster. The bourgeoisie and the gentry unanimous in their hypocritical reaction. As if I'd foreseen the Treibels and their ilk. One of the *Vossy*'s publishers even expressed outrage: 'Will this dreadful whore's tale never end...?' That pack of philistines did my Lene in. These martinets on their moral high horses! These afternoon preachers! Yet unlike Zola, whom I was reading at the time with a mixture of horror and admiration, I omitted anything ugly, any eruption of passion, even social misery. I avoided these things almost too timidly, because...Not until later, much too late, when the book was in print, did Schlenther and Brahm review it respectfully, with the result that my Lene, even if she didn't help my finances, at least achieved a certain *succès d'estime,* no more.... And now this eternal spy comes along, slaps an obsolete dossier down on the table, and says, 'According to our records, we're dealing here with...' Whispers, 'We have informants who tell us that the two of them were seen repeatedly, well into September, rowing on various arms of the Elbe, in still waters, in the course of which poems were heard being recited, which, however, didn't have revolutionary rhymes, and of which not one line can be attributed to subject Herwegh. Actually they expressed a certain bourgeois decadence. . . .' And this spy now wants me to take him out in a boat. . . . Wants to venture out on the water, of his own free will . . . I'd love to know if he can swim. . . ."

Thus tormented by memories, perhaps even thoughts of revenge, Fonty ignored Emmi's pleas and wore himself ragged on the Chinese runner, preparing for the impending boat ride. But it turned out differently. He had been heading in the wrong direction. Once again his day-and-night-shadow had stolen a march on him.

Few patrons at the Lakeside Café this early in the morning, but he, ever punctual, was already waiting by the pier, having paid in advance, so as not to have to surrender his identity card. He was a hodgepodge of colors, like a tourist. Fonty helped him into the rocking boat. And Hoftaller, who otherwise could handle anything, remarked, "Sorry, I don't know how to row. It's all yours, Fonty. You'll have to pull our weight. But watch out, I can't swim."

One in the stern, the other on the rowing bench. They sat facing each other, yet their knees never touched. Fonty stayed on course, down the narrow channel to the lake. Still Old Wives' Summer, the sun's rays slanting sharply. In the bushes along the banks, where the morning dew lingered, enormous spiderwebs glistened, each stretched around its own core, yet all of them woven together, as if the thread were endless, as if the spiders' dewy industry were calling out to the rower and his passenger: Look at this ceaseless labor! Admire our artistic know-how, our practical beauty. And we never give up. We're always searching for the hole in the system. There's always a gap to be closed. You can count on us. Yet we have a bad reputation. We're rewarded with curses. Only the prey that gets caught in our net can count on sympathy. Even the bluebottle fly, otherwise despised, is commemorated in rhyme. . . .

We are not guessing; we know: soon after that rowboat excursion, Fonty jotted down a quatrain, of which he penned a clean copy that he enclosed in a letter to Professor Freundlich, whose neck was on the line in Jena:

> *And so we see, caught in a single net*
> *Victim and perpetrator.*
> *Whether such proximity brings closeness, or happiness yet*
> *Poses an unanswered question only later.*

Perhaps it was because of this glistening metaphor, too close at hand, that Hoftaller urged the rower to shun the bank and—as soon as the arm of the lake opened up—steer toward the middle: "There we can let ourselves drift a little. Fantastic, Fonty, how good you are. Plenty of practice, eh? Not surprising. When you were a boy on Lake Ruppin, and all those times since then..."

A few more powerful strokes and space-gobbling pulls, and Fonty hoisted the oars and let the water drip off them. When there was enough distance between the boat, the bird sanctuary, and the lakeshore, he said, "Let's get this over with! Start the interrogation. Where did we leave off? Dresden, the summer of '42? Or must the club in Leipzig be operatively encircled again, observed, surveilled, skimmed, isolated, tapped, exhumed? Wolfsohn and Müller slipped through your net, but poor Blum was put up against the wall, and so was Jellinek, a wretched little student. Hasn't the spider had its fill yet? All right, Tallhover, suck away, suck me dry. I'm happy to be able to give up my last juices."

Hoftaller let his left hand slide into the water as he reclined in the gently drifting boat; he was plainly enjoying the ride: "Oh, come, my friend! Why take it personally? Leipzig, Dresden! A bagatelle! That proceeding was wrapped up long ago; it's of literary-historical interest at most. It could fill an archival gap, nothing more. But it's something else entirely when we come to the rowing excursions taken by a certain airman third class, then airman second class, by the name of Theo Wuttke, who later, much later, allowed himself to be widely known as Fonty, for which reason we had him down as an informant under that code name in Cultural Union days. And this soldier was rowing, not on the gently flowing stream of the upper Elbe, but first on the Rhône's turbulent current, with the proud, standoffish city of Lyon towering behind him, later in an area northeast of the city that was dotted with lakes. And, as I already alluded to, in the spring of that war year of '44, seated opposite him was no gardener's daughter but the daughter of the innkeeper Marcel Blondin. Like me, she let her hand trail in the water, patently blissful. They went rowing often. Dombes was the name of the area, with lakes full of fish. Sometimes the innkeeper's son, a certain Jean-Philippe, went along, not as a chaperone, but, rather... Let's not go into that. Let's chat instead about Madeleine, who, by the way, was pure ash-blond. What's wrong, Wuttke! Stop rocking the boat! You always had a thing for ash-blondes. Stop it! I told you I can't swim. And if this rocking doesn't... Don't want to wash up on the bank..."

Fonty ended his violent protest, but with fear-driven strokes he made for the bank, the weeping willows overhanging the water, the spiderwebs in the bushes, and between strokes he called out: "I don't want to hear this.... This story's been chewed over hundreds of times.... I already told you on Hiddensee.... Right, just a little hanky-panky... Happened all the time in those days, especially in the rear echelons... As sweet as it was harmless, when you get right down to it... Just a bit of rowing... A couple of excursions to Chalamont, where you could rent a boat from the fishermen... Besides, the invasion put an end to it.... And then in August, the uprising in Lyon... too late for Madeleine's brother... And I got my marching orders.... Retreat on all fronts... Was captured... Later sent to the camp in Bad Kreuznach..."

When Fonty, as if seeking refuge, made a move to halt the boat under the hanging branches of a weeping willow, near where we were sitting, Hoftaller turned tough, brandishing the familiar formula: "We can do this the hard way!" Then he ordered Fonty to stay away from the bank. What he had to say was meant not for the eavesdroppers to be found on every bank, but only for former Airman Wuttke. "We don't want to get ourselves into a situation now, do we?"

Back in the middle of the lake, Fonty drew up the oars, let them drip, took off his hat, set it beside him, and mopped his brow. "All right. Her name was Madeleine Blondin. Her brother, an electrician's apprentice, must have been a member of the *Résistance*. Was arrested at any rate. No, not by our people; the local gendarmerie took him away. Loved literature, like his sister. I read aloud to the two of them, right, in the boat. Yes, from *Delusions, Confusions*. But also Raabe, *The Black Galley*. A lovely time, but short. Occasionally on another lake. The last one near Bourg-en-Bresse. We had only a few months, then Lyon had to be evacuated. Besides, I was ordered back to Berlin, but wound up, as I said, a prisoner of war. End of mission. Over and out. Well, yes, memories, brief moments of happiness, but I request permission not to discuss those."

Hoftaller took his time, deliberately, even ceremoniously, lighting a cigar from his Cuban cache. In the drifting boat he followed the smoke with his eyes: "Fine, Wuttke. Or should I call you Fonty instead? After all, almost a year ago, on 4 November, a certain Theo Wuttke was called by that name on Alexanderplatz: 'Let Fonty speak!' Not a bad speech, by the way—confused and therefore in keeping with the occasion. So, my dear Fonty, I give in. Let's put an end to the rowboat excursions. Let's say nothing for now about your illegal outings to the Cévennes; let's merely hint at your contacts with the Resistance; let's just touch on your moments of happiness, for all I care. But please understand: it must be pointed out that in purely human terms your brief love affair bore consequences. Neither the invasion nor the hasty retreat, least of all your captivity, could remove from the world a piece of evidence that took a certain amount of time to come to full term; at all events, shortly after the end of the war a little girl was born, and was given the lovely name of Cécile by her mother. No, not Mathilde this time. But I see this is too much for you. Let's take a break, Wuttke. Let's drift for a while. Enjoy this September weather. No nicer time of year than late summer or early fall, whatever you want to call it. A terrific idea, rowing and chatting as we row about God and the world. A healthy child, by the way, little Cécile. She developed splendidly, even though her mother...had her head shaved in public...was chased through the streets...Shameful, Fonty...But I don't want to upset you, my friend...."

After that only the sound of the moss-green water gently lapping. From other boats came bursts of distorted laughter. Every breeze wafted the smell of shashlik over the area. On the lawn, a couple or someone sunning alone had turned up a transistor radio to blanket the area. The two in the rowboat were silent. As the sun rose in the sky, Fonty put on his hat again. His shadowed face revealed nothing. And as time passed, Hoftaller kept an eye on the growing ash of his cigar, as if something meaningful could be read from it, a coded message or a magic word.

But the moment he dangled his right hand, with the cigar, over the edge of the boat, this encrypted evidence of painstakingly even smoking dropped overboard in one piece, hitting the water with a hiss. Perhaps it had reached the breaking point, or perhaps a gentle tap had helped things along. After a slight sigh, Hoftaller said, "Ah, Germany," and then he suddenly reached a decision: "Let's change places, Wuttke. I want to row now. You can rest and listen to me for a while. Good God, what times we live in! History's being made every day. In just over a week the fatherland will be united. Bound to turn out badly!" And already he was on his feet. Fonty drew in the oars and stood up, too.

We think we heard the hissing of the ash. After that all was silence. From the lawn or from the shadowy banks, but also from other rowboats, a worrisome tableau could be seen: two old men changing places in a rocking rowboat. They were still waiting, as if for a command. They faced one another, one tall and lean, the other short-legged and squat, both with arms dangling in readiness, like statues, until the boat lay quietly in the water. "Go!" I whispered.

Viewed from the bank, the exchange was accomplished without words; and we shall refrain from assigning captions ex post facto to this pantomime, although there was much that had not yet been said. For instance, Hoftaller, after he had again announced that he could not swim—this time a little apprehensively—might have opened his secret coffer and fetched out memories of similar switches during rowboat excursions on the lakes northeast of Lyon, and Fonty would have had to admit that he had left the rowing bench in order to do a favor for the rower, Jean-Philippe, and his sister, Madeleine, seated in the bow: he moved to the stern and spoke, in a clear voice, into a tape-recording apparatus liberated from the Wehrmacht's inventory. All that on still waters. Hardly any background noise. But this secret was spilled only later, when Fonty received a decoration.

At any rate, the two of them stood facing each other without a word. No order was given, unless of course my whispered "Go!" was a help: now they began changing positions simultaneously. With small groping steps, which, however, could merely be guessed at from the shore, they moved a shoe's width at a time, at first free-hand, their arms still dangling, then joined together, each seizing hold of the other, for the boat had begun to rock, and they were now reeling along with it. Fonty's hands gripped Hoftaller's shoulders firmly, and Hoftaller hung on to Fonty's hips.

What could now be heard from the shore were instructions issued to Hoftaller, which he followed scrupulously because his subject was experienced at changing places in a rowboat. The linked pair pushed and turned clockwise. A solemn, groping dance. Or a ceremony of ritual seriousness. Or an embrace of the sort that is based on the well-known assurance: We're in the same boat.

That was true in every respect, and could have inspired Fonty to compose another quatrain, in which the rhyme for *asunder* would have been *go under*. But he was in no mood for such versesmithery.

Finally they had replaced one another. The tight grip was released. We breathed a sign of relief. I found myself wishing they would remain that way a while longer; and as if answering my wish, both of them stood still again, arms dangling, now that they had passed this test of courage.

When they then put some distance between themselves, stepping backward and taking their new places, it could be observed from the bank that Hoftaller, who was now seated on the rowing bench, had had his cigar, smoked down to a stump, clamped in his mouth during the entire place-changing ceremony; and apparently the Cuban stogie was still drawing, for he was sending smoke signals that we archivists could not interpret; where Hoftaller was concerned, we were limited to conjecture, except when the day-and-night-shadow actually spoke.

Fonty sat upright in the stern and tugged at his boater, which had slipped to one side. With fresh energy the rower placed the oars on the tholepins and with his very first stroke demonstrated how inept he was. The oars went in much too deep, then not deep enough or at an odd angle, which caused a lot of splashing. It was pathetic to watch. So much flailing to so little effect. So much effort schooled in futility. So much lost motion.

But he was rowing all the same. Short-sleeved, Hawaiian-patterned, he rowed in a circle, and with each stroke of the oar he launched words, sometimes bunched together, sometimes isolated—exclamations, bursts of laughter, abbreviated sentences, also longer ones, often incomplete ones—all aimed at Germany, all targeting the country's unification, all echoing across the lake, past the banks and over the lawn and the blaring transistor radio.

His speech sounded to us like dictation: "Mantle of history! Take charge! Had no time to lose...Had to act fast, so nothing could...Had been in the works for a long time...But they didn't want any part of it, those dodderers in Wandlitz, ha! Starting in '85, memo after memo...All for nothing...And the Russians totally unreliable...Nothing but glasnost and perestroika...But without the Soviet power behind us...Nothing but blahblahblah... Devil take the hindmost...Quite true, theoretically. But soon no stopping it. All that shouting: We're the people! Right, pure crap, but dangerous...Had to act, you know, because that Third Way stuff was even more dangerous...Doesn't exist, not anywhere: Third Way! Not over here, not in capitalism. In the West they realized that, too. So we opened her up—the Wall, I mean....Open Sesame! And down she went. Right-o. It was us. Wanted to create new conditions. On the skids, that Third-Way crowd. They could just forget about it. And we quickly made a little correction....Had to substitute just one word...First in Leipzig, then everywhere... See what one little word can do, Wuttke?...Not *the*, but *one* people! Tiny difference? Right! But it did the trick, it changed everything.

At first the West was speechless, but they caught on fast and grabbed the opportunity. The only bumps in the road were over here. Round tables—don't make me laugh! They wanted to place the people's property in trust, keep it from falling into capitalist hands, called it a democratic precaution.... Of course that didn't suit the West one bit. From their point of view, it was all individual chunks of property, whether residential or a factory, and all there for the taking.... Hundreds of bargains to snap up... But we weren't going to be left out. We're in the game was our motto. Of course over there they thought they should get it at rock-bottom prices. Began to haggle. So we quickly came up with a different slogan.... No go with tin money! If the mark won't come to us, we'll come and get it. That helped. Since then they've been paying themselves silly.... And it'll cost them more and more... and all borrowed money! I foresee a mountain of debt.... So what, Fonty, it's not our problem! We'll soften 'em up and break 'em down till they're scrunched up and ugly, you know, like us. Ha! Shriveled Aryans—the lot of 'em! That's the kind of unification we want. Just a few more days and there'll be no going back.... If they don't pay up, we'll tap another keg.... Normannenstrasse, I mean! There's plenty there in the cellar, tons of stuff, miles of files... operational proceedings, informants' babble, pillow talk, all siphoned off... and from both sides of the border, too.... Finally it'll pay off.... And us? We're gone, yet we're making ourselves useful.... We know exactly where the bodies are, and the time bombs.... That's what they're calling for now: the new openness! A new honesty! Naked truth, so to speak. We can do that: I mean, bring the past to light.... Ha! They want it, they can have it! Handed to them, for free and for cash... Big helpings or small. No, not all at once. We'll dole it out in tidbits.... They're panting for it. Germany's supposed to be cleaned up.... It will be, Wuttke! It will be! Unified and clean! Ha! And everything leveled, made equal, West and East. What we always wanted, theoretically. At last our Germany will be clean...."

We shall stop here, because at this point, or somewhat later in his speech, Hoftaller let the oars go and the boat drift. Whether conjec-

342

tured or actual: sweat was dripping from his forehead. He yanked off his cap: sweat-drenched spikes of hair. He had spat out the cold cigar stump shortly after he began speaking. Now he groped around under the rowing bench for the remains of his Cuban. He groped and groped. We surmised momentary exhaustion.

Fonty, who had been listening without moving a muscle, his posture upright and unchanging, stood up, pulled in the oars, which were lying dangerously loose in the oarlocks, and sat down again in the stern. He said not a word to any of this, although he could have clapped, or shaken his head, or defended the Third Way; no, he said nothing.

From our perspective on the shore, the most important part was over. When Hoftaller finally located the cigar stump and lit it, the boat was lying quiet in the water, hardly drifting. Only now, after he had removed his hat, did Fonty remark, "That's how it'll be, or something like that. No victory goes unpunished. Was no different in '71. German unification is always the unification of the Parvenooskis and Nogoodniks. Except that in those days there was the fourth estate, the working class. There was still some hope there. At least it looked that way. Yet even today we must congratulate ourselves that things turned out as they did, though old Frau von Wangenheim did say..."

Then he stood up and urged Hoftaller, who was still in a lather, to change places again. The day-and-night-shadow obeyed. Like a well-trained team they stood facing each other, embraced, switched oarsmen, slowly, surefootedly—the boat hardly rocked at all.

Since this tableau of dancing in place was by now familiar to us, from our place on the bank, we fixed our eyes on other boats. We heard laughter and noise echoing across the water, saw the pair of swans farther in the distance, several ducks close by. And then we watched with pleasure a solitary rower, whom Fonty would also have found striking, for on the bench in the stern the young man—he wore glasses, a student, perhaps—had set up a camera with timer. Against a variety of backgrounds he deemed himself, the spectacled rower, worthy of one snapshot after another. We thought we heard the shutter click.

Hoftaller and Fonty exchanged no more confessions. The past refused to well up. The boat ride was over. With calm strokes, Fonty made for the landing dock. I had hoped he would row toward one of the quiet side arms of the lake and there find the shadowed spot where just yesterday a ripped dress, a scarlet one at that, had borne witness to some act of violence, possibly a murder. But Fonty wanted to have the advantage of this one secret over his day-and-night-shadow.

They had hardly disembarked when Hoftaller, now smiling once more beneath a dry brow, remarked, "By the way, there's a surprise waiting for you. Company. From France. You have three guesses.... Well? When's the penny going to drop? Don't want to keep you in suspense any longer: it's your charming granddaughter, here to do research, but also for personal reasons.... Was delighted to meet her again, after a fairly lengthy correspondence. Name's actually Nathalie, but wants to be called Madeleine, after her grandmother, of course. Plans to go to the Archives, but means to meet her grandpa first. Brought something along, a trifle, maybe a present.... What's wrong, Wuttke? Pull yourself together! The girl's really charming. You should be happy—ecstatic, shout hosanna—whatever! What are you trembling for? If you want, I'll set up a meeting for tomorrow. Don't be so skittish. Your Emmi hasn't the faintest—how would she?"

Fonty stood there, looking stricken, as if an angel had laid its hand upon him. Nothing, not even a joking allusion to literary examples of happiness achieved late in life, in Marlitt's novels, for instance, could break his paralysis. Suddenly he made up his mind to pay for the boat ride, but Hoftaller had already covered the cost: "Goes on the expense account, Wuttke. So, how about it? All right, there we have a smile at last. About time, too. Let's say, tomorrow morning around ten. Same place, same face. I'm sure the girl likes rowing. And I've heard the weather's supposed to stay nice."

After that they had a beer under the chestnut trees of the Lakeside Café. It was not clear who picked up the bill. We didn't care about that anymore.

21

Rowboat Talk

All those girls: Magdalena, Lene, Madeleine. Actually we are in over our heads here, for in the Archives the information we have on the books pertains only to the seamstress with a flatiron; as far as Dresden and the consequences are concerned, all we can do is point to lacunae. The family, first and foremost Mete, painstakingly obliterated all traces, if, indeed, there were any to begin with. They wanted to pass the Immortal on to posterity free of dross. Nothing exists beyond that letter to Bernhard von Lepel that bewails "excessive strength of loins" and a second claim to support payments, with Dresden fingered as the scene of the crime.

And as for Lyon and the consequences, we had no information at all. But Theo Wuttke had a skeleton in his closet—otherwise Hoftaller could not have kept him on so short a leash for so long. And, because, as Fonty, he belonged to us, and furthermore was the most lively substantiation of our dry archival material, the Archives now received an assignment that we could not carry out by burying our noses in dusty files. We had to get out. Like Hoftaller, we were called into the field. Playing Peeping Tom, we crouched in the bushes or behind smooth-skinned beech trunks. We took turns. We passed on what we had heard: memoranda for later. The next morning I was supposed to be on duty.

To sum up, let us just say that the announcement of a meeting with the French granddaughter surprised us more than it did the grandfather. His face revealed little when he learned of this newest Madeleine. At most a touch of pleasurable anticipation could be surmised, after the initial shock wore off. After all, his sons had given him no heirs, and Martha and her belated Grundmann could hardly be expected to produce offspring. There were no little Wuttkes. But now word had arrived from a distant but not foreign land. At first Fonty must have felt shivers down his spine, but then he was flooded with emotion. To us, he said, "In the beginning I felt a tightening around my heart, but soon the iron ring burst asunder, as in the fairy tale."

So he tried to picture Madeleine. As he spent half the night pacing on the Chinese runner, she must have appeared to him in varying guises; or perhaps he saw her early the next morning seated at the kitchen table, where Emmi sat across from him, suspecting nothing. She may have noticed, however, that Wuttke had that look of his: "Sometimes he sees things that aren't really there."

It is conceivable that he summoned up her image from a mélange of longing, seeing her approaching, sometimes island-blond, sometimes ash-blond, but always in clothing of an old-fashioned cut with simple folds, no ruffles, nothing he would have felt compelled to disparage as "dolled up."

Perhaps he rehearsed the big apology scene before his imagined granddaughter, lining up sentences in his mind for a far-reaching confession, beginning with sin-ridden Florence on the Elbe and the Immortal's early missteps, pleading for leniency; for the confusion characteristic of a period lacking in liberty had led many astray, and not only in the field of politics. He could have taken a hundred-year leap from the Herwegh Society in Leipzig and its rebellious proclamations to the rumblings in officers' clubs behind the front lines in occupied France, and thus to his correspondence with members of the top Prussian aristocracy—von Witzleben, Yorck, and Schulenberg—and from there to the failed assassination attempt. In passing, he would have dropped purposefully lyrical allusions to rowboat excursions: just a moment ago, gently flowing arms of the Elbe could have rocked the lovers' boat, then a tranquil lake near Ambérieux.

Fonty could do this. To him the centuries were fluid. According to his inner geography, the Spree flowed into the Rhône. And with the help of the time-locks always at his disposal, he could repeatedly ruffle ash-blond hair with spring breezes and let sweet nothings whispered long ago drip from the blades of the oars. He could surely have dashed off a quatrain: What struck us there / Was love, no more, / Whether lake or river / Our small bark bore.... Or certain quotations would have acquired twofold meanings—heartfelt tones and their echo, delusions, confusions, time and again.

Not that a century's confession would have flowed trippingly and ingratiatingly from his tongue; rather, it would have come out haltingly, as if he were courting someone's trust; for, oh, how undemandingly, unselfishly, uncomplainingly, always cheerfully, with only a hint of wistfulness, the two of them, Magdalena Strehlenow and Madeleine Blondin, the gardener's daughter and the innkeeper's, had given themselves to the apothecary, the airman, entrusted themselves to the Immortal or his revenant, such that one of them could be memorialized as a model, the other adapt herself to the model. For did not Lene Nimptsch say, at once smiling and serious, "Believe me, having you, having this hour—that is my happiness. What comes of it doesn't matter to me." And Madeleine Blondin took everything absolutely literally.

Further anticipating this meeting with his granddaughter, Fonty could have accepted the blame for all the consequences of the rowboat excursions and asked for leniency. But because he knew nothing of the distressing events that had followed on the heels of his rear-echelon happiness in France, and had thus vaulted over that time, in the course of his pleading he would have begun to stutter. What knowledge did he have of the Dresden case except that support payments had come due? And he had survived the subsequent misfortune in complete ignorance.

Only Hoftaller, formerly Tallhover, knew the consequences born of the Lyon adventure; he had been and remained on the trail. For him no proceeding was ever wrapped up, no file ever closed. And where Fonty seemed clueless, his day-and-night-shadow had facts at hand.

With his knowledge he could have filled in several gaps in our Archives, for he viewed himself, after all, as a collector of missing pieces and a friend of written words, whose backgrounds, painted over here, retouched there, provided information even under the thickest layer of varnish; Hoftaller was fixated on everything literal, whether printed or spoken. Often it took only half a sentence to set Tallhover of yore, Hoftaller in a later iteration, on track, securing evidence, such as the incautious remark by the handsome but spineless Baron Botho to the effect that his Lene was "actually a little democrat."

We can testify that when the moment was right, whether in the paternoster or while they were treading water in the Baltic, Hoftaller pounded into his subject Fonty various pieces of information that the day-and-night-shadow characterized as "facts": "Fact is, the model for the literary Lene Nimptsch was a more robust democrat than her wishy-washy lover, who changed his beliefs like his shirt. Far into old age—Magdalena Strehlenow died in 1904—she remained devoted to the ideals of '48. Fact is, at the time of the Anti-Socialist Laws she was arrested four times for violating the ban on closed assemblies. But she didn't give in. Was in demand as a speaker, and not only in Saxony. Was said to have been acquainted with Clara Zetkin, if not friendly with her. Died without Christian assistance. And fact is, her daughter, Mathilde, was also a red, though more moderate, with leanings toward Bernstein. A typical revisionist. She spoke against the revolutionary wing at the Erfurt Party congress, was particularly dangerous for that reason. And even when her marriage to a layabout student..."

Hoftaller already had these and even more facts in reserve on Hiddensee, but it was only after the rowboat ride in the Tiergarten that he moved from the Saxon to the French details. They were sitting under the chestnut trees in the beer garden. Fonty pointed out the rich harvest promised by the splitting husks, and said, "The first will soon be falling." Then he wanted to hear more about the layabout student and the revisionist Mathilde, but Hoftaller refused to be deflected: "We'll talk about that later, maybe. Today let's prepare for the visit from France. Really, a charming person. Haven't promised too much. Her German is excellent. Talks like a book. Never fear, Fonty, you won't need to dredge up your rear-echelon French. She'll be a joy to you, a secret joy, if that's how you want it. By tomorrow, Wuttke, your heart will be jumping...."

We should have enjoyed the scene from farther away, but whatever the proximity, Nathalie Aubron, who answered to her grandmother's name, was truly lovely. Small and delicate, sometimes vivacious in a tomboyish way, then again very quiet, all ears, artlessly naive yet displaying a gregarious intelligence that fostered conversation and, as Fonty immediately perceived, boded well for a rowboat ride; even we archivists would have enjoyed being in a boat with Madeleine, that was how delightfully, no, how attractively, she bridged any distance.

When Fonty arrived, a little early, at the boat-rental stand, he used the time to drape his light summer scarf, which he usually wore carelessly, a bit more fetchingly: the tartan should show to advantage. Then he paced up and down, speaking in a low voice to himself, as if rehearsing words of greeting, for example: "We meet each other late, yet not too late." Or "May I count this surprise meeting as a gift of autumn?" Or "Mademoiselle, that you call yourself Madeleine like your dear grandmother awakens in me beautiful but also painful memories."

Yet suddenly Hoftaller was standing before him, and next to the agent of this family rendezvous stood *la petite,* a personage who instantly banished all anticipatory anxiety, and greeted him, moreover, with a ringing *"Bonjour, monsieur,"* accompanied by three utterly natural kisses on the cheeks, scattering the sentences he had been devising, so that all that occurred to Fonty was a repeated "So here you are, child." Then he looked searchingly at her face, and she at his.

Soon Hoftaller was superfluous. He hung around a little longer, while we gloated at his embarrassment, but then left, as if on command, after Fonty's granddaughter took leave of him, politely but firmly: "I am much obliged to you, Monsieur Offtaler, for opening the way to my grandfather. Likewise I find your discretion admirable: no one in Montpellier has the slightest suspicion. That is as it should be. Maman, who is still somewhat troubled, should be spared. One need not—how do you say?—shout everything from the rooftops, no? But now I should like to ask your indulgence, monsieur. Herr Wuttke and I have much to tell each other."

We think Hoftaller was glad to go. He knew enough as it was. In going, he left no gap behind. And Fonty, whom we have difficulty picturing without his day-and-night-shadow, was happy to be alone with his granddaughter.

As if there had been no other choice—a stroll through the Tiergarten to Rousseau Island, for instance—he invited her with a mute gesture to a boat ride. And Madeleine, who jumped into the rowboat first, offered him, as he climbed in, her small, childlike hand. With a chivalrous flourish, hamming it up a little, he expressed his gratitude.

Madeleine was already sitting on the rowing bench when, with a schoolgirl air, she asked permission: "Please, monsieur, may I row? I'm very good at it."

A lovely tableau, painted from the shore. The light kept changing as scattered clouds drifted across the sky. Dabs of color, play of shadows, aqueous transitions, as if in watercolor. Now and again a gust of wind rippled the surface of the water, then reflections again. First leaves were falling, faded. Dragonflies hovered over the duckweed. Already the lake was opening up. The two of them, in the dreamily gliding boat, toward which swept the pair of swans, as if ordered up for the occasion. And the bushes on the banks framed ever new tableaux.

Aside from the painted motifs, one could see that Madeleine's hair was not ash-blond but chestnut brown, with tight curls; the cropped head contrasted markedly with Fonty's frizzy white mane—he had set his hat next to him—especially when the boat glided through curlicues of light. Madeleine's dress, a loose frock sprigged with little flowers, concealed her boyish figure and flashed a predominantly blue signal. Only when she pulled on the oars could one see a hint of her breasts. She rowed with bare arms, her knees close together, as if this athletic posture had been trained into her. Her slim arms strong and muscular. In profile her pointed nose, as I remarked to my colleagues, looked a bit too pert.

Now she was rowing in a wide arc along the bank. At first Fonty tried to mobilize his rather sparse French. Because Madeleine spoke German so fluently, indeed hyper-correctly, as if according to some old-fashioned grammar book, the first thing the grandfather might have asked his granddaughter was where she had acquired her mastery of the language, which extended to the subjunctive, for as soon as she had found her rowing rhythm, she had remarked, "If I did not know that this was all happening, in fact and in broad daylight, I would have to think I was dreaming something most strange and wonderful."

Madeleine's reply to Fonty's question delved far into the past: the profound love her grandmother, who had passed away a few years earlier, had expressed for all things German; then her mother's prohibition on mentioning anything German at home or at table, even a VW or a Black Forest cuckoo clock; furthermore, the accumulated and undying resistance to the former occupying power, but also the secret connected with her grandmother's vanished lover, whom many remembered as a no-good, and no one as an antifascist hero; all that, and especially her grandmother's sequestered love, had motivated her while still a child, first out of defiance, then out of genuine interest, to learn this difficult and often illogical language, eventually to study it at the university, and—since her grandmother's death—to focus her studies on nineteenth-century German literature. "Monsieur can believe me, this was certainly no child's play."

And then Madeleine began, as she rowed toward the shore, to paint an idyll: In a lonely, now almost uninhabited village in the Cévennes, to which her grandmother had retreated of necessity even before the end of the war and the birth of her child, she, the devoted grandchild, had inherited a house. It was small and built of rough stone, but full of books, among them some that had belonged to her vanished grandfather, of whom no photograph, no letter, not even a postcard had provided evidence. And in the cottage in the Cévennes, with its thick walls and its deep storm cellar—"Monsieur knows, of course, that until late in the eighteenth century Huguenots sought shelter there"—she had read during school holidays—"and together with Grand-mère"—many stories by Storm, Keller, and Raabe, but had also begun to study *Delusions,*

Confusions, her grandmother's favorite book. That was how, early on, she had come upon the Immortal: "I was not yet sixteen when Grand-mère introduced me to Lene and Botho." To this day she could recite from memory the beginning of that beautifully sad but also somewhat stupid tale: "At the point where the Kurfürstendamm and Kurfürstenstrasse intersect, diagonally across from the 'Zoological,' there could still be found in the mid-seventies a large nursery garden, which extended far back into the fields. . . ."

Madeleine was still rowing her grandfather along the bank. The muscles in her upper arms and forearms were clearly visible. She rowed with stamina. She kept her back straight, her knees close together. Beneath the sharp angle of her nose, her small mouth smiled as she spoke, while her eyes, which seemed large in her little face, remained solemn, dark with so much intelligence and precocious knowledge: an alert gaze that could not be distracted from secretive happenings along the lake—on shore-hugging paths, behind elderberry bushes—a gaze that did not spare us, for she remarked, "*Attention,* monsieur! Here everything has ears, even the flora and fauna. Perhaps that is why they are talking so much about bugs these days."

Fonty, who was listening to his granddaughter voraciously, as though after a long fast, posed only occasional questions, cautious questions that seemed to be groping for details: Was the Perrache station in the heart of Lyon still in operation? He had read of high-speed trains that would get a person to Paris in just two hours. Was the Café de la Paix still there, in the suburb of Limonest, where in days gone by Monsieur Blondin had stood behind the counter, pouring first one pastis, then another for him, the godforsaken soldier?

And only then, after putting it off as long as he could, did he inquire anxiously about the horrors that the end of the war had brought in its wake, whatever the joy of victory: Had Madeleine Blondin been all alone with her child in that desolate village in the Cévennes; and why had the child—"I was told my daughter is called Cécile"—not brought her mother later to her house in Montpellier, thereby ending her banishment?

His granddaughter assured him that Lyon's railroad station was still in operation in that convenient location. Sorrow, trouble with the authorities, and finally illness were the reasons she cited for the sale of the suburban Café de la Paix. They had buried the widowed innkeeper in the early fifties. Right after *la terreur* had raged—an *épuration* amid the joy of victory—her pregnant grandmother had been shaved bald and had fled, under cover of night, to the Cévennes. The lonely house had been standing empty; it belonged to her father's family. And there she had given birth; only an old woman who had been out gathering herbs had been there to assist.

"But no, Monsieur Wuttke," Madeleine exclaimed, "Grand-mère never again became involved with a man, that is how deeply she had been hurt. And yet she always referred with much love to a soldier whom she recalled as a bit of a dreamer and absolutely unmilitary, and of whom she did not wish to speak ill, although he had brought her so much suffering after such brief happiness. *Mais non!* She did not want to leave that place. Nothing could persuade her. Maman, who had gone to Aix at seventeen, and then to Montpellier, and also my father, Monsieur Aubron, invited her time and again: 'Viens, Maman! We will fix up the attic just for you!' But she did not want to, did not want to be among people. And so she remained in the stone house, whose windows are as narrow as the loopholes in a fortress wall. I am certain, Monsieur Wuttke, that Grand-mère's fortress would please you. Everything there is full of secrets. There are little owls. On the hill behind the house stands a row of dark cypresses. One can see it even from afar. *Exactement!* An old Huguenot burial ground. And behind the hill more hills, becoming blue and then bluer. Durmast oaks, chestnut forests. We could go mushrooming or take outings to Saint-Ambroix, Alès, and even farther, into the Ardèche. That was something for which Grand-mère could be won over. In my *deux-chevaux* we drove to Barjac and then on to the caves, one of which is even called *La Grotte des Huguenotes,* because there the Protestants are said to have hidden from the Catholic militia, the dreaded *Dragonnades.* 'Missionaries in jackboots' is what the dragoons were called. Ah, yes! *La terreur* has a long history in France...."

Then we heard nothing more. Madeleine rowed the boat into that side arm of New Lake that smelled putrid, like a stagnant body of water, and in one of whose curves the ripped scarlet dress lay stretched out on rocks. But Fonty swore to us later that someone must have removed that rag, suggestive of murder; nothing alarming could cloud the mood, and his granddaughter did not find the dark branch of the water sinister at all. I can confirm as much: the boat was no sooner in sight again than we saw *la petite* chattering away, both asked and unasked.

She went on for a long time, painting for her grandfather a picture of the lonely Cévennes, the fortresslike house of Madeleine Blondin, the cypress grove, but also the misery of Huguenot galley slaves. She told him how an aging woman tried to recapture her briefly savored love from the heart of books left behind in a language that remained foreign, even after she had learned it, at first alone, with great effort, then later, much later, with her growing grandchild, who during school holidays mastered it quickly and could even read aloud to her in the lamplight as her eyesight grew dim in her final years; again and again the sad tale of poor Effi; the words in which wan Stine justified her renunciation; but also how decisively Lene Nimptsch commanded her heart to be still....

In contrast to her grandmother, who sought and found comfort everywhere, even between the lines, Madeleine Aubron was a critical reader. As she rowed her grandfather out of the gloomy arm back to the gleaming surface of New Lake and again drew close to the bank, she asked him to explain to her why the Immortal, whom she never called by name but referred to only as "our author" or, mysteriously, as "Monsieur X," time and again allowed class differences to kill off love in his novels, and why the prevailing order was allowed to record such sorrowful victories of reason.

"*Bien sûr!*" she exclaimed. "You will now explain to me the laws prevailing in a class-dominated society as arrogant but just, and, like our Monsieur X, will affirm the class order, while expressing regret and compassion for the unhappy lovers; but this tendency toward resignation has often irked me greatly. *Incroyable!* As a child I was already furious, when Grand-mère read aloud to me from her favorite book, that the tiresome Baron Botho took that stupid chat-

terbox Käthe as his wife—merely because she was of the gentry—
and not his Lene. And then, to make sure nothing would remain,
he burned in the fireplace all the letters, even the dried flowers,
which could tell tales of Hankel's Depot, and were tied with Lene's
hair. Grand-mère always laughed when I flew into a rage at our author. But one time she said, 'It's a good thing my Théodore did not
write me any letters. *Pas un mot!* They would have found them
when they came for me. And they shouted, *"La pute à boches!"* And
they would certainly have burned his letters, as they would have
liked to burn me. But to run with shaved head through Lyon was
worse than being burned at the stake.' When Grand-mère said
things like that, she was a little bit bitter. But otherwise she always
spoke of you with great fondness, and smiled as she did so. One
time, when I spent the entire summer with her, she said, as we were
sitting in the evening on the stone bench in front of the house:
'*Bien sûr*, my Théodore was a seducer and a dreamer besides. He
could speak with such empathy of this writer of French Reformed
ancestry who was his god, as if he wanted to relive every phase of
his life. Often, when he spoke of himself, describing his childhood,
for example, I did not know who was speaking to me. That other
one was always looking over his shoulder, so that, although in the
full bloom of youth, he often seemed to be from another time and
quite ancient. Perhaps that is why his radio broadcasts, which he
made secretly with us, were so successful. The *Résistance* owes him
much, oh, yes. My brother, who really hated the Germans, was
quite infatuated with Théodore. They were young, both of them,
and I was even younger. Like children, so silly. And yet we worked
very seriously for this partisans' radio. That was nice, the three of
us in a boat. One of them was called *La Truite*, but we called every
boat *Bateau ivre*. We had to change lakes often, you know, for the
sake of safety, which was not difficult, because quiet ponds were to
be found everywhere. And every time we went out in a boat,
Théodore would read aloud, in his soft but very clear voice. And
Jean-Philippe recorded everything with his machine. I was allowed
to row. Ah, that was such fun—until someone betrayed us, and
in the Mont-Luc prison they tortured and flayed to death our
Jean-Philippe, and the others, too, who did the broadcasts. Only

Théodore escaped, fortunately.... But later on no one wanted to believe that I belonged to their group, no one, not my sisters, not even my father. I was the whore of a *boche*, a *collaboratrice horizontale!*' That and more was what my grand-mère told me. Such things are painful, no? But that is not why I have come, Monsieur Wuttke! Or may I call you Grand-père, no, Grandpapa?"

He gave her permission. And now Fonty had a chance to speak. But since his granddaughter was rowing toward the middle of the lake as he spoke, we were left farther and farther behind. Several times she rowed the boat around the bird sanctuary, was out of sight, back in sight, once more behind trees and shrubbery, and brought herself and her grandfather into the picture once again.

Then from the shore we saw Madeleine Aubron draw up the oars. Fonty was still speaking, with sparse gestures. She was listening to him as the boat drifted gently. We could visualize her small, smiling mouth, her serious eyes, wise beyond their years. After listening for quite some time, she got up from the rowing bench and walked, no, floated, in her blue frock, to the stern where Fonty was sitting, now a bit hunched over. She embraced him. The granddaughter went down on her knees and put her arms around her seated grandfather. I should have taken a picture and yet another picture, but snapshots were not part of our modus operandi; even though, at the end of his long report, accompanied by cautious gestures, we saw Fonty embraced and then handed a small box by Madeleine, there is no record of the solemn moment in which Theo Wuttke, the former airman and war correspondent, received a French decoration, decades late, quite unofficially and in a private ceremony.

He must have told his granddaughter what Hoftaller confirmed: Fonty belonged to the *Résistance*, no, for a short time he was on the side of the French Resistance, or, to be more precise: starting in the spring of '44, Airman Theo Wuttke allowed himself to be used by a small group of partisans, working in isolation. Not that he went underground to dynamite munitions trains or bridges. But he did readings for a partisan transmitter that was in operation for three and a half months, half-hour readings targeted at the soldiers of the occupying force. In particular he read aloud from the Immortal's books, not only from the novels but also from the slim volume entitled *Prisoner of War: Experiences in 1870,* in whose chapters the Immortal balanced his love of France with his criticism of French chauvinism.

These morning broadcasts, which eschewed overt propaganda, are said to have been effective, especially once the Allied invasion began. The word is that the soldier read the dialogue brilliantly; he imparted irony to casual remarks, captured the author's sometimes clipped, sometimes chatty conversational style, could strike a tone of mellifluous delicacy but also one of Prussian curtness. And the soldier would interrupt his readings—from *Schach von Wuthenow,* say—with news briefs on the progress of the invasion or the assassination attempt in the Führer's Wolf's Lair headquarters. These reports were untendentious, simply factual, and the soldier skillfully established links between the battles raging around Caen and the Norman origins of the successful assassin Charlotte Corday, between the aristocrats involved in the failed assassination attempt and Prussia's glorious history. His pensive asides managed to weaken the fighting morale of the already bruised Wehrmacht, at least within the Lyon occupation zone.

Hoftaller assured us that this achievement was credited, only after lengthy research, to a German soldier who at first remained unknown. Yet, he noted, his agency could easily have been of service and identified the Luftwaffe airman. But not until the mid-eighties would the French side have been willing to take the name Theo Wuttke under consideration.

It must have been Hoftaller himself who wanted to see his subject given proper recognition; thanks to his outfit, he had contacts in the French Communist Party. And for the past four years he had been in touch with Madeleine Aubron, partly through intermediaries, partly face to face—on the occasion of an assignment confirmed for us by both of them as entailing a meeting at a specified place and time in March '87. The Workers' and Peasants' State was preparing to celebrate its fortieth anniversary, and when it decided to include, as a planning goal, festivities designed to buttress its continued existence, an official ceremony honoring Theo Wuttke was supposed to be featured in the program; yet when the moment arrived, the French voiced reservations, for there were already signs that the end was approaching for this state poised to celebrate itself.

This is the only explanation we can find for the handing-over of that tiny box, which took place during a morning boat ride, when the kneeling granddaughter decorated her seated grandfather and even handed him a document, certified, to be sure, only by Madeleine's signature, and not by any official stamp.

At any rate, from then on, on special occasions Fonty pinned to his left lapel a ribbon no bigger than the nail of a person's little finger. When we asked him what the fire-red dot signified, he maintained an expressive silence or spoke evasively of the painter Corot, in whose green paintings one could always find a cleverly concealed drop of blood; at most he would remark, "The *compagnons de la Résistance* felt they had to reward my oratorical skill. But this capability was praised early on in the Tunnel Over the Spree, for instance by Merckel, when I set the Tower on fire with my balladesque tone, and the assembled Tunnel brethren could not get their fill of the conflagration thus sparked in verse. '*Da capo!*' they shouted; even though the fire, as we know, left the Tower unscathed...."

Whatever else was recounted, reported, or merely chatted about between stern and rowing bench, we did not hear. Only once, when Madeleine rowed her grandfather back toward the shore, did we manage to pick up snatches of conversation that seemed to pertain to *Delusions, Confusions*. They were discussing a coach ride through the Hasenheide to the cemetery, and immortelles on the grave of old Frau Nimptsch. Later we heard Madeleine parodying stupid Käthe's remark, "Oh, that's just too comical for words ... the tree frog!" And Fonty quoted the novel's closing sentence: "Gideon is better than Botho!"

His voice carried across the water. *La petite* repeated this assertion, whereupon grandfather and granddaughter laughed in unison, and Madeleine's actually rather small mouth stretched to clownlike proportions. Then they exclaimed, in alternation or simultaneously, "Gideon is better than Botho!" Sometimes it sounded merry, sometimes despairing, finally even scornful. Time and again, as if a judgment had to be rendered or the inevitability of fate had to be invoked, both shouted, forming a megaphone with their hands, "Gideon is better than Botho!" Responses soon came from other boats and from the lawn where people were sunbathing: "Who d'you say's better?" "Something wrong, Gramps?"

We immediately comprehended the far-reaching double meaning of this conclusive judgment. Madeleine Blondin had refused to make a second choice like Lene Nimptsch; instead she had remained alone in the Cévennes with her cloistered love. But her daughter Cécile had barely turned seventeen when she ran away from her mother in her mountain solitude, to Montpellier and marriage to an auto mechanic named Gilles Aubron. Considerably older than she, he provided the child from the Cévennes with stability, and promised to be true to proletarian principles. Later, when they acquired their own repair shop, they even achieved a degree of prosperity.

When the only child of this evidently happy marriage recounted everything to her grandfather while rowing, painting a detailed picture of a painstakingly nurtured family life, down to table manners and principles of thrift, we heard him say, this time in a low voice rather than a ringing one: "Yes, yes. I suppose even a Gilles is better than a Théodore."

After that they changed places. It went very quickly and lightfootedly. As Fonty bent to the oars like a trained rower, Madeleine exclaimed, "Bravo, Grandpapa!" With her knees drawn up and her arms wrapped around them, she perched on the seat in the stern and displayed to us the sharp angle of her nose. In his head the elderly rower was probably working out a quatrain, whose final version was later enclosed in a letter to his daughter Martha:

> We found ourselves together in a boat,
> which long ago bore love on waves now gone.
> We count the wounds that ache still as we float,
> the hearts' sweet sorrow—and much that lingers on.

Not until the grandfather had all the rhymes together and felt, as he said, "in the mood for a coffee and cognac," did he row his granddaughter, who, as she remarked, wanted "to knock back a good beer," in the direction of the landing dock and terrace café, where I was already sitting under the chestnut trees with a glass of seltzer, my back to them, busy with my notes. *La petite* ended up having a second beer.

22

Three in a Boat

A handsome sight, the two of them making their way through the city: the old man striding along with his walking stick and the girl keeping pace with him; his seventy, her twenty-two years; he spry in his wrinkled linen suit, she delicate in her blue-on-blue flowered frock; his white hair ablaze in the midday sun, her close-cropped head dark with curls no comb could tame; grandfather and grand-daughter pounding the pavement—while we followed at a discreet distance.

They walked from Alexanderplatz—where they saved for another day the television tower, with its panoramic view from the top—to the Palace of the Republic, now officially closed—asbestos contamination!—then along Französische Strasse and past the cathedral, turned right onto Glinkastrasse, then left onto Behren-strasse, where the haughty Frau von Carayon had lived with her homely daughter, and that good-looking cad Schach von Wuthenow had been lured into the marriage trap; as they passed, Fonty delivered a lecture on the power of the ridiculous. And now along the last stretch of Otto-Grotewohl-Strasse to Pariser Platz, where Max Liebermann had had his studio, and then through the great gate, the gate of those victory-parade poems, which Fonty did not quote this time, the gate whose chariot was missing, removed since the beginning of the year for repairs. The two of them were headed for the Tiergarten.

Across from the Soviet war memorial, graced by the obligatory tank, a now obsolete symbol of victory, they turned left. He was leading her along old familiar paths. She took his arm for a while, let it go again, skipped on ahead like a little girl, then reached for his arm again, a young lady once more. He pointed out monuments and sculpture groupings with brief, sometimes dismissive gestures.

Fall was just beginning, determining the Tiergarten's coloration, but still the chestnuts refused to fall. Past Friedrich Wilhelm III, whose manner of speech, which hacked every sentence into kindling, we had learned to imitate. But Fonty was better at it: "Might deign to sit here . . . Or view of Luise preferable . . . benches aplenty there . . ."

No, they did not pause to catch their breath. Not until they reached the Great Way and then, by side paths, found the best view of Rousseau Island did Madeleine want to sit beside her grandfather, on his favorite bench. With him she enjoyed the antics of the diving duck, who was gone, then reappeared, unexpectedly, suddenly, according to whim; and with each reappearance its elegant crest remained unruffled. Madeleine called out, "Bravo!"

That, too, was a delight: to sit on a bench and comment, sometimes wittily, sometimes maliciously, on all the passersby, among them Turkish families, older ladies, and now and then a panting jogger. In between he chatted about Scotland and the Scottish clans, and she guided her travel-hungry grandfather through the limestone outcroppings of the Cévennes, all the way to her grandmother's padlocked house, on whose cool threshold a toad waited night after night. Madeleine had the key, Madeleine knew where the mushrooms grew, Madeleine was, like her mother, a child of the Cévennes.

They asked each other many questions, wanted to know everything precisely, and even more precisely. What technical arrangements had been necessary for the readings in the rowboat? "And the background sounds—the water, the birds in May, all the frogs?"

Had there always been three of them when the recordings were made? "Did Grand-mère really know anything about sound-recording technology?"

Who had suggested that he read chapters from the book *Prisoner of War* for the partisans' transmitter? "Were you the one, Grandpapa, who wanted to remind the German soldiers of Schiller's Joan of Arc?"

"No, my child; it was Jean-Philippe who insisted that I not omit any way station between Domrémy and the island fortress of Oléron. And the sounds of nature were not disruptive in the least. I even paused between sentences for an indefatigable cuckoo."

Then the question of betrayal: Who had talked? One of the sisters? And who was it who had come in the night? The Gestapo or the gendarmerie?

The soft responses, describing how Madeleine Blondin's brother died at German hands in the Mont-Luc prison. How no one from the partisan group survived but Madeleine. How at the end of August the prison was stormed and the survivors liberated. How Madeleine Blondin, since there were no witnesses to exonerate her—the others all dead, Théodore on the run—was shaved bald and driven through the streets of Lyon in sackcloth because she was pregnant by a German soldier.

Later, when she had settled all by herself in the Cévennes, she was even suspected of treason. And not until the Barbie trial did it come out quite by chance—"too late for Grand-mère"—what an injustice she had suffered. *"Bien sûr,* I did not rest until everything was cleared up and all the newspapers proclaimed her a hero. Yes, I also applied for the decoration for my long-lost grandfather, and I was the one who rammed everything through when the CPF tried to get in the way again. Not until the Wall came down was the award approved. In any case, I felt I was authorized to conduct a little ceremony. No, I am not a Party member, although that is the tradition in my family. I see myself as more of a Trotskyite, but what true Communism means I still do not know; perhaps it's rather like genuine Christianity...."

They sat for a long time on Fonty's favorite shaded bench. At their backs, birds were fighting over ripe elderberries. As always when the subject of Communism came up, Fonty was reminded of the Immortal's unfinished *Likedeeler* project, which he hoped to shape into an epic in ballad style and, if possible, complete: "Charged with piracy, they continued to call each other levelers, all the way to the gallows...."

But Madeleine pointed to the tiny red ribbon she had pinned on her grandfather and said, "Something like that cannot be shared, even among levelers. Not everyone earns such a distinction. I am very proud of my grandpapa."

Fonty put up some resistance to this praise: "All I did was read; didn't even know exactly for whom; was no hero!" He uttered this confession with an amused, bashful expression.

They watched the diving duck for a while. And because this waterfowl so suggestively embodied the principle of ducking under, they were soon back in the Cévennes, among the Huguenots and the Huguenot wars, and consequently among the fugitive Calvinists who had been forced to go into hiding, sometimes here, sometimes there. And already the grandmother's padlocked house, behind which, on the rounded hillside, a row of cypresses stood, was waiting for visitors again: "Such a *refugium* could be just the thing for you, Grand-père. And then the wide spaces, the emptiness, in which one can easily lose oneself. By the way, all the Blondins were strict Protestants, even if they considered themselves Communists, and the Aubrons still are—even me, a little."

Then they went on their way. Grandfather and granddaughter headed back in the direction of Queen Luise and on to Kemperplatz. Here, near Philharmonic Hall, which sticks up like a stranded ship, we might have lost them—for the many lanes of fast-moving traffic repeatedly cut us off and slowed us down—had we not been certain that Fonty could have but one thing in mind: he wanted to find the place where, according to the earlier location of Potsdamer Strasse, Number 134C had stood, the three-story building belonging the Order of St. John. Not far from the rear façade of the National Library, a bit more than a hundred meters from Eichhornstrasse, he pointed out several remaining lindens. Otherwise there was nothing, only a fenced-in area used by a breeder's club for training dogs. Dogs barking, snapped orders, dust, desolation, and several massive buildings looking imposingly forlorn. There was nothing for them here.

That probably explains why he proposed a little self-deception to his granddaughter—he spoke of "truth with a wink"—and exclaimed, as he led her up Potsdamer Strasse to a branch of Bolle's

Dairy and a generously laid-out video store: "As long as the street number's right!"

According to the new numbering, Number 134C was located between Porst's Photo and the Bülow Pharmacy. Nondescript postwar structures, which could be parlayed into significance only with the help of a historic address. What nonsense, we thought; but Madeleine played along and willingly let herself be persuaded by Fonty: "Let my footnote slaves put on their papery smiles; I say: It's a permissible dodge. Wuthenow Castle and the Tempelhof Church never existed, either. That's how literature is. Writers are allowed to do anything they want. Even deception is permissible, so long as it works. That's why, from a novelistic perspective, every swindler is a god—and only in other respects an abomination. At any rate, we have more associations with Number 134C than just dry-as-dust archival information."

Across the street from Number 134C, the two of them stood lost in thought, as if the traffic and its roar could neither disturb them nor recall them to the present. With a gesture that scooped up the void, Fonty pointed out everything that could be speculated into existence, and at once breathed life into the meaningless postwar structure: "And here, my child, stood, in accord with our winking agreement, the building belonging to the St. John's Order of Brandenburg, with a garret apartment on the third floor, a little garden out in front, a balcony over the entrance door, and a privy in the courtyard. Already dilapidated in those days. Was torn down at the end of the twenties. Not a trace left. Berlin's usual slash-and-burn method. Granted: we were very cramped there. Were happy when the sons left the house. Counting Mete's closet, only four rooms in all. Yet here, let it be noted, the foundation for immortality was laid, with hard-to-market books, both fat and thin. It was in the year '72, soon after the captivity and the second trip to France—when the Alexis essay had just appeared in serial form—that the family moved in—on 3 October, by the way. Kept having to change addresses up to that point. After the return from London, we were at 33 Potsdamer Strasse, then at 51 Tempelhofer. After the first book of rambles, it was the rather dreary Alte Jacobstrasse. Move after move. Only half a year later, on Hirschelstrasse, the first novel was in the works. That dragged on; *Before the Storm* took fifteen years to come to its final full stop; that was here, up there or thereabouts, in the hole under the eaves. And then, child, things really got underway, once the secretary's position at the Academy had been dropped. Over there, but also away on summer holidays or in hermitlike solitude—for instance, at Hankel's Depot—an old man's late harvest was brought in: from *Schach* to *Stechlin*. Sometimes it streamed forth, sometimes it just trickled. Often I was tormented for hours on end by a nervous cough. Colossally irritating when the family bewailed our 'wretched situation.' And then the reviews. A succession of insults. Wrote to my publisher, Hertz: 'Well, 510 copies sold, with 60 million Germans. . . .' At any rate, it was a good hundred years ago that *Delusions, Confusions* was finished. And *Stine,* my anemic darling, had just appeared when the first collected works came out, in twelve volumes, although the most important work was still in the inkwell. Next year *Irretrievable* will have its jubilee. At the time, the Treibel book, whose shabby cast of characters, by the way, would be perfectly at home today, was almost completed in manuscript. Ah, child, that whole world was captured on paper on this very spot, with ever-shrinking lead, on this spot, where nothing is left. I kept politics out, but it crept in through every crack. No, I didn't take part in the Reichstag elections, and we never hoisted the flag on Bismarck's birthday. Nor did Neumann, the Jew across the way. Wrote to Brahm or Friedlaender: 'Arm in arm with Neumann, I summon my century to the lists!' Then came illness. Started with Effi—anemia of the brain, the doctors said. Electric-shock treatment in Breslau—all balderdash. Finally the *Childhood* brought about recovery. Sold well, and not only at the Christmas market in Swinemünde. But what does 'well' mean: a second printing. Put the finishing touches on *Effi* right after that. It poured out of me, all of a piece. My Emilie could hardly keep up with the copying. Even before *Effi* sallied forth into the world to find an astonishing number of lovers, old Stechlin was already knocking at the door—not that he was all that old; in fact, he was considerably younger than I. . . . But now, child, I must sit down."

Fonty lowered his hand, which had been pointing at apparitions. At once the roar of the afternoon traffic drowned out all the magic he had conjured up with his words. He responded to Madeleine's questions, formulated with scholarly precision, in a nearby café, which humbly called itself a snack bar. They found a table for two by a window and ordered tea and a snifter of brandy for each. The proprietor, a glum veteran with a limp, brought tea bags, which they had to let steep.

Fonty seemed somewhat exhausted. Madeleine tried not to look worried. But when the granddaughter began to stroke her grandfather's hand, his writing hand, of course, and inquired in an equally gentle voice, "Do you mind if I ask you some questions?" he nodded: "Ask away, dear child, ask away... I just hope I'm not mixing things up.... You know, the worst part is not forgetting, but mixing things up, saying Moltke when you mean Bismarck, or vice versa...."

But Madeleine Aubron's questions did not focus on political matters or the Prussian military. For two and a half hours they sat in the snack bar, diagonally across from that singular house number. She would have done better to interrogate us; when she began to delve into the *Poggenpuhls,* more specifically into the function of the few pieces of furniture in the apartment belonging to that impoverished aristocratic family, the Archives would have been able to provide a more detailed response. Fonty merely called the meager furnishings "a mirror of poverty in keeping with their station."

We could have provided an annotated inventory. And if this conversation had taken place not at the Archives but on Kollwitzstrasse, and thus in what we called the Wuttkes' "Poggenpuhl parlor," Fonty would have responded more vividly, having the *trumeau* before his eyes; but no, it had to be the snack bar on Potsdamer Strasse and a wobbly table for two.

Then the conversation moved on to the late ballad about the "Balinese Women on Lombok," and after that to source material in general and specifically for *Effi Briest.*

Perhaps our response would have been too cool and objective. Madeleine's questions manifested as much fervor as if she had fumed firsthand—and only yesterday—at the newspaper accounts of the intervention by the Dutch colonial masters, and as if the Immortal had told her just the other week about the case of that Elisabeth of Ardenne who had served as the literary model but had then survived the publication of the Effi novel and lived on into the fifties of the following century.

We must acknowledge, not without envy, that the granddaughter was made of the same timber as her grandfather. Like him, she had no trouble inhabiting bygone times, living in the day before yesterday. They were matched as if made for each other, and would hardly have noticed the likes of us; no, we archivists would have been out of place, perhaps even subject to childish jealousy, if we had seen the two of them putting their heads together there.

Furthermore, Fonty had corresponded for years with the model for Effi, the ancient Elisabeth von Ardenne. Apparently the correspondence had been arranged by the physicist Manfred von Ardenne, whose research was done in the Workers' and Peasants' State. Fonty even raved about meetings they had had, in the days when it was still possible to travel with an interzone pass. The Archives could not compete with that. Madeleine was delighted to hear about Elisabeth, an Effi who had survived; life seemed to have proved more merciful than literature.

When her grandfather described a lecture he had given for the Cultural Union on the topic "Source Material and Fiction"—"That must have been in December '65, right after the Eleventh Party Congress, when literature was reeled in on the line"—he conceded that he had been faithful to his source material in his portrayal of Lene Nimptsch in *Delusions, Confusions*: "Both, the original and the copy, were allowed to survive; but Effi could not have been saved, unless, of course, she had burned the letters from Crampas. . . ."

"But no, Grandpapa, then we would have had no reason to cry!" Madeleine exclaimed. "And if you hadn't been faithful to the original, Lene might have died of grief. A most unnatural ending! All the interlocking motifs would have been in vain, or, as they say, down the drain, and probably my master's thesis as well; I'm writing on the artistic interlinking of motifs, the wreath of immortelles, for instance, the open fire in the stove, all the rowboat excursions.

I like these very much, because they are always seemingly inciden-tal details, not thundering leitmotifs. Forgive me, Grandpapa, if I remind you of the time when Lene, at Botho's request—this even before they spend the night together at Hankel's Depot—ties the bouquet of wildflowers with a strand of her ash-blond hair; but later, toward the end, the dried bouquet is burned, along with Lene's letters, by that stupid Botho, simply burned to ashes. Oh, yes! I cried, Grandpapa. I really had to cry when I visited Grand-mère in the Cévennes and read that aloud to her. I could still cry, thinking about it now...."

After they left the snack bar, they parted at the next S-Bahn station; but the following day Fonty was out and about again with Madeleine. The weather held. September was drawing to a close. Again and again the Tiergarten, that favorite bench. Often they strolled up or down Unter den Linden, perhaps to find the spot where, in Schach's time, snobbish officers of the Gendarmes Regi-ment had spread an extravagantly large load of salt so that they could enjoy a simulated sleigh ride under the summer sun.

Then they visited the French Cathedral, and the Huguenot Museum in the Tower House, where they could admire a glass-encased model of the siege of La Rochelle, as well as the plaster death mask of Henri IV, two tiles from the Cévennes depicting the Huguenot cross, many engravings and pictures, among them Chodowiecki's etchings of the terrible St. Bartholomew's Night, and the famous painting in which the Great Elector receives the refugees, furthermore a map of the commercial city of Lyon, a bro-ken harp, a church-collection canister made of tin, and hour-glasses used by preachers of the Calvinist doctrine of election.

And an excursion through the city took the couple to another destination: they rode the trolley to the Stadium of World Youth subway station, scheduled later to be called simply Schwartzkopff-strasse, to visit the nearby cemetery belonging to the French Cathe-dral's parish. In addition to the Immortal's grave, there were remains of the Wall worth seeing, especially where an unbroken stretch still hemmed in the Catholic part of the cemetery used by St. Hedwig's.

They stood for a long time before the restored gravestone, where Madeleine placed a wreath of dried immortelles, brought along for the purpose. "In France these straw flowers are still customary." Other bunches of flowers, some fresh, some wilted, lay in front of the stone, with its two names. A windy day. Clouds of dust rose from the desolate stretch that until a short while ago had been a dead-certain border.

Whatever they had to say, this much is sure: the grandfather and granddaughter spoke—he sarcastically, she sympathetically—about Emilie, née Rouanet-Kummer, and about the Immortal's difficult but enduring marriage. Yet Fonty avoided any comparisons with his civilian family life, just as, in the itinerary for farther-flung tours of the city, he deliberately avoided the area where the Wuttkes lived.

He did take Madeleine to see the Ministries Building, rode up and down with her in the paternoster, even past the turning points, but they never walked up Schönhauser Allee or visited Kollwitzplatz, and he never led his granddaughter past the former Schultheiss Brewery, now the Culture Brewery, to Offenbach's, or invited her to join him there for a glass of wine.

He did not take her to any of the spots that make up the Prenzlberg scene. We could have offered our services, and, drawing on our bits and pieces of knowledge, whispered to her a few more or less poetic tales of domestic espionage, but we prudently held back; the Archives had to remain above reproach.

This explains why Fonty and his granddaughter went no farther than the People's Theater on Rosa-Luxemburg-Platz. There he promptly turned historical again. And Madeleine stifled her curiosity. She asked only in passing about Prenzlauer Berg and its cultural-historical significance: "One reads so many ugly things about it. The sort of thing I do not want to believe. All these insinuations, Grandpapa, is there anything to them?"

Fonty had a reply to that: "In Prenzlberg no one could ever be sure of himself."

His married life was not subject to inspection. Anything that bore the name Wuttke simply did not come up, not even Martha, and Martha's wedding. Similarly, Madeleine's involvement with a married professor struck her grandfather as not worth asking about, although he sensed that his granddaughter was caught up in something; the student, who mentioned her professor only rarely and with studied neutrality, had hinted it was a "difficult relationship."

We knew more; but elsewhere the penny had dropped even sooner.

"Goodness me!" Emmi exclaimed. "How was I not supposed to notice when we hardly get back from the sea and my Wuttke starts going rowing every day. And he keeps saying it's good for him. At first I was thinking there was nothing to it, but then? He begins to talk about rowing in general, and what his one-and-only says about it, so I think to myself, I think: That's like before, no, way back at the beginning, when he got home from prison camp and was all run-down, even though he talked big about the new day that was dawning and such. I mean, about building a socialist society, 'cause now, at last, the working class... Well, we were engaged, had been since '41, but not married yet, 'cause my Wuttke wasn't there, you know, when our Georg came along. But then when he was home after the war, I say to myself, I say: Something must be up with the boy. Even his letters—they kept coming till the summer of '44— were kind of strange, even stranger than usual. Unfortunately, I burned them all—it was that time I got so mad at him 'cause he wouldn't let the Cultural Union give him a job, regional secretary in Oranienburg, even Neuruppin or Pasewalk, whatever. But nothing doing. Absolutely not, he said. I could tell him ten times over: Wuttke, we just can't go on this way. And then he went and 'jettisoned all the culture rubbish,' like he said, and—I'm sorry now— I crammed all those letters in the kitchen stove.... Must have been thirty or more... But I noticed right away: Something's wrong when he keeps talking about rowing in France, and in the boat it's always that Lene from the novel. What did he mean when he wrote, 'France's rivers and lakes are also good for rowing'? With who, that's what I asked myself. And what's he doing all this time down there in Lyon, when mostly his writing was about the area up around the Atlantic Wall, about all those bunkers, and at the end a few words about the final victory. After the middle of '44 nothing more came from him for the Aviation, so I'm thinking: Now the invasion's got him. But no. He was sitting pretty in Lyon and thereabouts. It's supposed to be real nice there. And when he finally gets home, thin as a rail, and shaking like a leaf and 'a nervous wreck,' like he always says, I didn't want to pry too much. Didn't want to make it even worse than it already was. I mean, me all alone with our Georg... And the air raids every night... And nothing to burn in the stove... But it was good we had those two rooms with my aunt Pinchen and got married before she died so we got to keep the apartment, 'cause then our Teddy came along. At that point his French souvenir, I mean, what came of all that rowing, was already one and a half, a little younger than our Georg. He could've told me that something happened down there. Exactly, he didn't know the rest of the story either. I'd've married him anyway, my Wuttke. But no, he always has to keep everything under wraps, so it gets worse and worse. You know how he is. See if you can find out what happened—that's what I'd've told him, if he'd just breathed a word to me. But the mother didn't lift a finger either. I guess that's understandable, 'cause in France they were dead set against us Germans at first, and the poor creature—she was no older than me back then during the war—must've gone through a couple of bad years, 'cause anything with a German soldier... Would certainly have had a right to child support, seems to me. Maybe she thought: He's dead. Or she only looked in the West and not over here, 'cause we were socialist. Or 'cause she didn't want to stir up memories. Or maybe she found somebody and had a chance to get married. Or maybe she had her pride. I could understand that. And when the child got older, it didn't want to hear anything about it—you know how kids are. Was the same with me, 'cause my father, the one who married my mother in Oppeln, wasn't my real father, but he was a sweet man, and that's what counts. No, Hering wasn't the name I was born with. And if you ask me who my real father was, all I can tell you is: He was a piano teacher and—

well, let bygones be bygones! Who knows what the mother, the one in France, I mean, told her kid later on: nothing, or just half the story, or some lie, like my mother; she always gave me a song and dance when I asked her. And now the Wall's just come down and no more communism, and this grandchild turns up and says: Whoops! I'm here! Anyway, that's what he told me. No, not at the kitchen table the next morning, and not of his own free will or on his own. I could've held my breath. Finally I'm getting suspicious, and I say to him, I say, 'Well, Wuttke, now I'm starting to feel like I want to go rowing with you.' Well, at that point he didn't want to, or not at first, even though he was all for it when the rowing business first got started. Right, that was when I didn't feel like it. But this time I didn't back off: 'Come on, Wuttke! The two of us in one boat. That's something I'd like to see, before the unification comes, and it's coming soon.' So a few days later, we actually did go, before all the bell-ringing and stuff. We took the S-Bahn to Zoo station, then walked along the Landwehr Canal to Lützow Bank, then over the bridge into the Tiergarten. Got a boat right away, too. Fantastic weather. And I rowed, 'cause he wasn't in the mood. Keeping to the bank and in a circle. All those ducks, even a couple of swans. And everywhere young folks out rowing, too. Must've looked kind of strange, two old folks like us. But my Wuttke didn't say a single word, just kept hemming and hawing. And finally, when we were out in the middle and I'd put up the oars to catch my breath a bit, he opens his mouth—"I've been wanting to tell you this, Emilie..."—and I knew what was coming. 'Cause when he says Emilie to me, not Emmi, it's usually something bad. Actually, I felt sorry for him, the way he kept swallowing, and his Adam's apple going up and down. 'You don't have to say much, Wuttke,' I says. 'Something's caught up with you from earlier, am I right?" And he smiled a bit, and then it just came pouring out of him, you know how he talks. First about the young thing, I mean the grandchild, and then about the war and what was going on in Lyon, just terrible, the whole thing. And why he has that red thingamajig on his jacket now, no, nothing to do with Communism, but for real achievements. 'But don't go thinking I was a hero!' he says. And then of course his one-and-only had to elbow in again, 'cause this Marlene—his grandchild calls herself that, too—reminded him of a certain character in a novel, that Lene Nimptsch, you know. And the story of this Lene goes back to Dresden and the revolution going on at the time, where they sang freedom songs and went rowing on the Elbe. But I could see my Wuttke only wanted to talk about those days, not about his war bride, so I say, 'That's all right, Wuttke,' I say. 'During a revolution or wartime, all kinds of things happen that no one really wants. Could've said something to me sooner; I can take it. I've had to take plenty already. I'm not so sure about our Martha... or when I think of our Friedel—with all his morals... or Teddy with his government career.... But I'll get over it. And maybe it's for the best that it's only coming out now. But I do want to meet her, this Marlene, your grandchild—now don't take on that way....'"

Emmi went on and on; and all this was of interest to us. In the beginning we collected such material more as a joke or out of habit, but later it became purposeful. In the days of the Workers' and Peasants' hegemony, maintaining the Archives had given us something to hold onto, but now, since that state had fallen off the face of the earth, our holdings had become of dubious value to us. More and more we found ourselves sliding into Fonty's story. He was more alive to us than the original compressed in our filing cabinets. We put ourselves not only in his hands, but also in those of his family.

And Emmi was happy to be able to unburden herself. Ever since I had served as witness at Martha's wedding, she trusted us, and me in particular. Who besides us would have been willing to listen to her so patiently? In this period of rapid change, we were, if not actually part of the Wuttke family, at least its ear and repository; we recorded even the most trivial details—for instance, the fact that out in the boat, as the conversation came around more and more often to Madeleine, Emmi suddenly began to sing the nostalgic "Lili Marlene," probably to needle Fonty, who was already taking things rather lightly again.

At any rate, two days later, on the afternoon of 2 October, they undertook a familial boat ride. Fonty had issued the invitation, this time as Theo Wuttke. At first the atmosphere was a little stiff. Madeleine rowed, all the while keeping her quick, probing eyes fixed on the couple seated in the stern. Sometimes they rested on her grandfather, sometimes on his wife. And when she leaned back slightly, after a powerful pull on the oars, she could see both of them at once: Fonty bashfully emotional, his eyes tending to tear up, although he sat bolt upright, as if, in spite of everyone's efforts to dissuade him, he had swallowed the infamous Prussian ramrod, Emmi comfortably sunk into her amplitude, with which she took up more than half the bench. She was not the slightest bit embarrassed, but actually seemed in control of the situation. He crowded to one side, she overflowing, he as if caught *in flagrante,* but with dignity, she all menacing good nature. A framed portrait, the icon of a bourgeois arrangement that had transcended all upheavals: Herr and Frau Wuttke.

And Mademoiselle Madeleine? We must now acknowledge that her darting eyes had a hint of a squint, and she went completely cross-eyed whenever she had to lean forward for the next oar stroke, the effect of which was that the seated couple came too close and confused her eyes, otherwise trained to see clearly.

Not much was said at first. As laden as the boat was, the middle generation was missing. Questions that Fonty did not dare to pose were passed over, for if he had asked how things stood with Cécile Aubron, née Blondin—"And how is your mother, my child?"—his belated interest would at most have met with polite evasiveness. Madeleine would have talked about her mother's work as a school social worker in an orphanage operated by the Protestant church, and would have hinted at periodic difficulties that her mother, now in her mid-forties, had with her nerves—a hereditary problem, it would seem—but little more. The distant daughter could not be summoned to join them in the boat, and if Madame Aubron had been a member of the party, she would have abruptly rejected any attempt at rapprochement on the part of her father, might even have called him "Boche!" and worse.

For that reason Fonty remained silent, and Emmi, who was likewise silent, explained to us later why she had kept quiet so long:

"Wanted my Wuttke to flail around a bit. It was up to him to start. Usually loves to talk." Then she conceded, "But then I started after all, out of decency. Someone had to take the plunge."

Suddenly, as Madeleine was guiding the family freight back toward the bank, Emmi asked the rower about her not yet completed master's thesis, as if she had a burning interest in the topic: "So what's it about? Been to Potsdam already, Marlene? Nice folks at the Archives. They know a whole lot!"

And the fourth-year student responded that her thesis dealt with interconnected motifs, locales, and narrative perspective, in *Delusions, Confusions* in particular, and that she was also including *Stine,* the early Berlin novel *L'Adultera,* and the late *Poggenpuhls* in her research, and that she furthermore intended to examine the author's Huguenot background. She had been in correspondence with the Archives in Potsdam for some time. "Even before the fall of the Wall, I was able to establish contact, thanks to an introduction from my professor," and of course she had used her stay in Berlin for a visit to Dortustrasse: "They're really very accommodating there, and not at all pedantic. You may be certain, madame, that whatever the personal motivation for my current visit, I shall not neglect my studies."

Only now did Fonty chime in. He referred knowledgeably to the part of the city known as Wilmersdorf, which in Lene Nimptsch's time had been bordered by open fields, to the Zoological Garden, rather wretched at the time, and to traffic patterns and road conditions—in conjunction with Botho von Rienäcker's coach ride through the Hasen- and Jungfernheide to the cemetery and the grave of old Frau Nimptsch. He waxed chatty, playing ironically on the immortelles motif, exclaiming, "In *L'Adultera* things turn out well after all for Melanie and Rubehn!" He said, "That was the Jewish element: there was either a lot of money or not much to speak of, but no class barriers," and then he began, without transition, to furnish the Poggenpuhls' apartment: "A few inherited pieces, along with a piece they acquired at auction that had to fit in with the rest: a white-lacquered pier glass, called a *trumeau,* with inlaid gold molding..." At this point he was interrupted by Emmi: "You know, our place on Kollwitzstrasse doesn't look any better than theirs on Grossgörschen. Most of our stuff is left over from Aunt Pinchen. Our mirror even has spots."

After Emmi had lamented other shortcomings and the general condition of the apartment house in Prenzlauer Berg, describing everything as "bad and worse than bad," she abruptly changed the subject, wanting to know from Madeleine what she, the Frenchwoman rowing with such concentration, thought of "the unification," scheduled to go into effect at midnight: "Maybe we'll go have a look tonight, when they start ringing the bells."

Madeleine ignored the change of subject. Still rowing, and not at all out of breath, she assured them that she had already visited Hasenheide a week ago, comparing the present beer garden with the description in the novel, had gone to the Zoo, and had used colored engravings of the period to compare the Wilmersdorf of the past to its completely urbanized character today. Of course she had sought out Grossgörschenstrasse in Kreuzberg. As far as the Poggenpuhl apartment was concerned, she would come back some other time to the loft that housed the old maidservant Friederike, and hence to the unbroached social question. "I know Monsieur X saw all that, but did not like to call it by name—as was the case with anything ugly." And only then, changing focus, did she take up Emmi's question: "On the subject of German unification, all I can say is this: From the French point of view, it is a normal development—if not precisely desirable, at least acceptable. In contrast to Grandpapa, who is full of reservations, me, I am happy about unification. I hope that you, too, Madame Wuttke, consider yourself fortunate. A great day!"

Seen from the bank, it appeared effortless. It was astonishing how easily that delicate little person moved the rowboat, sitting low in the water. The familial freight was in good hands. With solemn pleasure and real skill—two oar strokes to the left, one stroke to the right—she steered the boat past other boats. Often daring maneuvers were called for—by now there was a good deal of traffic on the Tiergarten's man-made lake. Anticipation of the scheduled unification set the tone. In some alarmingly overloaded boats, young men were already, long before nightfall, tipping the bottle. They drank to each other in beery unity. Throaty calls of "Deutschland!" from boat to boat. Bellowed assertions of harmony. People got closer and closer to each other—too close in the case of a couple of boats whose passengers were rocking wildly to simulate heavy seas.

Madeleine wasn't the only one who had seen this coming; we had, too: after a violent collision, one of the boats, a plastic model without a keel, almost capsized, and in the other, the three young women who had been recklessly standing on the rowing bench, arms around each other like the three Graces, pitched overboard, pulling each other down, with much screeching of course.

We laughed, too, for at first it looked comical, giving rise to much merriment and even louder shouts of "Deutschland!" from other boats and from the sunbathers on the lawn. But then it became clear that only two of the women could swim. The third was having trouble making her cries for help heard above the din of united hilarity. She had already gone under for a few seconds. Since all the others were utterly preoccupied with themselves, that went unnoticed. A disaster seemed to be taking its course unnoticed, for by now we had left the scene and were far away. The drowning woman remained alone with her now inaudible cry.

That is how it looked. And if Madeleine Aubron had not reached the nonswimmer with a few strokes of the oars, and swung the left oar over for her to grab onto, then towed the drowning woman close to the other boat, the one that had almost capsized, so that its crew, four young men no longer completely sober but still capable of lending a hand, managed to pull on board the blonde, now stripped of her hairdo, the happy anticipation of the one-fatherland-indivisible would have been tarnished by a tragic accident. But as it was, the male occupants of the boat could fuss over the young woman as if she were a gift. It almost looked as though they were trying to divide the booty. The two other women had swum to shore. No one paid them any mind.

On all the boats that had drawn near, lured to the spot by the accident, the rescue action was applauded. But Fonty found no pleasure in it: "They always have to exaggerate colossally! Have no notion of what unification means, yet they're celebrating. Acting as though it were Sedan Day!"

Emmi tried to soothe him: "They're just young, Wuttke!"

He continued to fume: "Nothing but would-be reserve lieutenants! Excess, excess *über alles!*"

"Well, it came out all right, 'cause our Marlene was paying attention."

"That's what I'm saying: One has to pay attention!"

And Madeleine, who accepted with a little smile the variation on her name, remarked, "That was droll. Could happen anywhere, no? Also in France, on the *Quatorze juillet,* for instance, when people get completely overwrought and think they must storm the Bastille again. Ah, yes! And not only in Paris, on the streets anywhere."

Already the lake showed no traces of the barely averted misfortune. There were beer bottles everywhere. People were trying to drown each other out in joyous anticipation again. Seen from the middle of the lake—for in the meantime we, too, had rented a boat—the delicate, yet also—as everyone had witnessed—highly capable person, rowed the Wuttkes along the shore. No, Madeleine rowed her grandparents, for more and more she was calling them Grand-père and Grand-mère; Madame Wuttke accepted the title graciously.

We called this "Emmi's good-naturedness." Or to be more precise: we credited everything she had been putting up with for years to the account of her capacious temperament. "Well, if Marlene really wanted a new grandma, she could have one, far as I'm concerned. 'Course my Wuttke and I called the little one '*du.*' But she insisted on being formal with us. Kind of old-fashioned, don't you think? But that's how they do it in France—they use formal address for Grandma and Grandpa."

Three in a boat. Rowboat talk: inconsequential comments on the run of lovely weather, on Turks in Berlin and Algerians in Paris, on immigrants in general, legal and illegal. This brought them to the Huguenots, those who had emigrated to Prussian Brandenburg, and those who had been forced to hide out for years on end in the Cévennes. And already Fonty's "one-and-only,"

"Monsieur X," the Immortal with Huguenot ancestors on both sides, was in the boat, describing Gascony and his blustering father—"a *causeur* from the old school"—who could name all of Napoleon's marshals by name. "My mother, on the other hand, was a child of the southern Cévennes, a slim, delicate woman with black hair, eyes like coals, energetic. . . ."

Madeleine had this quotation at her fingertips, but as the conversation edged into the dangerous vicinity of the Saône and Rhône rivers and then the region of la Dombes with its many lakes, and the risk arose that one boat ride might lead too obviously to another, because Fonty was once more beginning to short-circuit all the connections, Emmi remarked, "That's all right, Wuttke. Marlene and I know what can happen when you're out rowing and such."

As if on command, something else entered the picture. On the nearby shoreline promenade a stately gentleman was strolling along with a large dog on a leash. Madeleine exclaimed, "Look, Grand-père, a Newfoundland. I wrote a paper on the role that very breed plays in the works of our author. For instance, I discussed Hector at Hohen-Vietz Castle in *Before the Storm*. And Boncoeur in *Cécile*. And of course Rollo and *la pauvre* Effi at the very end, when Frau von Briest says, 'Rollo is lying by the stone again. It has affected him more deeply than us. . . .' And I wrote extensively about Sultan, the watchdog, though he wasn't a Newfoundland: the way he followed Botho and Lene with his eyes when they went out together, as if he knew all about life. . . ."

"A dog like that understands more than we think," Emmi said. "Back in the beginning of '62, right after the Wall went up, when our boys stayed in the West and we were all alone with Martha, we got ourselves a dog, too. A dachshund. A real city dog. But what a smart little fellow! My Wuttke always called him 'Ezechiel,' Lord only knows why. And not 'Hay-zu-keel,' like we say it in Berlin, but 'Uh-zee-chee-ul,' like in the Bible. But he answered better to 'Fifi.' And when he wasn't off traveling for the Cultural Union, he'd take him for a walk at night. We live three flights up, see. Go walkie, we say. Couple of times around Kollwitzplatz, till he'd had enough, and then he'd give three little barks. Martha didn't really like dogs.

But the boys sure would've . . . specially our Georg—Schorsch, the kids called him. . . . Well, we had to have Fifi put to sleep, back in '76. . . . A real bad time that was . . . When you think of all we've gone through . . ."

Fonty trotted out some more stories about the *Kreuzzeitung* editor to whose biblically inspired name the dachshund didn't answer: a steady stream of anecdotes. They all laughed, even Emmi, at the description of that arch-reactionary from Tunnel days whose bark wasn't as bad as his bite. And thus unified, and chatting without interruption, they finally pulled in at the dock of the boat-rental stand. That, too, the granddaughter carried off effortlessly and with seemingly innate skill.

Here we would gladly have brought the familial boat ride to an end, but there on the dock was someone who could not be avoided. We had noticed him much earlier, although he considered unobtrusiveness a virtue. He stood there as if by prearrangement, enjoying the tableau of the three in the boat as it approached land. His inexhaustible patience. That he always appeared at the right moment was likewise one of his virtues. He stood there with a cigar in his mouth and raised his American baseball cap by way of greeting. Ah, if only Professor Freundlich had been on the dock; but he was undergoing involuntary evaluation in Jena.

While Fonty paid for two whole hours of rowing and soon had his identity card, made out in the name of Theo Wuttke, back in his hands, Hoftaller said, "We have lots of time. Can go home and get some warm clothes. Might be chilly later by the Reichstag. There are huge crowds forming already. But we're bound to find a spot. It's going to be quite a show. This way, please. My Trabi's waiting by the Landwehr Canal."

23

Joy! Joy!

Before our foursome, a quartet drawn from different card games, sets out to join the celebration, in order to rejoice, merely be there, or bob listlessly in the crowd, we must fill in a few details, lest something get left behind in their rapid change of locale—first on foot, later in the Trabi. The deck needs to be reshuffled—or, to put it simply, we choose to postpone Germany's unity a while longer.

Even before the familial rowboat excursion, Fonty paid us a visit with his granddaughter. And soon after this *Anschluss*, this annexation officially termed a "voluntary accession," Madeleine came to the Archives without her grandfather, just as before the historic date she had sought us out on her own, for research purposes. This actual contact followed a good two years' worth of correspondence with the student, which did not emanate, as we had guessed, from the École Normale Supérieure in Paris, that elite institution where Paul Celan had taught into the sixties; but at any rate she was studying at the Sorbonne and was in the middle of writing her master's thesis.

One could say that Madeleine Aubron belonged to our regular clientele. Her exclusive concern in her letters, both those written during the end phase of the Workers' and Peasants' State, and those written after the fall of the Wall, was the Immortal and his literary field of reference, that is to say, the Platen, Lenau, and Herwegh Society and the Tunnel and Rütli poets' societies, as well as Theodor Storm's Potsdam period. She was also interested in half- or completely forgotten literary figures, such as Alexis, Scherenberg, even Wildenbruch. She wanted more information on Prussia's gentry, above all on Marwitz, than our holdings could supply. She wanted to look into the influence of Turgenev and Bürger, but was less curious about the acknowledged inspiration received from Scott and Thackeray. England was out of the picture; for instance, the case of William Glover and that greasy-palmed newspaper the *Morning Chronicle*. But the friendships with Wolfsohn, Lepel, and Heyse were important, likewise Gottfried Keller's withering comments on the Prussian mannerisms affected by the versesmiths who foregathered in the Tunnel Over the Spree.

Initially she inquired about the early poems from the Dresden period, which, as we have since ascertained, have been lost; later her questions, first written, then oral, grew out of her master's thesis, for which the so-called Berlin novels provided ample fodder. We must admit that we were impressed by her earnestness, by her scholarly approach, somehow a little old-fashioned in this day and age, but also by her logical, lucid judgment, its acuity sometimes tempered by emotional factors, or rather by the sudden intervention of emotion. It should not be concealed that from her very first visit she enchanted the Archives with her charm. One might say that Madeleine brought a bit of esprit to our old shop, which, for all our international correspondence, still had the claustrophobic narrowness typical of life under socialism. The minute she stepped inside, something of the Immortal's spirit wafted over us. Of the daughters of Count Barby, it was less Countess Armgard than Countess Melusine we heard, and she also sounded like Corinna, the saucy bourgeoise. She spoke like a book, almost as word-perfectly as our friend Fonty; thus we were not particularly astonished when she turned up on his arm to visit the Archives.

That was in the last days of September. She was wearing a simply cut dress of raw silk, cinched by a belt, like an elegant monk's robe. He, as always, had a bouquet in his hand: dahlias, the buds just opening.

Fonty exuded unmistakable, if ironically overplayed, pride when he introduced the student, whom we already knew, as "my granddaughter, a gift conferred late in life," and added, "But watch your step, ladies and gentlemen! Madeleine is not only clever and well read; she also has a prickly charm, or, to whet your appetites, she's like bittersweet chocolate. I'm willing to wager you've already had a taste."

When she was introduced to us under this memorable label— later, after his granddaughter had long since departed, Fonty yearned for the "bittersweet person"—Madeleine Aubron smiled, her eyes remaining serious, and said, "My grandfather tends to condense everything, much like Botho von Rienäcker, who condensed all the emotions that were unsettling his class consciousness to the epigram 'Order is marriage!' *Voilà!* If order can be defined so concisely, I'm happy to be your bittersweet person."

She reeled off a number of other quotations, giving her grandfather stiff competition. A well-drilled game, in which we archivists did not want to seem to lag behind. If Fonty exclaimed, "Palms are always appropriate!" Madeleine parried with: "Monastery clocks are always slow." We supplied "The more you bring along, the more you find is missing," and that maxim uttered by the Barbys' English coachman: "Widow is more than virgin." One of our colleagues came up with "Morality is good, inheritance is better!" I contributed that well-known insight of old age: "When life is silent, desire falls silent...." And the director of the Archives got the biggest laugh with "Breast of veal is all gristle." Finally it was Fonty who came up with a quotation whose context even we could not identify immediately, thereby bringing the rather jolly game back into the present: "But the Germans—whenever something opens up—always split again into two parts."

And that brought us to the topic of the day. It had to do with the soon-to-be-greater fatherland, that is to say, with the pretty gift we had been handed that would turn out to be impractical and unwieldy. What to do with it? What to do about ourselves? How to live with so much greatness?

Not that a general quarrel broke out, but the clash of views between grandfather and granddaughter became evident. From the French perspective, unification and the nation were a *fait accompli*. "And *basta!*" Madeleine exclaimed.

A declared enemy of "dusty Borussianism," Fonty was still enough of a Prussian to dismantle any unity into its smallest parts and dismiss the concept of the nation as a chimera, preferring a proper constitution, characterized, to the extent possible, by reason: "There's no question that what we lack is a constitution that would be a good fit for us, not merely for the West."

She charged the Germans with self-destructive insanity, he the French with self-righteous chauvinism. If she exclaimed *"Vive la France!"* he parried with "Long live Brandenburg!" The debate was heated, more bitter than sweet. And we, who were facing imminent annexation, kept our mouths shut.

What new ideas could we have added? No doubt we could have found quotations to document the Immortal's contradictory positions—"Germany is no longer merely a concept but a powerful fact"—but soon there was no getting a word in edgewise. Madeleine Aubron, in the heat of this battle of nations, resorted to her mother tongue; and Fonty surprised us by striking back in a Romance tongue. It did not sound to us like "pathetic rear-echelon French."

We were astonished to hear the conversation being waged so fluently over our heads. At most we could compete in a language that had been forced down the throats of all schoolchildren in the Workers' and Peasants' State: in our obligatory Russian, whose beauty we do not wish to deny. Quickly shedding any inhibitions, we gave it a try. One of us could quote Pushkin in the original. Now each of us spontaneously came up with something, one Turgenev, another Chekhov, I Mayakovsky. One of our ladies knew Polish and offered up a poem by Tadeusz Rózewicz, the other even remembered some Chinese from her broken-off university studies—"Mandarin," she said—and recited a short poem by the great Chairman Mao. The director called on his Latin: Ovid or Horace. Eventually we managed to bury the debate over unity and national identity in a welter of languages. Soon everyone was laughing, including eventually the grandfather and granddaughter, now reverting to German.

They stayed and stayed. Of course we brought out coffee and biscuits. We had plenty of time to discover how Fonty had acquired his language skills, which clearly could not be attributed entirely to the time he had spent as a soldier in France. Because Fonty had merged his life so completely with the Immortal's, he had gone to the same pains to draw up petitions while being held captive on the island of Oléron, petitions which, like all letters addressed to his wife, had to be composed in French to comply with the censorship. What is more, as Fonty, Theo Wuttke had derived personal benefit from this stay in France necessitated by the war; his love for Madeleine Blondin must have helped things along.

Toward the end of the visit, when the conversation came around to his release from internment, conflict broke out again. Grandfather and granddaughter went at it like lawyers. For the benefit of us, their audience, they brought to life a case to which we had made considerable contributions of our own with footnotes. Whereas Fonty was convinced that the Cardinal Archbishop of Besançon had been instrumental, after the Catholic von Wangenheim family turned to him for help, the student Aubron asserted that Bismarck's letter to the United States envoy in France, Mr. Washburne, had proved decisive. The envoy had promptly established contact with the French foreign minister, Jules Favre. The threat contained in the chancellor's letter had had the desired effect: he wrote that if the "harmless scholar," whom he characterized as a "Prussian subject and a well-known writer of historical narratives," were not released, the arrest of "a certain number of persons occupying similar positions in various French cities" could be expected. Madeleine exclaimed, "Our Monsieur X was freed by Bismarck!"

Fonty refused to accept that. His granddaughter was bold enough to shout "*Absurde!*" and bandied about the Immortal's favorite word, "*ridicule!*" We intervened, asking them to consider the fact that the writer Moritz Lazarus, like the Immortal a member of the Tunnel and Rütli literary societies, had communicated with the French minister of war, Crémieux, and had thus given the internment a push in the right direction; Crémieux was chairman of the Alliance Israélite Universelle, while Lazarus was president of the Israelite Synod. I stuck my neck out with the assertion "In Prussia and France, only Jews ever intervened effectively on the Immortal's behalf."

The director voiced the opinion that "Not until a commitment not to speak or print anything *'contre la France'* had been signed could the release take place, on 24 November 1870."

This more complementary than contradictory piece of information was not enough to put an end to the quarrel between granddaughter and grandfather. Sparks flew in both directions, until finally Fonty relented, exclaiming, "Was a free man again—that was the main thing!" Then he turned to us: "I'd ask you to confirm this: this is how she is, our Madeleine, delicate of form yet bitterly incalcitrant."

We were inclined to side with the student in this matter. But by the time she visited the Archives, alone, shortly after the union had been consummated, we had checked all the documents at our disposal and had become convinced that it would have been impossible for Fonty to give any credit to Bismarck, whom he called at every opportunity "a terrible crybaby." We reached the following agreement with Madeleine: "Monsieur X expressed himself with studied nonchalance where he himself was concerned: 'What matter who liberated me? It was either the Catholic party or the Jewish party, or the government party....'"

By the bye, the sketch *Prisoner of War* furnishes evidence that the Immortal kept his word. He recorded his memories of this involuntary confinement without casting any nationalistic aspersions on *"La France."* That certainly did not go over well in Prussia. Once German unification had been proclaimed, one could hardly hope for tolerance. Even his son George, who during the war against France was stationed with his regiment near St. Denis, was not prepared to tolerate the slim volume, which in the meantime had been published. In a letter from the field, he wrote: "I must express a small reproach to you, dear Father, in the name of all our rulers as well, because you mention so favorably the role the French played in your fate...."

The student Aubron regretted this familial conflict, but when we asked her, not straight out but in a roundabout fashion, about the boat ride with her grandfather and his wife, she said, "Our *tour en famille* went quite harmoniously. Madame and I got along splendidly. Truly, a kindhearted woman. When it came to Grand-papa, we were delightfully of one mind. After I explained that Monsieur Wuttke had received the honorary decoration on general principle, or, as they say here, theoretically, for he had proven himself, if not a hero, then certainly useful, she laughed most heartily and said, 'That's just what I was thinking myself. But it sure is pretty, that little ribbon.'"

Could one really expect Emmi Wuttke to be so understanding? Was everything that was painful to her buried under pounds of good-naturedness? Was she really so clueless, or was her indulgence toward her Wuttke the result of lifelong habit? Could it be that she knew even before Fonty did that France had a surprise up its sleeve?

When questioned about this, she said, "I hadn't expected the little one to be so adorable. When I think of our Martha, how moody she can be, and how stiff-necked...You should read her letters—you'd think Schwerin was the North Pole. Nothing but whining. And yet her Grundmann's given her a real villa, with a housekeeper, a terrace, and lake view. Well, compared to Martha, who's never satisfied, the little one's so refreshing. The way she rowed and looked at us with those saucer eyes of hers. And always cheery and sparkling, but not a flirt, I mean, like they say French women are. No, sometimes I think Marlene was actually brooding as she looked at us two old folks sitting there. But when the chips were down, she could be a tiger. I mean specifically when she locked horns with my Wuttke 'cause he didn't want to believe in the unification and kept bringing up '70–'71, 'cause that turned out badly, too, or so he said. That's how my Wuttke is. Always has to compare everything, the Parvenooskis from back then with the Parvenooskis of today, the soldier types and lieutenants with the riffraff that's on top now, I mean these gunrunners and expense-account leeches; that's what he calls them. First he always brings up those high and mighty Treibels, but then he also has it in for that shrewdy Krause, who wrote up the unification for us all nice and tidy. But the little one—Marlene—I mean, she explained to him, with that cheeky mouth of hers, that that kind of thing's perfectly normal, I mean, a little shadiness, 'cause that's life, at least in France anyway. She really got fired up when the show got underway down by the Reichstag. She was yelling so loud my Wuttke couldn't pretend he didn't hear her—that you can't always fuss about the details, you have to look at the big picture. And that the whole of Germany has to learn some time or other to be a real nation. 'Without a strong Germany, France will fall asleep!' she shouted. And guess who chimed in, 'Right, one hundred percent right!' No, of course it wasn't my Wuttke. Exactly! That stubble-head, Martha calls him. Well, he picked us up from the rowing and took us home so we could get our coats, and a sweater for our Marlene. And then we all piled into his Trabi and off to the Reichstag. Got as far as Glinkastrasse. Had to walk from there. And the stubblehead with us the whole time. Couldn't shake him. He always knows everything before you do. I mean, long before my Wuttke got sick, that one dropped some hints about him leaving the country by ship, heading up there to Scotland. You know, that was back in the summer, when the new money came. . . . And again, when we got back from Hiddensee . . . Comes around, worms his way in, and tootles, 'Dear Frau Wuttke, it's a little embarrassing for me, but we've recently received information that your husband . . .' Whispers that something's going on, that my Wuttke has some ghost from the past in France—he absolutely insists on coming along when I go shopping at KaDeWe, making it all suspenseful. First I told him to beat it, but he hung around, grinning like a bear with a tree full of honey. All right, let him talk, I think to myself. It's got to be something political, nothing new there. But I must admit I was shocked. First I thought it had to be something bad, like shooting partisans maybe. Was so relieved when it turned out to be just the business with the child. So what? I say to him, when we finally got out of the food section and he invited me to the cafeteria. So what? It was wartime. All kinds of things happen in wartime. And I know our engagement had dragged on pretty long by '44. I don't need you to tell me that. And if someone turns up, not his daughter but his granddaughter, it's not the end of the world, specially if the little one's been looking for her grandfather all these years, going back to when the Wall was still up, and we all thought it'd be here forever. Well, I say to him, if she only looked in the West, no wonder she couldn't track down any Wuttke. And he says, 'We were able to be of service....' Apparently the stubblehead got some kind of official tip-off from the bureau over there. And he showed up at Martha's wedding, too.... And just recently on Hiddensee, when I had that problem with my foot... You should've seen him—like an American overseas. And now he wanted to dig up all these secrets. You know, the old stories: what my Wuttke was up to in Lyon. And the stuff he put in his articles for the Reich Aviation—about the Huguenot wars and such. And that there was something in there about rowboat excursions, first on one lake, then on another. And that they don't just produce frog's legs in that area, but have a real fishing industry... 'So what?' I say to him, 'That's nothing new.' I typed most of those articles myself, see. But there was even more in his letters from the field. A lot happened in the war. And besides, I say, 'It's none of your frigging business, absolutely none, 'cause that's private.' That shut him up for a while, but then just the other day, when I was out shopping on Schönhauser Allee, he sidles up to me again: 'Just a moment of your time, Frau Wuttke, that's all I want. This'll interest you. She's here, that person we were talking about. She's documented as the granddaughter, no question. Determined to speak with her grandfather. Also brought something along for him. I'm certainly not betraying any secret when I tell you it's a decoration, a medal, after a fashion.' And then he says, 'An intelligent person, incidentally, and she's not making any demands, financial or the like.' Was polite, superpolite, to me, all 'My dear Frau Wuttke' and such, 'cause he wanted my permission, you know, for getting the girl and her grandfather together. Goodness me, I think to myself, he's actually turning out to be human, this weasel. And I say to him, I say, 'Be my guest, it's fine with me, don't let me get in your way.' But then I was curious about the girl. Course my Wuttke was relieved when I suggested the three of us go for a little boat ride together. Got all boisterous again. 'Rowing is always good!' he says, and then, 'It doesn't call for a lot of talking.' And it turned out nice, our afternoon on the water. Had a couple of hard rolls along, with cold cuts, you know. And you should've seen how the little one tucked into them. Just adorable, our Marlene. She said Grandmama to me, but still with the formal 'you.' And the way she stared with those black saucer eyes...But you know, I don't see my Wuttke in her at all. Anyway, after we went home to get some warm things to put on, we took a little stroll and stopped for coffee in between, 'cause my Wuttke didn't want to plunge into those crazy crowds right away, but first up and down the Linden, explaining everything to us, you know, what used to be there, Kranzler's Café and all those fancy restaurants and pastry shops. But we had that stubblehead with us the whole time, and he knew all about the old days, too. Just couldn't shake him. I didn't care for it one bit, nor our Marlene either. 'Miss-yeur Offtaler,' she says to him, real sweet, 'please understand that we wish to spend this historic night just amongst family and have no need of your help at this time....' We were almost at the Reichstag, and she wanted to send him packing. But you just couldn't get rid of him. 'I'm part of the family, too!' he says, and grins...."

Later we asked Fonty's day-and-night-shadow about it, and this is what came out: "It's obvious that you want to be with your wards when Germany's unity is being celebrated. Besides, the services did their part in terms of the decoration and conferring it as discreetly as possible. Came under the program 'Operation Family Unification'—all the rage at the time. I even got authorization for a trip to the nonsocialist countries. Of course I knew Lyon from before, but in the meantime it had 'decked itself out colossally,' as our friend would say. Rich city, everything in tip-top shape, impeccable. When I got there, the Barbie trial was underway. Huge brouhaha in the press over an old man, but under the surface it was also about the fellow who headed the militia at the time, Paul Touvier, and a certain Bousquet, who ran the police under Pétain. The French are still pretty touchy about these things. Even the comrades seemed quite embarrassed when we so much as mentioned the Jean Moulin case. Decided to leave that one alone. After all, we wanted something from them, nothing major. The case filed under the code name 'Fontaine' had been dropped long ago, and now needed to be reevaluated. But of course not! Why deny that I've known Fräulein Aubron since my visit to Lyon. It was at her behest that we finally received official assistance. We never could understand why the French kept dragging their feet. Basically it all came down to a formality—whether Airman Theo Wuttke had aided the *Résistance* knowingly or inadvertently. The veterans' associations were fairly prickly on that subject. The main thing, we argued, is that the readings he recorded on tape were subversive enough and had a destabilizing effect on several units stationed near Lyon, especially after the invasion began. What's insufficient evidence in a situation like this? As archivists I'm sure you know how much power words can have. No doubt about it: undermining battle-readiness, they called it at the time. Why? Your question amazes me. You mean you really don't know how dangerous words can be—no, are? Literature in general... certain books... sometimes all it takes is half a sentence... And these words had a particular impact because of the way they were spoken: the reader's voice—suggestive and insinuating and thus clearly insidious. Had the impact of a bomb every time they broadcast him. Just look at the statistics on defectors around Lyon. Still, the French comrades raised objection after objection. Mademoiselle Aubron was angry and let the Trotskyite show, which didn't help matters. So the decoration wasn't awarded in time, unfortunately. We'd have liked to see it done publicly, at the fortieth anniversary of our republic. The official rostrum! Red-carpet treatment! The leading comrades! The private ceremony was actually a breach of form, and the certificate, well... in a rowboat... an outrage, really... But he was pleased with the decoration anyway... doesn't like being out in public that much... big crowds... That's probably why he was so grumpy when things finally got underway and we all went down to the Reichstag to celebrate the united fatherland. Said he wanted to go home. Didn't want to wait for the bells. But we did our best to persuade him, especially Fräulein Aubron. He listens to her."

They did not get very far, no farther than the Western side of the Brandenburg Gate, because masses of people were packed in everywhere. The actual site could be seen only in the mind's eye: the Reichstag and the rostrum erected in front, where the speakers had already begun to gild this historic midnight hour, some laying it on thick, others more delicately. Nonetheless our little group stayed for the ringing of the bells, and for everything taking place against the sprawling backdrop—the speeches, the cheering with which the crowd rewarded certain utterances, the musical interludes—all carried by loudspeakers, albeit buffeted by the wind and audible only in snatches, yet intelligible, even captivating, because of its simple content; at any rate, a reverent mood was conveyed, and the solemnity created something like a feeling of togetherness.

And yet what Hoftaller told us was correct: from the outset Fonty had no desire to be where they were now standing, squeezed in, even though they were near the edge of the crowd. And as they found themselves swallowed up in the crush, he just wanted to get away, out of there, or, as he said, "Out of this colossal song and dance!"

But Emmi insisted on staying, because their granddaughter was determined to be there in any case, and until the ringing of the bells: "I beg you, Grandpapa, please show a little consideration for Grand-mère, even a little for me. For us, at any rate, the unification of the German nation cannot be a matter of indifference, no? We want to rejoice and give expression to our joy. For whatever reason, you may see Germany as incapable of unity, but we in France place the nation, *La France,* above all else. *La grande nation,* we say. Some with great pathos, as if echoing Général de Gaulle, the others a bit mockingly, but they all take it seriously. That is true, of course, also for me, a sometimes mocking little Trotskyite, who on the one hand indulges in her internationalist dreams and still hopes for a bit of Communism, but on the other hand most earnestly asks her grand-père not to spoil the joy of this night for her grand-mère and herself."

So they stayed. Fonty leaned on his walking stick, suffering in near-silence. Hoftaller, who claimed to be part of the family, made an effort to keep in the background. As it was, the sound waves bombarding the square did not admit of intimate conversation. The speeches wafting by in fragments had an incantatory quality, because formulated for repetition: "United in this hour... profound sense of gratitude... there will now grow together... in this historic hour... with profound satisfaction... what belongs together . . . unified and grateful . . . out of profound . . . out of deeply felt . . . but above all with joy and gratitude . . ."

And then, finally, the appropriate music. Proclaiming the great day, the notes offered up were challenging or uplifting, and left no one unmoved. Oh, yes! Voices were raised in song. Unfettered and chorally inspired, the German song-lust swelled in a deafening crescendo.

This music was so contagious that it was not enough merely to hear it. As all the loudspeakers around the Reichstag blared out the final chorus of the Ninth and, like some natural phenomenon, inundated the many thousands gathered there, even Madeleine Aubron joined in the chorus, in a delicate yet clearly audible voice, singing each word so clearly and correctly that soon Emmi, too, joined in, in a respectable alto. Then others standing nearby, among them we archivists, tried to add our voices to the "Ode to Joy," though not quite as clearly and correctly as the bittersweet person, who seemed to grow beyond her small stature with the up-lifting song.

Although surrounded by his family, Fonty remained aloof. He was wearing his fall coat with his light summer hat, while Hoftaller, who kept discreetly in the background, snatched his baseball cap from his head as soon as this song of joy leaped into the crowd, a spark divine, spreading like wildfire, as it was intended to spread. But the bareheaded day-and-night-shadow did not sing; singing along was not for him this time. Yet he glossed in his own fashion the repeated invocations of joy, the millions who were to be em-braced, the impending brotherhood of man, the sanctuary of peace: "Yes, yes, rejoice, you Wessies! We'll grab hold of you and hug you tight! Bears—ha!—that's what we are, real bears! Once we get our arms around someone, there's no shaking us off! You'll never shake us off! Millions, shmillions. This one'll cost you bil-lions. It's what you wanted, at any price. Unification! Joy! Just don't rejoice too soon. You'll get over it soon enough. Won't be much of a joy. Course it all went according to plan—Wall open: joy! Tin coin out: joy! D-mark in: joy! But the bill's in the mail. It's all scrap, you said, can be picked up for a song. That's what you think. Go ahead and rejoice. All brothers: rejoice, dammit! You're supposed to rejoice—go to it! From today at the stroke of midnight, nothing but joy!"

Fonty's mustache was trembling. But his stick supported him. Perhaps instead of listening to Hoftaller's cathartic outpouring he was cocking his ear toward his long-lost granddaughter, whose bright voice blended nicely with Emmi's warm one, or warm-hearted one, we would call it. This kind of familial harmony, this kind of euphony was more to his liking. Perhaps he was thinking how good it would be to have his daughter Martha there to add a third voice to the chorus of joy, Martha, who in her younger years had not only played the piano but also sung, and who had even bellowed out "Build up, build up!" at her wedding dinner. Usually no friend to music, Fonty liked this singing.

It wasn't until Hoftaller began to make smacking noises to augment the kiss-for-the-entire-world that had come over the loudspeakers, and shouted, "Yes, indeed! We sure will! Smooch the whole world! Global kissing only from now on!" then expanded the "Ode to Joy" with the cry, "Kissie, kissie *über alles!*"—it wasn't until this point that Fonty tried to throttle his immortal sidekick: "That's enough, Tallhover! You're frightfully right. Colossal balderdash, all of it. Can already see it: this unity is riddled with fission fungus. Now cut out that smacking this instant! It's sickening. Let's go, Hoftaller, come on, let's go!"

But neither Madeleine nor Emmi nor his day-and-night-shadow could be budged. The women's voices soared to the starry firmament above, while Hoftaller shouted, "Oh, come on, Wuttke! A joy like this has to be savored—it won't last long. And if we're all brothers, let's do it up right. They need to realize over there that we're contagious. They say we're scrap—we'll make scrap out of them. They're going to pay, and we'll pay them back, with Eastern viruses, ha! Yes, indeed. We're contagious—like joy. Let's grab them and embrace them—come, brother!—and before they know it, they'll all be infected. They want to in*west* in us, we'll simply co-*east* with 'em. Here's a kiss—smack!—there's a kiss—smack!—and before they know it, they'll be weak in the chest, just like us. A spark like that leaps the gap, a spark divine, whatever. I'm already all fired up.... Political parties be damned, we're just Germans, Germans everywhere...."

Hoftaller couldn't stop. He kept coming up with worse and worse diseases, epidemics even—plague, cholera—unifying and usefully contagious, all passed on through the fraternal embrace. He glowed with energy. "This is it. This is really it!" he shouted.

As the final chorus of the Ninth died away, and before rejoicing had time to follow the brief pause scheduled for profound emotion, Fonty used the respite—a few bells could be heard, but only far off in the distance, for not all the churches were willing to participate—to say, more to himself than to the family, "Too much joy takes you round the bend," and somewhat louder, "I don't expect much of this one-fatherland-indivisible."

He did not wait for the rejoicing to resume, but peeled himself out of the crowd and set out so decisively down Unter den Linden that Emmi and Madeleine, who at first had cried, "Come on, stay a little longer, Wuttke!" and "Please, Grandpapa, just two more minutes!" had to follow him, and with them Hoftaller.

Soon they had caught up with Fonty. Emmi took his right arm, and his granddaughter hooked her arm into his left. Hoftaller stayed close behind them as far as the corner of Glinkastrasse. When the family declined to ride home in his Trabi, which was parked there, and Madeleine took leave of "Monsieur Offtaler" with the curt instruction, "You should be satisfied now," he tore himself away from Fonty and his ladies: "Thanks so much all the same for letting me tag along. This kind of thing is best enjoyed communally. Isn't there a saying, 'Double your joy: divide it among friends'?"

But before he went, he pointed his pudgy index finger at the sky over Berlin. His gesture was so insistent that it had to be heeded. As Emmi and Madeleine looked skyward with Fonty, Hoftaller exclaimed, "Our chancellor can do anything! Hasn't a clue what's in store for him, but a full moon for unification, that he can pull off!"

We were no longer on hand when they all gazed up at the sky. As the crowd dispersed, we had lost track of them. But later on, in response to our questions, Emmi told us, "You can believe it, that business with the moon. It's true: when the stubblehead finally left, my Wuttke called after him, 'Full moon is good, but waning is better!' That's how he is. Always has to have the last word. If I put a cup of fresh-brewed coffee in front of him, he'll say, 'Hot coffee is good, but lukewarm is better.' And it was just the same with the moon when we got our unification. Always has to have his say... Can't help himself... He's like his one-and-only, I'm telling you. After that we walked our Marlene to the S-Bahn. She was staying over on the other side, in student housing in Eichkamp. Unbelievable crowds in the station at Friedrichstrasse and on the platform. And everybody pushing and shoving. But before her train came, the one that goes to Wannsee, my Wuttke started hunting through all his pockets. What? You'll never guess. It's not something you'd think of right away. Two chestnuts. 'Fresh ones,' he says, 'the first.'" And he hands them to her. From our courtyard—there's been a chestnut tree there forever and ever. Tickled pink, our Marlene was, and when the train pulled in, and she had to push and shove to get on, she called out, "They'll always belong together, Grandpapa, because they were given to me on the day of German unification.' But you know, there's not a year goes by my Wuttke doesn't stick those chestnuts in his pockets. That's why they're all so baggy. Anyway, we took the S-Bahn home, too, by way of Ostkreuz to Schönhauser Allee. Streets were completely empty. In our part of town no one was celebrating. Only in a couple of bars, where they had the TV on. They showed more bell-ringing than there really was, 'cause a whole group of pastors didn't want their bells rung, over there, and over here, too. But that business with the full moon, that's true. Even over our Prenzlauer Berg, there it was, clear as can be. Looked beautiful. And my Wuttke says, 'Now our republic is gone. But the moon up there, that's something no one can take from us.'"

BOOK 4

24

From Bridge to Bridge

And then everyday life set in. In its calendar-driven course, the labors of actually existing immortality took precedence again. Our responsibilities in the Archives, in addition to the usual trivia, included the sometimes stimulating task of attending to visitors from home and abroad. We had no time now for field operations such as boat rides and top-secret lakeside promenades in the Tiergarten. Instead we had to content ourselves with being what people like us are by profession, but also by inclination: sedentary types with bad backs, who find in the aroma of old papers a substitute for all those scents attributed in prose and poetry to nature—a range that extends from Prussian spruces and Brandenburg dunghills to the lilacs by the Queen Luise Bridge, also offers exhaust fumes from Potsdamer Strasse, and divulges fragrances here, stenches there.

Bringing her own characteristic aroma—bittersweet, from a perfume presumably based on essence of almond—Madeleine Aubron came to the Archives shortly before her departure to examine the correspondence with Mete, the sons, and the rest of the family. Text-focused as she was, she displayed a reserved demeanor that warded off personal questions; even while immersed in the letters to Emilie, born out of wedlock as Rouanet, adopted as Kummer, she would not tolerate any cross-references to Emmi and the Wuttkes. Only on her last visit did she wax briefly but firmly familiar: "Please allow me to express the expectation that you will continue to concern yourselves with Grandpapa's well-being. He has a tendency to make sudden decisions. Upon occasion he works himself into a state that he refers to as being '*abattu*' or suffering from 'nervous exhaustion.' *Bien sûr!* He must pursue his mission, which pertains completely and utterly to Monsieur X, through difficult and often murky terrain, and it is no secret to you or me that in the process he finds himself in very bad company, as it were."

And then—when "*la petite*" had just left us, or rather the Wuttkes and us—Hoftaller came calling, as if he wanted to even up the weights on the scale. "I was in an archival mood today. Excuse me for simply barging in."

In point of fact he had never let us know in advance that he was coming. He simply showed up. That he appeared all by himself could actually be considered atypical, atypical for the Workers' and Peasants' State, that is, whose watchdogs generally turned up in twos, one serving as security for the other. But since Tallhover's biographer had emphatically constructed his hero as a loner, we could not, and cannot duplicate Hoftaller; at most we are sometimes able to see him in multiples, lined up in a row or stacked, but always with his subject. Only Fonty broke his solitude.

But he always came to the Archives alone. He considered us part of his subject's ambient field, a kind of accessory. But that was not all: because his shadow fell on us, we—and all of our devoted predecessors in the Archives, who had viewed themselves, as we did, as living in the service of the Immortal—were under his care, the more so since his research often crossed paths with ours. Part of everyday life at the Archives was the certainty that we were under supervision.

What's more, Hoftaller saw himself as our unofficial collaborator. This explained his frequent variations on the now proverbial words of old Briest: "Our material covers too far a field. That's why we shouldn't get lost in individual operations...."

Thank goodness he did not come often. Actually his visits were routine. To declare the Archives off-limits to him would have had consequences; so we accepted his presence as part of everyday life. Only former colleagues recall his coming more frequently: during the period when we were building socialism, when we all took its promises to heart, not merely as slogans on banners. In the late forties and early fifties he maintained regular contact with the Archives, making himself useful. I can recall several times when he brought us letters thought to have been lost since the end of the war. They had, as he put it, "fallen into unauthorized hands." In addition, he had salvaged—again, in his words, "tracked down"—double-sided manuscripts, notes for the *Likedeeler* project, all sorts of treasures that we thought had long ago gone up in flames—for instance, the original of the only letter addressed to Wolfsohn. The locations where these documents had been found were never divulged. At most, if we questioned him persistently, he would allude to the enemy of the working class and the risk of "capitalist seizure," or he would refer again to "too far a field," a terrain that had to be paced off, surveyed, for it was constantly growing and threatening to expand to immeasurable dimensions. "Let's create an archival collective," was his offer, clearly made in the spirit of the times, an offer from which we timidly tried to distance ourselves—far too timidly by today's standards. We ask for forbearance, however, for understanding, because, at the time, he presented himself as collegial and knowledgeable; to have rejected his help would have been courageous, but in the Immortal's sense "colossally stupid."

After the period of building socialism waned, when things were just chugging along in their "socialist way," he did not turn up for a long time. It was his biographer who attempted later to explain why his partly oppressive, partly beneficial presence came to an end. At any rate, after the unrest in '53, the Archives received no more finds. We were already both hoping and regretting that we no longer lay within his field of observation. And after the building of the Wall, it seemed evident for a while that, thanks to the erection of that bulwark, the period of surveillance might be over. We were deceiving ourselves, as his biographer had deceived himself with the help of a fictitious obituary. Soon his shadow darkened our lives again, especially after the Eleventh Party Congress, when all hopes were smashed; and after the fall of the Wall, when many of us thought that enforced collective collaboration was gone for good, we were deceiving ourselves yet again.

For Hoftaller there were no historical breaks, no zero hours, only fluid transitions. He liked to speak in the plural: "We are engaged in a reorientation process. . . ." He said, "The services will be back." And: "Our concept of operational proceedings is beginning to take hold."

Everything continued on its way, though it was no longer the socialist way; and just as, after unification, Hoftaller's activity in the Ministries Building did not come to an end, but merely branched out into new activities connected with that building, so, too, he kept on Fonty's heels, and thereby on our heels as well, when, after the celebration, everyday life set in again.

He visited the Archives early in the morning. He did not bring flowers for the ladies. He smoked one of his Cuban cigars, which annoyed us. He said, "I've come on a matter of overriding interest. There are a couple of inconsistencies that absolutely must be cleared up. All regarding our mutual friend. We spoke recently about Lyon and the consequences; that was when the services intervened to assist with family reunification. But as regards the internment on the island of Oléron, located at the mouth of the Gironde, and the release of the war correspondent and Prussian subject, much clarification is called for. It wasn't the Catholic or the Jewish party, or, in spite of intervention at the highest level, the government party that effected the release of the person in question. No, it was us. In collaboration with our French counterparts, of course. War doesn't just divide; it also increases the value of existing connections, to the extent they can provide access to expertise. An experience we've had repeatedly. After the last campaign in France, for example. The services have seldom cooperated more smoothly, especially in Lyon. Don't want to downplay the efforts of the Catholic, Jewish, and government parties, but it's time your archival certainties were set straight: in every case we were the decisive factor. We swung into action. And in future we will also.... Please note this fact. Just a small point, but it furthers establishment of the truth...."

He talked and talked at us, with even the harshest statements accompanied by that smile of his—petrified, like his petrified expertise. "I'm well aware," he said, "that you gentlemen don't want to hear this—can't tolerate any fly specks on your image of the Immortal. There's no appreciation for our contributions. You can't wait for me to go. Yet I'm attached to the Archives. Would rather be headquartered here than anywhere else. I'm sick of standing around all the time. Such a grind, being out in the field in all kinds of weather..."

We had never seen Hoftaller so drained of purpose, so weary of his service. Suddenly he began to complain about everything: the ingratitude, the lack of respect, the bad reputation, the futility of it all. His own modest role and the marginal existence to which he had been consigned had become pointless to him. Altogether, he now had his doubts about all specialized state-security services: "The whole thing's a fiction!" Then he groused about his subject's whims, the way Fonty would suddenly leave the house and roam about aimlessly for hours. He asked us to help, and—like him— not let Fonty out of our sight: "Think of Domrémy, when he impulsively abandoned the Prussian troops to go and search for the Maid of Orléans. Or think of Lyon, when he put himself in harm's way with those boat rides. And just the other month, his most recent attempt to duck under and disappear somewhere into the Scottish moors. Believe me: our friend is a strange bird...."

For the time being, Hoftaller's field operations were impinged upon by bad weather. It remained autumnally mild after the third of October, and Fonty's walks stayed within bounds, because he was declared fit for service again. Right after the unification proclamation, he, too, found himself subject to the banal demands of everyday life. True, people were now officially calling the Workers' and Peasants' State the "newly accessioned territory," but in the former Ministries Building the employee Theo Wuttke was still in demand in all the offices and corridors of the many-storied building, for a new term had come into use: "winding down." In office after office and up and down in the paternoster, the ministries had lost their heads and had to be "wound down." The phrase began to make sense. The file courier could be observed in constant activity, because winding down meant clearing out, and clearing out meant making room for a new agency. Under the unification agreement, the "Handover Trust" law now went into effect, bringing with it the rehabilitation of a concept that had had far-reaching implications once before: for the duration of the Third Reich, everywhere in Germany the property and financial holdings of Jews in Germany had been placed under trusteeship.

This new agency had already been in existence for months, carrying out its business from a cramped location on Alexanderplatz. At the behest of the Round Table, it was supposed to protect the people's property. But now that the people's property had been declared an illusion, the Handover Trust had a new assignment. It was charged with "winding it all down," in the course of which it was supposed to outgrow itself. It demanded space for more than three thousand employees, whose goal was to privatize as quickly as possible all the assets rendered ownerless when the concept of people's ownership was declared invalid; in the Handover Trust's usage, this word "privatize" was the consequence of "winding down."

The entire newly accessioned territory was to be treated as a mass annexation. From the Oder to the Elbe, from the Baltic to the Erz Mountains, the national residual burden had to be inventoried. A task for giants—especially since this legislated necessity mandated throughout the land a radical downsizing, particularly wherever industrial plants still went under the name of "people's property"—which in turn required a central supervisory authority charged with "winding down" the centralization that until just recently had been in effect. This authority was the Handover Trust, which seized opportunity and property in equal measure.

The former Reich Aviation Ministry and later Ministries Building presented itself as the most obvious location. With over two thousand offices, the colossus won hands down. But before the Handover Trust could move in and make itself at home, the place had to be cleaned out, and that in turn meant "wound down." Fonty helped, and Hoftaller now assisted him with the winding-down, as previously with his everyday duties.

Since the Handover Trust retained some of the employees already in place, the core personnel, it was not surprising that the file courier was among them; despite, or because of, his advanced age, he was asked by the new bosses to play an advisory role. As they put it: Since he had been familiar with the building on the

406

corner of Leipzigerstrasse through every change of regime in its history, he embodied continuity; he belonged to the building, he was the mouthpiece of tradition and history; without him, they would be in danger of losing the necessary background.

This particular position came to Fonty from the highest level; it was confirmed, in writing, by the head of the new personnel division, and made palatable by Hoftaller, who had likewise been kept on, in middle management, in charge of field operations. Hoftaller's talent for frictionless transitions was sufficiently evident, for which reason his motto—"Without us, no new system"—could be considered one of the eternal verities.

And during a paternoster ride that cycled again and again past the turning points, Hoftaller persuaded the former file courier to accept the new position. "You can't really say no, Wuttke. Nothing to sneeze at. Western pay scale, of course. Soon we'll be an agency of the West, reporting directly to the Treasury. No one'll be looking over our shoulder then. Just us, Wuttke, just us. Besides, there'll be more than enough free time."

So it came about that Fonty no longer carried files from floor to floor, but served, at a good salary, in an advisory capacity. He was even promised, for a later date, an office in the north wing, which ran along Leipzigerstrasse—away from the frenzy of activity that had by now become the everyday routine: from the top floor he would have a view of the sky and one of the inner courtyards. Fonty was looking forward to this room of his own.

But for now there was the din of construction everywhere, while the winding-down proceeded in silence. Before the Handover Trust could move from Alexanderplatz to Otto-Grotewohl-Strasse, the cleared-out building had to undergo a thorough renovation, calculated to drive out any residual mustiness. House-cleaning was underway. A new broom was at work. Everything had to look right by Western standards. But Fonty, in his advisory capacity, made sure that certain things survived the sweep. Some of the potted plants left behind in more than two thousand offices, among them indoor lindens, rubber plants, ivy aralias, arrowroot, and tricolor saxifrage, were to be kept in suitable areas and tended for future lovers of horticultural decor. In an advisory function he wrote: "Governmental fondness for cyclamen and Chinese primrose is pan-German. What unites us Germans is the ever-blooming impatiens. What must go must go, but we should guard against brutally winding down potted plants that have outlived the Wall and barbed wire."

Furthermore, on Fonty's advice, they uncovered the linoleum that had been laid in the corridors during the time of the Aviation Ministry and was still shiny under all the worn-down socialist carpeting. As a result, the corridors gleamed like new when, after three or four months of housecleaning, Western standards of cleanliness had been achieved throughout. But before that point was reached, the Handover Trust consultant Theo Wuttke found time for excursions that took him far beyond his professional purview.

On afternoons and weekends Hoftaller invited him to join him for outings in the Trabi. Sometimes the destination was close by, sometimes they went far afield. Castles and Pückler-Muskau park, monuments and other sights were on their itinerary. Even when the weather turned unpredictable, their junkets knew no boundaries. And Fonty, who, since his granddaughter's departure for France, was often pierced by a sharp yearning for distant parts, accepted the invitations.

In this poor man's chariot, once coveted, now the butt of cheap cracks, known all over the West as "stinkpot," in this mobile emblem of scarcity, last year's model, in one of the thousands of products now declared scrap, with its two-stroke engine, the incomparable cardboard car, previously available only after many years on a waiting list, they drove, with Hoftaller behind the wheel and Fonty in the passenger seat, from Berlin-Mitte out past the city limits—toward Oranienburg, for instance, whose palace, hated by princesses of all kinds, had been wrecked by the border patrol billeted there during the Wall years. Or they headed for Cottbus, albeit without continuing their stroll around town into the nearby Spree Forest. And they also struck out for Neubrandenburg, where they paced off the remains of the old city wall, fantasizing about what it would be like to live in one old tower or another, remodeled into snug living quarters. Having served long enough to qualify as retirees, Fonty and Hoftaller thoroughly enjoyed asserting their right to government housing in their old age; yet the farthest thing from their minds was sitting around dozing.

Place after place brought memories to the surface. They tested each other, with word-perfect quotations, on Cultural Union lectures—for example, the innocuous one delivered in Cottbus on the local painter Karl Blechen—and also on the ticklish passages in the lecture Fonty gave in Neubrandenburg and again in Rathenow under the title "What Does Katte Mean to Us Today?" Its defiant topic—crown prince versus king, attempted escape, execution—clashed with the Workers' and Peasants' State's need for security. Both of them laughed at the fear-driven cuts in the manuscript that one of them mandated and the other, ad-libbing, flouted. However long the drive home, they remained in good spirits and planned further outings.

This particular trip did not take them far. In drizzle they set out for Potsdam, but not into Potsdam itself. They were headed neither for the palace nor for the Archives; they knew both well enough. No, there was nothing on the agenda in the service of immortality, not even Fredericus Rex's; they stopped short of Prussia's most famous garrison town.

We are not sure who suggested that they visit this momentous junction on the former border, the Glienicke Bridge. It was probably Fonty, who wanted to do something nice for Hoftaller, knowing as he did that his day-and-night-shadow had an interest in this destination quite separate from its architectural history—first wood, then brick, and finally iron—an interest of a sentimental kind. It was as the site where top agents were exchanged that the place attracted him. Filled with admiration, but also envy, Hoftaller gazed at the Glienicke Bridge, where, up to just a short time before the fall of the Wall, eighteen-karat spies, agents with years of deep-cover service behind them, sometimes even noted experts in the field of espionage, had been shunted from East to West, from West to East.

He parked the Trabi not far from where the bridge crosses the narrows between the two Havel lakes, on what might still be considered Western territory, to one side of the driveway leading up to Glienicke Palace. What Fonty merely hinted at was later confirmed for us by Hoftaller during a visit to the Archives: this bridge had cut him, Hoftaller, down to third-class status. For people of his ilk, this secret-agent sluiceway had been attainable only in dreams. "Glienicke!" he exclaimed. "That was only for the elite. Only top people were exchanged there. People like us, the so-called mid-tier, were out of the picture. We were fine for the dirty work: field operations, surveillance, care and feeding of informants, routine reporting, paperwork, now and then a little secret mission. Don't want to complain—it had to be done. But the bridge was always there—a fantasy, a dream destination, ultimate fulfillment. That really meant something. Theatrical—granted. But each of us secretly cherished this longing: Someday, maybe it'll be me...."

If we seem to be suggesting that Hoftaller waxed rhapsodic about the bridge, we are not exaggerating. And it is understandable that Fonty would want to do something nice for his suffering day-and-night-shadow. That is why we assume it was he who suggested they visit this noteworthy site. This time he had already planned the first move: no sooner had they stepped out of the Trabi than he invited Hoftaller to play agent-exchange with him on the bridge.

"You have to experience it in person."

"Out of the question! I don't have the right stuff!"

"Cut out the inferiority rubbish! You're not a nobody! After all, it was a Tallhover who had Herwegh under surveillance. Lenin's sealed train was your case, later even Lenin's brain...."

"Still, I'm a few sizes too small...."

"Stuff and nonsense! And what was I in '70–'71? Yet they took me off the island of Oléron and exchanged me for top people, as you call them: three high-ranking French officers, and me just a scribbler...."

"...who was assumed to be a top agent. They almost executed you for espionage. No, I don't measure up. A person would have to have Huguenot ancestors and a name like ... Guillaume, let's say...."

"Don't be a spoilsport, Tallhover. It's no accident you found a biographer so early on. If anyone displayed vision, it was you. There's a reason why you matured into the symbol of the immortality assigned to me. So chin up! Today it's your turn."

"So what do you want me to do, Comrade Commissar?"

Fonty set the ground rules. Hoftaller nodded: Got it. And then they played it out on the bridge, that junction of actual and invented spy stories and secret-agent thrillers, plots that had been filmed, documented, and repeatedly packaged as novels. We all recall scenes at the crack of dawn, in early-morning mist. The cold glare of arc lights. Suspense and shivers in a fine drizzle, at just the right camera angle. Two men in hats, their collars turned up, approaching each other one step at a time, only one of them coming in from the cold, although the other was freezing, too. East-West agent exchange. On film as in real life. And the world was watching.

They played out the familiar old ritual in the appropriate weather, beneath the handsome, swooping arches of the bridge. At first the day-and-night-shadow, now promoted to superspy, wanted to open his trademark umbrella, but Fonty objected: "That really doesn't fit." So they exposed themselves to the drizzle on this windless day.

Only the sidewalks had been ceded to them. They paid no heed to the traffic flowing, then slowing, in both directions. Hoftaller, who on Fonty's instructions had scurried across to the Potsdam side, in the East, advanced step by step toward Glienicke on the almost deserted sidewalk, keeping to the right. At a hand gesture from the far-off exchangee, Fonty had set himself in motion from West to East. Not in a rush, not too slow. At the midpoint of the bridge, above the spot where the two Havel lakes narrowed to a thin channel, they crossed each other's paths without a glance, each headed for the command center from which his orders emanated.

That called for an encore. Back and forth under arches that swooped gently from pier to pier. Initially on Fonty's orders, now at Hoftaller's behest. Under the bridge, single and double paddleboats passed by, then a motor launch; that was of no concern. Sometimes Fonty was the Eastern subject being exchanged for the

Western pawn, then the day-and-night-shadow would approach again, step by step, from the East, while Fonty left the West behind, until the two of them came abreast, frozen for a split second in a photo opportunity, unseeing, unspeaking, only to advance again, step by step, ever closer to one system or the other—world powers, mortal enemies, guarantors of deterrence: the enemy of the working class and the Red Peril—each entrusting himself to the hands of his own camp.

A game with few variations. Fonty for Hoftaller. Hoftaller for Fonty. Each validated the other. One could not exist without the other. They were playing for the same stakes, and for both the Glienicke Bridge seemed to stretch on forever like a nightmare. It looked monotonous. When the suspense began to let up, as during a compulsory exercise that dragged on and on, new variations would occur to them. Fonty, coming in from the cold, winked his right eye when they came abreast of one another, and Hoftaller, being handed over by the enemy of the proletariat, winked his left. Finally both subjects even spoke a few words during the exchange: "Be good!" said one. "Be better!" the other.

That may seem odd. In keeping with the systems to which they belonged, they might have sworn at one another, in more of a hiss than a yell: "Capitalist lackey!" "Red swine!" But no, they wished each other greater success for the next time. Two professionals, with the ethos to match, two realists unbeholden to any ideology, two specialists of equal rank, whose experience, subject to no statute of limitations, imbued them with confidence in their own immortality, even though Hoftaller, when the two of them were back in the Trabi, again insisted on his relative uselessness: "Compared to the top agents, I'm merely run-of-the-mill...."

"Come now, Tallhover. You were always colossally well informed, knew ahead of time...."

"But you had the real power—books, a whole army of words lined up behind you...."

"...words that chafed against the censorship—which is under your care—and were sometimes ground to bits by it. Without censorship..."

"Maybe it's true, Fonty, that we complement each other somehow. But we're equal only in the files."

Then he offered his thanks. Even more: he felt indebted. He almost hugged Fonty, but confined himself to squeezing his hand, stammering, "You have no idea how depressed I...was feeling superfluous...a pathetic figure...Did me a world of good, that silly game...Now I know what I used to know, had forgotten....I mean, how smoothly it goes, changing systems....You stay who you are... on either side of the bridge....Thank you, Fonty."

He let go of his hand, now smiling his familiar old smile. So good was his mood that Hoftaller would have liked to drive across the Glienicke Bridge into Potsdam and then to Dortustrasse, but Fonty felt he had done enough. He refused so gruffly to visit the Archives that Hoftaller capitulated, though with a remark at our expense: "No problem! Wouldn't do much good anyway. All they have is cabinets stuffed with boredom. Nothing new there. Even the topic 'Theodor Storm's Potsdam Ordeal' has been covered. Anyone who wants the real scoop has to come to us. As I said, without us, nothing gets done...."

The return trip through West Berlin was long—they got stuck in the afternoon rush hour. Again and again the jam brought them to a complete halt. They felt small in their cardboard suitcase, crammed in between mighty chariots of Western manufacture. It was the period when Trabi jokes were fashionable; the punch lines seemed to have been adapted from the once-fashionable jokes about East Frisians. Yet the driver and his passenger took comfort in the leveling effect of the traffic jam: whether Mercedes or Trabi, they could only creep forward. Fonty commented, "Colossal schemozzle! So much for the wonders of capitalism."

Since Madeleine's departure, he again found time for long, chatty letters filled with exhaustive accounts of daily events, and for mornings at the snack bar on Potsdamer Strasse, diagonally across from Number 134C. He kept an inkwell there.

Professor Freundlich, from whom he had concealed the existence of the granddaughter who had recently blown into his life, benefited from this letter-writing mood: he received a scintillating report on the "cinematic agent exchange" on the Glienicke Bridge, which Fonty dubbed "the Mecca of all secret agents ripe for retirement." And Martha Grundmann, née Wuttke, also received mail again. She read the following, which was turned over to us much later for analysis:

"...Enough about the weather, which for a long time was well disposed but then turned rainy; Mecklenburg's skies must have been equally patriotic on the night of 3 October. At all events, we survived the unification brouhaha—spotty bell-ringing and all—bravely, and thanks to the energy newly breathed into the family. Mama must have informed you from her own point of view, which I confess often baffles me, that Mademoiselle Aubron succeeded in winning our hearts in a *coup de main*; and perhaps my dear Mete has experienced much the same; for as I learned from an otherwise rather dry letter from Friedel, that at once the delicate and resolute young woman presented herself in Schwerin, Wuppertal, and even Bonn–Bad Godesberg before making her way back to Paris.

"I cannot help laughing when I think of my fine sons, especially Teddy, and picture him getting thrown off his high horse when confronted with this person, whom I like to describe as bittersweet. As for as my transgression, which has now attained a ripe old age, I shall have to leave final judgment on that to the family. But I am certain that my Mete will not put me on the rack; perhaps your newfound Catholicism will help you see your old father in a kinder light. 'We're all human,' as General von Bamme in *Before the Storm* puts it.

"Mama's good-heartedness in this matter came as a surprise. I feared a ticklish situation at home. She did seem flabbergasted at first, but then her curiosity got the better of her: she was determined to go rowing, with all three of us in the boat. As for this familial boat ride, which has surely been portrayed for you in detail, down to Madeleine's act of heroism, I have only this to add: it inspired me to compose the enclosed quatrain, for the rowing stirred up memories, anguished ones and animating ones, the kind that depreciate with time, and others that proved to have substantial book value. On balance, the animating ones put our account in the black.

414

"And just imagine: positively rejuvenated by the French injection, Mama and I celebrated our forty-fifth anniversary on the sixteenth, at Offenbach's, of course, since back when we tied the knot we celebrated rather wretchedly, with boiled potatoes and jugged hare (the main ingredient courtesy of the rabbit-breeder Max Wuttke). But this time we had Knight Bluebeard, at Mama's tactful request, which, translated from the Offenbachese, means filet of beef on a bed of vegetables, followed by crepes with stewed cherries. After this sumptuous meal—and made talkative by the wine— Mama confessed to me what I now impart to you in postal privacy: During the war, she, too, grew weary of waiting. Her engagement, as she said, had consisted primarily of waiting around. To make a long story short, she alluded to a first lieutenant on desk duty at the Aviation Ministry. Yes, yes, all those air raids. In the air-raid shelter they had grown more and more intimate.

"At any rate, we are now even when the transgressions are tallied, although Mama's wartime delusions and confusions bore no consequences, as she tipsily swore to me. Nonetheless I am left with a nagging feeling, an unremitting suspicion (as my punishment?) about our poor Georg, who, I was sure, until this anniversary at Offenbach's, gave proof of my strength of loins, as far back as my furlough in October '43. But let's leave that be. What is ever devoid of doubt?

"At the moment we are in the process of giving the seductively labyrinthine former Reich Aviation building, which, along with us, has become, as they say, history, a new, pregnant significance: in a few months the Handover Trust will move into its new quarters there. The advance guard is already in residence. And your old father belongs to it in an advisory capacity, handsomely remunerated. At the moment he is attempting, by means of an eloquent report, to protect the indestructible paternoster from modernization, which would mean brutal removal. Here the expression 'wind down' is in style; but so long as it is not my turn, the expression is good for laughs, and indeed we have an ample supply of those.

"Otherwise I am enjoying the better half of my half-day position. We, that is to say my trusty old companion (who understandably sticks in my Mete's craw), and your humble servant, have been going for drives in his factory-new Trabant. To Cottbus and Neubrandenburg; in the latter, during the era of ever-victorious socialism, I spoke on the painter Blechen, whom I admire; in the former, I got into some difficulty with my lecture on Katte and a few unauthorized digressions à la Marwitz. And recently we headed out to the Glienicke Bridge, a place conducive to flashbacks. My companion did not weary of reciting the names of top agents whose value was increased by exchange. In the end he felt so wretchedly mediocre that I had to help him back on his feet. If it hadn't been raining so gloomily, we would have done better to cross over to the Potsdam side. If you turn off to the right there, just past the bridge, you have a wonderful view far over the water to Peacock Island.

"But now to your Grundmann: you write that he is 'very forbearing' toward you, which on the one hand gives evidence of a good heart, but also signals to me that you are apparently supplying him with plentiful opportunities for having to show forbearance. I can understand that the waterfront villa is too big for you, but it must be better than the garret on Potsdamer Strasse, where my Mete had only a tiny hole in the wall. The trick is to be content with much.

"But to come back to my employer, the Handover Trust: its branch in Schwerin will certainly offer your Grundmann prime cuts of property; I just hope he doesn't heap too much on his plate...."

Hoftaller and Fonty had become loathe to subject the dowdy Trabi to the dense traffic of West Berlin. They had no desire to hear taunts, or even to suspect them. Excursions to Spandau—a tour of the citadel—or to Tegel's little Humboldt palace were stricken from the list. But they ventured from the eastern part of the city out to Frankfurt an der Oder, by way of the autobahn. They wanted on the one hand to gaze across the river to Poland, and on the other hand to search for traces of the first of the Immortal's novels at the chief scene of the crime.

During the drive, Fonty was already expatiating on the subject. And at the wheel, Hoftaller acted as if he were dying to hear what could have motivated a man of almost sixty—just liberated from the secretarial duties and intrigues at the Prussian Academy—to become a freelance writer, casting his family into financial uncertainty and—looking back to the period in France—committing to paper a mighty tome which, like the Oder Delta, branched off in far too many directions.

"While I was writing *Before the Storm*, other things were already gestating in the old noggin. The inner decline of Prussia, shortly before Napoleon came calling: *Schach von Wuthenow*, a novella. While in that expansive first novel the Prussian defeat has already occurred, the Corsican has likewise met his match in Russia. All signals are set for storm. Liberation from the foreign yoke! Reforms, cheaper by the dozen. And yet: it should have resulted in a constitutional monarchy. Stein, Hardenberg, Gneisenau, and Scharnhorst! 'From the General Levy to the People's Army' was the title of one of my lectures, delivered in Jüterbog. But your people, the ones who would later be called 'the leading comrades,' were against it. From the beginning, even before the storm. Those fawning courtiers! The people had barely liberated itself, and the vacillating king, too, when the Carlsbad Decrees were drafted, allowing your confrères to establish a state surveillance system, extending from the persecution of the demagogues to the most recent spy network, expanding it, tightening it, perfecting it. And it's no different today. Just yesterday the word was: We, only we, are the people! But now the wind has died down again. There's no end in sight. 'The new police state...' I wrote about that also, though under a pseudonym, in the *Dresdner Zeitung*, in '49. You're not saying anything, Tallhover, but your silence speaks volumes...."

Fonty liked such time-lapse foreshortenings. They parked the Trabi in the historic center of town and found a spot on the promenade along the border-marking river. From here they had an excellent view, one that lent itself to far-ranging observations. Fonty continued, "It's regrettable, but the fact is: here Germany has to stop, unified or not. True, I've always had a subliminal affinity for the Sorbians, but it's a pity, nonetheless, because now some of the novels have lost their hinterland. *Quitt* is set for the most part in

Silesia. For my Effi's Kessin there is no longer a Swinemünde. And after the botched attack on the Oder bridge at Frankfurt, young Count Vitzewitz was imprisoned in the fortress of Küstrin. That's where they shortened Katte by a head.... All gone, or known by Polish names now... Not to mention West Prussia, where Mathilde Möhring's layabout student eventually succeeded in becoming mayor. Nothing left. And as you see, not even the hint of a reflection of the old wooden bridge..."

At this, too, Hoftaller remained silent, or stood next to Fonty as if under orders to remain silent. While one of them pointed his long index finger to the north and Küstrin, and beyond that to Swinemünde, then to the southeast toward Silesia and the Riesengebirge, then due east to the lost Vistula region, the other stood with arms crossed: a grim Napoleon, still struck dumb by the retreat from Russia's far-flung expanse.

To their right, the railroad bridge linked both sides of the border-marking river. To the left, the postwar bridge now allowed the free flow of cars and pedestrians. As he sketched out strategic positions with the gestures of a Clausewitz, Fonty initially had in mind the battlefield of Kunersdorf, close to the east bank of the Oder—"Frederick's debacle"—then the precarious situation of the *Grande Armée* after the burning of Moscow and the defeat at the Berezina River—"Over there the pathetic remnants of French power were penned in, under siege by Cossacks"—and finally the battlefront in March '45, when the Red Army assembled on the eastern bank, ready to pounce and in plain view. "He who takes Frankfurt on the Oder has Berlin!" he cried, then, confirming once more the finality of the border with Poland: "It's a fact! No one will tamper with that again!"

Only now, after all the battles had been fought, did Hoftaller relax his crossed arms and say, more in passing than in a spirit of contradiction, "Oh, come on, Wuttke. No border holds forever. Day before yesterday everything was sealed up tight: Wall, Bastion of Peace, Iron Curtain, mines, barbed wire, death strip... and today? Everything's in flux. Nothing's certain anymore. Now we don't need a visa or a passport to cross—peacefully, of course. You just watch: even the services will become pan-European. Have to view it flexibly, the whole situation. Borders just get in the way."

Then he, too, pointed to the East, though with a stubby finger: "Still, it has to remain within limits. We have to shield these far-flung areas, I mean secure them, before the hordes descend. I'd call Poland a sort of boundary territory, or rather an outpost, because what's coming at us from out there, Wuttke, poses a real challenge. The East extends far, very far!"

Fonty agreed to some extent—"There's always something confining about the notion of the nation"—but he had just begun to warm to the idea of completely open, border-free conditions when the old reservations surfaced again: "In Deetz in 1806, a Frenchman was struck dead, the way a post is pounded into the ground, or with even less justification. And now it's Poles and Vietnamese who are being beaten to death on a whim. I know my Deetzers; in Germany nothing ever changes. . . ."

These words and more were heard by the Oder River, which was in no hurry, after a dry summer had left its water level low. With a flat toss, Hoftaller tried to make a few smooth stones from the riverbank skip across the water. When invited to try, too, Fonty proved himself more skillful. Later he admitted to us: "Was happy as a child when I managed to make my stone skip three times."

We were not surprised that they avoided the nearby Kleist Museum. After all, the Immortal had considered his fellow Prussian too eccentric, although he could respect Kleist's enduring greatness and was much impressed by that "colossal ode to hatred, *Arminius' Battle.*" Fonty remarked, "Birthplaces, whether Neuruppin or this miserable hole, as a rule have something behind-the-times about them." And Hoftaller commented, as they passed the museum, "That man Kleist would have been a case for us. But he was hard to keep under observation—too restless and erratic. . . ."

Instead they visited the city archives. There they stood for a long time in front of a primitive painting that showed the wooden bridge on fire during the French conflict, with the flames reflected in the river. At the sight of the conflagration, Fonty could not resist bringing up fires in a number of the novels and ballads, at the same time reminding Hoftaller of a lecture on this same topic that he had given during the sixties in Frankfurt on the Oder. "Was shortly before the Eleventh Party Congress…" As he warmed to the subject, he went from Tangermünde in flames to the castle fire in *Irretrievable,* not neglecting to mention the conflagration that devastated Neuruppin and the barn fire in *Childhood,* went on to speak of the futile effort to extinguish the great fire on Herr von Vitzewitz's estate, and finally produced the burning bridge in *Before the Storm* in a lengthy quotation: "…a shout of general astonishment went up. Across the river, the lumberyard and the planking shed were going up in flames, while off to the right the bridge was burning. The fire across the way rose high into the night sky, but above the bridge, which, because its wood was wet, was smoldering rather than burning, hovered dense clouds of smoke and haze, from which only now and then a dark glow flared up.…"

Fonty looked somewhat troubled as he stood before the painting. "The way it is painted here is not the way it was. Reality is always more banal. The whole business with the general levy failed miserably. The French held their ground. In barely a quarter of an hour, the *voltigeurs* had the pontoon bridge finished. *En avant!* Besides, the bugler from Protzhagen, as is written, blew, 'out of the fear in his heart, not the signal for attack but for retreat.' Soon there was no holding the position."

Given the trickle of border-crossers, they had only to show their identity cards. It may well be that Fonty captured the visit to the Glienicke Bridge and the final walk across the Oder bridge to the Polish side in a rhymed quatrain; rhymes came easily to him. As previously in the rowboat, he had come up with four lines on unification day. Yet it was not that historic event that moved him to poetry, but rather the two chestnuts in his coat pocket that he gave his granddaughter as a going-away present. In a letter to Madeleine Aubron that recounted at length the visits to the two bridges, with quotations aimed at Potsdam and Frankfurt, there were no bridge poems enclosed, but later he dedicated an autumnal quatrain to the bittersweet person:

For you, my child, these two hand-strokers here.
Chestnut brown tinctures this time of year.
Damp and floury from their husk expelled,
As pig feed and otherwise they've always excelled.

And because in his epistolary mood he always happened upon one or more "by the ways," Fonty was emboldened to ask Madeleine to give one of the chestnuts—"even if it has shriveled meanwhile"—to her mother in Montpellier, his still sulking daughter Cécile: "...in hopes of a forgiving smile."

25

On the Edge of the Abyss

Why all the detours? Why only second-rate towns? What reason was there for avoiding the actual spot, which was in fact close by?

Our guess was correct: Fonty would have liked to pressure Hoftaller to include a half-day journey to Neuruppin in his plans: straight to the statue of the Immortal. As they were driving back from Kleist's birthplace, the border town on the Oder, he suggested, just past the Müllrose exit, that their next excursion take them to the lake-dotted Ruppin area and that town listed on Theo Wuttke's identification card as his place of birth: "That would be something. The two of us posed in front of the seated bronze."

Hoftaller put him off—"Maybe later, no, definitely"—and justified the postponement by invoking the four- to seven-story structure at the corner of Leipziger Strasse and Otto-Grotewohl-Strasse: The renovations there were making good progress. It was important to be seen and to show interest. The watchword was being there, to make sure nothing went wrong: "They're capable of tearing out the paternoster while your back is turned."

And sure enough: there were proposals, even cost estimates, from West German companies for removing that allegedly accident-prone open-cabin form of transportation and replacing it with high-speed elevators, in the name of what was called "urgently required modernization." The feasibility studies offered statistical evidence that a large number of employees made adequate personnel-moving capability essential. The assertion was made, moreover, that "the homey quality inherent to the paternoster will negatively impact the institutional work ethic and result in dawdling and sliding into the old rut; an efficiency deficit can be projected."

But Fonty, who had scented danger even before Hoftaller, was already hard at work. In his report he stressed that the paternoster had survived a number of system changes and thus merited preservation as a historic artifact. He emphasized the usefulness of the reflective moments afforded by a slower means of transportation, terming it a "mobile moratorium." He praised the collegial dialogue fostered by the two-person cabins. He dismissed the absurdly small number of paternoster accidents with the adage, "Better to reach your destination with deliberate speed than to be whisked into the Beyond." He rang the changes on the name of the old-fashioned lift, asking himself and all users, "In times like these, who wants or is able to manage without a daily Our Father?" Although he suppressed references to leading party members of this or that ideological persuasion who, in the past and until just recently, had experienced their own rise and fall so vividly, he did invoke the "time-saturated aroma" of the wood-paneled cabins, calling it "worthy of preservation" for its accumulated richness; in point of fact, the ascending and descending compartments smelled musty to rancid from furniture wax.

Fonty formulated a strongly worded petition, and Hoftaller made sure it got into circulation. The signatures of individuals and groups helped give the paper added heft. Even the head of the agency that was now gobbling up room on every floor came out in favor of the paternoster, and released a publicity photo that confirmed him as a user of the cabin-lift. A dignified figure, whose rapid rise testified to his success, he was shown at full height, standing robustly next to a petite secretary. With such support, this conveyance in prayer-wheel form was saved from the barbarians' clutches, at least for the time being.

From all sides Fonty received the credit. In the corridors, in the lift itself, even in the lavatories, people were saying, "You really nailed that, Fonty."—"Stick with it!"—"After all, our paternoster's part of who we are."—"Right, we're not going to let them take that away."—"Nice going, Fonty!"—"Keep up the good work, Fonty!"—"How about a little kiss for taking the initiative?"

All this went on amid the din of construction. The success of the rescue operation carried over into the beginning of November. In a conversation conducted between the ground floor and the top floor, Hoftaller expressed confidence that the successful petition had solidified his own position as well. He was now assigned to the not unimportant personnel division, albeit in a mid-level position. He owed it all to Fonty; the last line of Fonty's report had struck just the right note: "May the paternoster henceforth remain at our service under the auspices of the Handover Trust!" That was the kind of thing they liked to hear. That sort of trust, that sort of trusting bid for protection was in demand. The boss wanted only the best—this was emphasized repeatedly. "Man, Wuttke, you read that just right."

During the weeks immediately preceding, we had observed that Fonty's day-and-night-shadow was looking increasingly ashen, but now he regained his bounce. On an ordinary workday he remarked, "We can risk a little outing again. Here we're just in the way of the workmen. Could be weeks, even months before the first rooms are ready for occupancy and the move from Alexanderplatz gets underway. There'll be added personnel, of course. More than three thousand positions have been authorized. Did six interviews today. The main qualification is field expertise. There's a shortage of people who know this quagmire inside out. Have a few on hand already. No doubt about it: this is going to be huge."

As they were leaving, he exclaimed, at a suitable distance from the colossal portal: "*Semper paratus!*" Then Hoftaller lowered his voice: "That's how it is, my dear Wuttke. Our battle slogan from the old days is still valid, even if the major tasks take an entirely different form these days. Frozen public property will have to become fungible private property. It'll happen! It'll happen! But not without us, Fonty! We'll have a hand in whatever is done."

They drove out to Lusatia. They left Kollwitzplatz in the morning. When they filled up the tank, Fonty paid half; he was quite flush of late. Emmi, invited as a courtesy, declined: "In a Trabi—never again!" They left without us, too, yet theoretically we were along for the ride.

In the Trabant, into sandy Lusatia. It was the second week in November when this outing took place. Emmi had lent additional emphasis to her refusal: "And absolutely not to that lousy place!" Since the back seat remained empty, our theoretical complicity in this trip was limited to hearsay; the most we could do was entertain a few visions wrested from the poor visibility.

After Hoftaller had rejected as premature an excursion to Neuruppin, located on the lake of the same name, postponing it to the spring, he wanted to make his "dear Wuttke" happy with a trip to the Wendish region known as Lusatia. They drove on 9 November, taking the autobahn toward Dresden as far as the Ruhland exit. We are familiar with this region, once an almost infinite resource to the Workers' and Peasants' State, and are even halfway versed in Wendish-Sorbian literature.

They turned off the Reich autobahn, path-breaking in the Führer's day, but since deteriorated into a patchwork of concrete slabs, and continued in the direction of Senftenberg until they reached that part of Lower Lusatia that will long bear the scars of large-scale open-pit lignite mining. During our student years, now long past, we became acquainted with this region in the form of an often-repeated warning: "If you don't toe the ideological line, you'll be sent to the production line. Then you can learn from the working class what it really means to sweat." And in the mid-sixties, when a colder wind began to blow again, I in fact had a chance to learn all about sweat during a year in the soft-coal mines.

They drove over back roads almost to the edge of the excavations. Everywhere they saw the earth's crust hacked open, and along the rim of the pits the remnants of abandoned villages, whose few remaining houses were slated for demolition. On this ninth of November, under a lowering sky, one could see all the way to the horizon.

They gazed out over a landscape that spread before them in descending terraces, saw conical slag heaps, bleached chains of hills encircling groundwater lakes, and sharp cones marbled with coal residue. They saw flat surfaces at the very bottom and the Lusatian hills submerged in the depths, but otherwise nothing— not a tree, not a bush, not a bird in the sky. Yet on the edges of the pits and in front of coal-bearing cliffs crouched huge power shovels made of some rust-prone material. Their sound would have been evidence of work and human activity.

We could have supplied the numbers to help complete the picture: cubic meters of slag removed, quantities produced, quotas fulfilled and exceeded, much-decorated brigades, collectives that had worked special shifts for peace, for progress, for the cause. We could have, but it would not have pleased Fonty.

On the autobahn he had already begun harumphing. When he caught sight in the distance of the chimneys and cooling towers of the Black Pump Combine, familiar to him from Cultural Union lectures in Hoyerswerda, he began to throw up barriers with cascades of words. He demanded that they halt, stop, turn back. "Don't want to go. Hate this area, always did. Like Emilie, I say: This is not for me. Letschin, the Oder Delta, even little Friesack, anything around the Ruppin lakes, gladly; Rheinsberg I could see again and again, or Mittenwald, for that matter, where the poet Paul Gerhardt was a provost, and if we must go into Sorbian-Wendish territory, then by all means to Lübbenau, into the Spree Forest, and on by boat into that delightful, bewitched region, blessed with cucumbers and wet nurses—but not here. Don't want to see it, not again, never want to go to Spremberg and on to Bitterfeld and into Saxony. No! The Cultural Union and the many fine memories be damned, I don't want to go there! I'll admit: the audience was excellent, the halls filled, the discussions interesting, not even ideologically rigid. For instance, about female characters like Melanie van der Straaten, Ebba von Rosenberg, and Mathilde Möhring, also Corinna Schmidt and the widow Pittelkow, all of whom have something emancipated about them. Was well received, my lecture. Lively debate afterward. Quoted from Bebel's *Women and Socialism,* and of course also something by Clara Zetkin. They liked it, even the leading comrades. So not a word against the Cultural Union in Hoyerswerda, but everything against this region here. Turned inside out and bled dry. Heaps of ugliness. Nothing the eye would care to rest on. Just abyss and moonscape. Would have been something for Zola: *Germinal* with open pits; but to me, the world of work, although essential for our existence, was always a horror. What's the point, Hoftaller? Do you want to count up for me the villages that have been swallowed up here, churches and all, kill me with production figures and overfulfilled quotas? Am I supposed to pray, Lord forgive them, for they know exactly what they do? Or what precisely is the point of my being here? There has to be some purpose behind it. A Tallhover doesn't just set out at random, and a Hoftaller even less, if I know him. . . ."

There was no objection that could halt the Trabi or lure it to some area that was charming or inviting, despite the November gloom. We would not have been drawn to the soft coal, either; the Archives were on Fonty's side. But who cared about that?

Hoftaller's grip tightened on the steering wheel, and he clung fast to his plan. We can safely assume that he was fixated on this anniversary of anniversaries, on this tragic, baleful, bloody date, as evil as it is accursed, this date to which one year earlier the calendar-maker responsible for Germany had tacked yet another meaning, this one betokening freedom. The abundance of historical events seemed to energize the driver. On pitted back roads, which seemed made for the sand-yellow Trabant, he kept finding, in the midst of this wasteland, ways to the rim of the excavations, some of which had been scraped clean, others of which had been used as unauthorized garbage dumps.

They got out of the car. He forced Fonty to get out and stare with him into the abyss, as into a calamity revealed. He led him over to the black tangle of discarded conveyor belts lying to one side of a pit entrance. Later, in a letter to Martha Grundmann, Fonty would describe this as "vomited dragon's guts." And even Hoftaller thought he was seeing more than simply fatigued industrial material: with his stubby index finger he pointed into the distance, indicating one power shovel and slag-mover after another, perched on the edge of the pit like giant insects or kneeling on the crater's floor. Although seemingly lifeless, they were at work, battering away, stripping, supplying intact conveyor belts, insatiable; and the wind that blew fine grit everywhere also carried their sounds, evidence of their activity.

What a sight! From Pritzen, whose last houses stood, picked clean, on the edge of the pit, awaiting demolition, the two of them could look out over the hole and the heaps of slag, stripped from its deepest layer, as far as Altdöbern, a little town with a church and a castle. "That's where we're headed," Hoftaller exclaimed, "right away, and from there we'll look back at Pritzen...."

Some of us recall that meditative spot. Everything there seemed to have come to a standstill, fallen asleep. That was before the lowering of the water table. On the castle grounds, the ancient trees, which included a number of exotic varieties, seemed eternal; only the seasons brought change. Enough work for all: sawmills, a distillery. Altdöbern lay surrounded by fields and forests.

Now there was no more wood-processing. The distillery's smokestack was blocked by an empty stork's nest. They parked the Trabi at the drive leading up to the castle, whose façade was crumbling behind forgotten scaffolding. Fonty wrote to Martha: "At some point, an heir from Prussia's dispersed aristocracy will turn up, and even here, where nothing is left for the taking, pound with brazen knuckles on the door...."

Only a few steps away from the church square and the cemetery, still tended, where three dozen Red Army soldiers killed at war's end were buried, directly behind the women's hospital and its wintry garden, where cabbages lay in rows, after a few more steps sideways from the last of the trees that had once lined the avenue, the earth's crust broke off. Their eyes leaped down giant stairs to the pit bottom, saw the gleaming black surfaces of groundwater lakes, here spilling out in all directions, there puddle-sized, onto which the clustered slag heaps cast their reflection. They could have counted receding tiers of mountain chains, but none of the conical peaks of the nearby hills rose higher than the edge of the pit that Hoftaller and Fonty were occupying, at the very end of the narrow but paved road that at one time had passed between fields of rye and turnips for a distance of four kilometers, linking the town of Altdöbern with a village called Pritzen.

They might just as well have stood on the edge of some other pit. There was abyss aplenty. We see them here, here, and there, a couple in multiple copies, cheek by jowl and staggered behind each other, in coats and under hats, different in build, a hundred and more day-and-night-shadows and their subjects, crowded and shoved perilously close to the edge; yet they stood there in such numbers only theoretically, and in reality alone. Over the whole scene hovered an oppressive sky, whose clouds seemed saturated, for in the distance, where they hung like sacks, a curtain of rain was falling; otherwise nothing was happening.

"Look over there, Wuttke! The few houses left. That's Pritzen, as I promised. From this vantage point you get a sense of what it means: open-pit mining, brown coal, real sweat. Incredible luck you had in '54, after the Cultural Union congress, that they didn't send you to the mines when you had to go and open your big mouth, specifically in regard to the events of June '53, all jumbled up with reactionary slogans from the Revolution of '48—'To put the democrats to rout, you have to call the army out!' And other provocations that could have earned you at least a year in the lignite mines. Yes, take a good look, Wuttke! If you look hard, you'll see not only black gold, but also a whole lot of future. You look into that hole and you get a sense how things will be, I mean, what's coming. That's all that's left of us—that's it. Relieved of our productive capacity, wasting away, totally exploited: we'll be human slag heaps, bigger cones and smaller ones that've been granted permission to see their reflection a bit—look, Wuttke, in the groundwater, way down there, not stirred by the slightest breeze, even when the wind is howling up here. And the same all the way to the horizon: in neat piles, orderly rows. Sorted residue, the dustheaps of history. Ah, Wuttke, what have they done to us? What have we let them do to us? Miserable relics. We're just leftovers, good only for scrap. They call us the 'residual burden.' Come on, Fonty! Take a good look! It's not every day you can see things so clearly. Who said anything about pessimism? It's your dictum, isn't it: To hope for little is always good...."

Hoftaller was standing right up against the fractured edge of the earth's crust. He pointed into the pit, with his thick index finger at the end of his short arm, as if he wanted to touch one slag heap or another. This was a new tone for him: remorse, self-scrutiny, conjuring up the apocalypse, let worldly things all go, simultaneous declarations of guilt and innocence. He stood there, legs spread, on what remained of the road to Pritzen, in his hat and flapping coat, while Fonty, too, stood there in his hat and flying coat.

And again we see them in multiples, crowded and clumped together as a group. Miraculously multiplied, their coats obey the stiff, intermittently gusty wind. You might think it would carry them off any minute now, with sails billowing over the abyss, the groundwater lakes, the slag cones, off to the horizon and beyond. But when we next saw them again as a single pair, something in their position on the brink had changed.

Fonty was standing with his back turned. He did not want to look into the abyss, did not want to stare into the pit and see more than was to be seen. This was nothing for Fonty. Even he could not breathe life into these remains of a landscape. No, he would not have wanted to banish poor Effi to this heaped-up wasteland. Not even wan Stine, in her abandoned state, could be pictured in this setting. No place for the chronically ailing Cécile. He would never have allowed Lene Nimptsch to undertake a rowboat ride with an infatuated lieutenant on this black groundwater lake. Frau Jenny Treibel would have been at a loss for poetic gilding in the face of this panoramic refuse heap. And even Mathilde Möhring's practical appreciation for the rewards of hard work was something he would not have wanted to test on such a lifeless production site. To Martha, his Mete, he wrote, "I'm no Zola! Never subscribed to *misère*! Could not bear to stare at so much soulless ugliness a minute longer. Abandoned not only by God—that would have been acceptable—but also by anything resembling beauty—I felt the void's pestilent breath on me...."

But the pits near Altdöbern did have some life in them, though not visibly. Suddenly a human voice rang out, amplified over loudspeakers. In Saxon tones it proclaimed that—wherever they might be—conveyor belts "two, five, eight" were in operation. The announcement was repeated. And now from far away, yet carrying across the distance, one could hear the crunching, screeching, and groaning of the conveyor belts on rollers. Again, this time piercingly defiant, the voice insisted on repeating itself, as if determined to prevail against the spirit of the times, which throughout the land was in a shutdown frame of mind, as if determined to say: We'll go on mining! We won't be wound down! You can't break us!

For the pit, although no longer in the people's possession, continued to yield brown coal in daily shifts. Where the maps had once shown Pritzen, lignite was still being scraped out fifty meters below the surface—despite the meager yield, only 9 percent—by functional reproductions of primeval monsters, steel dinosaurs spewing onto conveyor belts this end-product of organic decomposition. Hoftaller spoke of the fierce competition that had characterized production in the past, of extra shifts and bonuses, of the struggle of the heroes of labor against coal and energy shortages, of quotas exceeded; but Fonty wanted to hear none of it.

We see him with his back turned to the pit; he is gazing in the direction of the women's hospital and the church steeple. As if eager to distract attention from the pit, he can be heard chatting about the Altdöbern castle, which he calls pretty but dilapidated; the late Baroque façade can merely be guessed at. In the still usable interior, one of the block parties, "the one that calls itself liberal," has settled in. In the near future claims will no doubt arrive from the West, as is happening everywhere. Heirs always turn up. But there will be problems with the park, he says, which was inspired by the one in Muskau. The old stands of exotic trees are already damaged: "From the sinking water table. That's how it goes with strip-mining. No tree can survive if its roots are disturbed. But who cares about such things..."

In his letter to Martha, Fonty gave full rein to the sorrow occasioned by this state of affairs: "...as I stood there right behind my trusty old companion, which is to say, perilously near the edge of the pit, hardly daring to look down, I suddenly felt tempted to put an end to all this, to cast off, so to speak, this entire burden that had been oppressing me for years, simply to hurl it down to Orkus, whose depths were already filled with garbage and filth, even a dead horse, or its decaying head. What a stench! What a terrifying image! Certainly a mere chimera, yet you are well aware of all the torment to which I have been subjected. I wanted à tout prix—and even at the ultimate price—to get out of the whole mess: the coercion, the cripplingly tedious rehearsal of stale memories, which at best yields leering caricatures. But the realization set in that there is no abyss deep enough, and so no act could follow this murderous thought, however strong the temptation. It would have made as much sense for me to hurl myself into the pit—or he me.... Let's say no more!"

As regards Hoftaller, we would have been less delicate and would have been inhibited at most theoretically. My colleagues and I often chuckled at Fonty's itch to give a little shove—oops! there he goes! But the consequences had to be considered: was Fonty conceivable without his day-and-night-shadow? Wouldn't the latter's absence have put an immediate end to a story whose punch lines depended on an echo, a story that demanded to be sung in two parts, more or less out of tune? What is left, we asked ourselves, if Hoftaller drops out? Theo Wuttke, to be sure. But would his existence have been sufficient, and amenable to further development? No, Hoftaller was not mortal! We knew that his disappearance would at most have hastened a new birth; after all, Tallhover had not succeeded in putting an end to it all.

The letter to Martha Grundmann continued: "He who keeps his eye fixed on the void turns to stone. I told myself therefore: A person cannot stand at the abyss forever. After all, it was starting to rain. From the northeast, clouds were sweeping low over the earth's crust and its telegraph poles, roadside trees, and distant church spires. It looked almost as though the low-hanging clouds were going to scoop up all the shrubbery along the jagged edge of the pit and carry it off. A light rain was falling, turning the surfaces of the groundwater lakes from glassy to dull. My old bones were already fearing the onset of a cold that would be followed by a colossal barking cough. Suddenly I became aware that I was not alone. My trusty old companion was still at my side. He solicitously drew an umbrella out of his coat pocket and opened it over both of us. We should have left then, forthwith...."

With the push of a button, Hoftaller had extended and unfolded the protective umbrella, a so-called Pipsqueak, before opening it. But they did not leave. Rather, they stood rooted to the edge of the pit, knit tightly together, forming a compact silhouette. With his left hand Hoftaller held the umbrella high enough for Fonty's towering height. Now he could not turn away. The pit, the hole, was unavoidable. His gaze flitted down four or five carved-out levels; even so, he had to listen to Hoftaller's spontaneous tirade, sometimes fluent, sometimes halting. The hole furnished the cues.

"Right! That's how things looked everywhere when it was all over. The whole country bankrupt, last stop! Red ink everywhere. At least that's what our reports to the leading comrades said: nothing there, everything depleted to the point of no return. Well, some yield left, way out there, below Pritzen. And we could have kept on indefinitely putting up the concrete prefabs.... And certainly upped the number of Trabis coming off the line...And Olympic gold by the bucket.... Through KoKo and ITA we could've pulled off arms deals like the West.... And with more and more hard currency, Comrade Schalk could've...."

We let him yammer on. The litany was all too familiar. It was far more entertaining to multiply him and his subject, with and without umbrella. But even mass-produced, he refused to stop yammering; we heard a well-rehearsed chorus: "Those folks over there have done us in. No wonder! They set the pace, and we had to keep up. Didn't really have to, just thought we did, you know—compete, run the arms race till we were out of breath, sucked dry, scraped to the bone. Now all our beautiful people's property is down the drain.... The Handover Trust's grabbed it all and plans to auction it off.... They call that snapping up a bargain.... But it's a disgrace.... We're being reduced to nothing.... Honest, Wuttke, that's exactly what it said in our report—the enemy of the working class wants to reduce our value to scrap.... Let them have it, the scrap. They're stuck with it now, holding their trusty hand over it...."

And this lamentation was sung from the edge of the pit, like the chorale in an oratorio. We lined up umbrella-shielded pairs for miles: a black border around the sheared-off edge, which bulged here, straightened out there. Multiplied, they yielded additional profit, according to the latest theory of surplus value. Although looking small at that distance and bleary in the floating rain clouds, each unit stood there standardized, coupled with the next, each umbrella deployed in mass-produced uniformity.

"Want to bet they won't know how to deal with this? They won't be able to shake this millstone around their collective neck. Let 'em go ahead and swallow us. They're sure to choke. They never could get enough. Always wanted more, more, more. Now they'll get it all, and for free, too. Honest, Wuttke! that's why we told the leading comrades, 'Open up! Throw it all wide open!' But the folks in Wandlitz didn't want to, not till the pressure started growing from one Monday to the next . . . we were looking the other way on purpose . . . till there was no more holding back, and Wandlitz caved in. There were a few nonentities left, grinning to themselves, till finally, a year ago today, the shout came, 'Open the gate!' And open it did. . . ."

So that had been his plan all along. Here, overlooking the pit, above the abyss, he wanted to mark the ninth of November, but of course only the previous year's event: "It was gone, the Wall, as if swept away by a phantom hand. . . ." What did Hoftaller and his ilk care about the November revolution, Hitler's march on the Feld-herrenhalle, *Kristallnacht*, November's many casualties?

"No, Wuttke, ours went off peacefully. No bloodshed. The Wessies were meant to get us all in one piece, with everyone accounted for. It was our moment, right? We've never pulled off a coup bigger than the fall of the Wall. For years we were cursed or hated, or even worse. . . . They called us the firm of Eavesdrop, Peep, and Pounce. People told Stasi jokes, especially that loud-mouth of a songwriter we tolerated far too long, on the advice of the top lady comrade. And all those who followed his tune—primitive, always the same old song and dance, the same clichés: floppy hat, leather coat . . . Watch their smiles fade when we open up our bag of goodies. That crowd'll be amazed at our diligence, and to find out whom we trained to be diligent. All kinds of names, singly and by the dozen. Home delivery, just say the word. Truths, nothing but truths! We deliver. Let them tear each other apart; we'll be glad to help. We're not finished, not by a long stretch. We and our memory—ah, you know, Fonty, how far back we can go without forgetting anything—we've developed a special storage method. Besides, we're the only ones who've always believed, like our colleagues on the other side, in a united Germany. And that's what we're going to get, for sure. Honest, Wuttke! With our help, the Handover Trust will pull it off: an impoverished Germany, an equalized Germany, united in poverty, already hungering for a new order and for security. See, when the East overflows because the borders aren't secure...or a real ecological disaster...something like Chernobyl to the third power...And when everywhere else in the world they have nothing but crises, slaughter, refugees by the thousands...we'll be in demand again. With brand-new methods we'll seal up the cracks, tight as a barrel, hush-hush, on a global basis....But what am I saying? It's this pit here, this hole, that makes a fellow run off at the mouth. It's quite an opportunity—to look down into deeper and deeper layers. I mean, all the things deposited under the surface, not just geologically—this bit of coal—but in a deeper sense, metaphysically, so to speak....What we need, Wuttke, is a new source of meaning. Besides, it was a year ago today that the Wall suddenly opened. And we were the ones—honest—who undid the locks...."

Fonty waited a while, but nothing more was heard from Hoftaller except puffing and snorting. All the way to the horizon, the sky was drenched. Everything gray, in delicate strokes. "It was raining steadfastly," the letter to Martha Grundmann noted; and in fact the umbrella remained open.

As if he wanted to help the speaker, who had now fallen silent, Fonty provided cues: "You wanted to say something about immortality, right? Let's let that be. Lignite is immortal enough. Like her aunt Pinchen in the old days, my Emilie still burns it in a tiled stove and the little cast-iron stove in my study; so winter after winter she has to haul briquettes up three flights of stairs from the coal cellar, two buckets at a time. Yes, it's a wretchedly long story from its prehistoric origins to today and its final consumer. But what does final mean when all manner of things are going into the air, to be reminded of our blue planet from pretty high up and in a new form. Anyway, our minable product here began to form in the Late Cretaceous Epoch or even earlier, when dead plants... immense stretches of time...But let's get going now. The Trabi's waiting for us. It, too, is from an earlier epoch, but decidedly not immortal...."

This was going too quickly for the Archives. We would have come up with further variations on the theme of immortality. For instance, we could have supplemented Fonty's disquisition on stoves heated with lignite or with the inferior compressed coal slack. That was what people heated with, not only on Kollwitzstrasse but everywhere in Prenzlauer Berg. All of East Berlin relied on this fuel; and even the Archives derived their snug warmth from this material, which was sometimes plentiful, sometimes scarce. One could have spoken of the Workers' and Peasants' State as persistently overheated, for without lignite, and therefore without open-pit mining in Lusatia and elsewhere, this condition would have been unthinkable; yet we should not feel obligated to weave it any wreaths of immortelles, merely because its toxic residue will outlast it.

The two under the umbrella were standing, then, in the right place as Hoftaller delivered his November oration. And Fonty clapped at the right moment, and with both hands, for he had his free, whereas Hoftaller, who kept pointing with his right index finger into the pit and at the immortality layered there, had to hold onto the umbrella with his left hand.

The letter to Mete explained that Fonty had been applauding a "speech by the abyss." "None of my pastors could have done it better, perhaps Schleppegrell, but he was a Dane, and, where Germany is concerned, rather too far afield. Or possibly Lorenzen, when Dubslav von Stechlin was laid to rest: he might have let himself be inspired to invoke such a vision. Certainly not Pastor Seidentopf, when Hoppenmarieken, the old witch in *Before the Storm,* was buried near the end of the story with her crook and wading boots. No, my old companion was not to be outdone. He couldn't stop talking. I had to put an end to it with premature applause...."

"Splendid, Tallhover!" Fonty exclaimed. "Well done! You have not only got Germany back on its feet, poor but pure; you have even managed to resurrect the Stasi. We can now await any final catastrophes calmly. We'll be secure to the end. Congratulations, Hoftaller. All frightfully right. But you must let me have my share of the umbrella. A little more. I've already had a thorough dousing."

Only then did they go. Our theoretical presence allows a final image; that's the good thing about theory: you always have the last word, and in the midst of total destruction, theory remains intact—only the right one, of course.

As they went on their way, the two of them again offered the image that has been fixed ever since Fonty's visit to the French cemetery, of which we have given an account. Back when Fonty stood by the Immortal's grave, while someone was waiting for him at the gate, receiving him with an open umbrella because it was raining: two old men under one umbrella.

This time a succession of images formed. The pair of them yielded a sequence of frames as they moved farther and farther from the brown-coal pit. Past the women's hospital of Altdöbern marched a column of pairs, each pair shielded by an umbrella. Toward the front of the line, they shrank into smaller and smaller figures. Seen from the rear, they seemed to separate—gaunt from broad-shouldered—but at the head of the column back melted into back. The black coats billowing to one side in the wind, the black hats under black umbrellas appeared paler as the figures grew smaller, moving toward the church square: a cortege that followed no coffin.

We stayed behind them, passing the still-tended cemetery, its gravestones gleaming in the fine rain. Chiseled into their surfaces were the names of three dozen Red Army soldiers. We joined the procession until it broke up in the car park near the castle entrance, or rather evaporated. We had a firm grasp on only one remaining pair as Hoftaller shook his patented umbrella and snapped it shut, whereupon the two of them got into the Trabi.

The letter to Martha continues: "During the ride home, the windshield wipers did not rest. We sat next to each other as if safe and sound. And we had hardly got onto the autobahn when my companion began to sing. That old street song from days of yore: 'Mother, the man with the coke is here'—he sang it fervently in the pouring rain. 'I have no dough, you have no dough, who ordered the man to bring us coal....' In spite of the road construction and the traffic in the opposite direction, eventually both of us sang all the way to the outskirts of Berlin, 'Mother, the man with the coke is here.'"

26

A Room with a Desk

His letter to Martha closed with complaints about a cold coming on and about a dry, barking cough, as well as nervous symptoms that had been in the offing since the visit to Lower Lusatia; the overall tone was querulous: "...and besides, at home we now have the constant din from a crazy jumble of television programs; Mama sinks down reverently before this new acquisition. And to make things worse, the Scherwinski woman from next door comes over with her kids to sit and stare. The jolly jabber and aggressive noise find their way even into my study. It's enough to drive a person from the house. But where else can I discharge my epistolary debts, to Professor Freundlich, for example? In weather like this I'm in no mood to toil up Potsdamer Strasse and sit in the snack bar with my runny nose. What I lack is a quiet room...."

When he came to see us at the Archives, he complained in similar terms about the nerve-racking idiot box, the gabby neighbor, and the absence of the peace and quiet he needed for letter writing. Hoftaller, who also visited us, to give us an earful, "as one human being to another"—"Recently we were on the edge of the abyss, so to speak, in Lusatia"—confirmed that Fonty was in dire straits: "Oh, he'll get over his runny nose. But what our friend needs urgently is an office with a sturdy writing surface."

The wish went unfulfilled. To be sure, Theo Wuttke was praised for his report; to be sure, he had succeeded in persuading the head of the Handover Trust to keep the paternoster; and although the agency's move was not expected until the end of February, Fonty was already on the payroll. But the office he had been promised was not ready for occupancy. Perhaps the delay could be attributed to the circumstance that the former file courier was obviously far beyond retirement age, and thus functioned only as a "consultant." A similarly restrictive contract engaged his day-and-night-shadow for consulting services with the Handover Trust, since he, too, was ripe for retirement.

Yet that was not Fonty's complaint. Consulting suited him fine; it was the four walls he was lacking. And he was more than satisfied with the monthly stipend of two thousand marks. Besides, thanks to his position in the personnel division, Hoftaller had managed to secure for himself and Fonty what he called "the benefits nonsense they get in the West"—a Christmas bonus, paid holidays, and the like. That was ample reason for Fonty "to put a positive face" on matters and to assure the Archives that "except for the lack of an office and my heavy consumption of tissues, I'm so well off there ought to be a law against it."

And when the television was switched off for a few minutes, even the climate at home was much improved; Emmi Wuttke found that the monthly stipend sweetened the pot nicely, and certainly improved on their pensions. She saw herself taking a first small step in the direction of prosperity, and praised the Handover Trust as "real decent." She proudly told Inge Scherwinski, "My Wuttke's with the Trust now." Or: "The Trust couldn't manage without my Wuttke."

When she responded to our questions in greater detail, we learned the following about the Handover Trust in its role as benefactor: "...when he was just a file courier, we couldn't afford the TV. Just couldn't swing it. Besides, my Wuttke didn't approve of the tube. But this time I didn't really bother to ask, just went ahead... on installments.... Color, of course... Well, cable won't be here for a long time... but a couple of channels is plenty for me. And Inge Scherwinski from next door, that poor thing with her three kids, gets a lot out of it, too. No, my Wuttke still won't watch."

We should have responded, "Worse, much worse than that," for the idiot box drove Fonty out of the house even in bad weather. Since November's dampness had settled over all the benches, both in the Tiergarten and in the Friedrichshain People's Park, the Handover Trust was now his real home, even if there was little work for him there.

Occasionally he was assigned to pilot groups visiting from the parliament in Bonn through the construction mess and along the corridors. Or he was asked to present his report, now expanded into a memorandum, "On the Preservation of the Paternoster," to a special audit commission from the Federal Budget Office. People smiled when they heard the elderly man, whose dignified appearance commanded respect, call the indefatigable lift "a symbol of eternal recurrence" or allude to Sisyphus. He helped nervous visitors into the rising or falling cabins. When young ladies worried that failing to get off on the seventh floor would condemn them to making the descent headfirst, Fonty seduced them with his old-time charm into risking an uninterrupted trip at his side, all the way up and all the way down. The Lothario-like tendencies he had indulged during his younger years now stood him in good stead; he presented the turning point in the attic or the cellar as a harmless yet unforgettably exciting experience: "This is how I met my future wife, Emilie—long, long ago. How'd you like to try it again, dear Fräulein? Once around is not enough."

This customer service remained a sideline. And since Hoftaller was often out in the field on assignment for the personnel division, establishing contacts or conducting interviews, it was not only his promised office Fonty was missing. He therefore looked for another refuge. Since the Tiergarten was out of the question, he hiked all the way up Potsdamer Strasse, despite the wretched weather, with stick but no umbrella, to that dreary new structure between Bolle's Dairy and Porst Photo, which, simply because it had the right street number, inspired him to backpedal through time. It was this street number on which his eyes fastened as he took a seat by the window in the coffee-and-snack shop across the way. There he found a substitute for the four walls he still lacked.

Here he had laid out his earlier life for Madeleine Aubron's inspection. Here, as the biographer Reuter confirmed, the "man of long letters" had penned many epistles. On a scratched Formica table, with a snifter of brandy and many cups of tea-bag tea, Fonty discharged his epistolary debts. He attended to Professor Freundlich, then his granddaughter, and finally his son Friedel, bombarding us in between with written corrections—"in order that in every seemingly established truth the Archives may see the cracks." But before he got around to all that, he again traveled on the wings of words to Schwerin and the lakeview villa.

"Only now am I getting around to answering your troubled letter. I must say that your tendency to expect the worst first and foremost (a tendency you share with Mama to the point of ridiculousness) blocks my way like a wall topped with broken glass. I am forced to become a high jumper, taking a running start and then launching myself, as it were, over the obstacle, your own peculiar barrier. Here, from the other side, I declare straight from the shoulder: That is the way it is. When a person marries, there's often an unexpected wedding present, and, in your case, an unwelcome one. Apparently your Grundmann, who was a developer when you married him, is determined to live up to his family name by brokering all the ground he can, and 'underhandedly,' too, as you write.

"He probably has little choice. A broker has to grab while the grabbing is good. Just think of Fritsch and how cheaply he got his hands on those three lots in Waren an der Müritz. All with lake view! And because that is how it has always been, your Grundmann is out to get shoreline building lots. He is making his move before others make theirs, for nowadays, when anything that yesterday was certified by the Workers' and Peasants' State has been voided, brokers are springing up like weeds, of the fast-growing, deep-rooted variety. It's hardly surprising that your builder-turned-speculator calls himself a liberal, maintains excellent relations with the Schwerin branch of the Handover Trust, finding the door to its office always open, and, because he has access to excellent information, snaps up prime cuts in the heart of town, entire streets in washed-up Schelfstadt, and, to top it off, finds treasure along the Mecklenburg coast. As far as the new freedom is concerned, none of this is sinister. It is part of the plan. Your old father is likewise in the pay of this omnipotent agency, although at the moment he is still waiting for it to move from the Berolina Building on Alexanderplatz, which has become too small, to the colossus from the days of the Reichsmarschall.

"You complain of 'motorized robber barons,' but that is the way of the world, to which my Mete should long since have adjusted, relinquishing her once rigid adherence to principle and theory. Viewed in the light of day, nothing to be alarmed at: what yesterday called itself the people's property, and was sufficiently neglected to show it, is now slated to end up in private hands and with spiffy façades. I fear I must share your concern, however, that your Grundmann's cozy contacts with certain networks may make him an accomplice; I know how quickly such entanglements can catch a person in their meshes.

"Here, too, elements that ducked out of sight years ago and survived on the bottom are now swimming merrily on the surface, as busy as can be. It is remarkable how quickly the Western leadership—most of which is second- or third-rate—strikes deals with the local shysters.

"Yet this, too, dear Mete, is the order of the day in times pregnant with history. Was no different or better after '70–'71. There will always be Treibels, and their kin from the Tribe of Greed. Commercial-councillor riffraff, which harps of a Sunday on noble values and the general welfare, but during the week and behind one's back pulls off one crooked deal after another. And exemplary Münster Catholics though they may be, the Grundmanns, including Frau von Bunsen, have a tendency toward Treibeldom. Their family posturing left a bad taste in my mouth even at your wedding. (Didn't Frau von Bunsen already have her acquisitive eye on old Junker estates in the Eastern Altmark?)

"Wouldn't surprise me a bit if your Grundmann, despite all his liberal ballyhoo, turned out to be just the man for the successor party to Stöcker's Christian Socialists, in other words the Block & Court Chaplain Party. I'm thinking here of local politics, of course—the position of planning and development director, for instance. Be a good girl and read him a few pertinent passages when the moment seems opportune—for instance, over his afterdinner pint. I recommend the excursion to Halen Lake and the swanless swan shelters. Or, better still, Jenny Treibel's visit to the Schmidts, when Corinna gives her tit for tat. For you've always had that in you, too, my Mete, a bit of Corinna, although that young woman would probably invoke her Calvinist origins rather than your late harvest of Catholic communion wine. But as for Grundmann, tell him: planning and development director today is no better than commercial councillor in days gone by, not to mention Reserve Lieutenant Vogelsang and the renaissance of his type.

"But to turn to Mama. She sees herself on top of the world, now that I have become a henchman of the Handover Trust. I am tempted to believe that, aside from the monthly stipend I receive, it is the expression "Handover Trust" that she finds so gratifying. She is convinced that nothing can go wrong so long as we are in the Trust's hands. No doubt about it: Handover Trust is more than Cultural Union! In her eyes, and likewise in the view of your eternally naive girlhood friend Ingie, my value has increased since I was exalted to the rank of a Handover Trustee. Well, fundamentally she is right. For decades I was kept under ideological supervision and badgered. Using Menzel's paintings of industrial subjects (the foundries), I was supposed to backdate the birth of Socialist Realism. Partisan penny-pinching persistently robbed me of the best passages in my speeches. You are familiar with this red popery from your pre-Catholic period. Inconsistent with the interests of the working class, they would say. Or: Too conciliatory! Or simply: Reactionary!

"Nothing of the sort with the Handover Trust. My memorandum on behalf of the paternoster, which they wanted *à tout prix* to replace with a high-speed elevator, was commended at the highest level. And shortly I am supposed to be given my own office, and an assignment to go with it. Something along the lines of public relations, my trusty old companion told me on the q.t., and as you know, he can hear the grass growing. That obviously means propaganda. He sends his best, by the way. That should coax a smile out of you!

"A charming note arrived the other day from France, which I do not want to leave unanswered. I must also make sure today that Professor Freundlich receives his long-overdue response. The same goes for Friedel, whose current plans for his publishing house have global missionary ambitions, on a Moravian scale. From Teddy not a word. It remains to mention that the television set that has recently been billeted in my home, as a sort of lodger, compels me to go out on more walks than I care for, and in dreadful weather; but since of all forms of religion sun worship is the least to my taste, I am not terribly unhappy at the gray skies everlasting.

"By the way, I am writing to you from my now familiar old coffee shop, with a view of Potsdamer Strasse. The only thing authentic here is the street number diagonally across the way. . . ."

Scribbled around the margin of this Mete letter was the following addendum: "Friedlaender always wrote vividly. Even when there was nothing in his pen but society gossip, his comments remained clever and telling. I prized the Jewish acuity of expression in Nordau's articles for the same reason. And I feel similarly about Freundlich, who while still a Communist consumed far more wit than the Party had authorized. . . ."

Only to us did Fonty lament that the professor's letters written during the fall had sounded "quite morose beneath a surface of forced gaiety." "His daughters have left for Israel, which must be painful for such a dyed-in-the-wool anti-Zionist. I have urged patience; pampered as they are, the girls will find it too hot there in the long run. . . ."

In December he often dropped by the Archives, thank heavens without his day-and-night-shadow; but figuratively speaking, Fonty's granddaughter was present whenever he was.

Madeleine corresponded with him, as she did with us. After a few last questions about Hankel's Depot, her interest focused on the Immortal's Huguenot parentage. Since she was considering expanding her master's thesis in this direction, she pelted us with queries, mostly relating to Emilie Rouanet-Kummer, whose interchangeable French and Brandenburg origins were often commented on by her husband: "Today Mama is more from Beeskow than from Toulouse. . . ."

The student Aubron was collecting such traces, most of which could be gleaned from the letters. That was why, when Fonty turned up with his customary bouquet, the conversation turned to his granddaughter and her passion for knowledge. It was not without pride that he shared with us passages from letters written in her schoolgirl hand that demonstrated an unquenchable thirst for knowledge; and Madeleine's example provided incidental proof that the French educational system was characterized by a veritably Prussian rigor, something that went out of style long ago in these parts.

Since my male colleagues had assigned all correspondence with the student to me, I usually had the pleasure of chatting with our visitor, the Archives' friend Fonty, which was sometimes strenuous, especially when he played the lady-killer and wandered off the subject, indulging in occasionally risqué compliments. There was only one way to stop this: I would raise the touchy subject of the London period, and try to interrogate him on his understanding of the relationship between the Manteuffel government and the *Kreuzzeitung*, also on the mission of the "German-English Press Correspondence" and the role of the Danish agent Bauer. But our friend hardly ever blew his cover, and would attempt to distract me in turn by referring to the research done by Frau Professor Jolles, which he described as "thorough, at least by human standards," pointing out somewhat mysteriously that certain minor motifs remained unexplored. "Mere bagatelles, no doubt. But I understand: nothing entices archivists and secret agents more, since they derive most of their nourishment from such crumbs."

Then we got to the subject of his granddaughter's passion for knowledge. We were having tea and Bahlsen biscuits, which he had brought, along with chrysanthemums. He assessed Madeleine's correspondence with the Archives with ironic indulgence and devised a quotable formula to characterize our work, a formula inspired by a visit to the open-pit mines of Lusatia: "Much slag and little coal." Nonetheless, my exchange of letters with the student Aubron was a source of pleasure to him. He responded rather evasively, however, to the direct questions posed by his granddaughter, who always wanted to know everything exactly: "Much I no longer recall. The important details are missing. Happens more and more: that which was most part of one gets lost, sometimes through senile absentmindedness, often through forgetfulness aforethought."

446

One letter to me from the student asked why, if the Prussian Huguenots were generally noted for their industry and their knack with money, there should be, in the particular case of the Immortal's father, such clear evidence of chronic indebtedness, general lollygagging, and a tendency to botch his own life. Before answering, Fonty offered me Bahlsen biscuits, looked me up and down, as though he had a mind to flirt with me, and said, "Striking, the way you do your hair; I could take you for the former mistress of a prince." Only then did he turn to Madeleine: "Ah, well, this person I call bittersweet simply refuses to leave any stone unturned. To her even a bygone life is a freshly printed proof sheet that must be worked over again and again. She is never satisfied with what she finds between the covers of books. Only letters will do. In my next missive I intend to clear myself or—just between you and me—talk my way out. At the moment, my small volume of work at the Handover Trust permits me extensive correspondence. But as soon as I have my own office..."

That was taking its time. For now the coffee-and-snack shop on Potsdamer Strasse had to serve as a surrogate. Accordingly more letters went out than the recipients could or wanted to answer: to the daughter in Schwerin, to the granddaughter studying in Paris, to the professor who had meanwhile been evaluated into early retirement, to the son Friedel, busy with his publishing in Wuppertal, and to the government official Teddy in Bonn. Fonty's attempts to win back his second-born by means of solicitous letters failed repeatedly, and his inquiry as to whether Teddy, as a member of the defense ministry staff, had maintained contact in the past with a certain person went unanswered.

Theo Wuttke continued to be worried that this obstinate son, who had turned his back on the family, might be endangered by intrigues. Not a word of this in the letters to Teddy's sister and brother. Fonty knew how to keep embarrassing matters under wraps. But he communicated everything without restraint in an epistle of considerable length, written over brandy and tea, which we can reproduce here only in abridged form.

Since quite a bit was afoot in politics, he wrote, around the

447

beginning of December, to his faithful correspondent in Jena about the outcome of the parliamentary elections: "This result, to which I was absolutely determined not to contribute, confirms not only the numbers arrived at through anticipatory vote-counting but at the same time the pan-German economic relationships, in other words, the power relationships. Basically, one might as well entrust the business of government to the Federal Bank."

Far more worth communicating was the nature of his new assignment: "Just imagine, Freundlich, there is a publicity department here, and this department has given me an assignment that I find quite attractive, namely, setting forth the architectural history of the Handover Trust building. This monograph of mine is supposed to be used for friend-raising purposes. Now English expressions like 'public relations' and 'that's the message' just roll off my lips. I am supposed to make the history of the complex at the corner of Leipziger and Otto-Grotewohl-Strasse come alive. Perhaps your involuntary retirement will allow you to give me a tip here and there. Please understand this selfish desire on my part as a tribute to our many years of friendship. But as for your Israel-fixated daughters (and this twin tic of theirs), I am entirely on the side of your wife, whose advice, 'Wait and see,' seems frightfully right to me...."

He then turned again to his new assignment. Having had free run during several chapters of German history of the colossus that was now almost ready for its newest occupants, Fonty had been asked to bear witness to those times. In the letter to Freundlich, he enclosed a copy of the terse description of his charge, signed by the head of the Handover Trust: "Nothing must be repressed. In making no attempt to dissociate itself from the past and its residual burden, the Handover Trust argues for transparency. We are confident that with respect to your biographical data you, Herr Wuttke, are uniquely qualified to implement this assignment. We hereby request you to submit a preliminary outline of the proposed informational document."

Initially Fonty played hard to get. In his letter to Madeleine Aubron he lined up his reservations: "You know, dear child, that my interest shuns major events of the sort usually accompanied by

448

blaring trumpets. I live off unobtrusive details, that is to say, off leavings. What I find stimulating is not state visits and dry-as-dust ceremonial speeches but suggestive anecdotes, likewise amusing gossip and—admittedly—familial conflict. In the old days, as you know, my faithful correspondent Mathilde von Rohr, the lay sister from Dobbertin, was an inexhaustible source, for all the unmentionable subjects in the lives of Brandenburg's gentry flowed from her pen unvarnished. That elderly lady provided a wealth of excellent material for novels and novellas. Similarly, Friedlaender's letters were treasure troves; they may have contained no gleaming jewels, but they were packed with useful bric-a-brac. So-called subplots, which are always the main thing. You see, even in the case of tragic occurrences like murders and shootings, for instance in *Under the Pear Tree* and *Quitt*—a story provided by Friedlaender, by the way—the bloody deeds in question took up little space; yet it was the omnipresent sense of guilt, which continued to pulse even in far-off America, that determined the course of the plot. (What is plot? Often it is the slightest shifting of chairs, nothing more.)

"And now I am supposed to provide a commentary on historically decisive, in other words, earthshaking, dates. I would prefer to delve at length into cases from the immediate past, such as the case of Pastor Brüsewitz, who set himself on fire in protest, or the tragedy of the Wollenberger family, or the literarily rewarding and pellucid double life of Ibrahim Böhme. It would be an agreeable challenge to capture on paper the pastor's conflict with his congregation, or the tangled web in which the loving husband and punctilious informant was caught, between the state's concern for security and his conspiring spouse. As for the case of Ibrahim Böhme, the challenge would be to show how someone who lived literature literally—from Dostoevsky's lower depths to the middle position against which Brecht slyly plays both sides—can be celebrated as a saint and at the same time become a traitor to what matters to him most; a temptation, by the way, that is not foreign to me. All in all, much that was experienced in times past is being recapitulated in our day, for which reason the case of my friend in Jena—we spoke of Professor Freundlich when you were here—moves me more powerfully than any grand political theatrics; for if

449

he loses his daughters, who are named Rosa and Clara, and decisively so, to Israel—which is not yet certain—he will be left frightfully lonely. (If only his football club could manage to win an away game and cheer him up!)

"So many inner conflicts. Yet my task is to follow the dry trail of history and turn inside out the inner life of an abominable building; this they call transparency. Ah, if only my bittersweet person were at my side! We would know on what conversational journeys to set out. Yet as I see from your letters, the 'increasingly difficult relationship' in which you are entangled precludes a lightning visit over Christmas, a visit that would brighten my days...."

With similar eloquence he shared with us at the Archives some of his concerns and his ennui. He even confided to me that he was all written out. "No, no!" he cried. "Even if you took it into your head to descend on me in my almost ready new office, in a flight of Eve-like whimsy and as a flawlessly coifed muse, I should have to pass. My bag of words is empty. At the moment I am incapable of anything longer than those three and a half pages in support of the paternoster. There's no spark. And as you see, I can't even manage to play the lady-killer. A role, by the way, that never came easy to me."

Yet Fonty must have found a way to get started, probably more without than with a muse, for he wrote to his son Friedel: "Since yesterday my pencil has not had a chance to cool. A difficult birth, nonetheless. And certainly my most recent scribblings cannot compete with your publishing projects, which are assured a solid commercial foundation, through the grace of the Moravian Brotherhood and its worldwide mission. In my case there is little edifying to record, but much evildoing finds its way onto paper. Military and Party careers cut short, from the long-range bomber to short-term work, heroic traitors and knee-knocking heroes.... With continuing stories like these one could revive the old Neuruppin pictorial broadsheets that were so popular in their day; but even the most brilliantly colored windfall of scurrilous tales would be unsuitable for your publishing list; as you know, my son, I have no talent for tracts...."

Nevertheless he began to write. It may well be that Hoftaller cut the knot and gave him the last push to complete his assignment, if not with allusions to the promised office, then with frightening firmness. For when the consultant Wuttke expressed his intention of first sketching the Wollenberger case and as if incidentally reviving a subplot in *Irretrievable*, it apparently came to a confrontation.

Fonty's reasoning is easy to imagine: "What if the widow of Captain Hansen and her daughter Brigitte, that seductive Rubensesque beauty, were mixed up with the Danish secret service—which even poor Holk must have noticed, for he says to Pentz, 'And that fills my heart with trepidation. Is there really evidence of relations between a security agent and the daughter, or even between the police chief himself and the mother?' If so, then in the case of the Wollenberger family, supposing Normannenstrasse slipped a striking female agent into the mix..."

To that Hoftaller is supposed to have responded, "Listen here, Wuttke, the novel *Irretrievable* may be open to all sorts of speculation as far as the Danish security agencies go, but at some point the joke's over, even for a certain Fonty. We don't want to play with fire here. There are any number of variations on the Wollenberger case. For instance, there's material that could compromise your own family at the appropriate point in time. I'm thinking of that lieutenant and Starfighter pilot who went on supplying us with information even after his promotion to captain. And then I could mention a certain government official in Bonn whose expertise we were able to tap for years. The parents of these two gentlemen never had the slightest inkling. But all that can change, Fonty. I needn't tell you: We can do this the hard way!"

With prodding of this kind, the consultant Theo Wuttke had no sooner moved, a few days before Christmas, into a renovated office with a desk of his own than he began to take his assignment seriously.

As promised: on the seventh floor. The office's number was among the last of the building's two thousand numbered rooms and could be read as a significant birth year, even though, in conversation with us, Fonty liked to connect the year 1819 with Victoria, Queen of England and Empress of India: "A royal year. It marked the beginning of the Victorian era, of which, to be sure, little was noticed in Neuruppin, where shortly before New Year's someone with a famous name also came into the world. There, as in all garrison towns, the atmosphere was purely Prussian."

Soon Room 1819 was equipped with the bare essentials. Hoftaller helped, procuring bookshelves and a desk lamp in the style of the thirties. The only window looked out over the inner courtyard on the north side. To the right of the desk, which stood in the light from the window, a bulletin board hung on the whitewashed wall, with preliminary materials tacked up: reduced copies of Sagebiel's architectural plans, photos of soldiers presenting arms in the court of honor, and—right next to them—of striking workers who reportedly shouted down Minister Selbmann on 17 June 1953, likewise in the court of honor. In addition, resembling "wanted" posters, pictures of members of the Red Orchestra resistance group, active inside the Reich Aviation Ministry for a short time. And then photographs of adjacent buildings in the government district, all of which were reduced to rubble at the end of the war: the new and old Reich Chancellery, the Kaiserhof Hotel, Prinz-Albrecht-Palais, before it fell into disrepute as Gestapo headquarters.

A bit later another photo was added; Hoftaller had tracked it down from the Tallhover period. It showed Airman Theo Wuttke at about twenty-two, with his cap at a rakish angle and his courier's pouch. In the small picture, whose edges are somewhat bruised, he is standing in front of the wrought-iron fence that bounded the court of honor along Wilhelmstrasse and served the same purpose along Otto-Grotewohl-Strasse. Behind it one can see, flat as a backdrop, the limestone-clad colossus and the colossal portal. Upon close inspection, Fonty looked rather undistinguished in the guise of young Wuttke.

For the time being, the bookcase remained scantily equipped: a few statistical yearbooks, two picture books with architectural showpieces from various historical eras, a volume on architecture and urban planning in the Third Reich, something on the mission and organization of the Luftwaffe, a biography of the former Reichsmarschall by a British historian, and an Ulbricht biography in paperback. On an otherwise empty shelf stood two volumes of the expensive Hanser edition of the Immortal's writings and letters, which Fonty had purchased recently. At home on Kollwitzstrasse he had only the incomplete Aufbau edition and the Nymphenburg paperback edition. But now, as a consultant to the Handover Trust, he felt he could afford to buy the India-paper edition, one volume at a time. Soon two more would join those he already owned: the collected writings on German history; all the printed material yielded by the wars of 1864 and 1866 and the subsequent war against France; and the selected writings on art and art history, as well as book reviews—musty manifestations of a lifetime's effort, for which the Archives had been privileged to supply the commentary.

If it was just noted that the desk received light from the window, it must now be added that Fonty had spent a long time, with Hoftaller's help, shifting this new acquisition, a modest piece of furniture, back and forth. For a while the desk was to stand under the bulletin board; then Fonty put the desk at an angle, so that he could face the door. Two moving men at work. A desk seeking its proper place. Eventually Fonty and the desk settled in front of the window.

We never visited him there, yet we know that from where he sat he had a view; and at his back he had the door, as well as a washbasin, there since the thirties, to the left of the door. Hoftaller had succeeded in exchanging the modern office swivel chair for something resembling the old Thonet chairs, with bentwood arms. As far as the chair went, Fonty was sitting just as he would have in his study on Kollwitzstrasse.

No pictures graced the walls, but on the desk he had the family in frames: Emmi, Martha, the three sons, and, passport-size, his granddaughter. For Friedel and Teddy, he had had to make do with photos from their youth: the two boys shortly before the Wall went up, Friedel in his Young Pioneers uniform. Among Georg's things, a picture showing him in civilian dress had turned up; a mourning band was affixed to this photo. Madeleine's face was confined by a Biedermeier oval. Emmi and Martha stared straight ahead, one looking pained, the other grumpy. No photo of the

Immortal was at hand, but an unframed postcard showing the bronze monument in Neuruppin, surrounded by trees, leaned against a perforated brick like the one on the desk in Fonty's study. Here, too, writing utensils were stuck into the holes in the brick, among them two swan feathers and a half dozen Faber-Castell pencils. And the brass postage scale had been allowed to move with Fonty.

Fonty began to fill page after page. Preliminary notes for a commissioned work that he referred to disparagingly in our presence as "a puff piece." Hoftaller did not push him, but now and then appeared on the threshold after a gentle knock. He didn't stay long. Since they had forgotten to put a telephone in the office, none rang. When Fonty interrupted his note-taking, it was only to attend to Christmas correspondence. For letters he laid the pencil aside and picked up a steel pen, or sometimes a swan quill.

After the holidays, which went relatively well, despite the television set, he wrote to Freundlich again, in the quiet period before New Year's when even at the Handover Trust not much was stirring. He tried to "whip up a better mood" in Freundlich. Then he penned another Mete letter, thanking her for the lavish gifts, "especially the Oriental dressing gown." Finally, in splendid epistolary spirits, he wrote to Madeleine:

"I am touched by the combination of *arrière-pensées* and solicitude implicit in the authentic beret you foisted on me; it doesn't look bad, but I still subscribe to hats. Ah, if only I could pay back my bittersweet person as lucidly in French as she gave me a piece of her mind recently in the sprightliest German, scolding me for running around the Tiergarten and drafty Alexanderplatz in cold, damp weather with my coat open and my scarf hanging loose; telling me I should not lead Grandmama astray with swaggering gasconades; warning her grandfather to be wary of the attentive gentleman at his side; requesting that Grand-père not exaggerate the warlike rumblings in the Gulf to apocalyptic proportions, even though the ultimatum should not be underestimated. . . .

"And further admonitions. I promise, my child! I resolve to reform, if not retroactively to Christmas, then at least starting with

454

the New Year. It is not hard to heed the commandment regarding my coat and scarf (sometimes even the beret, by way of experiment), in view of the piercing though snowless cold. Now that I have an excellent livelihood, despite my seven-times-ten annual rings (soon to be plus one), a delightful truce has gone into effect at home, especially since I now have somewhere else to scowl; just recently (and at long last) an office was put at my disposal, from where I confess to you in postal privacy how much I miss you, with a piercing pain not unlike a toothache.

"To turn to the risk of war, which can certainly be written off as a footnote to history, but which might spread, as the Crimean War once did: unfortunately the television, placed practically on top of the Christmas tree, had overpowering offerings during the holidays, in which children's choirs competed with reports from the Arabian desert, such that my longing for solitude grew ever more intense, as did my desire to cultivate my cabbages somewhere or espalier a few plum trees.

"But as for Monsieur Hoftaller, whom you have so charmingly and inexorably lopped into Monsieur Offtaler by consistently leaving out the ho-ho-hoing capital *H,* we should remind ourselves that we owe our belated rendezvous to his good offices. Without him, there would neither be occasion nor address for this letter.

"True enough, caution is always in order. Hoftaller and Tallhover had, and have, their fingers in every pie. (Like Police Superintendent Reiff in *L'Adultera,* a mystery-mongering security agent lurks in the background in *Irretrievable.*) But in the final analysis, it is also true that a bit of secrecy is not all bad. Not everything should be allowed to see the light of day.

"By the bye, Hoftaller is better than Tallhover. And what is more, I have been acquainted since time immemorial with the surveillance practiced by one or the other, assuring the security of some state or other. I am tied to both with double knots, as it were. I know all their little tricks. Their stores of information—as a rule only incomplete information—are a familiar weight on me, although in the course of my cultural gymnastics on behalf of the Workers' and Peasants' State, that weight increased. My lecture tours crossed his path often enough. As much as he hindered the free flow of speech, he spread the safety net whenever danger threatened: after the fall of the Manteuffel government, for instance; after Stauffenberg's failed assassination attempt, for instance; after the workers' uprising on 17 June, for instance, to which I had carelessly attributed class consciousness; and likewise after the thuggish good-neighbor operation in Czechoslovakia— you were barely a year old at the time—when I almost talked my neck into the noose at a Cultural Union conference in Bad Saarow (charmingly located on Lake Scharmützel), by saying, on the record, 'Since Frederick the Great's day, lightning-strike marches into Bohemia have been a Prussian specialty, refined through the efforts of Bismarck and Moltke, then recapitulated in total fashion by a simple corporal from the First World War, whom we called our Führer for short; and lately Comrade Ulbricht has been doing full justice to this old Prussian tradition....'

"Ah, well, there was no appreciation for irony at Bad Saarow, or anywhere else, for that matter. I was disciplined. And if that Monsieur Offtaler, of whom you are so suspicious, had not put in a good word for your grandfather, I would have spent a few years safe and sound in the Bautzen penitentiary, known in these parts as 'the Yellow Peril.' And all that merely because I have a penchant for making far-reaching connections. From the Crimean War to today, no matter how tangled it may seem, history still forms such an easily perceived web that a war in the Gulf, if one should come, would not surprise me in the slightest.

"But apart from that, I now have an assignment gratifyingly suited to my foreknowledge. As you know (and from your French perspective may actually admire), the Germans have a proclivity and even a talent for the *Gesamtkunstwerk,* the total work of art. With similar genius (and as a counterpoint to Bayreuth), in the course of our unification, the Handover Trust was created, a model Valhalla for the gods and demigods and their machinations. And as a consultant to this all-inclusive construct, whose program now includes the twilight of the gods *en suite,* I am supposed to compose a piece whose purpose is to inform, that is to say, win friends. My task is to do justice to all the historical phases of this colossal structure, into which you had time only to poke your nose during your visit, alas too short. I am already sorting through material. Your grandfather, who thought he had been milked dry, already has plenty of ammunition. Already I am plumbing every depth—if need be with the help of memory-jogging rides in the paternoster.

"The room with a desk they set aside for me on the seventh floor is elevated far above all the renovation racket. One need only close one's eyes, and images begin to swirl. As you know, I came and went here as a soldier. For the last time when your dear, kind grand-mère had already grown fond of me, and in my happiness I really did not want to go home. Ah, France! That is the direction in which my longings carry me time and again, if not to the Scottish heath. They scour the banks of the Rhône, scan the lakes and ponds of the Plateau la Dombes for memories; they waft away to the heights of the Cévennes; they find refuge, as once the persecuted Huguenots did, in the wild Gorge l'Ardèche; and of late they have been knocking at the door of a house nestled at the foot of a hill dotted with cypresses, a door that you, as my Madeleine, have opened for me.

"And already the frivolous epistolary spirit has carried me on the one hand to the most recent subject of your industrious research, and on the other hand to your professor, and thereby into the vicinity of that relationship you are experiencing as 'increasingly difficult,' as your last dear little letter reveals. Both, the influence of the Huguenots on German literature and your relationship to a married man, the father of three children, take us too far afield: you will have a hard row to hoe.

"With all these worries, my bittersweet person should not remain fixated exclusively on the Immortal's gasconades—Schlenther calls him a 'New-Ruppiner and Old Frog,' by the way—but should also bear in mind the admirable Chamisso, likewise Fouqué. And in the process you should perhaps neglect your professor a bit, or exchange him for someone else, if your heart will allow that. Furthermore, let me commend to your attention a certain Willibald Alexis, forgotten though he is, whose family chronicle of a Huguenot hue has always been a cornucopia for me. . . .

"It remains to be hoped that the new year, come what may, will bring us together again. No matter how I revel in the peace and quiet of this office, the fact remains: I miss you greatly...."

Not all of his Christmas letters were of such length, of such weight on the postage scale. Since Fonty never penned a letter without first doing a draft in pencil, we are richly supplied with written documentation; and since we have meanwhile also acquired many originals of letters, and—thank goodness—everything concerning the family is available, comparisons are now possible that reveal how often he revised his first, spontaneous version and—true to his adage—in the end "spruced up the style," for instance, in that passage linking the festival site in Bayreuth with the Handover Trust as a "total work of art." In this connection, by the way, the Immortal's visit to Bayreuth—"*Parsifal* was being performed"—was invoked only in the first draft.

In the letters to Martha, the old-fashioned German orthography is noticeable, particularly the use of *th* where modern usage would call for a *t*. Even the Tiergarten, when it turns up in writing, is always spelled with a "*th*."

In other letters he makes do without the older spelling and expresses his expectations or even demands pointedly and concisely—for instance, when he repeatedly prods his publisher son to cast an expert eye on his father's Cultural Union lectures: "You have my word that my contributions to the cultural heritage are still fresh as the morning dew...."

The Archives could have confirmed the delight these texts afforded, but in the version of the collected writings we were editing there was no room to do so, because we were obliged to adhere to a narrow scholarly notion of relevance. Nonetheless we would gladly have helped fulfill his ambition to be published—if need be with expert opinions—but Fonty did not want any assistance; he was betting on his son. Although he mocked Friedel's publications as "Pietist drivel," he wrote him letter after letter, and at the end of the year this pleading epistle:

"I should have no objection to its being a slim volume. I'd like to see seven carefully selected lectures, unabridged. That would include the early historical sketch 'How an Apothecary Tried His Hand on the Barricades.' Wrote that in the fall of '53, under the impression of the previous June's events. No wonder major portions were deleted by the censors, portions that should be restored when it is printed. Something from that period must be preserved! I am appealing now not to my son, but to the publisher.

"The publishing houses here are in a more than precarious situation. They have been placed, for purposes of privatization, under the thumb of the Handover Trust, an enterprise as gigantic as the building complex assigned to it, and in whose service I now stand, to my joy and sorrow. At least I have been given a room of my own, with a view of a dreary inner courtyard. This view practically compels me to raise the aforementioned subject again in this year's-end letter to you.

"My lectures, which were neatly typed by Mama, are as good as ready to go to press. I have no objection to your issuing the accumulated sweat of your father's brow in paperback. No need for everything to reach the literary marketplace between hard covers. Since my contribution 'Why Should the Eskimos Concern Us?' makes passing mention of *Irretrievable,* and thus of the Moravian missionary enterprise, you should have no difficulty smuggling me in amongst your transcontinental heathen-saving tracts. On Holkenäs even Countess Christine, with her Moravian piety, had to swallow one reproach or another, whether Old Lutheran or Calvinist. To be sure, she condemned all the rest as heretical...."

After this letter, Fonty risked a glance into the lifeless inner courtyard. Then he exchanged his steel pen for a pencil.

27

In the Service of the Handover Trust

Neither in mid-November nor at the end of December did they go to McDonald's. Their seventy-first did not provide a sufficient pretext for "festivities," as Fonty assured us just after the beginning of the new year: "I'm weary of society, not only in a manner of speaking, but also in reality. Even celebrating my seventieth was *ridicule*."

The Archives' belated birthday wishes pleased him nonetheless. We gave him No. 42 in our "Papers" series, containing a recently discovered review of *Quitt* that we thought would amuse him—although it could not be entirely new to a memory such as his; after all, we had often heard him make fun of the critics' "hyper-cleverness," referring in one case to Julius Hart: "Actually he always knows in advance what he will want to say...." Besides, since *Delusions, Confusions* he had come to the general conclusion that "all reviews might as well be written by criminals."

He rather enjoyed the little brochure all the same, although he probably fell into a reflective mood upon reading the letters to Moritz Lazarus, who was addressed as "My most esteemed Leibniz" because he belonged to the Rütli poets' society: "From time to time there would be meetings with the Rütlions at home, so, too, in Lazarus's lodgings, which were on Königsplatz, the current Platz der Republik. A dreadful shame that this friendship had to end on such an ugly note ..."

When Fonty put on his reading glasses and skimmed a short piece on Friedrich Witte, the Immortal's boyhood friend, we learned as if incidentally that his day-and-night-shadow had presented him with the sixth volume of the Hanser Edition—the ballads, songs, and occasional poems: "A treasure trove, though with its share of mortifyingly sloppy rhymes." Yet the only gift Fonty had been able to think of for Hoftaller was the same as last year's—that diversion for old and young alike, a puzzle: "No, not of the blooming landscapes we were promised; my gift depicts, in thousands of pieces, the City Palace, which was blown up after the war. No big challenge for my old companion. I assume it took him only a few hours to slap together the front elevation of the building, a Schlüter design, by the way. He is fond of timing himself with a stopwatch, several times in a row. A pretty illusion, which he stirs into a hodgepodge of fragments again and again. I must renew his supply when I have a chance. Saw a colossal selection in KaDeWe. Much Prussiana in the mix—the Brandenburg Gate, of course, and Sanssouci. Would have liked to give him the old place on the former Wilhelmstrasse. That would be something: a Handover Trust puzzle! But they didn't have it."

Then we chatted about his new field of activity and encouraged him to do something playful with the name of his employer. In the best of moods, Fonty demonstrated to us how the Handover Trust could be converted by sleight of hand to a Landover Trust; and how at the Trust one hand washed the other, for which reason it would be no trick at all to get one's grubby little hands on the people's property with the Trust's blessing; and he came up with other puns, according to whose rules, for instance, one could avoid the awkward debtor's disclosure oath by raising one's right handover. Finally the whole conversation dissolved into silliness. One of us was scribbling down classified ads: "Handover seeks manicurist for fist!" "Closeout on waterproof Handover shoes!" and so forth.

As Fonty was leaving, he put his own activity in historical context for us. Already in his coat, he exclaimed, "Handover today is no better than Manteuffel in the old days, but it pays better."

We did the calculation later, comparing the buying power of the taler with the hardness of the mark. It was true: the Immortal could not afford any extravagances, in either London or Berlin— that was how tightfistedly Prussia rewarded its loyal subject.

———

He put in overtime. The consultant Theo Wuttke wanted to earn his stipend and did not restrict himself to the two specific regimes— one longer, one shorter—that had both ended ingloriously. The chronicler wanted to cover more than the mission of the Aviation Ministry during the Third Reich or the workings of ten or twelve ministries during the forty years of the Workers' and Peasants' State.

He began by looking at the prehistory of the streets flanking the complex. After Leipziger Strasse, which had not been forced to change its name, he paced off Prinz-Albrecht-Strasse, later renamed to honor the Communist Käthe Niederkirchner, this name, too, now subject to recall. He explored the length and breadth of Wilhelmstrasse, still named after one of the founding fathers of the short-lived but actually existing state, but destined soon to resume its course under a name shared by several Prussian rulers. And so he began to play with tin and lead soldiers. He brought Wilhelm-platz and its architectural transformations back to life. There was no end to things that once were.

His draft grew to a size eligible for the Prussian guard. Referring to the 1732 map of Friedrichstadt, Fonty sketched the grand parade ground used by all the regiments headquartered in Berlin. He made each one in turn, from the Alexander Regiment to the Gendarmes Regiment, pass in review and go through its paces. He counted off the busts of glorious generals erected in the years before 1800, from Seydlitz to Zieten; retraced the symmetrical layout of the square, designed by the architect Lenné; transformed the parade ground into a mammoth construction site with the building of the underground, begun in 1908; reeled off the names of all the palaces surrounding the square and strung along Wilhelmstrasse; mentioned with pride Prussian Brandenburg's noble families; and arrived by this route at the Schulenburg Palais, which from 1875 on had served as Chancellor Bismarck's private residence and official headquarters. He permitted himself to dwell long and anecdotally on the "Sulfur-Yellow Collar," sometimes revaluing, sometimes devaluing him with repeatedly sharpened pencils; he even saw him as the target of failed assassination attempts.

Then there were commissioned poems that insisted on being

quoted, for instance one celebrating the youthful Junker—"His head adorned in locks of gold, / Ever on horseback and nineteen years old..."—or the late poem "Where Bismarck Should Rest," which the Immortal, somewhat reconciled, and himself approaching the grave, penned at his son Friedrich's wish on 31 July 1898 to honor the memory of the founder of the short-lived Reich.

Founding of the Reich, the Founders' Era: a multitude of ministries demanded space, and, as enumerated by Fonty, turned Wilhelmplatz and Wilhelmstrasse into the hub of power. This subject carried him too far afield, and he had to retreat. But he did not want to give up the Grand Hotel Kaiserhof, which he needed as the locus of later events; for in 1933 the founder of yet another short-lived Reich would move from the Kaiserhof, where he had held himself in readiness, into an addition built onto the Chancellery during the brief Weimar Republic. At the same time, the Reich Minister for Enlightenment and Propaganda took over Prince Friedrich Karl's former palace, which underwent several expansions during the years immediately following, because propaganda was valued *über alles*.

He omitted not a single detail of this most recent will to power. In 1935 a "Führer's balcony" had to be pasted onto the Reich Chancellery. From here the crowds herded together below with increasing frequency were to be greeted with arm outstretched or bent, on the Italian model. The moment had come for far greater architectural ambitions. Fonty finally got to the point.

On a spacious lot bordered by Wilhelm-, Leipziger-, and Prinz-Albrecht-Strasse, site-clearing began for the planned Reich Aviation Ministry, intended to incorporate the existing building as well as the former Prussian House of Lords and House of Deputies. Several other monolithic building projects came to nothing, because of the war. Not much escaped its blows. It leveled every one of the buildings just named, all but the Reichsmarschall's complex, cast in stone.

We are going to considerable lengths not to name certain personages whose historical roles make them unmistakable. In this practice we follow Fonty, who found that it was adequate, or actually more expressive, to use designations such as "the Führer" and "the Reichsmarschall," but also sobriquets for former or current chancellors such as "the sulfur-yellow crybaby" and "the ruling mass." If we are not always consistent, that likewise mirrors Fonty's moods.

Only now did he turn his attention to the Reichsmarschall's career in construction. He called the entire project a "gigantic job-creation measure, which enabled many of the unemployed to find a livelihood clearing away 260,000 cubic meters of old structures while the new one was already going up. Demolition and construction went on in day and night shifts on eight different sites; from this one can conclude that criminals in public office like to legitimate themselves through acts of kindness."

According to the plans drawn up by the architect Ernst Sagebiel, who later built Tempelhof Airfield in comparable dimensions, such symbolic undertakings expressed the will of the Volk: demolition equals construction. Everything had to be done in record time. After only half a year—soon after the topping-out ceremony—a thousand offices were ready for occupancy. And after a year's construction the entire complex could be opened for use, with 250,000 square meters of space, not counting the former quarters of the two houses of parliament, which were reconfigured into the "House of Aviators."

Fonty withheld his personal opinion. He commented only sparingly on the architectural history of the Reich Aviation Ministry. At most he allowed himself an ironic "By the way..." with reference to job-creation measures the Handover Trust might launch in Zwickau or Eisenhüttenstadt. He merely nodded in the direction of the Cologne Cathedral, whose construction dragged on for centuries. But he quoted at length from official descriptions of the buildings or their functions: "The layout of the complex creates four courtyards open to the park and includes four interior courtyards. On Wilhelmstrasse a large court of honor leads up to the main entrance. The backbone of the design is the main structure, on a north-south axis; toward the park, the four expanded office wings, lower than the main building, are attached at right angles; the wings continue on the street side, but with more stories, the middle ones enclosing the court of honor...."

Since he viewed the piece he had been commissioned to write as historically conditioned, and to us often remarked on "my retrospective memorandum, which is devilishly bogged down in details," it seemed obvious to him that he should emphasize the peculiarities of the time in question, for instance the abundance of national emblems and the sheathing of the entire façade in slabs of eight sizes, delivered on short notice from some fifty Franconian quarries. He underscored quantities—for example, "30,000 square meters of silver-gray limestone"—and added in parentheses: "a stone whose color was as inanely monotonous as that of the Führer's favorite marble, travertine, but colossally cheap by the meter."

He lingered only briefly over the columns by the main portal, but did not neglect to mention the two bronze eagles perched atop two pillars, each with a swastika clutched in its talons, anchoring the tall wrought-iron fence in front of the court of honor by guaranteeing symmetry. Similarly, a stone relief by the sculptor Arno Waldschmidt was important to him; it adorned the open hall of columns before the entrance intended for ordinary traffic, and came into view from Leipziger Strasse: a column of steel-helmeted soldiers marching straight ahead with deadly certainty.

In the very next paragraph Fonty reported the destruction, occasioned by the historical moment, of the military relief, and described the wall decoration that had replaced it: a huge piece in tiles by the painter Max Lingner, twenty-five meters in length, showing a throng of people merrily manifesting enthusiasm.

With this monumental assemblage of tiny pieces, Fonty negotiated the transition from the Third Reich to the Workers' and Peasants' State, and thus to the Ministries Building. He continued to emphasize quantities, such as "without exaggeration, 1,715 tiles of Meissen porcelain, laid in fifteen rows." He characterized the mural—with its workers, intellectual and manual, but also laughing youths playing accordions and guitars as they march into the future, while in the background scaffolds and smoking chimneys stand for progress—as "the flattest exemplification of Socialist Realism."

Then he compared the soldiers marching off to death in Waldschmidt's relief with the proletarians gathered on the tiles, and without further transition moved on to other heroizing monstrosities—for instance, the huge painting by the Prussian court painter Anton von Werner, with its celebratory motif, the proclamation of the German Imperial Reich in the Hall of Mirrors at Versailles. Finally he surveyed all three commissioned works in historical order and added the marginal note: "Even if workers sweating buckets are better than soldiers sweating bullets, it was all balderdash in the end. It began with hurrahs and ended with a whimper. Forty-seven years of Imperial Reich were followed by barely thirteen years of Weimar Republic. And when the scant twelve and a half years of Third Reich are added to the four decades of Workers' and Peasants' State, all that remains when we do the final reckoning is German shortness of breath."

With the help of this balance sheet, he returned to the last of the states he had enumerated. The mural in porcelain tiles was created in 1952. Fonty then turned his attention to 7 October 1949. On that day, in the grand conference room of the former Reich Aviation Ministry, before whose ornate front wall the Reichsmarschall had once issued orders from an elevated leather throne, the Workers' and Peasants' State came into being as the German Democratic Republic; this step could be understood as response to the establishment of the Federal Republic of Germany in the West, that same state into whose hands the eastern rump state had now voluntarily commended itself, people's property and all.

"Whether one state is better than two remains to be seen," Fonty scribbled in parentheses in the margin of this marketing-oriented memorandum. He refused to leave it at that. The building was standing, true enough, yet the more than two thousand rooms seemed lifeless. By way of an experiment, he summoned heroes of aviation, recently decorated, with oak leaves added to the Knight's Cross at their throats; he ordered them to stroll along corridors and ride up and down in the paternoster. He allowed them to make snappy appearances in the reception hall, shuffled them around like tin soldiers, listed planes they had shot down (if they were fighter pilots), presented them now as blowhards, now as melancholy angels of death; came around to flying aces like Galland, Mölders, and Rudel; kept a dozen hard-hitting, bombproof, blitz-quick types in reserve; lingered over legendary Stuka and He 111 missions; reported on the air battle over England and the paratroopers on Crete; was familiar with all the fighter planes from the Me 109 to the most recent night fighter models, not to forget that reliable transport plane, the Ju 52; omitted neither the long-lasting rivalry between Generals Milch and Udet, nor the wear and tear on men and matériel, as well as the early loss of air supremacy over the Reich. He even sprinkled his overflowing account with whispered political jokes that took the Reichsmarschall as their butt; yet only the resting-in-state of those two heroic figures Udet and Mölders brought a little life into the place: the bombastic funerals held in the court of honor may not have been able to mask one ace's suicide and the other's accident, but at any rate the atmosphere was upliftingly spine-chilling.

Too much material. Fonty cut out more than he let stand. But the portrayal of the next phase also suffered from marching columns of numbers. Linguistic monsters patched together with genitives, produced on the assembly line by the Workers' and Peasants' State, swarmed over the scene. The accomplishments of the many ministries gathered under one roof could be documented only with drab or retouched plan-fulfillment data. Banners from one Party rally or another. Paper spewed out by the Central Committee. Our primary task is . . . At the Eleventh Party Congress it was resolved that . . .

And now the most recent phase was in danger of choking on numbers of its own: the Handover Trust was answerable for sums reaching into the billions. Its shadow fell on thousands of companies once owned by the people, on real estate, Party properties, collectivized Junker estates stretching over countless acres; it fell on seven thousand projected privatizations and two and a half million endangered jobs. Even the boss's pithy formulation, which was supposed to serve as the motto for Fonty's memorandum—"Privatize rapidly, reconstruct decisively, shut down cautiously"—could not spark life into anything, no matter how often Fonty repeated the words to himself; everything, even hope, was drowning in numbers.

"Seems dry as dust or reeks like a house of the dead." This comment and more of the sort could be found in a letter to Professor

Freundlich written in mid-January: "This time the celebration was more subdued than raucous. The air has gone out of us. The lies set afoot by the ruling mass are pretty lame; you can see them limping. We all felt pressed to the wall as the clock struck twelve; no comparison to the year before, when everyone thought there was reason to break out in hymns of joy, tap a keg, and light up the night sky with fireworks. As a substitute, the Gulf War, which opened yesterday, offers a spectacle that seems frightfully funny, at least on television, but must be terrifyingly close to your daughters in Israel. Everyone is justified according to his own premises. Victors on all sides. All killing in the name of God. Ah, my dear Freundlich, how am I supposed to produce a memorandum in such company?"

Yet he could have made it easy for himself. His chatty tone, which could bridge all the sewers of this world with equal élan, would have had at its disposal hundreds of anecdotes with hard-hitting punch lines. He would merely have had to open his private store: "In the days when I came and went here as an airman in the Luftwaffe..." Or: "During my many years as a file courier in the Ministries Building..."

After all, he was welcome everywhere and knew any number of receptionists who had served a succession of bosses without regard for historical turning points. He could even have woven into his narrative Emmi Wuttke's stories from the Reich Aviation period and her recollections of experiences in the air-raid shelter. Not he but Emmi Hering from the typing pool had been allowed to watch from one of the office windows as the official obsequies were staged in the court of honor for Udet and Mölders; and a decade later it was Emmi who saw the striking workers marching toward the entrance from Stalinallee, for, as an office worker, Frau Wuttke had found employment in the Ministries Building in the early fifties, long before Fonty. She was not fired until the end of '61, when her sons stayed in the West. This criminal offense was known as "Republic-desertion."

It was a long time before Emmi told us what had actually happened: "We were under pressure, see, and couldn't talk about it...." And that postcard-sized photo of the ace pilot Galland, dedicated and autographed, was something she showed us only recently: "He didn't look military at all, more the heartthrob type, with his little wisp of a mustache. That's why my Wuttke wanted to tear the picture up. Well, 'cause we were engaged, and he was always jealous. . . ."

Right, that was something else Fonty could have used to give his memorandum some sparkle: how he and Emmi first met in the paternoster. It was not in June '40, when Airman Wuttke returned from occupied France with his first richly atmospheric bulletin—"In Domrémy and Orléans our victorious soldiers visit Jeanne d'Arc . . ."—but earlier, in April, that Emmi was required to type up a travel piece from the Protectorate of Bohemia and Moravia as the first proof of her devotion.

Be that as it may: Fonty did not want to use personal material. For now, at least, he could not even heed the advice of his faithful correspondent in Jena, who had suggested before year's end that he give free rein to his familiar chatty style. The recalcitrant material got in the way. The limestone cast a gray pallor over everything. The colossus held Fonty prisoner. But in a paternoster epistle replying to the recently evaluated professor, we find a rough sketch of what would later breathe life into the memorandum:

"I can already guess, dear Freundlich, that you will urge me again to take an anecdotal approach, telling, for instance, the sad tale of that resistance cell in the Reich Aviation Ministry, which, when it was put on trial, the Gestapo dubbed the Red Orchestra. And I certainly do want to devote a brief chapter in my memorandum to Officers Harro Schulze-Boysen and Erwin Gehrts; for it was from a bathroom here that they maintained radio contact with other resistance groups. A foolhardy thing to do, as it turned out, for they were soon nabbed.

"By the way, I got to know Colonel Gehrts in person after my return from assignments in the field. When I had delivered my reports to the department in charge of me, there was time for a bit of a chat with this typical armchair officer, whom no one would have expected to show such resolute dignity, even in his death cell at Plötzensee. And truly well-read, too: like Liebknecht and the

469

historian Mommsen, he counted *Before the Storm* among his favorite books. Since I recklessly—and almost as an afterthought—allowed myself to be used as a courier, I often had letters for Gehrts in my pouch. I could also assume that some of the mail I was asked to deliver when I was ordered back to France might have been traced to Colonel Gehrts and Lieutenant Schulze-Boysen. Luckily I was not caught at a checkpoint. Altogether, I never realized the risks I ran during my military service, even though, when the trials began, I was summoned to Prinz-Albrecht-Palais, just around the corner from here, and interrogated several times in fairly typical Gestapo fashion. But they couldn't pin anything on me; or was it the guardian angel assigned to me for life—who in those days went by the name Tallhover—who was gracious enough to protect me?

"Was quaking in my boots. Always grounds for suspicion! You're familiar with these little life-or-death games, camouflaged as coincidences, from your youth in Mexico, when everybody could denounce anybody as a Trotskyite. But whatever danger the Red Orchestra may have got me into, the fact remains: Colonel Gehrts was absolutely first-class. Completely without the usual derring-do, yet colossally worldly.

"Unfortunately, this episode does not belong in the memorandum any more than my bulletins from the front, which tended to luxuriate in literary and historical atmospherics. On the other hand, there is one brief experience that probably must be included. It has to do with our Workers' and Peasants' State, though only tangentially—during its early years, to be exact, when we were full of hope, convinced that we were on the right path. I am speaking of the swarm of construction workers from Stalinallee that soon attracted vast numbers and was interpreted by our leading comrades, who were blind to reality—but also by you, dear Freundlich—as a putsch instigated by the West, or, in the official terminology of the day, as counterrevolutionary.

"And those rebellious workers, whom the West later celebrated to death under the phony notion of a 'popular uprising,' were at first only on strike. You recall, the issue was the government's decision to raise production quotas. But then they did revolt, and an estimated two thousand of them marched to the Ministries Building.

My Emilie, who was still working in the offices of the MB at the time, witnessed the whole thing: the crowd, more quiet than enraged, the workmen's overalls covered with plaster dust. They mistakenly thought they would find the secretary general of the leading party here, and wanted to speak to him in the court of honor. They chanted for him to come out. But the Goatee was somewhere else. Only one minister, probably Selbmann, had the courage to face the crowd. He wanted to speak, to calm the demonstrators, but could not get a word in edgewise. They booed him down and drove him from the podium. Instead a brick-carrier from C Block South spoke. Emilie remembers him shouting, 'Traitors to the working class!' and 'Down with the quotas!'

"That is all there is in the way of historic events. Yet I want this confrontation to add an accent to my memorandum—the striking proletarians here, the speechless minister there—although the minute I capture that 17 June '53 on paper, I get immediate interference from 18 March '48. You know, of course, how succinct a judgment the Immortal passed on these events in his old man's memoirs: 'Much cry and little wool!' And that, even though the young apothecary had been present when the barricades were thrown up and had even wanted to force his way into St. George's to sound the tocsin. But the gate was locked, which elicited from him the brief but still valid observation: 'Protestant churches are always closed!'

"That's how it is with memories. When you tell me stories from your early years in Mexico, and in so doing like to pay tribute to the odd nature of everyday life, I hear familiar notes. Looking back later, one enjoys skewering absurdities. The prize goes to the ridiculous. The hero becomes a figure of fun. Yet at the time of the events, my 'one-and-only,' as Emilie calls him, was viewed in the Jung Apothecary Shop as either a secret revolutionary or a secret government spy, and feared in either guise. Well, he was probably more a would-be revolutionary, observing with curiosity or even fascination the liberty-drunk thrill of the barricades while keeping an eye on the housewives lining up in the pharmacy for cod-liver oil. He knew full well that the cod-liver oil intended to prevent scurvy in children was actually being used to light their lamps. That led the writer, looking back fifty years later, to exclaim, 'Freedom was optional, cod-liver oil essential!' Of course cod-liver oil carried the day.

"And wasn't it equally banal, my dear Freundlich, the way we exchanged actually existing socialism for actually existing capitalism a little over a year ago? Except that instead of cod-liver oil, this time Western bananas were for sale. Not to mention the seventeenth of June. Of course at that point, too, freedom was declared to have the highest market value, but after Soviet tanks appeared on the scene, silence could again be had for a song. In a lecture for the Cultural Union that got me into a great deal of trouble, as you probably recall as well as I, I started out with the events of March '48, quoting the former would-be revolutionary: '...found myself more than ever convinced of the invincibility of disciplined troops in the face of any popular force, no matter how courageous....' Then I drew audacious parallels to the events of that June. For people were far too willing to count the government's retraction of the increased quotas as a victory. Likewise here of late, and yet again. Whether it is cod-liver oil or bananas on sale, freedom always gets shortchanged in such transactions.

"You are right, my dear Freundlich. Your objection is well taken. In '48 and '53, in March and June, there were casualties; this time it went off without bloodshed. 'Bloodless revolution' was the watchword. But the only reason no blood was shed was that the Workers' and Peasants' Power no longer wanted to be a state; it decided to let itself be absorbed. Now, thanks to our dowry, the blot on our biography, we will become a burden on the aggrandized western state. And eventually our communist system, which did itself in, will pull its twin brother, the capitalist system—at the moment still gloating robustly—into the pit as well.

"Of course this gloom and doom, otherwise so uncharacteristic of me, does not belong in the memorandum. But I do want to hint that if striking workers once demonstrated in front of the Ministries Building, the current occupant, the Handover Trust, may be in for more of the same. Beyond any doubt, a colossal privatization machine is to be set in motion here. In the long run, this sort of thing will not be taken lying down. And that is why it became painfully clear to me, as I looked back on the victims of March '48, that a rebellious people, even if it has nothing but its bare hands, is necessarily always stronger than the most heavily armed force of order, if not for today, then for tomorrow.

"Enough on that topic. As I gather from your letter, entertaining as always, Jena's Carl Zeiss Football Club is maintaining its position on the scoreboard (at the bottom, true), and you are beginning to find a certain piquancy in your regrettable situation, bringing your expertise in jurisprudence up to date and making yourself useful as a tax consultant. As it should be! Tax-consulting is essential! We shan't let ourselves be shunted onto a siding. No matter how telegenically the times are tuned to war, we must not cave in. Even to your daughters, Israel must be starting to appear questionable, no matter how enthusiastically they set out for the Promised Land. On the other hand, one never knows. Every war pieces together its heroes. For us there would then remain only a heaping spoonful of resignation, which, however, can be positively invigorating. . . .

"To answer your kind inquiry about my Emilie: she has her ups and downs. Yesterday she was feeling deathly ill, but she was up early this morning polishing all the windows with the chamois cloth. From my daughter I receive nothing but reports of Mecklenburg miseries. Marriage does not become Mete. But that, as you know, takes us too far afield. The best policy is to get used to it and keep one's complaints to a dull roar. After all, as they say in the West, there's plenty to be done, so 'Let's get down to business!' With this in mind, I shall return to my memorandum, for which I am still casting about for a vivid image, or, better still, a compelling one. . . ."

Fonty remained occupied with this task throughout January, a month that started out with storms, a month from whose midpoint on only weapons were doing the talking in the Gulf; new systems of destruction were tested; oil fields were set on fire; the stock exchanges rose with the outbreak of war, then fell; a prime minister generally considered clever resigned and hired himself out in Thuringia; Soviet tanks were dispatched to Lithuania to put down the protesting population; Gorbachev's star began to sink; and a sudden cold front brought snow. But in early February, when the Gulf War was threatening to become routine and the renovations at the Handover Trust were clearly making headway—the marble frames of more than two thousand doors had been polished to a high sheen—Fonty succeeded in finding the image he had been lacking. As always, when live inspiration was absent, simple reflection came to the rescue.

One day, on the ground floor, as he was waiting to get onto the rising paternoster but had two electricians in front of him, he saw, in a descending cabin, someone whose appearance was familiar to him from photographs: the head of the Trust.

Alone, but filling the cabin with his powerful build, he appeared, legs first, then from head to foot in gray flannel. He was coming from above, where he had probably been inspecting the future executive suite. A person who radiated strength of will. A person to whom success seemed custom-fitted, like his jacket and trousers. A fine figure of a man, so to speak.

The boss left the cabin surefootedly, and passed Fonty, whom he greeted and who returned the greeting. The electricians disappeared, going up with their toolboxes. Almost at once Fonty, who did not get on, but, rather, hesitated and watched the boss speeding away with his entourage, saw himself transported back in time by half a century. He saw himself in the blue Luftwaffe uniform, with his cap at a rakish angle, standing on that same ground floor and waiting for the next paternoster cabin; in front of him were two officers.

It was the Reichsmarschall descending from above. The gleaming boots came first, and bulging out of them the trousers with marshal's piping. Now the well-known figure appeared in all its bulk, topped by the fleshy head with a weak expression that tried to look tough. His costume matched the mocking verse that Berliners whispered to each other in those years: "Glitter left and glitter right, / But this fatty's not so bright."

Fonty, or, rather, Airman Wuttke, saw the chest studded with medals and the *Pour le mérite* decoration dangling from a ribbon beneath the fleshy, padded chin, saw, in that face familiar from newsreels and photographs, two actors called Bigshot and Milksop vying for position, saw, despite the attempts at cosmetic concealment, the signs of an insatiable morphine addiction marring the Reichsmarschall's publicly displayed mask.

Perhaps Fonty's retrospective vision had one eye on a photo he had pinned recently to the bulletin board in his office at the Trust: it showed the Reichsmarschall during the Nuremberg Trials, looking slack and deflated as he sat in the dock. After the announcement of the verdict, he had bitten the top off a cyanide capsule. Only in Fonty's retrospective was he present in the flesh.

An adjutant helped him get off. The next descending paternoster cabins brought the Reichsmarschall's entourage. The officers in front of Fonty missed their rising cabin and saluted crisply; Fonty saluted less crisply, lifting his right hand in a more-or-less automatic gesture to his cocked cap. Now the film was slowing down: slow motion, cut.

This segment was hardly over before Fonty began to film the historical transition, from the same perspective, but with a new reel. After all the uniforms, he called for the civilian dress appropriate to the postwar era, and directed the later chairman of the Council of State, Walter Ulbricht, whom the people called "the Goatee," to come into focus in a descending cabin: with his little potbelly and pinched Saxon expression.

Fonty pictured the Party secretary on 7 October 1949, immediately after the proclamation of the first German Workers' and Peasant's State, arriving piece by piece in the paternoster and getting off on the ground floor. On the bulletin board in his Trust office was a photograph of him as well, but this archival picture showed two persons: next to Ulbricht sat Goebbels; the Communist next to the Nazi, the Goatee next to the Clubfoot. In the early thirties both of them had been in Berlin organizing the transport workers' strike; from their point of view, the Social Democrats were enemy number one.

Fonty was no longer sure whether the later chairman of the state assembly—who much later, because of his first name, came to be alluded to, in a literary context, as the *Sachwalter*, or administrator—descended from above alone or whether, next to him, and

475

larger than he, stood his meeter and greeter, Otto Grotewohl. Had Wilhelm Pieck, the third comrade in the trio, been there, the cabin would have been too small. Fonty chose to focus on the Goatee.

He let the *Sachwalter* of the brand-newly proclaimed state come into the picture in his baggy trousers and get off with a confident hop. He, too, had an entourage on a leash. Since Fonty had not been an eyewitness to this historic paternoster trip, he was not required to greet the new arrival; but when Ulbricht's successor, the man with the little hat, whom both East and West called "Honni," visited the Ministries Building shortly before the end and the fall of the Wall, on the occasion of the Workers' and Peasants' State's fortieth anniversary, the file courier Theo Wuttke, called Fonty, witnessed this historic descent as well: shoes first, little hat last.

Now the series was complete. For the time being, no more historical scenes were being played out, although he would have loved to squeeze the ruling mass, visiting from Bonn, into a cabin and display him in a falling pattern. Fonty replayed the episodic film once, and then again. United in the paternoster. From the Reichsmarschall to the head of the Handover Trust. The memorandum had found its compelling quick-time image. He also saw himself, always waiting, through changing times, for an ascending cabin. He grasped the changeover mechanism in the guise of a tirelessly obliging elevator. So much greatness. So many descents. So many endings and beginnings. But to his daughter in Schwerin he wrote only: "Saw our boss getting off the paternoster the other day. This man has taken on too much. A colossal amount of power, which no one can really condone. Final decisions about people and property, which will make him hated—of that I am sure. At first glance: an intrepid fellow. Accustomed to success, knows how to take things in hand. Has something winning about him. But I should not like to be in his shoes...."

28

Posed Before the Monument

Her father's advice went as follows: "Pull yourself together if possible!" In addition, Martha Grundmann, née Wuttke, read the following in this rather long letter: "...Mama, who has been feeling exceptionally well for weeks now, has been in a grand mood of late, that is to say, ever since a television set has turned our kitchen into a theater of war. One might even say that her spirits have shot up like a rocket, even though her unfailing response to the surefire reports from the Gulf is, 'Isn't that awful, just terrible!' often seconded by the Scherwinski woman, who has to lob in her own commentary: 'Honest, it gives me the shivers. Go, USA!' Sometimes her little brats watch, too, as if it were a cartoon or a belated Christmas story. And Mama tolerates all this, and stuffs the boys with coffee cake; you know how fond she is of children.

"She is particularly impressed by the accuracy of the strikes. Just imagine: she explains to your friend Inge what antimissile missiles are. She talks about Patriots and about target coordinates as if she were praising the virtues of a new fabric softener. She may be sitting in there in her scuffs, drinking bladder tea, but at the same time she feels like an eyewitness on the front lines. Only once did I hear her express any concern: 'D'you suppose they have proper air-raid bunkers down there in the desert, like we had when we were in the war over here and had to sit there shaking in the cellar of the Reich Aviation, or down in our cellar here if they came at night?'

"Against my express will and wishes, she whisked the idiot box, which now plays a central part in our lives—a Western product, of course, with all the extras—first into the living room, and then, when I protested, into the kitchen, where it has ousted the old kitchen scale that once graced the spot and has turned that blessed corner into an altar. Hardly any consideration for me. And when I raised objections to the booming Schwarzkopfery and the remote-controlled saber-rattling, I was told, 'You used to always be for war, the blitzkrieg and such. Don't think I don't remember: the second of September was always Sedan Day!'

"That's all I shall say about this pictorial deluge. You understand, dear Mete, that this blithering boarder drives me out of the house. When there was still snow crunching underfoot, I would hurry through the Tiergarten, hoping to encounter Ludwig Pietsch skating around Rousseau Island. But now it just drizzles incessantly. I don't want to catch a cold, but on the other hand I cannot stand to see one more burning oil field, listen to any more panels of experts, and am hoping, if not for peace, then for an armistice, at least in our kitchen.

"For years we got along fine without the tube; we knew what was going on in the world. Not that we had exhaustive newspaper reports, for even my old *Wochenpost* kept us on a strict diet. But we stayed current with the help of our border-defying radio receiver—enjoyed listening to Bundestag speeches. Can still hear Erler's voice, and Carlo Schmid's. Or I remember how the two of us would listen to Radio Free Berlin or Radio in the American Sector, even though your Free German Youth forbade it, programs like Friedrich Luft on theater—'Same time, same station.' It was breathtakingly up to date. I was reminded of corner seat 23 at the Royal Theater on Gendarmenmarkt. Started with *Wilhelm Tell*, finished with *The Weavers*. Didn't miss a premiere, whether Max Haller's *Youth* or Ibsen's *Doll's House*...And if radio had existed in those days, perhaps I, too, would have been on the air—same time, same station....

"But that's not enough for Mama. There have to be pictures, moving ones, and in color, to boot. Since it came, I've felt out of place, the more so since the roar of war intrudes even into my study. To live in this world has become *dégoutant* for an old chap like me! As I wrote recently to Freundlich, 'The only thing I still enjoy is to sit in the sun with my eyes half-closed—if only it would shine....'"

The letter to Martha required double postage, because it kept getting longer, as he added to it day after day. And so February passed. We shall abridge Fonty's complaints about the new medium somewhat and pick up with the passage where he begins to fill his pages with memories again:

"...what times those were—when Polish uprisings, the Crimean War, and the carnage tearing America into North and South were brought home to us belatedly but vividly by Gustav Kühn's colored pictorial broadsheets. My father, of whose final years we were deprived by the malice of politics—you were barely ten when the Wall cut off your natural access to this most bizarre of grandfathers—Max Wuttke was full of broadsheet tales, because from his early youth, even before his apprenticeship with Kühn, he proved skillful at coloring the lithographic plates. I can already hear you raising objections. But what does this have to do with child labor? At least the little shaver was contributing to the household income. And in the twenties he could give me no greater joy than to bring me old prints that had been lying around at Kühn's or at Oehmigke & Riemschneider's, which he sneaked home—past the master, evidently—by rolling them up like scrap paper.

"I can still see before my eyes those broadsheets that transported the young rascal into raptures. There was one that portrayed Prince Friedrich Wilhelm and his princess driving in through the Brandenburg Gate. That occurred shortly before the Manteuffel government fell, when the Immortal was finally granted his long-awaited trip to Scotland. At the top was the date: 8 February 1858. And at the very bottom, in tiny print, was even the time: 'Five minutes before 2 o'clock.' A wedding picture! You could read about the thunder of cannon and pealing of bells for the newlyweds and about the welcoming speech by the mayor of Berlin, a man named Krausnick. Ah, well, the future crown prince was destined to enjoy only ninety-nine days as kaiser, and all the expense brought the people little benefit, only this lithograph.

"That reminds me of the gloomy sheet showing 'Napoleon Outside Moscow,' done only in black and white. And I have an indelible impression of that colorful sheet, dated 19 March 1848, reporting the Berlin uprising, with barricades and black-red-gold flags, with the freedom tree in the foreground and troops assembling in the background, complete with gun smoke.

"Now, in my late years, all this still lies before me as though it were fresh off the press. Those skirmishes at the barricades are as if imprinted. (Since then I've had a thing for revolution.) Today's images, by contrast, quickly cancel each other out. Nothing sticks. The deluge of images sweeps away with it anything it flashes before us. When I ask Mama after supper, 'Tell me, was there anything interesting on?,' she replies, 'Too much to take in. Just terrible what they show. When it's over, you don't know what was the worst.' Believe me, Mete, television is to blame for this pictorial amnesia...."

If we interrupt again here, it is to make Fonty get to the point of this letter, which was growing longer and longer with his vacillating moods. The point is Neuruppin. His thoughts headed off toward that destination after every tangent, and despite his fixation on the constant background noise at home:

"...I am certain, therefore, that we should know very little of the unfortunate revolution of March '48 and its casualties if, at the time, we had already had this memory-corroding kitchen television. But fortunately, in addition to Menzel's painting, which was never finished, we also had Gustav Kühn from Neuruppin! And I want to take a little outing to those parts. Very soon. High time I got out of Berlin, which is dreadfully fusty these days, divided no more, but unsure of what to do with itself. Once my compulsory exercise for the Handover Trust is down on paper and Mama has typed the manuscript for me—that much she wants to do, idiot box or no—I shall be off. A day-long outing in what I hope will be early-spring weather, and without my violent cold. Without Mama, unfortunately. Even though she is more from Beeskow than from Toulouse these days, the Mark Brandenburg does not tempt her in the slightest. Neuruppin? Ugh! You know how obstinate she can be. Of course, Alexander Gentz said the Ruppiners were philistines and dunderheads, one and all, but what really matters is that not only Schinkel was born there, but also…Ah, well, she cannot be persuaded. Furthermore, Madame refuses on principle to ride in the Trabi. 'Nobody's getting me into that thing!' she says. 'I'd rather walk on foot!'

"No, it's the same story with us as with you: not a word from Teddy. But the day before yesterday brought a curt letter from Friedel. A small volume of my collected Cultural Union lectures is still under consideration—a suggestion he himself made rather patronizingly across the table at your wedding reception, intended to raise my hopes. Of course I am entirely opposed—and not likely to change my mind—to business dealings between father and son, but I gave in so as not to offend him, and offered a few suggestions. But now he writes about 'necessary downsizing of our list' and about the 'drastic falloff in book sales across Germany.' He expresses himself like a colossally stuffed shirt. Quite unlike Professor Freundlich, who bristles with esprit even when he has a toothache. Yes, yes, I know: you have always said that the Jews' cleverness, their quick and waggish way with a phrase, gets on your nerves; but Germanic stolidity at best yields gloom.

"And that brings us back to your situation. I should like to see more sparkle in my Mete. Is there nothing that could cheer up your marriage a bit, difficult though it is? And if I now admit to you, in postal privacy, that I, too, have some lasting scars from bearing our Prenzlberg marital cross, I would at the same time ask you to take a quick look at Potsdamer Strasse: there, too, good cheer arrived only unexpectedly, and without knocking first.

"Thus the suddenly promised outing to Neuruppin has brought a ray of light into my life. And the same thing happened to me recently when I was in the Tiergarten—hardly any snow left—and again a child—it was a scrawny little kid of about kindergarten age—more demanded than requested that I tie his shoelaces for him. Had to squat down, with much creaking of the old bones, but it gilded the entire day and the following one as well; for which reason I say to you: Better to tie your shoes than to cry the blues. That goes for Schwerin, too, where, as I hear, the Handover Trust branch office is coming in for hefty criticism; your construction czar Grundmann, to whom I send greetings, certainly knows why...."

No letter for us. But a postcard tipped the Archives off: "Shall be paying my respects the day after tomorrow to the seated bronze...." That was enough of a clue.

Avoiding the western half of the city, they took the Berlin beltway to the highway heading for Rostock, leaving it before the turnoff for Hamburg, and in an hour or so, with no traffic jams to block the Trabi's way, they had reached the destination of their Saturday drive.

They made the trip on one of the first days of March. For a week now the Handover Trust had been moving its files and personnel from Alexanderplatz to the renovated colossus on the corner of Leipziger Strasse. Hoftaller had no sooner squeezed in behind the wheel than he hinted that the visit to Neuruppin should be interpreted as a reward. Because, "thanks to your dear wife Emmi," the memorandum "On the Progress of History" was ready in typescript, Fonty could indulge his yen for travel: "Now we can sit back and wait to see what the executive suite suggests in the way of cuts and revisions."

They set out in changeable weather; even intermittent hail showers pounded the roof of the Trabi. The desk back in Room 1819 had been left neat and tidy. The windshield wipers made sure, time and again, that the view remained undimmed. Only a copy of the memorandum, a mere forty pages, lay in front of the perforated brick in whose holes Fonty kept his writing utensils.

He was full of anticipation. He hummed a military march to the rhythm of the windshield wipers. He had tightened up the section on the paternoster, while adding further passengers: a steady flow of prominent personages rising and falling. He had even accepted some of Emmi's suggestions for deletions—for instance, taking out the anecdote about a highly decorated flying ace said to have tried out the corridors of the Reich Aviation Ministry as a roller-skating track.

When a white-on-blue highway sign announced the exit for Kremmen, he launched into a lengthy disquisition on the Briests' family history, especially the part concerning Luise: "Actually she is to blame. If she hadn't arranged that match between Instetten—with whom she'd had a dalliance as a girl—and her daughter, that charming yet foolish young thing..."

The rain was letting up. In the early-morning hours, cleaning women with their pails also used the paternoster. "I see it differently today: Luise von Briest, that frightfully solicitous mother...." And just as Italy's Count Ciano had once visited the Reich Aviation Ministry, later a Soviet Armenian by the name of Mikoyan had been a guest in the Ministries Building, where he was received with mixed emotions. And again the windshield wipers.

Then Fonty quoted from *Rambles*: the tiny province of Friesack. As Western sports cars zoomed by them, he found the tranquil garrison towns they were passing worthy of several digressions: he knew that the Third Hussar Regiment's Zieten Hussars had their barracks in Rathenow and a few squadrons of the Second Ulan Regiment had theirs in Perleberg. They patiently put up with being passed, again and again. "Never," Fonty exclaimed, "did I see Comrade Mielke use the paternoster!"

And then the passenger revealed to the driver that Effi had been called "daughter of the ether" by her mother, an allusion to Wildenbruch's play by that title. Effi on the swing. Effi swinging wildly, as she was lithographed by Liebermann. "Yet everything about Wildenbruch was capricious. And that's what the dumb masses call genius...."

But Hoftaller responded neither to garrison towns nor to the leitmotif introduced on the first pages of the novel. He was worried only about the head of the Handover Trust: no matter how confidently he presented himself, he made an increasingly troubled impression, and was under tremendous pressure, due to the hydra-headed scandals. The chancellor could keep out of it in Bonn, while he had to be the on-site whipping boy. The man already reeked of failure, even upwind. "The wrong man for the job!" Hoftaller exclaimed.

Suddenly the day-and-night-shadow was rocked by inner laughter. He gripped the wheel tightly to control the bigger and bigger shudders shaking his body. Then Hoftaller had to let it out, in bursts: "They'll never pull it off. Getting in over their heads. Didn't I say they couldn't handle it? Winding down, my foot; they're hopelessly tangled up. And who'll have to pay? The boss; who else? He can't see what's what anymore, our reconstruction-meister. Subsidiaries are being created everywhere, underhandedly, and then—right you are—run into the ground, ha! The wholesalers are playing grab bag with real gusto. And the insurance companies, and all the banks, ha! Why all the wailing and gnashing of teeth over foreign accounts? Or about rest stops on the autobahn? They're going like hotcakes. Interflug won't be flying anymore. And they'll shoot out the tires of the Wartburg in Eisenach. The same in Zwickau, where our Trabi came off the line. Mustn't allow any competition, oh no. This is what they wanted. Privatization, and the devil take the hindmost. And he's got him all right, sure enough! Just a matter of time before he has to step down, the ringmaster of this show. And if he doesn't, he's still finished, mark my words. Well, I just hope he signs off on your memo first. Took a quick look at it, Fonty. Reads well. Nice, the way you used the paternoster image, doing its job under any system. Something philosophical about how the three chiefs are all cut down to size as they descend from above.... Fabulous portrait sketches there... The Immortal's pen couldn't have caught them any better.... Or that crony of his, Ludwig Pietsch... Was an unreliable customer, but what he wrote about Menzel was just grand... You hit the nail on the head with the Goatee, too, but also with Hermann is his name-o, you know, the marshal's piping.... Something a little off when you get to the top man at the Trust, though. A bit too tragic, the way you've colored him in. He's no Winkelried! He's ridiculous, just plain ridiculous, a shooting-gallery target!"

This eruption and others as the traffic flowed smoothly. No construction, no backups. The two-stroker from Zwickau calmly consumed its blended fuel. The reliable windshield wipers went right-left, right-left. In changeable weather they glided past a landscape well surveyed in literature.

After Hoftaller had said his piece, Fonty put a date to one of his last visits to Neuruppin: barely fifteen years earlier, for the funeral of his mother, who had died long after his father, he had had to make the journey by train, which was complicated. "With Emilie, of course, who worshiped my mother, and who, by the way, took her side against my impossible but charming father..."

As they drove into Neuruppin, past military barracks, the sky cleared. The windshield wipers came to a rest. In fits and starts the sun shone through the clouds.

A small town within whose walls we would have liked to open a branch, to complement the Archives in Potsdam, in fact in the local history museum, small but well worth seeing, which Fonty and Hoftaller sought out at once; for Neuruppin was the birthplace not only of the great architect Karl Friedrich Schinkel, who imposed discipline on Prussia with simple restraint, but also of the poet of the Mark, the bard of Brandenburg-Prussia, furthermore an exemplary prose stylist, whose influence extended far beyond the Mark, the creator of immortal fictional characters, a master from whose school the author of *Buddenbrooks* issued forth, as well—we must concede—as the author of *Anniversaries*, whose writer's pantry was as richly stocked as it was cluttered.

Certainly he would have given them both top marks, with slight reservations, in a letter to Schlenther, let's say, just as he admired Keller, that "frightful Swiss," except for the poetry. He, the botched apothecary and turncoat revolutionary, he, the "man of long letters" and chat-fiend, living like a hermit in the garret above Potsdamer Strasse, he, whom we, too, following Fonty's habit, call the IMMORTAL, he, to whose service our Archives are dedicated, lived his earliest, and—after the return from Swinemünde—the last years of childhood here; Neuruppin was also the birthplace of a rather fine painter of oriental scenes, Wilhelm Gentz, overshadowed by greater names. It is to his son Ismael, by the way, that we owe a drawing of the Immortal preserved in the local history museum, a work whose quality was judged thus by its subject in a letter: "...I find it very good, but the others, my wife and daughter, are displeased...."

But because Fonty was more alive for us, also closer, as a sort of copy of a Liebermann drawing, we must emphasize once more—with the persistence of date-obsessed archivists—that it was here, one hundred years to the day after the Immortal, that Theo Wuttke was born, specifically on the corner of Klappgraben and Siechen-strasse, a few steps from the lake and the dock where the steamer tied up. Here he went to the Friedrich-Wilhelm Gymnasium, the same school, built shortly after the great fire of 1787, that Schinkel had attended. Shortly after his return from Swinemünde, the Im-mortal also had the opportunity, for a year as a fourth-former, and then in the lower third form, to study the Latin inscription above the entrance—a motto, by the way, that survived many political sys-tems, for which reason Fonty, right after the visit to the museum, as the two of them stood on the main square, with the old Gymnasium plainly in sight, translated the dedicatory inscription for Hoftaller, who had had to grow up without acquiring schoolboy Latin: "To the Citizens of Times to Come."

Now it must be said that the citizens of this changeover time we are describing did not want to see everything past and done with. The former Friedrich-Wilhlem-Strasse, which crossed the entire town from the Fehrbellin to the Rheinsberg Gates, was still called Karl-Marx-Strasse, and the larger-than-life bronze head of this most consequential of thinkers continued to stare at the two-storied school building with the small turret over its main entrance. Fonty and Hoftaller likewise looked in this direction, paying their respects to the citizens of times past and those to come.

There they stood, as if summoned to a photo opportunity. The blackened bronze made for an overwhelmingly menacing back-ground. The thinker's hair and beard were gleaming from the last downpour. But as the two of them stood so symbolically po-sitioned next to the bust of Marx, not a word was said of the worker-rallying manifesto; instead, Fonty insisted on quoting from *Childhood and Youth*: "The decision was made to send me to the Ruppin Gymnasium. The day after our arrival was a bright, sunny day, more March than April. In the course of the forenoon we went to the large Gymnasium building, which bears the inscription '*Civibus aevi futuri.*' Now I was supposed to become such a *civis....*"

Hoftaller, whose attention was fixed less on the boxy school and more on the bust of Marx, remarked, as if the moment had ar-rived to say good-bye to the colossal graybeard, "I ask myself whether the citizens of the time to come will soon have to melt this metal down for scrap. They won't get much out of it. And the street so fondly named after him is positively crying out to be renamed. They'll probably fall back on some Friedrich Wilhelm again...."

Meanwhile Fonty was hot on the heels of his extended school memories, those of the schoolboy Theo Wuttke: "Took my final exams here in '38. They called it an 'upper school' in those days— more Germanic. After that, Labor Service and the military. Of course you know, Tallhover, how I ended up at the Reich Aviation. It was duck duty. Always in the rear echelons. As a scribbler I didn't have to smell gunpowder. Am grateful for that, since fundamentally any form of heroism goes against my grain ... But never mind. After the liberation, this pedagogical barrack was called the Schiller School for a while. Then they tried the Immortal's name for a few years. But that didn't suit the leading comrades. Then they lit upon Ernst Thälmann. Now and for the time to come they're sticking with a temporary solution: 'Cultural and Educational Center'—don't make me laugh."

Having inspected the Schinkel monument on the square of the same name and waited out a brief downpour under the portal of the Schinkel church, they strolled through the dilapidated old part of town, along Siechenstrasse to the Cloister Church, then down to the lake and the landing for steamers, which, as a posted schedule promised, would ply the Ruppin lakes starting in May.

On the way back they looked for and found the spot where the father's Lion Apothecary Shop had once stood. Since everything looked unfamiliar, they paused only briefly. But close to the local history museum stood an old house, rotting away, where Gustav Kühn's pictorial broadsheets had been printed from stone plates. Here, too, only brief comments. They decided to skip coffee and cake, and instead walked—this time purposefully—back to the Trabi.

The sand-yellow Trabant was parked on Franz-Künstler-Strasse, close to the monument. We archivists must admit that this well-maintained park has not seen us often as visitors; but this time we cast a shadow.

As expected, they found the writer as a resting rambler, seated in bronze on a stone-hewn bench. He demanded to be viewed from all sides. Where he braced himself on his left arm, a metal plaque had been mounted on the decorative molding of the armrest. There one could read that this monument had been erected in 1907 to honor "the poet of the Mark Brandenburg."

He has been sitting there ever since, his coat unbuttoned, his right leg crossed over his left, his right hand, grasping a massive pencil, resting by his propped-up knee, while his left hand dangles casually from the stone shelf, holding open a notebook with the index finger. Next to the seated figure, who is bareheaded and stares off into the distance, the bench provides ample room for the metallic folds of the flowing coat and the hat, blackened over the years, which the resting rambler has put down. Its brim, turned up all around, forms a trench in which water from the recent downpours has collected. The crown, actually rather tall, looks flat because it has been crushed down. Over the armrest at the opposite end of the bench, where another metal plaque is mounted, giving the writer's name, birthplace, and two dates, the rambler through the Mark Brandenburg has tossed his famous scarf, into which, however, no Scottish pattern is woven. Furthermore, his hiking stick, cast true to life, leans against the stone armrest. The bronze gleams from wear, the hiking boots are polished. Suddenly a sparrow is perched on the hat, which, frozen in metallic form, now serves as a birdbath.

Perhaps the waistcoat revealed by the open coat should be mentioned, too—also that it forms horizontal folds—and likewise the cravat tied in a bow. We could lose ourselves in further details—maybe later.

As we did on our occasional visits, Fonty and Hoftaller gazed up at the monument, for it stands on a small mound, with boulders from the Mark scattered around the base, some of them overgrown with ivy. In addition, three stone steps lead up to the bench and the seated writer. Around the monument are trees, among them many birches. As the two looked up to this representation of the Immortal, taking him in first from one vantage point, then from another, crocuses and daffodils blooming at the foot of the boulders signaled the time of year. Again and again the sun asserted itself.

Although the likeness was larger than life, the question still arose: Is this really the man? The sculptor was Max Wiese, who made his home in Neuruppin and whose career did not begin until years after the Immortal's death. We know that he resorted to using his subject's son Theo as a model, even though Theo, at the time a military procurement councillor, bore only a rough resemblance to his father. If we quote at this point from a letter the father wrote to Mete, we do so not to say anything against the son, but to place the expressive power of the statue somewhat in context: "Theo is entirely his old self: well-meaning, good, decent, predictable, canny, and a philistine, but such a pillar of morality and righteousness that I could not bear to live with him...."

Fonty—who, we felt at such moments, was closer to us than the seated Immortal, because he had arrived in Neuruppin with his hat and scarf, his coat and his walking stick, to facilitate a comparison—smiled a little. He was probably thinking, as Theo Wuttke, of his own son, a section head in Bonn's Defense Ministry, that stickler for principle who for years had not sent his parents a greeting or a letter, and who, an official with security clearance, had got himself into trouble, or so Fonty feared. The day-and-night-shadow said nothing, so his subject spoke: "Reminds me colossally of Teddy; thanks to Friedel, I have a photo of him, also seated, which Emmi guards like a relic."

Since Hoftaller still remained silent, Fonty continued, "Of course when the monument was unveiled, in splendid weather, by the way, on 8 June, the good folks of my Neuruppin did not intend to honor the little-read novelist, but, rather—one could say, exclusively—the author of *Rambles Through the Mark Brandenburg* and also of Prussian-blue poetry. This is how the occasion unfolded: the festive procession had made its way from the reviewing area, which, as we have seen, is still called Ernst-Thälmann-Platz. They had assembled there and then droned their way through three victory-march poems. Needless to say: under black-and-white pennants and flags. That used to be schoolboy poetry. My father, who was doing his lithographer's apprenticeship at the time, was there, and often described this popular turnout to me. The publisher son was there, as well as a giant of a man, the monument's creator. But the person whose absence was striking was the daughter, Martha, who, by the way, is supposed to have thrown herself off a balcony ten years later—at least Reuter says as much in the biography...."

While Hoftaller lit a cigar from his Cuban supply, as if the news of this death had been his cue, Fonty inserted a brief pause to shift his thoughts into reverse: "Ah, well. It was her nerves. Just couldn't bear it anymore, this life. That's why I wrote to my Mete recently that even in Schwerin not everything could be utterly dreadful, and therefore, even if her husband were casting his eye on more and more properties, she shouldn't go off the deep end, shouldn't risk a nervous breakdown. I assume that explains why Martha didn't attend the dedication. But why Theo didn't come...And not a word from Teddy...But that's how it always was...."

Fonty, who was actually talking only to himself and hardly registered the cigar-smoker at his side, or at most as a natural shadow, suddenly seemed to mistrust his own words. He straightened up as if hearing a command from within: "At any rate, the whole business began with pealing of bells and the regimental band, directed of course by that fat Kapellmeister Heinichen. The normal-school and Gymnasium chorus sang 'Lützow's Wild and Daring Chase' and 'A Call Resounds like Thunder's Roar.' But also, as I would have wished, a song by the poet Paul Gerhardt. If I recall my father's account correctly, it was 'Go Forth, My Soul, and Seek Thy Joy....' Quite lovely...That sort of thing's always appropriate.... And after the obligatory wreath-laying there was a proper parade of all the Ruppin clubs and associations. Seldom had the town seen so many top hats in one place. The girls charming in white, under boaters adorned with ribbons. Sunshine bathing the entire scene. Of course afterward they had a monumental gala out by the Rheinsberg Gate. Went on into the night, with the weather holding....Yes, of course, with dancing...And no curfew..."

Hoftaller was still looking up at the monument. Above his uptilted chin his cigar pointed straight at the larger-than-life bronze. The poet seated on the stone bench gazed out over the heads of both visitors. "Wonder what he's looking at."

"He's gazing far into the distance, where else?"

"Don't think so. He's got his eye on something specific."

"All right, Hoftaller; my father always said he's looking in the direction of the railroad station. And he also thought the book in his left hand was the train schedule, and the poet had just checked on the next train leaving Neuruppin. . . ."

"Right. Off to Berlin. Where else?"

They both laughed. We would have liked to join in, and end their visit to the monument on a cheerful note. That would have been better for Fonty. We were worried about him, and loved him because in his mellowed elderly beauty he dwelt among us, while the bronze on the stone bench sat far removed; he was alive, while the Immortal merely demanded footnotes, cross-references, secondary labors.

But their visit could not end cheerfully with an anecdote. Before Fonty could unearth further memories of his father, once apprenticed to Gustav Kühn, something happened that Hoftaller had planned and worked out as the crowning moment of the trip to Neuruppin in the Trabi. Ah, if only a downpour had spoiled his scheme. Ah, if only a flood had intervened. But the sun seemed to have taken sides with the day-and-night-shadow.

The gap seemed made for it. Hoftaller invited Fonty—no, he ordered him—to climb onto the monument—over the Brandenburg boulders, up the stone steps, and once at the top to sit down between the poet and the bronze hat lying on the stone bench. And right away, pronto: "Get moving, Fonty!"

"What nonsense!"

"Make it snappy!"

"Not in my wildest dreams!"

"But in mine, and for a long time now."

"You want me to make a buffoon of myself? In my birthplace? In the place where I had to suffer, worse still, within whose walls he and I . . ."

"Oh, come now! Not a soul far and wide. Just so I can compare—it'll only take a second . . ."

"But I don't want to!"

"Afraid I must insist . . ."

"No!"

"Listen here, Fonty: this is the price you pay for immortality."

"No, no!"

It already looked as though Fonty would be allowed to stand his ground. Hoftaller seemed preoccupied with his cigar; apparently it wasn't drawing properly. Ah, if only the Cuban had gone out on him, but he licked the wrapping expertly—a professional in every respect—and was puffing away in no time.

"Makes me sad," he said, and then, "All right, we can do this the hard way. I guess I'll have to—contrary to my previous intention—bring up certain files that were stored till recently at Normannenstrasse, but are in a safe location now, whispering away to themselves, pretty embarrassing stuff...."

"Your threats are played out. Zoom right past me. Can't hit me anymore."

"Come on now. Who's talking about you, Fonty? This concerns a certain Section Head Wuttke in Bonn, who's been sharing his expertise with us for a good decade...."

"Leave Teddy out of it. Simply ludicrous. That stickler would never have..."

"That's what you think! Nothing earthshaking, of course. In Bonn he's responsible for uniform procurement, true, but even so, he gave us...And got a receipt..."

"That pillar of virtue! But sneaky, always was..."

"Want us to blow him sky-high? When the barn door's already closed? What would your poor Emmi say?"

"What do we care about that high-and-mighty son!"

"Up you go, now, Fonty! No more buts!"

What else could he do, standing there in his winter overcoat with his hat, scarf, and hiking stick, but give in, beneath the slightly piercing March sun. He knew only too well that Hoftaller never made empty threats. And even we would have advised him to play the fool in the spectacle now being staged before an almost nonexistent audience.

29

The Sermon on the Monument

What was at work here, besides mere whim? Why this humiliation? We puzzled over this for a long time, although obviously he was acting on orders.

As witnesses, and because Fonty was on terms of intimacy with the Archives, we suffered with him, the victim of all sorts of machinations and secret services. Our suspicion fell not only on Pullach and Cologne; we were sure that Normannenstrasse, although meanwhile sealed up tight, was still in operation, or in operation again. The suspicion, reflexive in the old days, that "the CIA must be behind this," would certainly have overshot the mark, and would hardly have been conducive to literary allusions; what did the Americans know about Brandenburg's aristocracy and the Prussian code of honor, about the Immortal's works or family, and hence about the tense father-son relationship perpetuated by the Wuttkes? Americans probably did not even realize that the less convincing half of *Quitt* was set in their own country.

For years, now, Fonty's arm had been vulnerable to twisting. In connection with his son Georg, for instance, of whose character as a child Fonty gave us a thumbnail sketch—"He was a dear boy, but marked by dejection. Even as a little twerp he liked to trot through Aunt Pinchen's living room with his hands clasped behind his back like Napoleon...." But when an untimely death cut short his career, the Luftwaffe captain was out of the picture. Friedel, whom his father described to us as a "dogmatic clod and truth-monger," had nothing to offer but pietist tracts. Aside from Martha—"poor little bird!"—and her actually rather banal cadre files, that left only the middle son, Teddy, who, because doubly exposed to incrimination, was under suspicion. He could be invoked at will and was thus present in front of the monument; on the one hand, as a ministry official on the informant list, and, on the other hand, as a procurement councillor who had modeled for the sculptor Wiese in his father's stead.

Eventually we concluded that it was none of the usual chicanery but rather the double constellation of the sons, Theo and Teddy, that forced Fonty to scramble over the boulders and up the steps; and the question that remained in our minds was only a hunch: could it be respect and affection that made Hoftaller want to see his subject elevated to such prominence?

So Fonty mounted the monument. "Utterly *ridicule!*" he exclaimed, yet made a fool of himself even so. Carefully, without crushing a single plant, he stepped over the crocuses and daffodils, then hoisted himself onto one of the ivy-wreathed boulders, was already on the next, larger one, then finally scaled more confidently the three stone steps, and now stood indecisively before the stone bench, whose seat was flanked by double armrests. Next to the sedentary, larger-than-life bronze he looked delicate, no, outrageously miniaturized. But whatever the proportions: Fonty had mounted his monument, on command.

"Sit down! Sit down now!" Hoftaller shouted from below. He pointed with his cigar.

"Haven't I done enough? This is mountain-climbing!"

"Sit down in the gap!"

"Feels so silly..."

"Move!"

So Fonty propped his much smaller walking stick next to the one cast in bronze.

"Now your hat! Put down your hat!"

So he took his hat, which had slipped sideways in the course of the climb, and jammed it on top of the casting, which was several sizes larger. The stone bench was too high for him, and he had trouble pulling himself onto it. Finally he succeeded.

"There you go!"

Some time passed, while he perched uncomfortably on the flat yet creased metal skirt of the coat belonging to Brandenburg's bard. It was funny to see the way his legs dangled, looking much too short.

"Now cross your right leg over the left!"

So he copied the statue's posture and awaited further orders.

"The hat's crooked. Straighten it! Now the stick: less of an angle! Perfect! Now take off your scarf and drape it over the armrest! There! We'll get it right. Looks great!"

Then Fonty was instructed to keep his legs crossed but to edge a little to the left, then a little more.

"Hold it there, Fonty. You're looking good."

But what to do with his hands? He did not dare to brace himself against the poet's bronze knee or reach for the bronze scarf tossed over the stone armrest; that would ruin the picture. Finally, without awaiting further orders, he assumed the preestablished position. He reproduced it approximately, though without pencil and notebook. Hoftaller seemed satisfied.

What gall! Now we could have shouted "*ridicule!*" But Fonty, too, felt the larger-than-life quality, now that he was seated arm in arm with it. Next to him, the original dominated the scene. Although there was no lack of similarity, the smaller version seemed like a shrunken model.

Hoftaller, standing with legs apart and cigar in hand, now instructed him to focus his eyes in the same direction. "Not just into the distance; look toward the station!" he shouted.

Now they both gazed in the direction where, once upon a time, at the Paulinenau station, as it was called then, railroad trains had arrived from and departed for Berlin. And that could have brought the performance to an end if, on this first rainy, then sunny day in March, chance had not decided to play its hand.

From the depths of the park, an audience appeared. An older couple, he clearly farther along in years than she, approached the monument. She was tall and slender, with a Gothic allure, he stocky and thickset. They looked a bit like people of yesteryear.

Although with his beret, slight stoop, and pipe, he presented the quintessential image of an artist on the lookout for subjects, it was she who wielded the camera. An idea that should have occurred to us was made a reality by a couple who now break into our report without regard for the posed scene. Barging in, yet as if it were the most natural thing in the world, they intervened in the flow of the narrative, for the duration of an intermezzo, as it were.

She snapped pictures, he gave instructions. His interest in details was suspicious. He seemed to be in a fine mood, the grumpy way he gazed out over his slightly askew glasses notwithstanding: "Terrific casting! Look, he's seated on granite. Clashes colossally, our friend up there would have said. Now from the front. Back up a little. Mind the focus!"

Since she called him *"Vadding,"* and he called her *"Mudding,"* the two of them seemed to come from along the coast, perhaps Western Pomerania. She was having trouble taking the pictures because her long, frizzy hair kept getting in front of the viewfinder. He grumbled under his walrus mustache, "That's what you get for refusing to wear a hat, or even a cap. Let's catch him in half-profile now, from over here."

Fonty sat as if cast in bronze; and Hoftaller, too, stood there turned to stone, cigar and all. The couple, however, refused to register either the day-and-night-shadow in front of the monument or his subject seated up above, the statue's double. They looked right through them. And to prove as much, the pipe-smoker exclaimed, "See, there's plenty of room next to our friend. Bet he was in Friesack earlier today and is about to set out for Rheinsberg. All right, let's get the inscriptions now, and that'll be it."

She must have snapped half a roll of film, frame by frame. His pipe kept going out. "Careful of the ashes," she said. Then they finally disappeared in the direction of the town: unequal yoke fellows who were living an entirely different novel.

But we were left to brood long and hard over fiction and reality, and Fonty, who had held admirably still, must have had thoughts of his own; he, too, had a tendency to overlook anything that did not suit him and to fill actual gaps with the offspring of his whimsy.

When the two of them were alone again, they acted as though nothing had happened. From Hoftaller's vantage point, the bronze and

Fonty were still displaying their respective half-profiles. As irritating as the size differential was, it became evident that the sculptor and art professor Max Wiese had succeeded in capturing a certain likeness, whether to the Immortal or to Fonty. First he had roughed it out in modeling clay, then stylized it in a plaster casting, and finally heightened it by chiseling the bronze casting. That proved that the son and war procurement councillor had served well as a stand-in.

The angular nose was convincing, as was the chin, receding under the bushy mustache, the forehead that seemed particularly high because of the absence of hair, and the gaze noted by many contemporaries—sometimes bold, sometimes quizzical. In comparison to Fonty's hair, which frizzed over the ears and crept down over his coat collar in strands, the bronze's hair was combed back and fell in two much too neatly coiffed waves over his nape, but as for the shaggy muttonchops, this hirsute detail was on the mark. Yet because the casting represented the rambler, a man of not even sixty who had not yet written any novels, and had put *Before the Storm* aside before it was properly begun, Fonty looked far older and more spiritual next to the bronze, with *Effi Briest* in his head, as it were, and after a prolonged spell of nervous prostration. Nothing robust, nothing dashing about him, only fragility, visibly accompanied by a nervous tremor. His gaze was also blurry, so much so that we could not suppress the ugly term "bleary-eyed."

"That'll do it, Fonty!" Hoftaller shouted. "Fabulous, the way you ignored those tourists. What a plague! Have to photograph everything. But actually look closely at something—that they'll never manage."

Then he waved him down with his cigar. But the old man remained seated. He sat there as if rooted to the spot, not budging. Ordered several times to hurry up and let go of the monument so he could climb down, he still clung to the bronze. We held our breath. He was resisting. No command, however sharp, could move him off the pedestal. Fonty refused to be ordered around, had settled in. And then he spoke from atop the monument.

At first disappointingly. We would have expected more, or something else—an outpouring, let's say, on the nature of immortality, seasoned with Schiller's eternal laurel-wreathdom and sprinkled with fatuous remarks on the idol of Weimar. And if not malicious swipes at others, we would have expected a panoramic survey of the complete oeuvre to be offered from atop the monument. We would have been satisfied with a passionate declaration of humanity's inalienable right to ambiguity. Or with something from *Stechlin,* when the old man, instead of an after-dinner speech on the occasion of Woldemar and Armgard's nuptials, mutters to himself, "Now in place of real men we have installed the so-called Superman; but actually the only men left are subhumans, and sometimes they are the very ones people insist on calling 'super.'..."

Yes, indeed! Couldn't he have stood up and, from that position, cursed the Prussian nobility once and for all, toasted the fourth estate, melted himself and the Immortal down, and literally recast them in a new posture?

Our hopes were misdirected. Perhaps he even disappointed his day-and-night-shadow. Nothing dramatic took place, not even something resembling a pantomime, although with Fonty clowning was still within the realm of possibility. He could have hoisted himself onto the lap of the seated bronze, Chaplin-style, hugged the rambler, showered him with kisses, flailing his legs all the while like a baby. A circus act would not have been too much to expect; and, as an audience suspended between dread and ecstasy, we would have loved to see him riding like an acrobat astride the rambler's shoulders.

No such scene was played out. Without theatrical gestures, moreover with a resentful undertone, Fonty first laced into the bronze seated next to him. Grouchily he took offense at the well-known fact that it was not the Immortal himself but his son, oh, no, not the bookseller and publisher Friedel, but the deputy procurement officer, then procurement officer, and eventually privy procurement councillor who had modeled for the sculptor and likewise, and with mulish tenacity, for the marble statue in the Tiergarten. Anyone could see it. The bronze radiated no spirit, no wit. Everything about it looked stodgy and leaden. The fellow sat there in borrowed trappings.

"A rustic squire in fancy dress!" Fonty exclaimed, now visibly agitated. But as indignant as he was, he remained seated. "And a self-righteous martinet, to boot. Sanctimonious, too, my fine son; he thought it was too much work to throw together a few rhymes for the opening of the French colony's festival. I had to do it all. Yet he complained that he never received real love from his father. As if our lives had ever been a bed of roses. On the contrary! My own old man never gave a tinker's damn about his *filius*. How could he or should he have? He himself lived the proverbial botched existence. One father like the other. But in the end, whether raising swine or rabbits, both of them were satisfied with themselves, though full of disdain for Neuruppin, this backwater garrison, this breeding ground for philistines, this German nationalist incubator for the Nazi plague. Old Wuttke never got over it that they fired him here, right over there, where the chimney of Oehmigke & Riemschneider is still standing, and all because he was a socialist. Lost one job after another from then on! And his marriage down the drain. And after the war, when he wanted to join the club and be a socialist again here, the Communists treated him like a mad dog, so he had no choice but to escape to the West. Neuruppin! A Schinkeled parade ground! Yet this is where it all started. Those first poems by the fourth-former. And then when it became unmistakable—I'm a poet; I want to be a writer—the old man just laughed: 'Well, go to it!' He was right to make fun of it: 'Just another pen pusher!'"

He forced all this out while still seated. But then Fonty slid off the stone bench, no longer wanting to be stuck to the cold, damp folds of the bronze coat. He positioned himself in front of the cast image he had just castigated. Now that he had had his tantrum, he was ready to exercise free speech. Before him stretched the park in its somber March dress, and below him, so to speak at his feet, lurked Hoftaller, an audience reduced to the smallest denominator.

We were on tenterhooks, expecting a major statement. But when he uttered the first words, announcing the topic, we were once more overcome with disappointment. He was drawing from an essay that appeared in 1891 under the pen name "Torquato," with the title "The Writer's Position in Society," in the *Magazine for Literature*. In the space of a few pages, the article laid bare the wretched condition of the members of the writing guild. Scandalous a hundred years ago, but today?

Fonty was of the opinion that in this country nothing had changed—"theoretically," he said. And so he spoke from the steps of the monument on the "Catalinian existence," as if he were discussing the current state of affairs; to make his point more readily understandable, and apparently with a larger audience in mind, he had the Roman conspirator Cataline join him on the platform as a literary precursor, and then pointed sternly down to where he could make out his adversary, "the overseeing opposition, the Tallhover principle." "Yes, indeed," he exclaimed, "What would we be without censorship, without supervision? You, my obtrusively unobtrusive sir, virtually serve as our good conscience!"

Having accepted this particular division of labor as right and proper, he turned to the terrible reputation of the entire guild. Still warming up, he quoted from a letter to Friedrich Stephany: "Fear is present, but no respect. And the most insignificant tax collector enjoys more status in official Prussia than we, who are simply consigned to a 'Catalinian existence.'"

Now he was no longer standing still, but was pacing back and forth in front of the seated bronze, as if he had the Red Chinese runner in his study beneath his feet. And in the course of this back and forth Fonty expatiated on the wretched position of the writer: "Those who trade in literature become rich, while those who create it either starve or barely scrape by. From this financial misery results something even worse: the ink slave is born. Those who work for 'freedom' are in bondage, and are often in a sorrier state than medieval serfs."

He then moved along to the great names of the "writer aristocrats," but after he had listed them, all in a jumble, from Gustav Freytag to Erwin Strittmatter, from the young Hauptmann to the late Brecht, he expressed the firm conviction "that good luck and occasional success do not improve the situation appreciably." After a longish lamentation—"Respect hardly ever comes the writer's way, always *blâme*. The entire métier has some screws loose"—he allowed a concession: "The writer's position is best when he is feared...."

And now, his eyes fixed firmly on Hoftaller, who was staring up at him, the cigar in his hand cold, he ascribed this fear of literature to a "certain detective quality inherent in the métier." On the one hand he celebrated the security watchdogs' fear of the "word, the clarifying, enlightening word that calls the emperor naked." On the other hand he found the "Poverty of Enlightenment" regrettable. He plunged Hoftaller, lurking below, into alternating hot and cold baths, promising censorship—an "unworthy and at the same time revitalizing institution"—a long life, and even "the lesser form of immortality."

But then suddenly, and with apparent good humor—he rubbed his hands—he made a suggestion for improving these conditions, a suggestion that he soon modified, however: "Approximately one hundred years ago it was still possible to assert, naively and well-meaningly: 'The state alone can effect a transformation here, if it attempts the unprecedented and declares one fine day: These unmannerly sons of mine are not really as unmannerly as they appear to you. And they are dear to my heart, they signify something, they are something....' Yet today, after the Workers' and Peasants' State spoke so paternalistically to its writers, pressed them to its broad breast, almost crushing them, and yet watched over them so solicitously, pampered them, kept them in preserves, like a prudent forest ranger, and placed all of them under the ever-vigilant supervision of its national-security apparatus, to the point that these previously despised writers interpreted such attention as respect, we see now to our horror that our wretched condition has remained the same. Even the most defiant pen can be suspected of having served the crown. Between the lines of the most courageous appeal one reads commissioned protest. And if the truth occasionally ventured onto the stage, these days its appearance is assumed to have had 'prior authorization.' There were advance warnings enough. Who managed to engineer poor Herwegh's audience with King Friedrich Wilhelm? 'I love a spirited opposition!' His Majesty fluted, and promptly ordered the hood-winked poet expelled from Prussia...."

Fonty had hit his stride. Now once more steady on his feet, he exclaimed with an accusatory gesture, his finger pointing downward: "That was your doing, Tallhover! You finagled that! You and your ilk always handled the shipping. Who put poor Loest behind bars in Bautzen? Who drove the best of them out of the country, chief among them Johnson, obstinate to the last? To whom does your own biographer owe the consequences of such intensive care? Who guarded our socialist fatherland like a locked institution and poured Kant's cynicism down our writers' throats like a categorical impera-tive whenever they acted up? It was you, you chameleon, you! In big-ger and bigger best-selling editions: you and you and you! And you always were an avid reader, because your love of literature, which I do not question, consummated itself in the endlessly hair-splitting censorship you practiced. We were so close to your hearts that their beating robbed us of our sleep. Your solicitude took the form of a large shadow. It was there around the clock. You're day-and-night-shadows, that's what you are. A whole host of shadows fell on us. You were appointed shadow-casters for the entire country. But it was us in particular to whose side you clung, and still cling. Therefore that essay from long ago needs to be revised, under the title 'The Shad-owed Writer's Position in Society,' for in the interim some things have changed, but in principle nothing has."

For just a moment Fonty let his final words linger in the air, then he scrambled down the stone steps and over the Branden-burg boulders, sparing the crocuses and daffodils, and not forget-ting before his descent to collect his hat, scarf, and walking stick, which he had placed or leaned, as ordered, on top of the bronze hat, over the armrest, and next to the bronze hiking staff. Slowly and cautiously he picked up his props and clambered down.

At the bottom Hoftaller received a trembling old man. After that resonant evocation of the state's undying solicitude, he em-braced his tottering charge. For a brief eternity he held him in his arms. And because the sun was still on their side, they cast a compact shadow. Then Hoftaller helped the exhausted speaker to

502

a bench, not hewn of stone but a normal park bench with bare shrubbery behind it. As he sat there, Fonty's shaking began to subside.

Had everything been said? Were there things left unsaid? We archivists do not want to contradict this idiosyncratic interpretation of the article on "The Writer's Position in Society," published under a pseudonym, but since we are not allowed to provide footnotes, we must now add some detail to the speech reproduced above in too abbreviated a form.

On the monument, the speaker first suggested curing the "Cinderella plight" of literature by means of "nationalization," then promptly added a warning: "But perhaps the remedy is worse than the current condition." And had a spell of weakness not brought him down from the monument, Fonty would certainly have concluded with the final sentence of that article dated 26 December 1891. Its suggestion was as follows: that for the good of the writers, any form of state solicitude be eliminated. After that we read: "The better remedy is: greater respect for ourselves."

A well-meaning piece of advice; yet perhaps in those days of changeover Fonty saw little basis for self-respect. In the West as in the East, writers were pillorying other writers. To avoid being incriminated themselves, they were incriminating others. Someone who had been celebrated only yesterday found himself tossed on the dustheap today. Things that had been said could be offset by things that had not been said. A saint was declared a whore of the state, and that singer who had once sobbed in pain could now manage only self-righteous squawking. Small minds took it upon themselves to judge others. Each and every one was under suspicion. And since the points of the compass continued to dictate the political winds, Eastern literature was to be traded henceforth at its Western scrap value. No, this was no time for "greater respect for ourselves." Fonty must have sensed as much as he clung, trembling, to Hoftaller, dependent on his encircling arms.

When he had overcome his spell of weakness on the park bench, they went on their way in accustomed concord. We were already familiar with this image: a special kind of team that grew smaller and smaller as it went, until it disappeared altogether.

Then, as chance, or the whim of directions from on high, would have it, the two tourists turned up again in front of the monument, he with his pipe, she with her camera, as though they had left something unphotographed. "Something's missing!" he exclaimed. But she said, "Doesn't look that way to me. You're imagining things again."

But she went back and photographed everything that was there, in the course of which her curly hair again blew over the viewfinder several times, and he rather grumpily surveyed the monument from all sides, searching for what was missing. Then they left.

Before we, too, went on our way, we had time to take a look across the way at the factory complex with its chimney. The brick walls, deserted and empty, gave no hint that soon after the First World War Theo Wuttke's father had found work there as a lithographer. Like the famous company of Gustav Kühn, Oehmigke & Riemschneider had printed the beloved Neuruppin broadsheets for over a hundred years, directly from stone plates; today these prints are collectors' items.

But that was not the reason Fonty remarked, more to himself than to Hoftaller, as they were sitting once more in the Trabi, rolling toward Berlin, "One should revive that kind of production. Could be done with the help of the Handover Trust. There's certainly no lack of material. Whether light-bulb manufacture or textile-working, they're closing up shop all over the country. Everywhere lives are going down the drain. Typical broadsheet tales..."

And then he is supposed to have added, "But otherwise it was pretty quiet in Neuruppin."

30

Yet Another Murder

The Bronze Age ritual chariot, the iron hand of Götz von Berlichingen, and other finds, as if Schoolmaster Krippenstapel had dug them up and Dubslav Stechlin had placed them in his cobwebby museum. Also the painting of an Abyssinian by Gentz, the bust of Voltaire, a chalice from the clothmakers' guild, and brightly colored pictorial broadsheets from the Kühn studio. And only then the gleaming, flawlessly dusted rooms, among them the Schinkel parlor, finely furnished against a background of red wallpaper, and the Immortal's blue memorial room, housing glass cases full of knickknacks, the folding table, a pier glass, and unused chairs reminiscent of a period on Potsdamer Strasse that had made do with a far more cramped apartment and worn seating arranged on a more meager carpet.

Back from Neuruppin, Fonty relived their short visit to the local history museum, which he described in a letter to his daughter Martha as "an instructive jumble." "Noted the absence of ridge turrets and weathervanes..." Then he got around to describing the encounter with the monument, which he referred to throughout as the "seated bronze."

"No new insights resulted, only much piffle about similarities, because this time I was not alone and could only stop by (as if on a flying visit), not luxuriate in a dialogue audible to us alone. You know, of course, that I seldom succeed in shaking off my day-and-night-shadow to venture forth, a second Peter Schlemihl.

"In times past, luck sometimes made it possible for me to duck out during a lecture tour and be alone for an hour or so with the seated bronze. Or meetings came about at my behest; for instance, seven and a half years ago, when I visited Rheinsberg, the Ruppin area, and along the way the garrison town that had meanwhile become unfamiliar to me; I had an appointment there that had been repeatedly postponed, and for certain reasons was difficult to schedule. The whole thing was treated as confidential, 'top secret,' so to speak. At any rate, I hoped to go unshadowed for this remarkable and still perplexing encounter, which took place in dry August heat, by the way. (At that time, as more and more often later on, you were probably on the Black Sea coast, on holiday.)

"For now I shall leave you to guess who could lure me, usually a rather cautious character, into such a conspiratorial meeting—and in such a prominent spot, too. We had agreed on it; it does not matter whether the suggestion came from him or from me. It turned out to be convenient that almost immediately after the meeting began, we had to share the view of the seated bronze with tourists, tour groups, and later even a class from a school in Perleberg; that left us quite inconspicuous on one of the park benches.

"Despite the heat, curiosity had led me to get there early. He arrived on the dot for our rendezvous, arranged, incidentally, through notes passed back and forth by a member of the Academy who was well disposed toward both of us.

"You will be wondering: Why that particular spot? Well, because he as well as I often sought the Immortal's counsel, although he made a point of doing it in a roundabout way, in riddles, saying, for instance, that he merely wanted to convey 'greetings from Ossian.'

"So I knew him from earlier meetings, when he was a tall, gangly youth, still with white-blond fuzz on his head and healthy; but even then—in the mid-fifties—I was confused (and amused) by his frightfully complicated probity. Now, my Mete, do I hear you uttering an 'Aha!' of recognition?

"As I said, I was there when he arrived. Perhaps the heat was affecting him. At any rate, as he came toward me, his bald head was bright red, and, as I soon noticed, he was in a pitiable condition. Imagine, if you please, a large, hulking man, stooped and sweating profusely, yet dressed from head to toe in black—not only a black leather jacket, but also a black leather tie—and that in the blazing sun.

"One could not miss the fact, to which I had been alerted, that within this overtaxed figure hid a far-gone alcoholic, whose strangely bloated appearance had something menacing about it; yet every phrase he spoke was delicately turned, sometimes tortuous in almost jesterlike fashion. He distantly reminded me of Theodor Storm and his obsessive Husumantics, of which this man's Güstrowisms were the equivalent, and equally crotchety.

"We had no sooner left the seated bronze to the tourists and sat down on a nearby bench than he began to question me about my earliest work for the Cultural Union. (He showed no interest at all in Theo Wuttke the file courier.) A stickler for detail, he wanted to know when and where I had given my lecture 'Melanie and Rubehn: Adultery with a Happy Ending.' After I had managed to satisfy him with more or less precise memories—it was in mid-May '52, in the Güstrow castle, that I presented my Berlin milieu study—he said with archangelic sternness that he found it impossible to accept an ending as conciliatory as that of *L'Adultera*. To him, the marital vows, written or unwritten, were sacred. 'A promise is a promise,' he intoned, looking troubled. At the same time he seemed to regret that he could not be a little lax (like me) on questions of morality.

"Then he began to speak in specific terms about Güstrow, offering the judgment that 'their lack of appreciation for the sculptor Ernst Barlach is a lasting blot on the people of Güstrow.' With that he drew a line, dissociating himself from the town, which, as he said, had been part of him since his schooldays. Of course, he was obviously still fixated on the place and its environs, indeed on all things Mecklenburgian. For that reason I found him happy, within limits, for in spite of his Republic-desertion—he insisted on speaking of a forced change of address—he had been granted permission to visit from time to time, probably with the help of intermediaries; in those days, our colleague Stefan Hermlin believed that as a highly respected member of the Academy he had the top comrade's ear. (Of course I refrained from mentioning Friedel or even Teddy, who never enjoyed such privileges, not to mention our Georg.)

"Then I had to give my companion on the bench information on the Cultural Union's third congress in Leipzig—he recalled the date, 19 May '51, with greater accuracy than I—and summarize for him the main points of the formalism debate raging at the time. When he attempted to entangle me, all too sophistically—it resembled an interrogation—in a pro and con on the subject of 'Lukács and the Consequences,' I confessed to my wavering partisanship in this matter, but conceded that at the time I had tended to disagree with the Brecht-Seghers line. Then I named for him all the laws adopted for the support of writers, listed under the rubric 'Our government supports the intelligentsia.'

"We laughed heartily at this dry-as-dust nonsense. He did not lack a sense of humor, but was tickled in a fiendishly inscrutable way, such that one could never be sure of the actual point of the joke. But because I had a certain 'liking' for this man, who enjoyed playing the Anglo-Saxon, I laughed with him, often without knowing exactly why. It was only on questions of morality that he could not take a joke. A Mr. Clean of the first water, he kept coming back to the case of *L'Adultera*, viewed in its day as scandalous, but at a farther remove as liberating; he insisted that adultery should be punished on principle. I let him talk, but made sure to tell him that the actual model for the character of Melanie, a woman from Berlin society, had lived a long and happy life up in East Prussia, surrounded by a swarm of small fry, and loved and respected by her Rubehn, whose extra-literary name was Simon. 'I know,' he said bitterly, and contested an idyll that in his eyes was undeserved.

"In the meantime, the seated bronze had to endure the wandering attention of a school group whose teacher was glorifying the 'cultural heritage' so loudly that one might have thought the Workers' and Peasants' State had of its own free will given birth to the Immortal, officially classified as 'bourgeois-progressive.' And then my colleague, so unhappy and so engaging, surprised me with—can you guess, Mete?—a present. He reached into his briefcase, black leather, of course, and pulled out some handwritten pages, from the fourth volume of his demanding, yet all in all outstanding, *Anniversaries,* pages that have my *Schach* as their subject; an episode of only a few pages, but a real gem! The character of the teacher splendidly realized. The ideological narrowness of the period captured with frightful accuracy.

"To whet your appetite for reading: the passage deals with a class from a school in Mecklenburg that in the fall of '50 reads the tale of the 'shirker' *Schach.* The reader discovers what a hornets' nest the teacher Weserich gets himself into with this assignment. The passage also deals with the significance of street names, and with the trouble the poor children have with all the foreign words; in this connection, I must admit to you that when I was still a newly certified teacher I had a terrible time giving up *nonchalance* and *embonpoint,* especially since the Workers' and Peasants' State had prescribed abstention from the Frenchified salon style like a cathartic.

"To make this unduly long letter even weightier, I am enclosing the manuscript pages I received from my Dr. Speculatius, hoping that they will give you more than just reading pleasure; for on the one hand he treats ironically the pedagogical compulsion to engage in social criticism, while on the other hand he finds in the sleigh ride organized by the officers of the Gendarmes Regiment an image for the enemy of the working class—the costly salt laid down in August to simulate snow, the haughty lieutenants.

"By the way, this episode contains quotations from several letters on the subject of *Schach,* among them the complaint I make at being eternally stigmatized as the 'Brandenburg Rambler.' Likewise there is mention of the all-too superficial praise of my talent for concreteness; of course, I invented everything, down to the smallest blade of grass: I never set foot in the Tempelhof church; Wuthenow Castle did not exist—in a letter to Mama I had a good laugh at a Brandenburg historical society that soon after the novella appeared announced a boat ride across the lake to that very castle. In the case of *Schach,* you can see with what precision one must lie and how the favorably disposed reader will spoon up the soup straight from the pot, so long as it has been well flavored with literary invention, and the seasonings have been expertly adjusted.

"Chance—to the extent it exists—would have it that the schoolchildren swarming around the seated bronze were fixated, like us, on this epitome and victim of ludicrousness; we heard the teacher droning on. Of course I politely expressed my gratitude for the very legible copy—to an author, by the way, whom they have also neatly categorized and put into a pigeonhole labeled 'Writers of Divided Germany.' That is as *ridicule* as all stereotypes. No, when it came to literature, he was number one, and without doubt a solitary, whose appalling death, reported not long afterward, left me feeling lonely.

"Ah, my Mete, what an outcast he seemed as he sat there, desperately trying to keep up appearances. The massive skull, where not a hair could grow anymore, beaded with perspiration. Ah, if only I had had laurel handy!

"True enough: there was much about him that was disturbing; his frightfully Teutonic manner was even off-putting; and yet, if a trip to England ever became possible for me, I would go to Sheerness-on-Sea, where he met his wretched death, and place a wreath of immortelles there....But as he sat beside me, imprisoned in his own rigidity, one could only feel sorry for him. I should add that around the time we had our 'conspiratorial rendezvous' in Neuruppin, his marriage was said to be on the rocks.

"And why? I suspect ordinary jealousy, which in his case had sprouted such luxuriant fictional images of carnal excess that the whole world, including his publisher, believed the hair-raising story. I, however, was not persuaded by even his darkest allusions, despite the fact that I knew, and know, what devious traps the state security imposed on us could, and presumably still can, set. He was lying in wait all too avidly for confirmation of his mania, the always convenient theory of betrayal; yet it was probably just a brief fling, as is usually the case in life. The story, however, had more literary appeal.

"For obvious reasons, our secret meeting did not go unnoticed. (No sooner did I get back to Berlin than this person and in particular that person knew all about it.) My day-and-night-shadow was gracious enough to view my 'unauthorized contact' with indulgence, and marked the 'Johnson Case,' filed in his papers under the code name 'Ossian,' with the label 'Agency Misconduct Due to Excessive Ideological Zeal.' Just recently, when we were standing together before the seated bronze, he said, 'That troublesome talent should have been given a chance to straighten out his thinking and develop over here, instead of over there, all alone and at the mercy of the market. We were guilty of inadequate solicitude.'

"He actually said that, 'inadequate solicitude'! Not a word about the way the man died far away in his solitary, self-imposed exile. Not a word about the obtuseness characteristic of that agency, and the Kantian imperative of categorical cowardice. And of course not a word about the broken marriage.

"That brings me to you and this Schwerin nastiness. You fret and fret, but believe me, elsewhere there are also people who have reason to fret. (For weeks now I have been alarmed by the desperate cries of my faithful correspondent in Jena, whatever the ironic finesse with which the professor broadcasts his SOS.) So when you bemoan the fact that lately your Grundmann has spared no effort to transfer Mecklenburg grazing lands the size of an entire agricultural cooperative into the hands of a Bavarian meat wholesaler, and that this far-flung land-taking has the blessing of your local Handover Trust office, it comes as no surprise to me. Ever since the move from Alexanderplatz, much larger scandals, originating in Halle and Dresden, have taken up residence in a central location, in other words in the Ministries Building. There is a colossal stench of legal fraud. Yet because I have been familiar with this smell since sulfur-yellow days, I hardly even wrinkle my nose. Fortunately, barely a whiff of it reaches me in my seventh-floor cell, where not a breath of wind stirs.

"Now and then I venture forth into the Tiergarten, which, in this mild spring with its overly punctual first buds, has instructed me of late that Germany is no longer merely a concept. It is a powerful fact; for when I was hoping for a little chat with Pietsch on my favorite bench—he failed to appear—three or four ruffians approached who could not bear the sight of me. They apparently took me for a Turk, whom they were determined to be rid of. Well, I challenged these scoundrels, calling them to order with stern Prussian admonitions, reducing them to a pitiful little band, and— like Seydlitz at Rossbach—finally putting them to rout.

"After this incident, the Tiergarten proved once more pleasant and inviting. But today is my letter-writing day. I want to, or absolutely must, write to Teddy, no matter how little hope there is of a reply. Rumors, or, worse still, suspicions have reached my ears that pertain to him (and thus to us all). It will never end.

"In France, writing must be taking another form, for letters are infrequent. Mama, although plagued with her chronic bladder problem, is enterprising during the day—taking in a movie with your chatterbox of a girlfriend, or going shopping. KaDeWe, however, has lost some of its appeal. And she's even had her fill of the idiot box, 'watched it to death,' as she says. Thank goodness no more work has been dumped on me, and the boss has not found time yet to review my memorandum. He rushes from meeting to meeting. I think he is in hot water, and in deep...."

That was indeed the case. It was in all the papers. The Handover Trust was under siege. A Moloch or a monster—that was what they called it. The word on the street was that the Trust was privatizing ruthlessly; it was a colonial agency, subject to no parliamentary control; everywhere, but especially in its outposts, telltale signs of networks, old and new, could be detected. Because here and there Western real-estate sharks and Eastern change ringers had made common cause, people spoke scornfully of "pan-German backroom deals." As for Halle, the term "Swabian Mafia" had come into circulation. Even in cautious editorials, tentative questions raised their heads: Will all competition be throttled? Will the motto "Line your pockets!" become liberalism's *dernier cri*? When will the head of the Handover Trust give thought to submitting his long-overdue resignation?

But he stayed put, and let the word go forth: We're just getting started; efficiently and without false compunctions, the residual burden must be wound down. That happens to be our thankless task: winding-down all of it.

And this verb became the word of the year. An ugly term, as if made to flow from the lips of colonial masters, a term long-suffering and imperious by turns. A term that made no mention of human beings; yet because winding-down caused the number of unemployed to increase from month to month, human beings could not be smuggled out of the picture, whatever the talk of necessary right-sizing or becoming lean and mean. And further linguistic monstrosities were unleashed, consonant with the regulatory mechanisms of the free market economy: investment barriers were to be eliminated, residual risk accepted, excess capacity capped, plants decommissioned, locational advantages seized.

Altogether, the term "location" began to undergo a shift in meaning. Later, as we know, in the absence of a nation, the concept of "Business Location Germany" got into circulation; and, quickly spreading to the West, all these terms turned out to be the pan-German mortar in the edifice of unification.

But at first it was only us, only the East. The Handover Trust and its well-known head made enemies. And this all-powerful agency and its centrally located boss had the reputation of being extraordinarily diligent—they set about winding down industrial complexes, real estate, publishing houses and their contents, slaughterhouses and holiday resorts, agricultural collectives and the people's castles, as if they had a quota to fill, meanwhile draping their diligence, which was rewarded with bonuses, in reports of success. No wonder they made enemies, perhaps a few enemies too many.

This and even more Fonty told the head of the agency, when they happened to find themselves riding in the same paternoster cabin. A conversation sprang up at once and without ceremony. They were on their way up as Fonty cautiously expressed his concern about the boss.

Two voluble gentlemen stood facing one another. Although nothing was mentioned about the memorandum, they had much to say. Something imponderable, something that went beyond mutual sympathy, was present in the cabin with them. And since their discussion did not break off, they spent a good quarter of an hour in the paternoster, and were closer to one another than a father and son can be.

They rode right past the turning points in the attic and the cellar, and after Fonty had unburdened himself of his concerns, they promptly fell into that timeless form of chatting that merely touches on everything and omits nothing. They would certainly have found even more material for this uninterrupted trip up and down if the security officers had not suddenly lost patience and done what they were trained to do: they pulled first Fonty, then the boss out of the cabin. The latter regretted this police action and apologized: "Too bad; we were having such a good time. Very convincing, your theory of the novel. Must continue this conversation some other time..."

Fonty, by the way, received a tongue-lashing after being dragged out of the cabin and patted down. But this security-service rebuke hardly troubled him, for the conversation with the boss in the paternoster marked the beginning of a friendship, which, despite its short duration, escalated into genuine fondness.

"Actually he is just a frustrated bookworm, distracted by excessive activism." That is what Fonty told us as he gave the Archives a blow-by-blow account of his "purely accidental yet seemingly providential encounter" with the boss. At first he had tried to give vent to various reservations he had about the godforsaken and hate-generating winding-down business, but then, because he had referred to "Treibelesque machinations and greed," they had gone on to discuss the Immortal's novels. "That is presumably why the boss expressed his frank curiosity about reading. When he was back in secure hands again and already being swept away by his entourage, he called out to me, with almost boyish enthusiasm, as I was about to take the next cabin up, 'I'm fascinated by that novel— for instance, why the poacher has to shoot the forester....' But he could barely make out my reply, because I had already half-disappeared on my way up."

Little suspecting the outcome of this friendship, we were amused at Fonty's literary adventure. But because this time there seemed to be no end in sight to his visit, we tried to get rid of him, before he became a pest, by making conspicuous reference to all the work waiting to be done. One of us advised him not to read so much into the meeting with the boss. What was so important about it? Actually the chat in the paternoster had had only the following result: thanks to the boss's simple curiosity, sparked by the story *Quitt*, a certain consultant to the Handover Trust, whom everyone called Fonty, had been brought face to face with one of his "problem children."

Who is familiar with *Quitt* nowadays? Even we give this hybrid work short shrift. At most we receive queries from abroad—France, America—pertaining to its genesis rather than to the question "Why does the poacher have to shoot the forester?" For the most part, inquiries focus on the influence of a writer of adventure stories named Möllhausen, now completely forgotten, and his once highly successful novel *The Mormon Girl,* in other words on the connection between its two settings on different continents. And because the Immortal met Balduin Möllhausen several times at Dreilinden, the hunting lodge to which, in the early eighties, Prince Karl Friedrich invited scholars and writers, but above all military aristocrats, for roundtable discussions, the field proved relatively fertile. Dreilinden is included in *Five Castles,* written at about the same time as *Quitt.*

Eight times the author was among the guests, many of whom had resonant names: von Schlieffen, von Caprivi, von der Goltz, von Bonin, von Wangenheim, von Witzleben....But this, as well as any discussion of influences, which could include von Bodenstedt or even Karl May, would take us too far afield.

Although even Fonty called *Quitt* unsuccessful, he considered the story interesting, whereas he viewed the detective story *Under the Pear Tree* as more accomplished, but dull; the latter also deals with a murder. To make *Quitt*'s fundamentally straightforward plot easier to follow, let us summarize its elements: a likable perpetrator who nonetheless defies the authorities; an unbearably self-righteous victim who tends to abuse his authority. From the beginning, the reader sides with the poacher, a murderer out of necessity, as it were. Since the poacher manages to escape to America immediately after murdering the forester, the crime goes unpunished for a long time. He starts a new life among the Mennonites and Indians, lives communally with the adherents of many religions, makes the acquaintance of another murderer, begins to fall in love with a Mennonite girl, and eventually atones for his crime in death, whereupon the reader is transported back to the scene of the crime in Silesia, among Berliners on summer holiday. Thus ends the tale of the hard-hearted forester Opitz and the poacher Lehnert Menz, a rebel against law and order. One could have answered the head of the Handover Trust thus: Where hatred confronts harshness, a motive is not hard to find.

The material for *Quitt* was provided in March '85 by the Immortal's faithful correspondent Georg Friedlaender. A local magistrate, with his residence and official post in the Riesengebirge, he was familiar with murders. In 1890, a prepublication version of the story appeared in the ladies' magazine *The Garden Bower,* but when it was published later by Hertz in book form, it attracted few readers. Yet because the Immortal had initially written full of hope to Friedlaender, enthusiastic about appearing in *The Garden Bower*— "...I am happy to eat from the same bowl out of which 300,000 Germans eat"—Fonty felt the urge to write to Professor Freundlich soon after the conversation in the paternoster. After reporting on his continued inactivity on the seventh floor, and on all sorts of familial matters, he got around to the problem child *Quitt* and thereby to his conversation with the boss:

"And again and again, for quite a few Our-Fathers. My dear Freundlich, you would have laughed yourself silly if our decidedly off-duty paternoster murmuring had reached your ears. Seven, if not nine, times we rocked along from the attic to the cellar, from the very bottom to the very top, without any fear of those admittedly always somewhat uncanny turning points. In the beginning, the talk was only of internal matters, i.e., fairly precarious cases; then it turned to murder. You will be thinking: What could be more obvious? And in fact this transition from one topic to the other did not require any memory-tickler.

"Once we had merely touched upon *Under the Pear Tree* and *Ellernklipp,* rather than discussed them exhaustively, we got around to the obsessive relationship between the forester and the poacher. 'One of them had to go,' I said to my boss, who is well read and a professed admirer of Effi's. He said, 'I must admit that again and again urgent redevelopment projects have interfered with my reading. And what's going on here at the moment is completely crushing the book lover in me.'

"'That I call intellectual suicide!' I exclaimed, which at once brought me to the topic of the many suicides in the news, usually ascribed to social hardship. But from there I promptly moved to literary suicides—for instance, in *Schach von Wuthenow, Count Petöfy,* and *Stine.* And then duels! He at once brought up the shots exchanged between Instetten and Crampas. Because he viewed the code of honor that led to that exchange as ridiculous but 'normal for those times,' I had to assure him again and again that *pistolero* cases like those in *Cécile* and *Effi Briest* were avoidable, if not in principle, then certainly on rational grounds. As indeed that dronebag and side-slapper van der Straaten in *L'Adultera* was able to muster the 'bourgeois generosity of spirit,' as I called it, not to shoot the adulterous Rubehn, but rather came around, after some choleric outbursts, to allowing his Melanie to experience the love he was denied. Certainly his Jewishness played a part—a circumstance, by the way, that also prevented the faithful correspondent Friedlaender from resorting to pistols in an affair of honor against an aristocratic adversary. Thank God! we would say today. That turned out for the best. But to my boss I said, 'The clash between forester and poacher was inescapable. Both are right. Both have plausible reasons for wanting revenge. No matter which of them falls, one of them must. That, too, is a law.'

"Then I had to concede that in this matter I often find myself vacillating. I said, 'Sometimes I weigh in on the side of the forces of law and order, sometimes on the side of the anarchic desire for liberty. Even though I basically favor order, in *Quitt* the forester had to be felled, because only the poacher could be heaped with so much guilt that in the course of the story he would feel compelled to carry this heavy baggage with him to America. If Opitz the forester had got off the first shot, and the poacher Lehnert Menz had fallen down dead, the story would have been over in a flash, for a state official always sees his actions as justified, and never experiences guilt; consequently he repeatedly provides grounds for others to kill him—in one capacity or another; the law may be on his side, but not life.'

"When I said that, my boss laughed in that boyish manner that comes so easily to all these driven, energetic men in their late forties who are determined never to grow up. (In the West they are called 'Sixty-eighters,' a reference to a pseudo-revolution that we were spared.) After tossing off a few jests about my 'killer logic,' as he called it, he was overcome by something like pensiveness.

"He wondered seriously whether the forester-poacher relationship I had painted on the wall for him could apply to his own situation. I tried to steer our conversation back onto a literary/ fictional track, mentioning the Communard L'Hermite, who likewise fled to America, after murdering, or rather executing, a bishop. Living under one roof with the poacher Lehnert, he, too, was consumed by guilt. But my attempt at distracting him only piled on further ambiguities and made everything 'even worse,' as my Emilie always says.

"'I understand you perfectly,' my boss said. 'It needn't be a forester who's cut down. Think of how the banker Herrhausen died or of how that Saarlander with the literary name survived only by sheer luck. But I could be in someone's crosshairs, too. I also stand for law and order, embody the power of the state, so to speak. Your *Quitt* offers a model, even if you regard this novel as artistically flawed. It's quite clear: in this scenario I play the target, but nonetheless must proceed strictly according to the law....'

"You can believe me, my dear Freundlich: that's how these gentlemen are—charming in manner, yet unrelenting in matters of business. By the way, I was coming from the seventh floor when he got on at the fourth. He opened the conversation straight off with an ingratiating 'May I call you Fonty?' (I wonder what you, as a certified jurist, think about these questions of law?)

"Yes, my dear friend, I often find myself reminded of your involuntary emeritus status. For what happened to you in Jena— when they forced you, an eminent scholar, to go back to school and submit to an examination used for accreditation in the West— is not that different from the winding-down being conducted here. One plant after another is being sold off for next to nothing, whereupon the buyer closes it down, lest any real competition spring up. That's what happened with the airline Interflug. The death knell for the Trabi in Zwickau will be echoed when the bells toll for the Wartburg in Eisenach. Our in-house theory goes as follows: by the light of day, everything is scrap! But it would be equally correct to say: In pure sunlight, everything burns.

"Yet all this involves human beings, does it not? (What a disdainful attitude toward life is expressed in their refusal to grant you the modicum of oxygen for which we are all gasping, big fish and little!) But no, such a simple insight merely gets in the way of the Handover Trust statute; from its perspective, everything is property. Would be no surprise if someone felt the itch to help a different law take effect. Without poachers, no foresters, and vice versa. But on that subject, more anon...."

Fonty's letter to Professor Freundlich contains a postscript, crammed into the margin: "You must not view your daughters' tandem decision in favor of Israel—whether right or wrong—as a step that compounds your already difficult position; as fathers we should know that we are going to lose our children one way or the other."

One virtue was interpreted positively on every floor of the Trust: with Prussian punctuality the boss arrived in Berlin early every Monday morning, stayed there through Friday evening, took the last plane out, and landed late in Düsseldorf, where he spent the weekend with his family on the left bank of the Rhine, quietly— provided he had not stuffed too many winding-down proceedings into his attaché case.

That is how we pictured this dynamic man, and Fonty confirmed the reports of his mobile work rhythm. Elsewhere, a bad habit was becoming widespread: other Westerners in leadership positions did not turn up until Tuesday, around noon, in Berlin, Erfurt, or Schwerin, in Halle, Dresden, or Potsdam, and headed west again on Thursday evening, for which reason they soon came to be called "three-day trippers."

Not so the head of the Handover Trust. His mania for work did not fit any "Wessie" stereotype. Often he did not fly back until late Saturday afternoon, and he frequently stayed at his desk far into the night, or paced through all the rooms in the secure area of the building, for which reason the main entry on the fourth floor was protected by a pane of bulletproof glass.

Yet it was not unheard of for the boss to leave the secure area at midnight, shaking off the security detail assigned to him, and rush alone through the deserted building, changing from floor to floor and speeding along the linoleum corridors as if they were running tracks; for he was not rambling around the building—he was on roller skates.

"Too much sedentary work, not enough movement" was the reason his doctor gave when he ordered him to exercise. Since the paternoster—like him—did not rest at night, the Handover Trust boss could change floors effortlessly without taking off his skates, thereby expanding his field of action.

And so it came about that late one Friday night—it must have been in mid-March—the consultant Theo Wuttke happened upon him on the seventh floor, shortly after midnight. The boss was skating along the particularly long corridor in the north wing, like a champion in training. He accelerated, settled into a steady pace, lowered his feet to glide, lifted one, then the other, to gobble up space, sped along in the posture of a long-distance runner, driven by ambition even as he sought medically prescribed relaxation, outdoing the previous night's performance by a fraction of a second, and probably had half a dozen kilometers behind him when someone in laced boots came toward him, returning from the men's room.

Although we know that the boss had addressed his consultant familiarly as "Fonty" in the paternoster conversation, we suspect that in this encounter, long past normal bedtimes, he greeted him with a jovial, "So, Herr Wuttke, still at work?" and not in passing; in fact, he immediately interrupted his training.

And Fonty could have explained his late-night diligence with allusions to the familial situation on Kollwitzstrasse: "My wife doesn't like me to be out so late. But it's only here that I can find the peace and quiet for gathering any thoughts that aren't mired in the present...."

We are certain that not a word was said about the roller skates. No astonished sideways glance, no "By the way...." Even if the boss had whisked along the corridor with wings, Fonty would not have made him into an angel. He merely noted briefly, "As I see, for you, too, Herr Doktor, there is no end in sight."

He discreetly overlooked the hardened rubber rollers, and the boss likewise saw no reason to explain his athletic activity, especially since he did his skating not in a warm-up suit but in ordinary business clothes, though without tie or jacket.

He found his own midnight restlessness perfectly normal, and could summon his youthful laugh at will. But then confessions came pouring out of him: "You can believe me, Herr Wuttke—or may I call you Fonty, like the other day?—the work they've piled on me...And then there's the responsibility...After all, we're dealing with people here, not just numbers....I mean, every signature impacts a couple of thousand lives....It's damned hard in every case, what's expected of a person....Should have refused, when this job...Am actually, or as they say here, theoretically, pretty much a committed social democrat...Was even an undersecretary under the socialist-liberal coalition...And only because major challenges have always attracted me....At one point it was steel production, at another point the coal crisis...But unfortunately this time there's no getting around the old heave-ho....Besides, I don't much care for the way our chancellor pawns off the dirty work on others...while he...Oh, well, it's understandable....As a historian, he wants to keep out of it...wants to avoid any speck of guilt....That's how he wants to appear in the schoolbooks....The unification chancellor, towering above everyone else...while I...But what's the point of whining...That's how they work, the laws of the free market....A person's got to know when he's...If you burn out, you can be replaced...."

Here Fonty, who found the boss's situation poignant, and in any case viewed the current chancellor as "a watered-down Bismarck," may have offered his nearby office—"my modest cell"—as the location for a nocturnal chat. Or perhaps he comforted this disheartened man, who seemed tired of the infernal redevelopment project he had been put in charge of, with one of his sayings: "Life often turns out this way: you set out to bag a quail and end up shooting a rabbit—the main thing is to hit something!"

At any rate, the boss accepted his invitation. Without having to unbuckle his roller skates, he was soon seated on the burgundy sofa, formerly located, if not in the furnace room, then in the attic. Only a few days earlier Hoftaller had succeeded in favoring Fonty with this piece of furniture, thought to have disappeared. And in the corner where his day-and-night-shadow had sat only a year ago, there now sat the head of the Handover Trust.

This gentleman extended his legs straight out, skates and all, stretched lazily in his sofa corner, and exclaimed, "Your office is so homey! Ours are wall-to-wall interior-decorated. Everything functional. The steel armchairs and fiberglass side chairs are supposed to encourage sober calculation. Maybe it works. But on this sofa of yours, I feel..."

Because the sofa's rustling inner life was a little irritating at first, Fonty put his boss at ease with one of the anecdotes he had in reserve for every occasion: "The stuffing of this piece of furniture has much in common with the poet Scherenberg's rustling pillow, where his wife hid her unpaid bills...."

And then they talked. The concerns of the head down-winder were received with sympathy. Whenever he seemed in danger of sinking into resignation, Fonty bucked him up with further anecdotes—for instance, the one in which the criminal about to be beheaded had his wish granted—to see his wife in her wedding gown once more. And when, despite all the anecdotal bucking-up, the grand redeveloper suddenly began to have doubts about German unification, Fonty expressed a comforting thought he had often tried out on Hoftaller: "Still, we must congratulate ourselves for the way it came about...."

Finally the host offered his guest a shot of Wilthen brandy, not without calling attention to the label of this people's enterprise. Now their subject was no longer the poacher Lehnert and the forester Opitz, but the arsonist Grete Minde. As they whiled away hour after hour, night began to give way to day. Not of his own volition, but on the urging of Fonty, who was concerned about him, the boss finally got back on his roller skates. He had no sooner emerged in the corridor again than he was off to a flying start, his powerful movements swooping across the entire width of his racetrack, and was so remotivated on his skates that some of his dynamic thrust found its way into all the offices of the Handover Trust, and eventually produced the desired results.

But this incident is treated further in a letter to Fonty's granddaughter, which, however, was not committed to paper until three weeks later, shortly after the murder.

Here we brake the onward rush of events with an interpolation, for we must back up and supply additional details before we quote at length. For instance: the sofa in question stood to the left of the office door, with a clear view of the desk and the window, through which the interior courtyard could be seen. Between the desk and the sofa was a cocoa-fiber rug, recently donated by Hoftaller.

This and more we must report from hearsay, since we were never allowed to visit Fonty at the Handover Trust; and certainly we would have been afraid to set foot there. "Anything not to attract attention!" had always been our motto. What would the Archives have had to offer, other than our endlessly piling-up expenses?

This much is certain: the boss paid him two more visits. The solitary roller-skater. Midnight chats. The crackling sofa. Shots of what was left of the publicly owned brandy. Thoughts and speculations about *Quitt* and the consequences. Retrospective reflections on the great fire in Tangermünde. Perhaps even a few small secrets allowed to come up for air in the wee hours of the night. Thus began a friendship that had little time to be savored. Afterward Fonty always spoke warmly of the head of the Handover Trust. "Nothing worse than being condemned to success," he said to us, only to relativize his comment immediately: "No doubt about it, speed was his element. That he could do: be tough. Yet he should be judged as a human being among human beings, and only on his own terms...."

31

Frau Frühauf's Potted Plants

"My dear child, now it has happened, the deed that cannot be undone. A thought, stubbornly convinced of its own correctness, went looking for a target, and a shot was fired; yet life goes on, as though this loss had been calculated in, as if the free market demanded this price; and indeed the stock market marches on.

"Of course everything is at half-staff, for appearance's sake. The official tears could fill a swimming pool. But no matter how longingly I rustle through all the available news-blotting-paper for a kind word, nothing speaks to the heart. Column after column is filled with dry husks; the murder was cowardly, or a stab in the back; the victim was not afraid to be tough, did his duty till his last breath. The editorials express shock, or dismay. The chancellor, on the other hand, seems quite annoyed. Now that his cardboard pal, who served as the target of all the hatred, refuses to play the sitting duck anymore, the chancellor is unmistakably responsible. He may (like the emperor in the fairy tale) feel exposed, naked as a colossal jaybird.

"Nonetheless, I am certain that nothing will happen to him; he is despicable, but not worthy of hatred. He lacks the necessary grandeur, no matter how much he inflates himself. For that reason alone, any comparison with Bismarck is off the mark. In his own day, we could malign the genius costumed in sulfur yellow (the color of the collar worn by the Halberstadt cuirassiers). Our own giant manifests a certain pettiness of character. Yet I would not deny that the ruling mass, whose genius is fueled primarily by lies, possesses sheer breadth of character. Indeed, this character is in such lavish supply that across the entire land—or, as the old anthem had it, from the Etsch to the Belt—it is forming mildewlike deposits. Everything that calls itself German is ruled by mediocrity, which finds its most stifling expression in 'his' ostentatious complacency.

"That protects him. Believe me, my child, no one will lay a hand on him. He and his kind have always been untouchable, which is terrible in itself. Ah, when one thinks of all those who have become targets of hatred. Assassinations were always the rule. They shot at the kaiser, several times, in fact. First the plumber Hödel took aim at him, then a certain Dr. Nobiling—two sorry figures; but when I leave aside our Prussian melodramas and cast a glance in your direction, toward France, my gaze is transfixed by an avenging angel of iconographic stature. I see Charlotte Corday. I see the dagger, and Marat in his bathtub. Now she is stabbing him. What passion, what grandeur, what hatred worthy of its object!

"Perhaps—no, surely—you will reject my comparison, and say that our German preoccupations, all the sorrows we have stirred into our unification stew, cannot be measured by the same standard as *la Terreur*, the guillotine, the reign of virtue imposed by the Committee of Public Safety; but I find the comparison apt. Millions of workers and employees are undergoing a process of beheading. True, it does not entail shortening an individual by a head, but the blade is chopping off his earning power, his job, which up to yesterday was still secure, and without which he might as well be headless, at least in this country.

"Lest I get myself in hot water with our modern suffragettes: when I say worker, I of course include women. Am by now familiar with the pressure to balance both sexes on one's tongue simultaneously by means of linguistic monstrosities. And because the situation often hits working women the hardest—indeed, they are the first to be dealt with cruelly—I am fairly certain that it was a single mother or young wife, who only yesterday still had her place on the assembly line, at a fish-boning machine, or in a lightbulb factory, and who now, today's Charlotte Corday, did not reach for a dagger, but rather pointed her pistol in the appropriate direction; only women follow through with such rightness of aim.

"I can see you assuming your bittersweet expression or shaking your dear little head with a sagacity beyond your years because this old curmudgeon seems so intent on picking a fight, borrowing a historical murderer and dressing her up in today's fashions, and because I also have such a gloomy outlook; yet I do not see things gloomily—I merely see them.

"Besides, as far as the daughters of Eve are concerned, it can safely be asserted that we succeeded in creating a dozen strong-willed female characters. Melanie van der Straaten will vouch for that, as will Corinna Schmidt and her nemesis Jenny Treibel, in a sense even Lene Nimptsch, and certainly Mathilde Möhring; their determination was made of stern stuff. And those of the women who are weak, and not so well armed with intellect, whether it be poor Effi or the ailing Cécile, are upright, despite being dealt a bad hand. Even Stine, no matter how wan and unconvincing she turned out—or, rather, how convincing in her pallor—displays a good deal of quiet pride. And for that reason I am certain that it was a woman who did the deed. No, not the widow Pittelkow; she sounds so radical merely because she has the Berlin mouthworks; but Frau von Carayon could certainly have picked up a weapon if deeply hurt, likewise Grete Minde in the frenzy born of pain. And certainly that paragon of sobriety, cameo-faced Mathilde Möhring, would have been capable of an execution, carefully planned and then carried out without any shilly-shallying.

"And that brings us back to your countrywoman, the dagger, and Marat. By the way, I saw the play years ago, not the Berlin premiere but the Perten production in Rostock. Ideologically askew as far as the relationship between de Sade and Marat goes, but the bathtub scene was brilliant: can still see the avenging woman slowly lowering the kitchen knife ...

"And fool that I am, on the repeated occasions when the boss of the Handover Trust honored me with a visit to my seventh-floor cell and sat on my sofa, I tried to warn him of male malefactors. Juxtaposing the claims of anarchy with the claims of law and order, I sent the eternal poacher from the unsuccessful story *Quitt* after the eternal forester. Time and again I played out for him the encounter on the road to the Hampel Hostel: 'One man's percussion cap failed, but now Lehnert leveled his gun and two shots rang out. . . .'

"A murder of the first water, certainly! But this time it was no poacher taking revenge on the forester, nor was it the resolute daughter of Normandy, who, whatever people may call her, was surely acting out of something other than madness; rather, she sought and found her target, this most nondescript of all the women avid for action, this woman who took a page from Mathilde Möhring's book. Ah, my child, there's nothing new under the sun!

"And yet our conversation could have continued, whiling away many a night. The last time the boss visited me in my cell—the night before Maundy Thursday, just before the first of April—we chatted about Bismarck's birthday, right around the corner, and joked about the fuss they always used to make over him in the Sachsenwald in my day. Then we discussed Prussia's glory and decline, the Kulturkampf, the persecution of socialists, anti-Semitism, but also the doubtful aspects of Communism and of Christianity, both of which constantly demand things of people that no one can fulfill. Finally we got to the twelve bad years, which had to include the history of the Handover Trust building, and the resistance group in the Reich Aviation Ministry, which was considered part of the so-called Red Orchestra, and thus also to the small part I had played as a courier, albeit unwittingly. Although I still heard not a word about the memorandum I had submitted to him weeks earlier, he exclaimed enthusiastically, 'Just terrific that you always came and went here. You belong to this building. I—I'm here subject to recall.'

"And when I described to him how things were long ago, and even longer ago, working my way back to the year '70, when I had just returned from French captivity, and all the Prussian officers I met assured me, 'Here you would have simply been shot for a spy,' he laughed like a little boy who has never known danger.

"I am tempted to call him naive. He could be amazed where there was nothing to be amazed at. I miss him very much. Grandma Emmi (who sends her best, by the way) was aghast—when I came home and found her in front of the television set—but she had nothing to say as the terribly meaningless images they were showing flashed by. Only later, when something else was on the screen, did she insist on crying for a moment. (She calls her tears 'heart drops.')

"I shall miss him for a long time. A man completely without pretensions. He must have often felt a powerful urge to clean house—no matter which. And just imagine, child, around midnight he often sped along the corridors on roller skates—colossally alone. For his health, he claimed, but I am inclined to believe he was running away from himself.

"Now it has caught up with him. What will happen next? They say a woman is being considered as his successor. That makes sense to me—if it was a Charlotte Corday who fired the shots. Only a woman could focus her hatred so precisely. Only a woman can bring to bear enough harshness for the winding-down required here. In the long run, he would have proved too weak, no matter how robust he appeared. But a woman will see this through...."

Then Fonty went on to speak of Madeleine's studies. He alluded only in passing to his granddaughter's relationship with her married professor—"I'm relieved to read that you see him seldom, and when you do, from an increasing distance." But he did not mention again the murder and the woman who had committed it, identified first as one person, then as another.

For a while Fonty must have dropped the idea of a woman as perpetrator, for when the memorial service took place in the Handover Trust's historic grand hall, and Hoftaller slid in beside him, his suspicion was aimed in another direction. They were seated in the very last row. The consultant Theo Wuttke said softly but insistently, "We have to talk."

But they did not have a chance until after the ceremony, when they got onto the paternoster: "Was it your people?"

Hoftaller replied just before getting off, "Why us? This system will do itself in."

Thus it happened that he followed Fonty to his office. Fonty pointed to the sofa and said, "Only a few days ago he was sitting in that very corner; he had premonitions."

"That's understandable when a person's at the very top."

"And has you people in the building and for an enemy, isn't that so?"

"Up to now we've been loyal to every system, and only when order was threatened..."

"...then you..."

"And a weak link showed up...."

"...for instance, the boss..."

"The services in Pullach and Cologne were responsible for him, whereas we specialize in seamless transitions, for which reason we view certain persons..."

"...as ripe for shooting down. Or am I mistaken?"

"A person could see it that way, Fonty. Anyone who puts himself at palpable risk and still thinks he can manage without our protection, shouldn't be surprised...."

"That's what I thought: an operational proceeding. A security breach had to be closed—your name is written all over it!"

"You're barking up the wrong tree...."

"Yes or no?"

"Just between the two of us: we're betting on the Red Army Faction. A bunch of clues have turned up, even a note claiming responsibility...."

"That doesn't mean a thing!"

"Besides, the careful preparation points to that...."

"No lectures on logistics, please! After all, you people aren't rank amateurs; you have..."

"All right, granted: there are hotheads everywhere. And the really dangerous ones are idealists who think the system isn't collapsing fast enough...."

"There we have it: he was too soft for you—am I right?"

"Well, there's a woman known for her toughness who's very likely to be moving into the executive suite soon. Here in the building people have been saying it for some time: The winding-down just has to move faster, because if we continue at this snail's pace, certain social-democratic tendencies are bound to..."

"So you just helped things along, picked out a couple of people who were suited for this dirty work...."

"You're spinning a novel, old boy. One of your bandit tales! Come on, Fonty, let's sit down. I'm tired, damned tired. I don't like the way this thing turned out either. Must have been the RAF, a typical product of the capitalist system; this is its modus operandi. The whole thing was by the book. At first I was thinking it must have been like last spring, some crazy woman with a dagger hidden in a bouquet, but the whole thing was too professional for that...."

They quickly found their usual positions and were sitting, as they had a year earlier around this time, in their sofa corners. We archivists were present only in a conditional sense, but we assert nonetheless that their sofa conversation could have lasted an hour or more. One should imagine the rustling of the upholstery. And Hoftaller with a Cuban, of course. And the cigar smoke may have coalesced into one suspicion or another, then dissipated into a haze.

Historical murders could have been brought up, for purposes of comparison. References to perpetrators who were apprehended, among them Dr. Nobiling, that bundle of nerves who, in 1878, picked up his shotgun and with one well-aimed shot unleashed the Anti-Socialist Laws. And passages came to mind that Fonty might have used to enliven dinner-table conversations— whether in the Treibel household or on old Stechlin's estate—in the course of which the topic of assassinations could have come up, preferably successful ones.

The most recent murder remained unsolved. When Hoftaller left, Fonty aired out the room.

Not that he fell silent, but he withdrew completely into final certainties. In a letter to Professor Freundlich we find the following remark: "Vegetating is the order of the day. Life here is becoming increasingly tedious...." And he wrote to Schwerin, "I have no more ammunition in my pouch."

We noticed that in the many-sided missives he was writing, he increasingly had in mind the historical Mete and the magistrate Friedlaender. The expression "Everyone is everything, and everyone is nothing" was followed by insights like "On his just deserts, everyone deserves to be hanged; yet we must portray the criminal in such a fashion that we can become reconciled to his character. . . ."

Since the murder, he saw his resigned state of mind mirrored a hundred years back: "My attempt to flee is an entirely natural reaction on the part of someone who in every possible situation proves anything unpleasant nonexistent, and goes to the utmost to do so. . . ."

At least he could still write letters. Only seldom did Fonty hear the static of everyday cases being wound down: the wailing and gnashing of teeth that rose to a incessant din. His room on the seventh floor protected him. Soon only the past made itself heard there—Hoftaller's sofa-contributions included—as if the most recent murder had the ability to revive old murder stories long since laid to rest. And because, in the case involving the poacher Lehnert Menz, which was on the books, the perpetrator managed to flee and disappear into faraway America, it looked as though the murder of the Handover Trust head might be destined to conform to the double shot fired at the forester Opitz and develop further along novelistic lines: they searched for the perpetrator—who, as Fonty was soon convinced again, was a woman—yet he or she remained unidentified; the security services could not piece together even a phantom profile. And since it was never determined who was responsible for solving the murder, the West German Federal Investigation Bureau was not the only service to be shown up; Pullach and Cologne were likewise making themselves look inept, for every newspaper Fonty could lay his hands on, from the *Wochenpost* to the *Tagesspiegel*, was filling up column after column with scorn. Even Hoftaller, when he stopped by briefly, spoke of an "alarming security vacuum."

Everywhere people continued to scratch their heads and speculate; only Fonty saw the matter clearly. That is to say, he saw a woman in her early thirties, whose passion-driven strength of will hid behind a nondescript exterior: "I see ash-blond hair, a muddy complexion. A gaunt figure, but always neat and proper in her dress. Many women look like this. That is why it has been so easy for her to duck under."

And then he said from his sofa corner, "Perhaps her profile has a specific quality, a contour with which the security services could do something, should they have an eye for such things: she has a cameo face."

Hoftaller waved the suggestion aside: "Even if there are certain things I wouldn't put past a modern version of your Mathilde Möhring, a well-aimed shot was never part of her repertory. Mathilde has other, more gradual ways; she's not the violent type."

We hear Fonty give a high-pitched laugh, feigning merriment. Nothing tickled him more than Hoftaller's knowledge of literature: "You should have become a professor—you're not all that sharp as a detective. You've never had what it took to work out more than a puzzle, that most ridiculous test of patience. You're slow on the uptake. Tallhover, too, according to his biographer, spent months following false leads. You hear the fleas coughing everywhere, but you can't even see through me—who am like an open book—let alone a certain person. Listen closely now, Hoftaller: she has prosaic eyes, watery blue, of course. But it wasn't the sun in her eyes but, rather, the soot of our current reality that induced her to act: bang! And already she's ducked under. Simply gone, surfacing somewhere else. We're familiar with this: the good old diving-duck principle. She's already busy doing something useful, as diligent and neat and proper as before, either working at the land-registry office or sorting tulip bulbs at a nursery. Teaching would be too obvious, or not obvious enough. No doubt right here in the building, in some department or other, she is busy attending to the brisk winding-down that's going on—armed with expertise and colossally industrious!"

This argument convinced not only us but also Hoftaller, who said, "That makes sense. The perpetrator—let it be a woman, for all I care—could certainly be located in or around the Trust. She or he's on the payroll. Maybe she—if it absolutely must be a Mathilde Möhring—works in the department handling publishing—when I think of all the state-run publishing houses that need to be wound down, the overdue personnel reductions, the many women editors who will soon be without a job..."

Suddenly Fonty's manner turned brusque. He leaped off the sofa, threw open the window, not in his usual quiet way but shouting, "I will not have you puffing on those cigars in my office anymore, even if you claim these are the last of the lot."

"I'm going, I'm going. Just one more thing: the guy who did this..."

"I keep telling you: It's a woman who has ducked under."

"All right, the woman who did this..."

"Put it out! Put out that stogie this minute!"

"Well, if you insist..."

Fonty sat down again. And Hoftaller, who was husbanding the last of his Cubans, tucked the cold stump in his pocket and took the liberty of suspecting that the perpetrator was a secretary or technical assistant: "Maybe it's someone who was brought along from Alexplatz. Not a former comrade, that's certain; more likely one of those Protestant church mice who were out there demonstrating Monday after Monday, always with candles and anguished faces..."

"That means you're betting on a woman in a position to know the effects of the winding-down firsthand, who therefore thinks she has to act on behalf of her fellow sufferers, in the spirit of radical Christianity...."

"You got it, Fonty! Ducking under doesn't have to mean 'Off to Lebanon!' It can also mean not budging, staying put, doing your duty without a peep, and continuing to bring the department heads cups of coffee. Like a plant on a windowsill, pretty, pleasant without being showy..."

"Not bad, your theory. The only thing that worries me a bit is her boyfriend. Because she has a boyfriend, you know, whom I picture as bearded, and clueless, not unlike one of those many bearded pastors now dabbling in politics. Dreamy and indecisive, he's a 'milksop,' as Mathilde Möhring recognized the moment she interviewed Hugo Grossmann as a possible lodger for the Georgenstrasse apartment. Someone who won't say 'Boo!' but is perfectly likable, although she told her mother, '...a big black beard, even a bit frizzy. Men like that are never good for much.' Anyway, having a type like that as her boyfriend could be dangerous, certainly in the long run, for the investigation will drag on for years. But we do know that Hugo Grossmann didn't live to be very old."

After they had enhanced the profiles of the unobtrusive perpetrator and her bearded fiancé with further details, Hoftaller left, and Fonty aired out the room as usual. He gazed through the open window into the inner courtyard, whose four-sided shaft had no exit. Then he looked up to the flat roofs. At least there was sky above the Handover Trust.

After the airing-out, the consultant Theo Wuttke paced off a considerable stretch on his carpet. We assume that during his glance into the courtyard and into the April sky, then on the carpet, and later at the desk, he was trying to trace, without paper and pencil, the contour of a cameo face that seemed to fascinate him.

The woman who succeeded the murdered boss brought a new tone into the building. The people's property was wound down more efficiently and at a more relentless pace: what had once been the East was transferred piecemeal to Western hands—they went by the name of private—and only the liabilities, which no one wanted to assume, remained with the Handover Trust.

The boss used incentives to boost morale. Winding-down accomplished especially quickly was rewarded with fat bonuses. No one took any pains anymore; everyone was in a hurry, and in the internal administration, too, everything had to be cleared off the table. Thus Fonty's historically layered memorandum on the repeated reuse of the building—that same memorandum whose evaluation the former boss had postponed so long, finally reached her desk and was promptly rejected.

The decision was not signed by the boss herself; that had been delegated to one of her male underlings. The curt explanation read: This altogether thorough study focused excessively on the past. It lacked a positive orientation toward future developments. As valuable as the treatment of the various historical phases was, it was still unacceptable to rank them as equal in significance to the building's third function. To speak of continuity was irresponsible if one failed to acknowledge that henceforth free market forces would take priority. Furthermore, the inclusion of the paternoster in this document, although an original touch, implied, especially in the portrayal of its high-ranking passengers, a principle of equivalence that could no longer be considered valid, given the free, democratic order now in force. Furthermore, the tragic death of the previous head of the Handover Trust, the result of a cowardly murder, commanded a high degree of respect; the memorandum's pervasive irony merely distorted the situation and signaled the absence of the desired attention to overarching values.

After enumerating the deceased head's achievements, and indicating that in future the building on the former Wilhelmstrasse would bear the name of this extraordinary public servant, the appraisal continued: "At the appropriate point in time we will revisit your rather interesting study for possible utilization in some other form."

Now Fonty had no work to do, but he kept his office. He wrote to Jena, "I've discovered how censorship Western-style operates. Since then I've been serving my time. It reminds me of the days at Hezekiel's *Kreuzzeitung* or in Merckel's Central Office. And the permanent secretary of the Prussian Academy likewise had nothing to do but twiddle his thumbs...."

He complained to his son, the publisher, with similar bitterness: "My dear Friedel: It turns out that I can now offer you my memorandum, which has been censored here in the most subtle fashion. Brought out in a case binding, it would certainly find readers. Yet I recognize how dreadful it would be if the sound basis of a publishing enterprise had to be a belletristic father. Just go on publishing your Moravian Brethren, and I shall continue to fill the desk drawer...."

And still more letters, for there was nothing to do; yet his inactivity did not attract notice. And it almost seemed as if the consultant Theo Wuttke had been forgotten, when one day he found a flowerpot on his desk, now swept bare: geraniums in full bloom. The following day a particular kind of evergreen appeared. On the Monday after a painfully long weekend, a new piece of furniture was there next to the desk, a plant stand, and on it, keeping the other plants company, a third pot: begonias.

Soon we were familiar with his blooming or merely creeping office decor. Fonty described the plant stand to us as an *étagère*. During a visit to the Archives he commented, "A colossally practical invention! In the form of a spiral staircase, shorter and shorter steps are arranged counterclockwise around a meter-high post, all properly pegged and braced. Six steps, and each of them load-bearing on both ends. Looks handsome in my sober cell. And yesterday I became the recipient of an African violet." Then he advised us to procure an étagère for the Archives: "Start with ornamental ivy. Never fear: plants will turn up."

After a potted calla lily had come on Wednesday, Thursday began with a blooming pelargonium, pink and white, and on Friday morning there was a knock on the door, which did not surprise Fonty; for he already suspected that there must be a donor behind the increasingly luxuriant display of bloom.

It was not Hoftaller who entered the office but a cleaning woman, officially known as a custodial specialist. In accordance with agency regulations, her smock bore a small tag that identified her as Helma Frühauf. Fonty also wore such a name tag, on his lapel, with the name Theo Wuttke inside a plastic holder; and even his day-and-night-shadow had to be legibly labeled.

Frau Frühauf did not come empty-handed. She had her arms around a potted plant of substantial proportions, and said, without putting it down, "So, Herr Wuttke? How d'you like the greenery? Was thinking to myself, it's so bare in here. Maybe he'll like this, the greenery, and some color. There's heaps left over from before. They just left them behind when they had to leave, all of them, because the place was being cleaned out. Lots of rubber plants and potted lindens. Don't care for that kind myself, but maybe you? But this one here, this one's a looker, don't you think?"

Fonty thanked her, but added a note of caution: "I'm not used to having so many plants." Yet he could not refute Frau Frühauf's "palms are always appropriate," especially since this quotation had become proverbial, not only at the Archives, but also as the title of one of his Cultural Union lectures.

The cleaning woman with the always-appropriate palm in her arms stood there in the middle of the room: "Gracious, Herr Wuttke, let's not be so modest. You were here before, and they kept you on, you know, like all of us from the custodial collective. Anyway, I say to myself, Look here, if anyone deserves flowers, it's him! But maybe you're allergic—then I'll have to get 'em out of here."

Fonty assured her that his only allergy was to a certain type of person. Then he took a few steps toward the palm-bearer. According to his description, Frau Frühauf appeared to be in her mid-thirties, on her way toward forty. Together they searched for a spot for the exotic plant. The cleaning woman was wearing a kerchief tied in a small bow over her forehead. The pot and its contents were too heavy for the plant stand. She was still standing there, weighed down by the palm.

"Over here, by the wall," Fonty said. "In the afternoon, the sun sometimes shines in here, you see—even plenty of it."

It took a while before the pot had found its spot. "Don't worry, we'll get it situated," she said, "maybe a bit closer to the window here."

The conversation might have been confined to this topic, but once Frau Frühauf was standing empty-handed next to the palm, Fonty wanted to hear more: how things were going for her, not only at work but also in her private life, if she didn't mind his asking.

"Oh, Lord, you get by," she said. "They pay us all right here, and even better on the fourth floor, you know, where they've got the holy of holies, and that new woman's in charge now. But they've got other folks does the cleaning there. Our crew's not allowed in. Security brought in those others, because of bombs and stuff, I guess. All we do's the north wing. In the morning after five, before anything really gets going around here. And at home, well, it's like it always was, except that my husband Erich doesn't have regular work now and usually just lays around the house."

Fonty wanted to know whether her husband had a beard and

whether Helma Frühauf had ever met the boss, even though she didn't clean the executive suite: "I mean before *that* happened, of course."

She smiled without opening her mouth, because of her bad teeth: "How come you know Erich's grown a beard since Narva laid him off? But it looks good on him. Naw, our crew never had anything to do with the boss. All we saw was the marks from his roller skates—we had to scrub those off. What a mess, all over the linoleum, even up here on the seventh floor, specially on the curves. Streaks everywhere. And he was in your office here a couple of times, too, with his skates on. Kind of strange, don't you think? Must've sat down on the sofa. Did you know about that, Herr Wuttke?"

Fonty mentioned briefly an "occasional exchange of views" with the boss—"He was interested in literature, to the extent time allowed"—and thanked her again for the potted palm: "I've seen splendid specimens like this only in conservatories, with their steamy hothouse air.... But now I must get back to work.... It was a pleasure, Frau Frühauf...a wonderfully speaking name you have there, since you really do have to be up early, at the crack of dawn..."

She said, "I'm going, don't you worry," and through the half-open door: "Maybe I'll bring you something real special tomorrow: a heliotrope, just about to open."

Only now, as she went on her way, did Fonty see her profile. Certainly a nondescript woman, prematurely aged, worn down by work, or, as they say, faded—yet a woman with a cameo face.

The heliotrope remained a vague promise, but he sharpened our picture of Helma Frühauf's profile with a quotation, the passage that describes Mathilde Möhring's experience as a young girl: "That had been in Halensee on her seventeenth birthday, which they had celebrated with an unmarried aunt. She had taken up a position at some remove but kept her gaze fixed on the skittle alley...." And then Fonty summoned one of the skittle players to be star witness. He confirmed that the ugly duckling had a bit of beauty after all: "She has a cameo face." He repeated this sentence solemnly and added, still quoting, "From that time forth, these words sustained her...."

After the cleaning woman had left, Fonty sat at his bare desk for a long time, trying to get used to the potted palm, as he had done his best in the last few days to accept the plants left over from the Ministries Building as an inherited burden. A bit of afternoon sun came to his aid. The shadow play of the palm fronds on the white wall. And the étagère, with its blooms and festoons, likewise cast a shadow.

Perhaps he also pictured Helma Frühauf's profile as a scissors-cut silhouette—the arch of the forehead under the kerchief's bow, the just barely protruding nose, the closed mouth, emphasizing the lower lip, the markedly strong chin, whose smooth, undoubled curve flowed into the sturdy pillar of her neck—for when he wrote to his daughter soon after this, he placed a quotation from *Mathilde Möhring* at the beginning of the letter: "In art, purity of contour is decisive...."

This short novel took a long time to finish. At seventy-two, the Immortal got the first draft down on paper, just after the publication of *Frau Jenny Treibel*. At the same time, a preliminary outline of *Effi Briest* was sketched out. Spells of depression and the major nervous breakdown ensued. And to top it off, *Stechlin* got in the way of his wrapping up this fairly straightforward story. After his death, the unfinished and barely legible manuscript was found, with all sorts of notes and corrections on scraps of paper, but when it was first published eight years later, it appeared on the literary market with many mistakes and distortions, even falsifications. These were not corrected until our colleague Gotthard Erler brought out his painstakingly edited Weimar edition; since then, this small work, whose main character for a long time repelled readers, has attracted more and more favorable attention, now among feminists as well, who find in Mathilde Möhring a kind of model. This phenomenon, too, was discussed in Fonty's letter to Schwerin. He advised his daughter to show some backbone: "Henceforth, your goal should always be to wring everyday victories out of life...."

The next day the Handover Trust consultant Theo Wuttke was

the recipient of a potted plant known as an impatiens, or "Busy Lizzy," and from noon on, he finally had work on his desk—delivered in-house. In a brief message he was requested by the Department of Public Relations and Communications to set off in search of words, to stake out word fields, in order to find a better term for "winding-down."

Fonty placed the vigorously blooming impatiens on the étagère, watered all the plants, and cheerfully hummed something Prussian. But then he said to himself, "Who wants to reach eighty and sit around shaking his head, with no one sure whether it's from old age or at the ways of the world?"

32

In Search of a Word

Sometimes his quotations were chosen for their topicality. At the end of April "Palms are always appropriate!" was in currency. Later he greeted us with the echo of a classified advertisement once formulated by the Immortal: "I am missing a word. But once I have it in hand, the rest will be easy," and as he was leaving, after a good hour, he urged the Archives to confirm for him that a certain title for a novel was a lucky find—as if the name were brand-new: "Effi Briest is pretty, because of the many *e*'s and *i*'s—those are the two most delicate vowels."

But otherwise he brought nothing but silence with him after the murder. He had even forgotten his seasonal bouquet, and sat there in our visitor's chair as if he had lost his place. Not until our director assured him that we knew how he was feeling did he say, "He could be seen as a friend," and promptly invoked his Scottish idol, as though seeking support: "While Walter Scott was working on *Woodstock,* Lady Scott died; he paced up and down in the garden for an hour, then sat down and wrote another chapter. That's how it must be."

Fonty had no unfinished manuscript lying around. His memorandum had been rejected. True, he was still hoping to complete one of the Immortal's fragments, the *Likedeeler* project, in the form of a balladesque epic, but he did not get beyond the intention. He had received only one assignment—to track down something that remained hidden, whether out of malice or out of shame: from the end of April, throughout May, and into June, the Handover Trust consultant Theo Wuttke pursued his search for a new term for the mandated process of winding down, a term that would be at once suitable and gentle, not abrupt or off-putting, but pleasant and euphonious. The discovery of such a term was supposed to serve the public. What was called for was not sweet talk, just a substitute that would make this process, which had acquired such an ugly name, sound friendly.

"It must have a pretty sound," he told us. "If possible, it should include those 'two most delicate vowels' praised in the title *Effi Briest.*"

We would have been glad to assist Fonty, especially since we, too, were currently in danger of being "wound down," as an unprofitable relic from the past. But our holdings did not contain any suitable substitutes, and expressions culled from the war books, such as "decimate" and "mow down," would merely have made the winding down seem the worse for the effort. Our suggestion was to consider quotations from the field of horticulture. Both in Dörr's nursery and in the prose works in general, references could have been found to activities like "pruning," "hoeing," or "weeding."

After Fonty, more word-perfect in his quotations than we, had taken counsel with himself and realized how little the Archives had to offer, he no longer appealed for our help. He sat out the workday in his office or paced back and forth between sofa and desk, his head bent, as if the missing word could be picked up off the shit-brown runner. So as not to be utterly fixated on the offensive, he devised a contrasting project of his own, for during his visit to the seated bronze, a thought had come to him that now inspired him to visualize brightly colored pictorial broadsheets.

He proposed to the Handover Trust that it enlighten the people as to its perplexing mission in an easy-to-grasp form. Using stone plates, diligent lithographers should print up simple pictorial stories for mass distribution. Without having received any such assignment, he wrote with hastening pencil, "Remember Neuruppin! Only in this way can this blasted winding-down business achieve respect, until a better term is found. Even stinging nettles can be turned into a tasty dish. It's all in the presentation, and besides, the medium would be message enough. After all, far worse stories were prettied up with the help of Neuruppin's pictorial broadsheets. For instance, a Zwickau broadsheet could follow the tragicomic passion of the Trabi from one station to the next, until finally, thanks to a prince called VW, it finds a fairy-tale happy ending...."

Then he was off again, canvassing for words. From the window he patted down the sky over the Handover Trust, but everything he found there was hazy. Now and then Helma Frühauf came by to surprise him with particularly luxuriant potted plants, an azalea or a tricolor saxifrage; but she never gladdened his heart with the heliotrope she had promised.

Around the middle of May she dropped in one day after work, this time as something other than a cleaning woman. She had removed her kerchief, and was wearing a pale green pleated skirt, a beige blouse, and a peat-brown jacket with a mannish cut to the shoulders. She brought a small pot of primroses and stayed for a glass of Wilthen brandy, which she sipped at now and then, after being invited to take a seat on the sofa.

"Gracious, Herr Wuttke, it's a good thing we saved the greenery, or it would've all ended up in the trash. That's the God's honest truth. Wasn't it your idea, I mean having a temporary home for the plants? At first we were fit to be tied, but then we did a good job of watering them, the whole time, in there where the canteen used to be. Looked like a greenhouse."

Fonty reported to his visitor on his new, thus far fruitless assignment: "Now they're begging for help, don't know how to get out of this pickle—those department heads and the lady running the show. First they go and bring a term into the world and wind down one company after another, until they have all the thread on their spool. And now it seems that 'wind down' won't do anymore; it's become suspect, sounds too negative. In other words, they want to continue winding down, but under another name. That's how it is with renaming. For instance, when they talk about 'freed-up manpower' and mean the unemployed, it certainly has a positive sound, but it doesn't change the end result one bit. It's nothing but adulterated wine and brazenly deceptive labeling. And now I, who've often been at a loss for the *mot juste,* am supposed to come up with something to save the day. I still have nothing in hand, and in general I'm opposed to contrivances, but perhaps you, dear Frau Frühauf, will be able to find something convincing."

She grasped the little glass with the fingertips of both hands and squeezed her knees together under her skirt. Even when speaking, she kept her faulty teeth out of sight: "Well, Herr Wuttke, like I was telling you, they let my husband go, too. He was with Narva, in light-bulb production. They don't need them anymore, have plenty in the West, Osram and such. Where my Erich was, the men on top started talking about a 'trimmed-down work force' and then 'thinning out.' And now he just lays around the house. But I've got him signed up for training already: computers and such."

Fonty reached for his pencil: "Trimming down is better than thinning out. Trimming down is always right." Then, on another sheet of paper, he jotted down the story of the Narva lightbulb factory as a possible candidate for a pictorial broadsheet: "One could begin in classic Neuruppin style with Edison, inventor of the incandescent lightbulb, and then show the spread of illumination from station to station throughout the world, forever threatened with short circuits, until everything goes pitch-black at Narva and elsewhere—ah, well..."

Meanwhile Helma Frühauf continued to sip her brandy. Later they chatted, without making any serious attempt to find a word. Fonty talked about his daughter and the real estate racket being perpetrated in Schwerin. He said that the Mecklenburgers' "dreadful pop eyes" had always annoyed him: "Even so, an Inspector Bräsig and a cabinetmaker named Cresspahl sprang from that soil." Then he came back to the Handover Trust and asked himself and Frau Frühauf: "Is it absolutely essential that everything be done so shabbily, with such utter contempt for human beings?"

She replied, "I s'pose so. That's what you always hear: This is how it's got to be done. And if you ask, Isn't there some other way? they say, Sure, there's another way, like socialism, and that means straight downhill. They're right about that. But it sure isn't going uphill neither, Herr Wuttke, I can tell you that."

Helma Frühauf was sitting on the sofa in her too-short skirt, her legs crossed, but Fonty assured us that it was not on account of her calves, which he described as muscular, "thanks to all the hard work," that he swiveled away from his desk for a side view of her. We were allowed to record the reason he gave, as had become our custom: "Was determined to catch her profile. It wasn't all that difficult, because she actually liked to show off her best side, even if it meant almost dislocating her neck."

Helma Frühauf had habits: she smoked. And one of her expressions, when she stopped by for a brief visit, was, "I'll just stay for a puff."

This is how we see her: the cameo face with the cigarette. She never sat in a corner of the sofa; she always occupied the middle. Whether with knees pressed together or legs crossed, she turned her head to the side as she exhaled. At the same time, she raised her round, slightly prominent chin.

Fonty viewed this intensification of her profile as a discovery, and at the same time as confirmation of his suspicion. Standing by the now fully occupied étagère—a Christmas cactus and an aloe were the most recent additions—he said, "At any rate, it can't go on like this. They're crushing everything. Someone has to shout Enough! Stop! Otherwise shots will ring out again, as they did a few weeks ago. That caused great consternation...."

"But not for long, Herr Wuttke. What came after that, the new boss of the whole show here, she really clamped down. You can tell, she doesn't bat an eye. She doesn't know what fear is. But what I was going to say—after the long weekend when that thing happened, I was tidying up here on Tuesday, real early, and I found the boss's roller skates under this sofa of yours. I just made 'em disappear. They're gone now. I was thinking, Better safe than sorry."

He was actually quite amused when he told us about this precaution: "Nothing can be proved with roller skates." But he drew incriminating conclusions from the cleaning woman's remark that she had been visiting her sister in Duisburg on that tragic Easter weekend, which meant she had been near the scene of the crime. She confirmed this supposition with the additional information: "Took the train back first thing on Tuesday and came straight to work from the station."

Then he asked us to keep it to ourselves and added, "Here I'd best stop; if I say any more, my words may expose me to suspicion, as an accomplice to murder. But thought should certainly be given to this: wouldn't the bloody end met by the head of the Handover Trust be the ideal material for a popular and effective pictorial broadsheet? One would have to begin with his childhood and youth, then illustrate his rapid ascent, showing him as somewhat radicalized in '68, soon thereafter as an undersecretary in the social-democratic–liberal coalition, then as a dedicated redeveloper, then portray the beginnings of the Handover Trust on Alexanderplatz, then the move, and a scene with the boss in the paternoster, finally capture his doubts, and, with the murder, convey a warning that points in all directions. Let me remind you of Kühn's pictorial broadsheet showing the story of Frederick the Great, starting with his youth, that is, with the beheading of Katte, and following him through all his battles and into old age, when he was bent double with gout. And even better, the mass-circulation broadsheet put out by Oehmigke & Riemschneider that illustrates the twisted existence of Dr. Nobiling, up to the moment he fires a shot at the kaiser and promptly turns the gun on himself. Yes, indeed! That must be shown. The murder of the Trust boss is a classic broadsheet story: at once tragic and instructive. Why should I go on grubbing for a word, trying to help these people out of a jam, when nothing, absolutely nothing occurs to them but 'winding down'?"

Yet Fonty did not call off the search. After Helma Frühauf's "trimming down" he wrote the word "liposuction." Then the term "liquidate" occurred to him, but he immediately crossed it out, even though this substitute word, as he assured us, contained the "delicate" *i* twice, like Effi Briest. He searched and searched, but no matter what he put down on his pad, "wind down" remained the most accurate expression.

At a loss, he wrote not only to his daughter but also to Professor Freundlich, and finally to his granddaughter. She was the first to reply, but offered only useless words from the culinary realm, such as "debone" and "fillet." Furthermore she wrote, "I'm afraid, Grandpapa, that you are stooping to do something far beneath

546

your abilities. Ah, if only I could raise your sights to a landscape in which a succession of mountain ranges, from the richest green to the palest azure, stretches to the horizon...."

Freundlich's response was bitter: "I'm in favor of sticking with wind down. This comes to you from someone whose thread has already been stripped from the spool. By the way, of late I've been falling back on quotations, as you have done for years: I'm on the point of making myself scarce...."

Martha Grundmann responded only indirectly to her father's request for terminological assistance; her marriage with the speculating developer was lending increased currency to the term "divorce." She wrote, "Of course, my conversion forbids any such a radical break, yet that which does not hold together must be put asunder...."

But when Fonty derived some relevant terms from this legal process, which normally dawdled its way through the courts, it occurred to him just in time that the connotations of any verbs referring to division might cast a dubious light on the recently accomplished unification of the nation.

None of the letters helped. "Wind down" it was. He left his desk and watered the flowers and vines, last of all the potted palm; but even the plants could not suggest a suitable word.

So he moved his search out of doors. The weather was with him: May everywhere. Because he had to spend only half the day in his office, there was ample time for lengthy walks through the Tiergarten and for the long overdue visit to the cemetery on Pflugstrasse, but also for impromptu trips by S-Bahn and underground back and forth across Berlin. It annoyed him that the Number 2 subway line still did not connect the two halves of the city; for his roving through the city he therefore had to rely on the S-Bahn, with its all-revealing daylight, whereas in fact he was profoundly in the mood for the underground and ducking under. The world, it seemed, had nothing more to say to him.

It did not escape our notice that since the death of the Handover Trust head Fonty had been in a condition that vacillated between paralyzing doubt and desperate restlessness. Whether surrounded by geraniums and impatiens or riding the S-Bahn between Erkner and Wannsee, he could not escape from the futile search for a better term. It constantly brought him face to face with the narrow confines of his own irreparable situation. As accustomed as he was to Hoftaller, of late he could not bear the stench of the man's cigars, even when the smoker abstained. Emmi's addiction to images, somewhat diminished now but still fed to excess by the color television, drove him out of the apartment on Kollwitzstrasse. Everything repelled him, even his study. Besides, he was very worried about Martha, whose letters now reported nothing but marital distress. And Freundlich's bitterness, cloaked in sarcasm, perturbed him to such a degree that he even admitted to us that he feared the worst: "He's cracking. I'm familiar with this. I'm afraid he's going to go off the deep end on us."

Sometimes a cheery message came from his granddaughter, but Madeleine was far away. Thus all he had left was the cameo face, but aside from finely silhouetted pallor, he could read nothing from those features. Helma Frühauf certainly responded so uninhibitedly as to be effusive, but Fonty learned nothing that would have confirmed his literarily well-grounded suspicion. It came as no surprise to him that the unemployed husband, prodded by his wife, was making progress in his computer training program and seemed generally willing to learn. And he dared not ask about the whereabouts of the roller skates, or the weekend in Duisburg.

For him the case was closed, the cameo face a dead-end motif. Even the smell of the flower pots on the six-step étagère was too intense for him. And when Frau Frühauf knocked briefly and came in with a pot of blooming myrtle—"Just for a puff"—he gave the custodial specialist to understand that too much was too much: "My dear lady, you are welcome to stop by even without more plants."

Actually it must have pleased him when he visited the double grave in the cemetery of the French Reformed parish to find it well tended, the rambler rose covered with buds. The wreath of immortelles that Madeleine had placed before the stone marker in early fall of the previous year had survived the winter well. And no sooner did he see these particular straw flowers than he was reminded of the wish expressed by old Frau Nimptsch, who liked to gaze into the open fire, for at least in fiction it had proved possible, with only gentle prodding, to persuade Botho von Rienäcker, otherwise not good for much, to make the long carriage ride out to the cemetery and place a wreath of immortelles on her grave. But when we pointed out that this once common practice functions as a leitmotif in *Delusions, Confusions* or tried to interpret it as an allusion to his life, our attempts to cheer him up were brusquely brushed aside: "Any battening on eternity and immortality is repugnant to me."

Now he stood before the double grave, saw the surviving wreath of immortelles, and searched for the word. Nothing seemed close at hand. Even this place of transitoriness stinted with suggestions. Because a few rows farther on cemetery workers were hacking away with shovels, the German concept of "rebedding" presented itself. But he immediately found himself wondering whether "rebed" was any more suitable than "wind down," when it would soon be a question of trimming down even more of the once publicly owned plants in Eisenhüttenstadt or Bitterfeld—suctioning out the fat, shrinking them to health, crushing them, or turning them into cash.

A group of chattering schoolchildren approached with their teacher. Fonty took them for an honors German class from "over there." He ducked behind some nearby graves so as not to be recognized. But he heard the teacher begin to invoke the Ribbeck pear tree, taking a brief excursion into history by way of Henricus de Ribeke, then calling the last owner of the estate a "victim of fascism," praising the land reform and the transformation of a good thousand hectares of former Junker land into an agricultural cooperative called "Young Life," and finally arriving at the pears, with the line in Low German, "My girl, come on over, I'll give thee a pear...." But even the cheery shouts of the boys and girls, who were calling this indestructible poem "a scream" and "adorable," as though it were a hit, could not raise Fonty's spirits. He slipped away without looking back.

No matter where he escaped to, desperate restlessness and paralyzing despair, his dismay at the general state of affairs, and his obsession with finding the right word dogged him. Even in the

Tiergarten, now coming into bloom, he found the birds' song and the bursting buds painful. On his favorite benches, whether close to the Luise Bridge or facing Rousseau Island, sat Dame Care, knitting him an interminable scarf that lacked any vitalizing pattern. His sighs were audible hither and yon, and even when he summoned companion spirits, hoping to distract himself, he could not find the right tone for a good chat.

He had hardly begun a conversation with Magistrate Friedlaender, which was easy enough, when he found himself compelled to deplore, "with the biting sarcasm of my advanced years, this stupid, avaricious aristocracy, its hypocritical or literal-minded religiosity, its everlasting reserve-officer mentality." He went on, as if his faithful correspondent from Jena were seated beside him, to equate the pillars of society from those days with the Parvenooskis, phrase-makers, and moral martinets of today: "Even when they know nothing, they know everything better. Nonetheless, you should not allow these Wessies to ruin life for you, my dear Freundlich. I'm not able to get up a full head of steam myself, but I refuse to let them wear me down. Courage! Just read in the *Tagesspiegel*, by the way, that your problem child did the name of Carl Zeiss proud by winning an away game. So you see!"

Thinking his English correspondent James Morris was sitting beside him—although at the other end of the bench sat only a droopy-mustached Turk of his own age—Fonty swore to them both that "world progress" was nowhere to be seen. He expressed his scorn so loudly and so globally that his Anatolian benchmate paused in telling his prayer beads: "The cannon and rifles are getting better and better, and seem able to guarantee *à la* Pizarro the continuation of European civilization, at least for the moment...." And the next sentence brought him to the "Gulf War with its new and improved destructive capability": "This most Christian orgy of killing ran simultaneously, and at reduced cost, on television. Even for my Emilie it was too much."

The Turk seemed to agree. Morris, on the other hand, continued to defend England's earlier contributions to world peace, whether in India, in the Sudan, or on the island of Zanzibar; he wanted to see peace imposed on the Gulf region in exactly the same manner.

Now Fonty brought up recent speeches by "Kaiser Wilhelm and especially his brother Heinrich in Kiel": "I am scared to death by all the hurrahing and the parades of ships, not to speak of the 'blooming landscapes' that the ruling mass has promised us, just in time for the elections. . . ." But with Bernhard von Lepel, whom he summoned as soon as his current and past benchmates had evaporated, it was hopeless to discuss the international arms trade and campaign promises, or even future threats to the human race, for he found this friend of his youth terribly ossified and narrowminded; and his old correspondent Mathilde von Rohr had nothing to report but the latest on Brandenburg's aristocratic families.

When Fonty imperiously commanded his anti-Prussian nemesis Theodor Storm to join him on the bench—"Get yourself over here at once, sir!"—the two of them soon reached agreement on matters literary, but when the topic of Germany's future capital arose, Storm was dead set against this "latest manifestation of Borussian presumption," while Fonty declared himself not in favor of Berlin but vehemently against Bonn: "Even Husum would be preferable, if you've no objection!"

The old quarrel from the frightful fifties broke out anew. We archivists must admit that it was the Immortal who wrote a letter on 11 April 1853, quite pedantically censuring Storm's poem "Epilog"—which called for revolution with a "final clap of thunder"—and refusing to publish it in the journal *Argo,* because the implications of this poem were "all too obvious to privy counselors, schoolmasters, and such people. . . ." And he went on to say, ". . . what smacks of a single, indivisible republic could be held very much against us."

At all events, the two of them were beyond help. If Storm saw emanating from Berlin a new bureaucratic—which to him meant authoritarian—state, Fonty was appalled at the prospect of musty provincialism: "Nothing more appalling than Pan-German Husumantics! Besides, the Germans will split in two again at the first bump in the road. . . ."

They spewed venom at each other, both of them equally touchy, and dredged up old stories from Tunnel days. First one, then the other took offense. Although old age would bring the two closer together—unfortunately, Storm died in '88—on the Tiergarten bench even we archivists could not have made peace between them; again and again ancient irritations welled up, and when Storm in his high, almost falsetto voice reproached poor Fonty for the *Kreuzzeitung*, all three war books, and his work as a censor under Merckel's rod, accusing him of being "an ill-paid but loyal and submissive state hack," Fonty fell silent and withdrew into himself, with spring crowing all around.

Fonty was looking wretched, as he did before or after a nervous breakdown; he was in the condition he referred to as *abattu*. No one could chat him out of his accumulated cares, neither Stephany nor the always amiable Schlenther, the last companions he summoned to the bench. They were a reliable pair. And just as they had previously in the *Vossische Zeitung*, both now praised the Briest novel. Fonty accepted their reviews as though hot off the press, but he could not shake off his sorrow. He thanked his friends, remarked, "Of course the Crampas letters should have been burned," apologized for the poorly motivated hiding place, saying, "But that is how banal life really is," and talked himself into a wistful mood: "Thus I say farewell to Effi; it will not come again, this last flaring-up...." Now alone once more, he decided, gazing at Rousseau Island, to fall silent for good. The birds sang all the more loudly.

Nature strutting her stuff. Everything so green that it dazzled the eyes. Far off, the roar of the city's traffic. If Freundlich had been there, with cares of his own, he would have referred to his mother, who even in Mexico continued to hum, "The month of May makes all things new...."

The only sight that could distract Fonty from himself was the diving duck, which was showing off its tricks among the ordinary ducks, as always providing an element of surprise. Not that this most deeply resourceful of waterfowl came up with the missing word in its beak when it reappeared; but the diving duck was good for ideas—be it a single, solitary idea, on which it held the patent in perpetuity.

On one of the first days in June, Hoftaller joined Fonty in the paternoster and spoke mysteriously of short trips to the West. He hinted at "new perspectives" and "renewed contacts," evaluated the services as "henceforth pan-German," and delivered greetings from son Teddy, the ministry official, who thanked his "Herr Papa for his accommodating assistance." But he had something else up his sleeve, and clearly thought that Fonty, who was on his way to the seventh floor, could be jolted by the news that the cleaning woman Helma Frühauf had given notice: "But what am I saying—given notice! She just left a note: 'Won't be coming back!' Simply up and disappeared, your cleaning and flower woman. Now you'll have to water all your plants yourself. You'll be getting a gardener's apron from me in the next few days."

Fonty assured him that he was not surprised. And Hoftaller, who got off the paternoster with him, offered to make up for this "bitter loss" by visiting often: "Me you can count on. And should I ever feel like a change of climate, you know: folks like us always turn up again, and again."

"*Sans* cigar, if possible. Neither the potted palm nor I can stand the pompous stench. And altogether, my plants and I like to be alone. If you'll permit me this old chestnut, I never promised you a rose garden. And as for Frau Frühauf—who, by the way, is a very bright person—she must have her reasons for quitting. Couldn't take the Handover Trust anymore. Maybe she got a good offer. She had other plans anyway: wanted to get retrained—go to night classes, study hard, eventually teach at a vocational school...."

"Nonsense! She's ducked out of sight. Not a trace to be found. We know the MO. But feel free to congratulate yourself, Fonty. I'll admit I thought your suspicion was far-fetched—the little gray mouse with an unerring sense of purpose—but there's something to it. Goes to show how dangerous literature can be. Just a shortish story, but with the impact of a time bomb..."

"Now the declared enemy of the written word is dreaming up new censorship rules that will take effect retroactively. Are you saying you want to place Mathilde Möhring in protective custody?"

"Not at all! I'm already looking forward to the next explosion. Actually none of this affects us anymore. We just watch while others go off in the wrong direction with their investigation. Simply ludicrous, this attorney general!"

"Not everyone's as well read as you...."

"He's grasping at straws. And in public, too! Well, it's no skin off our backs. You know my theory, of course: things'll start to slide, gradually at first, then faster and faster...."

Hoftaller sat a while longer on that sofa stuffed with special expertise, and added more and more details to his horrific picture of the Eastification of the West, a picture that had been painted over many times and was increasingly being drowned in darkness. He sat with a cold cigar in his mouth and sketched out a multi-tiered security system that included buffer zones here, bulwarks there, providing protective shields on all sides, especially to the east.

Once he had everything sealed up tight, he said, "That's the only way we can safeguard our Germany from being overrun by foreigners. The Western European hinterland can be included, but only—as I recently advised my new partners—if Germany receives special status. Think back, Fonty, not even all that far, just back to war correspondent Wuttke. You didn't concoct a single article in which you didn't celebrate 'Fortress Europe,' in between art-historical observations and landscape descriptions. Back then it was the Atlantic Wall you hailed, but your vision can be just as convincing today if the wall is erected against the East. Had to spell out the whys and wherefores in detail for the gentlemen over there. Otherwise we'll be Eastified, I said. You can already see what's cooking, and not only in the Balkans, but also in the Ukraine—no, everywhere in those parts and farther off in the Caucasus.... It's time, gentlemen, to give thought to all this, you know, the way Airman Wuttke gave thought to such things in his day on the Atlantic coast...."

Fonty was not prepared to contribute to the new security system. He sat at his desk. In front of him lay a proposal for reviving Kühn's pictorial broadsheets, and the meager list of substitute terms he had scraped together. He gazed out the window, over the square inner courtyard into the meaningless blue sky, then back at the étagère full of potted plants standing to one side of the desk, as if it could offer something to hold onto. Letting his eyes go from step to step, he named the plants to himself: the begonia, the African violet, the arrowroot with its rich variegated coloring, the ever-blooming impatiens, the azalea whose blossoms had long since wilted, the ornamental ivy, the old-fashioned primrose, the maidenhair fern, the myrtle, the aloe...

It is entirely possible that the sight of the fully occupied étagère or the potted palm by the wall on which sun sometimes shone led him to a word that evoked gardening and cultivating, a Frühauf word. "Repot!" he exclaimed. "She said, 'You've got to repot them.' Listen, Hoftaller, that's it: repot!"

During her last visit, the cameo face had suggested that by fall at the latest the fast-growing ivy-leafed aralia and the papyrus with its luxuriant shoots should be transferred to larger containers. She stood by the étagère, displaying her profile, and in Fonty's eyes had a Gothic look about her. He told us later, "Early Gothic, Upper Rhine school. But the Italian masters, too; think of Fra Angelico or of Giotto's women—there's a particular contour..."

When Helma Frühauf offered him her profile, she said, as if in parting, "And don't you forget, Herr Wuttke: a plant like this here grows and needs enough room, if not today then maybe tomorrow. Don't forget: repotting's important!"

Since the cleaning woman never called him Fonty, she was spared references to Dörr's nursery in *Delusions, Confusions,* where repotting took place from time to time. We archivists would actually have been the right ones to give this tip; for although the extensive gardens on the outskirts, with their view of the fields of Wilmersdorf, "lacked any elegance, with the exception of the asparagus beds. Dörr considered the most ordinary stock the most advantageous, and therefore raised marjoram and other sausage herbs, but especially leeks..."—even so, something certainly had to be potted or repotted for the weekly market, for instance gilly-flowers and geraniums.

After Hoftaller left, the consultant Theo Wuttke made a clean copy of the list of substitute terms, and ended it with the underlined entry, "Suggest in place of 'wind down' the word 'repot.' Out of the publicly owned, and into the privately owned pot." Then, after a pause, during which he held the quill a few inches above the paper, he added, in parentheses: "I'm convinced, by the bye, that the term 'wind down' will have to be retained; it has already put down roots and become proverbial."

Beneath the list he signed his officially registered name. Along with the signed and folded sheet of paper, he stuck into an envelope his proposal for reviving the Neuruppin pictorial broadsheet series with colored Handover Trust tales, and delivered the envelope to the Department for Public Relations and Communications.

Fonty felt relieved. He saw himself as having overcome a crisis, and, as one of his favorite epigrams had it, "Within this world of want, a person can live passably well."

Back on Kollwitzstrasse he found neither Emmi nor their neighbor Inge Scherwinski at home, but an opened telegram lay on the kitchen table. He read: "Must quote you at the end: If life is silent, desire falls silent. Yours, Eckhard Freundlich."

Not until two days later did the professor's wife confirm that he had died by his own hand. She wrote, "He had no will to go on. He asked me to follow our daughters to Israel. And because, alas, I must concur with the observation he repeatedly made of late, 'There is no room here for Jews,' I shall most likely honor his request...."

When the Handover Trust consultant Theo Wuttke went to his office the following day, more to water the plants than to sit out his hours of idleness there, he found a further communication on his desk. It contained not a word about the usefulness of the substitute expressions, likewise nothing about broadsheets portraying contemporary events, but he was informed in no uncertain terms that he had one week to clear out of Room 1819. His contract remained in effect. The consultant Theo Wuttke would be assigned to field operations. Detailed instructions would follow.

Fonty paced up and down. He could have said to himself, "It's not only Jews for whom there's no room here," but instead he said, "Well, all right, there's world elsewhere, too!" Then he watered the potted plants as though nothing had happened.

BOOK 5

33

False Alarm

After experiencing so much loss, he took his time saying his farewells. Certain parts of the city, such as Friedrichshain, Pankow, and
Kreuzberg, the Mitte district, railroad stations, his newspaper stand
on Alexanderplatz, the Gendarmenmarkt, and the Scheunenviertel, the former stable district, but also underground line No. 6 and
the S-Bahn line to Wannsee and Erkner, then his long-sat-upon
benches in the Tiergarten, for the last time the villa at Rabbits'
Run in the Grunewald—he traversed, traveled, and tarried in all
these districts, stretches, and rendezvous; and of course he went up
Potsdamer Strasse, then on by way of Hauptstrasse and Rheinstrasse to Friedenau, with a detour to Niedstrasse; and again and
again he stood on windswept Alexanderplatz or at the foot of the
Victory Column. But not one of the many theaters, not even the
People's Theater, was worth a glance, or any museum worth a visit.
Nor did he say good-bye to individuals—for instance, certain receptionists in the Handover Trust building, not to mention his day-
and-night-shadow. Only the footnote slaves toiling in the Archives
still mattered to him.

When he walked in holding a bunch of peonies, we could tell
that Fonty was visiting us on the eve of a journey. Dressed for summer, seeming cheerful and as if freed of burdens, he played the
chatterbox, reporting the latest from days gone by: ironic side-
lights on Wallot's Reichstag building, recently inaugurated with
much fanfare; the runoff election in the Rheinsberg-Wutz district,
from which someone in a balloon cap—Torgelow the file-cutter—
had emerged as winner; but not a word about the death of his

faithful correspondent and the funeral in Jena, which he had attended—apparently unescorted.

At most he opened up indirectly: "Something's afoot in the city. They're busy doing each other in. That's why I wrote to Morris, 'We see nothing but duels these days....'"

We did not interpret this as a clue to his intended destination, even though he repeatedly compared Berlin with London. But it was noticeable how easily he stripped off his identity as a Handover Trust employee, indeed his entire Theo Wuttke persona, stoking the conversation with quotations, effortlessly being the Immortal, without so much as a wink.

During the last few weeks he had made a leap in age. He had gained a number of years, and now appeared as the fragile old man whom Liebermann's drawing captures for us: with alert eyes but watery gaze—already not altogether of this world. It was as if he wanted to try out the cliché of "hovering serenely above the fray"—at least experimentally.

This time, unlike the last time he had ducked out of sight, the question did not even arise: Where should he go? The choice between France and England had become irrelevant. We speculated, just for laughs, that we might receive a postcard of the Empire State Building, for he quoted repeatedly from *Quitt,* and in the process brought the Wild West to life in Panavision: "Over there, the Mennonite settlement, bordering on the Indian territories—ah, the land of infinite opportunity..."

Then one of the women steered the conversation around to the ceremony that had taken place back in December, marking the establishment of the research society that we hoped would raise funds to support our work. Unfortunately, we had neglected to invite Fonty; or had he been taken off the list in deference to guests from the West?

To our astonishment, he was *au courant,* speaking of the event as if he had been there, and serving up quotations from the rather original keynote address by Charlotte Jolles, the professor who had earned her doctorate in German literature under Petersen but later emigrated to England. This lady, by now well along in years, had tried to pound some Anglo-Saxon business sense into us ivory-tower scholars: "The society we have established here today must have trading posts everywhere, as the British Empire once established dominance by means of such posts...." Fonty parodied the old lady's impassioned appeal: "Hence my motto: Let us invest in the Immortal!"

To our regret we were forced to admit that this appeal had thus far proved as good as futile: "But you know how it is, Fonty. Things are no different at the Trust. No one wants to invest, certainly not in culture. People want everything handed to them, or sold for a symbolic one mark. Yet Frau Professor Jolles went to so much trouble."

Fonty remained interested, as if it affected him directly, and repeated further passages from the keynote address: "This future society, ladies and gentlemen, will need money, money, money!"

To the delight of her listeners, she had canvassed the Immortal's characters for a patron saint with financial expertise. Fonty supported her efforts fully, whereas we had received her suggestions with a reserved smile or with the arrogance generally attributed to Ossies in those days. Like Charlotte Jolles, Fonty started with the manufacturer of blue alkaline salts and Prussian blue: "How about Commercial Councillor Treibel?"

Then Instetten was proposed, as a competent administrator, and rejected with an argument that could hardly be refuted: "Women members would be absolutely opposed, for, as we know from Effi, 'He did not know what real love was....'"

After old Briest, the eponymous characters Cécile and Stine were proposed, along with Melusine, whom old Stechlin prized so highly; then the two younger Poggenpuhl girls, and Lene Nimptsch, who, although very independent, was too young. But Fonty agreed with Frau Jolles that "Mathilde Möhring should not be dismissed out of hand. Of course she lacks the charm of the other female characters, but she has the practicality we need, and she masters life...."

But because Mathilde was insufficiently attractive, both were of the opinion that in this second Founders' Era only one of the many literary figures had the wherewithal to be the patron: "Frau Jenny Treibel is the one who will show us the way, for she alone managed to combine money and poetry!"

563

Did Fonty want to leave us this advice as his farewell gift, with the Immortal's assent? Suddenly our guest changed the subject. Rather coquettishly he reminded us that Major Dubslav von Stechlin (ret.), always called old Stechlin, had popped off at sixty-seven; he considered himself quite perky by comparison: "Because he was so attached to Prussia, Dubslav forbade his Engelke to sew a red stripe on the black and white flag flying from his tower; but I should like to hoist the Europa flag everywhere: Away with all borders! Down with all national rags! Europa is coming—monstrous offspring or no!"

Then he whispered to us the latest from Lake Stechlin: "You know, of course, that when the earth begins to shudder and shake anywhere in the world—whether in Iceland or in Java—the lake stirs, and a plume of water shoots up and falls back into the depths. As it did not long ago when Pinatubo erupted on the Philippine island of Luzon. I happened to be in the capital of Ruppin county, and after taking in several monuments—Schinkel, Marx, and so on—I paid a visit to Lake Stechlin, which had become accessible once more. It began to bubble. My companion—not exactly a hero—was terrified when, in addition to the plume of water's shooting up, as it often does, a red cock went flapping over the turbulent waters, its crowing echoing over the land."

Fonty waited to see the effect his anecdote would have. Then he looked at each one of us in turn and said, "That is a portent, gentlemen! Of course I regard the crazy weather we are having as a coincidence, but all the same: our old planet is beginning to rumble as if it would like to shake us off, as if we human beings had become a nuisance. Well, if the gentlemen didn't, certainly you, my dear lady, take my meaning. Time to close the books! Time to say good-bye."

Admittedly I shared his fears. I said, "But what should we do, Fonty? Jettison the whole thing? Simply take off? And where to, if I may ask?"

He went on his way. But before he left us there alone with the latest news from Lake Stechlin, he said in that familiar old sauntering tone, "By the way, the Handover Trust is sponsoring a contest. They are still looking for a better word for the unfortunate 'winding down.' It is open to everyone. Why not the Archives, since you are in need of cash, and the winner is assured a tidy sum. It all comes down to money, does it not?"

Where was he sitting when he put steel pen to paper? In the little coffee shop on Potsdamer Strasse, across from Number 134C? Or at Offenbach's, over salted almonds and a glass of red wine?

Fonty did not want to depart without having written something. To vanish without a word would not have been his style, and besides, he had a dozen or more letters composed in his head. Might he have been sitting on a bench in the Tiergarten, the inkwell next to him, turning the scribbled pencil version straight into fair copy, with exuberant loops, decorative garlands, and those almost closed ovals above the *u*'s?

Because his words of farewell were smuggled in among frightfully true epigrams and a good deal of horticultural ornamentation, he was presumably using the office from which he had been evicted. During the last few days before he had to clear it out to the bare walls, Fonty wrote letter after letter.

A letter to Professor Freundlich was already started, four pages in pencil, on both sides of the paper. Now its intended recipient was gone. Comparison makes it clear that he salvaged passages from this letter—for instance, the allusion to the potted palm and its connection with *L'Adultera*—for a letter to his granddaughter: "Facing me on the only moderately sunny wall of my hitherto windless cell is a date palm, to be precise *Phoenix canariensis,* which makes a fine potted palm. And, my dear child, whenever I think of your regrettably difficult relationship (between stools and probably also beds), my exotic sample in its rather bedraggled condition promptly reminds me of the van Straaten palm house, where the gardener Kagelmann remarked, 'Goodness, Frau Rätin, palms are always appropriate,' and a short time later the lovely Melanie and the infatuated banker's son Rubehn had a rendezvous with adulterous intentions. The conservatory was filled with towering palms, dracaenas, and giant ferns, through which twined intensely fragrant orchids. A colossal tropical forest under a glass bell. No wonder the couple were breathing hard in the languid air, while both of them whispered words, so hot, so sweet. . . .

"You know, my child, that I never allowed my scenes to become explicit, either in *Delusions, Confusions,* where a double room at Hankel's Depot provides ample opportunity, or in *Irretrievable,* before fire breaks out in the castle. I avoid that kind of infamous passage; most of them are the epitome of tastelessness. Effi's letter to Crampas and Crampas's notes to Effi say enough, and betray everything without becoming obvious. Therefore I shall not ask you questions about your professor that would promptly lead us to the sultry hothouse; but I would feel better if I could set out on my journey with the certainty that my Madeleine is free, and breathing fresh air.

"By the way, I shall soon be without a potted palm. They are taking away my office. By the day after tomorrow, the palm and I must clear out; the person who is writing this to you is in a sense homeless. They have, it is true, promised me 'further assignment to field operations'—but that cannot hold me.

"I must get out, get far, far away! I am in the situation in which my erstwhile faithful correspondent Friedlaender found himself when a court martial deprived him of his breathing room—some stupid officer's business, not to suggest a comparison with the Dreyfus Affair; of course the fact that he was a Jew (decorated with the Iron Cross after the campaign in France) played a certain role. Which brings me to Professor Freundlich: he is dead.

"Ah, my child, a void has opened up around me. Nothing could hold him here; and your humble servant, too, is about to take the leap. Everything tells me: Get out of this country, where, for all eternity, Buchenwald lies down the road from Weimar, this land that is no longer mine or allowed to be mine, in which too little holds me. Old Frau von Wangenheim had it frightfully right when she said in her quintessentially Catholic way, 'Prussian Germany is no Promised Land!'

"And therefore, just before the terrible news came (by telegram, by the way), I was about to write to Freundlich, 'Nothing to do but make yourself scarce! No one wants you here. The only use your westward-looking colleagues have for you is as a punching bag. They have evaluated you out of existence. Without ascribing too much to the—alas—weather-resistant anti-Semitism in this country, I can tell from what court-chaplainish direction the wind is blowing. Even I, who look more like a native of Brandenburg than I would wish, recently experienced an assault—and not the first—in the Tiergarten, as if Treitschke and Stöcker had been in command. So-called skinheads, four in number, did me the honor, near my favorite bench. Were suddenly standing there, with glazed eyes and honest-to-goodness clubs in their hands. "Jews get out!" That was the best they could do. Bellowing and beer fumes. I raised my walking stick, scraped together a modicum of courage and my rear-echelon French—*"Allez, mes enfants!"* and then, more distinctly, *"Imbéciles!"*—and they were gone.

"'You may laugh, my dear friend, but please consider that it could very well have turned nasty, for in the meantime everyone here is betting on force, with the Handover Trust leading the way. So look for a change of climate, before it is too late!'

"That is the advice I was about to give my correspondent of many years, when he took leave for good. (I then spoke in this vein at his grave, and called Germany 'a land of emigration,' in the widest sense of the term.) I imagine he still had his service revolver on hand, from his days with the People's Police—Freundlich was a lieutenant in the reserves.

"Now you will understand, my child, why your grandfather wishes only to get away, for here everything has again acquired the characteristic odor of pines and parade grounds. In short, I simply want to go 'poof,' as the Berliners say. But if I succeed in bobbing merrily to the surface somewhere else, as far from the German-German field of fire as possible, I shall send up my share of suggestive signal flares for you; without my Madeleine and her little letters, without you, my bittersweet person, I could not be happy anywhere...."

Even in his letter to Schwerin, Fonty did not suppress allusions to the upward-spiraling étagère. Two potted plants that Frau Frühauf had added to his collection shortly before ducking out of sight, a gillyflower and a petunia, gave him entrée to the Dörr nursery: "...diagonally across from the 'Zoological.'" At the beginning of the letter he reassured Martha: "Now you must not imagine that these potted plants are mere cuttings, like the fraudulent merchandise sold by that wizened old supplier Dörr, next door to whom the elderly Frau Nimptsch and her foster daughter Lene lived; rather, they were raised in their pots and are blooming splendidly, especially the petunia. So I should be in good humor. But as you know, the most important thing is always missing. For instance a heliotrope, which not only occupied a central position at the Briests' but turned up even in the Möhrings' modest milieu, where an overpoweringly scented heliotrope stood in the parlor for that reluctant learner Hugo Grossmann, who had come down with the measles.

"To be sure, I have everything here—a potted palm and impatiens—but I feel painfully the absence of the heliotrope, my true flower. And the general decrepitude is increasing. When I look around, only Menzel is still standing, completely ossified, to be sure, but for that very reason, nothing can touch him. I, however, am afflicted by many things at once. (Mama has certainly written to you about my most painful loss, which leaves me without words.) All that remains is to report on what remains: the clearance sale! Just as, from the point of view of Brandenburg's aristocracy—the Quitzows in the lead—the Mark was sold out to the Hohenzollerns, today the victorious hordes view it as nothing more than a bargain to snap up. I cannot bear to stand by and watch this commerce.

"In other words, your father is about to set out, if not in search of the Romantics' blue flower, then in search of the missing heliotrope. And I write this to you so frankly because I know that you alone understand me—my Mete's turn of phrase in her last litany of accusations was more than felicitous; you wrote about the 'many-threaded rackets' being spun by your Grundmann.

"I have had some more or less reasonable discussions with Mama, while in the background *Lindenstrasse* or *Golden Girls* was playing. Although she lacks real insight, she did understand that I have no choice. I know that comparisons are odious; yet I had to remind her that we have reached a point like that in the year '76, when I had to jettison the Academy rubbish—as I did with the *Kreuzzeitung* many years earlier—and set myself free, whatever the risk. No one wanted to understand me, even my Mete, when I was forced to bid farewell to the Cultural Union because of similar problems. Well, things are no less difficult today. The general situation, this shambles known as the present...

"Yet I worry first and foremost about you, for in your last letter you spoke of separation, even divorce. I will hardly be able to help with that. Of course, I know I am free of all pettifogging notions about 'marital bliss,' but as far as your husband is concerned, whom you took on as a seemingly solid and well-meaning developer, only to discover that he is now paying tribute to his name by grabbing the very ground others stand on, I can say only this: He, too, is a child of his times. For if he is buying up castles and manor houses by the dozen—whatever used to have a resonant name—such is the spirit of the age. It looks as though the victory over communism has made capitalism rabid. That is why I intended to urge Eckhard Freundlich, shortly before he commended himself to the grave, to make tracks, like me: 'There is no staying in Germany these days.'

"You will ask yourself: Where to? Why could he not have pitched his tent where capitalism erects its temples, in full confidence of God's favor? You recall that the grand old man of Weimar let out a heartfelt sigh, apropos of conditions here: 'America, you have it better.' I am assuming that still holds. (Besides, Freundlich would have been closer to Mexico there, the scene of his childhood.)

"I, however, am once again flirting with the island which afforded me mildly entertaining days in London, and several heroes for the novels to boot—for instance, the world traveler and cable-layer Leslie-Gordon, whose fate it was to end up with a pistol aimed at him by that skilled marksman and retired colonel St. Arnaud, and all for the sake of the both lovely and overwrought Cécile.

"You have often asked me why my female characters all have a screw loose. Well, that is precisely what makes me fond of them. This much by way of explanation for Cécile and Effi, but for my Mete as well. Please remember: every time you went to the theater, an opera glass fell on your head, or something of the sort...."

After he had interrogated the postage scale and stamped this last Mete letter, Fonty wrote curt, factual letters to his sons Teddy and Friedel. He told the former that they had nothing more to say to one another in any case: "Rather soon it may come to light that even you, the knight in shining armor, can no longer claim to fit any pattern of excellence...." He asked the latter to forget the book project, which had been talked to death in any case: "I daresay my Cultural Union lectures are unforgivably insignificant to today's reader, who lusts after sensational revelations. Besides, this way I spare myself the reviews...."

It should be added that he committed all the farewell letters to paper with flourishes, making dramatic loops on the capital *T*'s and *F*'s; he had laid aside the steel pen in favor of the swan quill. This was also true of his brief missives to important literary figures like the Wolfs and the playwright Müller, which we shall cite only sparingly. He warned the playwright, recently become a father, against naughty children who shave matchstick heads into the coffee and stick pins into pieces of bread. To the once celebrated woman of letters who had recently become the subject of withering attacks, he offered the sum of his own experience: "Often it is the selfsame outfit that sets up monuments and martyrs' pyres...."

Only to Frau Professor Jolles, to whom he announced his coming, and whom he described, almost giddily, as "a Miss Marple on the trail of my London days," did he speak plainly about his destination and date of arrival: "To save myself the ordeal of railroad and ferry, I have booked a direct flight...."

He did not write to Emmi Wuttke. She already knew the score. Later she told us, "Good lord, you should've seen how my Wuttke carried on at home. There was no keeping him. Didn't even try. When the Handover took away his office, it didn't just bother him, he took it personally. After all, he'd been going in and out of that old crate forever, starting with the Reich Aviation. And then there was that telegram. He knew right away what was up, even before we got the letter explaining everything. Terrible it was, just terrible for him. Just between us, he broke down and cried, my Wuttke did, real tears. But he wanted to get away earlier, too, get free, he said, and that meant from me, too, which really hurt me terribly, I'm telling you, and still does. But I say to myself, I say, if he needs a change of scene, let him have it. Let him go, for all I care. He'll be back...."

He buckled his seat belt at once. If we archivists can state that with such assurance, this is due not only to our image of Fonty but also to the services we had rendered: we were the ones who had booked the flight, reserved a window seat for him—nonsmoking section— paid for the ticket, and picked it up. We had even arranged for his transportation, by taxi from Zoo station to Tegel. One of us helped him check in. And one of our ladies walked him to the security gate. That had been his wish, uttered at the end of his farewell visit, almost as an aside: "By the bye, I'm a bit weary of Berlin, and would be most obliged if you could help me get away as inconspicuously as possible...."

He trusted us. And of course he reimbursed us in cash for the cost of the one-way flight. He did so promptly, when we found him, standing as arranged, under the clock in the railway station: ready for his journey with light bamboo cane, boater, and a new overcoat, which he carried folded casually over his arm. Next to him his suitcase and valise, as if he were setting out for a summer resort.

At that time we had already been absorbed, as per transfer agreement, into the Foundation for Prussian Cultural Holdings. This new accountability structure might have made him distrustful, because several of our recent acquisitions, such as the tabletop computer and the fax machine, had confounded him. Yet he thought he could be sure of our discretion; his link with the Archives had existed so long.

He even joked about the "colossal modernization," and during his last visit quoted old Stechlin: "I cannot bear telegrams!" But then he asked us to use our new machine to copy several articles by Frau Jolles on the Immortal's sojourns in London and his journals: "For the plane. Can't do any harm, madame, gentlemen, to see through one's own little game. I'm certain there's some frightfully good stuff here, and not only about the notebooks. But consider this, please: No one can get through life an innocent. What does Mister Robinson, the English coachman, say when he's visiting another coachman: 'But widow is more than virgin....'"

At his request, we dug out a photograph of Frau Professor

Jolles gesticulating eloquently at the lectern during the founding of the society. Fonty thought he saw a certain similarity to Mathilde von Rohr, "my dear old correspondent": "I wrote to her when I was working on the *Rambles* and had outlandish whims of an entirely different sort in my head—I think that was in July '74: 'Shall be traveling some time in the next two hours by sailboat to Teupitz, ten miles from here, passing Köpenick and Wusterhausen, heading upstream. The river is the Dahme or Sorbian Spree....'"

He recited these lines as if they were a Brandenburg ballad, but he had a distant destination before his eyes.

From Tegel directly to Heathrow. Everything went like clockwork: his window seat was waiting for him, and he could see the left wing of the jet. His first flight after so many trips by train. True, a few times Airman Theo Wuttke had flown by Ju 52 on urgent courier missions to Paris, or had landed on military strips in Brittany and Normandy, but these did not count. No Wuttke any longer; this was Fonty sitting there, buckled in; or, rather, it was the Immortal waiting for the plane to start, gather speed, lift off.... The wisps of his mustache were trembling slightly.

It took a while for all the passengers to find their seats and stow their hand luggage in the overhead bins. The British Airways plane was booked solid. In the rows in front of and behind him and on the other side of the aisle they were crammed in like sardines. As far as he could see, no one would have been able to find a last-minute seat. In the row in front of him sat a Sikh, recognizable by his towering turban. Next to Fonty was a little girl holding a doll on her lap. Apparently she was traveling alone, for the woman next to the child was leafing through a travel magazine without a glance or a word for the plump little beauty at her side.

Now all the passengers were buckled in, on instructions from the stewardess. The little girl, whose hair, by the way, was rust-colored, had even squeezed her slim, long-legged doll under her seat belt. Now the plane could have released its brakes and rolled toward the runway. Over the loudspeaker, the stewardess was explaining in two languages what was to be done in an emergency, miming each life-saving step. Now she floated down the middle aisle, checking everyone with a smile. She tossed an encouraging "Hallo" to the little girl traveling alone, walked jauntily to the curtain separating first class from tourist class, sat down, and buckled herself in as well. Fonty had both hands on his knees. Then the child said, "You're shaking, Opa. Are you scared?"

"Well, I'm flying for the first time."

"It doesn't bother me, 'cause I often have to fly to London for the weekend."

"So maybe you want to be a stewardess when you grow up..."

"Oh, no. That would be much too boring. Unfortunately, I have to fly back and forth so much because Mami and Papi are separated. But it's better this way. They really weren't getting along anymore, just fought all the time."

"And your Papi lives and works in London? I, too, was employed there for a while—that was a long time ago. Afterward I even went to Scotland...."

"No, it was Mami who left, and now she's opened a really hip boutique with her girlfriend Mary Lou, just off Portobello Road. It's doing quite well for a start, Mami says. But actually I live with Papi. It's better that way."

"How clever of you to see everything so sensibly."

"Oh, well. Sometimes I do have to cry. I'm only nine, you know. But then I always tell myself, it's better not to have a family than to have one where they just fight all the time. You're still shaking."

"Yes, my child."

"But there's no need, really."

"I know."

"In the beginning I used to shake a little, too."

"Tell me, what's your name? Why aren't we taking off?"

"Well, my name's Agnes. And we're not taking off because we haven't received clearance. That happens sometimes, and it can take a while. What do you think of the name Agnes?"

"I knew a child with the same name once. And this Agnes used to sit by the window overlooking the terrace and leaf through a picture book with castles, and lakes with swans, but also hussars. And the mother of this little Agnes, who had no father... I do wish we were in the air already...."

The child placed her chubby little hand on Fonty's right hand, which was shaking badly, despite his attempts to steady it on his knee. It helped a bit to have the child's hand resting on the back of his own, with its branching veins. He closed his eyes and narrated his way back into the past, told the story of the lake and the plume of water, of the weather vanes in the cobweb-filled museum, and then of old Stechlin, who had the odd given name of Dubslav, and of his servant Engelke and the old witch Buschen, but then he spoke only of the child Agnes, who sat very still in her red stockings, keeping the old man company, by the window overlooking the terrace, and leafed through a picture book, which was actually a bound volume of agricultural journals: "And when Dubslav was nearing death, the child said, 'Is he dead?' But the servant Engelke said, 'No, Agnes, he's just having a bit of a nap....'"

The other Agnes exclaimed, "I love the way you tell that. Tell me more...."

But Fonty's account of the death of old Stechlin was interrupted by a voice over the loudspeaker: "This is Captain Morris...."

There followed an explanation, first in English, then in German, concerning a piece of luggage on board that had to be checked again, for security reasons. Unfortunately, all passengers were kindly asked to exit the aircraft while this safety precaution was carried out. British Airways regretted the inconvenience.

While Agnes unstrapped herself and her doll, then helped Fonty unbuckle his belt, she said, "I've been through this before. It must be another bomb scare. Never takes long. And outside they'll give you a voucher for refreshments. Then you can finish the story about the old witch, who was really the grandmother of little Agnes, and about the teacher called Krippenstapel, and about Engelke, and the old man in his chair, and even more about Agnes in her red stockings. But also about the old man's sister, the one from the convent, who was so upset about the red stockings...."

We were not particularly surprised. Although we had kept our mouths shut, this intervention might have been anticipated. Or had one of us—in those days just about everyone was under suspicion—thought a little betrayal would be a good thing?

In the airport café—the stewardess escorted the passengers there and handed out vouchers that they could exchange for refreshing beverages in paper cups—sat Hoftaller, even though all the passengers booked through to London had already gone through passport control and were now in the duty-free area. He had received, as he said later, "special authorization—as a favor."

Dressed in new gray flannel, he came up to Fonty and the plump child with the doll, opening his arms in a welcoming gesture, and maneuvered his subject, without a word but with an unmistakable gesture, to one of the unoccupied tables. When Agnes wanted to join them, Fonty said, "I'm afraid you can't, my child. We have something we need to discuss...."

"I know," the child said, "something just for grown-ups. Mami always says, 'This is nothing for little ears,' and when Papi has company, he always says..."

"Maybe later..."

"I know."

"Then I'll finish the story...."

"No problem."

When the two of them were by themselves, Hoftaller said, "So, here we are again. What a coincidence!"

Agnes had sat down a few tables away with her doll and her backpack. She did not touch her orange juice. Her gaze, and the gaze of her doll, which she held pressed to her tummy, were of the same blue, and did not waver from Fonty or the other grown-up.

Hoftaller wanted to smoke, but that was prohibited here. Fonty offered him his container of juice. He polished it off in three swallows. Now only time was passing.

What difference does it make who initiated the conversation? They talked for a good hour. Finally only Hoftaller was left speaking. Other flights were called and departed: for Rome by way of Milan, for Paris. Fonty sat there ramrod-straight, struggling to maintain his composure. Sometimes he raised his hands, only to let them sink again. Several times he shook his head slowly. Once he was seen to nod. And only once did he raise his voice: "I'm familiar with the expression!"

For a moment he turned his bareheaded old man's face and

smiled at Agnes. She did not smile back. Then his entire attention was concentrated on Hoftaller again. His straw hat was lying on a vacant chair, against which the bamboo cane was leaning. Judging by his appearance, he could have been seen a little while earlier on Potsdamer Strasse, in the Tiergarten, at the Gendarmenmarkt, or in front of Zoo station: all in all, he seemed a figure from yesteryear. People looked at him and grinned; and in the airport café people swiveled their barstools in his direction. He stood out more than the Sikh in his turban or the plump child with her doll.

When the flight to London was finally called, and the passengers clustered around the counter, Agnes came up to the two grown-ups, who had remained seated. Her legs were sturdy, a little knock-kneed. Only now did Fonty notice that she was wearing red stockings and patent-leather shoes.

The child said, ignoring Hoftaller, "Just as I thought. It was another false alarm. That's better than something happening, though. And now we're really taking off."

Fonty, who wanted to stand up but then remained seated, said, "I can't, Agnes. Or I'm not allowed to, not yet. Maybe some other time..."

"But you're a grown-up. And grown-ups are always allowed, you know...."

"Not me. Or only now and then, for special occasions."

Agnes said no more. As she walked toward the counter, she let the doll dangle limply at the end of her stiff arm, so that its long legs and the child's patent-leather shoes scuffed along the floor of the departure lounge.

The Archives have long been at a loss for answers to the following question: Under what form of pressure, or what special pressure, and why (in case he was under duress for several reasons) was passenger Fonty forced to give up the flight to London we had booked for him? Even supposing one of us had not kept Fonty's intentions quiet, this betrayal would have made us contemptible, but none the wiser. What was reported to us did not allow us to formulate any definitive answer, for which reason we have, in the meantime, come to believe that it was several factors that induced him to reclaim his luggage, although the lightweight suitcase he had bought especially for this journey was not delivered to him on Kollwitzstrasse until two days later, when it found its way back from London. After deduction of the usual fees, they even reimbursed the cost of his ticket—through us. The expenses incurred on the abortive trip were hardly worth mentioning, but one thing is certain: after this experience Fonty was a changed man, though not outwardly.

Hoftaller took a number of different tacks with him. Presumably he began with that absurd if coherent story that made Theo Wuttke out to be the Immortal's great-great-grandson. The old Dresden business surfaced again—the rowboat excursions with Magdalena Strehlenow, the gardener's daughter, the Lenau poems, the thirst for liberty, moonlit trysts and their consequences: a child called Mathilde who had claimed financial support from the young apothecary, starting in the summer of 1843.

And in 1864, during the war with Denmark—the war from which the first of the war books issued—this Mathilde Strehlenow, according to the information Hoftaller revealed when questioned, is supposed to have married a rather down-at-heels teacher in training named August Wuttke, who later died of pneumonia, shortly after the birth of a son—Fonty's grandfather and the Immortal's grandson Friedrich.

That was near the end of the war with Austria, when August Wuttke had just been promoted to a permanent teaching position in Rheinsberg. The industrious Mathilde managed to secure a good education for her son. And in the three-kaiser year, Friedrich Wuttke, after advancing to chief buyer for Hirschfeld & Son in Gransee, married a teacher's daughter named Marie Duval, evidently of Huguenot ancestry; Hoftaller was able to lay his hands on a copy of the marriage certificate for us.

And among other children, and shortly before the kaiser sent his famous dispatch to Ohm Kruger, this marriage produced Max Wuttke, who is to be regarded as the Immortal's great-grandson and Fonty's father. That occurred shortly after the family's move to Neuruppin, where Friedrich Wuttke went into business for himself as a lumber dealer, but soon went bankrupt.

His son Max learned the lithographer's trade, joined the army in 1915, became a noncommissioned officer, surviving even the use of mustard gas, returned to Neuruppin with the few who were left from the 24th Infantry Regiment, and promptly married the daughter of a first lieutenant who had fallen at Verdun. Before their daughter, Liselotte, saw the light of day, Luise Wuttke, née Fraissenet, presented him with a son, whom they named Theo—the Immortal's great-great-grandson, our Fonty—whose only sister, Aunt Liselotte, was laid to rest in Hamburg's Ohlsdorf Cemetery in the mid-eighties.

And this hair-raisingly linear story—true or not—is supposed to have prompted the Immortal's distant relative to give up his flight to London after the bomb scare?

That we cannot believe. It seems more likely that Hoftaller traced the line farther into the present, putting into play the great-great-great-grandson from the Dresden branch, Teddy Wuttke, who was employed in the Ministry of Defense in Bonn, and here he did not have to spend much time on threats. No doubt it was an additional piece of information that provided a more powerful incentive for Fonty's renouncing the trip than the usual "We can do this the hard way": Teddy had apparently turned informant simply in order to protect his father and mother. Purely out of concern for his parents, he had shared his more or less secret expertise in dribs and drabs. A better son could not be found. "Just imagine," Hoftaller may have said, "what if Teddy, unlike his well-meaning brother, the pilot Georg, had been an obstinate, egotistical person who said to himself, 'What do I care about my family's situation? So what if they stick my nutty father in a factory, drum my sister out of the Party and even into Bautzen, and as for my mother...'"

That is how it may have been. And if not, then the account Hoftaller dished up in the airport café regarding Emmi Wuttke's attempted suicide certainly did the trick. Fonty had no sooner set out with his hat, cane, and suitcase, he said, than she had swallowed a whole handful of pills. Luckily their daughter Martha had left Schwerin as soon as she received her father's letter. She had arrived just in time to administer first aid, with the assistance of their neighbor Inge Scherwinski. "Of course they had to pump out your Emmi's stomach at the Charité. But I was assured just now by telephone that she's doing quite well, given the circumstances. Man, Fonty! You must have been out of your mind. A good thing I was tipped off. Anyway, your Emmi will be happy to have her Wuttke back as soon as possible."

That was sufficient. But if not, Hoftaller's promise to try to get the order evicting Fonty from his office perhaps not rescinded but at least postponed would have carried weight. He said, "Besides, a new perspective is taking shape. The Trust is going to commission you to show former castles and manor houses to interested investors. Tours to various locations. They're counting on your expert guidance. The people at the Trust know you're familiar with every nook and cranny. It'll be a sort of recapitulation of the rambles through the Mark Brandenburg. We're sure the purchasers you're supposed to butter up will appreciate your historical knowledge, which you often cloak in anecdotes. How about it, Fonty? There's a future in this. Off to the Mark! Strike London from the itinerary and take Kossenblatt Castle instead. Trips through the Spree Forest, Ruppinian Switzerland, swans on the Havel, the forests of the Mark. And everywhere ghost stories by the score. You can travel, Fonty, from castle to castle!"

And so Hoftaller succeeded in towing Fonty away. That must be taken literally. They had no sooner got through passport control than Fonty went limp. Several times he collapsed, gasping for air. With Hoftaller propping him up, they just made it to the front of the terminal, but he could not manage the few hundred meters to the taxi stand. Fonty stood there in his new overcoat, his knees shaking. His breath whistled. His hands were trembling so badly he could hardly hold his bamboo cane. Everything about him was aflutter.

Believe it or not: Hoftaller hoisted him onto his back. Without so much as a word, he turned himself into a pack mule. Thanks to his stocky build, he had no trouble simply picking up Fonty, who in his elderly decrepitude did not weigh much. The poor man was draped over his bent back as if strapped on. He sat on Hoftaller's hands, clasped in back to form a seat, and clung to his chest. His head, with his summer hat askew, dangled above his day-and-night-shadow's baseball cap, which clashed with his new flannel suit. Even Fonty's walking stick could be accommodated, jammed in somewhere. Thus they advanced, step by step. Two opposites unified. The beast and his burden. A moving monument to themselves, casting a compact shadow. And as we stood among other onlookers, we saw them working their way toward the taxi stand, which did not take long, although it seemed a small eternity.

He towed him away. "No," Hoftaller said, "I had to get our friend to safety...."

34

Under Alternating Care

It began with chills, so bad that during the taxi ride across town even the driver was worried—"Whew! Your friend back there's in terrible shape!" Then, after traffic jams and detours, Hoftaller had his work cut out for him when they reached Kollwitzstrasse, because Fonty could not manage two steps on his own, and had to be carried piggyback again from the first landing. By the time they reached the small apartment, Fonty's teeth were chattering uncontrollably, and he had fallen into a feverish delirium. Once Martha Grundmann and their neighbor Scherwinski had tucked the invalid into his bed, the thermometer showed 39.9° Celsius.

He was freezing under his feather comforter, which he kept throwing off. Like him, his dentures were unmanageable; his false teeth clattered against each other and had to be removed and put in a glass. Still, fragments of words and names could be made out. Fonty was calling for the friend of his youth. He was roaming the windswept heath in Scotland with Bernhard von Lepel. Then it seemed as though they had lost their way and wandered into a bog. Help was needed. He called out for Mathilde von Rohr, the friend and mother confessor who was always receptive to his troubles. Quieter now, and without the rattling of teeth, he first bewailed domestic strife, the most recent conflict in his marriage, and then laced into his colleagues with mumbled imprecations: how ossified Lepel had become in his old age, how Heyse in Munich had run out of material, and how "Wildenbruch has sinned with a dreadful poem again. . . . Many thanks for the asparagus, which stayed fresh even on the long journey by post chaise... They keep filling the news-blotting-paper with malicious gossip...."

Fonty's shaking and trembling ebbed. Finally, now with his post-permanent teeth in place again, he greeted his correspondent James Morris, as if he had made a safe landing at the London airport, and promptly drew him into an assessment of the world's latest crises: "And what do you say to the situation in the Balkans? Looks as though the Croatians and Serbs are about to spill blood again.... The Caucasus is falling apart. Worse still, the greater Russian empire is breaking up. Soon we will recall with nostalgia the terrible but stable state of affairs when the Soviet power still ruled with an iron hand.... Because nothing is permanent.... The world is out of joint.... As after Tauroggen, when the signals were all set for storm... And shortly before I departed, a plume of water shot up out of Lake Stechlin, higher and higher...."

After taking his temperature again—it had risen to 40.3°—Martha ordered the utterly miserable traveler's day-and-night-shadow off to the nearest telephone booth to call a number she hastily scribbled on a torn-off calendar page bearing the date 12 June: "And run, don't walk. Standing around isn't making things any better."

Dr. Zöberlein, whose polyclinic was due to be "wound down" any day now, but who was still the Wuttkes' family doctor, came at once, if two hours with a steadily climbing fever can be considered at once. One look was enough for the doctor, always frantically busy but never frenetic-looking: "The old story—he has a tendency toward anemia, nothing to toy with. But it seems much worse this time. The prudent thing would be to send him to the mental hospital in Buch right away. All right, I know: our patient will refuse. Would only cause additional strain on the nerves. So let's just rely on home care and our invalid's tried-and-true powers of self-healing. But it'll take a while this time. As for medicine, the usual. The main thing is to bring down the fever...."

Fonty lay there quietly, exhausted. In mid-sentence Dr. Zöberlein went from one patient to the other: "No wonder Mama Wuttke's stomach is acting up, when the old man pulls such stunts. Just taking off like that. Happens quite often these days, by the way. Must be something about the times..."

So the doctor looked in on Emmi, by whose bed Inge Scherwinski was sitting, adding her voice to the old lady's keening. Of course she hadn't really swallowed a handful of pills—the business about pumping out her stomach was entirely Hoftaller's invention—but she still kept to her bed, even though her Wuttke had been brought back. Hoftaller stood around in the kitchen, as if he were still needed.

"He'll be all right," Dr. Zöberlein said, and wrote out further prescriptions. When Inge Scherwinski asked him about her back pains—"I can't stand up straight anymore"—he suggested exercises and flat-heeled shoes. Then it was Hoftaller's turn. He was taken aback when the doctor asked him whether he had any complaints, but quickly pulled himself together: "Sorry, Doc, there are still a few healthy ones left."

Then the doctor departed, but not without promising Martha Grundmann that he would look in on the two patients the next day. "I'm counting on you. Mustn't cave in on us this time. You promise?"

Martha found the strength to run to the nearest pharmacy, but when she had provided her father and mother with fever-suppressing, nerve-calming, and stomach-soothing medicines, had shown her appreciation to Inge Scherwinski with a pack of cigarettes, and had set a bottle of beer on the kitchen table for Hoftaller, she began to feel "kind of queasy and worn out" herself. With sweaty brow and the beginnings of feverish shivers, she again showed that she was her father's daughter as she said, "My nerves've had it; I should be in bed."

When Hoftaller wanted to know, "So, what's it like living in Schwerin?" at first she just snapped, "What's it to you?" but then she modified her tone a little: "Well, what do you suppose it's like living there? Theoretically no worse than here. But I'm glad to get away for a few days. Can't take the way the Mecklenburgers talk—either they can't get their mouths open or they're bellowing. But it's not like things are a barrel of laughs here. First Mama's flat on her back, and now Father. And it looks as though it's getting to me, too. I have to lie down. Would you mind . . . I know Father would be grateful. . . . Just look in on him now and then. . . . Maybe tomorrow, too, till I'm back on my feet . . . I'm not good for much these days. . . . The keys? Oh, second drawer on the right . . . That's it. . . . There's more beer in the fridge."

The invalid was asleep. Emmi Wuttke had also dozed off. And soon after that, when Martha Grundmann managed to sleep a bit—her eyes were closed but constantly jerking under their lids in alarm—Inge Scherwinski remarked, "What a family! When one of them goes down, they all go down. It's a good thing you're here and can keep an eye on them. I've got to get back next door, honest, because otherwise my boys'll be tearing everything apart. . . ."

Hoftaller sat in the kitchen. When his bottle was empty, he fetched himself another. He noticed that Martha Grundmann had put half a dozen bottles of Schultheiss in to chill. They counted him in. He belonged to the family. As quiet as it was behind the closed doors in the apartment, he did not feel lonely. Aside from him, there was the kitchen clock and the television set, which, however, had been muzzled; the ticking of the clock with its enameled face said enough. How quietly Emmi and Fonty were sleeping, and even Martha seemed to be getting some rest, or if she was not sleeping, at least she was suffering in silence, listening to her insomniac nerves.

"Just want to tune everything out for a couple of hours, so I can get back on my feet, and you can be on your way," she had said before withdrawing into her old room. And Hoftaller's response, "I have time," showed that he was prepared for a rather long vigil. Now the clock ticked, and the refrigerator shuddered now and then.

Later Martha Grundmann told us: "Well, he looked pretty stunned when I just left him there in the kitchen. Wasn't used to nursing people and such. Must've thought I'd pull myself together in a couple of hours or maybe a bit longer. But then it dragged on with all of us. No way he could've known that when he said, 'I have time.' And it can't have been easy for him, with three people sick and all of us difficult, even though my friend Inge did the shopping and cooked up a big pot of chicken broth now and then. Right, I couldn't stand him, actually—well, because he . . . But you know all that. And when he had that grin on his face, for no reason, I could've . . . But you've got to give him credit; it was really touching the way he took care of us, for days—what am I saying, for weeks. . . ."

We archivists could not help gloating a bit when he reported to us from a telephone booth on his most recent doings: "Would never have thought this kind of thing has to be done around the clock. Fonty's not so bad, but the mother and daughter don't give you a moment's rest. Always asking for something or other. And it's always urgent. No, don't need any help, I'm managing. Sleeping in the kitchen, as best I can. But I've got to go now; the neighbor woman needs to go out in a few minutes, to various agencies, about family assistance or some such. . . ."

Not that he complained, but we could sense that the strain was telling on him. Yet Hoftaller must have been drawn to nursing. Perhaps he even felt responsible for the Wuttkes in a way, for he spoke of "my patients" and "my task, not always easy." In any case, Dr. Zöberlein was satisfied with his caretaking. To us he spoke of "a stroke of luck." "Everyone should have a family friend like that." And in early July, when the doctor was finally able to attend a seminar in the West—later, when the polyclinic had to close, he moved to the West for good—he could be sure that his three not-so-easy patients were receiving good care.

Altogether Hoftaller had to help out for almost four weeks. Down in the coal cellar he found a folding cot, left over from the bad old days. He set it up in the kitchen; apparently he was used to Spartan living. At least we pictured Hoftaller's home—for he had to have a residence of some sort—as furnished with only the bare necessities. In Tallhover's biography mention is made of a house and its kitchen, likewise the cellar in which he condemned himself to death—albeit in vain; there is also an allusion to an old woman who came to clean once a week. That was all—no district, no street. But we guessed that Hoftaller's address must be somewhere in one of those many indistinguishable concrete-slab apartment buildings out in the Marzahn district or Berlin-Mitte; it was there, in this legacy of the Workers' and Peasants' State, that the Party cadres lived cheek by jowl.

None of us ever visited him. Even Fonty made only vague references: "Presumably my day-and-night-shadow lives in changing locations and rather hand-to-mouth. Have no idea who looks after him. Never heard him mention women. And he certainly doesn't know how to cook. Have never seen him with anything but a thermos and mettwurst sandwiches in a tin box, his rations when he was assigned to field operations..."

It was therefore all the more astonishing that Nurse Hoftaller soon learned, with some pointers from Inge Scherwinski, to prepare a bland diet for his patients—for instance, hot oatmeal or chicken broth, which he called "Jewish penicillin." Later he even attempted lightly seasoned ground-beef patties with boiled potatoes and green peas, apparently with success, for Emmi Wuttke commented, "He did a great job with the cooking. Wouldn't have thought he had it in him. Even fixed veal fricassee with rice, and one time, when I was feeling a bit better, he popped a pork roast in the oven—the skin came out nice and crisp. And always did the dishes right away. The kitchen was spotless when I peeked in; that was when I started hankering for TV again, *Lindenstrasse* and such...."

But many busy days and restless nights had to pass before that point was reached. Fonty remained feverish, and Martha's depression actually worsened. Only Emmi was getting better, slowly but surely, and with much moaning and groaning. But in contrast to the two women, who lay in their beds in grim silence or apathy, Fonty was a voluble patient. That is to say, he talked in his fever, and whenever he could spare the time, Hoftaller drew up a chair next to his bed; even as a nurse he was a good listener.

Not much could be gleaned from it—delirious fantasies without beginning or end. Yet the hectic stream of talk, and even more the casual chitchat had a certain order to it, although it respected neither time nor place.

In the beginning, the invalid's long lament was fueled by the aborted flight to England. All the sights he had missed, whether the Tate Gallery or Westminster Abbey, were passed in review. The Pre-Raphaelites and the paintings by Gainsborough and by Turner, whom he described as an unsurpassed genius. Then he babbled passages from the London journals: "Wrote to Grover sitting in the Café Divan...Rap on the knuckles from Metzel...Concert at Covent Garden; main piece: *The Fall of Sebastopol*...Met Max Müller at the embassy...Glover business concluded for the time being... Sent letter to Metzel for Merckel...Saw *Othello*, a magnificent Desdemona...Two thousand taler per annum now assured by *Morning Chronicle*..." Then "sightseeing" was on the itinerary again, with and without Emilie, who had joined him and was now nursing her homesickness—"Bought a 'scotch plaid' for George...." After that, across the Thames bridges to Fleet Street or on to the grim Tower. And this pivotal site in English history brought the friend-in-need back into the feverish picture: Bernhard von Lepel. Off to Scotland! They traveled through County Kinross, stood side by side on the banks of Loch Leven, saw from there the island castle of the Douglases, named for the lake, and Fonty exclaimed: "Look, Lepel, however beautiful the picture unfolding before us is, I ask myself whether the day was any less beautiful when I went rowing on Lake Rheinsberg and saw the castle there...."

And already he was back, as he had planned in Scotland, rambling through the Mark Brandenburg, but now in anticipation of soon having to guide deep-pocketed purchasers from castle to castle, in the service of the Handover Trust: "But I don't want to! I'm no sellout! Never will I hawk the county of Ruppin, the little state of Friesack, the Oder Delta, to those Parvenooskis...."

But then England appeared in the foreground again, where, shortly after his arrival in London, his three-volume edition of *Vanity Fair* was confiscated, marginal jottings and all. One annoyance after the other. The cabby had hardly taken him, by way of his beloved Moorgate Street, to Finsbury Square, when he picked up the daily entries again: "Chat in Café Divan...Final break with the *Morning Chronicle*...Recruited Ingvessen...Answered Immermann's letters...Now it's the Danes who have put someone on my tail—me, the Prussian agent....A certain Edgar Bauer is spying on me. . . ." And after the fall of the government, further vexation made itself felt, which Lepel, as always, had to listen to: ". . . am neither a *Kreuzzeitung* man nor a Manteuffelian, but am simply the man I am, and this man has no desire to attack Manteuffel when he is down, for the aforementioned Manteuffel, although the way he outstayed his welcome and his police state were abhorrent to me, showed me personally nothing but kindness, for which reason I am also in no hurry, now that the Workers' and Peasants' State is gone, to play the hero and take out my anger on this state where things went passably well for me, at least under the Cultural Union, even though those dry-as-dust censorship guidelines . . . and even though I lost my sons . . . and we all forfeited any sense of meaning . . . and our prospects down the drain . . . Never solved the main task . . . and soon all pleasure in socialism was gone . . . so that now history has retroactively . . . Yes, indeed! Parades are planned. Public executions being simulated. Colossal greed at every turn! And once more it's an 'ism' we're supposed to place our faith in. Court chaplains preaching from every pulpit. But as for my credo, I was always ripe for the Lex Heintze, for which reason my reaction to Hauptmann and his *Hannele's Ascension* was, 'I could go on japing at this angel-making for the next two days.' A genius? The Sulfur-Yellow Collar was one, too. An ingenious trickster of a genius, one could say. No! On Potsdamer Strasse we and the Jew Neumann, who lived across from us, never displayed the flag on Bismarck's birthday, for which reason I still, arm in arm with Neumann, summon my century to the lists, even if, when we had landed safely—and the child Agnes had found her mother—I said to James Morris, who was waiting just past the customs barrier with Frau Professor Jolles: The last role I might be tempted to play is that of the war hawk. But fate takes its course, and on the next centennial of Trafalgar, or not much later, we will have a major clash, which will make the Gulf War look like a snap. . . . For just recently in Lake Stechlin, a plume of water . . . And because my Mete is married to a frightfully greedy castle-buyer-upper . . . And in Jena, Professor Freundlich, even though I wrote to him: Get rid of the pistol! That's *ridicule*! It would have made more sense for the head of the Handover Trust...But in his case, someone else got there first...."

Hoftaller, in his capacity as nurse, took all of this in. He told us later, "A complete muddle from start to finish. He even pleaded for a state pension, no matter whether from the Prussian state or that of the workers and peasants. I didn't say much, just held his right hand and patted it a bit now and then. At the very end—but there wasn't really an end, just pauses—I tried placating him: No problem, Fonty. We'll work something out with the pension. They know you've always been loyal. A little chafing at the bit was to be expected...."

That's the kind of patience Hoftaller exhibited. And when other parts of the invalid's life were illuminated, only to be extinguished by still others, which in turn flared up for only a short while, he remained all ears, and did not forget to stroke the feverish man's hand—the right hand—over and over again; he treated his charge so tenderly that we had to feel ashamed of ourselves, far off in the Archives, keeping our distance.

For that reason we are determined not to omit anything, no matter how confused Fonty's feverish ravings may look on paper. One minute he was groaning under the twelve-year weight of his war books and going at it hammer and tongs with his publisher, Decker, whom he castigated as a "stingy old grump." In the next sentence he was pleading with him, "If you could just pay me another three hundred and fifty talers, and soon..." And right after that, without transition, he was smack in the midst of family affairs, congratulating his son Theo, who had recently taken his final examinations at the Gymnasium—"You are the first *primus omnium* in the family"—only immediately thereafter to warn him, as his son Teddy and as a government official on Bonn's Hardthöhe, that he was in danger of seeing his years of activity as an informer revealed: "In the long run, I cannot protect you anymore....My own personal spy could....At some point, your less than kosher dealings will come to light....You should never have sacrificed yourself for us that way....Treason is treason....Bad enough, Mama says, that Georg, an air force pilot, used secret military information..."

Then his son Friedel and his publishing activities had their turn. He had just made the *Poggenpuhls* available to him for publication when he began twitting the Wuppertal publisher and his pious tracts: "What's this about showing pagans the way to God? Found it colossally pretentious that a shoemaker's son from Herrnhut wanted to convert 400 million Chinese, and now you, in your missionary zeal, want to take on more than a billion of them and wave the yellow peril onto a Christian track...."

Then he wrangled with Mete: "Why do you always complain of being shortchanged? It is a piece of good fortune to have an unrequited yearning; you can suck on it like a lollipop all your life...." And not until he had begun to bicker with Emilie "about that irksome Academy business"—"Today the kaiser finally approved my dismissal. For a moment I felt regret—for your sake. But *enfin*, it will be all right this way, too..."—did he fall, exhausted from all the arguing, into a silent sleep.

We see no reason to conceal the tongue-lashing he gave his nurse, taking Hoftaller for Police Superintendent Reiff or that Danish security officer of whom poor Count Holk in *Irretrievable* was so jealous: "Come on, you must admit you have that beautiful Brigitte Hansen on your informers' list. What do you mean, it's Copenhagen style? It's always been that way. At least you didn't succeed in milking Melanie for information, despite all your sanctimonious tricks, for as soon as Rubehn came home, his nose picked up your pestilent stench, and he warned her against having any more intimate dealings..."

Hoftaller swallowed that. With a smile, as if describing a sick child, he told us, "And just imagine: eventually, in the course of his feverish meanderings, old Fräulein Mathilde von Rohr and Frau Professor Jolles merged into a single person and mother confessor. To one he revealed his every misery—'My wife would have made an admirable wife for a preacher or a civil servant in a solid, well-remunerated position....' To the other he admitted: 'My Emilie, I must concede, is not disposed to spend a lifetime with me on the edge of the abyss, for which reason we should part ways. But recently, when I grew weary of the eternal carping and had our mutual friends at the Archives book me a flight to London, and told her at breakfast—'My dear wife, I have not only said farewell to the Academy; indeed, I am leaving for good'—she exclaimed, laughing: 'Go along then, go along, and bring me back something pretty....'"

The days and weeks passed in a constant whirl for Hoftaller. As much as he enjoyed listening to the feverish invalid, with his other ear he had to be constantly alert. Through the half-open kitchen door he could hear Emmi's moaning or Martha's imperious shout, "Hallo! Anybody home?"

He bustled around with ice bags and elastic bandages. Emptying the chamber pots was part of his morning routine. He took temperatures, changed sheets, shook out comforters, plumped up pillows. Since Martha winced at any ray of light, he darkened her old room so effectively that she lay there in eternal night, and when he went in to change the cool washcloth on her forehead, he tiptoed in on stocking feet.

Hoftaller's care for Emmi took an entirely different form. He had dragged one of the medallion chairs from the salon into the kitchen for her, so she could sit comfortably, wrapped in a blanket, as she watched television in the evening. And he had kind words for the neighbor, who did the shopping and sometimes relieved him—"Just for an hour, no more"—when urgent errands forced him to leave the house—"Have to pick up some books, nonfiction things." He would say, "Please, if you think of it, could you remember the papers, the *Tagesspiegel* and the *Wochenpost*. And if it's not asking too much, I wonder if you could pick up a six-pack of Schultheiss? Ah, dear Frau Scherwinski, you have no idea how grateful we are to you. You deserve a medal."

We archivists could not have been a better nurse to our friend, who was enduring the Immortal's nervous condition in exemplary fashion, as if he wanted every surge of fever to illustrate for us this lifelong vulnerability. Several times we came to visit, not all of us, but a delegation, two at a time. We could not help noticing the spotless condition of the kitchen. And one of us observed a foreign-language textbook lying on the kitchen table, also a notebook, a vocabulary booklet, and a pair of reading glasses close at hand. In response to our question, Hoftaller explained: "Well, a person has gaps in his education. It's important to keep on learning. And since my night watches here are stretching on, some of it is even sinking in: *se habla español...*"

Of course it was impossible to speak with Fonty, in the sense of real conversation, but we were permitted to witness his feverish fantasies. Unprecedented insights resulted, insights that went beyond the bounds of our expertise. We were sure we were experiencing the genesis of certain works in previously unknown versions. Sometimes he thought he had the manuscript of *L'Adultera* on the coverlet in front of him, and on the backs of the pages were handwritten copies of novellas he had already completed, such as *Grete Minde* or *Ellernklipp*. Then it was an essay on Katte, boyhood friend to the young Frederick the Second; he intended to edit Emilie's fair copy. What was more, Fonty meant to dash off a new version by the middle of the following month, for on 17 August the royal bones were scheduled to return home. The mortal remains of the father, the first Friedrich Wilhelm, also known as the Soldier King, and of the son, Old Fritz, were to be reinterred. And Fonty was looking forward to this day with feverish anticipation: "Must be on hand in Potsdam! Shall update my Katte essay by then, because executing Katte for pedagogical purposes is the essence of Prussia. I want to witness this elaborately staged joke, probably with military trumpets and similar balderdash...."

But in his feverish deliriums it was not only "Katte Today" but other new versions as well that took on contours that were absurd and astonishingly convincing by turns. Thus he faulted the ending of *Count Petöfy* as "bland with renunciation and religiously woozy," for which reason he wanted to suggest to the heroine, Franziska, since she came from a harbor town, that she begin planning her return from Hungary as a wealthy widow, now that the old count had committed suicide, and after the year of mourning marry a theater director in Berlin or, better yet, a ship's captain in Stralsund. "Enough of this Austro-Hungarian operetta milieu!" he exclaimed. "Out of the Catholic confessional and into that Lutheran institution otherwise known as marriage!"

Feverish variations on *Delusions, Confusions* occurred to him likewise. The aristocracy and the *Kreuzzeitung* should receive no consideration: "Away with class barriers!" In the new plot, Lene Nimptsch did not have to marry the boring conventicler and upwardly striving proletarian Gideon Franke, but actually kept her Botho von Rienäcker, who didn't give two hoots about the aristocratic ninny Käthe. Fonty caught fire: "Don't renounce him, Lene! If you want him, take him! The fourth estate seizes its heart's desire...."

His approach with Effi Briest was even more radical. "No doubt about it! It was the mother who set this awful business in motion, carrying on like a procuress. She should pay the price—retire to the lay convent in Dobbertin, for instance, while old Briest and his daughter and granddaughter take a long journey—no, not to Italy, but to China, to put an end to all the ghosts. And on the steamer, with its two smokestacks and long plume of smoke, which counts among its passengers a Dutch spice merchant, an encounter occurs, as accidental as it is consistent, between the honeymooners Botho and Lene von Rienäcker and the Briests, on which occasion the old man, egged on by Effi, finally gets around to making his after-dinner speech, in the course of which he publicly announces the social event of the voyage, the engagement of his daughter to Mynheer Koeneman. And later they all chat to their hearts' content...."

Fonty waxed enthusiastic about this ending, while his fever went back up to 40° Celsius: "A good thing Lene is on the boat and strolls arm in arm with Effi on the deck. By the way, the two are spotted later shopping in Hong Kong...incense sticks, lacquered boxes, silks..."

He was looking forward to serialization in the *Vossische Zeitung*, which had already had trouble with the original of *Delusions, Confusions*. He quoted the indignant reaction of the chief shareholder, Lessing—"Will this dreadful whore's tale never end?"—and provided a withering response: "No, Herr Geheimrat; in fact it will continue on happily. My Lene has earned it. I've owed her this since my days in the Dresden apothecary shop. And my Madeleine, whose criticism often has a bittersweet taste to it, will be delighted with this spanking new ending, which will stick a pin in all these sticklers' principles, especially now that Effi, that poor little thing..."

We archivists admit that Fonty's feverish variations had much to recommend them. "Effi's happiness" seemed adequately motivated, since Crampas and Instetten—as the invalid wished—had done each other in; we rejoiced to hear that the "remarried widow retained her merry ways far into old age."

Even Hoftaller was impressed by what he called the "Immortal's somewhat tardy change of perspective." Altogether, he was enjoying his role as nurse, and was not at all embarrassed to receive us with an apron tied around his waist, in clinical white, so to speak. He spoke with slightly exaggerated enthusiasm of his "round-the-clock duty," and even when he conceded that the two women had caused him more trouble than Fonty, he was full of understanding: "You have to feel for Frau Wuttke, and her daughter, too. The two of them certainly haven't had an easy time of it. The old man can be pretty hard to take. Often the only thing that did any good was for me to drop hints about a locked ward. It got really bad for Emmi and Martha when the three boys stayed in the West. The Wuttkes were subjected to endless harassment. Well, you know, because of mass Republic-desertion...Am kicking myself now because I didn't take good enough care of...Thought they needed a little object lesson...The spirit of the times...But in retrospect my official activities are becoming increasingly meaningless, if they ever had meaning....Actually I was already thinking of getting out in the mid-fifties....All those unresolved cases...Was living at the time all by myself in a house and often sat in the cellar...Settled accounts with myself...Had hit rock bottom...Yelled: Why doesn't anyone help me! It was a Sunday....The furnace stone-cold...Then I kept going after all, since the cause mattered to me, only the cause....But today..."

We had often heard him complain, but we had never seen him so remorseful, so unguarded. He rejected all systems of order and security. Hoftaller succumbed to doubt, then recanted his doubts. With some alarm we heard him stammering over Fonty, who had fallen into an exhausted slumber, "Back in Herwegh's day...didn't want to expatriate him, just get him behind bars... You see, I was born at the very moment Herr Staatsrat August von Kotzebue... at the hands of that student... It was five in the afternoon, as my mother told me.... Something like that leaves its mark on you.... We should never have allowed a certain Herr Lenin... in a sealed train... through the Reich.... But I never had anything to do with Prinz-Albrecht-Palais and Gestapo methods.... Was in Section 5 of the Reich Criminal Police; my boss's name was Nebe.... For which reason I also had nothing to do with Soviet prisoners of war, only with Dzhugashvili, as Stalin's son was really called.... And then, when I got to Prenzlauer Allee and eventually Normannenstrasse... All because Comrade Zaisser had misread the situation and wanted to avoid the word 'putsch'... Yet we were all convinced we were the shield and spear of our Workers' and Peasants' State.... Just as our colleagues in Cologne and Pullach are sure.... All for the cause, as I said.... And if a new assignment were to come along, I mean something meaningful, something satisfying, like this nursing I've been doing... There's nothing to hold me at the Handover Trust...."

We listened and understood that Hoftaller was in the middle of an existential crisis, one whose dimensions we could imagine on the basis of our archival knowledge; we assumed he had lost his motivation, as occasionally happened to us. He wanted to keep going, but he did not know for whom or against whom he should go to work.

It was in this condition that we left Fonty's white-aproned day-and-night-shadow and the invalids under his care. His invitation—"You're always welcome here on Kollwitzstrasse"—had a pleading ring to it. But the next time we were there, something occurred that caused the two women, at least, to recover—with lightning speed.

It was a Friday. The weather sultry and stormy. Outside you felt as if you had lead in your shoes. The news arrived as we were sitting by Fonty's sickbed. He looked so dear: worn down and almost transparent, the very image of the Immortal. When we heard the doorbell, he turned his head and followed Hoftaller with his eyes as he left the crowded study and went to answer the impatient ring-ing. When the nurse returned and hovered in the background with a yellow envelope in his hand, Fonty responded with old Stechlin's that's-that statement: "I can't bear telegrams."

Unsure as to whether he should open the urgent mailing, Hof-taller said that a telegram had arrived for Martha Grundmann. From the bed we heard Fonty's high-pitched, slightly bleating laugh: "Must be her divine husband confirming that he's snatched up the Villa Zwick on Lake Müritz. Finest lakeside location, of course..."

But when the envelope was opened and its contents read aloud in a low voice, Fonty lay there again with eyes closed, his hands twitching restlessly. Only once, when the decision had already been made to inform Martha, did he come up to the surface, this time with a visionary look in his eyes: "Plan to write a novel in telegram style...Messages hot on each other's heels...Abbreviations, bare minimum of words...Plot reduced to stutters..." But more than that he did not want to reveal, certainly not the actual plot. Our queries as to the new project received no answer. He was absent, completely in the grip of his fever.

Nor did Fonty react when noise penetrated into his study from the kitchen: banging of doors, shouts, a chair falling over. Some-thing had come to an end, something new was beginning. In the midst of the agitated family, we felt out of place. We left the sick-room before Hoftaller asked us to go, after a last glance at Fonty, who, though silent, was off on a journey again.

Martha's husband had been in an accident. One of the daily automobile accidents in the newly accessioned territory. It was a head-on collision, which proved fatal both to him and to the driver of the other car, a Trabant. It had happened on the highway from Schwerin to Gadebusch that continued across the former border to Ratzeburg. Heinz-Martin Grundmann had died on the way to the hospital. Apparently he had not been wearing his seat belt; but that last piece of information was not in the telegram.

Before we left the Kollwitzstrasse apartment, and while my col-league was putting the cut flowers we had brought into a milk can—they had been left lying in their wrapping on the kitchen table, next to the foreign-language textbook—we observed that not only Martha, but also Emmi, was already out of bed and dressed. In skirt and blouse, Martha was putting on water for coffee. No dismay, no tears; even Emmi Wuttke, who could cry at the drop of a hat, said good-bye to us dry-eyed and with an air that one could describe, if not as cheerful, then certainly as bustling.

"Couldn't have been any shorter!" she exclaimed. "It was his partner that sent the telegram; that's what it says here, anyway: Udo Löffelholz. We're going to have to keep an eye on that man. Don't have a minute to lose!"

She sent us on our way with this thought. Her zeal had brought color to her cheeks. And as we started down the stairs, she called after us, "Just had a feeling something like this was going to happen. Something terrible! It just couldn't be good, all that zooming around. But my Wuttke just said, 'You love disasters, that's all. Comes from watching too much television.' And look who turned out to be right!"

We shall resist the temptation to expatiate on the role played by telegraphy in *Effi Briest,* and the fatal contrast between von Instetten, that dispatcher of highly public telegrams, and Crampas, that master of seductively intimate letters. We shall also refrain from quoting other telegrams, for instance from *Stechlin,* and pass over that precipitator of political conflict, the Ems Dispatch. We shall concentrate instead on the situation in the three-and-a-half-room apartment, which had changed in a flash: from now on, Hoftaller no longer had three patients, but only one, in his care.

After the arrival of this telegram, which reported one person dead and made two others healthy, he would have been superfluous if Emmi Wuttke had declared that she was ready to take over caring for our Fonty; but Martha Grundmann, ready in no time to don her widow's weeds and pack her bags, wanted her mother to accompany her: "Well, I just can't manage—going to Schwerin alone, the funeral and all that, and then the will, which'll certainly cause problems. Not just because of his family—them I can deal with—but that man Löffelholz can be a real bastard. Exactly! I can see him making a grab for everything he can lay his hands on. Theoretically I'd rather stay with Father as long as he's still got this fever, but things are the way they are. We've got to keep an eye on them. I owe that to my Grundmann. You can see what we're up against...."

Hoftaller understood perfectly. "Out of respect for the unusual circumstances, but also out of long-standing friendship with the Wuttke family" he was prepared to stay in the apartment and tend to the remaining patient. "But of course. Your father means more to me than you can even guess. All those years...including some pretty difficult ones...A lot to be made up for...damage control... wounds inflicted by the times...omissions...saddening...You can rely on me, as your father's friend, absolutely and positively."

At this point something apparently happened that we learned of only secondhand: the door to the study was open a crack, and suddenly a shout was heard. Fonty allegedly sat bolt upright in bed, yanked his dentures out of his mouth, both the upper and lower plates, and stared at them in disgust, his now empty mouth open wide.

When Hoftaller, upon hearing the shout, hurried to his bedside, Fonty demanded that he do the same, whereupon his nurse obediently reached into his mouth and displayed his own false teeth: complete uppers and lowers. Imagine two old men like this, imagine the day-and-night-shadow empty-mouthed!

In response to our queries, Emmi Wuttke told us, "Oh, he just had a dream that they'd got their teeth switched around. In the dream they even fit right. What garbage! But all kinds of things happen in dreams. Course my Wuttke wanted his choppers back. And he was yelling. Could hardly understand him: 'What do you mean, friendship? What do I care about your tokens? My teeth belong to me, even if they are false. Come on, hand them over!' Well, we managed to get him calmed down. And I made like I was switching them, his and my Wuttke's. And then I say, 'It's all right, now, Wuttke,' I say, 'You've got your choppers back. Everything's going to be just fine.' And he accepted that and went right back to sleep, which was good, 'cause we were in a hurry and still had to pack...."

After Martha had crammed her things, only the absolute necessities, into a tote, she helped her mother. They were held up a bit hunting for clothes appropriate for their loss. Martha had come from Schwerin in summery things, including a blouse with bright polka dots. Mother and daughter rummaged around in their armoires. Emmi wailed, "Course no one thought of this when we went shopping at KaDeWe for the wedding—that was just a year ago. And when our Georg died—it's over ten years ago now—course they wouldn't let us go over...." And the widow screeched, "There's nothing here! It's all too bright! I'm going to go out of my mind...."

Finally they scraped together a halfway presentable wardrobe from the days of the Workers' and Peasants' State: an asphalt gray suit for Martha, a midnight blue jacket dress for Emmi. Hoftaller ventured the suggestion that when they got to Schwerin they should go out and buy what they needed, whatever the cost: "You'll certainly be the center of attention at the funeral, my dear Frau Grundmann. Not just at the wake. After all, your husband headed a major firm, one that's played an exemplary role in the rebuilding of the East."

Martha, who was standing there in her slip, utterly unself-conscious, apparently regarding her father's caretaker as some sexless being, replied, "Exactly. Löffelholz, no, the whole family from over there will be thinking: We'll just pay the widow off—the property on Lake Müritz and a little something in the bank. But that's not going to happen. Over my dead body."

Emmi, who had found some suitable shoes in the meantime, agreed: "We've been poor long enough. Usually got by, though. And my Wuttke always said: Poor but honest. That's true, but what we've got coming to us, we've got coming to us."

Had Fonty been in full voice, we would have let the Immortal speak through him, pithily, as was his style on such occasions: "Morality is good, inheritance is better!" Unfortunately, the Archives could not participate in the conversation, even though we saw ourselves as silent partners in everything that affected the Wuttkes.

Now the two women stood there ready for the trip: Emmi in a cloche that went with her ensemble, while the widow had chosen a beret whose label certified it as authentic; actually it belonged to

Fonty, a Christmas present from France, and smelled of mothballs and cologne. Both mother and daughter managed to assume suitably grieving expressions. Last instructions for Hoftaller: he should forward any mail. The two glanced through the half-open study door at their peacefully sleeping husband and father. At that moment the doorbell rang.

This time there was no panting telegraph boy. At the door stood the bittersweet person, her head cocked a little to one side. "Allo, I'm back," she said.

Hoftaller, who had opened the door, gave us further information: "She stood there like life itself, just overwhelming."

And Emmi Wuttke told us: "At first we were thunderstruck. But she was just adorable, the little one."

That's how it must have been. Madeleine's sundress, of a light material with a pattern of large flowers, left her shoulders bare. It announced to the two women in their mourning outfits that outside, on all the streets and squares, summer was still beating down with unrelenting heat; and, conversely, one look at the two women's dark outfits imparted bad news.

Hoftaller took it upon himself to dispel the alarm audible in Madeleine's exclamation, "Grandpapa?" While Martha and Emmi stood there in the middle of the kitchen, in unified expectation of condolences, the death in the family was properly identified and explained. In the course of Hoftaller's rather long account, Fonty's nervous condition—a long-drawn-out but not life-threatening illness—took a back seat to the fatal accident and the trip it had suddenly made necessary. Standing there in his white apron, the caretaker emphasized repeatedly that Herr Wuttke would on no account be left without care, even if Frau Wuttke had to accompany her widowed daughter to Schwerin: "I am at your grandfather's disposal around the clock, as I have been the last few weeks. Took a leave of absence for the purpose. Couldn't be any other way, Mademoiselle Aubron."

Madeleine quickly reached a decision: "'Err Offtaler, I am most grateful to you for your efforts. But from now on, I shall take care of Grandpapa. I would ask you to recognize also that my wishes in this respect cannot be any other way."

And with equal firmness she expressed her condolences to the widowed Martha Grundmann and to "Grandmama Emmi," using polite formulations learned from a text long since out of circulation: "Please be assured of my sincere sympathy in this time of sorrow...."

Martha thanked Madeleine for her sympathy with a curt nod, and then managed to find words after all: "Well, then, theoretically everything is taken care of. We can count on the girl. What are we waiting for, Mama?"

Madeleine went up to Hoftaller with unwavering firmness and fixed her imperious squint on him as she asked him to carry Emmi Wuttke's suitcase down the stairs and accompany the two mourners to the nearest taxi stand. He complied as if in receipt of an official directive. He promptly removed his kitchen apron—and with it his caretaking duties—cleared his possessions, among them the foreign dictionary and his reading glasses, off the oilcloth, stood there, now in his civilian gray flannel suit, and reached for not only Emmi's suitcase but Martha's tote as well.

Madeleine bade the two women good-bye with kisses on both cheeks. Only Emmi Wuttke managed to strike a cordial tone: "You sure are a good girl. Oh, this is so awful: snatched away in the middle of life....I just hope my Wuttke's fever doesn't go up too much again....My goodness, child, what a blessing that we have you...."

Immediately after the farewells, the door closed. We can picture Fonty's granddaughter in this new situation. Lest we wax rhapsodic, we shall confine ourselves to admitting that we were immensely grateful for her turning up at the right moment, for her resolute behavior.

The sudden silence in the three-and-a-half-room apartment. Hoftaller's folding cot in the way. The kitchen surely seemed alien to her: half-filled coffee cups, the shuddering refrigerator, the wall clock ticking too loudly. And then, too, the lingering smell of mothballs, the open doors to the other rooms, the sight of the unmade beds of two women who had been ill until just a few hours ago.

We presume that Madeleine sat down at the kitchen table for a moment. But then she took the few steps to the study door, opened it a crack, saw her grandfather tossing in his sleep, opened the crack wider, tiptoed very close to the bed with the four brass knobs on the corner posts, and perched on the edge, light as she was.

We do not know how long her gaze rested on his face, which she must have seen as alarmingly beautiful, ravaged by fever. A few quiet moments. His writing-weary hands. The structure of his skull plainly visible. His hair pasted down by sweat. He was barely breathing.

When Fonty opened his eyes, some time passed before he recognized Madeleine. But then it took very few words to say everything that needed saying: "Ah, child, you're here."

Soon after that his fever broke.

35

Mortal Remains

To us, Fonty's recovery was akin to a resurrection, as though *la petite* had said, "Take up thy bed and walk." At all events, by virtue of her mere presence Madeleine Aubron succeeded in bringing down her grandfather's fever, arresting his nervous twitching, gently getting him on his feet—in short, making him so well that the recovering invalid raved to us about a very special medicine: "There's something of the good witch about her. Must have learned her art at Buschen's knee, even if she didn't force burlap and cat's-paw on me—after all, old Stechlin couldn't be kept from dying, even by hot infusions accompanied with spells like 'Water draws out water,' or by Krippenstapel's honeycomb, although my Dubslav, who was far younger than I, certainly deserved to spend a few more years in congenial company. At any rate, my granddaughter must have brewed me an elixir of which it can only be said that it went down bittersweet and worked all the way to my toenails. Only yesterday I was tempted to say, 'It's all over with me, Buschen.' Today you may not find me ripping out tree trunks, but I could certainly jog around the Tiergarten. If I approved of jogging, which I don't. It's not healthy!"

No, he still had to take it easy, one step at a time. Once a day, toward evening, when the heat let up, he was allowed to go downstairs on Madeleine's arm, stroll slowly around Kollwitzplatz with her, and stop at the bistro on Husemannstrasse for a glass of Médoc with salted almonds, which he enjoyed nibbling.

Inge Scherwinski from next door marveled at the miracle, and saw in the newly arrived Frenchwoman the powers of a saint; at least she told us, "You could see it happen before your eyes, that's how fast the little one got the old man back on his feet. Honest, Frau Wuttke and our Martha had just left the house, because of the death and the funeral, and she goes and fires the old man's pal, just like that. And then the girl turned everything upside down: first she aired the place out good, then she stuck flowers all over, singing in French the whole time, you know, those chansongs by Piaf—still remember them from the old days, could have sung along. I'm telling you, she pulled off a miracle. And now she's living there and cooking up a storm for the old man, all those French-type recipes, naturally...."

Madeleine Aubron had brought very little luggage when she moved in. She did not want to sleep on Hoftaller's army cot, which stood folded up in the kitchen, but she liked Martha's old room, where the walls were hung with photographs from her Free German Youth days, crossed paper flags, a black-and-white photograph of Anna Seghers, and color postcards of the Black Sea coast. The photographs had tales to tell about choral groups, the Pedagogical Collective, May First celebrations, and world youth festivals. Seghers wore an expression that was at once stern and somnambulistic. The Black Sea was blue, with a sickly greenish tinge. And the little black-red-gold flags with the emblem in the middle wept for the Workers' and Peasants' State.

There was also a bookcase, whose top was occupied by various socialist devotional items, including a little plaster bust of Lenin, all gathering dust, as bric-a-brac will. The shelves held the classics of dialectical-materialist doctrine, as well as Russian and German authors. Madeleine leafed through *The Adventures of Werner Holt* and opened a dog-eared volume, *The Quest for Christa T.*

Before she got caught up in reading, she discovered a plywood cabinet with a phonograph on top and albums stacked or arranged in compartments: Bulgarian folk music, the singer Ernst Busch performing songs from *The Threepenny Opera*, but also wistful martial songs like "Neath Spanish Skies..." Finally she found a batch of classical music: Bach cantatas, Baroque trumpet concertos, and a good deal of piano music—solo or with orchestra—by Brahms, Schumann, Chopin, among them pieces Martha had probably tried to play herself when the piano in the Poggenpuhl parlor was still in tune.

Madeleine's old room in Montpellier could well have been decorated in a similarly class-conscious manner—although more in Trotsky's hue, and reflective of her cultural heritage. She probably felt quite at home. The only irritating feature was the picture, in a standing frame next to the photo of Rosa Luxemburg, of that most well-traveled of Poles; Madeleine promptly tipped the Pope on his face, as if he had given her a fright. And not until she had chucked God's deputy on earth behind a bundle of materials on teaching did she put on some records: first "And the shark has pretty teeth, dear . . . ," then a Bach cantata.

Grandfather and granddaughter worked out a modus vivendi, which is to say that Fonty had to put up with some music. He, who freely admitted that he understood nothing about symphonies—"I'm a tone-deaf Hottentot when it comes to music!"—and whose nerves could stand neither organ nor violin, learned to endure music as something tolerable, and even listened to the Brahms violin concerto Madeleine had found in the collection Martha had left behind, although he asked that the volume be turned down. He, who in the past had at most made sarcastic comments to demonstrate his distaste for musical settings of immortal poems—"Baron Senffl sang a Loewe ballad, the inescapable 'Archibald Douglas,' of course!"—and for chamber singers in general and, horror of horrors, Wagnerian tenors—now sat at the oilcloth-covered kitchen table and subjected himself to the St. Thomas Boys' Choir as well as the heavenly-praise-singing voice of a certain Adele Stolte, much admired by his granddaughter, who knew a goodly number of Bach cantatas by heart: "Praise the Lord in all the lands. . . ."

We were amazed, and he may well have been amazed at himself. Harmony of this sort was new to Fonty. The choral mode was foreign to him. A solo voice with a small accompaniment or a simple Lutheran hymn might be acceptable; when by himself and in a good humor, he would sometimes whistle or hum Prussian marches or old Berlin street songs. But this new music had a powerful effect on him, whether andante or fortissimo. He listened with head cocked to one side, breathing deeply, as if he had to inhale fugues or the cantus firmus.

Madeleine swore to us that the music had contributed to his recovery: "*Mais non, messieurs dames,* it was not I but Brahms who made him well." And he recalled, "At Stehely's or Josty's—it must have been in March '89, when we were sitting at *souper* after the performance of *Lady of the Sea.* Ibsen was there. Chatted briefly with him, one apothecary to another. But also Schlenther, von Bülow, and Schmidt at table. As well as a cigar-smoker who said not one word. Would not have expected such colossally euphonious melancholy from this Johannes Brahms. Could listen to it again and again..."

At any rate, the air in the three-and-a-half-room apartment was filled with a multitude of voices and many kinds of music. Whether the Dresden Holy Cross Choir or a Saxon trumpeter, the Gewandhaus Orchestra or the Thomas Choir, everything the Workers' and Peasants' State had had to offer in the way of music could be found in Martha's record collection, as well as a rich assortment of Chopin, of Polish manufacture. And when we brought up the subject of music's part in his recovery, Fonty thought back, then remarked, "Perhaps that unpronounceable Dr. Wrschowitz in *Stechlin,* who was often a guest at the Barbys' and who was dead-set against listening to anything Scandinavian, should have been portrayed less as a caricature, with more intelligence than wit. He says not a word about the three great Bs, but makes many telling and ridiculous remarks about Berlin: 'A verrry good city because it has musickk and it has critickk!' You certainly recall the scene in which the conversation turns on the 'Berlin madame,' and then on the uncommunicative brevity of the telegram young Stechlin sent to Czako, his regimental comrade, from London...."

All right, then: Fonty recovered with music; but when *la petite* began to sight-read an impromptu on the piano in the Poggenpuhl parlor, her grandfather protested: "The only good furniture is silent furniture!"

If Woldemar's telegram adhered to both the Prussian standard of terseness and Wolff's telegraphic language—"fifteen letters maximum per chargeable unit"—much the same could be said of the telegrams arriving in quick succession from Schwerin, which Madeleine had to answer, for, since his recovery, Fonty was in the mood for all sorts of things, just not for letter-writing.

The telegraphic contractions mentioned nothing about the funeral, but the opening of the will came across in supercharged units. The sender, Martha Grundmann, née Wuttke, was now a wealthy widow and could afford the expense. The bottom line was that the size of the estate made it possible to buy out the partner Löffelholz. The statutory portion was set aside for the children, of course, as rightful heirs. Further claims were barred. From this point on, she, Martha, would run the business as principal heir. After all, she was good with figures. Everything was going splendidly. Mama was doing fine.

Theo Wuttke remarked, in his capacity as Fonty, "Who would have thought that Mete, that poor thing, would turn out to be a financial genius?"

In the next telegrams hasty decisions—"MAMA STAYING. AREA APPEALING. LAKEVIEW VILLA SPACIOUS"—began to alternate with come-hithers: "FATHER URGENTLY WANTED. COME IMMEDIATELY. WILL SURELY ENJOY. TOWER ROOM READY. LETTER TO FOLLOW."

But no letter arrived. Martha was so preoccupied with the business that all she could manage was further telegrams, in which her father was begged, urged, baited with fresh air, and finally commanded, to leave behind the steep stairs, his study, the three-and-a-half-room apartment, the chestnut tree in the rear courtyard, and thus also Kollwitzstrasse, Prenzlauer Berg, Berlin altogether, along with the Huguenot Museum, the Pflugstrasse cemetery, everything the Tiergarten had to offer in every season, likewise the fictitious house number on Potsdamer Strasse, but also us, the Archives, and to take up residence in the villa of the now wealthy widow, along with his furniture, his books and writing stuff, the postage scale, and the Red Chinese runner. In a separate telegram, Emmi expressed her eagerness to have her Wuttke there: "COME SOON. WONDERFUL HERE. EVERYTHING MUCH BIGGER. AM HAPPY. BUT MISS YOU. GET MOVING. WILL COME FOR YOU OTHERWISE."

In the beginning Fonty had reacted with scorn: "Knew Mete wouldn't run around shedding widow's tears for long." Then he reduced everything to the Immortal's formula: "Morality is good, inheritance is better!" And finally he explained the women's megalomania, something never before manifested among the Wuttkes, with a glance back at the lean years: "Privation makes people petty."

No matter how promising the tower room sounded, he never considered, even just experimentally, moving to the villa on Lake Schwerin, which he had dubbed Bigshot Castle. He dictated a telegram for Madeleine to send: "AM UNTRANSPLANTABLE. DEEPLY ROOTED. TOO LITTLE BERLINWEARY TO BE MECKLENBURGFRIENDLY. MOODCHANGE UNLIKELY."

La petite soon learned to string words together into similar tapeworms. She telegraphed in a manner that was stallingfortime and syllablecounting. The word towerroomswindle was her coinage. The scholarly literature already included a dissertation on the historical significance of telegraphy in the novels and novellas, and we had often enjoyed parodying the abbreviated style of the Wolff Dispatch Agency with Fonty and his granddaughter. We were all convinced that the Prussian officers'-club tone and also the choppy speech of the monarch in *Schach von Wuthenow* were precursors of this telegram style. So the student Aubron must have particularly relished this stinting with words: "DECISIONPRESSURE STRESSFUL. FEAR CLIMATECHANGEFEVER."

Their neighbor Inge Scherwinski reacted more decisively when she likewise received a telegraphic invitation of very generous proportions. Martha, who shared with Inge wonderful memories of initiation ceremonies and potato harvests, offered her friend and her three boys the use of the gardener's cottage, the so-called annex to the lakeside villa: "DO COME. COTTAGE THEORETICALLY VACANT. . . ."

Inge Scherwinski was ready to move north: "Nothing keeping us here now. Honest, without the Wuttkes, we don't want to be here anymore. And besides, I'll have a job there. All in the telegram. Am supposed to take care of the household, in general and when they have to entertain. That's something I can do: make everything nice and pretty. Specially for our Martha. And it'll be better for my boys up there than here in town, where they just hang around or get into stuff."

Fonty advised his neighbor to seek the change of climate: even he found the outdoor life tempting. More and more often he yearned for distant horizons, he said, and for peace and quiet, away from people. But for the moment he still wanted to enjoy the city. "After all, there are still a number of things scheduled," he exclaimed.

The event took place on a gray day, suitable for the occasion: two sarcophaguses, each weighing half a ton, were loaded onto freight cars to be transported from the vaults of that Hohenzollern castle whose ramparts towered over the landscape in distant Württemberg, to Potsdam. The escort consisted of family members and officers representing all branches of the Bundeswehr. Hoftaller knew the particulars. He claimed he had once participated in the surveillance of the two coffins. Yet he was indebted to Fonty for the opportunity to be among those witnessing the arrival of the kings of Prussia, father and son, or, as it was expressed, their return home after a long exile. Fonty had interceded with Madeleine for his banished day-and-night-shadow.

For days Hoftaller had been making a nuisance of himself from afar. Whenever grandfather and granddaughter were out walking, whether on dusty Alexanderplatz, where the television tower cast the only shadow, or on Tiergarten paths, likewise oppressed by the August heat, a little man with a firm, stocky build trudged along behind them. Without his subject at his side, he cut a sad figure. On street corners he would walk in place, waiting, but remaining on their trail. He would duck behind bushes, could be surmised behind marble statues—Lortzing—then would come into view again: a man out for a walk or languishing on a bench with a view of other benches, both vacant and occupied—one in particular. He stayed put, leafing through a book that had recently found room in his briefcase, along with the thermos, the tin sandwich box, and the collapsible umbrella.

From both benches one could see Rousseau Island. Enlightenment, that ambiguous word, that elastic concept. Even one of the Prussian kings now being allowed to come home was often described as enlightened. For a time he kept Voltaire at court, as a kind of jester, and he abolished corporal punishment. He imposed religious freedom and is said to have introduced the potato into Prussia. But Hoftaller, too, who was now poring over vocabulary words through his reading glasses, viewed himself as tirelessly active in the service of enlightenment. Like a truffle pig, he dug into the meaning of underhanded utterances, he uncovered subversive elements, he brought things to light. Nothing remained hidden from him.

On the other Tiergarten bench Madeleine remarked, "I gather Monsieur Offtaler never calls it a day?"

Fonty cast his mind back: "As long as I've known him—and that adds up to quite a few years—he's always been on duty."

The granddaughter would have preferred to see Hoftaller over the hills and far away, playing the tourist: "But in August everyone takes a holiday; why not he?"

Her grandfather smiled: "My companion wouldn't know what to do with himself at the seaside or in the mountains. As it is, he's suffering from withdrawal. How could he survive something like a summer resort, left entirely to his own devices?"

After an interval during which the silence between the two benches was broken only by the pond and its grandly named island, with their bickering birds and quacking ducks, Fonty remarked, "Let's do the humane thing, my child, and take him with us to Potsdam, if only *par piété*."

We presume that Hoftaller was waiting for this invitation. Madeleine delivered the welcome tidings from one bench to the other: "...but I beg that you not torment Grandpapa with unnecessary questions. He must still be spared. So nothing official, Monsieur. You are welcome only in a private capacity."

And so they were able to take the Trabi the next day. In keeping with the occasion, they followed a historic route: from Potsdamer Platz, where they had arranged to rendezvous quite early, they drove by way of Potsdamer Strasse, Hauptstrasse, and Rheinstrasse to Steglitz, then along Unter den Eichen, all the way to Wannsee. From there they planned to proceed to the Glienicke Bridge and on into the festive throng. Hoftaller had advance information: "They're expecting quite a crowd, a hundred thousand and more. The Autonomists will try to disrupt the event. But the actual interment won't take place until midnight, under tight security, of course. Friedrich Wilhelm will be placed in the Friedenskirche, Friedrich below the palace terrace. It was always his wish to be buried far from his father.... No grand tattoo, only a small ceremony, but with television, the chancellor, Hohenzollern princes... it'll take a while.... Actually all supposed to happen two years ago, when we were still in the driver's seat... but didn't work out. They were moved in March '45... salt mine, more than five hundred meters underground... but then... it started right after the war... from Bernterode to Marburg... endless back and forth... loading, unloading... from one vault to another.... Must look pretty bad inside the coffins... but now, in unified Germany, the mortal remains can finally..."

To hear Hoftaller talk, you would have thought he had been there for each stage of the odyssey. He knew exactly when the caskets had been moved, shortly before the war's end, from the Garnisonskirche in Potsdam, where father and son had had to endure each other's company far too long, to another location. He knew where they had been taken afterward, suffering increasing damage in transit; but we do not wish to accompany this complicated search for quarters, in whose often hectic course the royal bones had been thoroughly scrambled. Nor do we wish to waste words on the Workers' and Peasants' power's futile efforts to recapture Prussia's mummified legacy. All these matters, which Fonty repeatedly referred to as a "violation of the last will and utter hogwash," must go unremarked upon. But at the point where the Trabi has barely reached the Wannsee railroad bridge, we must interrupt the trip to Potsdam, more on command than according to our wishes.

The student Aubron was bound and determined to visit another grave that lay on their way, so to speak: "One of my favorite writers is buried here, *n'est-ce pas*, Grandpapa? Kings do not concern me, even the French ones, but I do want to pay my respects to the author of *Penthesilea*, if you will permit."

Hoftaller obediently parked the Trabi. And Fonty complied with his granddaughter's wish, though rather crossly. Kleist struck him as an overwrought genius. Kleist made him uneasy. Heinrich von Kleist was the other Prussian. As is often the case with immortals, despite feelings of respect, there was no real closeness.

This sense of distance already informs the essay "Kleist's Grave," in the *Rambles* volume titled *Five Castles*. Although he had written at great length about Scherenberg and other forgotten figures, in this case he kept it brief.

One immortal visited the other in May 1882, and found a "much frequented pilgrimage site." Initially his attention was drawn primarily to a group of ordinary people, "four persons and a terrier, who, the terrier not excepted, were carrying out their pilgrimage with the good humor that from ancient times has characterized visits to graves...." Only then, and after he had expatiated on the group's "bourgeois character," did the focus shift to the double grave, surrounded by a wrought-iron fence between four stone corner posts: "A blunted obelisque from earlier days and a marble stone from more recent times, slanted like a drafting table..."

He did not mention by name Henriette Vogel, whom Kleist shot before shooting himself; but he quoted the writer's dates, although not quite accurately, as well as the inscription on the stone, which the Nazis later removed because their author, the writer and physician Max Ring, was a Jew: "He lived, sang, and suffered in a dark and trying time; here he sought death, and found immortality."

Leaning on his granddaughter's arm and accompanied by his escort, Fonty followed the marked path to the memorial above the Kleiner Wannsee. The most recent stone bore the words "Now, o Immortality, thou art all mine," and Madeleine, who read the line out loud, knew that she was quoting from the play *Prince of Homburg*. "What's wrong, Grandpapa? One can't take him at his word any more shortly and sweetly than that. You're usually all for immortality, as questionable as the notion may appear to us today."

Fonty immediately took his place in corner seat 23 at the Royal Theater. Over the years, the eagle-eyed observer of opening nights for the *Vossische Zeitung* had seen three of the man's plays from that vantage point, and with varying degrees of approval, first the *Battle of Arminius,* then *Prince Friedrich of Homburg,* and finally *The Broken Jug,* a comedy. We know how much the German-Roman carnage impressed him; such dramatically heightened hatred could be construed at the time the play was written, after Prussia's defeat at the hands of Napoleon, as hatred for the French. Despite the somnambulism in the early scenes and all the "romantic caprice," he praised the prince, but he was annoyed by the "abominable village magistrate," calling the play about the jug "suitable only for reading." He applauded some of these plays' details, however—for example, the "economy of characterization" in the last, the "clarity and consistency of intention" in the previous one, and in the first the "absence of clichés"—but because the genius's acknowledged greatness found expression in all the plays with alarming intensity, Fonty averted his gaze not only from Kleist but also from this gravestone that so insistently invoked immortality.

"You're jealous, Grand-père!" Madeleine exclaimed.

Hoftaller attempted to stand up for his subject: "He's annoyed by the lack of moderation. Because everything's so exaggerated, really pathological. This Kleist belonged in the loony bin...."

Fonty said nothing. The gray day concealed the view: no panorama of the lake, hardly any sailboats. Finally he said, "I see it differently today. It was the period he lived in that was sick. He was the better kind of Prussian, a Marwitz Prussian, hence a disobedient one, one they would have hanged at Plötzensee after a summary judgment, like Witzleben. From him one could have learned to disobey orders, to say no, to risk saying no, to express defiance, even to murder the tyrant—and to pull it off. I must admit: it's not easy to achieve—hatred of great aesthetic finesse. He could do it. On the other hand, among my small virtues is that of not aspiring to change human nature."

On the way to the grave, Madeleine had already picked a few flowers, or rather, flowering weeds. She added them to the faded wreaths. If you did not confine yourself to the lake, veiled in gray, you could catch a glimpse of the city's fashionable outskirts, a large expanse of villas set amidst lawns and trees, and hidden among them a particular villa, once the site of the Wannsee Conference, now a museum of terror, awaiting visits from schoolchildren.

Hoftaller was restless because Madeleine's request had taken him to the wrong burial place. Other visitors appeared, among them two women, still young, who were interested only in Henri-ette Vogel. A solitary Japanese tourist had Kleist's grave on his sight-seeing itinerary. A father explained to his wife and children in local tones: "Well, first the two of them had themselves a nice picnic here, and they didn't do the shooting till they were fin-ished...."

Still facing away from the grave, his eyes fixed in the direction of Dreilinden, Fonty said, "It doesn't get any more immortal than this." We would have been happy to hear more, but Hoftaller was impatient: "The coffin-viewing on the palace terrace is already starting. High time we got going. They're letting the public in...."

On the way back to the Trabi, Madeleine, who had taken her grandfather's arm, said regretfully, "What a pity that he had to hate us French so much."

Meanwhile the special train, pulled by a historic steam engine, had rolled not directly into the dilapidated old Kaiser station, but into the Wildpark freight station, where its cargo had immediately been unloaded. Engineers from the Bundeswehr made sure the opera-tion ran smoothly. Prussia's black and white was draped over the two sarcophaguses. Muffled drumrolls. Shouted orders. Every phase of the unloading and reloading took place in simple, ritual-ized moves.

After the military band had played "The Deeds of God Are Deeds Well Done," the solemn procession, led by two teams of horses pulling their heavy freight, set out past the New Palace, down Maulbeerallee, and, with gawking spectators lining the route, stayed on schedule, while a Trabant with three occupants was having a hard time making its way across the Glienicke Bridge, through the eye of the needle.

Toward midday, when the son was finally separated from his unloved father, and the first Friedrich Wilhelm lay in state in the Friedenskirche while the coffin with the remains of the second Friedrich lay in Sanssouci Palace's court of honor under a black canopy with white tassels, Hoftaller was trying to find a back way that would get him close to the palace. He managed to locate a parking place right in Potsdam. They walked along Voltaireweg straight to the palace, without further delay.

There people had already begun filing past the sarcophagus of the royal misanthrope and dog-lover, which was flanked by eight officers. The chancellor went first, then the ordinary people were allowed in. Thousands shuffled by, a long line kept at a respectful distance by a fence, including older people, familiar with queuing up from earlier days of scarcity, when the main attraction had been potatoes or nylon stockings.

Fonty did not want to join the line. He stood off to one side, detached. Although there was a good-sized audience nearby, he was even unwilling to recite the poem written in honor of Adolph von Menzel's seventieth birthday, "On the Steps of Sanssouci," in the course of which the king, with hat, star, and greyhound— "Biche, if appearances were not deceptive"—mocked the stammering writer: "*Poète allemand!* Yes, yes, Berlin is becoming a metropolis. . . ." "It was a complete debacle. Menzel did not express his thanks until later, and then stiffly, because I, speaking through the king, had promised him only ten more years. That's how it is with birthdays. . . ."

Suddenly everything revolted him. He refused to participate, and wished he were far from that mass of people queuing up. But he was barred from the New Palace, where in early afternoon the official ceremony was slated to get under way, and where what remained of Prussia's aristocracy was gathering, with invited guests, the chancellor in the lead. The man who had celebrated in prose and in verse this aristocracy's early blossoming was not included. Fonty was not part of the event. All those poems honoring Prussia's warhorses, whether Seydlitz or Derffling, even the printed fact that old Stechlin always insisted on flying the black-and-white flag, could not get him admitted; and even if he had had at his side his Bülows, Poggenpuhls, Rex and Czako, Botho von Rienäcker, Vitzewitz and Briest, even von Instetten, the kaiser's protégé, all this love's labor for Prussia—three war books' worth—would have been lost; nothing could have turned him into a guest of honor with a front-row seat.

"What's the point!" he exclaimed. And: "What are democracy and the ruling mass doing here?"

Fonty turned his back on the queue, not without a touch of bitterness. Madeleine was likewise disappointed: "In France they would have staged the spectacular *funèbre* as a state ceremony with a grand parade, like the one they had for Napoléon when he was brought back from St. Helena to be buried."

Hoftaller said nothing. Not until it began to drizzle did he say, "Whoops! Afraid I left the umbrella in the car, because we were running late. Let's get under some trees before we're completely soaked."

There was no dearth of trees on the palace grounds. Finally they even found a pavilion, with columns for supports and a stone bench inside. In the deserted park the rain was washing the dust off the leafy canopies. They looked like people who had fallen out of history. And since Hoftaller opened his briefcase and invited the others to join him for a snack, which consisted of café au lait from the thermos and mettwurst sandwiches from the tin box, the three of them formed a civilian tableau, regal and nearly rococo though the pavilion sheltering them might be.

Here, far from the royal bones, Fonty set the tone, which is to say, he chatted his way into the past, taking Madeleine and his off-duty day-and-night-shadow on a tour of other castle grounds. He did not allow himself be irritated by Hoftaller, who pointedly reminded him of the Handover Trust's assignment—conducting acquisitive gentlemen on tours of Brandenburg's castles. No, he was not interested in buttering up potential investors; rather, Fonty was venturing far afield to visit the Dreilinden hunting lodge, and his itinerary also included the Marwitz family seat of Fredersdorf, then Kossenblatt Castle, of course, and the Oranienburg and Köpenick castles. Finally he reached Rheinsberg, which brought him to the young crown prince and—quickly leafing back—first to gloomy Küstrin Castle, in whose courtyard Friedrich saw his friend's head topple, then to the village of Wust, where Katte's crypt is still located and his coffin rests among stacks of other coffins.

And as they sat there having their café au lait and mettwurst sandwiches on a stone bench, protected from the drizzle, which had now turned into pouring rain, around them the king's park with all its trees, Fonty began to expound on the story of the harsh father and the weakling son, which he deemed a tragedy: "Yet the core of the story is not Frederick, but Katte. He is the hero, and he's the one who pays for the crown prince's malfeasance...."

The Archives had refused to close for the royal bones. This televised vultures' feast was nothing for us to celebrate. There's nothing as superfluous and at the same time despicable as yet another "Potsdam Day," was our motto. We chose to concentrate on our everyday minutiae. It was quiet, so invitingly quiet, in our place that we wondered where, if not in the Archives, they could have found a better refuge from the pouring rain and the masses milling in the streets. Madeleine would have been glad to examine the manuscripts on Wust and Küstrin. Even Hoftaller would have found this case of high treason and attempted escape interesting, especially the conversion of the court-martial's sentence of "everlasting incarceration" to the king's declaration that "he should be brought by the sword from life to death." The first Friedrich Wilhelm had made the following finding in the Katte case: "Better that he should die than that justice perish in the world." That was how his Majesty's fine judicial mind worked. The king even dredged up his schoolboy Latin: "...Once learned the saying *Fiat justitia et pereat mundus!*"—which, according to Büchmann's collection of famous quotations, means "Justice must run its course, even if the world perish."

Would that not have made sense to Hoftaller? He could certainly have agreed with that sentiment, for reasons of state. Forcing the crown prince to look out the castle window and see Katte being led to the block and beheaded could be viewed as an exemplary pedagogical measure: a harsh verdict like this laid the cornerstone for Prussia's greatness. No matter how moved the actual culprit might have been—according to a contemporary report he exclaimed "*Mon cher* Katte!" and blew a kiss to him, the victim of the prince's foiled escape from paternal strictness—"*Je vous demande mille pardons*"—in truth this was the only way—right, Hoftaller?!—he could be transformed into a king, a Fridericus Rex, that same

Frederick the Great whose grievously damaged bones were now finally being allowed to come home, grist for television's mill and the chancellor's.

But they did not come to the Archives. We were somewhat hurt when we learned later that Fonty had chosen instead to reel off his horror story in a delicate pavilion more suitable for pastoral tales. He led his listeners to Wust, to Katte's crypt. Even in those times, mortal remains were moved. Upon the family's petition, the coffin with Katte's head and body was dug up in Küstrin and hauled along miles of sandy roads on a narrow wooden cart pulled by two scrawny horses, all the way to his father's manor.

Fonty probably asserted again that the Katte case would have provided ideal material for a play along the lines of Brecht's *The Measure Taken*; but did he also mention that Wust was near Jerichow? And did he reveal in passing that Uwe Johnson's Jerichow is no invention, but is based on that other Jerichow, transplanted to Mecklenburg, and that the author of *Speculations about Jakob,* in a late book dealing with himself, the casualty, brings to literary life a character called Joachim de Catt? Even for Fonty that might have been venturing too far afield.

Perhaps, because Madeleine wanted to hear more and more, and Hoftaller showed an entirely unofficial interest, Fonty described that bright day in August when the Immortal had paid a visit, ducking out of the glittering light into the crypt and glancing into the open coffin. He explained that grave-robbing souvenir-seekers—for instance, a traveling Englishman—had stolen the vertebra severed by the executioner's sword, while others had pulled out the dead man's teeth. Or Fonty went on without transition to his own visit to the crypt in the early summer of '67, for which he had found time after Cultural Union lectures in Tangermünde and Rathenow. His daughter Martha, already wearing the Young Pioneers' blue shirt, was allowed to accompany him; the place had given her the shivers. The village church was in disrepair, which was not particularly noticeable because throughout the Workers' and Peasants' State the dilapidation of older structures was making rapid progress. Fourteen coffins in all, among them two children's coffins, were stacked up there. Enough material to allow Fonty to chat for hours about all the Kattes—the field marshal, the cavalry captain, the marshal's second wife, née von Bredow, and "Katte in Boots," the family jester, whose riding boots had held up better than the mortal remains.

At any rate, all attention was now focused on this most Prussian of stories. When the rain slackened and then stopped altogether, they decided to follow Madeleine's suggestion and stroll through the town as a way of ending this 17 August, the most recent Potsdam Day. Here they again encountered the beheaded Katte, as though he, and not one or the other of the two kings, were the central figure in the day's events.

It was almost impossible to get through the streets. There was congestion everywhere, because individual groups were staging their own contributions to the festivities and attracting onlookers, who chose sides with applause and whistles. Here members of student fraternities were parading in full regalia as saber-rattling Prussians; there militarism was being carried to its grave in a cardboard casket. Aside from stands offering bockwurst and roast chicken, still referred to as "broilers," a group of gay men cross-dressed in courtly splendor were drawing a particularly large crowd: they were expressing their devotion to the second Frederick in the finery of his time. Wearing puffy farthingales below towering powdered wigs, generously bedizened with beauty patches, and constantly flicking their fans, the entourage circled His Queer Majesty. In better weather, all this could have made for a real people's festival, especially since there was plenty of security, and skinheads as well as the Autonomists had been preemptively barred from the scene.

Hoftaller and Madeleine had placed Fonty between them. Perhaps his dignified demeanor, with hat, walking stick, and light-weight overcoat, commanded respect. At any rate, even in the densest crowd a path opened up for them. Older people greeted him. Some even doffed their visored caps. There was the impression that the incarnation of Prussian virtues was in their midst. The word "aura" seemed fitting. Even shouts of "Fonty!" could be heard. And Hoftaller, who was basking a bit in the glory, said, "You see, mademoiselle, here your grandfather's a somebody. Here people really appreciate him. He, and only he, should have been the one to deliver an address on Prussia's greatness and decline before the Hohenzollern princes and all the invited guests. But that can still happen. Before a large crowd. I already have a place in mind...."

As the shouts of "Fonty!" multiplied—someone yelled, "Fonty's our king!"—it became too much for the object of this adulation. He asked his granddaughter to take him by way of side streets to a quieter part of town. They accordingly made their way to the Dutch Quarter, an area of modest structures dating back to the era of the first Friedrich Wilhelm, who had welcomed Dutch artisans to Brandenburg for the sake of the skills they brought with them. The reasons were fairly obvious: since the time of the Great Elector, the royal family had had a Dutch Calvinist branch and had felt like strangers amid the narrowness of Brandenburg's Lutheranism. Only the Huguenots paid court to them without religious reservations, while the Prussian aristocracy rejected these infidel interlopers and obeyed them only under duress.

Fonty rummaged around in his historical stockpile. And Madeleine was in her element. The thesis she had recently submitted for her master's degree had earned her a *"mention très bien."* When we add that the conclusion of her observations on the Immortal's Huguenot underpinnings had also marked the end of her affair with her married professor, we say this with relief, and entirely in Fonty's spirit; as the trio finally found itself alone in the Dutch Quarter, he reached for his granddaughter's hand: "Ah, my child, you know there isn't a trace left in me of kisses so glowing they can warm the entire room, but your love does warm my old bones."

He did not let go of her hand even to point out with his walking stick some of the unpretentious matching buildings that had been undergoing renovation since the days of the Workers' and Peasants' State and were now supposed to be turned into little jewels: "Look! Scaffolding everywhere! It's enough to make one think things are moving along apace."

And something was going on in front of one of the scaffolds. Actors, apparently mimes, were performing a play; it was not clear at first whether it was a comedy or a tragedy. Only a few onlookers, whom the trio now joined, were standing in a loose semicircle around a platform made of metal drums supporting scaffolding planks. According to the sign on the side of a VW bus parked to one side, these were students who had come from Küstrin, known since the end of the war as Kostrzyn, to celebrate in their own way, in black jerseys and with white-painted faces, the return of the royal bones. Nothing was happening yet, except that a drum was sounding, jaunty and mournful by turns. The drum was supposed to follow the course of the action. Later there were rolls and single notes to mark the transition between scenes. Everything else had to be done in complete silence.

As if Fonty had arranged for the performance by the Polish ensemble, the play recounted the tragedy of the Gendarmes Regiment's Lieutenant Hans Hermann von Katte. This was announced in red letters on a white banner that was now suspended between two uprights on the scaffolding. Since all the mimes were identically dressed and made up—their eyes ringed with black against their chalky faces, their mouths widened in strawberry red—at first one had to guess who was who: over here was the corpulent soldier king, who smashed the flutes his son was forever playing, tore up his books, and threw them into the fire; over there—apparently it was a woman playing the role—was the crown prince, whom the royal father now beat with such fury that Frederick's purported comment—"You treated me not like your son but like a common slave"—could have served as additional motivation for the crown prince's mimed attempt at escape. Yet the gestures and facial expressions said enough and more. There was no need for a flute, a book, or a rod as props.

Only then did Katte appear, betrayed by a misdelivered letter. Faced with the crown prince's incompetence, he wrung his hands, for he had been identified as abetting the escape; but he did not want to flee alone and leave the crown prince in the lurch.

First the father had the son arrested, then came the scene in which Katte was apprehended; the sentence the Immortal had quoted in his account of the tragedy called for particular expressiveness in the pantomime: "Katte handed over his sword without changing color."

After muffled drumbeats, Princess Wilhelmine, lovingly devoted to her brother the crown prince, made her appearance. She was sorry to see Katte arrested, and when he was taken before the king, he mimed what the princess was supposed to have said of him: "He was pale and distraught." Again the audience saw Friedrich Wilhelm in a rage. He snatched something from the prisoner's chest—it was the St. John's Cross—and flogged the unfortunate man lying at his feet. He also kicked him until his victim shuddered under the mimed blows and kicks.

Drumroll and a single beat: a larger group of mimes gathered to represent the court-martial, their heads clustered together in consultation. The verdict on Katte was promptly ripped up by the king. His punishment was to be not everlasting incarceration, but death by the sword. Just as the Immortal had asked in a letter to the lieutenant's descendant, Marie von Katte, while he was doing research for his Küstrin essay, "Above all, what about the executioner's sword?"—the mimes now faced the following question: Is a sharp, decapitating gesture sufficient, or is a prop needed to sever the head from the body? As the trio and the other spectators who had joined them experienced Katte's execution, the scaffold in Potsdam's Dutch Quarter had to represent Küstrin Castle, and the mime Katte, while he knelt, was beheaded so impressively with a well-aimed chop that in the silence—for the drum kept still— you thought you heard the head bounce onto the boards.

Before that the crown prince had been forced up into the scaffolding, so that he could see what was happening. He had only enough time to blow his poor friend the famous kiss, which Katte caught with his last glance. Then Frederick, with Wilhelmine standing beside him, collapsed: a blubbering bundle of misery.

The drum beat out a sluggish rhythm. Madeleine wept. Fonty said, "It happened much like that, colossally heartrending, and as legally correct as it was unjust." Hoftaller felt the tragedy had failed to convey the pedagogical effect of the punishment. But then, after a brief, military drumroll, the play continued.

While a white cloth was spread over the executed Katte, the crown prince, who had just been lying brokenhearted on the plank, picked himself up and began to transcend himself. The girl behind the mask reveled in being a young man, swinging acrobatically on the scaffolding. He carried on like a clown, leaped onto the platform, suggesting the flight of an eagle, hopped over the covered corpse of his friend, walked on his hands, executed double somersaults and backflips, and in between launched symbolic wars, tore up treaties, pillaged provinces, fought battles by the dozen, strode with now practiced leaps over corpses, shooed the pantomime chorus—Prussia's numerous foes—first here, then there, was shooed in turn, yet did not surrender, was indeed regal through and through, as his father would have wished, had grasped the lesson he was taught, ruled with a stern hand, but in the end, no matter how cynical his silent grin, he offered the image of a deeply tragic hero who took no pleasure in plunder, despised himself and mankind, and finally, trembling and bent with gout, only played with his dogs.

The drum punctuated his slowing heartbeat in macabre fashion, then fell silent. As the mimes bowed, several in the sparse crowd had already left. Fonty, caught up in Madeleine's enthusiasm, clapped, and remarked over the head of Hoftaller, who did not move a finger, "I still say, my hero is Katte." As the trio left the scene of the tragedy and at the same time Potsdam's Dutch Quarter, he again reached for and found his granddaughter's hand.

The ride home in the Trabi proved uneventful, aside from the traffic jam at the bridge and various detours. The former garrison town, now capital of the state of Brandenburg, was emptying out; for the solemn burial of the king, scheduled for midnight on the castle terrace, was closed to the public. Only the remaining Hohenzollern princes, the chancellor, and the television crews would be allowed to break yet again the provisions the second Frederick had made in his will.

For us, a normal day at the Archives was coming to an end. And Hoftaller, who gave us a full report, confirmed that we had done well to stay away: "There wasn't much to it, nothing of lasting value. Not a trace of the 'spirit of Potsdam.' My passengers were pretty quiet on the way home. Tried to cheer them up. Even quoted your bread and butter, the Immortal: 'Much cry and little wool.' Didn't help. Mademoiselle sulked: 'If they put on a carnival, they should do it right, with a rollercoaster and Ferris wheel,' but she acted as if I wasn't there, or just the chauffeur. Really lousy mood. Not till we drove down Schönhauser and I stopped at the corner of Knaak and Dimitroff, was I able to pull off a little surprise: at the entrance to the Culture Brewery they already had the poster up, hot off the press. Yes, well, I wanted to do something nice for Fonty. For such a long time he wasn't allowed to speak before an audience, and now he could do a lecture: 'Childhood and Youth,' the piece that helped him get back on his feet last year. And in the Boiler House, which holds a ton of people. He was so happy to see it: his name in bold letters, and next to it 'Fonty'—in parentheses and italics. Of course he immediately let loose with one of his sayings: 'I'm no speaker, you know, but if I absolutely must...' Only Mademoiselle seemed worried, supposedly because of the strain on him. But then she suddenly seemed to have a change of heart: "And as soon as it's over, we'll go away for a little rest and relaxation, right, Grandpapa? To me she said rather sharply, 'I assume you have no objection.' I replied, 'Why should I? Be my guest. Far be it from me to interfere with travel plans....'"

36

Various Fires, or Who Struck the Match?

It was not Fonty, but Madeleine, who invited Hoftaller for tea at the apartment on Kollwitzstrasse. They had to discuss details of the lecture scheduled for the Culture Brewery; for instance, whether there should be a table or a lectern. But when the three of them were seated in the Poggenpuhl parlor and Hoftaller had reached for his first piece of crumb cake, the granddaughter broached a question of a different sort, since her grandfather remained silent. As always, she chose her words carefully: "Might we inquire, Monsieur Offtaler, about your future plans?"

About to take a bite, he offered them his ancient retroactive smile, but held the delicate pastry suspended, did not want to speak with his mouth full, and, ravenous though he seemed to be, displayed excellent manners; before Hoftaller said, "A good question," he took a sip of coffee.

Only then did grandfather and granddaughter discover that their guest had recently gone back to school, signing up for an intensive language course being offered during the semester break: "Just imagine, me at Humboldt U. I'm sitting in class, and at my age. Thought at first they'd laugh at me, but the young folks there are friendly. All beginners like me. People always say Spanish is easy, but that's not my experience, especially the pronunciation...."

As if to prove his point, he lisped. He rolled his *r*, practiced guttural sounds. He had no problem with short sentences like "*Hasta la vista*," but pronouncing the word "*información*" gave him trouble. No wonder Fonty called his day-and-night-shadow's pronunciation exercises "*ridicule*." He wanted to change the subject and get to the lecture, which was just around the corner, but Madeleine refused to relent: "And may I inquire—not that I want to seem indiscreet—where and for what you will be needing these language skills?"

Now Hoftaller took his time chewing. He chewed with his mouth closed. The two others seated at the round table saw their guest chewing. Fonty was sitting on the sofa beneath the Gross-görschen engraving, Madeleine on one of the medallion chairs, when he said, his mouth not quite empty, "Nothing like crumb cake. But if I praise the pastry first, it's by no means because I want to avoid your question, Mademoiselle...."

Now Fonty, too, reached for a piece. He did not hesitate to speak with cake in his mouth: "Out with it! You wouldn't be thinking of taking a holiday, on Majorca, perhaps. It's supposed to be packed year-round...."

"You know I'm not one for holidays, and hate nothing more than sweet idleness...."

"May we then assume that Monsieur Offtaler has fallen for an Andalusian señorita? You smile. Is that so far-fetched?"

"Maybe after this little interrogation it'll be enough if I simply admit that my interests have shifted a bit, in light of recent geopolitical changes, let's say in the direction of Latin America. True, the East-West perspective isn't completely irrelevant, but..."

"And when, if I may ask, are you departing? For Nicaragua, let's say."

This and further questions Hoftaller left unanswered, with a smile, of course. He admitted that for his part he was somewhat curious about where Fonty would be going for his rest-and-relaxation trip, in solicitous company; or was he seriously considering joining his wife and daughter in Schwerin, moving into a tower room with a view of the lake? Fonty, too, remained vague, merely saying, "No need to worry about Mete. But Emilie? She knows my little ways. Is insisting that I put in an appearance. Misses me colossally, she claims. Well, the thought is tempting. Everything up there along the coast is redolent of England, Scandinavia, trade; whereas in Brandenburg everything smacks of pines and parade grounds. But as stifling as the air is here, the north can't draw me away from Berlin. Have a better place in mind... Don't subscribe to holiday resorts...What I'm seeking, you won't find in any summer resort...peace and quiet, just peace and quiet....But first I plan to sing here; that is to say, I plan to bring them to their feet with my lecture. I think I'll have a lectern after all. If you have to speak, then straight from the shoulder!"

Then they chatted, without asking each other any further or even any follow-up questions. Hoftaller applied himself to the crumb cake. Madeleine described how happy her family in Montpellier had been when she passed her exam with flying colors: "Even Maman, despite the fact that my thesis is written in German!"

The news from Schwerin sounded positive, even in telegram style, at least as far as the business end went. They heard that Emmi was now being chauffeured when she went shopping. And Hoftaller, who felt included in the familial conversation and was visibly pleased, was able to supply the information that the cornerstone for the Culture Brewery complex had been laid exactly a hundred years earlier for the Schultheiss Company: "You recall, Fonty. The whole scene played itself out shortly before your seventieth, with tremendous whoop-de-do...."

"And how! But there was also genuine theater. *Before Sunrise* was put on, and there were some small publishing sensations as well: the rough draft of *Jenny Treibel* was finished. Friedel brought out *Stine*. And then the first collected works appeared in twelve volumes....Altogether, much was afoot, construction sites everywhere...noise, dust, shouting on the 'change....They called it the Founders' Era....And every evening you could run into the director of Schultheiss, a certain Patzenhofer, having a drink at the Hops Tavern....Those were the days...."

"And the Schultheiss Brewery was no sooner finished than the lay nun Mathilde von Rohr died. A bitter loss, I know. Soon after that, the nervous exhaustion came to a crisis. Even the family was considering a mental institution. Anemia. Nothing to fool around with. You were lucky, Fonty...."

"Oh, yes!" Madeleine exclaimed. "And that is how *Childhood and Youth* came to be written, from which Grandpapa will now read, standing at a lectern, as we have decided. Fabulous to think how a brewery of vulgar beer has been transformed into a brewery of culture. *A la bonne heure!* A very nice job you did there, Monsieur Offtaler. Everything planned so carefully. Grandpapa and I owe you a debt of gratitude. . . ."

Not only Prenzlauer Berg came; all of Berlin did. And of course we, too, were in the audience. What a labyrinth of walls! Following the plans drawn up by the architect, the same Franz Schwechten who a short while later would design the Kaiser Wilhelm Memorial Church, a great deal of brick had been mortared to stack these buildings together. Plenty of room and plenty of rooms. With towers and turrets, as if the idea had been to build a Staufen fortress: the boiler room, the washing and changing rooms, the former stables, the warehouse, and whatever else was necessary for a brewery, for instance, the smokestack towering above the entire complex—all surrounded the large inner courtyard where audiences gathered for various cultural events. In other courtyards, plaques on the old walls explained that this had been the hayloft for the brewery horses, while over there, in the spirit of social responsibility, had been a workshop for the disabled. Now galleries and theaters offered their wares here. But all who had come on this particular evening wanted to get into the Boiler Room, where the lectern was waiting. Outside, people stopped for a quick beer, then hurried on in. Everybody wanted a good seat.

It was only a few months earlier, in mid-May, that the Culture Brewery had been incorporated as a management company, ltd. But during the last years of the omnipresent Workers' and Peasants' State, artists had begun using the buildings—which had suffered little damage in the war and were hardly touched by the hard-fought final battle for the center of the city—while some spaces that were standing empty functioned as a furniture warehouse. Since the fall of the Wall, the place had been jumping: live music festivals, cabaret, readings, exhibitions, street theater, workshops, panel discussions—whatever was cutting-edge (especially in this period of changeover), and sometimes things that were willfully alternative. But celebrations were also accommodated: a Turkish children's festival, the Jewish New Year, and a banquet marking the end of Ramadan.

Fonty's lecture, which took place, by the way, just a few days after Gorbachev's overthrow in Moscow, was therefore only one of many events scheduled. And yet it was a notable event, because the older members of the audience knew that the speaker, Theo Wuttke, had survived the gray years as Fonty; and even the younger people were aware, though perhaps only by hearsay, that there had been something special about this man, long ago, when everything here still went by the book. Said things he wasn't supposed to, made ambiguous allusions that the boys upstairs didn't like. Got in trouble for that. Anyway, if this Fonty was speaking, you had to be there.

So they all came. Even some of the young talents from Prenzlauer Berg—who had meanwhile found a livelihood, or at least a focus, running bistros or diligently engaging in self-denunciation—were sitting in the audience, far apart, because they were all furious with each other. Many former staffers from the Ministries Building had paid for tickets. Cultural Union functionaries grown old and gray were there to demonstrate their affection. Members of the Academy were present, luminaries as well as dimmer lights. Pastors from nearby churches—a minister from the Corpus Christi parish and a priest from St. Hedwig's—had come. There were even members of the press, in reserved seats. Only the western part of the city was not represented. And evidently the Handover Trust did not have a presence there, although this piece of real estate, including the Boiler House, also fell within its purview. Nonetheless the event was sold out. Fonty was a draw.

Because of the many thematic links to our own work, we had been urged to give the introduction and celebrate the speaker as proof of living, outliving, immortal literature. But our director had recommended restraint; the attendance of several staff members would have to suffice. Instead a woman from the Culture Brewery management spoke. She wanted to be brief, and she made it brief: "Fonty needs no introduction. Fonty, as we know, speaks for himself. I'm willing to bet everyone would like to be a little like Fonty, honestly! To all those who know about him from bygone times, and even more bygone times, but also to the young people who've come to the Boiler House today because of something they heard, our Fonty is an icon. Let's give Herr Wuttke a big hand!"

What applause! As if people wanted to burst the walls of the brick temple, the source of long since dried-up streams of beer, the Boiler House. We were sitting in the first row and could only guess who was clapping behind and above us. Later we heard that the Wolfs, old Hermlin, even Müller had been there; but what was said later does not count; later one heard only opinions and rumors.

Madeleine was sitting next to us, silent, her knees primly together, the tip of her nose lowered, and her fingers clutching a handkerchief in her lap. Hoftaller had found a seat off to one side under the "Emergency Exit" sign. The lofty space was lit mainly by spots mounted high up on iron rigging. The plaster on the towering walls was bare and splotchy. The audience sat arena-style in three rising blocks. Crackling anticipation.

And then Fonty, who had had his place of honor on a chair up front, stood up slowly, straightened his back, a venerable graybeard, and walked, relying completely on his yesteryearly appearance, up to the lectern, holding the manuscript in his right hand. There he stood, the light full upon him, and bowed slightly, whereupon applause once more swelled the walls of the Boiler House. Now the house lights were dimmed, leaving only the lectern illuminated.

With his first words, "By the way," and the following flourish, "I'm really no public speaker," he already had some laughs on his side, but when Fonty made the fundamental declaration, "Having to speak in public has always held extraordinary terrors for me, hence my aversion to the parliamentary system," the merriment ebbed. Then he executed an about-face—"But from birth I have been a *causeur,* that is to say, one who likes to chat"—and that brought him to the manuscript, the beginning of "Childhood and Youth."

The microphone helped project his voice, which did not carry particularly well. He lectured by reading. Now, in his reading glasses, he looked somehow different, distant. He cast a glance at Neuruppin from a dual perspective, compared the bourgeois ménage and the Lion Apothecary Shop, always threatened by bankruptcy and gambling debts, with the family subsisting in proletarian straits, amidst the reek of cabbage soup or fish. This brought him to the lithographer and socialist Max Wuttke, and thus to the Neuruppin broadsheets and their perennially current educational value, which still, after the move to Swinemünde, where yet another apothecary shop barely eked out an existence, exceeded that of all private instruction, even from the beloved tutor Lau. The same was true of Neuruppin's grammar school, from which only his mother's ambition and talent for penny-pinching succeeded in getting the boy Wuttke promoted to the Gymnasium.

Fonty skillfully employed the lithographed mass production from the Gustav Kühn and Oehmigke & Riemschneider workshops as a historical template. When he came to the Wuttkes, he cut to Fox's Movietone News. He vaulted from the events in Potsdam—Reich President Hindenburg shaking the hand of a former corporal, now decked out in top hat and tails—to the cholera, and how it stopped just short of Swinemünde and the dignitaries gathered around the apothecary's counter; and then another temporal leap brought him to the fascist-brown plague. In either case, he was highlighting the thirties of one century or another. He blended the odors of the apothecary shop with those in Kühn's print shop. He let the mothers vie with each other in strictness. He added dashes of color: here the sky-blue house on the Baltic, there the paintbrushes wielded by Brandenburg children doing piecework. First Lake Ruppin, then the Baltic again was enlivened by sailboats and steamers. He dealt only briefly with major events, but lavished detail on the milieu of ordinary folks. Fonty was at home both here and there; and his double-entry bookkeeping came out so even that the audience could follow without any difficulty.

And now he built a monument to the two fathers. From this elevated vantage point, the changing times could be observed like a fashion show and could provide the subject matter whenever he engaged the two fathers in dialogue with each other. The topic might be Napoleon and his marshals, and at the same time a vision of worldwide cooperatives; experiences with raising swine and breeding rabbits were exchanged; the gambler confessed to the drinker in passing how debts had dogged him from place to place, and the drinker indicated to the gambler the size of his swollen liver. They laughed at philistines of every stripe and cursed reactionaries and traitors, aristocrats and civil servants, Bourbons and Hohenzollerns, and black, red, blue-blooded, and brown riffraff.

But the two fathers also traded anecdotes. They tried to outdo one another. And it may be that the unerringly aimed gasconades, of which both were past masters, seduced Fonty into departing suddenly from his script and speaking straight from the shoulder.

He shoved the stack of paper aside, took off his reading glasses, and tucked them in his pocket. Standing erect, because he no longer had to bend over the linear text, he stepped to one side of the lectern and abandoned the microphone, now confident of his voice. He gazed into the audience as if looking to start a conversation across the rows of seats, and in the half-darkness found several individuals he could address directly. Both hands became eloquent as he quoted from *Between Twenty and Thirty*, backtracking to the Revolution of '48—the failed attempt to sound the tocsin—and then, after another light-footed temporal leap, standing on Alexanderplatz and addressing the crowd of five hundred thousand. In the process he skipped over various things—for instance, the Reich Aviation Ministry—but kept everything that followed firmly in focus. Not that he mirrored every phase of the Workers' and Peasants' State—its building-up, crumbling, and demolition—rather, he continued to take leaps, lingering at once over the pre-March period and the seventeenth of June, saying: "This is something I could not have kept in my manuscript in Hoyerswerda or anywhere else after the Eleventh Party Congress, but it still holds true today: In the long run one cannot keep any people on a leash. . . ." To him, nothing was buried in the past. He mixed the Sulfur-Yellow Collar's newly founded Reich, "adulterated with blood and iron," with what he described, his anger escalating as he spoke, as "the oversweetened blend brewed by the ruling mass," mocked a minister named Krause, "whom they would have ennobled at once after '71," and suddenly he was hurling darts at writers; as he took aim at Wildenbruch or Brachvogel, contemporary figures came into view—he called the last president of the Writers' Union a "hack whom God created in His wrath."

After that Fonty glided back into calm waters, but the audience was growing a bit weary, and it got worse and worse as he set out to retrace his rambles through the Mark and in lengthy digressions visit a dozen of Brandenburg's castles, defoliating Prussian family trees in passing and losing his way among obscure aristocratic feuds and now tumbledown manor houses.

The hall began to stir restlessly. Hecklers made themselves heard. Someone yelled, "Wrap it up, Fonty!" To that he responded, "All this and more is now in the hands of the Handover Trust. On orders from the Trust, all this, one castle after the other, will be put on the block and will no longer belong to the people; the Trust makes it possible!"

We were worried; like Madeleine, whose fingers were clenched around the handkerchief in her lap, we feared that Fonty might go completely astray. Should one of us feed him a cue? Madeleine whispered in the direction of the lectern, "Get to the point, Grandpapa...."

"Right," we chimed in, for up to now he had kept back the most important part, the Immortal's late works, the novels and novellas, as if saving the best for last. "I'm not very conversant with literature," we heard him saying coyly. All he had said on the subject up to now was, "The royalties for *Delusions, Confusions* came to three thousand fifty marks." And right after that, more as an aside: "Wrote at the time to Schlenther: 'A woman of about forty-six was just here, claiming that she was Lene, and I had written her story....'" Nothing more about Lene Nimptsch, except the remark, "She must have been very pretty at one time." But now that Fonty had provided his own cue, with the Trust that made everything possible, he began to conjure up an unparalleled literary celebration.

Looking out over the audience, he stood there in his threadbare lecture suit, his frock coat, and spoke without notes. On his lapel, he had the droplet-sized ribbon of the *Compagnons de la Résistance.* Every bit the embodiment of his originator, and armed with immortality, he exclaimed, "Were you aware of this? Did you know, ladies and gentlemen, that today, at this very hour, in the former Ministries Building, which was once the Reich Aviation Ministry, our present and omnipresent Handover Trust has assembled an illustrious company? For a special occasion. You see, the one-thousandth winding-down is due to be celebrated. A reason if ever there was one! And the guests are coming in costume. The invitation read, 'Frau Jenny Treibel requests the pleasure of your company...,' and people are gathering on every floor, in the corridors, and in the conference rooms, decked out with Chinese lanterns. Guests from the novels and novellas, even from the minor works, are welcome. I can hardly name them all—that's how many are doing Frau Jenny Treibel the honor of appearing. But there's time to mention a brief selection. I see a mixed company of the high-ranking and titled, whether in cutaway or uniform. For instance, Lieutenant Vogelsang is speaking with Commercial Councilor Treibel about election strategies and how best to capture the vote. Rex and Czako have dragged along young Stechlin. Now they are on the lookout for Armgard and Melusine. Of course Gundermann must be on hand, the man for whom everything is still grist for the mills of social democracy. Look! There are Effi and Lene, the former in a hat with veil, the latter in a little bonnet, exchanging the latest Berlin gossip, as if there were no difference in social station. Even Stine has allowed herself to be persuaded by Widow Pittelkow to appear in public. She is wearing her dotted guinea-hen dress and is hoping to dissuade young Count Waldemar from using a pistol to put an end to her story, which in any case is falling victim to consumption. And there he comes now, with a hole in his head already, alas. And believe me, dear listeners, none of the pastors is absent: Lorenzen, Niemeyer, Schwarzkoppen, even Schleppegrell the Dane has come in his preacher's robes. There is no shortage of pedagogues, either: hardly surprising that Professor Schmidt has answered the summons of his boyhood friend, but that Krippenstapel was able to overcome his reluctance.... Ah, the tutor Lau is there, from *Childhood and Youth*. And who else is there, dressed to a T as characters from the novels, in buckled shoes or laced boots, with simply parted hair or coiffures piled high? Who trusts himself to try to fill Briest's shoes? Who, in a minor part, will appear as the maid servant Friederike, housed for decades in the Poggenpuhls' loft? Who is sporting the Gendarmes Regiment's dress uniform? Who fancies herself a pastor's daughter or a wet nurse from the Spreewald? Who wants to be a coachman or a house steward? It is the Handover Trust's department heads and secretaries, the technical experts and receptionists, but also those who reek of money or have a nose for money, powerful investors and major buyers, who have dressed up to match the literary originals. As Vitzewitz—that may be acceptable. But one asks: Who was brave enough to subject himself to ridicule as Schach von Wuthenow, almost a caricature? Who had the nerve to present himself as Melanie's bankrupt lover? Who is hiding behind the often invoked Luise, who behind Count Petöfy? Who are these three graces playing the Poggenpuhl sisters? And over there: which executive suite has produced the two smartly attired gentlemen who greet each other as von Instetten and von Crampas? How much financial power is lurking behind that family doctor who keeps writing out prescriptions for trips to the spa? But there is no mistaking Frau Jenny Treibel: she is the head of the Handover Trust. She alone manages to combine money and poetry. Only she could have come up with this socially respectable way of celebrating the thousandth winding-down. And just watch: in a moment Corinna will appear on the scene and give Frau Treibel a piece of her mind...."

The audience was carried away. Fonty trotted out an unending succession of characters. More and more shouts rang out: "Where's Alonzo Gieshübler, the noble apothecary?" "Too bad Hoppenmarieken's not there!" "If you have Czako, the Schmargendorf woman has to be there!" "Didn't anyone invite Frau Kruse, the one with the black hen?" And someone asked a typical archivist's question: "Did beautiful Brigitte bring along her Danish security assessor?"

Fonty took up all the questions and could assign his personnel almost without limitations. They were on call: where Schach was, Bülow couldn't be far behind; with his daughter came Captain Hansen's widow; and Frau Dörr was there, bickering with the wizened gardener Dörr. Madame Trippelli sang "The Boy on the Heath." All of them spoke their lines, and with all the chatter, General von Bamme never got around to ordering the signal to attack the Oder bridge. Fonty even made the dead Chinaman appear, to give a bit of a fright to Effi, who promptly obliged. But when someone in the audience called for Cécile, Fonty responded, "Sends her regrets. She's suffering from a migraine. But her gentlemen are alive and well, although here with loaded pistols. And other project-makers and professional bankruptcy-artists have answered the call of the head of the Handover Trust. When they catch a whiff of fast money, the monetary gentry assemble in a flash. But poor devils, too, panting to make a fortune. Just look: here comes Hugo Grossmann, a bearded mayor looking for investors. And surely—no, without a doubt—Mathilde Möhring has a finger in the pie somewhere. There she is, working her way toward Frau Jenny Treibel, to propose, with her innocent cameo face, the thousand-and-first winding-down: a particularly nice little bargain. What a crowd! Chests studded with medals, dress sabers, high collars. Privy and commercial councilors out in force, with the directors of the major banks behind them, and likewise the Sulfur-Yellow One, recognizable by the collar of the Halberstadt Cuirassiers; he has brought along his man Bleichröder, a Croesus, nowadays backed by the Dresdner Bank. Credit sharks and defaulters, incorrigible borrowers! You may be assured: Rubehn, yesterday still down and out, is in a festive mood today and riding high...."

More and more characters making a grand entrance. We archivists noted the absence of one or another, yet we did not dare to add our shouts to the others to ask about, say, Lissauer, the homeopathic veterinary from *Irretrievable*. We were worried about Madeleine. She was sitting there as if ready to leap up at any moment and put an end to the hocus-pocus. When I, seated next to her, expressed my concern, she whispered, "*Bien sûr.* Grandpapa certainly has something else up his sleeve. This is no joke. He is completely serious about this, and will push the scene to the limit, *à l'outrance.* I fear he will stop at nothing...." Her paper handkerchief was by now completely shredded.

Perhaps we should have intervened. Or someone else—but over by the "Emergency Exit" sign there was no Hoftaller. And we did not intervene because, from Fonty's point of view, the scene at the Handover Trust was still merry.

Now he brought the paternoster into play. The audience was shown the old-fashioned lift with an amusing cast. Fonty forced old Stechlin into one cabin with his dreadfully stern and pious sister Adelheid. Dubslav muttered his standard "Monastery clocks are always slow," and the Domina repeated, "Keep your French to yourself. It always depresses me," or complained bitterly about a timeless problem: red stockings. In the next cabin the widow Pittelkow insisted on having a word with the count, that old lecher: "My little Stine is not the kind of girl who latches onto someone or forces her way into someone's favor...." Then came the maid Roswitha with Frau Kruse, who was holding the black hen in her arms. Right after them Botho von Rienäcker was compelled to listen to Käthe's mindless chatter: "Isn't that just too, too funny, no, isn't that just too, too funny?" Then one of the Poggenpuhl daughters was having a stern word with Leo, their impulsive brother, who was dying to set out for the African colonies in search of adventure. And in another narrow cabin Corinna exclaimed to the disguised head of the Handover Trust: "I find that ridiculous! Who are the Treibels, after all? Manufacturers of Berlin blue with a councillor's title, but I, I am a Schmidt!"

Pairs of characters who belonged together or butted heads were squeezed into paternoster cabins: Rex had to be better than Czako. Fonty condemned his cast of characters to ride, thus yoked up and down for all eternity. And all of them uttered their signature phrases. The trusty old paternoster rumbled from floor to floor, sighing and squealing—"but always reliable!," as Fonty declared from the lectern. It made its way through the novels and novellas, even transporting, in a somewhat macabre pairing, Lehnert Menz the poacher and Opitz the forester past the turning points. One saw those constantly bickering businessmen Baruch and Isidor Hirschfeld, father and son, come once again into view, and now finally Buschen and Hoppenmarieken followed them.

And whom else did he submit for our inspection, either rising from below and disappearing on their way up or in a downward trend? Two man-crazy pastors' daughters; coachmen yoked together; the Barby daughters, prettily contrasted; family doctors disagreeing violently over diagnoses; and finally Briest and Luise, he with his famous catchphrase. Van der Straaten remarked casually, as if it were a business matter: "You want to leave me, Melanie?" And she replied, "Yes, Etzel." The mighty word "Renounce!" was followed, a little sheepishly, by Count Petöfy's question to Franziska: "Can you do that?" When Holk, who had come from Holkenäs just for the occasion, appeared from above, only to disappear below with Baroness Christine von Arne, he was wailing, "The more you bring along, the more you find is missing." And she responded with pious indignation, "If you had your way, the cows' troughs would be as spotless as baptismal fonts."

But with the appearance of these two characters from *Irretrievable,* promptly followed by Brigitte Hansen and Ebba von Rosenberg in the next cabin, Fonty's presentation entered the realm of pure speculation. Police Superintendent Reiff and a mysterious unnamed Danish security assessor exchanged findings they had listed on paper. Grete Minde was then seen descending completely alone. After that Fonty left the Handover Trust celebration to its own devices for a while and returned to his manuscript. He immersed himself once more in "Childhood and Youth," and the audience in the Boiler House was with him. He portrayed the fire in the stables outside the Rheinsberg Gate as a blazing spectacle. Then, before the last sparks had scattered, he went on to the huge stable fire in *Before the Storm* and to the burning bridge over the Oder, added the bright glow of the blazing lumberyard, summoned the arsonist Grete Minde, who had appeared at the costume party just in time to make the town of Tangermünde go up in flames—"and in the next moment a shower of red sparks shot up over the rooftops..."—then, after this conflagration, returned to the Handover Trust to have fainthearted Botho burn the letters he had received from his Lene, spelling errors and all, until nothing but ashes remained; then he quickly recited some lines from his ballad on the "Burning Tower"—"See the thirsty flames aleaping / Now from lofty tower to tower..."—and next asked Ebba and Holk, Holk and Ebba, that impossible couple, to replay the chimney and chamber fire in Frederiksborg Castle; and they obliged, before the eyes of many illustrious guests, in one of the woodpaneled cabins of the tireless paternoster.

Fonty stoked the various fires so energetically, the flames leaped so high, the smoke was so acrid, the kindling so dry, so many passions flared and were mutually enflamed—broke forth, consumed and were consumed in turn, crashed down in showers of embers, spilled their glow, died down, and built up such an all-encompassing heat—that the audience, and we with Madeleine in the first row, felt we were there as eyewitnesses outside the Rheinsberg Gate, in Tangermünde, by the Oder bridge, and in the castle courtyard; no wonder we assumed the sirens approaching outside were part of the lecture. People thought the Immortal had ordered the Berlin fire brigade to deploy en masse and participate in Fonty's fiery performance. At that moment, someone outside tore open the emergency exit and shouted: "It had to happen. The Handover Trust's burning!"

It was Hoftaller who shouted that. As the presentation was reaching its climax, he must have sneaked out. "A major fire!" he shouted, and was gone again in a flash. He had come with the red-hot news, and since the audience took the burning Handover Trust for the end of the presentation, crackling applause was the upshot. Still clapping, the people all pushed and shoved their way outside to search the sky for the glow of fire. At once cheerful and flushed, the audience dispersed. They had enjoyed being at the party in the costumes of their choice—each in a favorite role—and they shouted their approval when they heard that the celebration's blazing finale had been validated by real life.

In the Culture Brewery's Boiler House, as the crowd surged toward the exits, shouts were heard: "So the old crate is burning down at last!" "About time!" "They should put a match to Normannenstrasse while they're at it!" "Well, there's plenty of tinder there!" Someone spontaneously came up with the rhyme: "The Trust and Stasi are burning / At last our luck is turning!" And someone else asked himself and the crowd, "So, who was playing with matches?"

Unmoved by the applause and the noisy departure of the audience, Fonty was still standing behind the lectern. Someone had thrust a bunch of flowers—fire lilies they were; how prescient!—and an envelope into his hand: his honorarium. He put down the bouquet and the discreetly concealed five-hundred-mark note on the lectern, took a sip of water, sorted the manuscript of "Childhood and Youth," felt for his glasses, actually wanted to continue his talk, did not understand the commotion, looked, now unspectacled once more, astonished, and said, more to himself than to the audience, which in any case was thinning rapidly, "They must have all gone off the deep end. The whole thing is fiction, and real only in a higher sense. They always clap too soon. Should have waited for the end of the Handover Trust party, when the Immortal himself puts in an appearance. Suddenly the paternoster brings him up from below. He has the Order of the House of Hohenzollern on his jacket. And the boss, Frau Jenny Treibel, greets him effusively and cordially on the fourth floor, as is her wont. Whereupon the two of them lead off the dance for the guests swarming in all the corridors."

Only we and Madeleine were listening to him. Only we and *la petite* saw his handsome old head glowing, hot from speaking, and his fuzzy white hair blazing. Yes, his gaze was lit by inner fire; no wonder, after such a blistering talk.

When his granddaughter went up to the lectern and took her grandfather by the hand, we held back, but I heard her say in a small voice, "*Excellent, Grand-père, vraiment excellent.* But now I'm afraid we must go. You will be under suspicion. I know, it is all an invention, like the church at Tempelhof or Wuthenow Castle. But we must hurry away, before they come looking for us...."

I saw Madeleine stuff the manuscript and the envelope with the honorarium into her bag, pull Fonty away from the lectern, skillfully insert herself and him into the remaining crowd, and disappear with her grandfather through the nearest emergency exit.

The bouquet of fire lilies, whose funereal scent Fonty could not bear in any case, remained lying on the lectern. We took it with us, on his behalf. When everyone had left, I was the only one who stayed behind. I hunted and hunted...

At last: he was wandering about outside in the dim light. I found him between the Boiler House and the former stables, squeezed into an alcove. When he saw me, he pounced, refusing to let go: "Have you got him?"

I mumbled something about "having a drink with the management," and said, in an attempt to placate him, "Our friend looked exhausted. He needs peace and quiet. You should be more considerate, too...."

The orphaned day-and-night-shadow would not be mollified. "No doubt the little one has towed him away. Theoretically not a bad idea, because he absolutely must be taken to safety.... And without delay. The search for the perpetrator is sure to have begun by now...."

I warned against exaggeration: "Well, a person really couldn't have a better alibi...."

"Rubbish! The Archives are playing naive again. But I could tell what was coming when he pushed his manuscript aside and began to speak straight from the shoulder.... That's what always happened when he... uses some dodge to get away from the prepared text—'What I wanted to say, by the way...'—and promptly comes to the real point. He calls it 'naming the horse and rider.' And now the clock is ticking. Alibi! You've never heard of remote ignition? I've got to find him.... Whatever it takes!"

He stopped haranguing me. So I left, left hesitantly, turning to look back again and again. He was standing there, at a loss, now completely alone with himself in the large inner courtyard of the former Schultheiss Brewery.

I stopped in the shadow of the exit, which had the dimensions of a castle gate, and saw him pacing back and forth. Sometimes closer, sometimes farther away. The sparse light cast by the arc lamps pulled him in, spat him out. There he was, exposed, then gone again, but his voice lingered. He was talking to himself. I picked up some fragments: "Saw her in the audience... right section, third row from the rear... a hardened criminal... that bitch... Of course, the flowerpot woman... it was her profile, I'm sure of it... Comrade Frühauf... unreliable... pathologically unstable, always was... they'll duck under at her place... there's no way around it—they'll have to duck under somewhere...."

Hoftaller seemed to have completely lost his bearings. Suddenly he shouted so loudly that it echoed through the inner courtyard: "I've had it, had it…these endless field operations, field operations…I'm signing off, signing off…Getting out of here, out of here…"

Then I could no longer see him. All I could hear as I left was that someone, probably a drunk hidden in the night shade cast by the brick ramparts and towers, perhaps where the brewery's smokestack rose skyward, began to sing that old revolutionary hymn "*Ça ira, ça ira—ça ira, ça ira …*"

37

With a Little Luck

By the light of morning, everything looked different. The Handover Trust had not burned to the ground, even though the fire alarm had indeed gone off on the evening of the lecture, toward seven-thirty, summoning a number of brigades to the scene. In the building at the corner of Wilhelm- and Leipziger Strasse, a fire had broken out, filling all the stories with smoke, but easily confined, brought under control, and eventually extinguished. Shortly before eleven the incident was over, but a fire watch was set up in the building.

The paternoster had caught fire. Because it remained in operation all night, the fire made the rounds and managed to ignite most of the cabins and burn them out; those remaining were charred to a greater or lesser extent. One could speak of a total loss, as far as the open-cabin lift was concerned; the Trust itself walked away with a bad scare.

Rumors of arson began to circulate immediately; the winding-down headquarters had certainly given plenty of provocation. Despite official denials, the newspapers refused to let the story go. Each new article outspeculated the last, naming possible perpetrators and responsible groups. At the time the blaze broke out, leading staff members were having a drink in one of the conference rooms in the otherwise empty building—on the fifth floor, to be specific. They thought the moment had come to celebrate the successful winding-down of a round number of residual-burden cases. But those participating in the little party, where alcohol flowed freely, by the way, could hardly be considered suspects; as the leaders of various agency teams and their administrative assistants, they were part of a system that had always known how to provide its own alibi.

A short circuit was identified as the cause of the fire. The wood paneling, impregnated with wax and furniture polish, had gone up like kindling. Later it was suggested that the lift hadn't been serviced properly. Nonetheless doubts remained: there was no getting around the fire department report, which mentioned empty canisters found in the cellar, as well as charred rags discovered in four adjacent cabins. But since no note claiming responsibility turned up, the press assumed that this time it had been an individual perpetrator, not the Red Army Faction; Stasi network members who had ducked out of sight were suspected. Nevertheless, neither the Federal Investigation Bureau nor any other higher-level agency launched an investigation. At the government level, the word was: Downplay the incident. The authorities wanted to get back to business as soon as possible, and this they did.

The paternoster was not restored. It was considered an obsolete model in any case. Only recently an inspection team had classified the lift as "extremely user-hazardous." The plan called for its rapid replacement with a modern high-speed elevator, which presumably has already been done.

In summary, the following may be said: The fire hardly impeded the work of the Handover Trust, and brought that work only briefly into the glare of the headlines. Fonty's lecture, which elicited a response that ranged from benevolent to mocking in the culture pages of numerous newspapers—including small-town ones—was not linked in any serious way with the burning paternoster. Here and there commentators glossed the "symbolic parallel." In one mass-circulation paper, a headline read, "Speaker Poses as Clairvoyant." The article itself filled no more than a column, for at the end of August there was no shortage of sensational news items: Gorbachev's star had fallen; the Soviet Union was coming apart at the seams; murder had begun in the Balkans; and the stock market was going crazy.

In such exciting times, who would care to launch a manhunt for an elderly gentleman, still carried on the Handover Trust's payroll under the name Theo Wuttke, but known only—if at all—as

Fonty. He would not have had to duck out of sight. No one gave a criminological damn about him. Besides, he had an alibi: the Boiler House at the Culture Brewery. So many eyewitnesses on his side. Only the power of fiction placed him under suspicion. But he stayed away, and was considered missing.

Not that we would have gone so far as to close the Archives, but we did search for him high and low. Some of us were always out looking, and I, too, repeatedly signed up for field duty. We had reason enough for our search: after only a few days, we found we missed Fonty terribly. It was as if whole piles of valuable papers were turning yellow in our hands, as if his life-giving, dust-stirring breath were absent, as if we had to invoke him to make him seem real again; as if duty called us, now that he was gone, to take up immediately the collective task of capturing on paper the story of our vanished friend.

Ah, how bleak it was without him. We called out favorite sayings of the Immortal's to one another, sayings that pithily summed up summer holidays gone awry: "So many things that can drive one away: mangy dogs, crowing roosters, people..." Or: "Through the open window stream the blended scents of liquid manure and gillyflowers..." Also the famous epigram: "The question 'Why keep going?' keeps growing..." And when someone sighed, "I wish the little Brahm would come by for a chat," we all looked toward the door—but Fonty never came.

We searched every corner of the Tiergarten. We did not even find wet nurses from the Spreewald (those nurses who "all smell of sour milk"), only Turks of his age, who had no information. Nothing occurred to the diving duck but endless repetitions. Rousseau Island offered no higher meaning. Yet we never felt tempted to abandon our efforts.

At the cemetery of the French Cathedral parish, we tucked a note under the wreath of immortelles: "Request confidential meeting." We tramped along Potsdamer Strasse to the imaginary house number and left another coded message in the snack bar that we hoped would lure him out of hiding: "New material found for *Likedeeler* project." And on Alexanderplatz we sought out his favorite newspaper stand, where we posted a lost-and-found notice.

Whether in the Scheunenviertel or on the bridges over the Spree, we left none of his favorite spots out of consideration. In between we repeatedly toiled up the three flights of stairs to the Kollwitz-strasse apartment, rang the bell, pushed notes under the door, even put our ears to the keyhole: nothing stirring. The new neighbor had no clue, the building superintendent was merely loquacious. We were just about to put an ad in the *Tagesspiegel* saying, "Seeking someone who writes with brevity on great matters, at length on small ones," when, on our last attempt, the door to the three-and-a-half-room apartment opened.

We found Emmi and the widow Grundmann there. It took us a moment to recognize them. Both had just come from the hairdresser's. Their clothing fancy, but with no trace of nouveau-riche vulgarity; rather, this was Hanseatic chic, as if mother and daughter had had their clothes custom-made in Hamburg. The plump, rather slovenly Frau Wuttke we had known had turned into a stately matron, while Martha was now the self-possessed business-woman; even her perfume smelled profit-oriented.

The two women had taken charge of the kitchen and the other rooms, the older sizing up the furniture they had left behind, the younger looking about with a bored and almost distracted air. Only when they opened their mouths did the old Kollwitzstrasse make itself heard; no beautician could powder over that tone. This sometimes grumpy, sometimes lachrymose, then again good-natured rambling could not be cut to order. No perfume could cover the cooking smells of the live-in kitchen, no change of backdrop transform the women's familiar music-hall patter into grand opera. Fundamentally, mother and daughter had remained the same, and at first found everything as bad as could be: "That my Wuttke would go and do something like that to me...." "Well, this is just the kind of trick Father would pull...."

Invited to join them at the kitchen table, we reported on the event at the Boiler House, on the large audience, the important people in attendance, the speaker at the lectern, the applause during the presentation. Although we suppressed Fonty's digressions and emphasized the quality of the speech, especially the verbal wit and the complex interweaving of word-perfect quotations, Emmi remarked, "He just can't leave it alone, always has to open his big mouth, and folks just laugh themselves silly at him. That's how it was way back with the Cultural Union. I told him a thousand times, I told him, just say what they want you to say, and don't go quoting stuff. You mustn't do it, Wuttke, you get caught up in too many other things, I say, it just runs away with you. . . ."

And Martha, who had listened impatiently to our account, commented, "Nothing new. We heard the whole story ages ago. Was even written up in our paper, that Father'd hoisted himself by his own petard again. Quite clever, too, what they had in the *Mecklenburg Times*: 'The talk began with the smallest of details and ended with the largest of fireworks.' Must have been pretty funny in the beginning, but in the end he flipped out, like always. I know the routine. Exactly. Saw it as a child—at some point Father always opens up a can of worms. And then when we read the article about the fire at the Trust, I knew the score and thought to myself, I wouldn't be surprised if Father's involved somehow. . . ."

But Emmi saw it differently: "My Wuttke? He'd never do a thing like that there. He just talks. It's just like before, when he talked himself into hot water and just made everything even worse. He should've come to us. One telegram after the other, and cost us a bundle. But Martha always said, Never mind trying to save money. If it's got to be, it's got to be. And we had everything ready for him, you know, wallpaper and all. All we got to do is move this stuff. Can't wait any longer. Tomorrow we'll get everything packed up— not everything, but most of the stuff he's attached to. Even the old curtains and drapes; I'll have them taken down and put up in his new room, so he'll feel at home sooner, when he shows up. . . ."

"First he's got to come up for air!" Martha exclaimed. "I'm sure this is something that girl engineered. She wants him all to herself. I know the type; theoretically they'll stop at nothing. And Father? He just went along. Exactly; this is the kind of thing he likes: giving us the slip. 'Making yourself scarce,' he calls it. And the girl just eggs him on. . . ."

"Now don't you say anything about our Marlene. She's taking good care of him, that's for sure. Besides, she's part of the family now, whether you like it or not. Don't be so hard on her, Martha.

She's just a lot different than you; I mean, she has a little more zip...."

When the daughter fell silent and assumed a grim expression, the mother began to run her hand over the oilcloth-covered table: "Lordy, lordy, that Wuttke of mine. There were times we could even be a bit proud of him, like when they gave him something for activism, in silver even. And we had some real happy years, certainly in the beginning. It was just so crowded, with the three boys all in one room. And Martha, when she was little, slept with us. No way to live in the long run. That was bad, how we were crammed in here. But when the boys were gone, and we finally had enough room, it seemed like the place was empty. And then my Wuttke moved into the study with his bed, so I slept all alone in there, all those years...."

Emmi shed a few tears. We sat there uneasily on the kitchen chairs. Martha claimed to be "steamed" because Madeleine had taken her room, had put away some mementos and in general poked her fingers into everything. "She even got her paws on the piano. Saw that right away. And moved my records around in the cabinet. Oh, well, what do I care! She can have all this garbage. I can't stand to look at it anyway, all the junk here! That surprises you? Well, that's how it is now. You've got to be able to start over, not always be looking behind you. What we used to have here is over and done with anyway, though I always say that not everything about our republic was that bad. It just wasn't efficient. Planned economy? Sure. But only when it really works and pays off. This is what we've got to learn, I told the comrades in Schwerin just the other day: 'Not till your production is market-driven, not till the bottom line's healthy and you're making a profit can you think in terms of socialism....' Me? Of course I've joined again. The Party needs people who know something about business. It's got almost nothing to do with belief, only with conviction. That's exactly what I wrote to Father Matull—you know, the one who spoke at my wedding. I told him that in the Party, now that it's got a different name, we make room for something like doubt, theoretically. And I told the comrades, 'If you don't have doubt, you don't believe in anything!' And even some of the old guys, who used not to be able to take a leak without checking the Party line, yelled, 'Right you are!'

Come on now, Mother, stop bawling. That won't make things any better!"

Emmi soon finished crying. We promised not to abandon our search. We turned down Martha's offer to cover any costs associated with looking for Fonty—she said, "We really don't have to worry about money anymore." But finding Fonty was a point of honor with us, we said.

We noticed that the businesswoman was wearing a cross around her neck on a simple gold chain. When we asked how business was going, she said, "Pretty well, considering we're just getting started. My Grundmann was more for improvising; I'm just the opposite, I like to get things organized. I said to my girlfriend Inge, who's taking terrific care of the house for us and also has this tendency to jump into things, I said, 'Risk's all right, but it should be calculated.' Oh, well, she'll learn...."

We weren't offered coffee, but we were allowed to glance into Fonty's study, which still looked unchanged. Only the Red Chinese runner had been rolled up into a sausage and was leaning against the desk, ready for the move. No flowers in the long-stemmed vase. The Russian green pencils sharpened to different lengths. The swan feathers ready at hand. Everything in its place. Nothing seemed unfamiliar. Yet on the desktop, half covered by the Cuban cigar box with its rubber bands, stamps, and pencil sharpener, lay a note that Martha and Emmi must have overlooked. In handsome, looping script were the words: "Over the hills and far away"—nothing more.

My colleague didn't hesitate; she promptly secured this clue for the Archives. I would have liked to take the postage scale as a souvenir. In the end I slipped a steel pen into my pocket.

Just as we were leaving, Father Matull from St. Hedwig's stopped in to "stand by the family, if only with the feeble powers at my disposal," as he said. He remembered me from the wedding. At a loss for something to say, since after his first utterance he preserved a deafening silence, I brought up a Catholic expression that was secretly intended to take the sting out of my little theft. It was an expression that alluded to "venial sins," a practice of abatement common in confessionals, about which the Immortal had read with amusement in a Jesuit rulebook; for which reason Fonty, too, was wont to file away past and repeated lapses under this heading.

Matull did not take me up on this Catholic initiative. He was there only for the family. Consistent with this pastoral duty, he gave us the tip, as we were leaving, to inquire at the French Cathedral as part of our search for our missing friend. "Exactly!" Martha called after us, and Emmi was positive: "That's where my Wuttke must have hid with our Marlene—that's where she's from, you know...."

We found confirmation for our doubts: not at the Reformed Church, the New Synagogue, or any of the churches we canvassed, in no temple we visited had the grandfather and granddaughter sought asylum, let alone taken cover. We even checked the Salvation Army, though by then we were filled with despair.

Days passed. Emmi and Martha had left. Before departing, they managed to "take care of moving the couple of old things," as the widow Grundmann said on the telephone to us. When she went into detail, we learned that the Poggenpuhl parlor had been cleaned out by a secondhand furniture dealer, with one exception: "I just couldn't part with that old piano. Maybe I'll feel like playing again someday. Exactly. A couple of easy pieces, Schumann's *Kinderszenen*, that kind of thing..."

Then we were given instructions. The minute any information turned up, we should send a telegram. But even the police, who promised to act on Emmi's missing-persons report, had no luck; actually, as is usually the case in large cities, they had plenty of such reports, more, as they admitted, than they could handle. We were already trying to get used to the idea of finding meaning in our work without Fonty's support. We were already beginning to set up a parallel archive for him. We were already speaking of Fonty as if he were dead, and as if it were a matter of composing a eulogy, after preparation both broad and deep. We were already getting started on the writing, when Hoftaller came to the Archives.

He just wanted to say good-bye. He was about to set off on a long trip. The assignment that had presented itself of late could no longer be postponed. He could give us only this much of a hint: ex-

650

pertise like his and experience spanning several regimes, of which he had no shortage, was more urgently needed than ever, what with the world situation totally askew, while the need for security remained unaltered: "Just as I've always said: fundamentally nothing changes."

Our guest had spiffed himself up: suiting in a fine small check. No doubt there was the label of a London firm in his silk hat lining. Instead of his scratched briefcase, he was carrying an attaché case. He looked somehow rejuvenated, or entirely renewed; only his smile had grown old and tattered in the service. It was dangerously close to a smirk—that was how cheerful our visitor seemed. He even came up with cracks such as "Really enviable, the peace and quiet you have here" and "I'd have loved a position like this, with no field duty at all." When we offered him the visitors' chair, he said, "But no more than fifteen minutes. Still have something to take care of, just a formality. Then I'm off. Been sick of Berlin for a long time now."

We tried to guess at his destination: "You wouldn't be headed for Yugoslavia, would you, where chaos has the upper hand?"

"Has Moscow come calling, now that after the putsch..."

"I've got it! You were taking that intensive language course— you must be going to Latin America."

"Could it be Columbia, into the heart of the drug swamp?"

Hoftaller's smirk was the only answer we received. "My biographer," he said, "who dealt so thoroughly with Tallhover's long-term prospects and wanted to dictate a self-inflicted death for me, would be amazed to know...."

"CIA!" we all exclaimed, and I added, "Why should we be surprised?"

Other secret agencies occurred to us, even Mossad, the Israeli service. Now that his departure was assured, we thought we could ask him anything we liked, without fear of the consequences. He let us flail around and bark up the wrong tree. We sent him off to hunt down the last surviving Nazis or into one Mafia jungle or another. Clueless as we were, we promoted him from his lifelong mid-level position to top agent. He put on a show of modesty—"All a few sizes too big"—but then, as he was already getting up, Hoftaller started a sentence with an expression very familiar to us: "By the way..." he said, and we already knew whom he had in mind.

"By the way, I have greetings for the Archives from our friend. Wasn't that easy to track him down. Followed a lead that turned out to be a dead end. You know, of course, that flowerpot woman, the one who ducked out of sight long before him. Right, Helma Frühauf. Didn't leave a trace. Was carried in our files as 'Cameoface.' Initially, when we still had things pretty much in hand, she was reliable, but toward the end...Anyway, a bum steer...Fortunately, I remembered something Mademoiselle Aubron said to her grandfather several times when we were in Potsdam in mid-August: 'All these kings. And everything so deadly serious. I'd be in the mood for something really droll. Ah, Grandpapa, could I ride the carousel with you?' Well, she could. And now I'll reveal to you— but this is absolutely just between us, and as a friend of the Archives—where I had the pleasure of running into our Fonty and his charming granddaughter. A real surprise. You'll be amazed. Just a few hints before I go, but then I really must..."

He had found them in the Spree Amusement Park, which in the days of the Workers' and Peasants' State was called the Culture Park and formed part of Treptow Park, where the Soviet Memorial stands. He said, "As a senior citizen, I only had to pay half. Pretty pricey even so—Western scale. But you can go on all the rides as often as you like, even the roller coaster. A bargain—you should give it a try."

And on this rickety roller coaster, creaking in all its joints, shuddering, yet free of accidents from the time our children, now grown, were in school, he spotted the missing pair, easy to pick out at a single glance. They sat there among the teenagers and screeched like all the other passengers on the curves, on the abrupt descents, while whizzing through tunnels, where they leaned way back, and on the twists and turns of the route that bit its own tail. He had to wait quite a while—"The two of them couldn't get enough"—because Fonty and Madeleine made three more trips, experiencing four times altogether a pleasure whose very sight could turn a person's stomach.

"Wasn't really up my alley," Hoftaller said, his hands tracing curves as he mimed the way the roller coaster crept uphill, then zoomed down from the peak and sped toward the last loop. He even imitated the squealing on the curves. Finally the two of them had had enough, but they hadn't staggered a bit as they got off, and hadn't been the least bit amazed to find him waiting there by the exit: "I was hard to miss."

Apparently Fonty was ready with a quip: "It's taken a colossally long time for you to find us. Looks as though the bloodhound is losing his nose." And Madeleine had been quite impertinent: "May I invite you, Monsieur Offtaler, to a little jaunt through hill and dale? Only looks dangerous. You're a man of courage, *n'est-ce pas?*"

Hoftaller's smile took on kindly dimensions as he recalled for our benefit the adventure in the Spree Park: "Never fear. I only let them talk me into a harmless carousel ride, and that was bad enough."

Although he was in a hurry and kept leaping out of the visitors' chair, he gave us a thorough description of all the attractions with which the amusement park was equipped, among them a ride called "Flying Carpet," which Fonty and *la petite* had tried out numerous times. There were even swan boats that glided along, following, by means of a pulley system, a meandering path down a man-made arm of the Spree; in one of these they could have chatted in peace about all sorts of things, even about plans for the future.

"But that was not for Mademoiselle. She wanted to do something wild, or show us her sure aim. Just imagine, there was a shooting gallery with lots of artificial flowers in little tubes. With one hand free and with just a few shots, she won a rose for her grandfather and a tulip or something for me. Unfortunately, I couldn't return the favor. Always was a bad shot. But Fonty—who would have thought it?—took only three shots and was able to present her with a corn-flower—of course he promptly cursed subversively: 'The kaiser's favorite flower. When Wilhelm had his birthday, every assessor, every lieutenant wore one in his buttonhole. Actually dislike cornflowers myself. A stupid, meaningless blue, and no scent, but just right for shooting galleries.' And on we went, from one attraction to the next. There was even a circus act: a motorcyclist on a high wire..."

Finally Hoftaller did manage to get Fonty away from his grand-daughter, if only briefly. We would have liked to witness the familiar pair, the day-and-night-shadow and his subject, climbing into the gondola; at Hoftaller's wish and with Madeleine's permission, the yoked pair managed to spend a quarter of an hour on the Ferris wheel.

Of course Madeleine joked when she heard this particular wish: "Monsieur, I harbor the suspicion that you are a bookworm. Could a certain Graham Greene, your colleague, so to speak, have coaxed you onto the Ferris wheel by literary means? Or was it the film—the famous scene in which Orson Welles philosophizes about cuckoo clocks and Michelangelo?"

"Typical *la petite!*" we exclaimed, enjoying Hoftaller's lingering embarrassment. He was allowed to be alone with Fonty in the gondola for three rides in a row. Along with the air up there, Hoftaller praised the view, and enumerated for us all the things they could see: the Spree, of course, and Stralau, situated on a peninsula between Rummelsburg Lake and the river. "That's the spot where you have to picture Lene Nimptsch and Lina Gansauge out rowing." They could see past Neukölln and far out over West Berlin. "Could make out exactly where the Wall once stood. Oberbaum Bridge in the haze, but still distinct. You should try it some time, the Spree Park—the view from up there's really worthwhile. The city stretches on and on. You can even see Karlshorst, the harness-racing track, all the way to Köpenick, even Müggel Lake, when there's no haze. A feast for the eyes, really..."

He was still impressed by the distant prospect that the giant wheel had afforded him. Not until we asked what had been discussed with Fonty at the very top and in the course of the ride did his smile reappear, nicely realigned and oiled: "Oh, well. I had to say good-bye to him, too, which wasn't easy for me. By the way, our friend wasn't curious in the slightest, unlike you. No prying: Where are you off to? 'Go!' he said, 'Go wherever you're going. You're needed everywhere.' And then, as I said, we enjoyed the view. In silence. A happy minute... or maybe even longer... Doesn't happen often, that kind of thing... In the west, a storm was brewing... a mass of clouds, pretty sinister.... But way down below we saw Mademoiselle standing and waving. We waved back. Oh, right, I had a bunch of papers with me, old stuff from way back when, but also documents relating to the Wuttke family, especially their son Teddy, responsible for uniform procurement.... Not a big fish, but still...We had fun tearing the paper into smaller and smaller pieces—rip, rip, rip. Then we let it all fly away, like confetti, up and away in the direction of the Spree. There was quite a breeze up there. What a sight! Were both relieved, even somewhat giddy. 'A thing like this has to be brought to a close,' I told our friend, 'one way or another....'"

"Did any poems get shredded?"

"And the letters to Lena? The traces of the Dresden period?"

"Maybe the poem where the apothecary's apprentice rhymed oil of cod-liver with boat drifting on the river?"

"All gone?"

Hoftaller let us flounder in uncertainty: "Already told you, out-of-date materials, mere residue. Time for you to face up to it: no archive without gaps!"

That was all, or almost all. When the three of them were once more standing by the giant wheel, they decided to get something to drink. According to Hoftaller, they drank fizzy lemonade at a bar table beneath a cluster of trees. And there, between one gulp and the next, Madeleine apparently hinted that after the sudden ending to the event in the Boiler House it had proved easy to find cramped but acceptable lodgings. As Hoftaller reported, she said, "We were lucky. The little room was offered to us by a simple housewife, whose husband is unemployed and who showed great enthusiasm for Grandpapa's speech. That's how we found a hiding place. Really cozy, with a view through a skylight. No need to be worried, Monsieur Offtaler. Though I must say, the many houseplants were a bit of an annoyance, for me more than for Grandpapa, who even discovered a heliotrope, his favorite flower, in our *jardin des plantes*. Well, it'll be bearable, the sharp scent, I mean. We're out of the house a good deal, and will certainly not be staying long...."

The farewell took place across from a Minol filling station, where Hoftaller ordered a taxi for himself. Fonty and Madeleine were walking across Puschkinallee in the direction of the S-Bahn when the first drops fell and the wind began to blow. But we were not satisfied with the sentence, "And so we parted company."

We wanted to know how it had really been, this parting: "Just like that, without further ado?"

"We went our separate ways."

"Without saying anything special?"

"Nothing more to say."

"But there must have been something, some gesture of farewell?"

"Well, yes..."

We could hardly believe the picture Hoftaller conveyed to us, with some embarrassment, just before he left the Archives: "Imagine: at the end Fonty gave me a hug."

And so a day-and-night-shadow, which had also fallen on us, vanished into thin air. He remained gone, but we continued to speculate: In what direction was he going? What could possibly lure away from us this specialist in changes of system? So many possibilities for launching operations—wherever television directed our eyes, there were glaring gaps in security, situations teetering on the brink, immediate intervention called for. After the usual back and forth, we settled on Cuba, and not only because he had run out of cigars. But for a long time the question remained open: On which side would he be working, in Havana or from Miami?

And finally, we must confess that in parting he left behind an envelope for the Archives. It contained a few documents from the Leipzig period—relating to Dr. Neubert's apothecary shop, the White Stag, on Hainstrasse—and two early letters from the Immortal to Wolfsohn. Happy occasions like this have become rare here. Nothing sensational, but one of the letters has a very revealing passage in which he vehemently dissociates himself from Herwegh, reestablishing the connection with Lenau; at any rate, this farewell gift enriched the Archives' holdings.

We heard nothing from Fonty, except for a postcard with greetings from Spree Park. The picture showed the giant wheel, and noteworthy was a self-quotation scribbled with a felt-tipped pen: "Nothing more tyrannical than old people!" In brackets he had added, "I have warned Madeleine, for I have the feeling I'm about to prove that true." And in her schoolgirl handwriting: "Grandpapa is exaggerating again. Perhaps five trips on the roller coaster were too much even for him. We're having a wonderful time."

So at least we could consider Hoftaller's report on Spree Park to have been substantiated. It was not until several more days had passed, with paralyzing slowness, or so it seemed to us, that another postcard arrived, this time showing the television tower on Alexanderplatz. We read that grandfather and granddaughter had been in the restaurant atop the tower, which revolves constantly two hundred and seven meters above street level; they had eaten "stuffed cabbage, very reasonable, with a terrific view." And all the things they could see from up there: "The Playhouse on Gendarmenmarkt, the French Cathedral, the State Opera House, the Friedrichstadt Palace, the Charité, the Bode Museum on the water, and then, toward Prenzlauer Berg, the People's Theater on Rosa-Luxemburg-Platz. In the west it was fairly hazy, but we could make out the Reichstag, the Brandenburg Gate, the Tiergarten, and the Victory Column, looking minuscule. Simply fantastic!" Madeleine wrote. From her grandfather there were merely greetings.

The following day we received a further postcard, postmarked 12 September, showing the death mask of Henri IV and apparently purchased in the Huguenot Museum. We realized we were being pointed quite openly in the direction they were headed, because Fonty, this time in pencil, mentioned only "two particularly pretty tiles from the Cévennes," among all the museum's holdings. Furthermore the message included the highly ambiguous sentence: "Without doubt I myself am now becoming the youngest child of my fancy."

Then nothing for a long time. We had given up on field duty. To put to rest any further uncertainties, the director wrote to Frau Professor Jolles. A reply arrived promptly from London: "Regrettably, the missing gentleman has not turned up here. Perhaps your friend, familiar to me from correspondence, will have felt drawn directly to Scotland and the highlands. There are still solitary hamlets there, even heather and witches' dens, although modern tourism leaves no stone unturned. . . ."

Weeks passed. We began to get used to having to take care of our minutiae without help incarnate. No, we did not get used to it; rather, we were sure we had fallen into a bottomless pit, because along with Fonty, the Immortal had left us. All our papers seemed lifeless. Our thoughts refused to sprout wings. Nothing left but footnotes and a lifeless wasteland. A void wherever we looked, with at most secondary rumblings. It was as if all meaning had been stripped away. Fonty, our benevolent spirit, was missing. And only after we began to fill page after page, conjuring him up, alone or with his shadow, did he once more acquire contours, become recognizable, call on us with flowers and quotations, embody, every bit the figure of yesteryear, the old gentleman drawn by Liebermann's hand, close to us, yet already with that far-away gaze, about to slip out of our hands again. . . .

To make things worse, financial worries were preying more and more on the Archives' mind. As everywhere else, more had to be done with fewer employees. My position was reduced to halftime. I was already sending futile applications to the National Literary Archives in Marbach and elsewhere; it already looked as though the only thing left for me was to escape, late in the day, into so-called married bliss—ah, yes, "marriage is order!"—when, toward the middle of October—the chestnuts were falling—a postcard arrived—the last, as we now know.

It said everything. The shiny picture side showed a hilly landscape, green in the foreground and growing blueish toward the horizon. The back, with an illegible cancellation mark on the stamp—a carmine-red Marianne!—bore a few words, this time written in ink.

We read: "With a little luck we find ourselves here in a colossally unpopulated region. *La petite* asks me to greet the Archives for her, a request with which I am happy to comply. We often go mushrooming. When the weather is calm, one can see far. By the way, Briest was wrong; I, at least, believe that although we have gone far afield, an end is in sight. . . ."

Translator's Note: I wish to thank Christian Thorne-Miano for his invaluable assistance with this translation. I am also grateful to Petra Crosby, who helped me with questions of German idiom. Responsibility for the final form of the text rests with me alone.

—*Krishna Winston*

If you enjoyed *Too Far Afield,* look for
these other titles by the Nobel Prize–winner

GUNTER GRASS

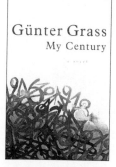

0-15-601141-7

$13.00 / Higher in Canada

0-15-615551-6

$13.00 / Higher in Canada

0-15-615340-8

$14.00 / Higher in Canada

0-15-675830-X

$15.00 / Higher in Canada

0-15-626112-X

$17.00 / Higher in Canada

0-15-123816-2

$35.00 / Higher in Canada